I0660526

The Voyages
of Lord Seaton
to the
Seven Planets

The Voyages
of Lord Seaton
to the
Seven Planets
or, The New Mentor

by
Marie-Anne de Roumier-Robert

translated, annotated and introduced by
Brian Stableford

A Black Coat Press Book

English adaptation and introduction Copyright © 2015 by Brian Stableford.
Cover illustration Copyright © 2015 Fleurine Rétoré.

Visit our website at www.blackcoatpress.com

ISBN 978-1-61227-446-1. First Printing. December 2015. Published by Black Coat Press, an imprint of Hollywood Comics.com, LLC, P.O. Box 17270, Encino, CA 91416. All rights reserved. Except for review purposes, no part of this book may be reproduced or transmitted in any form or by any means, electronic or mechanical, including photocopying, recording, or by any information storage and retrieval system, without permission in writing from the publisher. The stories and characters depicted in this novel are entirely fictional. Printed in the United States of America.

TABLE OF CONTENTS

Introduction

Voyages de Milord Céton dans les sept planettes [sic], *ou Le Nouveau Mentor*, here translated as *The Voyages of Lord Seaton to the Seven Planets*, was first published in four volumes in The Hague in 1765-66, with the by-line "*traduits par Madame de R.R.*" It was subsequently reprinted in volumes 17 and 18 of Charles Garnier's collection of *Voyages Imaginaires, songes, visions et romans cabalistiques* [Imaginary Voyages, Dreams, Visions and Cabalistic Fictions] in 1787, with the spelling of the title adjusted to render the seventh word as "planètes," although "planettes" is retained within the body of the text.

"Madame de R.R."—who was the author rather than the translator of the work—was Marie-Anne de Roumier-Robert (1705-1771). She was born into an aristocratic family that had already come down in the world considerably by the time she was born; her paternal grandfather was a provincial prosecutor but her father was obliged to go into commerce to make a living; her mother, whose maiden name was Bourée, was the daughter of an advocate. Her father was acquainted with Bernard Le Bovier de Fontenelle (1657-1757), author of *Entretiens sur la pluralité des mondes* (1686; tr. in 1687 as *Conversations on the Plurality of Worlds*), the enormously influential popularization of the Copernican theory of the solar system. She met Fontenelle on more than one occasion when he came to dine in their home, and retained a sufficiently elevated idea of his importance to grant him a place of honor on the world of the Sun featured in her own work, where all the great minds of Earth and other worlds go after death to live in the City of Philosophers, but if she ever read his masterpiece she does not seem to have taken its lessons aboard, as her own account of the solar system is extremely confused.

Marie-Anne's parents died while she was still young, and the debts her father left caused a posthumous bankruptcy that left her devoid of any inheritance; the relative who became her guardian put her into a convent, from which she only emerged to be married off to an advocate named Robert. The only brief biographical memoir written by someone who apparently knew her, Joseph de Laporte, contained in volume five of *Histoire littéraire des femmes françaises, ou Lettres historiques* (1769), has nothing to say about Monsieur Robert except that he was highly esteemed in his profession, and does not make any mention of his death, but the preface of *Voyages de Milord Céton* finds her alone and "without support" in struggling with her tribulations, and strongly suggests that she was a widow by then. Laporte also reports that her health was apparently poor and she was often ill.

Whether she was a widow or not, it was not until relatively late in life that Madame Robert decided to try her hand at writing. She might have taken some inspiration from the examples set by Madeleine de Scudery and Madame de La Fayette a century earlier, in the days when the de Roumier family was peripherally associated with Louis XIV's court, and from the slightly more recent success of Francoise de Graffigny, but she was undoubtedly also aware of some of the contemporaries featured alongside her in Laporte's volume on the works of living writers, where she takes second place behind the former actress Marie-Jeanne Riccoboni (1714-1792) and ahead of Madeleine de Puisieux (1720-1798), an occasional collaborator with Denis Diderot. Madame Robert's works follow a pattern not dissimilar to theirs, including both naturalistic "sensibility novels"—the ancestors of stereotyped modern love stories—and fantastic "moral tales" borrowing motifs eclectically from Antoine Galland's pastiches of Arabic folktales, Madame d'Aulnoy's *Contes des fées* [usually translated, dubiously, as "fairy tales"] and Classical mythology.

Madame Robert published two sensibility novels prior to venturing into new literary territory in *Voyages de Milord Céton*, the first of which, *La Paysanne philosophe, ou Les Aventures de Madame la Comtesse de* *** [The Philosophical Peasant Woman] (1761-62), detailed the complex but relentlessly moral love life of an orphan peasant girl adopted and brought up by an aristocratic woman. That novel was reprinted three times, and thus appears to have been considerably more successful than *La Voix de la nature, ou Les Aventures de Madame la Marquise de* *** [The Voice of Nature] (1764), another tale of an orphan in quest of true love; the plaintive preface to *Voyages de Milord Céton*, as well as certain comments in the account of life on the Moon, suggests that the relative failure of the second novel might well have impelled her to attempt something more eye-catchingly unusual. The text of *Voyages de Milord Céton* contains some passages suggesting, somewhat disingenuously, a strong disapproval of the public's liking for such fantastic works, but if Madame Robert felt some resentment at the fact that she was pandering to that appetite, it certainly did not prevent her doing so wholeheartedly, and at great length.

Voyages de Milord Céton belongs to the tradition of lunar satires spectacularly launched in France by the posthumous publication of Cyrano de Bergerac's *L'Autre monde, ou Les États et empires de la lune* (1657; tr. as *Comical History of the States and Empires of the Moon*) and more recently carried forward by Charles-François Tiphaigne de Le Roche in "Zamar" (1754 in the second edition of *Amilec*; tr. as "Zamar")[1] and *Le Voyageur philosophe dans un pais inconnu aux habitans de la Terre* (1761; tr. as *The Philosophical Voyager*) signed "Monsieur de Listonai."[2] Madame Robert had definitely read the latter work, as she borrowed a passage from it, rather clumsily, to shore up a description of laboratory apparatus in which she was clearly out of her depth, and she almost certainly read Tiphaigne's novel too; both works carried forward, in their own idiosyn-

[1] Black Coat Press, ISBN 978-1-61227-033-3.
[2] Black Coat Press, ISBN 978-1-61227-367-9.

cratic fashion, the traditional notion of the Moon as an abode of folly, which is reproduced, with an equally idiosyncratic twist, in Madame Robert's satirical depiction of that particular "heaven."

It seems probable, too, that Madame Robert was familiar with the Chevalier de Béthune's *Relation du monde de Mercure* (1750; tr. as *The World of Mercury*)[3]; although her account of Mercury is very different from Béthune's, the patchwork narrative strategy she employs, including both allegorical and anecdotal inclusions, is similar, as is the stratagem of an introductory account with a salamander. Her novel's subtitle, however, indicates that its principal literary model is not an interplanetary fantasy at all but François Fénelon's *Les Aventures de Télémaque* (1699; tr. as *The Adventures of Telemachus*), in which the protagonist is taken on a educational tour by his tutor Mentor, who gives him extensive lectures on the kind of government that he ought to adopt when he succeeds his father Ulysses as King of Ithaca. Madame Robert's account of the more far-ranging educational tour to which Zachiel subjects Céton and Monime is to a large extent an homage, and certainly echoes many of the criticisms that Fénelon made of the court culture of Louis XIV's reign (which resulted in his expulsion therefrom) but also rebukes the earlier Mentor to some extent for the implication of *lèse-majesté* contained in his more radical ideas about parliamentary government.

After publishing *Voyages de Milord Céton*, Madame Robert went on to publish a third naturalistic novel, *Nicole de Beauvais, ou L'Amour vaincu par reconnaissance* [Love Vanquished by Gratitude] (1768) in the same year as the fantasy novella *Les Ondins, conte moral*, here translated as "The Water-Sprites," three years prior to her death. *Les Ondins* bears a far closer resemblance to the whimsical fantasies produced by contemporary female writers than *Voyages de Milord Céton* does, but it is more extravagant than the general run of such stories, packing in far more incident and a greater abundance of disparate motifs. It also makes an interesting stylistic contrast with the early novel, cramming more action and color into its 33,000 words than *Voyages de Milord Céton* contrives to accommodate in more than 200,000.

The antiquity and eccentricity of both texts caused various problems of translation, of which not the least was posed by the strange title of the earlier volume, Céton being a blatantly impossible family name for an English aristocrat. The logic of its selection is very difficult to detect, although it surely has nothing to do with the fact that its pronunciation is oddly similar to the English pronunciation of "Satan." It is arguable that I ought to have left it as it stands, in spite of its absurdity, but I decided instead to substitute a more plausible equivalent. (There was no Lord Seaton in the English peerage in the 17th century, when the story is ostensibly set, nor in the 18th, when it was written, although a Barony of that name was created a century later for Field Marshal John Col-

---

[3] Black Coat Press, ISBN 978-1-61227-410-2

borne.) In general, Madame Robert's names—many of which are obvious adaptations of common French words, following a familiar pattern—give the impression that all of them ought to contain slightly-veiled meanings, but if that is true of Céton, I confess to being unable to determine what lies behind the veil—and the same is true the name of his partner in adventure, Monime.

A second vexatious problem arose with the term *génie*, which I have translated in this instance as "genius," although many English translations of French *contes philosophiques* that borrow Gallandesque materials (including one of mine) have preferred "genie," Galland having translated the Arabic *djinni* into French as "*génie*," thus adding to the existing confusions in the meaning of the world, which already signified both genius in the sense of a kind of spiritual being and genius in the sense of intellectual prowess. Madame Robert's use of the term is unusually profligate, her eclectic hierarchy of spiritual beings including the equivalents of Christian angels and demons as well as pseudo-Paracelsian elementals. I have annotated a few other problematic decisions of minor significance.

It has to be admitted that *Voyages de Milord Céton* is not the most readable of texts, even by the standards of its day; it is not only prolix, repetitive and inconsistent, but is certain respects remarkably lacking in seemingly-necessary intelligence, although certainly not in boldness; it requires a defiantly eccentric courage to set out to write an interplanetary novel if you not only unsure as to whether the Ptolemaic model the solar system or the Copernican is the correct one, but not even sure as to why it makes a difference, and to offer an account of the population of the City of Philosophers on the Sun when you only have the slightest idea what any of the philosophers in question discovered, believed or opined, or why it was significant.

Like many writers of philosophical extravaganzas, however, Madame Robert appears to have been using the writing of her novel as a means of clarifying her own ideas about various matters, and attempting to fix her own moral compass by working on some difficult issues. That is undoubtedly the explanation of some of the story's inconsistencies, and also its incessant repetition of the conclusions it attains. Not all the issues in question were resolved, and it is arguable that the remaining ambiguities and ambivalences are more revealing of her own state of mind and the confusions of her historical moment than the firm commitments she makes. Her attitude to war is one interesting instance, as her occasional polemics against it—and famous warriors receive remarkably short shrift in her allegorical account of the Temple Of Glory on Mars—are counterbalanced by her account of Céton's preparation for a military career and by the striking intervention of Monime in the battle fought in the climax of the plot. It is notable that the gushing depiction of the utopian world of Saturn takes it for granted that the planet's inhabitants still fight regular wars, even though there does not appear to be any possible source of their provocation.

As well as the interesting and partly-redeeming features of what might be regarded as its faults, the narrative also has some striking compensatory virtues. Not the least of those compensations is the sheer bizarrerie of the narrative, both in terms of the intensely exotic imagery of some of its odder passages—the visit to a comet, for instance—and in the reckless mingling and confusion of the literal and the metaphorical, especially in the ventures into pure allegory on Venus and the Sun. Then, too, there is its underlying plot, with produces some very strange side-effects along the way, most especially in the extraordinary love-affair between Prince Petulant and the temporarily-amnesiac Monime, as monitored by the perversely-conflicted Céton in the form of a stinging fly.

The somewhat tormented relationship between Céton and Monime eventually reaches its conclusion in the context of a strange alternative history, which employs variants of the names of several actual historical individuals—the novel is set in the mid-17th century, although some of the visits to other planets involve dramatic chronological inconsistencies—but moving therefrom into a spectacularly counterfactual account of the history of one of the nations of Eastern Europe. Although it is not really an "alternative history" in the sense that the term was later attributed to a subgenre of fiction, its innovations in bold historical invention are nevertheless of some note.

Most of the anecdotal inclusions inserted into the main narrative as asides are relatively straightforward, some of them being stereotyped exercises in sensibility fiction, but a few push that envelope quite considerably, including the most substantial ones related by secondary narrators on Venus, Mars and Saturn. The Saturnian chapters entitled "Le Triomphe de l'amitié" [The Triumph of Amity]—echoing the title of a 1751 novel falsely represented as a translation from Greek and signed "Mademoiselle de ***" (subsequently attributed to Marianne Falques, although Madame Robert could not have known that)—are particularly striking by virtue of a subtext that modern readers cannot help noticing, although contemporary ones might not have done so. Echoes of the Falques' novel also seem to be detectable in the tales inserted in the section set on Venus, although the ultra-respectable Madame Robert would surely not have borrowed anything therefrom had she known that the novel was the work of a defrocked nun who was forced to flee to England and whose subsequent literary works became increasingly scandalous and seditious.[4]

---

[4] Marianne Falques (c.1720-1785), who routinely introduced particules into various spellings of her own name and various supplements thereto, including de Vaucluse and de la Cépèdes, subsequently worked with William Beckford on his translations of Arabic materials and on the composition of *Vathek* and its episodes, originally written in French, which contain echoes of her own Oriental fantasy *Abbassai* (1753). Most of her works, in English as well as French, were published anonymously, and some undoubtedly remain unattributed.

Les Ondins, being—in spite of its subtitle—a pure entertainment, perhaps requires fewer apologies than its predecessor. It is certainly less ambitious, tackling no issues beyond the author's intellectual scope, but it makes the most of her undoubted imaginative scope in its hectic and zestful eclecticism. The story eventually gets lost in the maze of its own complications and leaves dozens of loose ends dangling, but its narrative exuberance is quite extraordinary, and it deserves to be reckoned an eccentric classic of fantastic fiction, which has closer affiliations with modern fantasy fiction than most contemporary works in a similar vein. It makes one wonder what the author might have produced had she shed her narrative inhibitions a little earlier in life and allowed her imagination that kind of free rein when she was closer to her prime.

It is not easy nowadays to sympathize with Madame Robert's intransigent monarchism and her absolutist views on sexual morality might also seem a trifle manic. Both attitudes were more than a trifle old-fashioned in her own day, but no one who read her works in the 1760s really wanted to be Mentored in that fashion, and undoubtedly found the two fantasies translated here interesting for much the same reasons that modern readers can still find some interest in them: their strangeness, their fervor and their occasional sarcastic wit. It is hard not to regret that the feminist opinions that crop up occasionally in both texts are not extrapolated more fully, and are sometimes flatly contradicted by the course of the narratives, but that very ambivalence and contradiction help to make the leading female characters, especially Monime—the real hero of *Voyages de Milord Céton*—a little more interesting than the stereotyped heroines of sensibility novels.

All of these features help to make the elaborate patchworks contained in both of the works translated here into uniquely fascinating collages. Although undoubtedly long-winded and sprawling—in a manner far from unfashionable in its day— *Voyages de Milord Céton*'s panoramic view of human life, divided up in order to emphasize different features in turn, does add up, jigsaw-style, to an original and worthwhile whole, and the far more economical condensation of a similar whole featured in *Les Ondins* makes the latter into a useful and charmingly playful supplement to the longer work.

The translations of both stories were made from the versions contained in the Garnier collection, from the copies reproduced on the Bibliothèque Nationale's *gallica* website. I also had to consult the version of the first edition of *Les Ondins* available at *archive.org* in order to fill in a small gap in the text of the *gallica* version.

Brian Stableford

THE VOYAGES OF LORD SEATON
TO THE SEVEN PLANETS
or, THE NEW MENTOR

EDITOR'S PREFACE

I was meditating profoundly in my study one day, very anxious about the success that certain works I had recently given to be printed might have.

"Oh, you silly woman," I said, slapping my hand, "what possessed you to advertise yourself as an author? Do you have the intelligence and talent to sustain that title? You live a tranquil existence, almost devoid of anxieties; is it necessary that glory should come to trouble your repose, and that, in order to acquire it, you should choose the thorniest of paths? Why have you entered that labyrinth, without a guide or support?

"Would it not be better to limit yourself to your distaff? People pay you a thousand compliments a day, saying that you resemble one of the Fates; one assures you that he would have liked the thread of his life to have been in your hands; another flirts with you; you're regaled with a thousand light comments that signify nothing, and which are nevertheless the substance of the majority of conversations; you're regarded as a pretty automaton, from which no one demands sentiment, delicacy, wit or common sense.

"Who could imagine that those drugs could enter into a little bourgeois head? Is it made to have even the slightest idea of what is known as good taste? What pretentions, then, can it have? Ought one pay attention to someone who has neither status, nor a title, nor wealth? That is the reasoning of certain simpletons, of whom, unfortunately, there are a great many in the present century, which is that of people whose pride, self-regard, caprice and imbecility guide them in all the actions of their life; of people who would regard themselves as dishonored if they dared to regard as friends persons who have no other entitlements than virtue, candor and honesty.

"What are you getting at? That those qualities ought to make them blush internally at the baseness of their sentiments. However, there are some of those people whom you castigate with so much liberty who will be your judges, and judges who will be all the more rigorous because the title that you are daring to take seems to demand that you only open your mouth to utter witticisms. You were not obliged to have wit before, but it will be demanded of you in future."

I was interrupted in my reflections by the sound of an explosion, which caused a prodigious number of sparks to fly from my hearth. I pushed my arm-chair back precipitately when I saw a little fiery man emerge from the midst of the flames, who seemed dazzlingly bright. That man started to leap and caper with such great energy that I felt scared. My first impulse was to flee, but I was seized by a tremor so universal that my legs refused me service. I am naturally cowardly; I confess to you willingly that I am not made to ornament myself with the audacity appropriate to warriors.

Meanwhile, the brazen imp was knocking over everything in my study. He perceived the disturbance that he was causing me, and took delight in augment-ing it by a thousand further mischievous pranks; then, with a nimble leap, he came to sit astride my neck.

"Oh, great God," I cried, excited by an increase in fear, "free me from this infernal spirit!"—for I took him at first to be one of the most malevolent of de-mons.

That made him burst out laughing.

Far from imitating him, I said internally all the prayers that I knew by heart. I even think that, in order to try to rid myself of him, I combined them with a few invocations, always holding my hands in front of my face. It is true that I was peeping through my fingers to see what became of the fiery man or demon; I feared that he might reduce everything to ash.

Exhausted by his vivacity, I was ready to faint, when I saw him approach my table, on which, after throwing off everything that was on it, he placed a large scroll of paper, which he unrolled and arranged with a great deal of atten-tion.

When I saw that he was quiet, I made an effort to compose myself, in order to show him more boldness and firmness, and said to him in a tone that revealed even more obviously the disturbance I felt, but which I nevertheless thought to be imposing: "Malign spirit, I implore you in the name of the great living God, who is my master and yours, to tell me who you are, and by what audacity you take pleasure in frightening me with your fire and the rapidity of your move-ments."

The effort that I made to express those few words occasioned a cold sweat, which prevented me from continuing. I awaited the imp's response with an ex-treme anxiety; I feared his accolades horribly. Fortunately, he finally took pity on the distress in which he saw me.

"Be tranquil," said the fiery man. "I am a salamander, who, far from seek-ing to harm you, has no other intention than that of giving you advice that might be useful to you. You ought not to be unaware that fire is the element destined for us and in which we live; that is what dictates that we can only show our-selves while fluttering incessantly. But should you not, having been occupied in the study of the sciences[5] for a long time, have freed yourself from the weaknesses of your sex? Why, then, has my presence intimidated you so much? You ought to know me, by virtue of the accounts that a number of philosophers have inserted in their writings on the qualities of different genii."

"That is true," I replied, reassured by those words, "but is one master of one's first reaction? In any case, I confess to you that it required this adventure for me to believe in genii; I know that it is very rare for them to deign to communicate with feeble mortals, and cannot imagine by what good fortune I have been able to merit such a favor. You have dissipated my fears; continue instructing me; I am ready to listen to you tranquilly, always provided that you can moderate your vivacity somewhat."

"I consent to that," said the salamander. "Learn, then, that hazard put on to your fire a log that attracted me; I have been witness to your anxieties; they have excited my pity and caused me to emerge from my element in order to aid you with my advice and commence to give you evidence of my protection.

"Firstly I warn you not to take offense if high-minded Messieurs take the trouble to criticize the boldness you have already had in advertising yourself as an author; those great geniuses always honor those they have the generosity to slander; be persuaded, therefore, that there is nothing like the glory of being criticized to add to the success of your works.

"Nor should you worry if they lack brilliant comparisons, bold metaphors, borrowed ornaments and fashionable phrases—in brief, the wit that is so envied and so sought-after, since it is almost as ridiculous to want it as it is difficult to acquire it. Follow naturally the fire of your imagination, without being put off and without being embarrassed by the judgments of certain censors, unaccustomed to applaud anything that does not emerge from their own pens.

"Limited minds never suspect the intention of an author; those which are too keen always exaggerate; they want to find allegories of which one has not thought. It is only people with common sense who grasp accurately the point of view that the author has adopted. Your intention ought to be to instruct while amusing; follow that project exactly; it is the only means by which you can acquire glory and reputation."

My salamander did not say any more; he went back into my fire, and left me to dwell on new reflections.

At first I concluded that I must have fallen asleep in my armchair, and that everything I had just seen and heard was nothing but the effect of a dream produced by my imagination and inflamed by my anxieties. But what new phenom-

---

[5] When Madame Robert refers to "the sciences," as she often does, she does not mean, as we would, physics, chemistry, biology and so on. She sometimes uses the phrase to refer to knowledge in general, with more emphasis on practical skills than theoretical understanding, but also employs it as shorthand for "the occult sciences."

enon presents itself to my eyes? I cannot understand it. Everything in my study is turned upside down. I can even see that scroll of paper there, which I know is not mine; I begin to suspect that I might still be asleep. I rub my eyes, and I drink a large glass of water; nothing is dissipated.

I've never been a sleepwalker, I say to myself, going to my table. *And yet there is a manuscript that is completely unknown to me. My door is locked; who, then, can have brought it if not a spirit? Let's see what it contains... but the writing is exactly similar to mine....*

Then I scan it rapidly, and I find that the manuscript contains a perfectly coherent story, which is nevertheless nothing but folly; but that folly appears to me to be very singular in kind, giving me the desire to impart its contents to those who are curious about novelties.

I am therefore doing so, without changing anything within it. I have only removed a few citations because they annoyed me; perhaps a few rather modern anecdotes will also be found therein, which might well have emerged from my pen. That is a privilege that it is necessary to forgive a female editor, who cannot let others talk for long without mingling with the conversation. It is, therefore, in the capacity of editor that I ought to render an account to my reader of the plan that is proposed in this work, which is entitled *Voyages of Lord Seaton to Various Worlds*.

Lord Seaton, raised by the cares of a genius of the first order, commences his voyages with the Moon. That globe immediately furnishes him with ample material to exercise his curiosity. It is of that world that he depicts for us the character of frivolity, the love of novelty and the inconsequence of conduct of the inhabitants of that planet, which, as is well known, is subject to a thousand variations.

From there he passes to the world of Mercury, which only offers to his eyes a world filled with citizens who sacrifice everything to interest and fortune.

Venus, a small, bright planet full of fire, only contains voluptuous people sensitive to pleasures; love reigns there everywhere.

The Sun, the abode of Apollo and the Muses, presents us with a world of scholars.

Mars announces glory; one sees nothing there but heroes; it is on that planet that our hero thinks it appropriate to perfect his understanding of the military art.

Nobility shines on Jupiter; everyone there is only occupied with titles, grandeur and the honors that are due to them.

Saturn represents the golden age, the good old times of the patriarchs; it is on that world that one sees the reign of the noble simplicity, candor, love of truth, obedience to the law and the respect so legitimately due to sovereigns. That world ought to serve as a model to all the others, but unfortunately, none of them resembles it.

That, in brief, is the whole plan of the work, which also furnishes many more little stories analogous to the way of thinking of the inhabitants of the different worlds where they live. I shall not add any reflections to it, and leave my readers the pleasure of taking their imagination as far as they wish. I shall not try either to support or strive to give a footing to my ideas, in which the author doubtless had no other design that to make it evident there are no opinions, however ridiculous they might seem to a sensible man, that one cannot support with the authority of a few philosophers.

Some might feel that the serious matters distributed in this work ought not to have been treated with such gaiety, but it is necessary for you to understand, dear readers, that in imitation of Democritus, who often laughed alone at the follies of the world, the editor, far from wanting to don the title of a serious individual, is doing likewise, and invites you to follow her example. In giving you this work, she has no other ambition than that of amusing you. You will fulfill her expectation perfectly if you take pleasure in reading it. If you encounter a few malicious remarks therein, perhaps you will not be far removed from the author's idea.

INTRODUCTION

The revolutions that arrived in England under Cromwell were the source of disorder for my family. I owe my birth to Lord Seaton, who, strongly attached to the King, found himself, after the tragic death of that monarch, in the dire necessity of taking flight in order to escape the tyranny of Cromwell, who, by virtue of disguised self-esteem, had just adopted the pompous title of Lord Protector of the realm, after having refused that of king.[6]

Lady Seaton, in despair at such a precipitate departure, would certainly have liked to be able to accompany her husband, but he formally opposed her design, by making her aware of all the inconveniences that might result from it.

"I am leaving you," my father said, "with two children, who will perhaps one day cause the glory of their ancestors to be reborn within our family. It is to your tenderness that I confide their days; occupy yourself with their education. I demand of your love that you put your care and attention into engendering within their hearts the principles of wisdom, virtue and reason with which you are so thoroughly penetrated yourself. Do not surrender yourself, my dear spouse, to grief or vain regrets, which can only serve to make your health deteriorate. We owe it to one another, my dear, to rise above our misfortunes and demonstrate, by our confidence, in suffering them, a heart greater than all the evils that are heaped upon us. Hope that in time some fortunate revolution will reunite us; in the meantime, conserve prudently the few friends who remain to us in London, in order to take advantage of any favorable circumstances that might produce the changes that must eventually arrive."

After my father's departure, the Lady, surrendering herself entirely to the bitterness of her grief, was unable to support the burden. A wasting malady took her from us within six months. My sister and I were still in adolescence, and were unable at first to sense the loss that we had suffered.

One of our closest relatives was appointed to be our guardian. That relative, a hard, severe and caustic man, abhorred all pompous titles, which he regarded as vain and frivolous. Attached to the sect of Quakers, he never called anyone by name without adding to it the title of Milord, or some other, and although he was himself one of the foremost lords of England, he never called himself anything other than James, with the result that one never saw anyone in

---

[6] Oliver Cromwell assumed that title in 1653, so the ostensible setting of the novel is the mid-seventeenth century, although that is not consistent with the description of the City of Philosophers on the Sun, which features numerous individuals active in the eighteenth century, and there are occasional anachronistic references in the other sections.

his house but Georges, Williams, Charleses and Simons. However, in spite of his prejudices against ceremony and politeness, he did not neglect any of the talents that ought to serve the education of well-born persons.

Monime was the source of all my pleasures; that dear sister had scarcely entered her fifteenth year than she seemed a prodigy of intelligence and beauty; the graces and the talents were combined in her person; it seemed that her prudence was in advance of her age; nothing escaped her penetration, but the enlightenment of her mind only served to make her more sensitive to the harsh empire that James exercised over us. For my part, recently emerged from the hands of a tutor, I tried to drive my annoyance away by means of hunting.

One day, having gone astray, I found myself at nightfall in a somber pathway that led me to an old castle; the drawbridge was lowered, and I went into it with the intention of asking for a guide who might put me back on the right path. Not encountering anyone in the courtyards, I went up a perron that separated the apartments. Hazard led me to a large room, which I assumed at first to be a temple.

Two marble colonnades supported the vault. I advanced into the middle of the vast edifice, from which, parading my gaze around in order to contemplate all its beauties, I perceived to the right, under one of the colonnades, several paintings, the figures of which seemed to me to be animated; I saw a quantity of grave individuals moving and walking. How surprised I was, however, when I perceived the most apparent among them advancing toward me in a grand and majestic manner.

I confess that his aspect penetrated me with a sudden fear; my hair prickled and my legs felt unsteady, seemingly ready to buckle under me; but, not perceiving anything hostile in the gaze of the old man, who offered me his hand with a gracious smile that restored calm to my soul, I had courage enough to present mine to him.

He took it, shook it, and advanced his head as if to invite me to kiss his cheek, which I did with the same confidence. The venerable old man then passed his arm around my neck. "By that noble courage," he said, "I recognize the blood of the Seatons. Oh, my son, I see with pleasure that you have not degenerated in any way the value of your ancestors. You see in me the first of your race. I have learned of the misfortunes afflicting our family, and those by which you are still threatened, the harshness of the Quaker, and the troubles of the charming Monime.

"A genius of the first order has guided your steps to this castle; that same genius would like, in response to my prayer, to take you both under his protection—but in order to merit his favors, my son, it is necessary to give him a second proof of your intrepidity, by consenting to spend the night here, in the midst of the spirits that inhabit his castle."

"Venerable old man," I said, in a free and assured manner, "if the blood that runs in my veins was immediately known to you, believe that the love of glory and that of virtue will always be the first motives of all my actions; I am not unaware that a noble boldness must be their base."

"Oh, my son," said the old man, hugging me to his breast, "how I love to see such magnanimous sentiments in you." Then he made a signal with his hand, which caused a troop of genii to advance to take my weapons.

When I was disarmed, the old man took me to the genius Zachiel, who was clad in an advantageous stature and the most handsome face in the world: a privileged physiognomy, a tender gaze and an affable expression prejudiced me in his favor from the outset; at the same time, the grandeur and majesty of his person inspired respect and confidence in me.

That genius, after having given me the most gracious assurances of his protection, made a long speech on the calamities of the world, and added that Monime and I were still under the threat of the greatest misfortunes. The pursuit of Lord Seaton had only been deferred until now, in the form of taking vengeance against the family of the individual who was out of reach, out of consideration for a few of Lady Seaton's relatives who had so far enjoyed Cromwell's confidence, but, the latter having been disgraced in their turn, the minister had sent orders to arrest the only offspring of a family proscribed by the tyrant, with a view to putting them to death in the Tower of London.

"Make haste," the genius said, "as soon as dawn breaks, to go and impart to Monime the important information I have given you; enjoin her to come here to put herself in my hands; calm her fears, and neglect nothing to convince her that this castle, abandoned and deserted though it might seem to you, is nevertheless the only place in England where you will be sure of finding help and protection. Assure her that I am able to defend both of you against the forces of the realm."

The genius left me, inviting me to yield to sleep for the remainder of the night, but my mind was too agitated to obtain any.

The twilight that announced the return of day had scarcely begun to appear than I left the castle; a well-harnessed horse was waiting at the door; I mounted it without fear, and it took me of its own accord to the Quaker's house.

I ran to Monime's apartment; she had spent the night in mortal anxiety.

"Alas, dear brother," she said to me, "is it possible that concern for my repose touches you so slightly? I would never oppose myself to whatever might amuse you, but for pity's sake, at least, devote a few hours in the day to an unfortunate individual who has no pleasures or dissipation except those you procure her. Help me to support my misfortunes. Alas, if your heart were penetrated by the same sentiments that I experience, would I need to make you perceive that two days have passed without your deigning to remember a sister who is occupied with no one but you? Can you suspect all that I have suffered, for fear that someone had made an attempt on your life or your liberty? Useless plaints! I am no longer loved, and no pretention to repose remains to me."

Monime could not hold back her tears.

21

Penetrated to the depths of my soul by a reproach that I hardly deserved, I said: "Stop, dear Monime; cease to insult a heart that is devoted to you alone; do not condemn a man who adores you.... What am I saying, while trembling? My reason is going astray; a delirium, no doubt, is taking possession of my senses. Oh, forgive this trouble that your unjust suspicions have engendered in my mind. I don't love you? Oh, Monime, dear Monime! How has such an injurious thought been able to find a place in your heart?"

Monime, surprised and nonplussed, looked at me without daring to respond.

After a quarter of an hour of silence, I added, with slightly less emotion: "I love you, my sister. You could not doubt that without being unjust; I have come expressly to give you proof of my attachment."

Then I told her about the adventure of the castle of the genii. At first, Monime had great difficulty in believing it, but when I had described the new misfortunes that were threatening us, I saw her forehead covered by a mortal pallor.

"Dear brother," she said to me, in a tremulous voice, "I see with that I can no longer doubt the story you have just told me; our misfortunes are all too real; thus, the dark mystery is clarified. Know, my brother, that James left precipitately yesterday without seeing me. One of my chambermaids, whom I interrogated regarding his departure, protested that she could not divine its cause, 'All I know,' she told me, 'is that James has received letters brought to him by an express courier, and that he did not read them without shedding tears. He immediately shut himself up with Simon, his man of confidence, and on emerging from his study, I heard him say to him: *It is to your fidelity and care that I confide these unfortunate residues of a family ever prey to dolor.*'"

However afflicting Monime's discourse was for me, I nevertheless felt a secret satisfaction, since the story confirmed that what had happened at the old castle was not an illusion; that the old man and the genius were no longer hypothetical individuals; that their advice was only too well-founded; and finally, that I could confide myself to the amity of which they had already given me evidence.

I pressed Monime to depart immediately; the same horse that had brought me could take us back; but it was only with infinite difficulty that I could succeed in making up her mind; a thousand difficulties that it was necessary for me to combat took us until dusk. Finally, finding no other retrenchments than in the concern of deceiving the vigilance of the chambermaids and Simon, I seized the opportunity and proposed that she disguise her sex by putting on one of my coats. She could not refuse that expedient, and we departed at nightfall.

When Monime saw the castle drawing near, she was gripped by such a great fear that she begged me not to force her to go inside.

"I'm not unaware, my dear Seaton, that with you I ought not to fear anything, but is one master of one's impulses? Why do you want to ask of me things beyond the strength of my sex? I can no longer sustain the idea that I have formed of living with genii. I would prefer the misfortune of being imprisoned in the Tower of London to all the advantages that they might bring me."

"What have you to fear from genii?" I said. "Is it possible that the enlightenment you have received cannot yet serve to make you overcome vain prejudices? Do you believe me capable of risking the life that is so precious to me? No, Monime, be certain that I would defend it at the peril of my own life."

During this speech, Monime, trembling and bewildered, had not perceived that the horse, increasing its speed, had brought us to the entrance of the perron. The genius advanced to receive us.

"Come, charming Monime," he said to her, presenting his hand to her in order to reassure her. "You will enjoy here the peace and tranquility that ought to be the lot of pure souls."

"My Lord," said Monime, in a tremulous voice, "my brother has informed me of the generosities with which you want to honor us; I know that it is to the concerns of the first of our race that we owe favors so scantly merited."

"It is true," said Zachiel, "that I rendered at first to the instances of the great Seaton, but, beautiful Monime," the genius added, gallantly, "who could know you without being keenly interested in your happiness?" Then he took us into the great room.

I was surprised to see another old man appear, who emerged from a gap in the colonnade to the left. His tall and majestic stature imposed respect; his head was ornamented with a crown, his eyes were sharp and brilliant; a white beard hung down to his waist, to which was attached a saber garnished with carbuncles that seemed to illuminate that marvelous room with their gleam.

That venerable old man came to stand before Monime, who, far from showing any fear, ran to throw herself into the arms that he had opened to receive her. An action so bold on the part of Monime was bound to surprise me, especially after the weakness she had shown, but it was only to the presence of the genius that she owed that courage. I could not hear what the old man said to her in pointing out to her several grave individuals who were walking under that colonnade. Afterwards, he looked at me with a great deal of attention; I perceived that he was talking about me; what he said made such a great impression on Monime's mind that I saw joy and satisfaction shining in her eyes. She turned her head to look at me, and they all disappeared in an instant, leaving us alone with the genius.

He took us to separate apartments. In hers, Monime found several chambermaids to serve her. I found similar help in mine. A large cabinet full of books was adjoined to Monime's apartment; that room was designed by the genius to serve for our education.

"I don't believe," Zachiel said to us, "that you will ever have occasion to regret your Quaker, but I read in the eyes of the tender Monime that she would like to know how he received the news of your flight. Know, then, that in order to spare him a futile search, I had him told that a superior power has taken you both under his protection, and that he will only be informed of your fate when Lord Seaton returns."

"What chagrin he must feel," said Monime, "for, in spite of the harshness of his character, he loves us."

"You do him justice," said the genius. "Be certain that the person I employed to inform him of your departure was able to tranquilize him and calm his mind."

The next day we went with the genius into the library cabinet.

"I have formed great plans for you," he said, "but it is necessary for you to prepare to merit them by an attention worthy of the care I want to take in educating you. I am convinced that the charming Monime is able to follow the most elevated discourse; the heaven that has given her grace and beauty has also give her the spirit of order, the common sense and vivacity that are the marks of an honest intelligence equipped to receive the best education."

"I desire that ardently," said Monime, "But my Lord, will you have the patience to reply to all the questions that I anticipate being required to ask you, by virtue of the certainty I have of my ignorance?"

"Be certain of it," said Zachiel. "It will prove to me the interest that you are taking in our conversations. I shall begin be asking you both to banish the title of Lord, which only belongs to the supreme being; it is for his glory that I want to work for your perfection, and you can only attain the degree of perfection I demand by assiduous application, in order to try to grasp in the sciences what is true and essential.

"It is necessary to begin, my dear children, by disengaging yourselves from superstition and the odious dread of death, clarifying the idea of virtues and vices, and trying to grasp accurately the distinction between virtuous and wicked individuals. It is only by following those principles that one can attain the pure sensuality that procures human beings two inestimable pleasures, the only ones for which ambition ought to aim: wisdom and health; because wisdom is to the soul what health is to the body. You will sense that better by means of this analogy.

"Imagine sensuality as a beautiful queen, ornamented by her beauty alone; her throne is made of gold, and the virtues, in their best clothes, make haste to serve her; her virtues are prudence, justice, strength and temperance, all of which are careful to pay court to her, to anticipate her slightest wishes.

"Justice prevents her from doing wrong to anyone, for fear that insult might be returned for insult, without her being able to complain. Strength restrains her if, by chance, some sharp and sudden dolor obliges her to try to make an attempt on her own life. Prudence watches over her repose and safety. Finally, temperance defends her from all kinds of excess and warns her assiduously that health is the greatest of all possessions, or at least the one without which all the others become futile and can no longer make themselves felt."

It was by means of such instruction that the genius enabled us to pass several months in the castle without tedium. Monime familiarized herself so well with Zachiel that I was tempted to take her for a sylphide herself. His reflections were always just, often playful, but full of good sense.

One day, the conversation fell on the subject of the genii. Monime, curious to know their origin, asked Zachiel to inform her.

"For that," he told her, "it is necessary to reveal secrets that are only known to a few philosophers, but I know your prudence too well to fear that you might misuse that knowledge. Know, then, beautiful Monime, that there are several sorts of genii. The ones that are called sylphs are widespread in the air; others, known as gnomes, inhabit the earth; the waters are filled with undines, and fire is the element of salamanders;[7] finally, others are distributed in various planets, and bear names appropriate to their attributes. Those kinds of genius ought not to emerge from their element; it is only those of the first order to whom that liberty is accorded.

"You ought not to be unaware that God is the author of everything in nature; that he is the unique source of light; that he is an intelligent and supreme being. As humans find themselves find themselves at an infinite distance from that primal being, and they can neither perceive nor approach him because of the immense void that separate them from him, God wanted to replace that void with an infinite number of inferior substances—which is to say, demons or genii—which participate to a greater or lesser extent in the light of which God is the principle, or in darkness, from which humans cannot disengage themselves.

"Those genii are of two kinds, the superior and the inferior. The former have only benevolent inclinations; they carry the prayers of humans to the Supreme Being and bring back to them the benefits and graces accorded to them. The inferior, or those that hold to the earth, jealous of that commerce, oppose it ardently, because they have no other goal but to do harm; that is why it is prudent to bind oneself in narrow amity with the former, which are the superior, and try to render the inferior favorable, in order to engage them not to trouble that commerce with their malice."

---

[7] This taxonomic scheme of elemental spirits owes its popularization to *Liber de Nymphis, sylphis, pygmaeis et salamandris et de caeteris spiritibus* (1566), an alchemical text published under the name of Paracelsus, although Paracelsus was long dead by then and it is almost certainly apocryphal. It acquired the reputation of being one of the key texts of Rosicrucian lore, and many supposedly-Rosicrucian works, including the widely-read quasi-documentary fantasy *Comte de Gabalis* (1670) and novels drawing on it, such as the Chevalier de Béthune's *Relation du monde de Mercure*, employ variations of the ideative framework.

"I cannot conceive," said Monime, "how you can fly incessantly from the earth to heaven and from heaven to earth. Tell me, then, dear Papa, what you do with your body during these voyages, for I imagine that with good telescopes it would not be difficult for our astronomers to perceive you, unless you hide in a cloud."

"As our bodies are only fantastic," said the genius, "simple desire disengages us from them or put them on again, as the occasion requires, and simultaneously gives us the facility to take on whatever form we please."

"What a pity," said Monime, "that we do not have the same facility!"

"Would you like to change form?" asked the genius.

"Yes, I would like to have yours. What a pleasure I would have, my dear Zachiel, in imagining that Seaton and I could be with you incessantly, and that, flying here and there through the air, we would no longer have to fear the unjust pursuits of the tyrant who oppresses us! I sense, however, that those are vain wishes, whose accomplishment would be impossible."

"Not as impossible as you think," said Zachiel, "and if you feel sufficient courage to accompany me to different worlds where my presence is absolutely necessary, I might well be able to procure you the advantage you desire, enabling you to acquire fantastic bodies like ours."

"What?" said Monime, showing her surprise. "Are there several worlds? Oh, you delight me; how much pleasure I would obtain from that! Perhaps we would find protectors of oppressed virtue in others. Have no fear, my dear Papa; be certain that I would follow you anywhere in all the vast universe, without showing any weakness. Undoubtedly, the stars that I perceive, which appear to me to be attached to the sky like diamond nails, are as many worlds that must be different from ours."

"Yes, beautiful Monime," said Zachiel, "and you ought to know that between the earth and the ultimate vault of the heavens to which the fixed stars are attached there are several worlds at different heights that are not attached to the same sky. Those planets have unequal movements, relating to one another and forming various collective figures, whereas the fixed stars are always in the same situation. But I shall stop, as I do not want to give you a lecture on astronomy; it will suffice to tell you that those first principles were discovered in this world by shepherds living in Chaldea. Similarly, geometry was born in Egypt, where the inundations of the Nile confusing the boundaries of fields were the cause of everyone striving to invent exact measurements in order to discriminate his own field from that of his neighbor. Thus, one can say that astronomy is the daughter of idleness and geometry the daughter of self-interest. If I were to speak to you about the talent of poetry, I could not give it any other father than love."

"I am very glad," said Monime, "to have learned that genealogy of the sciences, but as it is a question of voyaging in the highest regions of the air, I shall focus for the present on that, and would even like to renounce geometry forever.

But let us return, if you please, to our genii; it seems to me that that knowledge has some connection with astronomy, since the majority are inhabitants of the heavens. Tell me, then, my dear Zachiel, why they have the facility of taking on any form they please?"

"It is," said the genius, "by habit that they have conserved it. It is necessary for that to give you an idea of the various sentiments of several philosophers; some have asserted that the Supreme Being had permitted genii to prepare bodies in order to place the souls of the first humans therein. Others have asserted that, if the first humans had conducted themselves with wisdom and decency, respecting the dignity of their being, the voice of generation would have been totally unknown in the world; neither amour not the distinction of the sexes would have been known, nor the flattering attraction that draws one sex toward the other."

"In truth," said Monime, "I beg the pardon of Messieurs the philosophers if I find their theory utterly extravagant. A fine project, if it had succeeded! What would one do in the world, if you please, if one banished amour, desires, amity and sentiment? Which is to say that these great individuals only wanted to compose statues as cold as marble."

That quip made the genius smile, and he continued his discourse.

"Men having fallen into vices and shameful deregulation, those philosophers made the genii act again, to transform the culpable into birds, quadrupeds, fish and mollusks. But without going into the detailed circumstances of those metamorphoses, I will only say that the first men, who, during their lifetimes, showed too much weakness and timidity were changed into women or mollusks; those who wanted to examine the divine sciences with too much curiosity, seeking to pierce the mysteries of nature, were made into birds; those who plunged into base and gross pleasures became quadrupeds; and finally, those who spent their lives in stupid ignorance were changed into fish.

"That, beautiful Monime, is the detailed succession, or, if you prefer, the genealogy, of the beings that fill the universe. The desire of each soul is to return to its fatherland, which is the star dominant within it, and the retardation of that return is the punishment for their follies.

"What I have just told you about the different theories of those philosophers is not universal, since it is appropriate that souls that have conducted themselves well during life should not be obliged to pass through those ordeals. Monime is of that number, and I am convinced that she will return to the star that is most dominant within her."

"In that case," I said, "she can only inhabit the Sun, which I regard as the most beautiful and purest of all the stars."

"Gently," said Monime. "It appears to me that you want to lodge me very warmly; you doubtless mistake me for a salamander, in suddenly pushing me into that globe of fire."

"What, dear Monime, would you prefer to inhabit the Moon?"

"Why should I not go there? I think it must be a very agreeable abode, especially for fops and coquettes, for there is no doubt that it is the star that is most dominant in them and to which they will surely return after death; that is what makes me think that life is more amusing there than on other worlds.

"Permit me, my dear Zachiel, to ask you another question. Why, in the story you have just told us about the metamorphoses of men, did you not say a word about the metamorphoses of women. Can one conclude in consequences that they have always made more use of their reason than men, since there has been no obligation to punish them? Doubtless those men changed into women presently form all the capricious, the foolish and the immodest, and those canting women who form a class in society more amusing than estimable.

"I agree that in the genealogy you have made for us of the first humans, it appears that the soul has no sex; in accordance with that thesis, if the genii had prepared as many male containers as female ones, a soul that is presently enveloped in one of those first containers—I mean one of those reasonable souls that have not yet failed the dignity of their being—must be very surprised only to encounter, in the majority of human figures, weaknesses, ignorance and caprices: pride, vanity, self-love and knavery, men devoid of religion, morals and good faith. One might think that they are those first male sinners, who, for want of being able to place themselves in female containers, because they were filled with reasonable beings, have been obliged to resume their original forms."

"I listen to you with pleasure," said Zachiel. "I confess that I had not expected that definition. It is true that women know admirably well how to turn everything to their advantage."

"Now you are mocking me," said Monime. "However, you are forced to agree that the greatest of men have often been unable to resist the power of their charms. And your Socrates whom you were lately praising to Milord, for all that he was one of the wisest philosophers of antiquity, found their commerce so agreeable that, in spite of his wisdom, he could not content himself with only one."

"It is true," said the genius, "that Socrates had two wives, Myrto and Xanthippe,[8] which contributed more a little to testing his patience. Thus, when someone joked about their humors, he replied, smiling, that he emerged from his house fully acquainted with the bizarreries and disparities of those he might encounter—an advantage of which he was often able to take advantage."

"Hold on, Mister Zachiel," said Monime, "I cannot suffer you; you are making bad jokes and doubtless think that they will give me a taste for the theses of your philosophers."

---

[8] The notion that Socrates, famously married to the shrewish Xanthippe, also had a wife called Myrto originates from an apocryphal work attributed to Aristotle. As Plato makes no mention of her, we can be reasonable certain that she never existed.

"Well," said the genius, "let us leave the philosophers in order to follow our genealogy; I am curious to know what you think of the quadrupeds."

"I shall excite your pleasantries again," said Monime, "but no matter; let us continue, since it amuses you. I can tell you, therefore, that I find it very pleasant that a man might do his penance in the body of a deer, a dog or a horse. I see in Lord Seaton's dog an instinct so singular that I'm tempted to believe, having learned our genealogy, that it was some gnome who had taken that form on your orders. In fact, it has talents so particular that it's necessary to assert that it is animated by the soul of some great philosopher. Tell me in confidence, my dear Papa, whether it is not that of Descartes, of whom you spoke eulogistically a few days ago? I confess that, in spite of all the suffrage you grant him, I would not be sorry to know that he was punished for the temerity he had in sustaining that all animals are machines similar to clocks—a thesis that I shall never believe and against which my reason revolts. It is a hypothesis whose falsity is evidently demonstrated by natural enlightenment, and to which all the animals give the lie every day in a convincing manner.

"For example, how could anyone persuade me that my dog, in which I observe memory, conception and reasoning, is not sensible not only to the passions that act directly on the senses, like hunger, thirst, pain and pleasure, but also to those of which the principal operations are in the mind, which include amity, tenderness pity, gratitude, fidelity, affliction and jealousy? How, I say, can I imagine that my dog is merely a machine, which cries without pain, although I see him mourn, eats without pleasure, desires nothing and fears nothing? And yet, he obeys my voice, and is afraid of my displeasure.

"I have reflected for a long time on the instinct of animals, and I am charmed that you have relieved my mind in imagining that they are the souls of the first men who are doing their penance in coming to animate the bodies of beasts. With regard to the rest of our genealogy I can say nothing, except that there are in the world a great number of those bird-men, who torment themselves in vain to discover things that are beyond their knowledge. As for the fish and the mollusks, I think you will dispense me from talking about them; I can imagine nothing in their favor, but I believe nevertheless that we might well be in the century of their reign, for how many of them does one see allowing themselves to be caught by hooks, as birds are by snares?"

After we had spent several months in the old castle, during which the genius continued his instruction, he said to us one day:

"You have not forgotten what I have told you about the plurality of worlds. It is a question now of convincing you of that by enabling you to visit some of them. You are not unaware of the different opinions of ancient philosophers who admitted their infinity; I have already told you that the planets and the fixed stars are as many worlds inhabited by creatures of every species, and that it would be as ridiculous to think that there might be only one ear of wheat in a field that seems covered with them as to believe that there is only one world in infinite space.

"Nature has not produced anything that is unique in its species; she loves to copy in her works; and by multiplying the copies she has made, she takes pleasure in varying them in an infinity of different ways—which is to say that her works resemble one another broadly and not in detail. Why, then, should she belie herself in only producing a single world? It is certain that there are many. I shall not pause on the differences between certain scholars persuaded by pride that they have penetrated the mysteries of nature, who have counted as many as three hundred and eighty-three worlds, nor those who have advanced that there are as many as there are days in the year.

"As you are sufficiently instructed," the genus continued, "to know and distinguish the marvels that I am preparing to develop for you, and I want to give you the benefit of all my power, it is to a number of those worlds that I want to take you. We shall commence with the planets, and, if you wish, with that of the Moon, which is the nearest to the Earth."

"Oh, my dear Zachiel," said Monime, "you fill me with joy; let us depart immediately, I implore you. In fact, dear Papa, it seems to me that I can already hear the sound of the celestial worlds, and can see the active and laborious inhabitants of the planets, and those of the brilliant stars, applied to their ordinary occupations. At this moment, my delighted soul is ready to break out of its prison to enjoy in advance the precious advantages that you are preparing for us."

I joined in with Monime to beg the genius not to defer granting us that favor. "Our hearts are known to you," I added, "and I believe that you will render us sufficient justice to be persuaded of the sentiments of the keenest gratitude with which they will be penetrated."

"It is true," said Zachiel, "that I know you both better than you know yourselves; I am content with your way of thinking; it does not belie the care that I have taken to instruct you, and it is that knowledge which determines me to distinguish you from other mortals. There is, therefore, no longer any question at present than that of the operation of metamorphosis into the tiniest forms. I believe that of a fly would suit Monime well enough, and as you love one another too much to be separated, I will cause you to take the same form."

"My God, stop!" said Monime. "Tell me, my dear Papa, before operating the change you are about to make, whether there are any spiders in the worlds to which you are going to take us. I shudder in advance in thinking about the dangers to which we will be exposed is we have the misfortune to allow ourselves to be caught in their webs, for if they are large, they will only make one meal of our poor little individuals."

"Have no fear," said Zachiel. "The fantastic bodies, far from attracting them, will cause them to flee."

"Oh, there is yet another embarrassment; in sum, my dear Zachiel, it's necessary that I confide all my fears to you. I will tell you, then, that I do not like the idea of only being dressed in a fantastic body, which, probably, can only be lined with criticism, embroidered with curiosity and ornamented by hopes; I confess that such a garment is scarcely solid, and appears to me to be a little too light for the modesty of my sex."

The genius could not help smiling. "Have you already forgotten," he said to her, "that I command a multitude of genii who are subordinate to me, and that it is in my power to send them from one end of this vast universe to the other? It will therefore be no more difficult for me to have a complete wardrobe of palpable fabrics made up for you in no time at all. So, beautiful Monime, all your difficulties being alleviated, we can now prepare to leave."

"Oh God! Give me another moment; you're not giving me time to breathe; at least think that it's necessary for me to talk, that I conserve all the faculties of my soul. Alas, I'm shivering, I'm dying, and can no longer travel."

She said no more, and our metamorphosis took place instantly. Monime then appeared to me as the most delicate little fly that one could ever see.

"As you've renounced travel," said Zachiel, "we shall relegate you to this cabinet."

"It's true that in the moment of our metamorphosis, I was afflicted by a mortal fear, but now that I'm a fly, I feel myself all audacity and lightness, and I protest that if I were presently in the seraglio of a great lord, nothing would prevent me from landing on his moustache."

THE FIRST HEAVEN: THE MOON

Chapter I
The Character of the Lunarians

We finally departed on Zachiel's wings. As we rose into the air, our Earth gradually shrank, soon appearing to our eyes as a dot similar to a comet. The genius, ever attentive to our education, first made us admire the perfect symmetry with which the stars were arranged.

"Look," he said to us, "at the Milky Way, in which the stars seem to be heaped up without order upon one another."

We discovered it to the right and the left, seemingly emerging from the depths of the firmament, which I could scarcely perceive as yet. My imagination launched forth in that direction, so to speak, in order to scan all the worlds, of which I formed a delightful idea; it seemed at the same time to be engulfed in the vast concavity of the heavens; already I was savoring the delight produced by the contemplation of an object that occupies the entire soul, but without fatiguing it.

The genius enabled us see distinctly all the beauties that nature has dispersed to ornament the thousand various worlds; we saw the suns shining and moving that appear to us to deploy around them the banner of the skies; I thought then that nature, newly hatched, was embellishing herself with the freshness of spring, in order to paint all the beauties of the first day of the world.

Monime and I were gripped by admiration at the sight of so many marvels, whose grandeur, fecundity and variety fixed our attention by turns. Zachiel, continuing his flight with greater rapidity, made us traverse a part of the immeasurable desert of the void, which excited a horrible fear in us.

When we approached the large silver ball that some ancients called the sun of the night, we began to discover the form of the Moon that appears to our Earthly eyes sometimes as a cheek and sometimes a nose, with an eye or a ear to the side, or sometimes as an entire face, which our imagination surely composes, and which our most famous astronomers regard as patches that are nothing other than chains of mountains, large rocks or great cities.

Unaccustomed as we were to traveling in those high regions, the vivacity of the air had almost suffocated u; we were scarcely breathing when the genius descended on the rocky peak whose summit rose up as far as the clouds. After having reanimated us both with a divine breath, which had the same effect on us as heavenly dew when it dampens a newly-blossomed flower, the genius invited us to admire the fertility of the country.

"This world," he said, "contains all the follies of the others, and it seems that all opposites are united here. You shall see reigning, at the same time, the most sumptuous opulence and the most deplorable poverty, science and talents often debased, ignorance and stupidity always recompensed."

"They doubtless have astronomers," said Monime. "Tell me, my dear Zachiel, what they think of our Earth, and whether we have acquired among them the brilliant quality of a star; whether they regard us as a luminous body, and whether we appear to their eyes as the Moon appears to ours."

"I give you my word," said Zachiel, "that your Earth becomes a planet for the Moon, in the same way that it is one for us. As the planets can only be luminous because they are illuminated by the Sun, which imparts its light to them in proportion to their distance, that which the Moon receives is sent back to illuminate your nights, and the light that you receive directly from the Sun, which makes your most beautiful days, is sent back in its turn by the Earth in order to render the Moon the same service. Although they do not see the Earth describe a circle around them, it appears to them nevertheless to perform the function of stars regularly enough."

"I suspect," said Monime, "that our Earth, instead of showing itself to the astronomers of the Moon in the form of a crude face, might only appear to them as a backside, in which, applying their noses and eyes thereto, they seek continually to make new discoveries and serious discoveries, as ours do with the patches on its face."

"It appears to me," said Zachiel, smiling, "that the air is already influencing your reflections; I would not have imagined that in speaking of such serious things, they could inspire such follies."

"I don't know why you're condemning my reflections," said Monime. "They appear quite natural to me. But I'm docile, and don't like dispute, so I'll abandon my thesis, and, in order not to displease you, will resume a grave tone in order to beg you to explain to me of what substance that great vault of the heavens is composed."

"I ought not to reply to you," said Zachiel, "but as I do not want Seaton to bear the burden of your extravagance, it is to him that I shall address myself, to tell him that a few lunar philosophers have explained the movement that the celestial bodies make above the sky that you see, some by establishing crystalline heavens that impart movement to the inferior heavens by passing light through all the crystals."

"In truth," said Monime, "I can no longer hold back; you're giving me a horrible fright; my heart is palpitating and my senses are troubled when I think that if, by some unforeseen accident, all those heavens were to break, the universe would collapse and the poor inhabitants of all the worlds would be sliced into pieces."

"Be reassured," said Zachiel. "Their thesis is quite false, since the heavens are formed of a fluid material like the air; but as the empire of the moon is not conducive to science or philosophy, I shall transport you to the bottom of this mountain, in order to enable you to learn the mores and customs of the Lunarians."

The genius then took us down to a plain enameled with flowers, where he caused us to adopt other fantastic bodies similar to our own. Gnomes were summoned at that time to serve us and procure us all the things that might be necessary to us. The genius always used the same resources in all the worlds we visited, while giving us intelligence of languages.

An admirable caleche was ready; we climbed into it and Zachiel took us along one of the most beautiful highways in the empire of the Lunarians. The roads seemed to us to be very pleasant, by virtue of the variety, the beauty and the fertility of the countryside; I admired the richness of their fields, covered with the precious gifts of Ceres and those of Pomona. Further on we saw vineyards, whose grapes were almost ripe, preparing and abundant harvest for the growers.

The landscapes were varied by pleasant houses, which, in truth offered nothing to our eyes but pretty houses of cards. The houses had no depth, they were all doors and windows, but the windows were ornamented by blinds or shutters, some painted blue, others green or red—which, in the midst of trees, had the most delightful effect in the world. At first, Monime took them for decorations of perspective that the Lunarians had placed there with the intention of ornamenting the roads to spare travelers from tedium.

On the slope of a hill we encountered a young courtier who was going to one of his trains. He was in a kind of filigree armchair drawn by a horse, which he was guiding himself, which seemed to me to be flying like a bird, and I could not help asking Zachiel why the young man was risking himself like that in a vehicle that the slightest shock might reduce to dust.

"What can oblige him to such imprudence? Are the inhabitants of the Moon formed of a different matter than those of our world? Or do they have enough presumption to be convinced that nature ought to respect her work in regard to them? Speak, my dear Zachiel, explain to me the reason for their temerity."

Without replying, the genius showed me the young man crashed, his vehicle shattered, his horse fallen and the domestic who was at the rear thrown by the impact astride his master's shoulders.

Monime, sensitive to that misfortune, uttered a piercing scream, and we ran to help him.

It was fortunate for the young man that he had encountered us on the same road. After he had been given all the necessary assistance, Monime came forward graciously to tell him that she was sorry for his misfortune and asked him whether he was injured.

"I am very grateful, my Lady, for your obliging concern; I believe that I only have a few bruises; my fall will not have any unfortunate consequences." To his domestic, he said: "Frontin, the pendant of my ear-ring has become detached; it's absolutely necessary to find it. Give me a lick with a comb. Do you have a brush? My coat is covered in dust, my beauty-spot has fallen off and I'm in a horrific state of disorder. In truth, my Lady, I'm devastated by the necessity of appearing before you in this state; go back to your carriage, I implore you."

"Nothing prevents me, sir, from offering you a place therein and taking you wherever you intended to go."

"You are heaping me, my Lady, with offers to precious for me to be able to refuse them; will you only permit me to search for my ear-ring? I have a singular interest in finding it."

"I can't see it, sir," said Frontin, "but here's one of the trinkets that was hanging from the chain of one of your watches. I don't know whether it's the left one or the right. It's a little windmill, very prettily worked."

The young man, whose name was Damon, delighted to recover that bauble, hastily pulled out his two watches in order to see which one was lacking; we observed that the chain was attached to an infinity of little trifles, including a weather-vane, a key, a cabriolet, a trowel, rings seals, little birds, a monkey, a Moor, cassolettes, grotesque faces and a thousand other puerilities, which seemed to be the attributes of their characters.

Damon then took out a traveling case full of little bottles filled with essences of different odors. He rubbed some on his head and hands, and sprinkled some on a white handkerchief, took a beauty-spot out of the box and placed it on his face, simpering. And, after having been combed, rubbed, wiped and brushed, he climbed into our carriage, where we were waiting for him, and Frontin on to the horse that had been pulling the little armchair, which Zachiel called a cabriolet, and we set off for Damon's manor.

Monime, judging from the scrupulous search that he just made for a trivial item the chagrin that he must feel over the ruination of his cabriolet, asked him whether it might not be possible to repair it. "I'm touched by the loss of those lovely paintings with which it was ornamented. Could they not be made to serve another, by touching the up with new varnish?"

"Fie!" said Damon. "It's a horror; it had done its time You wouldn't believe that it had served me for more than a month; I didn't dare to appear in it in town any more, and I had destined it for my little trips to the country. Oh, if you had seen that of Baron Farfadet! It was radiant. It appeared yesterday on our ramparts, to the delight of all persons of taste; I've ordered one that will be delightful!"

When we arrived at Damon's manor house, he invited us with a singular grace to spend a few days there, while an apartment was being prepared for us in his house in the city. "You are foreigners," Damon added. "It would be ridiculous, after the obligations I have to you, for me to suffer that you should lodge anywhere else but with me. It's the sole means I can find to procure myself the advantage of expressing my gratitude."

We could not refuse such a kind offer.

I was delighted by the open manner of the young lord. It is true that the Lunarians allow themselves to be penetrated easily; they exhaust the efforts of artistry in supplying their tables, in their furniture, their adornments, their pleasures and their ostentations, without conserving anything that might conceal their thinking from a stranger. Doubtless they believe that it is not worth the trouble of hiding today a sentiment that they might longer have tomorrow, for it is certain that they have an ever-active reinforcement in their language much more rapid than thought.

During our sojourn with Lord Damon we learned to know him; he was one of those fops who is affected by nothing except pleasure and dissipation. Damon had no other employment than that of pleasure, no other thought than that of amusing himself, no other taste than that of novelty. He possessed to the highest degree of perfection what passes as the art of being "good company" among the Lunarians—which is to say that he had as many fashions of presenting himself and as much variety in his expressions as is necessary in that society not to appear uniform among the various lords that admitted him to their society.

He combined with all those talents a repertoire of little stories, curious or malicious, and, in his terms, struck in good coin. He claimed to be informed of everything that was happening at court and in the city, and even boasted of being significantly involved in all those adventures. It was easily appreciable that with such extensive acquaintances, he was the first to acquire all the new songs, verses, epigrams and pamphlets, of which he made an indigestible heap, to which he added all the minutiae and bagatelles that appeared, as well as having the most profound knowledge of fashion.

We were occupied the day after our arrival in visiting Damon's manor, which appeared to us to be very well constructed. Monime could not help admiring the magnificence of the furniture, the variety of its gardens and the vast extent of its park; nothing so beautiful had yet been offered to our eyes. Monime thought that it was only polite to tell him how pleasantly surprised she was by the countless beauties that she encountered at every step.

"Fie!" said Damon, interrupting her. "It's easy to see, beautiful lady, that you still conserve the taste of our nation, but if all countries resembled one another, it wouldn't be worth the trouble of traveling. Know, then, that this manor has an utterly Gothic appearance; it's true that my father had it built at great expense, but I've come here with the intention of giving orders to have it demolished; my architect has given me a new plan, which is divine and much better imagined; you'll surely applaud it when I've explained it to you.

"Firstly, on the site of my manor house I'll have beautiful avenues planted, which will abridge my route when I got to court by almost half a league; I'll build another where my flower-beds are, from which I also count on getting a forecourt. To the right will be my stables, to the left a similar building where I shall lodge my dogs and my servants. I also want to fell all the trees in my park in order to pierce new pathways, which will give a much more extensive view from my apartments.

"Consequently, it will be necessary to change my furniture, which, although quite rich, has entirely lot the taste of novelty; those massive designs are no longer fashionable; they'd be taken for items of jewelry. My upholsterer has given me some new ideas, which are seductive. You'll agree, when I've had the pleasure of your company for some time, that there is no land in which the sublime in every genre is assembled as it are here; here, everything is of the most perfect excellence, everything is miraculous and divine; one spends one's life in the midst of luxury, one moves through pleasures and enchantments; a thousand agile and elegant hands are incessantly occupied in working with a ravishing dexterity one everything that might flatter the taste."

Surprised that so much extravagance could enter the mind of a thinking being, who ought to be make use of the reason supplied by heaven, Monime could not help saying so to Damon, by means of a sensible discourse, but which made no impression on the young lord, whose petulance and vivacity caused us to regard him as a Proteus capable of taking on different forms. The fecundity of his imagination regarding his new projects, the contrast of his passions, the inconsequence of his conduct and the rapidity of his movements made us believe that the influences of the air must act with much greater force on him than others.

When Damon had recovered from the contusions caused by his fall, we left together for the capital city. The roads that led to that city were charming; hills, plains and woods rendered the view very agreeable. We traveled along a beautiful highway garnished with a double row of trees that formed beautiful avenues.

The environs of the city were ornamented by beautiful manor houses with gardens that seemed to have been designed by enchantresses, forming a delightful spectacle. The gardens offered double terraces to the view in the form of amphitheaters; to the sides were beautiful trees shaped trees shaped into parasols or fans; trellises sculpted by expert hands, well-designed; beautifully winding hornbeam hedges; bowling-greens of every form; yew-trees shaped into dragons, pagodas, marmosets and various kinds of monsters; and flower-beds in which the flowers were enclosed in filigree baskets, with designs represented by variously colored sands. To the ornamentation of the flower-beds large bronze vases and beautiful marble statues had been added; cascades and pools of water surrounded them, whose surfaces presented crystal mirrors in order to double the view.

"It seems to me," I said to Damon, "that taste reigns everywhere here; these gardens are a charming visual feature; but I see nothing useful. For myself, instead of those little pines so carefully sculpted I would plant good fruit trees;

instead of the horse-chestnuts, I would plant walnuts; and instead of those sad yews that cover the walls one could establish espaliers."

"Fie!" exclaimed Damon. "I can't stand it any longer. It would be a horror; fortunately, that folly has never entered anyone's head; it would be the ultimate in ridicule to put in gardens what one finds in the country; one does not tolerate plants or shrubs here; one only sees porcelain flowers and marble fruits."

"I cannot see," I said, "that it would be so foolish to mingle the useful and the agreeable, and I would find it very pleasant to be able to pick a fruit to refresh myself while out for a walk."

"In truth, my dear sir," said Damon, "your reasoning has a coarseness that aggravates me; it revolts good taste. Fruit trees in a garden, picking them and eating them! Never praise such burlesque ideas. But you don't know, my dear Milord, that in order to be fashionable one should only esteem that which comes from far away, even if it only a vegetable, in order to find more taste therein. One ought to least to obtain it from more than fifty leagues away."

"You do not, it appears," said Monime, "have the pleasure of eating fresh produce."

"As fresh as your complexion, beautiful lady; it is a matter of a day."

"Tell me," I asked Damon, "What prevents your lands being equally cultivated; I have seen several of them that appear to me to be fallow."

"That," said Damon, "is because our peasants have long sensed the abuse to which they were once subjected of staying in their villages to work there with the sweat of their bodies without being able to profit from the fruits of their labor. By working in the cities they are almost always sure of living there in repose and comfort, and well-fed, because it befits the dignity of a lord to have a large retune of domestics, whom he maintains at great expense, the majority of whom only serve to ornament his antechamber. It is a custom established among us, which everyone wants to imitate, even at the expense of his fortune.

"You see, my dear Milord," Damon continued, "that one is forced by custom to work for one's own ruination, and if one has any talent, it will soon be annihilated. You might believe, by examining my exterior, that I am the most fortunate man of the world; I confess to you nevertheless that I am not without chagrin. My family persecutes me incessantly in urging me to choose a profession; they want to prescribe me the tedious role of a sensible man. It is not that I cannot flatter myself with being able to succeed in that as well as the next man; but I'm rich. I confess that I have a marvelous inclination for the sciences, but I would never dare to indulge it. I read nothing but novels and comedies, for fear of passing in society for a pedant.

"It's true that one would perish of boredom if it were necessary to imitate the majority of scholars, who exhaust themselves in the ancient authors; those men, bristling with dead languages, cannot please us. They work laboriously in the wellsprings of science; more skillful than them, we find it complete in newspapers and dictionaries, which one can even dispense with reading, since one has the assistance of almanacs, which represent all the sciences to us in miniature; add to those resources our bureaux of intelligence, where it is distributed almost for nothing.

"With that I have as much erudition as I would need to fill twenty positions; I have ambition, hopes founded on my birth and my talents, and I flatter myself on having a fine figure. I'm very popular at court; more than twenty women protect me there, to whom I try to prove my profound veneration; in truth, if I renounced such sure pretentions, my creditors would think me ruined and I'd have no more credit. I'm therefore forced to make great expenses in order to sustain it, gambling and spending nights with women, in order to keep myself in their favor. You can see, my dear Milord, that honor would require me to sacrifice the greater part of my wealth to attain any considerable position; and do I not still have the resource of an advantageous marriage? That, however, is what the Gothic common sense of my aged parents cannot comprehend; they dry me up with ennui and disgust with their antique reasoning, so I try to keep as far away from them as I can."

"I would not have thought," I said "that one ought to complain about listening to the counsels of reason. I would have thought, on the contrary, that in taking it for the guide of our actions, it enables us to enjoy interior satisfaction, which ought to be the source of sovereign wellbeing."

"Oh, what folly!" Damon exclaimed. "One can scarcely pardon those people, as insipid as possible, who find themselves reduced by their tedious reason no longer to being able to live with themselves. Fie! I'd a hundred times rather conserve my uselessness and be in fashion. In any case, if I wanted to waste a few moments in the study of laws and government, it would be stealing them from pleasures, and on my honor, I am not the master; I'm never left to myself; I'm incessantly embarrassed by the choice of the invitations made to me, and I'll tell you in confidence that I'm tyrannized by women; they vie for the pleasure of possessing me."

"I congratulate you for that," said Monime, with a malicious smile. "After the story that you've just told us of your good fortune, I believe that one can, without displeasing you, compare you to those new jewels that caprice brings into fashion and curiosity causes to pass from hand to hand in order that it might be examined more closely. Thus, in this world, it seems to me, according to your account, there is little difference between being a fine monster and a handsome man; both are mechanisms with springs, very easily put out of order, whose merit lies entirely in their form and movement."

Far from being annoyed by this mockery, Damon made a lively exclamation. "It's inconceivable," he said, "how striking, clear and luminous that definition is; its cuts to the quintessence and extracts the subtlety of everything. Do you know, beautiful lady, that you are adorable, and that you inspire in me a very serious taste for your charms? But I shall reserve for another occasion instructing you as to the impression you have made on me."

"Oh, I dispense you from that," said Monime. "You're far too busy to attempt to please me."

While Damon and Monime continued to converse, my curiosity caused me to look around. The city was already visible, when Zachiel pointed out several partly-constructed houses that had been abandoned by virtue of the inconstancy of the populace. I saw half-built edifices, here a manor house only lacking a roof, there various building in the process of demolition to give them a new form. Elsewhere, a prodigious quantity of workers were laboring to dig up a road in order to make another ten feet further away along the same line.

That examination brought us insensibly into the city.

Chapter II
A Description of the City

At the entrance to the city was a palace whose architecture seemed to me to be consummately tasteful. I had our carriage stop in order to admire its beauty, proportions and symmetry. Pilasters of the most beautiful marble in the world, ornamented with festoons, decorated its façade. Nothing could be seen more agreeable than the gardens, their situation and their distribution. In sum, everything about the edifice was charming; it seemed to me to be worthy to lodge the master of the world. I had no doubt that such a magnificent palace must be the abode of the Queen.

"This is doubtless the place where your sovereign resides?" I said to Damon.

"You're mistaken," he said, with a disdainful smile. "It's true that the palace was once destined to lodge one of our Princesses, but as its improvement has been neglected since, tastes have changed entirely. It's only small apartments that are in fashion; those have nothing pleasing; they're too vast and they lack an infinity of cupboards, little boudoirs and wardrobes; for in truth, my dear, I only know what can form comforts that one can't do without. That's why this old palace no longer serves for anyone but a few officers, who are granted lodgings here, as well as the Queen's workers."

Several magnificent houses were then offered to our gaze, and we eventually reached Damon's, where sumptuousness and the latest fashion reigned everywhere; nothing was more elegant than the furniture, nothing more ornate than the cabinets, nothing prettier than the boudoirs, and nothing more comfortable than the wardrobes, where everything was in the finest taste. After Damon had taken each of us to the apartment that he had destined for us, he left us in order to see to his toilette, in order to go to supper with the Queen.

The next day, Damon offered to take Monime to see the most beautiful places in the city. Charmed by his proposition, we got ready to accompany him, in order not to seem entirely new in various companies, and to be able to get a little closer to the taste of the nation, trying to present ourselves a good light.

Having traveled through various quarters, admiring the beautiful squares with which the city is decorated, and visiting a few of the temples, Damon took us to a beautiful promenade; several ranks of chairs bordered its pathways, which were occupied by the most brilliant people of the city. Monime thought at first that the location was destined for the pronunciation of some eloquent discourse in honor of Folly, who is the goddess most revered by the Lunarians, and to whom their finest days are consecrated. Informed of that idea, I saw her hasten to take a place in the rank of the persons who seemed most apparent.

"What, beautiful lady!" said Damon. "Scarcely have we come in, and you already want to sit down?"

"It's necessary," said Monime, "in order to hear."

"To hear what?" said Damon. "The conversations of all these ladies? But you're right; they're sometimes quite pleasant, always witty, feminine and light-hearted; they electrify the silliest individuals and often draw sparks; one learns the most interesting news there. In any case, there's nothing like the fortunate contrast of the fashion of acting with that of thinking to give birth to those sparkling sallies, luminous asides and intoxication of sentiment."

After that witty tirade, Damon began criticizing all the people that passed before us; no one escaped his satire; he had the secret of lending them all ridicule, telling us about their adventures, and in less than an hour we were instructed in the entire chronicle of the court and the city.

"I'll leave you momentarily," he said, interrupting himself in mid-sentence. "I've just perceived Faustine, and I need to talk to her. She was present yesterday at a scene that occurred in the home of the Comte de Merluche, by which she was greatly intrigued."

We saw him go immediately to join a number of people whose reputations he had just been shredding pitilessly, whom he nevertheless heaped with kisses, with demonstrations of amity that surprised us greatly.

I asked Zachiel whether Damon's mind was not slightly unhinged. "I cannot understand the young man's extravagance," I said. "Is it possible that all Lunarians think so ridiculously?"

"Damon is one of the most reasonable men in the empire," said the genius. "The ridiculousness of the Lunarians is manifest everywhere; it extends through their ways of thinking, their works, their tastes and their fashions; they have an affected language, an arrogant tone, free and unserious manners; they kiss one another all the time, address one another informally, swear and lose their temper; pride is their ordinary vice; the necessity of enjoying the moment is their maxim.

"You can, my dear Seaton, compare them to theater decorations, which always lose by being examined at close range, because their minds have no consistency, all their passions being vivid, impetuous and temporary; vanity drives them, inconstancy varies them, and moderation never controls them; they know no other measure than excess. You can see them become intoxicated by a mediocre success, and fall into depression at the slightest reverse; but their frivolity and love of novelty soon consoles them with songs and epigrams.

"They also have the resource of numerous periodicals, which always promise them an imminent triumph in times when they are at war; that is what keeps the fecundity of the greatest wits of this world shining. I shall not say any more, in order to allow your intelligence and penetration the care of developing the character of the Lunarians fully. I recommend you, above all, to be careful in your speech; for, in order not to make enemies, one must never deviate from sentiments received and authorized by worldly custom, even if they are contrary to your principles."

Damon came back to join us. He was accompanied by a young man whom he introduced to us, announcing him to us as Baron Farfadet I cannot express the degree to which the Baron pushed impertinence, ridiculous airs, false glory and the critical tone so scornful and so commonplace among the Lunarians; half of that society is occupied in slandering the other half. We did not require half an hour to familiarize ourselves with his brilliant qualities.

On returning to Damon's house I was very surprised to find the large drawing room full of people he had invited to supper; as it was nearly eleven o'clock when we returned, I thought at first that his petulance had caused him to forget them, but I soon learned that it was the height of elegance and fashion not to be at home when guests arrive.

When supper was announced, every man presented his hand to the lady who pleased him the most, took her into the dining room and placed himself next to her unceremoniously. I followed the example and sat next to Monime. The fare was delicate, served in little dishes of everything new that it had been possible to find. There were fricassees of cherubim, accommodated in camailleu, little turtles in blue sauce, green oysters with wallflowers, swallows with pistachios, escargots in roses, grasshoppers in cheese, and how do I know what else?—for I cannot list the prodigious quantity of dishes that were served with a neatness that was thought delightful.

At dessert, the table was covered with a flower-bed mingled with castles, forts, bastions and towers; all those little buildings were made of sugar, and everyone took pleasure in smashing them and hurling themselves upon the ruins. They were replaced by others immediately, filled with precocious fruits that Damon had imported at great expense. All the guests praised them to the skies; they found them divine, perfect, marvelous and enchanted. Personally, I bit into a few that I found detestable, insipid and tasteless.

When the sparkling wines were serves, the joy began to develop, and we suddenly saw a torrent of puerile banter and insignificant bagatelles unleashed. From the excess of license that reigned in their discourse they passed on to accounts of interesting news; an enameled box in the latest style was examined, filed with creamed tobacco. It was said that the return of the officers promised an ample crop of adventures.

"By the way," said one coquette, "did you know that the brilliant Mademoiselle Pomponet has finally married the fat senator who has bought the earldom of Lourdaud? It's said he paid fifty thousand in diamonds of the first water for that sepulchral spout."

"The woman is doubtless very pretty," said a young officer. "I must pay court to her."

"She's a provincial beauty," replied a precious individual, "devoid of a soul; a melancholy assemblage of features, which might be regular enough, but graceless, devoid of physiognomy, merely sculpted; one of those shameful faces that blush at every remark—so I believe that, in spite of the elegance of her attire, it will be quite difficult to make an exhibit of her in high society. In spite of that, would you believe that she's already had more than one adventure? That's why she would have done better to conserve her liberty."

"For myself," said Damon, "I find that marriage to be a perfect match."

"I'm of the same opinion," said Licidas. "I was at their wedding, and I thought I was seeing Lucifer espousing a Gorgon."

"Have you ladies seen the Earl's carriage?" said a woman who had not yet spoken. "It's necessary to compliment him on it; it's sparkling."

"It's true, said the Earl, "that it's radiant; it's a new style. Did you notice my varnish and the paintings? They're divine. But what's the matter, beautiful Baroness? You have a dark expression that petrifies me. Is it necessary to electrify you today to extract a few sparks of your wit?"

"I'm good for nothing," said the Baroness. "I have a darkness in the soul, and I'm repulsively stupid; I shouldn't have come here with such a tragic physiognomy. What do you expect? I'm seeking to distract myself from a chagrin that I can't forget; my bitch, the pretty little rascal, the most perfect things there was in the world!"

"Why, my Lady, what's happened to her?"

"She's dead, alas."

"Oh God, beautiful lady, the poor little beast!"

"What folly had she committed? Can she ever be bettered?"

"Oh, I want to give you another to console you."

"Here, beautiful lady, you see me being playful; on my honor, I'm furious. I had the most beautiful parrot in the realm, which spoke as well as one of our Academicians, which was all my delight. My servants let it die; those rogues are thoughtless; domestics are a scourge; they're insolent, libertine and give themselves airs that counterfeit ours in every way."

"I forgive mine all their stupidities because they're tall and well-built, look good and have sufficient intelligence; I like to be surrounded by men of intelligence who understand me at the first word. Besides which, when one has more than one affair, one needs a fellow with a little understanding, in order that he can help us to understand, in order to avoid the quibbling that might excite the jealousy of women who are attached to a young man."

"For myself, I'm sick of it. The Duchess of Nausica, who, has been impassioned for a week for a few talents that I've been granted, would like to keep me incessantly by her side, and I'm constrained to yield to the impatience she has to have me painted in miniature. It's necessary to be obliging enough to lend my face for three hours; it's enough to make one perish. No matter, I can't refuse her that consolation."

Monime, who was extremely bored by such conversation, employed the charms of her wit to try to steer it in a new direction; she finally succeeded in rendering it brilliant, amiable, dull of enjoyment and quips; nothing resounded of the indecency of the initial conversation; modesty, in concert with wit, seemed then to dictate all remarks.

The ladies, animated by Monime's example, caused the delicacy of their thoughts to shine admirably. They combined with it the graces of a purified language; fashionable terms were employed to render the frivolity of their ideas with more energy. The men, in their turn, put a little less conceit into what they were saying.

The conversation soon fell back into the recitation of pompous bagatelles, however, very importunate for individuals who were not amused by them. After having spouted a host of pointless things, they started to sing and to praise one another for their beauty, flexibility or range of the voice.

Although it was after three o'clock when they left the table, it would have been the height of ridiculousness to go to bed so early; a card game was proposed, and a part of the company began to play. Monime and I remained chatting with Damon and Licidas.

"By the way, what's become of the Marquis?" asked Licidas. "I no longer encounter him anywhere I expected to find him here; he's your friend."

"Fie!" said Damon. "What do you expect me to do? He's no longer recognizable. You don't know, then, that he's completely lost the tone of good company? He's become a uniform, tedious individual! It's fatal; nothing more can be done; I tell you that he's a horror, that he's not presentable. His little cousin assured me yesterday that he's now devoting himself to be sublime; he's decked out with all the defects imaginable—she gave me details; they're infinite. You can't imagine the extent to which he's taking extravagance; did you know that he's left his singer?"

"What? No, I don't know anything," said Licidas.

"Oh damn it," said Damon, "you must have been living in the belly of a carp to be so out of touch with the news. Know, then, that the Marquis, in order to put the cap on the ridicule, has paid his debts; that he's going to marry a virtuous young woman full of talents, whom I'm assured in miraculously beautiful, whom he's chosen himself; and that he shuts himself way with her every day. That's where his soul transports him, ecstatically, to sublimity and divinity. In sum, my dear, that's the only idol to which he sacrifices. What do you think of that metamorphosis? Don't you find it astonishing?"

"Oh, stop it," said Licidas, "you're exasperating me; do you know that your account paints a sorry picture? In truth, it's necessary to be stunned by the charm of such a rapid and radiant narration. You're divine, my dear, and I must kiss you. But in good faith, can you believe that the Marquis is taking his folly so far? If he is, I don't think he'll ever dare show himself in society again?"

Chapter III
Theaters

We spent several days making visits and receiving them; that is one of the great occupations of the Lunarians. A lord came one day, very simply dressed, whose face did not reveal any trace of make-up. A superbly-dressed groom gave him a hand; a number of domestics made up his retinue, clad in red coats with gold braid, with hats similarly trimmed and ornamented with beautiful white plumes. Monime's valet, who thought that all those gentlemen were officers, announced Field Marshal Cati, followed by several colonels; at the same time, he brought forward armchairs, and thought about shoving away the master in order to put the groom in the first place.

Monime, who did not know the lord in question, seemed embarrassed, not knowing at first to whom she ought to speak, but the Field Marshal sat down, after having paid her his compliments, and as the groom withdrew respectfully she observed the scorn of her domestic, and made her apologies to the lord, who made his visit rather a long one.

The following day, Damon proposed to take us to see a comedy. We had all the difficulty in the world getting there. It was a new play, which was loudly applauded. Monime and I, however, found it pitiful, the subject frivolous, devoid of intrigue and interest, lacking in regularity and plausibility, the denouement trivial and the declamation forced.

Doubtless the majority of the poets of that planet have forgotten, or perhaps have never known the talent of depicting the passions; it is to be presumed that they have never had among them a Terence, a Menander, and many others who have worked usefully to perpetuate good taste by pouring ridicule on various vices or the different passions of humans, in order to make them visible in all their deformity.

Monime asked Damon whether their theater was never occupied with finer and more interesting plays.

"We have old ones," said Damon, "which would doubtless be more to your taste; for you ought to know, beautiful lady, that no one in the universe has taken further than us the force and beauty of the tragic, as well as the agreeable and instructive in comedy. Those works could have their beauty then, though; that was the taste of our ancestors. Today, that taste has become Gothic; people perish of boredom at all those plays. We need the new, and it is necessary to agree that our poets are superior to the ancients. Everything that is given to us at present is superlative; there are frivolous intrigues, pretty tales of enchantment put into elegant verse, sublime phrases unintelligible to the vulgar."

"You have no poets, then," I said, "Who work to correct mores by means of light badinage, who make sensible the ridiculousness of a bizarre and peevish

47

character, that of a foolish coquette—in sum, that of a miser, a prodigal, a poseur, a liar, a schemer, and that of those people who lose themselves in false politics? It seems to me that all these ingenuously-formed characters might make a considerable impression on your fellow citizens."

"That might be," said Damon, "but don't you think, Milord, that with all our fine portraits, there are people who might find it very annoying that another was taking the liberty daring to make fun of them in public?"

"I understand," I said. "Which is to say that a poor poet who fears for his reception is obliged to retain his wit, in the anguish of a perpetual torment."

"Precisely," said Damon. "That's the fact; and I can tell you that I would trade all the fine actions reported to us by past centuries for the lightness and frivolity of ours. It's necessary to perish at all those great speeches, and Harlequin alone amuses me more than all philosophers; my heart dilates on seeing him, and merely reading the others petrifies me to the point that I dread turning to marble."

I understood by Damon's discourse that the Lunarians are annoyed by the beautiful, the true and the natural, since one sees them lavishing monstrous chimeras with the same applause that might be given to the finest pieces. Such is presently the taste of those people; one sees them stupidly admiring any novelty. I noticed that the ordinary resource that their poets employ to acquire their suffrage is extraordinary fictions replete with the marvelous and outré. The Lunarians allow themselves to be easily seduced by anything that bears any mark of singularity; noble simplicity, exact resemblance in mores and sage conduct in incidents have less impact on them than unexpected events lacking plausibility.

The next day we went to the fair. "I want to take you to see my little street-merchant," Damon said to me, "who is lovely, well-mannered and as sprightly as can be. Good day, beautiful child, what a pink complexion! How pretty she is! What a lovely hat! Truly, she has graces all the way to the ends of her hair. Look at her mischievous eyes; they're significant—and her eyebrows, as if they were designed, and that mouth, so prettily ornamented. Do you know, my lovely angel, that I adore you? You have a divinely-formed neckline. On my honor, one has never seen lace of such an appetizing design. Is she a blonde? Permit me to look more closely."

"Stop it, my Lord," said the vendor. "I can see that you're only here to flirt. I'm only here to sell my merchandise, and I don't have time to listen to all your nonsense."

"You're in a bad mood, it appears, my little charmer."

"Bad mood! Oh, one doesn't have time here to make bile; one scarcely has enough to have a bite to eat, and we have no need of Monsieur Purgon to chase away our humors."[9]

---

[9] Monsieur Purgon is one of the physicians in Molière's *Le Malade imaginaire*—a play evidently familiar to adolescent market traders on the Moon,

"How singular she is!" said Damon. "So you still refuse to relent? Do you know that you'll be the death of me?"

"Too bad, my Lord. I don't want to kill anyone."

"Well, what must I do to please you?"

"To please me, buy everything in my shop and I'll find you an adorable man. Stop it—no jostling. Here are novelties of every kind; look at this, which might suit my Lady; I'll give you a good price for cash."

I cannot estimate how many trinkets filled that shop; Monime furnished herself with several new adornments there.

"I find nothing so agreeable," Damon said, "as the variation one encounters at a fair: those cries, those compliments, those vendors of every species, in which one sees the effort of art in all the seductiveness that they present to our eyes Don't you find that it forms a spectacle that is interesting, striking and enjoyable, combined with the diversity of the games one encounters at every step?"

Damon took us to the comic opera, where we found Licidas, who had become one of Monime's admirers. He came into our box, where, after telling a few insipid jokes, he told Damon about the loss of a great battle, in which a part of their army had been cut to pieces, and was said to have been a complete rout. He named several of his and Damon's relatives who had remained on the battlefield; others had been taken prisoner. In sum, the consternation was general. We were sensibly touched by the misfortune that had occurred and Monime expressed to Damon and Licidas the part that she took in their grief, in the most touching terms.

When we returned to our apartment with Zachiel we spent a part of the night deploring the unfortunate fate of a number of families. Monime, scantly informed of the customs of the nation, mourned for all the widows who had lost their husbands, and would also find themselves ruined by the excessive expenses they had been obliged to make, proportionate to their position or their dignity. Others lost an only son, the sole support of their name and the hope of an entire family.

On the following days we did not see Damon. We thought that, uniquely occupied with the common misfortune of the nation, he was working in concert with the other lords on the means of finding some expedient that might remedy the loss it had just suffered.

It was true that he was fully occupied, but for a motive very different from the one we attributed to him. His days were spent running between the court and the city, in order to visit all the people of his acquaintance. That difficult exercise is customary among the Lunarians; one might think that they were the

---

although doubtless out of fashion with the aristocracy. Its familiarity is all the more remarkable given that the play dates from 1673, more than a decade after this scene is supposedly set.

49

nephews and cousins of all the important people in their society. It is necessarily the case that they have two complimentary formulae, one of congratulation and the other of condolence. Like an actor who plays several roles in the same play, they are seen sad or cheerful as many times as the different occasions require it on the same day.

The genius told us that discord between the generals had caused the loss of the battle. Far from acting in concert to attack the enemy, they had allowed themselves to be taken by surprise in their positions, each one blaming the negligence of someone whose position he desired. Far from punishing a fault that might have brought the State to the brink of disaster, however, they had been promoted and awarded considerable pensions.

"There are," the genius continued, "impenetrable secrets that it is forbidden to the citizens of this world to examine in depth. It is thus that those who are at the head of the council take every opportunity to ensure themselves of the impunity of their faults, and obtain by that means the same recompenses that they have awarded to others; for here, everyone takes his turn as chief vizier; it is a law established among these people since their creation.

"Meanwhile, the queen who governs them is endowed with all the talents imaginable; but such is the misfortune of sovereigns that the truth escapes them whatever cares they take to seek it out. The mouths of courtiers are not made to present it to them; they never expose things are they are. If no individual can boast of a thorough knowledge of the disorders committed in his own house, how can it be possible for a prince, almost always seduced by the number of flatterers that surround him, to be enlightened with regard to everything that troubles his estates? One ought not to accuse him, therefore, of the faults that are committed in his kingdom, since it is impossible for his sight to extend over the different objects that stir there, and is obliged to rely on the good faith and enlightenment of those he charges with the detail of its affairs.

"Thus, the science of a sovereign consists of being able to choose his viziers and generals well, and then to place them in accordance with their capacity or the extent of their enlightenment, distributing his favors and recompenses in proportion to the services they render him, showing strength and firmness in punishing them when they are derelict in their duty. Excessive clemency is often dangerous; an example of severity, made appropriately, retains the subject in obedience, prevents vexations, maintains order and avoids great evils."

"It appears to me," said Monime, "that these people follow a very different maxim, since recompenses are not accorded either to merit or prudence, but to the extent of their stupidity. It is to be presumed that courage, bravery and the advantage of vanquishing enemies are presently regarded as ancient chimeras, which are no longer fashionable here. It would doubtless seem ridiculous to dare to manifest the indefatigable activity that is the true character of conquerors. Perhaps those who are foolish enough to carry out some striking action that makes the enemy tremble are regarded as imbeciles.

"Furthermore," Monime continued, smiling, "you have told me, my dear Zachiel, not to castigate received usages. Thus, it is necessary to believe that there are good reasons for conforming to that new fashion, when recompenses become the fruit of poor maneuvers. Who would not allow himself to be defeated, at that price? For, in addition to the glory one acquires therein, they combine it with the advantage of conserving their existence. Is that not what is known as being heaped with the favors of fortune from all directions?"

Chapter IV
Portrait of an Old Coquette

Damon came to Monime's dressing-room the next day.

"You're very cruel," she told him, "to leave us so long in anxiety. Has the bad news been confirmed? Things are often exaggerated."

"I don't know what you mean, Madame," said Damon. "What is this news?"

"That is a singular question," said Monime. "I have every reason to be astonished by our security. Have you already forgotten the loss of that battle, which must have spread consternation through all hearts? What! You aren't touched by the desolation of a large number of families, the despair of widows and orphans?"

"Oh, Heavens!" Damon exclaimed. "Stop, beautiful lady; one cannot resist. That commencement is so tenebrous as to darken the imagination, and if you had been required to make the funeral oration of all those poor deceased you could not have acquitted yourself any better. On my honor, one has never seen anyone take her anxieties so far. Oh, we're more reasonable; that matter has already been forgotten. What do you expect? We hope to have our revenge soon. By the way, I have several couplets of a song that I need to show you; the tune is very pretty, the rhymes rather nice; they've arrived with the post; they're being sung everywhere. I'm in despair at not having been able to bring them to you yesterday; it's only novelty that's pleasing."

Damon set about singing the couplets with a gaiety that would have disconcerted the gravity of a rector.

Far from applauding those trivia, Monime was indignant. "What, Monsieur," she said. "Is it with songs, then, that a good citizen ought to console the misfortunes of the State? Is it thus that people of distinguished rank occupy themselves in the concern of repairing the misfortunes that ought to overwhelm everyone? You, for example, Monsieur, who flatter yourself of having your sovereign's ear, who claim always to be heard favorably, I believe that, in order to merit that confidence, it is at least necessary to be more interested in the public good."

"Oh, damn it, I can't hold back any more," said Damon, bursting into laughter. "Those are reflections that seem to be to be exceedingly rare. Permit me to tell you, beautiful lady, that you're a trifle misanthropic—but if so, at your age, in truth, it's shameful. I'm petrified to hear you; I'd be tempted to believe that you're not of our world. I don't know the customs practiced in the climes that saw your birth, but know that here, our reason serves us infinitely better.

"When some event occurs that interests the fatherland, we immediately open our eyes to what it will produce; often, that event gives birth to the thousand others, which similarly capture our attention; one can compares them to clouds that are gathering; the first is borne away by the winds; a second succeeds it, which amuses us; a third appears, which absorbs the first two, but it will be annihilated itself in an instant by an intrigue at court.

"Thus, new projects amuse us; we seize them avidly without reflection, and do not worry about the consequences that might result therefrom; the concern for our pleasures is the only one that flatters and occupies us. You are, in truth, too amiable and too witty not to conform to our customs. Good day, beautiful lady, I'm sorry to be obliged to leave you, but it's absolutely necessary for me to be present at the Queen's *petit lever*.[10] If I learn any news there, I'll be sure to make you party to it."

Damon left without waiting for Monime's response.

"I cannot conceive the reasons for such extravagant conduct," said Monime. "Tell me, then, my dear Zachiel, why their laws and customs are so different from ours."

"It is not in the empire of the moon that one ought to talk science or politics," said the genius. "All that I can tell you is that here, no one can follow the talents he receives from nature and education; everyone emerges from his sphere, quits his estate, in order to be employed in things of which he has no knowledge. The folly of the Lunarians is to want to pass for universal; they do not want to limit their sciences, which makes them commit new stupidities every day, but their passions are a labyrinth in which the further they walk they less they know where they are. The great are sometimes constrained to yield to that by their status. Always agitated, they agitate their society by the extravagance of their visions. That is what excites the hatred of reasonable people, who like order and peace, against them. In any case, you see in all worlds such a great mixture of wisdom and folly among humans, that one cannot admire sufficiently the inequality that makes them seem so self-contradictory. The one who appears to you to be the wisest in one matter is extravagant in another. It's not in the turbulence of this world that one ought to criticize their folly; there are too many people interested in maintaining and defending it."

In the afternoon, Licidas came to pay court to Monime; he told us that he had held an extraordinary council. The custom of those people is to begin by acting; reflections come later; the council had therefore been assembled in order to examine what had just been done. Opinions had been divided, as usual, and

---

[10] Although I have translated most of the original text's conventional French phrases into English, because they are supposedly translated from that language, this one has no equivalent; it relates to a convention established at Louis XIV's court, where the Sun King always rose twice; his *petit lever* was an intimate early morning affair restricted to a few friends, to which it was a great privilege to be admitted, prior to his official emergence into the wider court. The practice appears to have inspired the monarchs of several other worlds.

everyone went their separate ways without being able to resolve anything for the present, or anticipate anything for the future, either because no means was found to remedy disorders or because the difficulties put them off. It had only been decided that it was necessary to leave it to the generals to get themselves out of it as best they could. I believe that was the best decision they could make.

Licidas urged us with such ardor to spend the afternoon with him, and a few other people he had invited, that we could not resist the young lord's insistence.

His house ceded nothing in magnificence to Damon's. Licidas began by showing us all the apartments; he made us admire the distribution and the furniture, which was in the latest fashion. It is true that everything ornamenting them was admirably elegant: beautiful cabinets filled with bronze figures, precious vases, grotesques, little dolls, puppets, cut-outs he had made himself, which he claimed to be portraits in profile of all the people of his acquaintance; prints representing indecent figures. Pot-pourris of different shapes were distributed in all the corners of the apartments, and spread delightful perfumes therein.

In sum, I could not count the prodigious quantity of useless things with which the house was filled, and which were all extremely costly—but there was not a single book, nor anything that might announce the taste of a man who took advantage of the time that he ought to have for self-education. Only a few recent pamphlets were scattered in the boudoirs, because it was fashionable to know their titles.

Monime opened one of them, entitled *The Foppish Ape*. She had no doubt that it was the story of some lunar gallant, which ought to be curious and interesting. She asked Licidas whether it was well-written.

"Superbly written, Madame; it's divine."

"Such complete praise," said Monime, "suggests that you have read it very attentively."

"Me? Not at all; I assure you that I haven't taken the trouble; at a glance one can see what a work contains, and when the title pleases, that's sufficient. Besides which, it's by Enthusiasm, who is incontrovertibly one of our best authors."

Damon came in, interrupting us. "What the devil are you doing there? What! In a boudoir, a lovely woman has a book in her hand? Oh, damn, it's too comical. Do you now that your large drawing-room is full and that Miss Nayle has arrived? Madame, that's a gallantry of Licidas; he likes to surprise, and always does it agreeably. It's in your favor that this party is being held. You're going to hear the most beautiful voice there has ever been. The young woman is presently the delight of the court and the city; she combines the flexibility of her windpipe with the most noble, tender and touching declamation; her sounds, gestures and all her attitudes put the soul into a kind of delirium. Oh, Mohammed, if the houris destined to perform the music of your paradise resemble her, what delights for your blissful!"[11]

That's an enthusiasm," said Monime, "that announces to us a person of great intelligence, since she has the talent to awaken the passions with so much force."

"You're mistaken, beautiful lady," said Licidas. "The actress is nothing but an imbecile; she scarcely vegetates; she's merely a species of automaton, whose most perfect organs are those of the throat. As regards the rest, the fibers of her brain are too coarse for one to get a spark of common sense out of them."

While chatting thus we found ourselves at the door of the drawing room, which was filled with a numerous company. Monime was received there with the graces that high society gives; her hair was thought delightfully arranged; her attire was examined and her ornamentation found to be in the latest fashion. She did not receive this praise ungratefully; she knew the custom and returned it a hundredfold.

We had no difficulty distinguishing the admirable actress among the number of the musicians, by the urgency shown by all the young lords in anticipating her caprices; they suffered in turn fifty impertinences on her part before she consented to honor them with a song. The kindnesses that it pleased the young woman to demand of them were pushed as far as countless abasements. I suspended judgment as to who was the most imbecilic, the actress or the people she commanded with such great authority.

Hazard placed me beside an old woman who was heavily ornamented. She irritated me at first with gallant remarks, which she accompanied with little simpering grimaces appropriate to complete the ugliness of those aged individuals that nature has never favored, and cause everyone who looks at them to remark the folly of their pretentions. When they try to assume a gallant and child-like expression that was never made for them, can one not say that they are the only ones at that moment who are blind to their worth?

Attentive to the music, I received the irritations of Cornalise—that was the old doll's name—rather poorly, which seemed at first to offend her; it caused the irritating manner she had adopted, and which could not have been less becoming, to be succeeded by a certain piqued expression that did not suit her any better.

---

[11] This historical reference lends credence to the suspicion, which many readers might already have formed, that Seaton and Monime are not really on the Moon at all, but still on Earth, which is merely being viewed through a distorting lens in order to highlight one of the many aspects of human folly. That might explain why the Moon and all the other "planets" have exactly the same gravitational attraction and atmosphere, and why the nights on Venus and Mars are moonlit like Earthly nights; but if it is the case, Zachiel never admits the deception.

Monime, who could not tire of examining her, called my attention to her ridiculousness and stupid vanity by means of a smile and a wink.

"I believe," she said, whispering in my ear, "that that woman, who seems so proud and mannered, might well have been the nurse of the first woman born in this world."

I looked at Cornalise then with the eyes that Monime's quip had just animated, but she appeared to interpret that glance in her favor, and I saw her smile in such a hideous fashion, displaying a set of false teeth, that I had difficulty remaining serious. She took out a box of bonbons.

"Milord," she said to me, affecting a husky voice, "have one of my pastilles; they're the very best."

I thanked her rather coldly.

"I believe," Cornalise went on, opening her pocket mirror, "that I must look a fright. There's a perfidious wind today, which disturbed my hair as I was getting down from my carriage."

She readjusted the curls of her wig, plumped up her plume, pinched her lips in order to make them redder, put rouge on two prominent bones beneath two little holes in which one could perceive, on looking at her closely, eyes that seemed to be lost in the concavity. Those two holes were heightened by exceedingly thin crescents, but of the finest black that one could ever find; one might have taken them for silken thread that had been artistically stuck to her plastered forehead. From the middle of those two arches a nose descended in the shaped of a parrot's beak, the tip of which came negligently to repose on a sharply pointed chin, which, charmed by that advantage, advanced toward it to mark its gratitude for the little caresses it obtained every time that Cornalise closed her mouth—which happened often, for the reason that, in order to have the pleasure of opening it, it was necessary for it to be closed.

But let us leave those two friends to kiss as many times as they find the opportunity, in order to finish painting our Sibyl, or at least her bust—I shall go no further. I shall therefore say that beneath that divine chin, one observed a wrinkled skeleton, covered with a yellow and oily skin, whose backcloth had a slight hint of green in spite of all the whiteness that she had striven to impart to it. To all those decorations was joined a hump. It is true that it was not one of those large villainous humps that come with impunity to plant themselves in the middle of the back, but an obliging hump that had attempted to move in my direction for the facility of seamstresses. I am extending myself slightly; how can one not be prolix when one is making the portrait of a new conquest?

When the concert finished, we went to table, where I had the advantage once again of finding myself seated beside my infanta, who hastened to have me served with the most delicate dishes. Monime who was sitting opposite, between Damon and Licidas, examined all that simpering, which amused her to the point of not thinking about eating.

Damon, who perceived my distracted and expression and Cornalise's aggravations, said in the gravest tone that he could contrive that it was lacking the politeness that was owed to the fair sex to affect such cruelty toward a beautiful lady, who did not appear to have too much time to wait, and that I had the appearance of subjecting her to a sequel to the torment of Tantalus.

At that joke, Monime could not help bursting into laughter, which set an example to the whole company. At first, Cornalise and I were the only ones not to join in the chorus. I looked at her, with the design of making my apologies for my lack of attention, but I found her so risible and so disconcerted that, losing all my gravity, I could not help laughing in my turn, will all the more force because I was excited by the example.

Cornalise's fury then burst forth against me and against the entire assembly; she forgot her dignity, respecting neither herself nor anyone else; she would have liked to have a hundred tongues in order to be able to employ them in multiplying the insults that she hurled at us. As she was the wife of a man who held a considerable rank in the State, and also belonged to the highest aristocracy, no one wanted to attempt to respond to her, for fear of aggravating her further, with the result that after having spoken for a long time with a great deal of vehemence and volubility, she was constrained to fall silent by exhaustion and the dryness of her throat.

Old coquettes are not rancorous when one flatters their follies appropriately; it was essential to appease this one. I saw that I was the only one who could attempt that. Her weary lungs occasioned a dry cough that lasted a quarter of an hour; to soothe it, I offered her a glass of ambrosia, which she initially had some difficulty in taking.

"You have too much intelligence, my Lady," I said to her, "to be seriously offended by a poor joke that escaped without reflection. The feigned anger that you have just affected has intimidated us all, and I protest to you that joy will only reappear when you are willing to show us a more serene face. Do you not know that youth sometimes makes errors that it is necessary to pardon?"

"No one knows it better than I do," said Cornalise, "for it happens to me often. I am so lively that most of the time I don't know what I'm doing." As she said that, in order to give me an example of her vivacity, she made a movement on her chair that almost knocked it over, and caused a waiter to drop a dish that he was about to place on the table, which was tipped entirely over her dress.

"Good," said Cornalise. "There's another of my blunders."

At those words I had all the difficulty in the world preventing myself from laughing. I got up hastily in order to wipe her skirt.

"Fie," said the child-like Cornalise. "Don't take the trouble; it's a misfortune that will be to the advantage of my maids. I can assure you that they won't be sorry about the adventure, although they often have similar ones. You don't know me; I'm so foolish that I tear and pull and get myself caught everywhere. My husband is sometimes annoyed by my vivacity. It's true that I'm not what I was; sometimes I lose my make-up, sometimes my pocket mirror; another time, one of my diamonds; in the end, all my jewels go astray and my servants spend all their time searching for them. That puts them in a bad mood; they often take the liberty of quarreling with me; I laugh at it, and that cheers me up. Sometimes, too, I hide them, for it's necessary to amuse oneself with those animals."

"I'm sure, Madame," Damon said, "that your husband is delighted with all your mischief; one might say that your little follies, since it pleases you to name the most brilliant of your sallies thus, are very agreeable, and certainly make you the charm and amusement of all the companies that you honor with your presence."

I feared that Cornalise might take offense again at that sarcasm, which even I thought a bit strong, but, far from being offended, her self-regard allowed her to take it as a delicate and clever compliment. Damon continued to flatter the extravagant woman's folly by praising her for her beauty, her figure, hr youth and the ornaments that were distributed over her entire person; we made a list of her talents, especially praising that which she had for declamation, added that they ought incessantly to be playing a comedy, and that it was necessary for her to choose a role therein.

That was another of Cornalise's follies; she often put on plays at home, in which she was always insistent in playing the leading roles. A part of the night was spent deciding the next play that was to be performed there. That is a mania of those people; all of them have a theater at home, no matter what the cost; the bourgeois, who always imitate the aristocrats, put on performances too. There is no reputable house where people do not assemble to perform all the new plays that appear. No doubt they believe that they are honing their talents and graces by that exercise.

Chapter V
Portrait of a Fake Worthy Man

Several days went by, during which we were invited to the homes of various people, in which we only perceived the same ridiculousness and the same conceit.

Zachiel asked us what we thought of the societies encountered among the Lunarians.

"I have noticed," said Monime, "that they often make very uncomfortable visits, in which I believe there is almost always more politeness than amity; the majority only entertain with indifference or coldness. I don't know why they seem so desirous of getting together in order to sow such little cordiality and sincerity."

"It's because the inconstancy of these people ordinarily makes them renew their society every three months," said Zachiel. "Their friends in summer are no longer those of the autumn. They have lost even the idea of their former acquaintances. They encounter one another without any prior knowledge; they are very ardent to see one another. In the early days, they go for walks, go to plays, meetings, balls, to the country; the habit of seeing one another becomes tedious. As they have neither esteem nor amity in their hearts, they quit one another without regret. Familiarity soon destroys the seed of affection to which novelty gave birth.

"There are not enough resources in their minds to sustain long commerce; their inconstant moods soon lose their taste for the same objects. The charm of conversation requires wit and common sense, for in order to recount agreeably and listen to what is said with complaisance, it requires a mildness of character; one has to avoid obscenities, piquant mockery and furnish others with opportunities to shine in their turn. Those qualities have no impetus in these people, because they require judgment and they only have folly, to which, in order to increase their ridiculousness, they add a pernicious itch to want to pass for clever: precious diction, excess of liberty, imperious tone, esoteric words, insipid topics of conversation and a great deal of emphasis to say nothing. You must have noticed that all their conversations revolve around fashion; the spirit of criticism reigns over everything, and the decisions of their bravest individuals are often turned to ridicule."

We were interrupted by the arrival of Damon, who came in followed by Baron Fanfaronnet, whom he had already seen in several houses.

"I've finally found you, my Lady," said Fanfaronnet. "I would almost have renounced that advantage, without the passion that you have inspired in me. The Sun, which you resemble, and to which it's said that the universe permits no repose, is nevertheless fixed in your eyes to illuminate the victory that you have won over my heart. I love you, my Lady. You're laughing! Oh, damn it, you're disconcerting me. I protest that I've acquired, in truth, such a keen appetite for your charms, but so constant and so serious, that it has, I believe, been nearly eight hours that I have been thinking about you uniquely. Be accessible, therefore, to expressions of veneration and protestations of love on the part of a man who is not entirely unworthy of meriting a favorable welcome. You ought not to be unaware that goddesses always receive with pleasure the smoke of the incense that we offer them every day; something would be lacking in their glory if they were not adored. As you are far above all of them, since you combine in yourself alone all the perfections divided between them, it is certain that your attributes must be adorable."

"In truth, my Lady," said Damon, "I defy you to resist such a radiant declaration. What! There, if I know it, is the sublime and the marvelous! To stop the course of the sun in my Lady's eyes! That, on my honor, is the most brilliant compliment."

"And that's where you're in error," said Fanfaronnet. "You interrupted me precisely in the middle of my speech."

"Do you have something to add to it?" said Damon. "Believe me, I might be doing you a service; you were about to intoxicate yourself with incense, and inevitably, by approaching the sun too closely, you would have burned your wings."

"Lord Damon," said Fanfaronnet, "You're making a bad joke; your pride ought to be reined in. You'll have news of me tomorrow."

"Which is to say," said Damon, "that Milord is picking a quarrel. Your conceit believes itself to be invulnerable; doubtless your épée is made from a branch of Atropos' scissors, the wind of which alone can stifle your enemy. Wouldn't one think that he's going to devastate the shoulder-blades of nature? I fear that the earth might not remain motionless in admiring his prowess; everything ought to tremble at the aspect of his wrath."

"I can at least," said Fanfaronnet, "make you feel all the weight of my vengeance."

"I believe, gentlemen," I said to them, "that you're forgetting Milady's presence, and the respect that you owe her."

"I have not failed in that," said Damon, "and think that she ought not to disapprove if I reject the insults that a rogue offers me in my own house."

"Please, gentlemen," said Monime, getting up to stop Damon, "stop, I beg you, a discourse that frightens me, and whose consequences might offend me. Is it necessary to make a serious affair out of something trivial? In truth, I would be in despair to be the innocent cause of a duel."

"You are too good, my Lady," said the Baron, going out, "to interest yourself in the days of a man who ought, in truth, only to employ them in your service."

Damon tried to follow Fanfaronnet, but I joined in with Monime to prevent him from leaving.

"I'm keeping you under my guard," said Monime, "and will not tolerate your going to risk your life on a false point of honor. The Baron is your friend; why do you want to shed his blood for a word indiscreetly uttered, which you ought to forget?"

"You're taking this affair very seriously, from what I can see," said Damon. "I beg you not to worry about it. Be sure that all that racket was just a rush of blood to the head. I know Fanfaronnet, and I can assure you that he loves life to much to expose himself to the risk that he might be reproached for being dead. I'm perfectly certain that he'll wait for letters from the god Mars, which will indicate to him the moment at which our duel ought to begin. The Baron isn't one of those people who seek to die promptly in order to quit existence; he's in no hurry to visit the somber manor. More generous than you think, he'll scorn all the disgrace that might arrive in order to live a little longer. He finds the daylight so beautiful that he doesn't want to sleep underground for a cause that isn't obvious."

"You've reassured me," said Monime, who understood by this speech that the quarrel would have no unfortunate consequence. "I perceive that Baron Fanfaronnet is a magnificent man full of foresight; he doubtless dreads falling in the meadow and embarking indiscreetly for the other world. What can one do? Lords are prone to have many creditors; perhaps his would seize the opportunity to accuse him of bankruptcy. Now, as he's full of honor, he wants to avoid that reproach.

"Agree, though," Monime added, "that you were wrong to attack him, since you can see that he's limiting himself to the quality of a good talker, without being ambitious for that of fond memory. What do you know? Perhaps he's composed his epitaph, the point of which will only hold god as long as he lives for a long time."

"In truth, my Lady," said Damon, "I find your wit so sparkling and sublime today that I'm overwhelmed."

"Do you think, my Lord," said Monime, smiling, "that I'm beginning to acquire the right tone?"

"On my honor, my Lady, you're unrecognizable; I can't express to you the prodigious effect this change produces in my soul; I find your beauty miraculous."

Damon was interrupted by the arrival of the Earl of Frivole, who entered in a noisy fashion without being announced.

A fine figure! He had a doll-like face, with hair arranged like a swallow's wings that did not overlap. The back of his hair was enclosed in a purse ornamented with clusters of ribbons. A coat the color of a nymph's thigh, decorated in the latest style with doubly ruffed sleeves, embroidered stockings, red heels—what do I know? In sum, he was the distilled essence of all fops.

Frivole talked to us about his horses, his servants, his dog pack and his good fortune; took out various boxes which he turned in his fingers with so much artistry that the raises fingers simultaneously showed off two large diamonds, whose gleam as augmented by their continuous movement. Eventually, he got to his feet, performed a few pirouettes, looked in all the mirrors, simpering, came to sit down again, talked about the nobility of his ancestors, came back to his pretty face, which he could not weary of admiring, bowed three times, departed without saying anything, and flew away to plunge himself into a surly mood in order to go and be seen at court.

The Earl of Frivole was one of those fops all of whose carriages are elegant, the horses always spent, the runner always exhausted, who presents himself at thirty houses every day, promises to have supper at several and arrives at eleven o'clock to ask whether he was not expected, in order to repeat the news that he has heard, and have himself admired for five or six erudite remarks, although he does not understand their meaning himself. To those rare qualities he added a perpetual applause on his own account, and the noble ambition of wanting to appear the lover of all women, whereas he only had recourse to those who were decried. He was the victim of coquettes, the slave and imitator or their mannerisms, and the scourge of good company, which only received him as a marionette with which one could amuse oneself briefly.

Left alone with Zachiel, I said to him: "I cannot accustom myself to the lunar character; I find an eccentricity and a perpetual contrast in all their actions. I would like to know what the reasons are for a conduct so different from ours."

"It's because they are too mercurial and too scatterbrained to submit to the advice of reason," said the genius. "Far from profiting from the stupidities of others to avoid committing them, they are similar to birds, who let themselves be captured by the same trap into which they have seen a thousand others fall. That is why the stupidities of the fathers are lost on the children. These people have always had the same penchant for folly, over which reason has never been able to establish its empire."

"Since we're alone," Monime said, "I beg you, my dear Zachiel, to explain to me why one century differs so much from another? Can one not believe that nature declines in strength and momentum, and that a time of repose is required before great men can be reproduced?"

"That philosophy is a trifle lunatic," said the genius. "It's an error to believe that nature can decline; she modifies herself variously, but changes nothing in the immutable order, which allots all beings their places and their functions; the form of substances does not change; the gifts of nature are always the same; one can only look at humans as wild trees, which only produce bitter fruit if they are not grafted by a good gardener. It is the same with science and talents, which are only acquired by a good education; that is what improves humans and renders them able to contribute to the mutual wellbeing of society; but in the empire of the moon it is almost impossible to find reasonable people.

"If the fashion of being a scholar, of being sincere and disinterested could take hold among them, they would be much more fortunate. I'm sure that among the prodigious number of people who allow themselves to be governed by caprice and folly, nature has perhaps produced two dozen reasonable men in this entire world, which she has spread out in all the parts of the planet. You can well imagine, charming Monime, that a great enough quantity are never found in any one place to give birth there to a fashion for science, virtue and reason."

Chapter VI
A Description of the Sublime Manor

The next day, to satisfy our curiosity and simultaneously diversify our pleasures, Damon took us to the home of a lord of his acquaintance whose folly was paintings. The man was a curious individual who believed himself to be a connoisseur and who had dissipated the better part of his wealth in assembled the most beautiful works of all the painters of antiquity; however, although his house was full of them, we only noticed one original, which was undoubtedly himself.

Damon then proposed to exercise our charity in favor of a philosopher, whose research had consumed all his wealth. He took us up to the top of a house, where we found in a kind of attic a man so stiff and so black that Monime compared him to a stout stick of charcoal.

The man, once very rich, had found the means of passing all his effects through the crucible. Chemists, by whom he was still surrounded, as ragged as had become himself by virtue of their operations, had nevertheless conserved sufficient empire over their minds, in spite of their knavery and ignorance, that they still maintained him in the false idea they had inspired, that he would one day find the secret of the Great Work, which would compensate him amply for the loss of all his wealth once he had the facility of changing copper into gold. We saw no other furniture in the poor imbecile's home than furnaces, crucibles, and charcoal.

The same house lodged a poet with a great reputation among the Lunarians; conclude therefrom that purpose and thought were banished from the composition of all his works. It is true that in order to make his ideas heard he employed phrases so singular that one was forced to admit that he must have a very superior mind and talent to be able to assemble the twenty-four letters of the alphabet in thousands of different fashions without saying anything at all. Monime could not help comparing the poet to a sorry frog who mingled in profaning the divine art of Apollo by croaking incessantly at the foot of Mount Parnassus.

Damon, who was one of those fops who think themselves very knowledgeable because they have brushed all the sciences, of which they have only retained the name of each, took us the following day to the home of a geometer, who seemed to us to be a madman of the first order. The man talked to us about his science with so much enthusiasm that we did not understand a word of what he was saying to us. He assured us that he had discovered the quadrature of the circle, wanted to demonstrate to us that one and two only make one, and that the smaller fraction is equal in dimension to the larger one.

Finally, that man, whose abstract mind neglected terrestrial knowledge in order to contemplate the movement of the celestial bodies that surround the globe of the universe, added that, by means of his calculations, he had discovered that al is predecessors had been mistaken in their operations regarding the distances between planets by more than half a league; that he had spent several years calculating the different degrees by means of infinity, and that by means of those same calculations, he had counted exactly the number of the atoms of Epicurus. He told us about a thousand other discoveries almost as interesting.

To put some order into our observations, Damon, who had raised himself to the rank of mentor, took us to the home of an astronomer, who assured us that he had made the most beautiful discovery in the world by the surety of his navigation, which no one before him had yet been able to find. It was, he told us, the longitudes. He had to give us a very long lecture to set out the knowledge he had acquired regarding all the others. The man took us up to the top of his house; there, in a cabinet, where the scholar ordinary made his observations, he showed us, with the aid of a telescope, a prodigious quantity of stars, of which he knew all the names. It seems that he kept an exact record of everything that happened in the heavens; all destinies were known to him—but he did not know his own, which, Zachiel told us, was to drown in a pond while trying to discover a long-tailed comet that had been announced and had not appeared.

Damon wanted to take advantage of the opportunity to have his horoscope drawn up. The astronomer, after having asked him for the time of his birth, examined his books, leafing through them for a long time, drew various diagrams, and told him, with a great deal of emphasis, that he found in the signs that had presided over his birth, the house of Taurus; that in considering the bases and aspects of those signs, the saw clearly therein that he could not avoid bearing the antlers of a deer.

"Because," the scholar added, "in the fifth house, in which you were born, all the malign aspects are encountered in battery, all the signs bearing horned weapons, like the Aries the ram, Capricorn the goat and Scorpio. Venus and Mercury are dominant over the rest, which means that you will be very fortunate."

We then went to the house of a mechanician, who showed us a prodigious quantity of bagatelles that amused Damon infinitely. The man assured us that he had discovered the secret of perpetual motion; it was a curious kind of pendulum, all of whose mechanism was visible. Unfortunately for the honor of that beautiful discovery, however, the machine stopped as we were examining its springs very attentively. The author of the curious piece seemed to us to be extremely disconcerted; he nevertheless assured us that he could see the defect, and that he was only mistaken very rarely, about things that he found it very easily to remedy.

The next day, Damon, who thought it almost a duty to amuse us, proposed that we go to visit the Sublime Manor, the name he used to designate the lodgment of all the theoreticians and all the makers of projects who were entertained at the expense of the State. Monime, curious to hear the sublime geniuses reasoning, accepted the offer.

When we arrived at the Manor, I examined the structure, which appeared to me sufficiently baroque to dispense with giving a description of it here. After we had traversed a large courtyard we encountered a pale, fleshless man with black hands, a muddy face, a very stiff coat, with dirty linen and wild eyes. The man accosted us with a grave expression and told us, by means of a vague discourse, that he had been working for more than ten years to invent new tools appropriate to serve in all manufacturing processes. He added that, by means of those implements, he claimed that a single worker could do the work of more than a hundred.

Another came to meet us and took us to one side, in order to tell us in confidence that he had found a new and very useful method of cultivating the soil; the method consisted of moving a plow without the aid of horses or oxen, by means of attaching it to sails that would go where the wind blew, drawing the plow like a ship. It would be of great utility to the citizens, in view of the savings that would result by suppressing a large number of animals that were currently employed for that purpose, and the upkeep of which was very costly.

We went into a study thereafter, where was saw a grave physician, whose principal subject of study was the science of government. That man, wrapped up in his new system, believed himself to be the only citizen in a position to discover the causes of all the maladies of a realm, and the only one who could find the remedies appropriate to cure it. He claimed that the natural body and the body politic were perfectly analogous, and that both could be treated with the same remedies. That was the method he intended to employ.

"It's necessary to remark, sirs," he said to us, "that the people at the head of the government always have humors more bitter than others, which often causes them obstructions of the heart, weakens their head, renders their mind debilitated, and occasions frequent convulsions followed by a canine hunger, which necessarily causes indigestions, combined with a contention of the nerves in all their limbs, which puts them continually in movement. Now, to remedy all these ills, I intend to give them astringent remedies, palliatives and laxatives, and to reiterate them at each of their assemblies. It is only by that means that one can bring about a unanimity of votes, conciliate different opinions, render speech to the mute, close the mouths of declaimers, calm the impetuosity of young viziers, reheat and reanimate the blood of the old, in order to put them in a state to give weight to the authority of the law, which is confided to them.

"It will also be necessary," the doctor added, "that in each of the assemblies, after an opinion has been offered and supported by the strongest means, that the sovereign resolves, for the good of the state, to conclude the contrary proposition."

Damon complemented the doctor on the vast extent of his new system, which he thought delightful, and added that he would speak to their sovereign about it that very evening.

After leaving the physician, we traversed a large galley in order to visit two Academicians who had been occupied for a long time in discovering means of levying new taxes without causing the people to murmur. The project of the first seemed to me to be rather singular, in that it involved establishing a tax on the vices and follies of humans. It is certain that the method in question, directed with prudence, might perhaps contribute to rendering people less vicious, but how can one go about establishing taxes on sins and vices when people in this world think that they are all perfect, as they do in all the others?

His colleague's project, entirely opposite to the first, appeared to me to be much simpler in its execution. I thought the idea so good that I asked him for a copy of it, which he was pleased to give me because it flattered his vanity. I shall translate it here without changing anything.

The project consisted of levying a new duty on all subjects that was to be proportional to their income or to the charges and dignities with which they were decorated, but the tax would only be established on the virtues, talents and good qualities of the mind and the body. Each of the citizens would be his own judge, and the duty would only be applied to the advantages he agreed himself that he had received from nature; his own disposition would set the level.

The heaviest duties would be imposed on the minions of Venus, proportional to the favors that they had received on the part of that goddess; one would rely for that article, as for the others, on the good faith of fops: wit, valor, flexibility, intrigue, exterior graces, stature and figure would be estimated at the same rate as honor, probity, wisdom, modesty and good faith in contracts. In brief, all the moral virtues would bring in nothing; the people of the world were not in a good enough condition to be driven to excel in that manner. Women, old and young, would not be exempt from those duties; the father of a family would be obliged to pay the tax imposed on his children, in accordance with the declaration he made of their perfections.

Several bureaux were established for the execution of that project, in which the clerks appointed for the supervision and receipts of various taxes had to have the graces or talents annexed to the duties that their positions demanded. It was believed to be necessary, in order to prevent partiality or fraud, to attach to the door of each office a large tariff, in which all the inhabitants could read the price that their condition or fortune imposed on the talents, graces and merits to which they laid claim. By that means, no one could rightfully complain about their lot, since they themselves were its arbiter.

On leaving the academicians, we passed through a large hall where several pashas were occupied in composing music. The hall was filled with various instruments, to one side was a cabinet whose walls were garnished with large folio volumes. Several financiers were visible within it ranged around a table, each holding one of the large volumes, which contained their code, their laws and their customs, which they were amusing themselves annotating, in order to confuse them in such a way as to enable them to confuse judges and force them thereafter to follow their decisions.

Several further visionaries were offered to our curiosity, but their new systems appeared to me to be so absurd that I shall dispense with reporting them.

Monime, who could not get over the folly and extravagant ideas of the individuals we had just visited could not help talking about it to the genius.

"It is thus," he told her, "that the majority of people stray into falsehood, in trying to raise themselves above their sphere. No one in this world follows the talent appropriate to him. If men fulfilled their duties, there would be nothing false in their way of thinking, their taste or their conduct; they would show themselves as nature had formed them; they would judge things by the light of reason; there would be justice and proportion in their views and their sentiments; their taste would be true, it would be simple; it would come from them and they would follow it by choice and not by custom or hazard. But beautiful Monime, you must have perceived that all these people seem to have made it a duty to trouble the harmony of their estate by false ideas that draw them insensibly away from the fixed point to which they ought to be attached. No one any longer has an ear sufficiently accurate to hear that cadence perfectly.

Damon did not see us for a few days; he spent them at court. He came with Licidas; after a rather frivolous conversation, they proposed to Monime to make a tour. She agreed, and, climbing into the carriage, she instructed the coachman to take us to the Elysian Fields.

"Oh Fie!" cried Damon. "But we'll die of boredom there; do you know, lovely lady, that one no longer sees anyone on the promenade but souls in pain? Please, wait until we're dead to send us there. You haven't yet seen our ramparts; it's presently there that all the important people assemble. Why not follow the fashion? Don't you want to make that generous effort in our favor?"

"Gladly," said Monime.

Those ramparts, so vaunted, are bordered on both sides by very tall buildings. The buildings in question limit the view, and one can only breathe noxious air on that promenade, produced by the filth brought there from all parts of the town. It was, nevertheless, in that arid location where, in magnificent carriages, we saw the wife of the aristocracy and the bourgeoisie shining, along with the Marquis and the financier, who were not distinguished either by their arms or their livery. Where did that come from? It is fashion that prohibits it; so that estates are confused, and it is permissible for all citizens to find the fashion most agreeable to them of ruining themselves.

It is, therefore, to those famous ramparts that the Lunarians go in a crowd in order to have people admire the paintings that decorate their carriages; it there that the women one takes for figures in pastel, by virtue of the different colors that illuminate their faces, show off the gleam of their diamonds and display all the elegance of their adornment; it is there that men, lying nonchalantly facing one another, show off the richness of their attire, with their hands in the air to make them seem whiter, and also to show off large diamonds, or the delicacy of a fingertip, to whom flowers seem to be attached for no reason; those men, as dressed up as women, who believe themselves more beautiful than the god of day, look down from the height of their conceit on the simplicity of the people who admire them, and present to the eyes of a rational spectator, if there are any in that world, a living depiction of their folly.

We cast our gaze over those who were strolling on foot. The men, like the women, have an affected gait, cadenced and twisted steps, head held high, nose in the air, bowing deeply, smiling at the fops who, with one hand on the hip, raising one shoulder and lowering the other, gazing at the women through lorgnettes, muttering between their teeth a few new couplets from the vaudeville in fashion. Others, with long hair, which descends in a point to the lower back, dare not impart any movement to their bodies for fear of disturbing one of those hairs, which they doubtless believe that amour has attached to them expressly to captivate women, whom they want to honor them with one of their glances, provided that they are facing them; for, like wolves, they cannot turn their heads without turning their entire bodies.

Chapter VII
Which Contains Nothing New

The genius, who had absented himself for a few affairs that had summoned him to another world, came into Monime's apartment one day. Her maids withdrew, and we remained alone with him.

"Oh, my dear Zachiel," she said to him, "your absence seemed long to me; do you think one can amuse oneself without you on a world where we have as yet encountered nothing but fools and imbeciles? Can I, then, not have the satisfaction of seeing a rational man? Please, before we leave this planet, take us yourself to see a few men of letters."

The genius consented to that, and took us the following day to the home of a man full of intelligence, who received us very affably. He took us into a study which was filled with neatly-bound books. I picked up one of them, whose title was: *A Digest of History, with notes, in which one sees the Commencement of the Splendor of the Empire.*

Curious to look through it, I fell at first on the origin of sofas and chaise-longues; the same year, the women of high society had adopted skirts garnished with hoops, and, in augmenting the elegance of their adornments, had learned to paint their faces in several colors; they had also introduced the vapors, which, by the succession of time, had passed to men.

The second chapter informed me in which year the fops had invented the variety of carriages and their costumes, scatterbrained airs, light compliments pronounced in a drawling voice, divine sighs, amours of a day, small houses, puppets, flowering turnips and thousand similar petty curiosities.

I visited several others, which appeared to me to be rather interesting, but which reduced my curiosity considerably.

It was surprising to find there only fairy tales, more appropriate to amuse children than to satisfy the mind of a scholar; not a single book on morality, not one history, nor anything instructive. There was nothing but stories, little works of fiction full of fantasy and hyperbole, which, we were nevertheless assured, had an allegorical meaning.

"I cannot conceive, sir," I said, "that a man of intelligence, a scholar, can amuse himself with such nonsense. Have you no authors here more zealous for their compatriots, who can occupy themselves with the concern of instructing them, by putting the most memorable features and the most singular events that happen in the world before their eyes? A delicate and light critique might perhaps make some impression on their minds; when something ridiculous is well-described, I believe that one ought to be ashamed to find oneself in the situation that is being reproached. Thus they can be corrected while being diverted."

"You speak like a sensible man," said the scholar, "but in our world people do not reason; people only like novelty; the natural inconstancy that reigns among us constrains a man of letters incessantly to engender new ideas. Here people prefer the singular to the beautiful, the agreeable to the useful, because it makes a more vivid impression. That is why ridicule is dominant in everything; the curiosity of readers causes the number of bad books to increase.

"A singular title is a trap for a curious person, easy to deceive, the name of a fashionable author increases the price. I have two large bookcases filled with large volumes that have only been written with the intention of clarifying a point of mythology; I defy you, however, however much attention you bring to reading them, to be able to understand the subject that might have formed the dispute, or the objections that they employ to combat their adversaries; in sum, they are books that are produced in order to animate the zeal of partisans.

"In general, people are only avid for criticism, puerility and trivia. The greater number of people would think that they were degrading themselves if they occupied themselves with studying the fundamental laws of the empire; only a few people of reason and good faith any longer know their rights and privileges. Philosophy and pedantry are for them synonymous; they have a sovereign scorn for anyone who, in occupying themselves usefully, finds more perfect pleasures than sleeping by day, spending the night at table with women, or displaying the face of a doll in the evening, at some theater or steam-bath, chatting mechanically there about a number of stupidities. It seems that nature, informing them, only wanted to produce a kind of animal, half human and half ape; their lives pass without a single moment's reflection, nothing but a sequence of debauches in which, believe me, they consult neither the public good nor their own.

"You, Monsieur, who are a foreigner, whose customs are doubtless very different from ours, will agree with me that when it is not animated by honor, praise or any other motive, the heart of a scholar sinks, and the desire to distinguish oneself languishes.

"What is the point, a man of letters will say, of devoting myself to incessant labor, exhausting my health in late nights, in order to procure the utility of the public good, in wanting to impart the knowledge that I have acquired by assiduous hard work, if that unjust public makes more of a wretched ruffian, fattened on the blood of widows and orphans, than all the scholars in the world, and if, by a deplorable abuse, wealth honors a boor who barely vegetates, while true merit cannot render the same service to an honest man?

"That is why one only sees here men of talent carefully cultivating the puerile talent of arranging words, in which there is nothing but sounds, cadence and harmony, as in an opera, when one probably ought to expect things that respond to the pompous and interesting title under which they are announced. But those sounds are so soft, those words adapted to one another in such a singular and extraordinary fashion that it requires a very particular talent to excel in that art, and one that is even more admirable to divine what they mean. For there is every reason to believe that those authors have not understood themselves, especially when they strive in their writings to prove to us that intelligence and judgment only consist of a certain conformation of fibers in the brain, which bring us to science, talent, virtue or debauchery.

"According to those fine minds, you see, everything is due to chance. But ask them to what you owe the fact that you are not born stupid or bewildered. Almost nothing, they will tell you; to a slight disposition of imperceptible fibers; ultimately, to something that the most delicate anatomy can never perceive."

"Which is to say," I put in, interrupting the scholar in order to give him time to catch his breath, "that your fine minds try to sustain that there is none of them who can have merit or talent independent of hazard; that, no doubt, is where they obtain the noble privilege that accords them the right to be scornful of all men. But if, before appropriating something and extracting vanity therefrom, they would make sure that it belonged to them, there would not be so much pride in the world."

The scholar took us into another room filled with excellent books. "I think, my Lord," he said to me, "that these will be more to your taste. Would you believe that the majority of our fops condemn, without having read them, a large number of books by our ancient authors? It is taste, they say, that informs them on the first page of a book that all scholars were nothing but fools, and taste is born in them without study and without care; is that not marvelous? They all credit themselves with erudition, but you must have noticed that their principal occupation is the table; the second is calumny and the third saying stupid things and talking continuously about themselves. Furthermore, the things that happen in that society are not made to be treated seriously; it follows necessarily that all our works resemble perspectives, to which one must give several points of view."

"From what I see," said Monime, "your treatises on morality must be regarded here as speculations on wisdom, which can only be boring. I've perceived that no esteem is accorded to merit, and that virtue counts for nothing."

"It's true," said the scholar. "That is why our most celebrated authors are reduced at present only to composing allegorical tales, because any more elevated genre of works becomes suspect. The high sciences are banished from the world. The mind always hindered by the dread of displeasing someone, one dares not expose one's thoughts to daylight, one does not trust one's reason. Why? It is because wisdom is only founded on temperament and nature conserves all her rights here.

"You can judge by that how the reason that honest people cherish has lost its credit; it is, in consequence, no longer in a state to make use of its authority, since people do not hold it in high enough esteem to make use of it; but one is constrained to conform to fashion, often praising that which appears ridiculous. Among us, dissimulation is the tightest bond of our societies. As one often finds oneself in the necessity of frequenting people that one cannot like or esteem, artifice takes the place of verity, politics substitutes for cordiality, and the necessity of reaching agreement renders that disguise excusable for people who think differently.

"All our citizens, however, think they are happy; they make every effort to persuade themselves of it; but I am not duped. Why? It's because I know that superior happiness consists of three things, which are virtue, health and the necessary. What does it matter, in order to be happy, that the body is fed on delicate foodstuffs, if the mind only drinks bile and absinthe? That is my morality in brief; it is not to the liking of the Lunarians because their minds allow themselves to be seduced by self-esteem rather than persuaded by reason and the majority of rich men are knavish, tyrannical, presumptuous and ignorant."

Monime and I were delighted by that scholar's conversation, and with the choice of the genius. We quit him with regret, groaning over the extravagance of the people.

We took our leave of Lord Damon, who seemed very put out by our departure. He made a thousand entreaties to get us to stay longer, but our sojourn on the planet was to be limited, and we were obliged to depart in order to visit various other provinces, in which we observed the same mentality and taste for fashion, that of novelty being the dominant passion of the people. Everywhere, a fop wants to pass for a fine mind; it suffices for him to criticize, well or badly, all the theatrical productions and new tales; he even often extends his acquaintance as far as novels, provided that they have no moral point, for then he finds them insipid and deadly boring; he scarcely turns a few pages before condemning them without appeal.

One can say, after mature examination, that their life is as uniform as the course of the sun: in the morning, at the Queen's *petit lever*, or in the antechamber of a vizier; the rest of the day at table, at play or on the promenades; it is then considered good to run around all the theatrical performances in the same day; in one there is a new actress who is to appear in one act; in another one wants to see an *entrechat* or a *pas de deux*; the rest of the time concludes in debauchery in one of their small houses. In general, one can compare the Lunarians to chameleons, servile imitators of the virtues or faults of those who govern them. Sad individuals, devotees, gamblers or debauchees, one sees them immediately honor those various vices, similar to real automata, which a single machine or identical mechanisms cause to move.

Chapter VIII
An Academy of Women Skilled in the Art of Inventing New Fashions

I forgot to say that in one of the capitals of the Lunar world an Academy of Women has been established, who claim the title of Ingenious Women.[12] Those women hold their assemblies twice a day, in order gravely to discuss the fashions they ought to invent. No one can appropriate the right to make one appear unless she has passed the examination of that Academy.

Before that institution, ladies of the aristocracy and the fops of high society were enthusiastic to fulfill the functions of ingenuity themselves, but that introduced into fashion as much variety as there were different caprices, and brought a great deal of confusion into it, because each of those ladies wanted to give her name to the coiffure she had invented and the new adaptations of her ornamentation. In order to avoid the disputes and altercations that arose every day on that subject, the person who was then at the head of the Council—I cannot remember whether it was a man or a woman—instituted the Academy. It is certain that it is of great utility for these people, and that it produces large sums for the State by the taxes imposed upon it.

It was therefore determined by a decree of the Council that fashions would be uniform, and would last for at least a week, along with the interest taken in a pretty face, which everything suits, and without any regard to the others. It was ordered that all women and fops would henceforth appear coiffed very nearly in the same style, and that they would wear the same adornments, but that each would nevertheless be permitted to vary the colors, provided that one of them would be dominant throughout the time that the new fashion lasts. By that means, rose, jonquil, violet, bronze and all the other colors would reign in their turn. All those reasons determined the creation of that Academy of Ingenious Women, in which no fashion could be passed without a majority vote.

Since then, schools have been established to perfect the talents most useful to the coquetry and inconstancy of all the citizens of the Moon. It is in those famous schools that one learns to arrange ribbons, indentations and assortments for new adornments, and the pompoms, necklaces, tiaras, headbands and handbags that are also part of the equipment; and for men, shell-like purses, swordknots in pink bows, ruffed sleeves and a thousand other ingredients that are the ornamentation of a fop, as amorous of his face as a pretty woman.

---

[12] *Ingénieuse*, as the feminine counterpart of *ingénieux*, does translate straightforwardly as "ingenious woman," but it is worth noting that if the dictionary of the French language had permitted a female equivalent of *ingénieur* [engineer] at the time, that too would have been rendered *ingénieuse*.

These schools are distributed in various classrooms, some for the composition of jewelry, for it is necessary, in this society, for men and women to be loaded like mules; one must carry cases of every sort, filled with various tobaccos, pocket mirrors, rouge and bonbons—the fashion is presently to present them to oneself—and also liquids of every species, for which one must have numerous bottles. I do not know how they can walk with their pockets full of so many trinkets, unless it is to balance them on promenades and to serve as subjects of conversation in their circles.

Nothing is lacking in those schools for public utility; it is there that one learns to compensate for the unpleasantness of deformed statures, where one studies in depth all the facial expression, with the art of taking advantage, by turns, of blonde and brunette hair, turned up noses, long faces, asymmetrical faces, and, in sum, forming a respectable appearance. When one has reached that degree of perfection one can be admitted to the Academy; its places are sought avidly for a long time, by virtue of the immensity of wealth they procure for those who acquire them, for I cannot express the interest that all Lunarians take in their beautification, nor how much attention they bring to procuring new pleasures.

Nothing is too costly to satisfy their vanity; all their self-esteem is tied up in exterior graces; that is where they derive all their glory. Their vanity does not extend so far as seeking to acquire talents, ornamenting the mind by cultivating the sciences, according graces without exhibiting them, helping the unfortunate, rendering a heart content, filling a soul with joy, anticipating extreme needs, or even remedying them; they are incapable of that.

Of all engagements, the one contracted with the least precaution throughout the globe of the Moon is marriage. Everyone seizes blindly the first object presented, whatever faults it has, provided that it is rich. Interest embellishes; it is by that alone that all conventions are formed, and nothing else is consulted. Intelligence, heart and sentiment play no part in it. The similarity of humor and sympathy of character that ought to be the principal bonds of marriage are entirely neglected there. All grandeur consists in wealth; it is to such base maxims that the majority of Lunarians have attached their honor.

Some of those people, however, in order to correct that abuse in some measure, have introduced among them a kind of novitiate, with which they precede the solemn vows for several days; others contract determined leases, at the end of which it is permissible for the two parties to separate. One can judge that they are not stubborn regarding a chastity of which certain peoples deem all their happiness to consist; it is certain that the virtue in question scarcely figures among them; they respect it far more than they like it, since one sees them take every day, without any scruple, women who have already passed through several proofs, always provided that they have the talent to enrich or to act as protectors, because the presents they demand are regarded as a tribute owed to their favors.

In order to travel more comfortably and with less difficulty, Zachiel made us resume the form of flies. We traveled through various provinces of the Moon like that.

Having arrived at one of the extremities of that world, Monime was frightened by the deformity of the people inhabiting it, who made such a great contrast with the others that she asked Zachiel whether it was not in that place that the genii fabricated their fantastic bodies, because all the people seemed at first glance to be gross masses of formless flesh.

Nothing can express our surprise when we saw men without heads, who have, in consequence, no eyes, no nor nose, no ears; of the five natural senses, they are scarcely able to enjoy one alone, which is, I believe, touch. However, they have a mouth in the middle of the chest, which is so prodigiously large that one might take it for an oven. Their arms are very long, their hands large and always ready to receive what is offered to them. Their feet are similar to those of donkeys, of which they only make use in order to make backward leaps.

Those people are called Fibulars; they are dependent on the Lunarians, and although they are almost always at war with them, they nevertheless take pleasure in imitating them in everything and seizing with an infinite care all their folly and ridicule.

Monime did not want to quit that part of the Moon without witnessing a ball that the steward of the province was holding for all the nobility. In order to get into it with greater security, we placed ourselves on the steward's shoulders. That lord opened it with the Marchioness of Sarabante. That lady was then taken by the Earl of Entrechats, who subsequently led the Baroness of Contredanse.

I have never seen anything as grotesque as that assembly, in which all the men and women had employed the greatest efforts of their imagination to disguise themselves in a singular fashion. Several among them had fitted themselves with fake heads, which they had copied exactly from the model of the Lunarians.

As there are almost always a few singular events in large assemblies that amuse some people and are the torment and humiliation of others, however, this one, which was very numerous, gave rise to several very serious disputes between the masks, the majority of which has lost their heads in the crowd. Those heads were mostly cardboard, but a few were made of glass, which, doubtless when they fell, had broken; perhaps people had also stepped on them. What is certain is that they were obliged to bring large brooms in order to sweep away the debris, which was pushed into a corner in order that everyone could recover the pieces that belonged to them.

That accident put an end to the square dances, and they spent the rest of the night talking about the consequences the event might have. It did indeed give rise to many troubles, with proved very difficult to remedy, because all the affairs that required reflection, or those that could only be understood by linking ideas together and only solved by reason, were entirely beyond the scope of the Fibulars.

We quit the assembly at daybreak and went to find the genius, who was waiting for us to continue our voyage.

Monime was very dissatisfied only to have encountered throughout the extent of the Moon's globe stupidity, foolish pride, vanity, obstinacy, errors, blunders, projects poorly conceived and even more poorly executed.

"In general," she said, "the planet is filled with weak individuals, frivolous, anxious and passionate for new bagatelles—in sum, people whose inclinations are base, puerile, foolish or ridiculous, which they nevertheless mask under the names of purified taste, frankness and probity, while one sees them every day sacrificing their best friends to vile interests, and in the quarrels that they have with their families nothing reigns but animosity, and knavery in their arrangement. There are tastes and liaisons that hazard alone has formed; resemblances of character that they strive to pass off as the consequences of sage and useful reflection, and a thousand other things that weakness, illusion or extreme ignorance causes them to regard as beautiful, heroic and striking, although fundamentally they are worthy of nothing but the most sovereign scorn. Can one not compare the majority of the inhabitants of this world to the mad and the insane, more worthy of pity than anger?

"Is it in vain, then," Monime continued, "that I had hoped that this planet might procure us amusement and satisfaction, since, after having traveled all over it, we have only encountered one reasonable man? I would like to know the cause of that dearth of sane men, and why that which ought naturally to amuse me has irritated me so much."

"It's simple," said Zachiel, "since people who have the use of their reason can never amuse themselves for long with fools, imbeciles or the capricious. Whatever they do, their character engenders hatred and scorn; they are displeasing in all sorts of ways: their limited minds, their inconstancy, their frivolity, their affectation, that awkward politeness, that insipid complaisance, can never make them likeable. Don't conclude from that, beautiful Monime, that all human beings are naturally vicious and wicked; these have only become so by virtue of the need to satisfy a multitude of passions, which are the product of their societies, where the appetite for fashion and frivolity reign everywhere.

"But it is not by sumptuous attire, frivolous decorations or studied speech that one ought to recognize humans; it is only by the use they make of their intelligence and their reason. Here, the habit that everyone has contracted of never reflecting on anything ensures that lies and errors have taken the place of truth, which has been finally rendered captive, and which is regarded among these people as an unfortunate stranger who encounters nothing within them by disgrace and opposition. No one dares reveal what they think, and the ancient enmity that has always reigned between talent and wealth will not end soon. One can say that stupidity, extended to ridicule, is encountered throughout this planet, and that its inhabitants compose the nature of everything contrary to reason; one sees them every day appearing at spectacles, making fun of them and heaping censure upon them without perceiving that the ridicule falls on themselves, and without thinking about reforming their defects.

"You must have noticed in these people, beautiful Monime," the genius continued, "nothing but an assortment of comic vices, piled up methodically. There are four good mothers of whom they only recognize the children, including the truth, which every sane person honors and respects, but which in them engenders nothing but hatred. Prosperity engenders pride and self-esteem here, severity peril and familiarity scorn. Why? It is become in becoming familiar they make their defects known, giving their inferiors the right of comparison, their peers the right of authority and their superiors the right of chastisement.

"So, my children, you ought both to regard the Lunarian way of life as a useful lesson that might make you aware of the dangers to which such errors lead, in order carefully to avoid any occasion to fall into them. It is good to know evil in order to be able to guard against the severity of the wicked and flatterers.

"I can see," Zachiel added, "that nothing ought to keep us any longer on this world; thus, we can now go on to the plant Mercury. In order to go there more comfortably, however, I shall take you into a vortex;[13] they are the vehicles of which we shall make use for all the voyages that we shall be continually obliged to make in all the possible worlds, to which we are incessantly summoned for the utility of the people who inhabit them."

We followed the genius, although slightly alarmed by the aspect of the vortices, which might be compared to chaos.

---

[13] The present text is inconsistent in its use of the term *tourbillon* [vortex], although that translation is clearly licensed here and elsewhere (rather than the more commonplace "eddy" or "whirlpool") because it derives from René Descartes' theory of vortices, which hypothesized that space was entirely filled with matter in motion, rotarory disturbances in which were responsible for the movements of the planets, including the "epicyles" with which pre-Copernican astronomers attempted to explain eccentricities in the apparent movements of the planets around the Earth. The vortices here invoked as a means of interplanetary travel are smaller scale phenomena, the notion of vortices also being applied to individual atoms—as evidenced by subsequent references to travelling by means of "hooked atoms."

Chapter IX
The Genius has them rest in a Comet

We did not have time to admire a thousand new beauties that were offered to our gaze by the rapidity of the movement of the vortices. It is certain that the lightest Scaramouche cannot take as many tumbles in his life as those monstrous vortices caused us in very little time by their continuous whirling. I would not advice vaporists to embark in such carriages. Monime and I thought we would both be stifled there, in spite of the smallness of our persons, and we soon had need of all Zachiel's skill to get rid of the little void that separated them for us.

Whatever Descartes, who is their inventor, says about them, if I had had the advantage of knowing him when he was composing them, I would have taken the liberty of giving him my advice. I am not unaware that those vortices cost him many sleepless nights and much application; although his theories were not much liked and several people opposed them forcefully, he always put his glory at stake by sustaining them, and his dear vortices, on which the genii set themselves astride in order to travel with more promptitude to the different worlds to which they are summoned, brought him a considerable return by virtue of the new ideas with which they furnished him every day.

Perceiving Monime's weakness, Zachiel feared, rightly, that she could not resist the violence of vortices; that is why he caused us to pause in a comet that had appeared several years previously, showing itself sometimes over the Moon but more often over Mercury. Descending into that comet, the genius commenced, in order to fortify us, to rub us with a spirituous liquid, which gave us a new vigor, reanimated our strength and excited within us desires of curiosity that he promised to satisfy.

Zachiel, after having told us not to be frightened by the extraordinary things that were going to appear before our eyes, took us down to a somber and arid plain. That place began by inspiring horror in us; we saw the sky strewn with stars, which put out a blue-tinted light; the Moon, which appeared in its fullness, only rendered a light much paler than usual; it finally disappeared and left us for a long time in a frightful night.

Boreas, Coecias, the noisy Argestes and Thoucias,[14] all covered in ice, snow and frost, were enclosed in their brazen prison, and seemed to have become paralyzed there. Nothing could be heard of the soft murmur of springs; they were mute; the birds had forgotten their songs; the fish believed themselves encased in glass; and all the other animals had no more movement than what

---

[14] The first three terms in this list are all Greek names for various winds—northerly, north-easterly and north-westerly—but the fourth is enigmatic and idiosyncratic to this text.

they required to tremble—and the horror of a frightful silence seemed to announce that nature was ready to give birth to something terrible.

When the Moon reappeared, we advanced into that plain, where we only encountered owls, crows and other birds of ill-omen; the earth was filled with nothing but toads, serpents, and huge spiders, which caused Monime such great fear that she hid herself under the wings of the genius; finally, we saw nothing on all sides but thistles, poppies and hemlock.

On the far side of that plain we saw a tall old man emerge from a frightful lair, class in white. He had a tanned face, long crescent-shaped eyebrows, haggard eyes and a long, thick beard. A verbena hat covered his head and his waist was circled by a broad belt, woven from spring ferns and four-leaved clover, woven into tresses. At the place of the heart we saw a bat attacked to his robe; his neck bore a collar in which seven different precious stones were embedded, each of which bore the symbols of its dominant planet. With that mysterious attire, he carried in his left hand a triangular vase full of lustral water; in his right a hazel wand, one of whose two ends was garnished with a composition made of the seven metals, the other serving as the handle of a little censer.[15]

The old man, after having kissed the entrance to his lair, took off his shoes while pronouncing certain mysterious words; then he moved forward, retreating beneath the branches of an old oak, which seemed, by its size, to have been planted at the creation of the world. Beneath that tree we saw him hollow out three concentric circles, and the earth, obedient to the orders of the necromancer, took on of its own accord, quivering, the figures that he wanted to trace there. He engraved there the names of intelligences of all the centuries, those of the year, the season, the month, the week, the day, the hour and the minute, with their different numbers, each of which he put in its place, and incensed them all with particular ceremony. Then he placed his vase in the middle of the circles, removed the lid, put the pointed end of his wand between his teeth, lay down with his face turned to the orient, and went to sleep.

During his sleep, real or feigned, we saw five fern-seeds fall into the vase. When the old man had woken up, he took them, and put one into each of his ears, one into his mouth, plunged another into the vase and threw the fifth out-

---

[15] This passage and the next seven paragraphs are translated from a story that was first published in English, in an issue of the *Royal Lady's Magazine* from 1831 under the title "Passages from the Diary of a Late Lunatic," which is unsigned. The dream recounted in that story goes on to introduce the dreamer to a considerable number of individuals from history and mythology. An abridged version of the story was reprinted in William Mudford's anthology of *Tales and Trifles from Blackwod's and Other Popular Magazines* (1849), where Madame Robert might have found it. The back-translation into English does not reproduce the mannered archaisms of the original, because that would have jarred with the style of the translation as a whole.

side the circles—but scarcely had it emerged from his hand than we saw it surrounded by more than a million animals of ill-omen.

The necromancer then touched with his wand a screech-owl, a fox and a mole, which immediately came into the circles, uttering an abominable cry. He seized them, cut open their bellies with a stone knife, and tore out their hearts, each of which he wrapped in three laurel leaves, and swallowed the, making a few grimaces; afterwards he separated the livers, which he pressed into a hexagonal vessel and incensed them, after which he mixed the blood with the lustral water in another basin, and steeped therein a large scroll off virgin parchment that he held in his right hand.

Then we heard him utter frightful howls; he closed his eyes and commenced his invocations, almost without moving his lips. All that was audible was a buzz in his throat, which might have been taken for several voices mingled together. We soon saw him rise up from the ground, more than six feet, while always looking attentively at the nail of the index finger of his left hand. His visage was inflamed, his veins swollen, his hair bristling; finally, he became agitated, making different contortions, which frightened us extraordinarily.

The old man, whom I believed to be possessed by some evil spirit, called for help; then, rising up to more than a hundred feet from the ground, he fell back again on his head, which he split, while moaning. He continued nevertheless to ask for help, but as soon as he had articulated three magic words the ground opened up; a troop of malign spirits emerged, some armed with swords, others with forks and large clubs; some had hammers and nails, others crowns of thorns which they forced on to his head, while others were occupied in piercing him with their swords and driving nails into all his limbs; others, finally, struck him with large sticks.

They all seemed to be striving to rend him to pieces, but all those torments, far from weakening him and doing him harm, reanimated his strength and put him in a state to sustain without vacillating the frightful shocks of a terrible wind that blew over him, sometimes in gusts and sometimes in swirls. It seemed that the obstinate wind was trying to make him emerge from his circles; for an instant we saw the three of them spinning beneath him. Then a hail as red as blood fell, with torrents of fire that dazzled as they whirled, and divided up into globes, each of which burst explosively, like thunderclaps.

Then we saw a bright white light spread, which drove away the fanatical wind and dissipated the dismal meteors completely. In the midst of that light a young man appeared who had his right foot on an eagle and the other on a lynx; in one hand he held a trenchant blade, with which he struck the magician and all those surrounding him, who fell at his feet; and the young man disappeared.

The necromancer was stunned for some time by the blow he had just received, but, gradually recovering his strength, we saw him run away into the frightful ruins of an old castle, where the centuries had been working for a long time to put chambers into the cellars.

Monime, gripped by fear, did not want ever to go in there, whatever the genius might say to reassure her.

"For pity's sake, my dear Zachiel," she said, "let us get out of this comet, which announces calamities, as quickly as possible. I am tempted to believe that it is the Moon's Hell, since it is full of goblins and magicians."

"It is true," the genius said, "that this comet, which appeared a few years ago and is seen to dominate the Moon and Mercury, is only formed of the black exhalations that it draws from those two worlds, and by virtue of the attraction between it and Mercury, several of the inhabitants of that planet have been rapidly abducted therefrom. Their brains, empty of sense and reason, did not have sufficient confidence to retain them, and those minds, yielded to fanaticism, easily allow themselves to be seduced by the most primitive visions. Most of them, ignorant or facile, are led to believe great absurdities.

"The necromancer you have just seen is the one who dominates them in this noxious world; it is here that he makes himself feared, revered and obeyed by all those poor imbeciles, whom he draws every day into a thousand new extravagances. They are all convinced that he is immortal, and regard him as a god, who can, when he pleases, dispense wealth and abundance or famine and misery. The intelligence that the magician has with the infernal spirits facilitates all the extraordinary operations that you have just witnessed.

"It is by means of those charms that he provokes wars, igniting them beneath the evil genii that govern the Moon and Mercury; he commands the demons to inhabit the abandoned castles, to batter with various instruments those who try to lodge there; he teaches people how to harm their enemies by making wax image that resembles them; he finds hands of glory for those who want to enrich themselves; his distributes candles made of the fat of hanged men to thieves in order to put masters, valets and dogs to sleep; he fabricates flying coins and rings for fugitives that allow them to cover a hundred leagues in a day; he teaches curing with magic words; he informs shepherds of the wolf's prayer and the herbs that they ought to pick on an empty stomach at a certain time of the year; he wrings the necks of those who read grimoires without carrying out the requisite ceremonies.

"When travelers are stranded in the country at night when are witches going to the Sabbat, he makes them appear as a troop of cats, or forces them to kiss the hindquarters of the goat; with others he rubs their hindquarters with honey and has them licked by flies. Often he causes incubi and succubi to be found in the beds of his favorites; he sends the nightmare, and provokes the spirits to break, to impale, to roast or to crucify, to drive in nails or the points of iron spikes; he sends toads under the doors of sheepfolds or stables, with curses that cause all the animals to perish. He gives a secret virtue to certain words when they are recited backwards; he lends magicians of both sexes a familiar demon which accompanies them and prevents them from undertaking anything if they have not made their prayer to Master Martinet,[16] who often obliges them to dress in an extraordinary fashion.

"The necromancer also offers information regarding the making of little triangular cakes on a certain day in order to break the strong; he cures those with the werewolf disease by striking them with a sword between the eyes; he makes witches feel his blows when they are imprudent enough to be helped or struck by persons not initiated into their mysteries; he teaches diviners the fashion of turning a sieve to find what is not lost; he excites enchantresses to dance naked in the moonlight, with lubricious and indecent poses, to invite those who witness their indecent ceremonies to participate in their indecencies and extravagances. He makes ardent spirits run over rivers and streams to drown travelers. He teaches the composition of warrants, spells, charms and talismans, magic mirrors and constellated figures. He enables the finding of the new year mistletoe, the misleading herb, gamaches and magnetic plaster; he sends the goblin, the iron-shod mule, King Hugon, the black men, the white women, ghosts, farfadets, larvae, lamias, shades, manes, specters and phantoms.

"In sum, that famous necromancer is known on the Moon and throughout Mercury under the name of the Wandering Jew. The secret that he has acquired by science of the composition of an elixir, made with serpents of the same species as the one that Tiresias struck when he changed sex, also gives him the facility of changing it as many times as he thinks appropriate, and, in consequence, that of presenting himself in different forms, according to which one he finds more or less advantageous."

"Of all those secrets," said Monime, "that is the only one I would be ambitious to have in my power. As I am convinced, my dear Zachiel, that nothing is hidden from you, I beg you, when we return to our world, to give me a phial of that elixir."

The genus promised it to her, while teasing her a little for the desire she was expressing to change sex.

All your jokes," said Monime, "cannot extract me from the melancholy in which I have been plunged since we arrived on this comet. That is why I'm begging you at least to get me out of a world where extravagance seems to be in its ultimate period."

"I consent," said the genius, "to satisfy you this instant."

---

[16] This esoteric appellation of the Devil is almost certainly derived from Laurent Borderlan's skeptical comedy *L'Histoire des imaginations extravagantes de Monsieur Oufle* (1710; tr. as *A History of the Ridiculous Extravagances of Monsieur Oufle*), although some of the other details given in this passage are copied from the work cited in the previous footnote, whose necromancer similarly claims to be the original of the Wandering Jew. Borderlan's reference is immediately followed by Monsieur Oufle's summary of the pseudo-Paracelsian taxonomy of elementals, and might have the source of Madame Robert's account.

84

THE SECOND HEAVEN: MERCURY

Chapter I
The Planet Mercury

The genius transported us to the second heaven, which is, as you know, the planet Mercury. The rapidity of the attraction that drew us toward it carried us away with such great violence that we dared not respire—which prevented Monime and me from admiring a thousand beauties that were offered to our gaze.

We arrived on the new world extremely fatigued. Our gnomes, which had gone on ahead, were waiting for us on the frontier, with carriages appropriate to the dignity and expense that foreign lords ought to display. In spite of our impatience to find lodgings that could procure us some repose, however, we were obliged to traverse great forests and deserted and arid plans.

In order to dissipate the tedium of a somewhat unappealing route, the genius tried to give us an ides of the customs observed on that world, and the way of thinking of its inhabitants.

"This," he said, "is the abode of opulence, luxury, ostentation and all sorts of magnificence. Sumptuous edifices ornament all the cities, beautiful manor houses and admirable parks embellish the countryside. Throughout this planet, money is the only god, the only friend, the only merit that is revered; that metal ennobles; it gives status and intelligence to the most stupid individuals; it also enables them to succeed to the highest dignities, even though they have no sort of talent to fulfill them; that is because no one in this world is occupied with anything but the means by which to acquire great wealth.

"To succeed in that, everything is employed; the passion for wealth forms the dominant character of all its peoples, who call themselves Cillenians,[17] but

---

[17] The term Cillenien [Cillenian] appears to derive from the poem "Des Amours de Diane" in *Les Oeuvres poétiques d'Isaac Habert* (1582), in which that is the name attributed to the god of "the second heaven," which is unnamed but must be Mercury, given that the Sun is the first in that poem's schema, and Mars is named as the fourth, Jupiter the fifth and Saturn the sixth. Habert (1560-1615) was a baroque poet, not to be confused with the later theologian of the same name; the work in question combines mythological, religious and astronomical materials in an eclectic allegorical mix.

they changed their manner of using it a few years ago. Once, their great principle was to conserve what they had amassed; they thought it just to protect carefully what they had taken so much trouble to gain, and that it was sufficient to have full coffers to make friends.

"Today, that way of thinking would be regarded as avarice. They have changed their method entirely. There is no longer any question of treasures or coffers, or, if there are any, they certainly have no bottom; for, in spite of the prodigious quantity of gold that goes into them, they are always empty. Thus, there is no world in the universe where one finds more people who appear simultaneously to be powerfully rich and extremely poor, because the majority of those who show the most brilliant figure are heavily in debt, and although they leave the most beautiful heritages after their death their children nevertheless find themselves forced to repudiate the heredity. To have debts is a title of nobility, and even of grandeur.

"However, listen to the reasoning of their maxims, which are admirable. They never speak about probity, honor, right and humanity; they even sometimes avoid praising confidence and religion; all those virtues are regarded by the greater number of citizens as prejudices of opinion, prejudices of which they can soon rid themselves. It is nevertheless by the appearance of good faith that they commence their reputation; unfortunately, they often end it by corruption. Among them, duty, amity and gratitude are no more than old chimeras or ancient errors, which are the bonds of the stupid or the weak, because the influence that dominates them drives them and determines them is the true genius of interest, that of rascality and brigandage. They cultivate those odious talents by study, and fortify them by experience.

"The avidity for wealth has the same effect on them as on other worlds: ambition, honors and power they amass in various fashions, which are as many fruits of industry. You scarcely see one of them who does not have more than one adventure to his count in which probity has been wrecked. Their great secret, for making creatures, is to promise much and deliver almost nothing. They have for a principle that the surest route one can take, and the most gracious, to obtain the esteem of others, is that of fortune. It is certain that in this world, with money, one has science, intelligence, status, credit and courage; in sum, one has everything, one sets the tone, one makes the law. In consequence, it is an abuse only to want to acquire the consideration of others by means of talents and virtues; that path is too long and too difficult."

Meanwhile, as we advanced into Cillenia, we first encountered a few wretched villages, whose semi-ruined houses with thatched roofs only offered frightful hovels to our gaze, more appropriate to serve as retreats for wild animals than to lodge reasonable beings. A multitude of individuals of both sexes bore the seal of indigence imprinted on their physiognomy. The rags in which they were dressed, their pale and emaciated faces, their sad and languid gait and the grim silence they maintained all announced individuals withered by despair and languishing under the burden of need. Then came women surrounded by several children, whom they dragged along with difficulty; they only seemed occupied with the means they could employ to appease their hunger; the poor unfortunates seemed to regret internally the times in which milk was sufficient for their subsistence, and when they found in the breast the nourishment that was refused to their cries; and those poor little individuals, who had scarcely begun to live, had already lived too much.

Monime and I could not look at those wretches without being penetrated by a dolorous pity; we had some relief distributed to them.

Further on, our pity was excited again by the most frightful spectacle of poor peasants, from one of whom his cow had been stolen, the sole resource he had to supply his needs, and the other whose workhorses had been stolen. On the other hand, we saw young men forced to follow soldiers and abandon their fathers, depriving those worthy old men of the help of their arms, and by that means making it impossible for them to pay their impositions—which did not prevent a barbarous tax-collector, in the name of the sovereign, having their bed and a few other poor items of worm-eaten furniture put up for sale. To that was also joined a few measures of grain destined for the nourishment of a woman whose age and infirmity made it impossible for her to provide the subsistence of four or five daughters who were only at the age when one can do nothing but suffer.

"Alas," exclaimed Monime, "the heart fills with bitterness at the sight of so much misery. What pleasure do you obtain from deceiving me? Why, my dear Zachiel, do you want to abuse my credulity? Since we have been under your guardianship, I have always regarded you as my father, my guide and my support; you possessed all my confidence, but you have made a game out of abusing it by means of depictions so far from the truth. Is this, then, the wealth and opulence that I ought to see reigning everywhere among these peoples? Tell me, my dear Zachiel, what judgment I ought to make when I see, in the contrary, that nothing is so wretched as the Cillenians?"

"Far from being annoyed by your reproaches," said the genius, "I congratulate myself that your impatience has attracted them to me. They call my attention to the tender interest you take in the fate of the unfortunate. If only the persons who govern them had as much humanity as you on showing one to the other. Be sure, my dear child, that I have not thought to impose upon you. It is true that nothing is comparable to the misery of the peasants, but know that in Cillenia, it is only by the total ruination of a million souls that one can succeeded in becoming rich. A favorite of Plutus spends more on a single meal that the annual income of an entire village. It is to furnish that sumptuousness that a thousand unworthy vexations are inflicted on them every day, and what you have just seen is merely a feeble indication of the misery that presently reigns throughout the rural areas.

"Recover, beautiful Monime, your cheerful humor," the genius continued, smiling. "Accustom yourself to adopt the fashions of the world, and be sorry that here, all hearts are hardened against charity and humanity. No one gives alms here. In the midst of a luxury that advertises the greatest opulence, people say tranquilly to a poor man that they have nothing, and far from being touched by his distress, they only offer him the relief of blessings."

We finally discovered a great city, which Zachiel told us was one of the capitals of Cillenia. Having arrived at the entrance to an outlying district, I was extremely surprised to see all our carriages stopped, and some of our trunks opened and emptied.

Monime, who took them for thieves, seemed at first to be gripped by fear, but the genius, in order to reassure her told her that the men were posted there in order to examine everything that was entering the city.

"I find the curiosity very extraordinary," said Monime, "that causes these people who do not know us make an inventory of our effects. What use do they intend to make not it?"

"Know," said Zachiel, "that these men are seeking to take possession of a part of your effects, which they regard as a capture that might enrich them, and on the pretext that they are prohibited merchandise they will deprive you of them fraudulently by seizing them."

"Why do people suffer such injustices?" I asked. "Can one not complain to their superiors?"

"That would be futile," said the genius. "If any of the Cillenians were to try to claim the justice that is due to him he would be ruined before being able to attain it. These people here are supported by those who employ them, the majority of whom have been valets, and they are not unaware that the person who has put them in that post has been one himself. That is what gives birth in them to the spirit of cupidity and the idea of the fortune to which they hope to succeed."

Meanwhile, to satisfy Monime's impatience, I took a great deal of care in requesting the gentlemen to let us through quickly—but they replied to me in a brutal fashion that their office was cluttered, that the multitude of our baggage would require at least three or four hours, and that our urging would not make them go any faster.

Zachiel, who remarked our anxiety, soon found a means of liberating us, by adroitly slipping a few gold coins into their hands. Then they softened their tone, telling us that they did not want to delay lords like us any longer, and giving our coachmen leave to pass.

We traversed a part of the city in order to reach the most beautiful quarter, where a very well-furnished house had been prepared for us. I admired the height of the houses in certain places, which one might have taken for as many towers of Babel; perhaps the people who lived in them spoke in various languages. Having arrived at our house, we spent a few days resting, and our domestics occupied themselves in unpacking our trunks. Although they contained the most gallant costumes, our steward assured us that they were not rich enough to be able to pass muster on this world. That is why Zachiel proposed that we go to the shops of the merchants who had the reputations of employing the best manufacturers, in order to select the richest and newest fabrics.

The brilliance of our carriage and the number of our domestics immediately set the merchant, his wife and all their assistants in movement; several old fabrics, known as shop stock, were unrolled, while they protested on their honor that they were new. The greatest princes were cited as having similar ones, and the ladies of the court for making their most beautiful attire therefrom. As they were not at all to Monime's taste, however, they were obliged to show us newer ones, which they assured us no one else had seen as yet, the crates having only just arrived.

The merchant employed all his eloquence, which consisted entirely of the terms "probity," "conscience," and "honest man"—terms that the Cillenians use in almost every sentence, about which signify nothing other than the desire they have to dupe you.

Monime, unused to those customs, would have allowed herself to be taken in by them if Zachiel not warned her that they were overcharging for the fabrics by half. After a long contest, the price was agreed and the total added up. Monime, slightly embarrassed, signaled to Zachiel that she did not have enough in her purse to pay it; he smiled at her anxiety and, without replying to her, told the merchant to put it on account and sent his bill to the house—which caused no difficulty.

When we had climbed back into our carriage with the merchandise, Zachiel said: "What simplicity you showed in wanting to pay in cash. Know that people of a certain quality must always obtain goods on credit, and that if one does not owe money everywhere, one is regarded a person in which it is necessary to have no confidence—and, what is worse, an orderly person, which is the ultimate ridicule here. So, my dear Monime, if you want to conform to the fine manners and follow the maxims of this world, you ought always to dispute with the greatest ardor when anyone asks you for the price of your expenditure, and never pay without saying harsh and disagreeable things to the merchants."

We were soon in a state to appear with sufficient magnificence to be well received in good company—for it is as well to know that among Cillenians, it is only clothes and carriages that are honored; a man, often of the basest extraction, who announces himself noisily, is the most esteemed, prosperity hiding all defects and all ridiculousness. If he is an amiable man, he is rich, his table is well served, his carriage well gilded, numerous domestics accompany him, he spends lavishly, and gambles for high stakes, that is enough to merit all their esteem, but it is necessary that the true merit in question takes possession thus of their veneration; his charms will always attract the envious and criticism; all the admirers will follow his fortune and consecrate themselves to being among his favorites.

Thus, we were easily introduced into the most opulent houses. Monime, who liked to talk—like all witty individuals, to whom people always listen with pleasure when they have the brilliance and lightness that make conversation pleasant—was very surprised and even slightly annoyed to see that in all the places we went, there was almost no question of conversation. Scarcely had the reverences been made and returned than a valet brought tables and arranged three or four chairs around them; then you were made to draw little sticks of nacre or ivory; you went to sit down in the place that fate had designated for you, and everyone took out a package containing pieces of cardboard daubed in different fashions, some in red and others in black, to which were given the names of Caesar, Alexander, Hector, Pallas, Judith and others apparently appropriate to the picture they represented.[18] Six or seven hours at a stretch were spent shuffling these cards in turn, which were then distributed around, and equal number to each person, which they were then obliged to throw on to the table one after another, and sometimes all together. Someone else picked them up in order to recommence the distribution—and that puerile occupied lasted, as I say, for a substantial part of the day.

What I found singular is that all that was done with the greatest seriousness in the world; it seemed that the fortuitous arrangement of all those pieces of cardboard ought to decide the fate of the nation; scarcely a word was spoken, and that word, as if it had escaped, only concerned the fashion of throwing one's card. Some manifested an extreme gaiety; others, sad and chagrined, had a great deal of difficulty dissimulating externally the violent transports by which they were agitated internally; sometimes they became annoyed with one another, and argued fiercely, and the session always ended by counting money. I regarded that occupation as mental labor, but it pleased the Cillenians to call it play; some spent the greater part of their lives on it; one can say that gaming is, among them, one of the sovereign passions that often lead them to ruin.

Those little cards are found in all houses, where they are employed in a hundred different ways. In general, it requires neither industry nor intelligence, nor a knowledge of all the games; it is only cupidity and the hope of gain that drives them to play them. It is true that considerable sums are risked in them. Some have made immense fortunes therein, but others have been completely ruined.

There are houses that are only sustained by hosting games; it is the resource of a quantity of people whom luxury, gambling and good food have ruined. In their homes several cheats assemble, who form an association; it seems in many houses that gambling ennobles; estates are confused there; that of the player puts everyone at the same level; he is in society with the great, he is an

---

[18] Playing cards were given individual names in eighteenth-century France; [Julius] Caesar was the King of Diamonds, Alexander the King of Clubs, Hector the Jack of Diamonds, Pallas the Queen of Spades, Judith the Queen of Hearts.

honest man; he plays nobly, and the imbeciles that passion blinds do not perceive that he is duping them and shining at their expense.

One day, I went to one of these academies, which seemed to me to be a true den of cut-throats; games were played there that were called games of chance. I saw some there who swallowed ivory squares because they had lost a hand; others bit their fingers and chewed cards that they had folded and creases in several corners, swearing and cursing the bad faith of the world. I also noticed some who, cleverer than the others, knew the secret of rendering fortune favorable by means of subtleties and supple tricks. But if the gain is not always legitimate, it is always assured. Among the Cillenians, gambling debts are the privileged debts, paid in preference to all others; they are called debts of honor. To go bankrupt, to disappoint creditors, to ruin one's family, to violate one's oaths, to betray one's friends is regarded there as amiability or mischief, but not to settle one's gambling debts is a dishonor.

Chapter II
Subsequent Observations

Zachiel advised us to continue for some time yet in circulating in what is known as high society. We saw there, as elsewhere, little sincerity, a great deal of bad faith, affectation and grimacing, with the difference that the courtier is more subtle, acts with more finesse, bends himself with more artistry, and disguises himself with more skill in order better to hide the baseness of his sentiments.

The Cillenians link themselves together willingly; interest engages them to see one another frequently, but the pleasure that society offers is nothing to them; they frequent one another for political reasons, with a view to learning how better to deceive those who have need of them; the strive to pass of lies as truth, and knavery as kindness. The satirical spirit spreads its venom. One only sees people in order to criticize them; from that irreconcilable hatreds are born. Can people love one another when they know one another so well? However, they continue to see one another; card games or trips to the country bring them together regularly; one brings to them a great deal of finesse in wit, a quantity of quips and aphorisms, and an extreme politeness whose basis is dissimulation.

One day, I was invited to supper at the house of a woman who lived in the neighborhood and who cut a very grand figure. The woman, whom I encountered in all the best houses in the city, had assembled a numerous company in her house. Everyone showed a great deal of joviality. The mistress of the house excited them to joy herself, with a thousand playful remarks, in which satire played the leading role.

An officer came to announce that dinner was served; we went into a dining room where there was a table well garnished with the most delicate dishes; numerous bottles of different wines ornamented the sideboard. When everyone was seated and everyone's plate was full, I asked my domestic for bread. All the guests did the same, thinking that someone had forgotten to put it on the table. The external domestics set about fetching it from the sideboard, and those of the house looked on, smiling.

The mistress, impatient, flew into a temper, scolding her servants, especially the butler, who, leaning close to her ear, said by way of excuse that she had been told several times that no baker would any longer give her credit; that she was not unaware that those who had been supplying her for a long time were demanding absolutely to be paid, and that they had warned her.

"They're great rogues," she said. "Who would believe that anyone would be bold enough to refuse credit to a person of my status?"

I was sitting beside her; the butler had not spoken quietly enough not to be overheard; I thought, therefore, that it would be polite to offer her my purse, which contained fifty gold coins. She accepted it unceremoniously, slipped it to her butler, and without being disconcerted, made her excuses to the company for the stupidity of her servants. No one was duped, however, except for me, who had lost fifty gold pieces.

That adventure amused Monime a great deal when I told her the story.

A young marquis came to take us to pay a visit to the Earl of Minucius, who had just won a considerable lawsuit that had lasted more than fifty years. We departed together, and found a considerable number of lords in the Earl's house, who had come to congratulate him. There was no talk about anything but his triumph, and a few poets who presented themselves had already exercised their verve in order to mark, in verse as well as prose, the extent that they shared in his joy.

Zachiel, who accompanied us, did not want the opportunity to escape to make us see how far the imbecility and stubbornness of the Cillenians went. He therefore asked Minucius what he subject of such a long contention had been.

"It was the right to a quit-rent that one of my neighbors disputed with me," said the Earl. "The object, in truth, was not considerable, but if a lord does not sustain his rights, he has no esteem in the province and attracts the scorn of all is vassals. It was, therefore, essential that I sustain the suit ardently. I have spent the whole of my fortune on it, for I cannot hide from you that, although I have won the case, I find myself absolutely ruined by the reiterated sums that it was continually necessary to furnish the leeches who are occupied solely in giving birth to and perpetuating the most odious quibbles, and who, with no pity for the poor citizens obliged to have recourse to them for the arrangement of their affairs, employ their intelligence and their science solely to the ruination of widows and orphans, taking charge of the for and against in order to favor the one who pays the most, suppressing the best pieces of evidence of the unfortunates they have the intention of defeating, extorting signatures from some, of which they make use under false names, in order to lead them to their ruination when they are unfortunate enough to place their confidence in them.

"In um, there are no ruses or embezzlements that they do not employ in order to appropriate the wealth of their clients. It's with one of those men that I have been dealing for a long time. His son, who has succeeded him in his responsibility, as rascally as he father, has followed in his tracks; neither of them has spared me; where only one simple signification was required they had thirty; and so on. Judge, gentlemen, whether I can find myself comfortable in spite of the award of costs."

"But my Lord," I said, "since you were informed of all these rascalities, would it not have been better to settle the matter than to let yourself be eaten away by those scoundrels?"

"One always hopes for a prompt and definitive judgment," said the Earl. "One pays the money, one wants the result. One is animated against the opposition; one has friends to support one's rights; time goes by, which, instead of softening you, only irritates the passion one has to triumph."

"You see," the genius said to us, as we left the Earl's house, "that a clever Cillenian, when he undertakes a lawsuit, ought to begin by ensuring protections, without which, even if his case is incontestable, he ought not to have any confidence in his right; for if his party is more powerful, it is certain that he will win,. Recommendations have a weight that always tips the balance. Justice, dazzled, has no regard for the law. One might think that the goddess in question, following the example of coquettes, only becomes sensible to flattery or the sight of gold."

A few days later, we asked the genius to take us to the court, but he declined, and assured us that it was not permitted to him to appear in any court in Cillenia. He advised us to ask Amilcar, who was reputed to be very well received there, to introduce us.

Monime judged by the luxury and ostentation that reigned in the city that nothing ought to be comparable to the brilliance of the court except the glare of the sun. She was extremely surprised to see that the greatest lords, in spite of the efforts that they made to shine, were very far from approaching the magnificence and superfluous expense of new favorites of fortune.

The Prince received us kindly, and said the most agreeable things in the world to Monime. As our objective was to examine the customs of the court, we stayed there for some time. I noticed that Cillenians from everywhere assembled there with the design of making a fortune there and advancing their families. Some flattered themselves that they would lead a delightful life there, but did not take long to realize their error; the place was not made for liberty; establishments there were very uncertain; it seemed that fortune had erected her throne there in order better to display her inconstancy. It was there that the majority of courtiers spent their lives in feverish intrigue and solicitation, while obtaining nothing.

"What a tedious occupation," said Monime, "to be incessantly making petitions that are not read, trying to bribe a valet to be introduced to his master, whom one often reaches only to be refused."

"It appears to me," I said, "that those who seek support and protectors here in order to obtain employment ought to arm themselves with patience, since everyone makes you promises without any intention of keeping their word. I notice that everyone shows a great urgency in wanting to serve you, while in the depths of their heart the resolution has formed to do you harm. Those who frequent the court are incessantly tormented by ambition; it is necessary to sacrifice their best days to fortune, without any hope of peace or tranquility, and if hazard raises them up, envy soon precipitates their fall."

Amilcar drew our attention to an old courtier who occupied one of the largest houses in the city. That lord employed a despotism toward his family and servants that made them all tremble before his gaze; they were all submissive to him and hastened to anticipate his slightest desire. Far from enjoying all those advantages, however, tormented by ambition and the desire to acquire great wealth, he quit the respects that were rendered to him and the magnificence he enjoyed in the city to come to restrict himself beneath the roofs of the sovereign's palace, in a little paneled chamber where he could scarcely stand upright. Attached to the footsteps of the Prince, he put all his efforts into attracting a few favorable glances from him.

"I cannot conceive," said Monime, "what advantage that man can obtain from the care that he invests in acquiring great wealth, if servitude and slavery prevent him from enjoying it. What contentment can be obtained from having fine lands, beautiful houses and lovely forests if he does not have the liberty to stroll there?"

"It's true," said Amilcar, "that a favorite torments himself continually to obtain that which flees before him; he can never savor the sweetness of true repose, and by virtue of an inconceivable blindness, his ambition always causes him to desire that which is accorded to a few others, removing from him the veritable usage of what he possesses. That man, however, who seems to you so humble and supple in the presence of the Prince, seems to want to compensate himself for his servitude when he is at home; by the abuse of his grandeur, one sees him look at the people who need his protection as if they were some kind of animal far below his being, on whom he takes pleasure in inflicting sensible insults, using them as playthings, like children who martyrize dogs and cats by tormenting them."

During our sojourn at court, several fêtes were held there, in which the monarch paid marked attentions to Monime. I also shared the favor of the Prince, who was kind enough to admit me to various pleasure parties.

The welcome that we received from the Prince made many people think that we were well advanced in his favor. That news spread to the city, and when we returned, we were besieged from all directions by a multitude of petitions.

One entrepreneur of food supplies, having amassed immense sums at the expense of poor soldiers, still had the right to obtain payment of several millions, for which he affirmed that he had supplied the value, and in order to achieve the reimbursement of the claimed debt, he offered to share the sum with us.

A thousand new projects were presented to us, in which not only did people want to interest us for considerable sums, without furnishing the funds, but also our domestics, two of whom were given sums of money in order to engage them to speak to us in favor of their projects.

Our reputation thus established, we were overwhelmed every day by a host of interested visits, for among the Cillenians, the great and the small devoted themselves furiously to new projects. Amilcar, who was obliged, in accordance with his false principles, to make considerable expenditures, wanted to persuade us to present some that had been proposed to him, in which he had hopes of a considerable interest. Delighted to find an opportunity to oblige him, we agreed that he could come the following day with the author of one of those projects, to hear it read, in order that we could examine together the advantages that might be obtained from it.

The young courtier came the next day with the man of the project, who addressed himself to Zachiel.

"My lord," the man said, "I am taking the liberty of presenting to your grandeur this new project because I regard you as the most enlightened citizen in the realm. You know, my lord, that all gifts are variously divided; you ought not to suspect me of vanity, although I dare say that I am the foremost man in the world in the science of projects. Lord Amilcar, who knows my talents, has doubtless spoken to you about my work, and the vast extent of my ideas. You can judge them by this project, which will surprise you.

"I shall begun by announcing to you that it tends to the general good of all the people. Don't think that I limit myself to the mechanical art of augmenting the revenues of the state, cutting back superfluous expenses and regulating the prince's affairs and those of the nation efficiently, not of putting an exact order in everything. My design is far more extensive; you will easily conceive that when I have informed you about this new project, which has the objective of taking advantage of the enlightenment of our forefathers, from who we inherited the deadly art of tearing the entrails of our mother with an impious hand in order to search for treasures therein, which the wisdom of nature has carefully hidden there.

"You understand, my lord, that I am talking about gold, silver and precious stones, which presently cause the misfortune of almost all the citizens by the luxury that those metals have introduced into the cities. But it would be too difficult to remedy that luxury, gold and silver having become absolutely necessary to all human beings; for it is demonstrated that those metals, well applied, can change people to the extent that they are no longer recognizable, since they make a fool out of an intelligent person; they confer nobility and change bourgeois women into women of quality; finally, they cause people to forget what they have been, only retaining the memory of their present fortune.

"It is, therefore, presently only a matter of establishing a just circulation, which ought to be communicable between all the citizens—for you will remark, my lord, that it is only by a movement that can never be interrupted, until it has completed the circle that it must follow to bring it back to its point of departure, and only by following that maxim, that you can enrich the entire realm. But to succeed in that, the greatest difficulty will be unblocking all the channels that have impeded circulation until now.

"It is from your enlightenment, my Lord, that one ought to expect the secret of tendering the execution facile, and I dare to hope of your generosity that it will want to give me a little money, which will aid me to subsist until the entire accomplishment of my project."

We sent away that poor overheated brain, giving him what he requested. Amilcar, embarrassed by having presented such a madman to us, made us many apologies.

"That is the way that the majority of men think," said the genius. "the activity of the passions gives birth to new ideas, making them want to do great things, and it can happen that, aided by chance, they discover a useful one that has escaped the research and profound meditation of the human race. You will also agree that there are moments when, in the calm of nature and the senses, intellect instructed by the study of the sciences, seems to ferment by reflection; then one extends one's ideas in an immense circle, which can embrace all four elements."

Chapter III
A Description of the Temple of Fortune

All the arts flourish among the Cillenians; one could believe that they are their inventors. It is certain that on that world mechanics has been taken to its highest perfection; marvelous automata can be admired there; they appear to imitate, as closely as it is permissible for humans to approach it, the secret art of the great workman. Here one thinks one sees marble live, there a painting whose subject seems to be breathing; elsewhere, birds move, sing and digest.

In sum, new discoveries are made there every day, by virtue of the curious efforts of a thousand fine minds, some of whom are occupied in nothing but measuring the universe. Others are seen who, in order to roam the heavens, cross in bold flight the limits of their world; doubtless they believe themselves to be clever enough to steal a portion of nature's secrets.

"You must have remarked," Zachiel said to us one day, "the difference that exists between the Lunarians and the Cillenians. Among the former, commerce and the cultivation of the land, which ought to be the two principal pillars of a state, are often neglected, and seem only to be regarded as a ornament of their empire, or a superabundance of their wealth; instead of which, among the Cillenians, commerce is considered as the sinew, the life and the soul of the state. Accustomed to negotiate all the seas, following the example of the sun, they say, they visit and stimulate all the parts of the world, in order to enjoy and extend as far as they can the advantage that industry gives when guided by the avidity for profit. It is in this world that necessity, the mother of all art and all vice, extends its power with the greatest empire; the cupidity of men makes them bold; in whatever can be done to acquire wealth, they employ all kinds of means.

"Navigation seems to them to be the most prompt; it gives them the facility to travel all over the world; it is by navigation that they have found the means of communicating their environment, and by that combination that the knowledge of the earth and the heavens has been perfected. It is also by that means that all the treasures that nature has dispersed as assembled every day by commerce."

"Could one not add," said Monime, "that it by the same route that their vices are communicated, since it is true that commerce, in multiplying treasures, seems also to have multiplied needs? That is what gives birth to luxury, the primary source of all human corruption. But one cannot deny that in the political order, navigation is necessary."

"It is for that reason," said the genius, "that all the nations that have cultivated naval force have enriched themselves on the spoils of the peoples they have conquered. Athens acquired superiority over all the states composing Greece. Carthage disputed the empire of the world for a long time, and Rome only extended its conquests when it began to equip fleets. Venice made peoples tremble by its power, and enriched others by its industry. Spain, in discovering a new world, almost obtained universal monarchy, and you are not unaware, my dear Seaton, that England, in spite of the storms of its government, has often swung the balance of Europe.

"All these examples, although unknown to the Cillenians, seem nevertheless to authorize them to cultivate a commerce that, in opening up all treasures to them, engages them to equip numerous vessels, in which they bring back the rarest and most precious things that the islands produce, of which they make an exchange for that which they export of the superfluity of their provinces. It is also by that means that gold and silver circulate in their cities and the citizens have the further advantage that those who are without wealth or employment can easily find both in navigation, which puts them within range of making considerable profits in commerce, commencing with very modest sums, and one sees that the fortunate success that responds to their hopes gives birth every day to a quantity of ship-owners attracted by the double profit that they find not only in the merchandise they embark but from the product of those that they receive in exchange.

"The inhabitants of this world recognize no other divinity than Fortune, whom they claim to be the daughter of the ocean, because that is where the goddess in question exercises her power with the most empire and force. They believe that she alone presides over the distribution of wealth and honors; that she overturns, when she pleases, cities, kingdoms and states; that she raises them up again and gives them a new vigor. In sum, they make that goddess act like a pilot guiding a ship at the whim of her caprice; good and bad results are imputed to her; one hears them heaping her by turns with praise, insults or maledictions.

"Meanwhile, to honor that goddess, the Cillenians have built her a magnificent temple; sixty high priests serve her there and are charge with addressing to the goddess every day the prayers, incense and offerings that every citizen comes to present, in order to obtain one of her favors."

When we had visited the principal curiosities of the city, Zachiel proposed that we go to the Temple of Fortune.

The temple is built on the top of a steep mountain, and seems to bear its dome into the clouds. Sixty columns of transparent marble sustain its vault; none of its doors is closed; a thousand paths lead there, but the majority are rugged, filled with precipices, and are difficult of access; others resemble labyrinths by virtue of the different detours it is necessary to take to reach the foot of the mountain. Nevertheless, people flock to the mountain from all over the world, and for every individual who is seen to climb it with a degree of facility there are a thousand who stumble and break their necks.

On the road that leads to the temple we saw several vast buildings, which, the genius told us, were the Cillenians' schools. One of the schools is destined to teach all the ruses and all the tricks of the most venomous chicanery; in another, merchants fortify themselves in the art of deceiving their correspondents and that of enriching themselves at the expense of bankrupts; in a third the pupils learn to seduce and deceive their best friends by means of false promises and captious notes, whose execution is studied; the fourth is for gamblers. In sum, one finds one for every species of theft and rapine.

Advancing further along the road, we discovered a great forest, which we were obliged to traverse. The forest in question is very dangerous, because a quantity of brigands are encountered there, who, under the pretext of guiding you to fortune, only seek an opportunity to steal your money and jewels. Often, those wretches have no scruple about taking your life, perhaps believing that they will this avoid the pursuits of the law.

When we arrived at the bottom of the mountain, the genius, by means of a rapid flight, lifted us up to the middle of the temple, where there is a square pedestal a hundred cubits high, on which stands a magnificent throne, on which Fortune sits. The goddess is depicted as Amour is depicted, with a blindfold over her eyes. She also appeared to me to resemble Mercury, in that she has winged heels. In one hand the goddess holds a horn of plenty, in the other, the helm of a vessel. One of her feet is supported on a wheel, which she seems to be able to turn at her whim, taking a malign pleasure in overturning those whose boldness has allowed them to pass through all kinds of dangers to reach the summit of the wheel, in order to cause wretches to rise, whom she lifts up rapidly by hooking their undergarments.

The latter seem so stunned by their sudden elevation, their pompous titles and their great qualities that if Ovid had known them, he would have found ample material to compose a new chapter in his book of Metamorphoses. One could put them in the confederacy of golden asses. However, one sees them at the summit of the wheel, where they believe themselves to be secure, grazing with disdainful scorn on those whose place they occupy, until the goddess, by virtue of a new caprice, takes pleasure in putting the movement of the wheel into reverse, which knocks them down in their turn and sends them back to the oblivion from which they were snatched. It is thus that, in the world in question, the fortunes that seem the best established are often overturned.

We then examined several individuals who had just prostrated themselves at the feet of Fortune, in order to implore the favors of the goddess. I heard some of them begging her to rid them of a father whom death had doubtless forgotten, or an eternal uncle, who was making them languish in anticipation of a considerable succession. Others prayed to the goddess to favor them in gambling. One implored the ruin of his neighbor, in order to obtain his position; another, more devoted and interested, asked her for the favor of being admitted to the number of the sixty priests charged with all the offerings of the citizens. Some expressed a desire to obtain a stewardship or a government post, others a financial receipt or the administration of a hospital. In sum, I cannot recall the number of all the indiscreet pleas that the cupidity of the people and their love of wealth impelled them to make.

"What, then, is the folly of these people?" I asked the genius. "How can they justify such bizarre conduct?"

"You see, my dear Seaton, that all their glory is limited to living in opulence; it is only to fulfill that vanity that they continually address prayers to Fortune. It is to that goddess that they sacrifice their honor and their repose. It is in this world that one sees the fidelity of a friend die in the arms of interest; it is here that one sees luxury and envy shine, stifling the virtue of a young woman, who wants to participate in the favors of fortune; it is here that commerce extends over everything; you see here people in high positions making a traffic of their authority, the great a traffic of their protection, and women of their charms.

"Everything here is for sale, including intelligence, of which one makes shoddy goods for all the different nations that inhabit the globe. A man who can profit from his industry can easily, with fifty gold pieces, make an annual income of three or four hundred by distributing them in modest sums to the wretched poor, who come to pay him interest every week. It's certain that the citizens of this world have nerves so sensitive that the slightest appearance of profit sets them quivering.

"As great lords can only become rich at the expense of the people, they try to persuade the latter that intelligence, courage, sentiments, the shame of the heart, purity of language and wide knowledge are found innately in persons of high status, and that it is their prerogative to profit from the pains and labor of the poor, so one sees at every step people pursuing you and begging for bread.

"But how many of these leeches have to employ sleepless nights in reaching their goal? What cunning, what finesse, and what deceit do they not employ to distinguish themselves by their sumptuousness? It seems that they dispute with one another the pernicious advantage of having put more skill or subtlety into the maneuvers of which they make use to exploit dupes.

"The Cillenians honor the deregulation of their imagination, one sees nothing in their conduct but violent ferments and false protestations in which honor is always compromised; pride and interest are the only springs that make them move, because there is nothing except opulence that obtains respect, while true merit is scorned, when it only appears to be accompanied by indigence.

"Ask a Cillenian what he needs to make him happy; he will reply that one cannot be without possessing a large income, beautiful houses, superb furniture, a well-decorated carriage, spirited horses, a table served with delicate dishes and fine wines, cheerful friends, and lavish suppers with actresses—but they refrain from any mention of probity, morality, moderation, justice and good faith in keeping promises. Accustomed to neglect them at every opportunity, they regard those virtues as imaginary."

Monime and I were curious to visit the ports; we saw that they were very advantageous with regard to the shelter fund there by vessels obliged to put in there, either because they were taking on water, were short of food supplies or had been damaged by some storm.

The harbors are preceded by large and beautiful havens of vast extent. We went along the shore for a considerable time, which was filled with entrepreneurs and laborers employed by people whom the lure of riches leads to the extremities of the world, and who risk all sorts of dangers to acquire them. I do not presume, however, that they were exempt from dread and fear.

One could say that the Cillenians always have the precept before their eyes that Fortune, as a woman, likes to be importuned. It seems, in fact, that it is necessary to use violence to ravish the favors of that goddess. The most enterprising are almost always those who have most success. She often grants to the importunate that which she refuses to others who are more modest; boldness hides the bad qualities of the former; all their steps tend toward the goal that they have adopted and they never deviate therefrom; that is what ensures their success.

Approaching one maritime city, surprised to see the inhabitants emerging in a crowd to take flight, all charged with whatever they could carry of their most precious possessions, we had our carriage stop in order to enquire as to the reason of an old man who was prevented by the weakness of his legs from running as fast as the others. The poor man, who appeared to us to be full of common sense, told us with tears in his eyes that his compatriots had just suddenly discovered in the bay of their port a considerable number of vessels armed for war, bearing an enemy flag, several of which had already entered the harbor, and that the enemy was preparing to take the city by force.

He added that as soon as they had perceived its arrival, the inhabitants had alerted the governor in order that he could assemble the troops appointed to guard the coast, but that he had only found a few lame old soldiers in no condition to fight. In that extremity, all the citizens, stimulated by the necessary of defending their property, liberty and life, had offered to take up arms. They had first run to the arsenal, where they had only found a few poor cannons without gun-carriages, and wretched rusty rifles that were unusable, but no powder, mortars, or bombs.

"That negligence," I said to the old man, "doubtless comes from your governor's conviction that you had no strong enemies to dread."

"Pardon me, sir," said the man, "but for a long time we have been menaced from all directions; perhaps it's the fault of those responsible for the care of the artillery. The powder-merchants also neglected to renew the stocks; that was as much profit for them. Alas, my dear sir, there were many abuses in need of reform. I suspect an underside to the cards that will only be discovered at the end of the game; but it's not with a poor wretch like me that it's appropriate to reason on matters so delicate."

The old man left us to continue his route, after we had given him something to console him for the loss he had just suffered, which drew a thousand blessings from him on our behalf.

The city was taken without it costing the enemy a single man; no one thought it a duty to render assistance, with the consequence that the pirates, after having seized considerable booty, returned tranquilly to their vessels without encountering any obstacle. However, that city was one of the most flourishing in Cillenia, because of the extent of its commerce and the advantageous situation of its port.

"What do you think of the conduct of these people?" I asked Zachiel.

"It's no longer possible to form any judgment for the future," said the genius. "A more enlightened politics goes astray and gets lost in the new and incomprehensible maxims that are followed today throughout Cillenia. It seems that these people have invited their own loss by acting directly contrary to their veritable interests.

"What they see happening every day no longer teaches them to suspect anything; their intelligence has changed into a petulant fire, which prevents them from reasoning; their conduct, strayed from the fixed point of ancient government, resembles a machine detached from its pivot, which no longer has any certain basis or assured confidence. The superiority that they brought to the domination of all their allies, in whom it was necessary to instill dread and respect, no longer touches them. The time when they gave, not charitable advice, but laws and orders that brought others to obedience, is past for them; that was their Golden Age.

"Thus, my dear Seaton, you can compare the conduct of the Cillenians to that of a demasted vessel whose pilots, in poor accord with one another, instead of occupying themselves with the general maneuvers that might save it, are only thinking of their own interests and their personal salvation."

Chapter VI
The Portrait of a High Priest of Fortune

As our objective was to visit the principal cities of Cillenia, we took the road to another province. At the end of the day we perceived a manor house which, by its beauty and the vast extent of its park, gave Monime a desire to visit it. She asked Zachiel the name of the prince to which it belonged, and whether we could, without lacking decorum, request shelter there until the following day, because we were a long way from the city. Monime was horribly fearful that we might encounter thieves and brigands, with which all the roads in Cillenia were filled. The genius found no difficulty in satisfying Monime, and we sent one of our domestics to ask the permission of the master, who sent back word that he would be honored to receive us.

We entered into a long and beautiful avenue, the trees of which formed triple rows. In order to give us an idea of the house, the genius told us that it had once belonged to a great lord, whose son, by virtue of the decadence of the family, was nowadays only too glad to be admitted to the table of the man who had become its possessor, although he was not unaware that he had once poured drinks for his father. Such is the caprice of Fortune in that world, who is pleased to humiliate some in order to favor others.

"The individual you are going to see, in order to succeed to that high degree of fortune, commenced with the vilest employments: first a lackey, then a name-lender, and something else that is easily guessed, which is of great utility to a Cillenian who wants to get on in the world—in sum, base and unworthy services that led him to have petty interests, from which he obtained such a good profit that he had himself appointed as one of the sixty high priests in the Temple of Fortune.

"The man acquired immense wealth there, which gave him a great deal of credit among the great, especially those who have the liberty of drawing on his treasures. His table is always delicately served; he distributes employments and obtains graces; that is why everyone hastens to cultivate his acquaintance; they forget what he has been in order to attempt to obtain a share of his opulence. It is true that it is necessary to crawl before him; he imagines that everyone has lost sight of his low birth and the oblique paths that led him to the Temple of Fortune. The man has no character of his own and the superiority he has acquired by his wealth has become a harsh tyranny for the people who form his society; but that is the prerogative of all the dullards that fortune has raised up; many people despise them but nonetheless render them homage and respect. An honest man who is indigent sometimes complains, but far from offering him a helping hand to alleviate his difficulties, they flee him and always try to avoid encountering him."

We eventually arrived at the high priest's house. All the domestics had insolent expressions; they were already anticipating their master's conceit; they had copied his arrogance and pride and received us in a curt and disobliging fashion as they introduced us into the apartment of the Lady of the house. She, nonchalantly lying on a chaise-longue, honored us with a nod of the head.

The woman was what is known as a Validated Sultana—which is to say that the high priest had once distinguished her sufficiently to honor her with his name, for throughout Cillenia, highly-placed individuals have acquired, by their opulence, the privilege of entertaining several young women, whom they lodge in magnificent houses, and when they become tired of them, they marry them to one of their protégés. The validated individual also acquires the right to furnish certain plumes that have the advantage of pleasing her with all the money that she requires to shine in the world; by that means, everything is compassed and no one has any right to complain.

The high priest, who was a fat, wheezy little man, took a few steps forward to greet us, and said to us, raising his voice as if he were talking to someone deaf, that he was charmed to have the opportunity to oblige us, indicated seats to us with his hand, and, without waiting for us to sit down, plunged into a capacious armchair filled with pillows.

Monime, who had not yet had the privilege of encountering one of those favorites of Fortune, was extremely surprised by that brusque politeness; she nevertheless offered an apology for the liberty we were taking in coming to ask for shelter, but explaining the distance from the city, the awkwardness of the poor roads and the fear of me unfortunate encounter had obliged us to do so.

"Of course," said the high priest, moving his armchair closer to Monime and gazing at her in a brazen fashion. "You could not have done better; our goddess must have inspired you. I would like you, for the honor of her religion, to spend a few days here. Tell me, my charming lady, what business you have. I feel inclined to render you service." He looked at me over her shoulder, and went on: "Is this your husband? You could not do better than to address yourself to me to obtain a position for him. It's doubtless for that reason that you're going to the city. Rely on me, lovely lady, and don't go any further."

The fop added a tissue of more impertinent proposals, accompanying every sentence with loud burst of laughter. Monime wearied of his grossness, and to put an end to his trivial discourse replied that we had no need of protection or any position. "We're strangers," she said, "led by simple curiosity; the desire to learn alone has determined us to visit different courts."

"That must cost you a great deal," said the impertinent Validated Sultana, who had not yet deigned to speak. "Do you have a considerable retinue?"

"No," Monime replied, coldly. "Thirty domestics compose almost all of our following."

"That appears to me to be respectable enough," said the favorite of Plutus, darting a cold glance at us for the first time.

She was interrupted by a woman who came to present herself with a humble and modest expression; her husband had just been dismissed—I do not know the reason—and he had fallen ill with chagrin. The woman had come to implore the pity of his protector, who was perhaps the most pitiless man in the world. He commenced by speaking to her in a harsh and barbaric fashion, making all his authority felt with an arrogant expression, threatening to have her husband imprisoned to punish him for his negligence.

The poor woman, disconcerted by those threats, could not imagine at first any other means to soften him than to paint, in the most touching terms, the extreme poverty into which they would be reduced if he abandoned them. She combined that with a long genealogy, by which she proved clearly that she had the honor of being related to him by blood ties, since they had the same grandparents.

I believe that if the high priest had had the thunderbolts of Jupiter in his hand at that moment, the poor woman would have been reduced to dust; given her imprudence in daring to declare before strangers that a man who had once had no other employment than taking donkeys to the mill was the ancestor of an Earl, which was surely laughable. At any rate, that new Earl is decorated with men-at-arms; secretaries fill his cabinets; valets ornament his antechambers; he has a butler, cooks, doubtless stables, and who knows what else—more than forty men in livery, a huntsman, a pack, coats of arms; he buys all the marquisates and earldoms that are up for sale, and a duke has long ago sold him his daughter. I thought that the high priest and his wife would choke with anger.

The poor woman was thrown out and treated as a lunatic for coming to tarnish thus the glory of a man at the moment when several genealogies have been purchased in order to work in concert to make him descend from one of the most ancient nobilities in the realm: a man who thinks that no mortal is capable of calling himself his equal; a man, in sum, who believes himself to be of a nature much superior to others by virtue of his pride, even if it his artificial, rascally, cunning and deceptive. Ought one not to forgive a man simultaneously virtuous and unfortunate for the secret spite he feels in seeing that it is only the wicked who prosper?

I confess that I was not sorry that the man had suffered that petty mortification, for I believe that if the presumptuous man had not been needed, he would be left to contemplate himself, his horses, his house, his stables, his apartments, the furniture and the decorations with which they are ornamented, the harness, his table and his set of false teeth. Little envious of his fate, no one would take the trouble to congratulate him; but he lends money; it is true that it is at his interest, but no matter; he is always a resource.

It is certain that among the Cillenians, that man is regarded as one of the public thieves, who, under the false pretext of the onerous advances they have made for the needs of the state, furnished with edicts, declarations, similarly rob the sovereign of his rights and the people of their substance. Unfortunate instrument of immeasurable ambition! Unjust usurper, who sacrifices friends and enemies indifferently, who takes possession of their property by violence when trickery does not succeed!

Barbarians, who only take pleasure in the disorder of which they are the authors: such is the character of the noble society of the high priests of Fortune. I had no need of instruction by the genius to recognize it.

We quit the high priest in spite of the efforts he made to retain us and in spite of the cold politeness of his Lady, who had humanized herself slightly since being informed of the number of our domestics.

We continued our route, while Zachiel made us a not very advantageous portrait of the province we were about to visit.

"That city is swarming with partisans hungry for gold and silver, which the perversity of their mores and their frenetic appetite for superfluous expense was already causing their eyes to devour. That appetite has corrupted their heart, their reason and their mind, substituting knavery and bad faith in treaties; they are seen to betray the confidence of the sovereign, and to take possession of all his treasures by felonious actions."

Before entering the city we saw a vast building, which attracted our admiration by its extent. Monime mistook it at first for the dwelling of some great prince, but Zachiel, smiling at her error, told her that the superb edifice had only been elevated with the design of assuring the poor a retreat, in order to finish the days that labor and poverty had entirely enfeebled, rendering them incapable of earning a living.

Monime could not help praising the prince whose generosity and charity, full of zeal for the wretched, extended as far as providing for their subsistence.

"It is true," said the genius, "that if the intention of the Prince had been fulfilled, nothing would be more edifying than that establishment. The house enjoyed considerable revenues, not only from the benefits of the prince, but also from a large number of donations that rich citizens made to it, perhaps with a view to restoring to the poor the wealth that they had unjustly acquired. However, in spite of those immense revenues, the poor scarcely find what they need there to prevent them from dying of starvation, in consequence of the rapine and the maladministration of the people charged with supplying their needs, because the concern of enriching themselves is the only one that occupies them. That is the goal to which every Cillenian aspires; their conduct is always marked with the stamp of interest. Devoid of humanity, rectitude and honor, cruel to the unfortunate, hardened to their misery, they sell their services, deceive their masters and make a shameful commerce of their authority."

To hide us from the attention of the curious, Zachiel only kept one carriage, with the number of domestics that was absolutely necessary to us. He found us lodgings with a widow whose only income came from a house that she let fully furnished; it as in the best quarter of the city. The widow only lodged people of quality; she was pretty and had acquired by their frequentation an air of ease and politeness that gained Monime's amity.

The day after our arrival she came in familiar fashion to invite us to spend the afternoon with her. Scarcely had we entered her apartment than we heard a carriage stop. The widow ran to her balcony and signaled to us to accompany her.

"Look at the elegance of that carriage," she said. "Its paintings are very fine, as is the varnish of the most fashionable of men. It's Baron Friponot, who will amuse us with his witticisms."

Friponot entered in a buoyant and familiar fashion; although he had a very bold manner, we judged nevertheless by his fashion of introducing himself and his low and trivia discourse that he was, at the most, only an aspirant to the favors of Fortune. He played the part of an important man before us, talking about a project that he had presented to the ministers, saying that he was sure of its success, and reeled off a great many insipid pleasantries, which the widow applauded. She wanted to engage him to make up a party with Monime, but he excused himself on account of the prodigious quantity of affairs by which he was overwhelmed, which obliged him to go, in order to shut himself away in his study to reply to fifty letters that could not be put off.

"Who is that cavalier fellow?" asked Monime, when he had gone.

"He's a Baron of recent manufacture," the widow replied, smiling, "who owes me a great deal. Would you believe, Madame that I kept him here for more than a year, to shield him from the pursuits of his creditors? He's the son of an honest merchant, who left him considerable wealth when he died and great credit in commerce, which he had acquired by a recognized probity, living as a good bourgeois, distanced from ostentation and any superfluous expense.

"Having become his own master by the death of his father, that one, far from following his example, doubtless dazzled by his treasures, immediately began to try to imitate the greatest lords. The paternal house could not contain the inflation of his pride; he bought a much vaster one; he needed garages and stables, numerous domestics, a porter, not yet daring to hire a guardsman with a moustache, a town carriage, a country carriage, horses, dogs trained for hunting, even though he could not yet handle a rifle, an opera girl, little suppers, balls, parties at home, elegant furniture, well-ornamented cabinets.

"That sumptuousness attracted a number of lords to him, who only came with the design of sharing his opulence. Everything flattered his vanity; he needed a title to shine in the world, so he bought a barony and several other fine estates. His treasure dissipated, he could not pay for any of them; so his goal was merely to defraud the owners if a few years of income. Those were the maneuvers he employed to succeed. As he had the reputation of being a very rich man, when he bought some land he began by renewing the leases, even letting the same farm to two or three different farmers and demanding half the price of the lease in advance; then he devastated the manor houses, removing the most precious furniture and paintings to sell them cheap, and appropriated all the merchandise on the pretext of negotiating in foreign lands: curtains, fabrics, furniture, wine, wheat, hay, straw, oats—in general, everything tradable—which he sold at half its value in order to obtain prompt payment.

"Finally, after having accumulated considerable sums by several illicit means he disappeared one day and came to hide in my house in women's clothing, while the rumor was put around that he had gone to some remote island or country in order to spend the money he had taken away. Baron Friponot was soon declared bankrupt, unfortunately taking twenty others with him. A year passed in negotiations with his creditors, who finally accepted ten per cent of their credit and Baron Friponot reappeared in society more brilliant than ever."

"In truth," said Monime, "that man is more guilty than a highwayman. How do you dare to be in commerce with such a rogue?"

"I can assure you, Madame," said the widow, that the man is very well-received everywhere; it's only his first bankruptcy, but I suspect that he's making arrangements for a second that will complete his enrichment. Furthermore, you know that opinion is everything among men; everyone pays for his own. The one that is most in vogue here is to honor the rich; everyone is in agreement on that point; the poor honor them because they find their profit therein, and the rich their satisfaction; thus, everyone has his turn."

Several days were spent visiting the most beautiful places in the city and when we returned in the evening we were sure to find a numerous company in the widow's house, because she often hosted card games. It was not people of quality who gathered in her home but people who were studying to counterfeit them; female shopkeepers newly prosperous on the fruits of their industry, others that the caprice of Fortune had extracted from the vilest estate to heap them with favors.

One of those princesses, a former seamstress whose husband had become a cashier some time before and who knew admirably well how to get full value from the coins in his till, was precious, intense, swollen with the pride of her new dignity, mocking and scornful of anyone who did not have a carriage or numerous domestics. She took ridicule, false vanity and even impertinence so far as to want to take the high ground in very company she encountered.

That woman took it into her head, during a card game, to snipe at another, who was in truth very simply but decently dressed, who appeared at first to pay little attention to what she said. Occupied with her game, she allowed her tranquilly to reel off all her insipid pleasantries, while winning her money.

When the former had emptied her purse her remarks began to slow down, her face became longer and her mockery ceased; in order to try to win her money back she asked for chips in order to continue playing. The other, seeing a large gold casket, which she might yet appropriate of fortune continued to favor her, wanted to take it as surety for her chips, but when she had enough for the value of the casket she took possession of it, returning the chips. The imprudent cashier's wife, wanting to recover the casket, got carried away, saying that she was well able to pay the value of the chips, and that one did not offer such an insult to a woman like her.

"Eh? What are you, darling?" said the other. "Since you've been here, you've only shown a great deal of impertinence and ridicule. It would have been lowering myself to respond to your gibes; women of your species only merit a sovereign scorn. If I seemed to listen to you patiently, it was to punish your pride. Try to profit from the lesson, in order to correct yourself."

She departed then, leaving the other very humiliated by her adventure.

Chapter V
Portrait of a Libertine

The house facing ours lodged a young man named Specade, who was reputed to be one of the richest lords in the province. His father had been the governor and had left him immense riches and several beautiful lands yielding a considerable income. The young man maintained the expenditure of an ambassador in the city, which amounted to double his income. His steward and his butler formed a conspiracy to profit from his dissipation and his lack of experience, working together to enrich themselves at his expense, and although they each had a mistress maintained in style, they succeeded in that easily by the secrecy of their industry.

Following the example of the other two, the cook did not fall asleep; he went every day to take all sorts of provisions, which he doubtless thought superfluous to his master's table, to his nymph. One can imagine that such economies contributed not a little to the ruination of the young man.

One day, Specade perceived Monime on her balcony. Immediately smitten with her beauty and her graces, he sought an opportunity to pay court to her; their proximity furnished him with the pretext. He rendered several visits to Monime, in which he showed his passionate sentiments, and a great deal of vivacity and urgency in paying court to her.

In order to cement the liaison that he wanted to establish between us, he said to me one day, he invited me to come and see him on a familiar basis, because he wanted to introduce me to several houses where I would be well received. I could not refuse such an obliging offer.

One day, I was in Specade's house when a jeweler came in carrying a little coffer full of jewels and a case containing the most beautiful diamonds.

"Those, Lord," he said, in presenting them to him, "are the most perfect in the realm."

Specade chose several of them, as well as the jewels, which, the merchant said, came to twenty thousand écus, for which Specade gave him a credit-note. When he had gone, he summoned his steward.

"Here, Forban," he said to him. "Go and have these diamonds turned into gold and come back immediately, bringing me the value."

"Lord," said Forban, assuming a hypocritical expression, "I can't prevent myself from telling you that I foresee, sadly, that if you continue making such bargains often, they will infallibly lead you to your ruin. You're not unaware that your beautiful lands are mortgaged for considerable sums, and the bourgeois who lends money to you at high interest has finally jibbed and is threatening to seize your income."

"Mr. Forban," said Specade, shifting his weight in his armchair, "your reflections annoy me furiously; you're playing the role of pedagogue, which displeases me; go carry out my orders, without worrying about the consequences they might produce."

Forban withdrew without daring to reply. He came back two hours later with a hypocritical air to say to his master: "Monsieur, I'm in despair; money is so scarce that no one wants to give you any but a very modest sum for your jewels; the usurers are true tyrants; I dare not tell you the price they offered me for your effects; the bad faith of those men is a horrible thing. I've gone to all the ones I know. I'm exhausted by fatigue, and haven't been able to do better. But Monsieur, how can one resolve oneself to abandoning a good effects for a fifth of their value?"

"Oh," said Specade, "enough of your lamentations; let's take it. I'm engaged this evening for a card game. You know that I lost heavily yesterday; it's a revenge I'm being given; if Fortune favors me, we'll get them back tomorrow. Give them to me."

"I didn't want to accept them, Monsieur," said Forban, "but since you're determined to sell these jewels for a fraction of their worth, I warn you that they'll be totally lost to you, because tomorrow, there will no longer be time to recover them."

"No matter; go fetch them. Don't waste any time; take my carriage in order to go more quickly; my credit isn't entirely extinct and I might be able to find other resources."

Forban, who knew his master's impatience, came back in a quarter of an hour. He had not gone far to find the sum, since he had made the acquisition himself with his master's money, and the jewels would serve to ornament his mistress.

After leaving Lord Specade, I went to see a woman in order to make a purchase that Monime had asked me to make. The woman was one of those schemers who often mingle their intrigues with a métier. As she did not have what I wanted, she went out to look for it. I was placed near the door of a neighboring room and I heard two people arguing hotly.

"I'm a man of honor and probity," said one of them. "Good faith is the basis of all my actions. I only have one thing to say. That is the proposition that I've made to you, which is certainly the most advantageous to you, since you're not unaware that I can get two hundred thousand for my master's land. However, I'll let you have it for a hundred and fifty thousand, on condition that you give me an advance of thirty thousand, to be paid in cash before the signature of the contract of sale."

"I'll agree," said the one who wanted to make the purchase, "to give you the thirty thousand in advance, provided that it's stipulated in the contract, or that you give me and authentic recognition; otherwise, you can see that if the land is reclaimed by withdrawal, that sum would be entirely lost to me."

"I see that," said the other, "but for want of reaching an understanding, we'd be losing a bargain profitable for both of us. Firstly, sir, it's essential that my master has no knowledge of the commission I'm demanding, because he'll want to take possession of it and might perhaps do me the injustice of withdrawing his confidence from me. Now, to obviate that inconvenience, there's a sure means of tranquillizing us both, you with regard to the fear of withdrawal and me for the discoveries that my master might make in this affair, which might make him think that I prefer my interests to his. To avoid any embarrassment, we only have to antedate the sale; I'll take care of that—provided, of course, that you bear the expense."

The acquirer appeared to like that plan, and they left together, doubtless with the design of concluding their affair.

On returning to Monime I found her with Zachiel. I gave them an account of my day, deploring the blindness of young Specade, whom I saw lowering himself to the unworthy role of fraudster in order to procure the means to furnish his crazy expenditure and, at the same time, satisfy his stupid vanity.

"In all Cillenia, my dear Seaton," said the genius, "you will only find men, even those of distinguished birth, who trample probity, honor and good faith underfoot. The majority have recourse to the most unworthy ruses in order to procure money; such is the deadly fruit of pleasures. Pleasure-seekers appear at first to be walking over flowers; everything is smiling, everything is delightful, everything presents an agreeable form to seduce them, while they do not deign to make the slightest reflection regarding the future. They believe that their days will be an incessant sequence of new pleasures. Fatal illusion! Those pleasures abandon them, after having led them to the precipice. It is then that the blindfold falls and they recognize the error that has abused them. They have ruined themselves to satisfy their ostentation; the appetite for pleasure that still subsists in them drives them to continue in the same excesses, at whatever price is required to succeed therein; honorable sentiments are renounced, to fly the flag of intrigue and knavery. In the end, they only sacrifice to the god of wealth, and it is Plutus alone to whom their prayers and offerings are directed."

"Your reflections," I said to Zachiel, "cause me to dread that Lord Specade will become the victim of his bad conduct, and will fall from the bosom of his opulence and grandeur into poverty, obscurity and scorn. This province furnishes far too many examples of that, which leads me to believe that the influences of the air must act more forcefully here than in the other provinces of Cillenia."

One day, the widow in whose house we were lodging introduced us to a man of an illustrious family. His name was Prodigas. That name, known throughout the province, caused us to receive him with distinction.

That first visit was followed by many others, which began to be burdensome to us. Monime, wearied by the tedious individual, whose conversation revolved entirely around his birth, the high dignities and honorable posts his ancestors had possessed, without ever his having thought of rendering himself worthy to sustain their brilliance by means of virtues, nor any of the talents that might distinguish him from ordinary men, asked Zachiel to find a means of getting rid of him.

"That's easy," said the genius. "I'm surprised that none has yet sprung to mind. I'll indicate one that is sure. The assiduities of the man are only tending toward borrowing money from you; he won't take long to broach the subject. Seize the opportunity; agree to lend him a hundred sovereigns for a week, and I give you my word that you'll never see him again."

Monime was able to follow Zachiel's advice that same day and we were rid of him.

Although somewhat surprised by that lack of good faith, which is all too frequent in Cillenia, Monime nevertheless mentioned it to the widow, who appeared very sorry to have procured us that acquaintance.

"But my Lady," she added, "I only did it after many solicitations on his part, presuming that he would not be so bold as to borrow money from you. It's true that I neglected to warn you that the lord in question is a man drowning in debt, but he only does it to sustain his rank with all the brilliance that connects an illustrious birth with a magnificent fortune.

"That Lord, whose lands were in forfeit, had conserved nothing of his ancestors but the name and the good fortune of making, a few years before, the acquaintance of one of those men that Plutus, the god of riches, had heaped with his favors. The man in question, who was seeking to ally himself with an illustrious family, in order to shield himself from the investigations that might be made of the immensity of his wealth, offered his daughter to Lord Prodigas, with a very considerable dowry, in order to enable him to repair the disorders occasioned by a poorly regulated conduct, provided that he would regulate his expenses in future and adapt them to his income.

"Prodigas, who would have been completely ruined without that alliance, promised everything that was demanded of him, and the marriage took place with the most brilliant trappings. But can you imagine, my Lady, the surprise, shame and chagrin that the young wife must have had on her wedding night, when Prodigas, in a tone of offensive scorn, declared to her that it was in vain that she flattered herself on seeing her marriage consummated, if her father did not add a further two millions for a wedding present. Aurélie, sensible to such an insult, after having responded to her husband's tender compliment with a great deal of bitterness, ended up by protesting that she would go to beg her father to take her back to his house and keep his money, in order to have a marriage annulled in which the torches of the furies had served as nuptial candles.

"When the father heard about his son-in-law's evil maneuvers he was rightly carried away; the affair made a great deal of noise in society. Prodigas' family involved themselves to reconcile the parties, and in spite of Aurélie's tears, they finally succeeded in persuading her to return to her husband's house. The father, believing that he was contributing to his daughter's happiness—or, to put it more accurately, the ambition of seeing her take up a considerable position at court—paid the sum that his son-in-law had demanded. Prodigas, content with that expedient, far from making it his duty to execute the new promises he had made, departed for one of his estates, where gambling, women and debauchery have ruined him for a second time, and are presently forcing him to live on intrigue, after having sustained a long lawsuit against his wife, who has separated her person and her wealth from him.

"Since Prodigas has returned to the city, he has employed all the means imaginable to reconcile himself with Aurélie, but the young lady, outraged by his indignities, his bad faith and the baseness of his sentiments, is allowing him to consume himself with futile regrets. Unafflicted by his fate, she is tranquilly enjoying the gifts that nature, in accord with Fortune, has lavished upon her in profusion. The sole advantage she has obtained from that alliance is a great name, which she sustains with nobility and dignity, and the charming Aurélie has made friends with all of her husband's family, while his bad conduct has made him as many enemies."

Chapter VI
A Singular Adventure

Next door to the widow lodged a man who possessed immense wealth, but who was so miserly that no domestic could live with him for long. The man in question always searched for pretexts to exempt himself from paying their wages.

Woken up one night by a frightful racket that I heard outside that house, I got up and went into a cloakroom that overlooked the courtyard. I perceived by the faint light a man in a nightshirt, begging for mercy from a groom who was belaboring him with a pitchfork and crying: "Thief!"

The domestics came downstairs in response to the noise that the groom was making, and the racket stopped as soon as the lantern appeared.

It was Monsieur Chicotin himself that the groom was maltreating thus, pretending to mistake him for a thief.

"Damn it, Sire!" said the servant, "So you come every night to steal the oats from your poor horses, in order to accuse me afterwards of selling it to my own profit?"

Chicotin, confused at having been discovered, was then obliged, although he was badly bruised by the blows he had just received, to ask his domestics not to divulge anything regarding the adventure. In order to engage them to be quiet, he gave them a few coins, which he took from his fob pocket one by one, and to complete the disgrace, he had a surgeon called to bandage his wounds, which kept him in bed for some time—and poor Chicotin had the misfortune of not being pitied by anyone.

We left that city to go to another province, but the influence dominating the world was the same everywhere. Hardly anyone says what he thinks; no one can distinguish amity without interest; sincerity and knavery are mingled and one might think that virtue and hypocrisy are daughters of the same mother.

Having arrived in a big city, Monime wanted to see whether common sense and reason might not be relegated to the people, which caused the genius to lodge us with a tailor, whose wife was an embroiderer. There, we mingled with all kinds of workers, who were all following the court, and I was surprised to see on the awning of a cobbler the glorious title of "Shoemaker to the Queen."

A young woman often came to that house whose father had no other employment than that of schemer. The man played all kinds of roles, sometimes a charlatan, sometimes a magician, at other times and actor or juggler; he tried by means of these different professions, to dupe people.

One day, the young woman came, in a panic, to beg our hostess to hide her father in the grain-loft.

"What has he done now, then?"

"Alas," said Finette, "one of his friends engaged him to play the necro-mancer, and unfortunately, he took the role a little too far, for you know very well, my dear Louvette, that when it's a matter of snaring a dupe, he always wants to extract the very blood from his veins. But I'll go fetch him and he can tell you the story himself."

Finette came back a quarter of an hour later with her father.

"Hey, my poor Mr. Fourbison," said Louvette, "what made you play the sorcerer?"

"Oh," said Fourbison, in a mocking tone, "if I had as good a trade as your husband's, I wouldn't have to talk to the devil to make money."

"Good," said Louvette. "You only have to get yourself appointed as a prosecutor; those fellows make money; it's necessary to see how their wives act like duchesses. Look, here's a dress I'm embroidering, the design of which was made by a president's wife, but as I couldn't make it for less than a thousand shillings the president's wife found it too dear, and the prosecutor's wife, for whom nothing can be too beautiful, came to give me a hundred pounds in advance. Anyway, tell us your story, then. Can you really talk to the devil when you want? Step away from me a little; I'm afraid that you might have a little one in your pocket that might leap on to my collar."

"Have no fear," said Fourbison. "They don't extend their malice as far as my friends, but they take pleasure in troubling the tranquility of a mother who thinks she's taken all the necessary precautions to ensure the virtue of her daughter. I trouble that security; I put the young person in despair, and I cause the fortunate lover to lose all the pleasures that he savors in the rendezvous that his mistress grants him. To husbands who possess indolent wives, who appear not to care for any pleasure and have languid eyes, vaporous wives, or those whose adornment announces an exterior model of little baskets, big butterflies, no rouge and perennially modest color in their clothing, who tear apart the reputation of other women bitterly—I say: refrain from drinking from the enchanted cup, for not enough remains therein to moisten your lips."

"Good, we have trouble enough with all those goblet tricks," said Louvette. "Just tell me about the adventure that obliges you to hide."

"Gladly," said Fourbison. "First of all I ought to tell you that Arlequin and I have more than one drinking den in the city and the suburbs where we hold sorcery shops, and it's there that all the women who tell fortunes with cards, coffee-grounds or bottles come to learn and to tell us about the disposition of the houses where they go, and a thousand little intrigues that happen in the city. One of these women came one day to tell us that she'd discovered a very rich woman very desirous of becoming even richer, and that there was a good coup to bring off because she had got it into her head that one of her husband's country hous-es, nor far from the city, contained a treasure guarded by an evil spirit, and she was convinced that no one could dig for the treasure without conjuring it. The woman added that she had advertised me as a great magician and that it was necessary for me to prepare to play my role, because people would soon be sent to search for me for a consultation.

"The very next day I was asked to go to the woman's house; she talked to me about the treasure and asked me a great many questions on the subject. After she had revealed an ardent desire to possess it, I judged that I could find a much surer one for myself than the one she wanted to have, by finding a means to draw for as long as I could on her purse. So I told her, with an air of good faith, that in order not to involve her in needless expense, it was necessary first to consult the spirit in order to be better assured of the truth of the matter; that as those sorts of spirits were very self-interested, I would not presume to be able to talk without offering it more than a hundred pieces of silver; that it might take a hundred and seven, a hundred and eleven or a hundred and thirteen, as long as the number in excess of a hundred was odd. She gave me a hundred and thirteen in order to obtain a favorable response.

"Furnished with that money I went to find Arlequin, it being agreed between us that we would share the good fortune we had. Honesty is necessary in those treaties, and I can say that mine has never been lacking. I told my comrade everything I had just learned, and we agreed that he would assist me in the enterprise. I went back to Mr. Oronte's house."

"What!" said Louvette. "That's who you're dealing with? Oh, I have the honor of knowing the wife. The old Argine,[19] who was once a mender, examines everyone's clothing every day to look for wear and tear. Truly, it's that lady who produced it, in several houses, where she did very well. Well, my dear, has the treasure been found?"

"Patience," said Fourbison. "I said to Mr. Oronte that the spirit had replied: *dig*; and that on that response I had no doubt that there were considerable sums buried in the earth. I then saw joy shining in the eyes of Sir and Madam, nothing being done except on her orders. She promised to make my fortune and that of my children. I added that it was necessary for me to see the house that contained the treasure. The coachman was ordered to hitch up the horses immediately and I was taken to the house.

"I was equipped with a hazel wand, with which I made several circuits of the garden, and then assured them that I believed that the treasure was in the cellar. We went down there and I placed a silver coin in each corner of the cellar, and one in the middle, assuring them that the place where a coin turned over would mark where the treasure was, but that it was necessary to leave it there for nine days and to make sure that no one could go in; that they had only to come back after and see whether the coins had turned over. In spite of their care and vigilance, I nevertheless had the skill to turn over the middle one.

---

[19] Argine was the name given to the Queen of Clubs in a deck of cards, the name being derived as an anagram of Regina.

"That expedition done, I gave an account of it to Arlequin, who put several of our people on campaign in order to be informed on all the steps they took. When the nine days were up I went to find Mr. Oronte and told him that the spirit had announced to me that the treasure was in the middle of the cellar, but that it would not permit digging there unless it was given as many pieces of gold as I had already given it of silver. As Sir and Madam had just visited their cellar, and had indeed found the coin in the middle turned over, they made no difficulty about giving me the hundred and thirteen pieces of gold the spirit demanded; I even got a couple on account of the fortune that had been promised to me.

"Not seeing me return, Mr. Oronte came to find me. 'Oh, my dear Sir,' I said to him, weeping, 'the devil is a great liar; he accuses me of having stolen half the sum that you gave me to give to him, and maintains that it was two hundred and twenty-seven gold pieces that he demanded of me.' I showed him an old coat ripped to shreds. 'Look, Sir,' I said to him, 'this is how he treated me; I'm still bruised by his blows, and if you don't have the generosity to add what he demands, my life isn't safe and you're running a great risk of never getting the treasure, in which I can assure you that there are several millions: what prejudice can that do to you?'

"Mr. Oronte left without saying anything, to go and consult his wife, but when he told her that I had assured him that there were several millions there, she decided that it was necessary not to spare any expense in order to render themselves masters of it, and I was invited to come and get what I'd requested.

"We should have stopped with that last bleeding, but Arlequin, who's insatiable, didn't want to. 'It's my turn,' he said, 'to appear in the play. Go back to Mr. Oronte and tell him that the spirit seems content; that it's no longer anything but a matter of conjuring it to render it obedient to your orders, but that, unfortunately, someone has stolen your grimoire, and that there's only one man in the region who has one. If you're asked where he lives you'll simply say that it's in the north, but that you don't know his name or his face.'

"I followed Arlequin's advice. Oronte, like those gamblers who finish ruining themselves by chasing money they've lost, didn't want the advances he'd made to be a pure loss; that's why he determined to make a search for that new magician, and, beginning to be suspicious of me, he kept me at his house until the man who had the grimoire was found. Not seeing me come back, Arlequin guessed what had happened. He immediately sent several emissaries to Oronte, who indicated the shepherd of a village situated ten leagues from the city.

"Oronte left at daybreak the next day; encountering a peasant on the road he asked whether he was far from the village. The peasant said that he was only half way. 'There's no point,' the man added, in taking the trouble to go any further; I know what brings you here; I'm the person you're looking for. Is it not about a treasure in the cellar of one of your country houses?'

"'Yes,' said Oronte, surprised by the man's science, 'and since it's you that I'm looking for, you have only to climb into my carriage.'

"'I'd like to,' said the villager, 'but before then, it's necessary to go into the inn that's a short distance away, in order that I can write a few words to send for my grimoire, without which I can't do anything.'

"Oronte consented to that, and when Arlequin—for it was him—had felt all his pockets he scribbled a few figures on a piece of paper, screwed it up and threw it in the air, saying: 'Don't take long to come back.' Oronte, who couldn't see anyone, wanted one of his domestics to take the note. 'Fie,' said Arlequin. 'It'll take six hours for your domestic to go and come back, and mine will be back in ten minutes. Let's have a drink while we wait.'

"A quarter of an hour later, Arlequin, who's the cleverest trickster there ever was, got up to go. 'I'm waiting for someone to bring you your grimoire,' said Oronte.

"'There it is,' said Arlequin, showing him a book that was on the table. Our man, surprised not to have seen anyone come in, couldn't help shivering. He climbed back into the carriage with the sorcerer, who was difficult to recognize even for me; he was disguised in such a way that he looked to be more than a hundred years old. Madam Oronte was frightened, and thought she was seeing the devil in person.

"The new magician assured them that I was stupid and ignorant, that it was necessary to dismiss me because I'd allowed myself to be taken for a fool by the spirit, and that it was necessary to start my operations again. 'In order to show you that I'm incapable of deceiving you,' said the sorcerer, "I'm going to force the spirit to bring the treasure to your apartment himself, in order to avoid the difficulty and expense of transport.'

"That new plan seemed delightful to Sir and Madam; they gave him the largest and best room to carry out all his operations. First he made three invocations, which lasted nine days, in each of which it was necessary to hand over ninety-three pieces of gold and as many of silver. The devil, who likes order, declared at the third signification that he had been guarding the treasure, which contained more than ten million in gold, along with several vases of the same metal, for more than three hundred years. The magician then conjured him to bring the treasure to the middle of the room.

"The spirit refused, and in order to force him, it was necessary to have a prodigious quantity of perfumes, yellow wax candles and several machines that he said were necessary to the enterprise. Arlequin thought he would put them off by asking for things that were almost impossible to find, but nothing was refused him. Mr. Oronte, impatient with all the delays, pressed the magician to redouble his invocations and to give no rest to the spirit until it finally brought the treasure.

"The sorcerer assured him that on the third night, between midnight and one o'clock, he would hear a loud clap of thunder, which would be the signal for the obedience of the spirit to his orders and the arrival of the treasure, but that it

120

was necessary to make sure that all his servants were in bed and that no one appeared at the windows—which was scrupulously done.

"During the three days, Mr. Oronte and his wife began to enjoy their treasure—which is to say that they were already distributing it. They sought appropriate charges, in sword and attire, for their son, chose among the nobility the greatest matches for their daughter; Sir wanted to be a magistrate and Madam wanted them to shine at court, which caused a considerable dispute between them, and was doubtless the reason why the spirit, in order to bring them into accord, had refused to yield to the conjurations of the magician—who had only demanded that delay in the hope of finding a means of escape.

"His hopes were in vain; it was necessary for him to keep up the farce until the end. Finally, that night, so much desired on the part of Oronte and so much dreaded on that of Arlequin, arrived. Everything in the neighborhood seemed calm and tranquil; everyone, including the inhabitants of the gutters, were enjoying a perfect repose; but my dear comrade and I were in a furious embarrassment. I had never ceased prowling around the house, and that night, in the skin of a big black dog in which I'd wrapped myself, I was lurking on all fours near the door, fearful of being recognized, when I saw Madam Oronte appear, who, bolder and more curious than her husband, was looking through the attic window to see whether she could see the spirit arrive, in what form it would come, and in what carriage it would bring her treasure.

"More than two hours had passed in tedium when she heard the cries and lamentations of the magician. Gripped by fear, she went down to her husband's apartment—who, frightened himself by what he had just heard, was getting ready to go to hers, both of them imagining that the devil had the sorcerer by the throat. They made the resolution to expose themselves to all sorts of perils rather than permit a man to be murdered in their house, for one might say that they were the best people in the world. So they went into the room where they had locked up the magician, and nearly fell over when they saw him lying full length in the middle of several circles he had drawn on the floor, his face, hands and shirt covered in blood. The room and the furniture were also covered with it.

"Arlequin, pretending to be possessed, started bellowing like a bull; he seemed terrified. 'Alas, Sir and Madam,' he cried, 'the spirit will wring my neck if you don't extract me from his hands. He's rejected my offerings, and yet I swear to you that I was only mistaken in two commas in the terms I employed.' Redoubling his screams, he went on: 'Look, he's coming in: he's that big black cat, it's him who's bloodied everything.' By chance, the house cat, which was black, finding the apartment open, had come into it in search of some prey. Arlequin, making several bounds into the air, with grotesque grimaces, put such a great fear into the cat, that it fled, spitting, over the rooftops and was never seen again.

"In order to render the scene even more touching, my comrade reproached them, weeping, for being the cause of his giving himself to the devil, and that he had only done it to render them service; that the spirit was a rogue that that deceived him. In sum, he made such a terrible racket that Mr. Oronte, fearing that such an affair might be talked about, causing a scandal that could only fall on him, set the pretended magician free, threatening to have him burned if he dared to divulge the adventure. Arlequin promised not only to keep quiet, but also to extract himself, if he could, from the devil's claws and never to have any further commerce with him.

"However, Mr. Oronte, annoyed to have lost his money, although he was not yet entirely cured of the opinion that had been given to him of the power of magicians, has, unfortunately for us, confided the adventure that had just happened to him to one of his friends. That friend, surprised by his credulity, took it into his head to make us return a part of the money that Arlequin and I had obtained from him by trickery. After being informed of a few of our glorious deeds, he made a complaint to the judge, who has just issued an arrest warrant against us, which is why I need to hide until the affair has died down."

The boldness of that rogue surprised me greatly; I could not convince myself that there were people simple enough to be taken in by such absurdities— for if one cares to reflect a little, should one not wonder why these pretended sorcerers or magicians, do not use their power for themselves? Why are they all vagabonds, when they only have to draw from the entrails of the earth or the profoundest abysms of the see more wealth than all the potentates in the world have ever possessed? However little one reflects on such follies, so many ideas crop up to combat them that I am astonished that they can be in anyone's head— but on examining the conduct of the Cillenians, I believe that a general stupidity must have struck all the inhabitants of the planet, in order to make them act directly contrary to their veritable interests.

Monime, who was bored, decided that we would leave that city in order to take the road to the province of the Merces.

Chapter VII
Vice Confounded and Virtue Recompensed

Having arrived at that new capital, we obtained lodgings in a furnished house near the entrance to the city.

When I had retired to my apartment and sent away my domestics, I heard some sounds through the wall of my dressing room, which made me anxious. I lent an attentive ear, and distinguished the plaints of a woman; the sighs and sobs she was uttering testified to a great desolation.

Two hours passed without my being able to decide to go to bed; softened by the chagrin of the unfortunate, I could not get rid of the desire to go to offer her some consolation. I opened my apartment door quietly and went into a small room next door, from which someone had neglected to remove the key. But what did I see? A young woman, whom dolor had almost stifled, was lying back in an armchair, her arms extended, not moving. A mortal pallor was spread over her face, which appeared to be bathed in tears.

That spectacle caused sympathy to spread through me; it fixed all my attention, and in spite of the state in which I saw her, I found nobility in her physiognomy, graces and an air of gentleness—and I thought, in sum, that I was looking at dolor personified. First of all, I was tempted to summon Monime's maidservants to help her, and save me at the same time from the dolorous interest that she was beginning to inspire in me in her favor, but I could not liberate myself from the pity I felt; it would have been necessary to harden my heart too much—and that concern for myself would have put me more ill-at-ease than the sad sympathy for her misfortunes.

I therefore approached her, with the intention of consoling her. "Forgive my boldness," I said to her. "I haven't come here, Miss, with the intention of causing you any difficulty; penetrated to the depths of my soul by the state in which I see you, I would like with all my heart to be able to lessen your grief. Have pity on yourself, relieve your pain by confiding the reason for it, if you can, to a man who, far from wanting to abuse it, wants do everything in his power to try to diminish its bitterness."

The young woman, doubtless surprised by my appearance, looked up at me, and then lowered her eyes with a confused and embarrassed expression. She only replied to me with further sobs, her tears flowing more abundantly.

When she had pulled herself together somewhat, she looked at me more attentively. "Great gods!" she exclaimed, uttering a profound sigh, "will you have pity on my troubles? I believe, sir, that you are incapable of abusing my confidence, and since you have the kindness to take part in my affliction, I shall, by a sincere recitation, inform you of the evils that are its source.

"I am the daughter of a family whose father, ruined in service, died ten years ago. My mother, left a widow with two children, for whom she had a great deal of tenderness, initially sustained our misfortune with sufficient firmness. We lived on a little plot of land, the only property that remained to us from the debris of our fortune, but, my father's creditors having seized it, we were obliged to come to this city in order to sustain the rights that we had enjoyed, and which were in dispute. We came to stay in this house, where for more than nine years we have endured all the delays of an impenetrable chicanery, which ended up consuming all that we had left.

"Finally, by dint of solicitations, we succeeded in having a judge appointed to examine the affair, which was so confused by the malevolent quibbles of the prosecutors that our judge could not understand it at all. To complete our misfortune, his secretary, avid for money, had allowed himself to be seduced by our opponents, better informed than us with regard to the means to employ to obtain a favorable judgment.

"It was impossible to approach our judge, for want of protections, our poverty and the simplicity of our attire always causing us to be turned away by domestics who only recognize those whose clothing advertises opulence. If we ever got as far as the audience hall, a host of claimants prevented us from getting to him. Perhaps we would have been able to make him understand the justice of our rights by simply telling him the facts; the truth would doubtless have struck him; the disgraces fecund in touching expressions might perhaps have led him to examine our case more carefully—but sir, how can unfortunates dare to imagine that they will be welcomed and heard? No, that privilege is reserved for people who, by the richness of their clothing and the cortege that accompanies them, announce ostentation and opulence.

"Useless reflection. What can I say to you, in sum? A definitive judgment ruined us entirely. When my mother learned that our suit had been lost, her spirit and virtue buckled beneath that last blow of our misfortune. She could not support its rigor: the harsh economy that she had had to maintain for a long time in order to live and support the expenses of an inevitable procedure, the complete retrenchment of a thousand small delicacies to which she had been accustomed, and whose privation became a surplus of evils, the chagrin of seeing her children become domestics, and perhaps even those of others, a mute and shameful sadness that she observed in us and which misery paints clearly on the faces of honest people when they are humiliated, the sadness more painful to see in people who have sentiments than the most obvious pain. All of that threw my mother into a despair of which she was no longer the mistress, and which led her to the tomb in a matter of days. I cannot, sir, express to you the grief that I feel at her loss, and in which you see me.

"My brother, whose mind had been formed at any early age by our misfortunes, found my one day in my room, my face bathed in tears. 'Alas my sister,' he said, tenderly, 'spare a brother who loves you, and who only expects consolation from your amity. Shall I always see you prey to the bitterest dolor? It's true that the loss we've just suffered ought to be very sensible to us both; in the first days I didn't condemn the excess of your affliction; you surrendered to it, and that was just; overwhelmed myself by the blows that had struck us, I couldn't do anything to console you; it isn't surprising that reason buckles at first beneath reverses as crushing as those we have suffered. I know that the movement of nature must take their course. But my dear sister, one recovers, one calms down, one comes round, and reason eventually gets the upper hand. However, I see you still the same; I've devoured my chagrin for fear of augmenting yours, but you have the cruelty to make me perish of ennui. You're crushing me with your dolor, without being touched by mine. Oh, you don't care about it; do you think that what happens in my heart isn't sufficiently sensible? Do I not have enough chagrin, then, without doubling the bitterness? Is it necessary that despair follows us to the tomb? Believe, my sister, that there are people who have more to mourn than us; there are those who have hollowed out the abyss into which they have fallen themselves; at least we don't have that reproach to make to ourselves; that's a reason for consolation—but you don't employ any for my tranquility, and all are lacking to me.'

"'Alas,' I said to him, stop heaping me with unjust suspicions. It's wrong of you to criticize my amity for you; nothing can weaken it. My brother, if you could read the depths of my heart, you would see that this dolor, whose excess I cannot moderate, only comes at present from the tender interest I take in our fate. The saddest reflections on the future carry me away in spite of myself. Forced to yield to them, no kind of hope offers itself to my mind. How much we have to mourn: without relatives, without protectors, without friends, without help, what will become of us? Who attaches themselves to honest people when they fall into indigence? Is there any object in the world more disgraced and abandoned than a woman both poor and virtuous? For a long time I have perceived only too clearly that all hearts are icy toward us; everyone avoids us; we're strangers in nature, whom no one wants to recognize. Rogues might be more scorned, but they are better received, less rejected; perhaps they even gain by not being either esteemed or estimable. They employ all their strength in baseness; they crawl, and that flatters the vain; they enjoy their triumphs; they have the pleasure of priming and satisfying their foolish pride—but us, dear brother, what can we do? What course can we take in such great abandon?'

"'Be tranquil, my sister,' he said, 'I've found a means to get us out of the extreme poverty to which fate has reduced us; it's a project that I've been meditating for a long time, since I have nothing better to do. It's necessary to decide to follow it; at least by that way we can procure the necessities of life, and if Fortune looks upon us favorably, the idea I have is one of the routes that often leads to benefits.

"'You know that I have acquired a smattering of medicine; I sometimes studied anatomy on our land, and the knowledge of simples. I have a little Latin

125

and a few Greek words leaned by heart. To that feeble enlightenment I have only to join a great deal of assurance, a grave bearing, a long wing, a staff like a crutch, and that's more than is needed to render me skillful. Many doctors have probably begun with fewer talents. Our landlord seems disposed to oblige us; he's a simple and interested man, to whom one can promise a recompense in order to engage him to tell all the strangers who come to lodge with him that I'm a very clever young man, who got him out of a very dangerous malady. Anyway, he knows a very rich lord who lives a short distance away; the man is attacked by vapors that are all in his mind, whose ills are entirely in his imagination, and whose constitution is weakened by the quantity of remedies he believes himself to be obliged to take. If I can gain access to that visionary, I'm sure of curing his folly; me prescription is certain; I'll give him nothing but good clear soup.'

"I applauded my brother's ideas; he left with the design of going in search of what was necessary to carry out his plan, and I went down to see our landlord to engage him to favor my brother in his new establishment. The man promised to put everything to work in order to procure his success.

"But sir, good and ill fortune are divided; one rarely sees them unite; everything ordinarily goes in the same direction: to the fortunate further prosperities; to the unfortunate, new excesses of disgrace. No one in the world has undergone crueler ordeals than my brother and I. Our life is a nothing but a chain of troubles, which succeed one another without interruption. Always the target of the injustice, the bad faith and the tyranny of men, I can no longer resist.

"Just Heaven!" the young woman cried, "if it is in the extremity of peril that you are pleased to signal your power, have my woes not arrived at their completion?"

The unfortunate young woman's tears interrupted her discourse; I employed what I believed to be the most consoling to tranquilize her.

"Alas, sir," she continued, "if you were born sensitive, this is the time to bring your soul into play and to signal your generosity. In the name of all that you hold dear, deploy the nobility of your sentiments in favor of an unfortunate woman whom everyone flees and abhors."

So saying, the young woman threw herself at my feet. I picked her up immediately, almost as emotional as she was.

"Don't be surprised by my action," she said, sighing. "Those unjust men have taught me to humiliate myself to the utmost depths of my heart. All of them have rejected me; I have suffered everything from their injustices, and they still push barbarism to the extent of wanting me to lose even the consolation of self-esteem. But Monsieur, I am not confusing you with those perverse men, enemies of humanity. I perceive, by the sensitivity that you are showing, that my story has touched you; I ought therefore to regard you as a divinity who will put to flight the troop of wild beasts that has surrounded me thus far. I expect anything of the generous pity that makes you sympathetic to the unfortunate; I dare assure you, sir, that I merit it. Know, then, what is presently the subject of my despair, which is confounding and overwhelming me.

"The unfortunate destiny of my brother led him, on leaving the house, into a side-street where three men were attacking one with such great fury that his generous and sensitive heart could not refuse to take the side of the one who was being beaten so badly. 'Oh, sirs,' he said to them, 'what can have been done to you to drive you to commit such an unjust action. Can you be cowardly enough to set yourselves three upon one? For the sake of your honor, abandon such an unequal combat.' Then one of them, without replying, turned the point of his sword in order to pierce him with it. My brother, taken by surprise, only just had the time to put himself on guard to parry the thrusts of the hothead.

"Meanwhile, one of the other two received a thrust that felled him, and of which he died instantly. The noise they were making finally attracted several people; the guards came and arrested them, and took them to prison. Unfortunately, the man my brother had tried to help died a quarter of an hour later of the wounds he had received, without having had time to justify my brother; the other two, who belonged to persons elevated in dignity, were released immediately, after having taken injustice so far as to charge my unfortunate brother with their comrade's death. Imagine, sir, my despair when I learned that evening that he was detained in a frightful cell.

"Although overwhelmed by that final blow of the fate that was pursuing us, I have not ceased for more than six months to solicit his judges. Alas, I flattered myself that I had touched one of them by my door and my tears; he even appeared to listen to me at first quite favorably, giving me permission to speak to my brother, from whom I obtained all these details . I informed the judge of all the facts that could serve for the justification of my brother, and pleaded his cause myself. Dolor, when it is justly animated by motives of honor, seems to be naturally eloquent. The judge appeared to allow himself to be persuaded, but it was only with a view to seducing me.

"Oh, sir, dare I tell you that that inhuman being only offered me my brother's liberty today in seeking to cover me with shame? Yes, it is only be satisfying his infamous desires that I can obtain the justice due to an innocent man, without which his doom is sworn, and I shall see my wretched brother dragged to a scaffold like a criminal in order to suffer the most shameful death thereon. In that extremity, I have been to throw myself at the feet of those who have made themselves his accusers, in order to implore their pity, but they have all refused to see me; no hope is offered to me. Rejected everywhere, the blow that will cut short the days of my unfortunate brother will pierce my bosom. Alas, what have we done that the gods should pursue us with so much vigor?"

The young woman interrupted herself with sobs, and marks of such great despair that I feared for her life. Penetrated to the depths of my soul by the misfortunes that she had endured, and those that she had yet to dread, and indignant at the injustice of the Merces, I did my best to calm her down.

"Cease, Miss," I added, "a despair that your reason ought to condemn. Be persuaded that there are still men who cherish virtue, who love, respect and protect it. Honor and probity have always been my rules; rely on my cares; count on finding in me a protector all the more zealous to help you promptly because he is sensitive to all the misfortunes that are overwhelming you. I can protest to you that you will see tomorrow the brother who is the cause of your alarms today, and that his presence will reestablish tranquility in your soul. To serve you efficaciously, I shall employ a man whose power is limitless."

The young woman thanked me in the most touching terms; those assurances calmed her, and I left her, after having slipped a purse full of gold behind her armchair.

Moved by the dire fate of the unfortunate woman, I did not think of resting. I went to Zachiel's apartment; the emotion I was experiencing did not surprise him; without rendering himself visible, he had witnessed our conversation.

"I've come to beg you," I said to him, "to interest yourself in favor of a young person whom a chain of misfortunes has reduced to despair. I could not hear her troubles without offering her your protection."

I wanted to tell him the sad story then, but he stopped me.

"I know the injustice of the Merces," the genius said, "and I am not astonished by what this family has experienced on their part. Day is beginning to break; you have promised this victim of intemperance to work for the deliverance of her brother; moments are precious when it is a matter of abridging the pain of someone in the anguish of an imminent death that he believes to be inevitable. Let us hasten to render two souls content, by procuring his liberty; it's time to go."

"Yes, my dear Zachiel," I said, "but the promise I dared to make is only founded on the help I expect from you, for I can do nothing myself."

I followed the genius to the Pacha. The sun had scarcely begun to appear when we went into his study. The genius had rendered me invisible, as well as him, to the eyes of all his domestics.

"I have come," he said to him, in a majestic and severe manner, "to prevent you from committing the blackest of all injustices. You have held in a frightful dungeon for more than six months a young man whose innocence is known to you. Why have you delayed in setting him at liberty?"

"I find it rather singular," said the Pacha, "that you dare to ask me questions. I do not, I think, have to account to you for my conduct. The young man is condemned; the proofs of his crime are complete; it is necessary for him to submit to the fate reserved for those like him, and your audacity makes me suspect that you might be one of his accomplices; on that basis, I could have you arrested."

"Ah, wretch!" cried Zachiel. "I can read your soul and penetrate all its blackness; you are but half of a human creature; you have the form, and the penchant for evil, but you have neither the dignity nor the nobility. I have no fear of your anger or your vengeance; both are impotent with regard to me. I therefore order you to listen to me, vicious man. You have only condemned the young man because his sister had the misfortune to excite your lubricity, and the justice you owe to her brother could only be purchased at the price of her honor.

"In any other circumstance, I would not be astonished that her youth, grace and beauty had inspired lust, but that her face afflicted by despair, its features changed by dolor and its graces withered by tears, was unable to disconcert your lust, and has not made you a protector for that unfortunate; that that lust, far from sympathizing with all her misfortunes, has only received a more brutal confidence; that her misery, fecund in touching expressions, has only determined you to outrage and not to benefits; that at the sight of such an object, that lust has not melted into generous pity; that charity has not caused you to sympathize with the perils to which these misfortunes expose her; that you have listened to the tale of her misfortunes without comprehending their excess, without sensing any confusion of your desires and without being frightened of catching yourself in the horrible design of taking advantage of it; I confess that that I cannot understand how one could bear the weight of such iniquity. One can only regard it as an intrepidity of vice that the imagination of an honest man cannot attain.

"Tyrant that you are, the youth of that woman, prey to all that dolor has of the most bitter, has not been able to touch your soul or excite your compassion; you regard her as a victim come to offer herself to your lubricity; the help that you offer her is as much opprobrium—which is to say that, in order to obtain justice, it is necessary for her to become infamous. In sum, I perceive that you have stifled within yourself the honest man, to set the monster at liberty. Believe me, it is time now to look into yourself, and if you want to merit henceforth the precious title of a just man, reflect on the nobility of our duties in order to fulfill them with equity: cease to protect crime and prostitute justice by the abuse of the authority confided to you; cease to violate with impunity all rights; instead of being the ravisher of a tender ewe, become her protector; and finally, cease looking beneath the bandage the blindfolds you to discover whether those who solicit you share favor, or whether they are soliciting you with hands full of gold. As a final advice, remember that the Supreme Being always has his eyes open to the conduct of a judge, and if he suspends the blade that ought to fall on the heads of wicked and unjust men, it is only to punish them with more severity."

The judge, surprised by the boldness of the remonstrations of the genius, thought that he was seeing and hearing justice personified. Astonished, confused, humiliated and overwhelmed, he could not find any words to justify himself; his pride seemed confused; with his eyes fixed on the floor he maintained a bleak silence. The genius, who perceived that his discourse had made a deep impression on the judge, encouraged him mildly to follow the routes that justice, honor and probity indicated to him. In fact, he had touched that heart, which had previously allowed itself to be drawn away by the torrent of its passions, so effectively that it persisted after that adventure in the sentiments of the most exact probity.

After leaving the judge we went to liberate the young man, whom we took back to his sister.

At first the young woman could only express her joy and gratitude by tears.

"It is to this gentleman," I said, introducing Zachiel to her, "that you owe the liberty of such a tenderly beloved brother."

Then, recovering from the disturbance that our presence had caused her, she expressed herself with natural and touching grace, which depicted so well what was happening in a tender soul sensitive to benefits.

Afterwards, I took them to Monime's apartment, to whom I gave an account of all the misfortunes they had experienced. She was touched, and asked the genius not to leave his work incomplete, and to contribute with all his power to render them happy. The genius established both of them very advantageously, and heaped them with wealth.

Chapter VIII
The Story of Tacius

The expenditures we made, the brilliance of our carriages and the large number of our domestics made the government anxious. Everyone reasoned variously as to our quality and the views that we might have. People naturally given to deception are always suspicious. That is why Zachiel urged us to visit a man who held a high rank in the state.

"You can scarcely dispense with that duty," the genius told us, "because they are very intolerant in this realm of strangers, the purpose of whose voyage is unknown to them. I know that they are beginning to suspect you; it is dangerous to inspire mistrust when one cannot make oneself known, and equally difficult to escape the observation of an old man, always superior by the advantage of his position and that of his experience. This visit will tranquilize him on your account; he certainly possesses the confidence of the prince; it is from him that all graces flow, and his court is much more numerous than that of his master.

"However, even though he has acquired immense wealth, he still sells his favor; it is true that he does it in an oblique fashion and disguises his avarice with his exterior magnificence, which might be imposing if one did not know him, but his head valet sells all the graces and gives him seven eighths of the money he obtains. By that means, neither responsibilities nor employments are distributed to those who have the most merit and talent, but to those who pay the highest price—with the consequence that in this part of Cillenia, one often sees eminent posts occupied by persons whom nature has deprived of the virtues necessary to fill them, which they only owe to their opulence, their cliques or their intrigues."

In order to reach that vizier we were obliged to traverse several antechambers, a long gallery, an audience hall, a bedroom and a dressing room. That entire sequence was garnished with domestics whose rank increased the closer one came to their master. We were finally announced by an old Officer, who introduced us into a private study. Our visit was spent in vague discourse, many questions on the part of the minister and a few offers of service, and concluded with the compliments customary almost throughout Cillenia.

We then left the audience and saw several large rooms filled with individuals of all estates, some of whom had come to pay court, others to request graces or employment. I noticed some who had sad and timid expressions, which interested me in their favor. The recent history of our unfortunates caused me to suppose chagrins. Curious to learn whether or not I was mistaken in my conjectures, I proposed to Monime that we go into the embrasure of a window in order to be able to witness the audience without being noticed.

"I've come to a conclusion," I told her, "which is that an honest man is almost always humiliated, almost always devoid of wealth, and almost always sad. He has no friends, because his friendship is not useful for anything; people avoid him, are disdainful and scornful of him, and they even blush to find themselves with him. Why? It's because he is only estimable, and I do not believe that quality counts for much in this world."

"I can only admire the justice of your remark," said Monime. "What a difference for those on whom gold and silver shine from all directions! One would think that they spread more virtue over them than those who have no income. Look at their free and bold physiognomy, their bold gaze, that tranquil and satisfied attitude; everything, including their plumpness, announces opulence."

As soon as the vizier appeared, all the rich people advanced toward him in a free and easy manner; he listened to them calmly, and replied to them in a gracious and affable fashion; but to those poor people whose timidity announced indigence, he turned his back; his domestics moved them away, and although they tried to run after him, and several tried to vanquish, by the force of the lungs, the difficulty of expressing oneself while walking too fast, it was a waste of effort; they articulated poorly, and were not heard. When one asks for grace, if one's heart is in the right place and one has nobility in one's soul, one is always short of breath.

We left, feeling compassion for the lot of those unfortunates.

"How humiliating it is," I said to Monime, "for a man of merit to be obliged to make petitions of the great. You must have noticed the welcome given to all those rich people; that proves that wealth is the only advantage that distinguishes a Cillenian. That is what serves to repair the lack of merit, to fill the frightful void of a man distinguished by birth or elevated by fortune, and everything yields only to the gleam of riches; they put up for auction dignities, responsibilities, nobility, favor, reputation, alliances, and finally set the price of virtue itself."

As we were about to climb into our carriage, we saw a young man come out of the vizier's house whose pale and emaciated face, sad, defeated, confused and humiliated expression made a deep impression on us. His physiognomy announced the candor of his soul. Monime, animated in his favor by a sentiment of pity, pointed him out to me. Inclined, like her to render him service, I advanced toward him.

"Might we be useful to you in some way, Sir?" I said. "It isn't curiosity that engages me to ask you that question; we're strangers, doubtless moved by sympathy to take an interest in you. It's true that, not having the honor of being known to you, the proposal must appear singular to you, but sir, virtue carries with it a certain character, which is imprinted in the hearts of those who cherish it."

"Alas, Sir," he replied, uttering a deep sigh, "your sensibility makes the nobility of your soul evident; far from being offended by the offer of charity you make in my favor, I regard it as one of those evidences of providence that are only manifest in the extremity of a peril. I don't want to stop you here for long; we're not in a place here where I can inform you of my troubles, and since you have the generosity of taking an interest in the fate of a poor man whom fortune never ceases to persecute, do my the kindness of indicating to me your residence and a time when I might, without being importunate, have the honor of seeing you."

"If your affairs don't summon you elsewhere," I said, "give me the pleasure of climbing into our carriage with us."

The young man seemed very appreciative of my proposition, and made no difficulty about accompanying us.

Having arrived at the house, Monime, in order to put him at his ease, lavished politeness upon him.

"In truth, my Lady," said the young man, "I am so deeply appreciative of your kindness, and my Lord's, that I lack expressions to testify my gratitude."

"Wait," said Monime, "until we have effected the desire that we have to oblige you. Speak, sir, have no fear of deploying your soul; misfortune does not depreciate merit at all, and only serves to add luster to virtue. We're ready to listen to you."

"I obey, my Lady," said the young man. "You see in me a gentleman whose misfortunes obtained their source as soon as his birth. Left at a young age under the supervision of a guardian, who had need of one himself, that man, far from conserving the income of a sufficiently honest property that my parents had left me, dissipated the funds after having ruined himself gambling. His wife and their only daughter, who was almost the same age as me, were obliged to seek refuge with one of her relatives, only too glad to be taken in.

"As for me, then aged seventeen, left to myself without any resource, my first idea was to enlist in the army, but hazard led me to encounter a young man with whom I had made part of my studies. The young man remarked an alteration in my spirits and asked me for the reason. I had no difficulty in confiding my troubles to him, and the predicament I was in. 'I'll get you out of it, my dear Tacius,' he said. 'Let's begin by having dinner; afterwards, I'll take you to a lady who is the favorite of a high priest of fortune.' I went with him to the lady's house; she received us politely.

"After a few days, my friend came to tell me that I had been appointed to an employment of two thousand pounds, on condition that I gave twelve hundred to the woman who had obtained it for me. Although that condition seemed to me to be rather onerous, I nevertheless expressed my gratitude to him. We immediately went to the lady's house to draw up our agreement there.

"I came out with my friend and thanked him, not only for having obliged me, but also for the promptitude and zeal with which he had done so. 'I would have liked you to enjoy the whole of the income of the employment,' he said, 'but that woman, who has chosen me to be the high priest's substitute, and who,

133

between us, does not fail to furnish me with considerable sums, has never wanted to be consent to relax her customs. It would therefore have been necessary for me to quarrel with her, and I confess that she is a great resource to me.' I assured the young man that I was only too glad to be able at least to subsist.

"In spite of the mediocrity of the income I obtained from my employment, I nevertheless found the secret, by means of my economy, of being appropriately dressed. After a few years, while out walking, I encountered my guardian's widow; she was with Rosalie, her daughter. The elegance of their attire initially caused me not to recognize them, but the lady advanced toward me. 'Is it really you, my dear Tacius?' she said to me. 'How many anxieties you've caused me. I've been searching for you for me time, in order to make some reparation for the wrongs my husband did you, by sharing our good fortune with you.'

"During that speech, my eyes were attached to Rosalie; my heart was moved by the sight of the object of my first love. Rosalie, who had once been animated by a similar sentiment, could not hide her disturbance either; her forehead was covered by a blush that announced to me that absence had not altered the tenderness she had always felt toward me.

"That mute conversation did not interrupt her mother's, who informed me of the death of the relative to whose house she had retired after the disaster. That relative, who was very rich, had nominated her as her sole heir. She gave me a long account of the cares and complaisances she had employed to capture the old woman's benevolence and lead her to the point of making a testament in her favor. She ended up by inviting me to supper at her house.

"During the supper, Clia told me that she wanted me henceforth to have no other table than hers, and that she was going to prepare me an apartment in her house in order that we would no longer be separated. I accepted those offers unhesitatingly, which enabled me to see my dear Rosalie every day. I went, therefore, to live with Clia, her mother, for whom I had always had a great affection. I only quit those two amiable individuals to satisfy the duties of my employment.

"Clia, who had made considerable inroads into society since her opulence, introduced me to all her acquaintances, and eventually obtained, by means of the number of protectors she employed in my favor, a very considerable employment for me. As soon as I was installed therein, I asked her to complete my happiness by allowing me to marry Rosalie. She agreed joyfully, and our marriage as concluded within a week.

"Three years passed in a union that love and gratitude had formed. But how dearly I paid, my lady, for that time of tranquility! Soon, that happy calm was succeeded by storms. My guardian's creditors discovered that his widow was living in opulence, and that she enjoyed a considerable income, by virtue of a rich succession. They immediately obtained information as to where her properties were situated, and had them seized, without our having had time to react. I tried to intervene in the suit, but their claims were anterior to mine; they were preferred, because Clia was unfortunately engaged for considerable sums.

"In consequence, she had the dolor of seeing all her property sold, without them acquitting her of all her obligations. Although in despair after her disaster, she at least found reasons for consolation with us, since my employment was more than sufficient for us to live comfortably. Nevertheless, the loss of our suit determined me to cut back on our carriages and a few of our domestics. That reform distanced the false friends who surrounded us, who, far from sympathizing with us for an unmerited misfortune, had the cruelty to calumniate us, by spreading false stories on my account and representing me as a wastrel. Those rumors eventually reached the ears of my protectors, and I was dismissed, without being able to justify myself.

"For the more than ten years that I have been soliciting, I have not been able to obtain anything. Rebuffed everywhere, I have been gradually forced to sell the effects we had in order to support my mother-in-law, my wife and three children, whom I see perishing of need, finally reduced to frightful poverty. To complete my woes, my dear Rosalie, unable to bear her troubles any longer, has fallen ill; she has been in bed for six weeks, deprived of all help. But what am I saying, my Lady? Bed? It's nothing but a poor mattress; the rest has gone to pay our rent, and we no longer occupy anything but a grain-loft, from which we'll soon be expelled.

"A week ago I presented myself to the memory of one of my former protectors, to whom I gave a frightful depiction of our situation. I had no response but rebuffs. If I had had money to give to one of his secretaries, I might perhaps have been able to obtain employment, but of all those inhuman individuals deigned to say to me distractedly, the most consoling was: "I'm sorry; there's nothing vacant"—while I see considerable positions given every day to people whose entire talent consists of including them in a concert party, or lending themselves to complaisances unworthy of an honest man."

Monime was so touched by the gentleman's misfortunes that, in order to remedy them immediately, she took the decision to present him with a purse full of gold. "I do not intend, sir," she said, "to limit myself to that feeble assistance. You ought no longer to regard it as an effect of my charity, but as a tribute to all that honest people owe to those humiliated by fortune. If I did not fear humiliating your family by rendering myself a witness to their misery, I would not defer for an instant bring them the consolations they merit. Go, sir, fly to their aid; and when you have put them in a more appropriate state, and you judge that they can receive our visit without importunity, do us the kindness to come and fetch us."

Tacius, transported like a man beside himself, received the present that Monime made him with a tremulous hand. "Oh, my Lady," he cried, falling to his knees and kissing the helpful hand respectfully, which he bathed with tears that he could not hold back, and which gratitude caused to flow, "what idea ought I to have of such a noble and tender fashion of being kind? Ought I to believe that sentiments so generous can be the prerogative or a mortal? Perhaps there is too much vanity in thinking that a divinity has wanted to humanize herself and descend as far as me in order to alleviate my despair and change my distress into delight, but my Lady, whoever you are, you will always merit the respect and adoration of all those who have the good fortune to approach you."

Chapter IX
The Conclusion of the Story of Tacius, and an Encounter with Ashtaroth

Monime and I were still deploring the unfortunate fate of Tacius when Zachiel came in. We gave him an account of our visit, the encounter we had had on leaving the vizier's house, and all the injustices the young man had suffered.

"What a world this is!" Monime added. "How hard, cruel and barbaric its people are! It seems that the further we advance in Cillenia, the more we see vice triumphing over virtue."

"It is true," said the genius, "that an honest man cannot succeed in this world without attracting jealousy; envy is unleashed, a thousand obstacles are raised against him; competitors betray him, enemies thwart him and succeed themselves by means of intrigue, dishonesty and crime; then incense is offered to them everywhere; the voice of the public gives grace to their faults; it waits, to reproach them, until others have taken their place by virtue of their fall. A man discredited by an unexpected check, all of whose projects of elevation have been overturned, must expect to see all his friends disappear; even his relatives will not recognize him, and seem ashamed to be associated with him. But if he comes back into favor, he will see them reassemble and honor themselves by including him in their companies.

"When one wants to succeed in Cillenia, the first step that it is necessary to take with regard to a man in position is to seek information as to the friends he consults and the women who govern him. It is only by following that path that one can succeed, and it is only by spreading gold in his channels that his graces can be obtained. Here, wealth ill-acquired is possessed without remorse. A guilty party hardly ever reproaches himself for his injustices; he finds his excuse in his industry and believes himself to be infallible in his success. A fortunate ambition always seems innocent; the end justifies the means and their cause. In sum, a certainty of hard work is worthless to a man of intelligence; the slightest of advantages gives favor to a fool.

"In Cillenia, and in this province above all, virtue, morals, probity, good faith in treaties—all of that—is merely useless furniture; no attention is paid to it; everyone thinks only of his fortune; provided that one is a good calculator, and that one is prepared to venture all or nothing, nothing more is necessary in order to be rich."

Tacius came back a few days later to ask us or permission to introduce us to his family. "The hope of a happier future," he told us, "by virtue of the protection that you have kindly accorded to me, has helped Rosalie to recover, like a penetrating balm that has cured her completely, apart from a sight weakness."

"I shall not permit your wife to go out so soon," Monime said, "since you tell me that our presence will not cause her any emotion injurious to her health, you will not mind if I anticipate her."

She ordered the horses hitched up, and almost without any response to Tacius' thanks, who seemed confused by that excess of generosity, we climbed into the carriage, after which he indicated the location of his dwelling to the coachman.

We found the unfortunate family in a state of languor, which made us see how much they had suffered. I shall not report the conversation that we had with them; suffice it to say that Clia and her daughter employed all that gratitude could dictate to them of the most tender and the most touching in order to let us know how sensible they were of our kindness. Rosalie, especially, charmed me; she expressed herself with the simple and natural eloquence that easily finds the path to the heart. The young woman, without being conventionally beautiful, combined a fine physiognomy with graces, an air of gentleness and nobility that her troubles had been unable to efface. Monime lavished many caresses on her, distributed several valuable jewels to her children, and we left them, both very satisfied.

Tacius and his family paid court assiduously to Monime while we were resident in the city. The genius, knowing the purity of their hearts, assured them of a fortunate and independent future, which they enjoyed in tranquility.

We then traveled through various other provinces contained in that globe, but we saw nothing anywhere but people oppressed by the fraud and rapine of the high priests of Fortune, or by the politics of the great, families ruined by the impenetrable rubric of prosecutors and their odious chicanery, and citizens imprisoned as a result of the unworthy plots of their enemies. In sum, all of Cillenia is filled with nothing but spies, paid informers, calumniators, crooks, gamblers, pickpockets, fraudulent bankrupts, thieves, seducers, fake scholars, partisans, hypocrites, slanderers, mockers and rogues enriched at the expense of the poor.

Monime, distressed by encountering nothing but knavery and bad faith wherever we went, asked the genius to take us to another world.

"In the name of the amity you have for us, my dear Zachiel," she said to him, "let us not remain any longer with men of wrath, injustice and menaces, who, if it were in their power to have their tyranny forgotten, as it is easy for them to prevent protest by the fear of unjust punishment, would further reduce those poor people to the equivalent of a clock with no driving mechanism. Let us hasten, then, to spend time on another planet, where nothing is prohibited but crime. Let us seek examples to follow, which will cause us to lose the memory of these; take us to the world where the gentle peace that once reigned among humans has taken refuge. Why do these people no longer enjoy it? Is it a scourge of heaven, or an effect of the vicissitudes of time? Tell me, my dear Zachiel, will the time come when every created being will have to bear the seal of misfortune from birth, and will the One who submerged the lands under a deluge of water submerge them again under a deluge of misery? Hasten, then, to transport us to the place for which we have been hoping for so long."

"It is not yet in my power to satisfy you in that article," said Zachiel. "Subject as I am to the order and the plan that I have drawn up, it is necessary for you to conform to it. Thus, you will not be able to arrive at the world that ought to satisfy and fulfill your desires without passing through more than one proof; but, assisted by my advice, I flatter myself that you will resist them all."

Night having overtaken us, we stopped at the entrance to a city, where several people had climbed up to a large, high dome in order to examine the stars. Each of them had a large telescope resting on the shoulder of another.

"What is that ceremony, then?" I asked Zachiel.

"Those people," he told me, "believe that the firmament encloses precisely the figures and resemblances of everything that is born and which shines in their world; they affirm that all the parts of the universe have between them a beauty of relationship and assortment, which leads their astronomers in all their observations. Those whom you see on that dome regard the heavens as a veritable book, in which everything that happens in nature is written in legible characters, traced with great exactitude, forming separate words and lines, but that the celestial alphabet in question is very difficult to decipher. Thus, their greatest study is astrology, mathematics and geometry.

"From that comes, no doubt, the penchant they have for magic; it is from this planet that I don't know how many subtle and mysterious inventions are obtained, such as astronomical mirrors, or the art of hearing what is pronounced by the Moon, the wheel of onomancy, or the relationships between names; the sphere of divination; the particular system of colors, in which one finds that they are all signs of possession when they appear during sleep; the magical and superstitious medicine that consists of sympathies and antipathies or in the reciprocal combat of elementary qualities, and a thousand similar follies, which they combine with astrology—a vain science, in truth, but which flatters two human passions: curiosity, by promising to pierce the future; and pride, by insinuating that destinies are written in the heavens.

"One ought, however, to note one thing that never escapes the penetration of a clever Cillenian, and that is that there is ordinarily found in every person something definite, either in the physiognomy, the bearing, the mannerisms, or in a certain enchainment of the passions, which can permit the divination of what ought to happen to them, and that it is only that examination that astrologers study in order to produce their horoscope."

We were getting ready to quit the planet when we perceived the figure of a gigantic man, whose appearance surprised Zachiel infinitely. He recognized him immediately as Ashtaroth, one of the greatest captains of Pluto.

What are you doing here?" asked the genius, stopping him. "I am no longer astonished that the greater number of those inhabiting this would have become so rascally and wicked; doubtless, you and your legions are flying incessantly around the Cillenians in order to blow the pestilential venom of their noxious and corrupt tongues into their ears?"

"You're mistaken, "Ashtaroth replied. "It's true that I have brought several of my legions here; you're not unaware that our intention has never been to work to make humans better, but be certain that these, naturally inclined to evil, have no need of us to be corrupted, since this world has always furnished us abundantly with as many subjects as the Prince of Darkness can desire for the maintenance of his table and that of his ministers. You will perhaps be surprised to learn that I am here by order of Pluto, in order to teach enable his troops to learn new lessons in the art of catching humans. I only arrived two days ago, and in order to bring you up to date with my commission, it's necessary to tell you what has happened in Hell.

"For a number of years, hosts of people have descended into the tenebrous empire driven there by Discord; those individuals, similar to serpents, have so increased in their number and grandeur, that they thought themselves strong enough to act as masters, commencing by exercising the same functions that they had on Earth. All the inhabitants of those subterranean places, whether demon or damned, surprised to be overburdened with assignations and requests, indignant at such a vexation being introduced into Hell, joined forces in order to take their complaints to the infernal judges. To begin with, however, Rhadamanthus, Aeacus and Minos made no effort to stop such infractions, doubtless regarding them as trivia that did not merit their attention.

"Emboldened by that negligence, believing themselves authorized to vomit all their peculations and knaveries; animated by Discord, excited by the three Furies, who never ceased to shake their torches over them in order to inflame them more and more, they finally pushed their audacity so far as to threaten Pluto, the sovereign of Hell, that his realm might really be seized and divided up between them. At that threat, all Hell assembled, and everyone took a side. The bankrupts, the gamblers, the traitors, the trimmers and all the thieves, great and small, rallied to the standard of the wretches, forming a vast army. In vain we tried to return the rebels to their duty. Several battles were fought, without any advantage on our part.

"When Pluto learned about all this disorder, which we strove to hide from him, he was foaming with rage and wanted to expel his three judges, but on the advice of Proserpine he took no action against them. In order to remedy the disorder his council proposed to gather all the most battle-hardened demons, and the Prince, seated on his throne between Aeacus and Rhadamanthus, addressed this speech to us:

"'Listen to me, demons, and let all Hell tremble at my voice. I have learned with righteous anger of the outrage done to my glory, that you have had the laxity of allowing yourselves to be vanquished in blackness and malevolence by this vermin that has been introduced into my empire. I cannot believe that you have had the weakness to betray me by ceding them our rights, but is this the way that you maintain the reputation of my troops? What will they think henceforth on Earth, where you are not unaware that people obtain news almost every day of what is happening here? I foresee, to your shame, that many mortals will no longer fear you; you will be regarded as wretched petty imps, who pale by comparison with these men of discord and chicanery before who you have been obliged to lower the flag; they alone will be feared; it is already known that they have taken possession of all your ruses, and I have received reliable information that they are presently more feared on earth than several legions of my troops.

"'You, Lucifer, Beelzebub and Ashtaroth, whom I have always regarded as my best generals, what were you doing during the battles that have put my armies at a disadvantage? Doubtless you were amusing yourselves in the hypocrites' quarter, to which I relegated that new sect of fanatics that the Cillenian world has produced for us and who are descending here in platoons. Your most agreeable exercise is to perform the same exercises on them that they perform on earth; to see them crucified, beaten, roasted, threaded with hot irons and a thousand similar follies is a charming spectacle for you.

"'It's not that I want to criticize you for amusing yourselves with those comedies; the mind needs relaxation. On the contrary, I know that they fulfill a moral role, which educates you as to a thousand subtleties and tricks of finesse of which you were previously ignorant, capable in future of being useful to you when you employ all the things you have learned to the entire human spaces, against whom, like all my troops, you have sworn an implacable hatred. But as recreation ought not to prejudice duties, in order to punish you for having neglected concern for my glory, I exile you from my presence and order you to take several legions of my soldiers, which you will take to the planet Mercury, in order to put them in garrison in all the bodies of those men of chicanery and discord.

"'You will also send into them hypocrites, traitors, gamblers and all kinds of malefactors, in order that they can undertake a new apprenticeship in rascality, blackness and knavery—after you have first had crushed in the great mortar of Hell all those men who have debauched Tisiphone, Megaera and Alecto, in order to make them serve their bold enterprises against the rights of my empire. I want to see them pulverized, with all those who have revolted, in order to make a mustard that will revive the demons' appetite. I order that a corrosive sublimate should also be added, for I think it a very good purgative against cowardice. With regard to the hypocrites, fanatics and bigots, let them continue to be caramelized; I'll reserve them for my dessert.'

"When Pluto had pronounced this judgment, which made all Hell tremble, he descended from his throne in order to go and unwind with Proserpine for a day—or, to put it better, a tiring night—leaving it to Rhadamanthus and Aeacus to have his orders carried out. The infernal judges acquitted themselves in that matter with all the zeal that the Prince of Demons expected. As for us, after having completely satisfied the orders of the sovereign of the empire of the dead, we immediately left for the world of Mercury, with the design of abridging our exile, if possible, by profiting from the ever-varied and ever-new examples one encounters there at every step. I've distributed my legions in proportion to the extent of the provinces. I flatter myself on finding amusement there, and occupation for my troops, whom I shall be careful to keep on their toes, in order to restore them to grace."

Zachiel, who perceived that Monime was ready to faint in terror, sent Ashtaroth away; he disappeared instantly, and left us in an indescribable surprise.

THE THIRD HEAVEN: VENUS

Chapter I
The Genius Takes Monime and Seaton to the Third Heaven, the Planet Venus

The space that it was necessary for us to traverse in order to pass from the planet Mercury to that of Venus gave us time to admire the new perfections of the heavens. I thought I saw other heavens shining around them, which might be compared to officious lamps spreading light over light; their precious radiance and their sacred influences appeared to be converging on the world of Venus.

The genius took us down on to a plain decorated with the most precious gifts of Flora. On one side of that charming spot the River of Delights could be seen flowing, and on the other, that of Sensuality, which maintained by their gentle warmth the plants with which their banks were embellished; and the sun, joining its gilded redness with that glow, made them shine like a sea of jasper receiving a new honor from those garlands.

Swans could be seen floating on the two rivers, with arched necks and their white wings lifted up like a royal mantle, carrying their majestic bodies forward. Sometimes they were also seen the quite the water to cleave the median region of the air. In sum, I immediately perceived, on entering the world of Venus, that all of nature respires nothing but pleasure, joy and voluptuousness there, and it seems that the entire universe pays tribute to its obedience and is forced to render homage to the preeminence of its empire.

"I don't know," said Monime, "whether the new air we're breathing is already having an influence on me, but I confess that I have the loveliest, most cheerful and most agreeable idea of the planet Venus. Those we have visited have offered me objects of scorn are compassion; this one will at least furnish us with amusement. What a pretty world Venus is! How charming it must be! Why, my dear Zachiel, it seems to me that I'm on the isle of Cythera so lauded by our poets. In fact, is it not Venus herself who is its Queen? That court is surely the assembly of the Graces, and I'm convinced that it's made to fix here the most indifferent philosophy. That must be the case in this world where Hebe, the goddess of youth was born, since it's to Zephyr and Aurora that she owes her life. Laughter, games and all the mischievous little gods cannot fail to inhabit that court; I even believe that Voluptuousness makes her ordinary abode hers, and that Amour, the god that animates nature, governs all the pleasures of this world."

"It's certain, beautiful Monime," Zachiel said, smiling, "that Amour makes himself more keenly felt in this part of the globe of Venus, which is named Idalienne.[20] He is on all the worlds, however, and holds the middle ground between heaven and earth; but he cannot be a god, because the gods are essentially happy, and Amour is incessantly seeking to achieve that. There are moments when he elevates humans to the felicity of the gods, and others when he reduces the gods themselves to the level of humans.

"Amour," Zachiel continued, "takes his birth from two genii that hazard brings together; one presides over abundance, the other poverty. From his father he obtains audacity, vivacity of spirit, confidence in his strength, the art of setting ambushes, a certain manner of insinuating himself, persuading and vanquishing; the contrary qualities come from his mother—which is to say, famine, the fear of revealing himself, the indigence that drives him incessantly to make demands, the timidity that often causes him to miss the best opportunities and an inexhaustible fund of desires. It is by virtue of that mixture that he passes without perceiving it from life to death, and from death to life; he is incessantly sighing after voluptuousness, and stakes all his happiness on the game."

"In truth," said Monime, interrupting the genius, "I don't understand. Since we have entered the empire of Venus, I believe, my dear Zachiel, that your discourse might well be analogous to the mysteries of the goddess, for I cannot comprehend anything of what you just said. What does this new genealogy that you are giving to Amour signify? Is he not the child of Venus? Why, then, are you employing a different allegory today to make him descend from genii? That implies that there are celestial spirits that have amused themselves by fabricating Amour. But tell me, I beg you, whether, in that agreeable pastime, they have thought about the happiness of humans. I would be curious to know how they express their fires; is it by gentle commerce, by tender gazes, or rather by…?"

"Stop," said the genius. "Don't take your curiosity any further. Let it be sufficient for you to know that genii are perfectly happy, that their felicity lacks nothing, and that there is scarcely any true happiness without veritable love. It refines thoughts and augments courage; when it combines the union of hearts with that of innocence, its seat is in reason, provided that it is judicious and does not allow itself to be absorbed by sensuality; individuals ought to unite themselves by pure desires that do not soil the soul, by a mutual confidence, and by sweet smiles that are an overflowing of the heart, and which serve to reanimate the fires frequently."

---

[20] "Venus Idalienne" is an epithet employed in French translations of Virgil's *Aeneid*; the reference is to Mount Ida, where Venus was awarded the golden apple by Paris in the famous beauty contest that led to the Trojan War.

"You can say what you like, my dear Papa," said Monime, continuing her pleasantries, "but all your grave reasoning can never prevent me from regarding you as the father of that malign Amour who only takes pleasure in making nests, for you strongly resemble the portrait you have just painted."

"Well," Zachiel replied, "to punish you for your allusion, I shall cause you to take on the form of an Idalienne; I shall allow the forces dominating this world to act upon you, and we shall see how you treat my so-called son, and whether you have strength enough to defend yourself against his arrows."

The genius immediately transformed her into a nymph; he gave her the stature and the majesty of Diana, the youth of Flora, the beauty and the graces of Venus, with the smiling expression of Amour.

"As for you, my dear Seaton," said Zachiel, "I don't want you to quit Monime for a single instant; as I know the range of your strength, I believe that it is prudent not to expose you to temptations that it is almost impossible for a man to resist."

I confess that I was very annoyed with Zachiel for the preference that he had just accorded to Monime.

Why, I wondered, *is he giving more strength to a sex that everyone accuses of so much fragility? Is it possible that the sex that seems to our eyes to be so delicate and so feeble nevertheless retains more firmness on occasion? What, then, is the injustice of men?*

Then, looking at Monime, her beauty and graces gave birth in me to violent desires, without the bonds of blood being able to put any brake on them. I forgot them, and imagined that in appearing in my natural form, I would at least have been able to drive away lovers. I thought that it would have been much safer if Monime had remained a fly in the empire of Venus, if I were not to be in the form that the genius had just made her take on. I rightly feared the influences of that planet, and although we had both escaped that of the Moon, this one seemed to me to have much more dangerous consequences for the interests of my heart. Even so, I dared not make known to the genius the violent agitations of jealousy by which I had just been animated.

Zachiel gave Monime the most beautiful carriage; it was in the form of a shell, ornamented by the most beautiful paintings, which represented the different attributes of the goddess Venus. On one side one could see her rendezvous with the god Mars, and several little amours that appeared to be frolicking around her; on the other the despair that the death of Adonis seemed to cause her, and her retreat to the island of Lesbos.

More than fifty Gnomes and Gnomines were summoned to ornament Monime's retinue and to serve her. Not being able to distance myself or lose sight of her, I placed myself in a curl of her hair, and we set off.

When we reached the bank of a canal, the night star had already traveled more than half of its course; the sister of the god of day was mirrored in the transparent waters, which were stirred by a light zephyr, making the surface quiver with an agreeable murmur. Swans whiter than snow were floating majestically on the crystal liquid.

It was the month of April, a time consecrated in that empire to public rejoicing, because that season reanimates all nature, causing pleasures as well as flowers to be reborn. The mild and temperate air that reigns in the world then inspires a cheerful and frolicsome humor in Idalians, which attracts them to the banks of the canal, which form a delightful promenade. We saw them arriving from all directions, and I noticed that the men and the women were uniquely occupied with their adornments, their beauty and their graces; joy and pleasure were equally evident in their faces, but their attitudes were too affected; one did not see the noble simplicity or the amiable modesty that are the greatest charm of beauty, and which alone can fix an honest heart.

The impression of laxity, the artistry of composing their features, their vain adornments, their bold gazes, which they sometimes strove to render languishing in seeking those of men—in a word, everything that I saw to begin with in their behavior—seemed to me to be vile and despicable.

The genius told me that in this world libertinage renders the men and women illustrious. "It makes heroes and heroines of them; it is displayed at promenades and spectacles. Those women you have just seen, who appear to you to be similar to divinities, and which one might mistake for goddesses educated in the art of pleasing rather than mere mortals, have all renounced the virtue and modesty that is the most beautiful ornament of the sex. They are only formed for debauchery; they have acquired the talent of insinuation; the graces of speech seem to make honey flow from their lips; nothing is more persuasive than their conversation. They combine a becoming exterior with a provocative attitude that subjugates men, and the mind, ever attached, puts up all the less resistance because it finds pleasure in allowing itself to be vanquished.

"The gentle violence of those flattering objects tames the most savage natures, softens the most ferocious, intoxicates the strongest; it is a magnet that attracts the best-tempered steel. It often happens, however, that they fall victim to their own lures. It is only for these sirens that the Idalians ignominiously prostitute their virtue and renown, however. Sometimes, repentance cases them to expiate their insensate transports; then reason returns as soon as they cease to be their admirers; the charm is broken; the arrows shot by foolish Amour are no more than blunted darts carried away by the wind; a scornful glance renders such weapons futile; they are no longer anything but feeble minds that have allowed themselves to be dazzled."

As we approached the queen's palace, I thought I was seeing Armide's enchanted island or the gardens of Flora. First we entered a beautiful avenue; the trees that composed it compelled admiration by the enormous height of their crowns; on raising one's eyes to their summits, one doubts that the earth can support them, or suspects that it might be them that are carrying the earth suspended from their roots; one might think that their proud brows have been forced to furrow by the weight of celestial globes, and that they only support their burden while groaning; their arms, extended toward the sky, seem to be embracing it and requesting the stars for the pure benignity of their influence, in order to receive it without having lost any of their innocence in the bed of the elements.

On all sides in the delightful place one sees flowers that, without having any other gardener than nature, emit an agreeable odor that stimulates and simultaneously satisfies the sense of smell; one is often spoiled for choice between the rose and the jasmine, the honeysuckle and the violet.

Further away, one thinks one can hear streams, by way of their soft murmur, recounting their amours to the pebbles that surround them. Here the birds cause the air to vibrate with the sound of their songs, and the soft chorus of those melodious throats becomes so general that one might think that every leaf had acquired the voice of the nightingale. The variations of their songs form a concert so perfect, the echoes take so much pleasure therefrom that they seem to be repeating the tunes in order to learn them by heart.

Some distance away, a jealous river grumbles as it flows, irritated by its inability to imitate them. It is only in this world that Amour reigns imperiously over all of nature, and the sky, the earth and the waters recognize his domination.

To either side the palace there are two carpets of grass that form an emerald expanse as far as the eyes can see, combined with the confused mixture of colors that nature attaches to millions of little flowers whose shades are confounded therein, and whose tint is so fresh one has no doubt that they have escaped from the amorous kisses of zephyrs that are hastening to caress them. It seems that places so charming would like to engage the heavens to unite with the earth.

Through the middle of those vast and perfect carpets runs the seething silver of a rustic spring, which seems very proud to see the edges of its bed enameled with orange-trees, myrtles and lemon-trees, and those little flowers cluster as if to dispute the glory of being mirrored there first; one breathes an embalmed air in that place.

We finally went into the queen's palace, which is made of transparent marble. The edifice has an exceedingly majestic appearance. Above the architecture on each side is a massive fronton, on which one sees sculpted in relief the most agreeable adventures of the goddess Venus, who is represented there in the nude. All the apartments are full of mirrors, as are the ceilings. The display of the palace is the most agreeable one can imagine, as is the distribution of the gardens, where art and nature appear to collaborate obligingly to embellish such a delightful abode.

Zachiel introduced Monime to the queen under the name of Taymuras, Princess of Georgia.[21] I was very surprised by the quality and the rank that the genius made her take, but he assured me that the dignity in question was justly due to her; she sustained it with grandeur and majesty. She was accorded in that court all the honors merited by such a distinguished birth, especially when it is accompanied by the rarest qualities. The queen wanted her to be lodged in her palace, and heaped her with amity.

Monime appeared in that court as a new divinity, and her dazzling beauty soon attracted the suffrage of all the fops, who are very abundant on that planet; one might think that they are birds of all worlds; they made haste to pay court to her. I do not know how I did not die of jealousy, dread, anger or chagrin; it is certain that all those emotions agitated me by turns during our sojourn in that court.

---

[21] I have retained the spelling of "Taymuras" used in the original in the account of Venus, although the author subsequently alters it; I shall add the necessary explanatory footnotes to the name and its implications at the point in the text when they become crucially relevant; it is simply used here as a convenient alias..

Chapter II
The Mores of the Idalians

In the empire of Venus it is women who govern the state. The most important negotiations are made by them; all the changes that happen and great events are their work. They dispose all responsibilities, all employments, all eminent positions and all governments, although only men appear at the head of their councils.

The Idaliennes, more skilful than the women of our world, do not recognize the rights that men have judged it wise appropriate to claim for themselves, nor the severe rules that are imposed upon them; they say that they are almost impossible to observe. It is true that on our world men think they have the right to demand everything. They take their generosity do far as to attribute to women a great deal of weakness and more vivacity in their passions, and simultaneously demand more strength than they have themselves to surmount them; I would like to ask them whence comes that exclusive privilege of being able to anticipate all their desires, yield to all their impulses and only listen to the voice of nature, while they scarcely accord to women the faculty of vegetation; they only regard them as automata, who should only serve as the ornament of a drawing room , which they would like to decorate with various changes.

It would be necessary, to judge with equity the weakness and flighty humor that is said to be the portion of the fair sex, to reduce things to a fair equality, in order to be able to examine, setting prejudice apart, whether, in spite of the frivolity attributed to women, they are not a thousand time less inconstant than men. It is well known that when a fop becomes unfaithful, his conduct is justified all those of his species; no one bothers to protest against his perfidy, and the mistress he has abandoned becomes one triumph more for him; but if that mistress wants to avenge herself on the infidel by substituting a new lover for him, it is settled that she is a coquette, fickle and perfidious, and the entire nation of lovers condemns he without appeal. The same action that adds to the glory of the man dooms forever the woman who has been unfortunate enough to conceive a liking for him and confide herself to his probity.

Meanwhile, women are incessantly decried; they are accused of inconstancy and infidelity; a virtue proof against anything is demanded of them, and the unjust men who have made the laws want to reduce them to a harsh slavery, while they accord themselves a complete liberty. The consequence of that is what one sees every say, which is to say that a surly, jealous, eccentric, bigoted or miserly husband imagines a thousand chimeras and mistakes the frenetic visions that agitate him for realities, which he publishes loudly; then all of marital society takes his side, condemning the wife without a hearing, and all women in general find themselves engulfed by the devastating verdict that the jealous senate delivers against them.

I am always astonished that women do not band together, that they have not imagined forming a separate society, in order to avenge themselves on the injustices that men do to them; may I live long enough to see that fortunate usage of their courage! But until now they have been too coquettish and too dissipated to occupy themselves seriously with the interests of their sex. I have noticed on almost all the worlds that it is nothing but self-regard and vanity that enchains them; personal interest comes to the rescue of a heart already seduced by the lure of the pleasure they promise themselves, and which often only resides in their imagination; those are doubtless the reasons that prevent them from banding together, and which make them abandon the common cause.

Among the Idalians the law is egalitarian, and amour, far from being a torture, only serves to assure their happiness. A man who dares to boast in that empire of always being insensible, would be regarded as stupid or an automaton, and they even try to purge the country of them, in order to avoid the scandal of their conduct.

Among that people, a tender heart is the most noble gift they can receive from Heaven; it is only the delicacy of sentiments that distinguishes them; it is to the ardor to please that they owe their most beautiful knowledge; they claim that it was Amour who first gave them the idea of writing; the art of painting was also invented by him. It is certain that on examining the most considerable events there, one sees that they almost all owe their source to tenderness.

An Idalian believes that without Amour, everything in nature languishes, that the god in question is the soul of the world, the harmony of the universe, and that Heaven, in creating man, gave him the penchant that draws him toward women, that the love that they have for one another is a gift of the divinity, who orders them to love a sex that has been created from the purest clay, since it is more sensitive and softer. Why, they say, should we blush to follow the impressions that nature gives, especially when there is nothing criminal therein except when they are corrupted by vice or debauchery?

Those grave philosophers of eighteen or twenty years would try in vain to combat their passions, though; they are too vibrant, too dissipated, too weak and too exposed to have a serious desire to tame them; they attach their hearts with all the more advantage because they appear to have contributed to it themselves by stimulating it with ever-renewed temptations; and it is only by fleeing them that one can listen to the counsels of reason and procure the tranquility and peace of the soul, so sweet and so necessary, without which the heart becomes a tyrant itself and left a martyr—but the Idalians do not recognize those principles; their indelicate imagination is filled with cheerful ideas that prevent them from reflecting.

When an Idalienne combines generosity of heart with pleasure, however, which is fairly rare, she is dominant, she forces the soul and, so to speak, drags it along in spite of itself. I am assured that most of them make use of a philter that they know how to compose, to persuade great lords and those who, possessed of great wealth, and spread it in profusion, that gold, diamonds, jewels are the richness of furniture are the only proofs of love that ought to be deployed to please them, and that they have a right to be loved without them being obliged thereby to make any return.

The constellations that Venus pours into that world are very dangerous for women; the most virtuous can scarcely resist her influence and are often at risk of an unfortunate catastrophe; one might think that chastity were regarded there as a chimera that men have only recommended to them in order to satisfy their self-esteem.

Monime soon felt the malignity that reigns in the atmosphere. It did not take long for me to see her taking on all the mannerisms of the most refined coquetry. She became unrecognizable; her spoken remarks were free, her gazes provocative. Brought to love by example, I no longer saw her occupied by anything but the concern of pleasing; all of nature offered to her eyes nothing but a living depiction of the amour that was passing through her heart.

In despair at that change, I placed myself in the curl of her ear in order to make her the most stinging reproaches, but either she had forgotten the language of flies or her heart had changed completely; she had the cruelty of turning her head away every time I tried to get closer, and even of chasing me away with her fan. Annoyed by such a procedure, I took the decision to go and settle on one of the trinkets ornamenting the mantelpiece, and there I deplored my unfortunate fate—without, nevertheless, being able to cease gazing at Monime. I examined her with the dolor of a man who believed that everything was lost for him.

A crowd of fops arrived and I saw her smile at one of them, while a distracted and languid gaze was directed at another. She advanced toward a mirror in order to adjust a diamond brooch, which she moved several times, only to return it eventually to its original position. That little maneuver was simply in order to enable the beauty of her hand and the whiteness of her lovely arm to be admired; then, changing her stance in order to shift her skirt, in order that, by raising it slightly, the bottom of an admirable leg became visible, and the prettiest foot in the world. Then she began talking in a low voice, with a frolicsome expression, in order to give birth in those who were listening to her to the desire to hear her, and simultaneously satisfy her own self-esteem by the pleasure one experiences in being applauded.

Monime seemed to be to be the most accomplished little flirt on the planet Venus; not only had she taken on the mannerisms of the most gallant of women, but she also seemed equipped to give them lessons on all the refinements that a coquette can apply when she wants to subjugate a lover.

As can be imagined, I was not at my ease, but I could never resolve myself to quit her. I followed her one day to the Queen's apartment where they were playing cards. When Prince Petulant came in, Monime was immediately struck by his fine manner, the air of nobility and grandeur that high birth gives. She had not seen him before. The prince, absent for six months in order to impose discipline on a province in revolt, which had caused a great deal of anxiety, had returned covered in glory, after having fulfilled the expectations of the Queen, who had given him command of her troops in the expedition. The Princess, wanting to show him marks of satisfaction in the presence of her entire court, gave him the most tender welcome, and heaped him with the most flattering eulogies.

A number of courtiers surrounded the young Prince in order to combine their eulogies with the Queen's, but, perceiving Monime, the Prince scarcely took the time to respond to them. Enchanted by her beauty and the charms distributed throughout her person, he exclaimed to one of his courtiers: "Gods, what an adorable object! Is it Flora or Hebe? How vivid and touching her expression is! Heaven is in her gaze; every gesture marks dignity and grace; what a voice! It bears amour into the heart. Has she been at court for long? Does anyone know what she has come to do?"

"I don't know," the courtier replied, doubtless annoyed because he foresaw that the prince might steal from him a conquest of which he already felt sure.

"But her heart isn't disposed in anyone's favor?" Petulant went on, full of his amour. "Oh, if it is, I shall die of chagrin; I need to find out."

Prince Petulant was at the age at which everything inspires love and lust. Pleasure seemed painted in his eyes, tenderness in his physiognomy and persuasion on his lips. One could not look at him without sensing that amour must be a delightful sentiment made to triumph over the grimmest virtue. He had run after women who had spoiled him somewhat by granting too many of his desires, which had rendered him vain and a trifle reckless.

When the game had finished the Prince approached Monime and offered her his hand, in order to escort her to her apartment, telling her all the most tender things that love inspired in him. He expressed himself with the charm of an intelligence seeking to please.

The ardor shining in his eyes intimidated Monime to begin with; her astonishment caused her to remain silent.

"If my importunate gaze wearies you," the Prince added, "at least endure my adoration, Can you be offended by my liberty? Your eyes, which seem more serene to me than the heavens, must be the seat of gentleness; why arm them with severity? Oh, reassure a man whom the majesty of your face has already confused; if I have committed a crime in declaring my love to you and contemplating your allure, it is the crime of your charms. Everything that I respire must adore your beauty. Who can compare to you in the entire universe? You are worthy to command the gods themselves."

Eventually, the Prince began to make the most of the passionate sentiments that he had for Monime, He swore a hundred times to love her eternally, caused his impetuous flame to shine, and in the transport that animated him he took one of Monime's hands, squeezed it, looked at it tenderly, and when he saw that she was not thinking of withdrawing it, he applied a burning kiss to it.

That kiss increased his disturbance and his desire. Emboldened by that favor, he had no hesitation in showing them. But what became of me when I thought I perceived that he was causing her to experience something similar in her turn?

Gods! I cried. *I'm lost!* Everyone knows, however, that flies do not have loud voices; I was not heard.

In sum, to please, to love, and to say so, was for those two lovers the work of a single evening. Their hearts communicated more easily because they sensed what they learned by speech; their disturbance and their gazes serves as expressions of the mysterious thing that true lovers and friends feel, which I had felt myself for Monime, but which I could not express.

People are right to say that Princes move quickly in amour. It is a law generally received and followed in almost all the worlds I have visited, but that of Venus holds sway over all the rest. As those people do not live for long, they abridge all inconvenient ceremonial as much as they can; constancy seems banished from that world; sensuality, the love of pleasures and good food are their dominant passions; they add to those rare qualities ostentation and magnificence.

Suppleness is a natural character among them. An Idalian employs all his skill in dissimulating his faults and exaggerating his good qualities. All of them want to pass for having morals, probity, intelligence, knowledge, judgment and reason, but all of those pretentions are chimerical, since they have more brilliance than solidity; they are more superficial than profound, more vain than proud, more lustful than delicate, more weak than sensitive, and more occupied with the desire to please than the means of attaching themselves to a person of merit; one can say that all their steps are inconsequential. As for the women, they are only jealous of their beauty, their grace and the preference they obtain over their rivals, without any concern for their reputation.

Chapter III
The Love of Petulant for Monime

Idaliennes in general are very clever; they have subtle and cunning minds, affecting disinterest although, deep down, they are only occupied with the means that they ought to employ in order to work for the complete ruination of their lovers. The more fortunes they overturn, the greater is their triumph; it is then that their reputation extends everywhere and men compete for the glory of ruining themselves for them.

Nothing is bought so dearly in that world than the company of women, but it is true that one has the liberty to purchase it like a box of bonbons and it is certain they always deliver themselves to the highest bidder. An Idalienne will let you off sweet talk; long declarations bore her. Be rich and liberal; that's all that is required to please. Instead of delicate and refine cares, give her money, jewels, diamonds, a beautiful carriage, a well-furnished house, numerous domestics; with those advantages you are certain of preference. But it is necessary not to believe that in return they will be faithful to you; you will be fortunate is those beauties do not give you more than half a dozen associates. A man is often maintained by the mistress of a great lord; he maintains another himself; they are, so to speak, sub-lettings, in which their merit is surely affirmed far more than it warrants; it is thus that the favors of the simulacrum of amour are caused to circulate.

In that world, lovers are indifferent individuals who see one another for amusement, for appearances, out of habit, or momentary needs; the heart plays no part in those liaisons; only interest, convenience and certain external appearances are consulted. That is known as "knowing one another," "having an arrangement," "seeing one another" or "living together;" those liaisons of gallantry last little longer than a visit. They have very sagely found that it is necessary to provide desires with the faculty of immediate satisfaction; that is why they hardly ever make any other choices than the ones that come most easily to hand; however, their lovers swear eternal constancy, even though they are sure to perjure the oath as many times as they change object, and every defeat prepares for the one that will follow. The habit that they acquire of vice effaces in their eyes all its horror. Drawn to dishonor and infamy, they find no reason to pause, and one sees them taking as many falls as they make false steps.

One can compare the Idalians to the ostentatious glamour of a superb tomb, which art has decorated with a thousand trophies, but inside it, worthy of pity, is nothing more than a magnificent carcass or a skeleton of true amity; all their merits are exterior; when utility disappears, they close the door of their hearts after it.

The intelligence of Idaliennes bursts forth in several circumstances; one sees them at first employing all the mechanisms of their coquetry to fix a lover who has been able to please them. Cunning and artful, they have refinements of which they alone are capable; but if they discover that that lover has betrayed them, if he directs his attentions to another object, if he leaves them or scorns them, the dolor they conceive from an infidelity they believe they have not merited soon changes their love into an irreconcilable hatred, and the lover must expect to endure all the darts of an implacable fury; all the mechanisms of vengeance will be employed to doom him, and the conditions of any new treaty will only be made with that end in view.

"What a difference I find," I said to the genius, "in the way of thinking that presently reigns in our world. Among us, a great heart is less touched by beauty than intelligence; one wants sentiments and delicacy; one regards it as the salt of gallantry. It is true that at first, a pretty face engages, but a good character arrests. Without fine discernment and solidity in intelligence, beauty becomes insipid; it is necessary, in order to please for a long time, to add the finest qualities of cheerfulness, politeness, complaisance and even temper; it is only by those combine qualities that one can flatter oneself that the most inconstant man can be fixed, if he is reasonable enough to prefer the pure pleasures that can only have their source in the mixture of souls, and can only receive their perfections in a mutual confidence and complaisance.

"Those qualities, so desirable for the wellbeing of society, are often found in a pretty woman, above all in one who has morals and education. I have noticed that almost always, caprice, eccentricity, spite, anger, jealousy, an abrupt and disobliging humor, a spirit of criticism and calumny are faults attached to the ugly, or to old coquettes who can no longer make use of their outdated allures, and who, for their consolation, amuse themselves by speaking ill of the entire human race and poisoning the simplest actions. Might one not believe that ugliness is the inferno of certain women, since it makes as many demons, whose sole concern is tormenting others?"

Prince Petulant continued to pay his assiduous court to Monime.

"Why, charming Taymuras," he said to her one day, "do you doubt the passionate sentiments that you alone are capable of inspiring in me? Do you still fear my inconstancy? If the love that I feel had been able to pass into your soul, a thought so injurious to a Prince who adores you could never have found a place in your heart; cease, then to suspect me of frivolity. Render more justice to the fire you have ignited, and be convinced that it can never be extinguished. I confess that before you appeared at court, I have often sought opportunities to amuse myself; like the zephyrs that are incessantly in search of new flowers, I have only fluttered, without being able to settle upon any object.

"That confession ought to prove my sincerity. Alas, I regret all the expressions of tenderness that I have lavished on women who merited them so little. Could I swear to be faithful to passing fancies? No, divine Taymuras, it is only in your eyes that one can find the impression of a veritable amour, and only by union with you that that one can experience its intoxication. The entire universe pays Venus the tribute of its obedience; must you be the only one whose resists her sweet influences?

"I thought I perceived at first that you were not insensible to my love. That would be to accuse it of the weakness that fears inconstancy. What a difference I perceive between my Princess' way of thinking and that of our Idaliennes! I have learned only too well that they do not know how to love. It is never tender amour that determines them; one only sees them yield to ambition, the attraction of wealth, to coquetry or to nature. How can a Prince flatter himself on being loved, when even he is only seeking amusement? Their facility is repulsive and disgusting; their vivacity is troubling; their self-interest and inconstancy renders them despicable; but one is sure that a soul like that of my Princess only surrenders to the choice of her heart. Shall I be fortunate enough to have been able to touch yours?"

That speech by Prince Petulant was accompanied by the most enthusiastic transports. The occasion became pressing, and I believed that I saw in Monime's eyes that she shared the Prince's desires.

"It is time," she said, "to let you know my true sentiments. Yes, dear Prince, I love you; I have sensed in seeing you that true love links hearts by a delightful sympathy. Don't abuse the confession I've just made to you; let it suffice for you to learn that you alone possess my tenderness; don't hope for anything more."

"Oh, divine Taymuras!" cried Petulant, falling to his knees, "no mortal in the world is as fortunate as me; you love me; you deign to tell me so; after such a confession, my lot, if it were known, would be envied by the gods themselves. Oh, I no longer feel or listen to anything but love! How can I resist the pleasure that I feel in hearing your mouth pronounce it? You love me: what charms those words are? Repeat them, I implore you, my adorable mistress."

Petulant added a thousand more passionate statements, mingling them with digressions and expressions of tenderness, which completed my despair. Then I forgot the impotence I was in to take my revenge on Monime; I flew to her bosom furiously, which I stung sharply. Then I attached myself to the nose and eyes of my rival, into which I plunged my sting with a great deal of animosity.

The pain that they both felt made them extremely impatient, which satisfied my vengeance somewhat. Monime chased me away with vivacity, and Petulant did everything he could to catch me; but, subtle as he was, I escaped to the height of a cornice, very content with my courage, and having given Monime, by means of that exploit, time to recall all her virtue, which I thought ready to collapse; it was perhaps at the critical moment when I had the joy of thwarting the Prince.

Monime blushed then at Petulant's transports, resumed a severe expression, made a crime of his temerity, and no matter what he was able say in shifting the blame on to the force of his amour, in order to punish him for it, she did not permit him to see her for several days.

That interval seemed a century to Prince Petulant; he could not hide his chagrin, and everyone rationalized it in accordance with their ways of thinking. He came to the Queen's apartment one day; Monime was there; she perceived that he was seeking an opportunity to talk to her, and withdrew immediately. Joy and graces followed her, and left in their place regret for her departure. Petulant, rendered desperate by that mark of coldness, left a moment later and went to lock himself in his apartment with one of his favorites.

"I'm the most unfortunate of men," said the Prince. "You know my amour and the object that gives rise to it. Would you believe that the ingrate is punishing me for a crime that her charms provoked? Taymuras has banished me from her presence, and what completes my unhappiness is that I cannot moderate the impulses that draw me toward her. The enjoyment of all the honors that surround me has abandoned me and I become insipid apart from my Princess.

"You know that before she appeared at court I found pleasure in all the brilliance it presents to my eyes every day, but I admit that those pleasures never produced in my mind any of the vehement desires or any of the delicacies of sentiment that I find in the presence of Taymuras. Every day I discover new charms in her, and she seems to me so perfect, so full of knowledge, that what she does or says always appear the most wise; science is disconcerted in his presence; her beauty is so brilliant that it takes wisdom apart and causes it to resemble folly; one would think, on seeing her, that authority and reason were only made for her, and that the graces have taken up their chosen residence in her person; her charms attract tenderness, esteem and amour, and nature has formed her so perfectly that one can love her without weakness.

"Would you believe that, with sentiments so pure and so perfect, one can displease the person whom one loves? And yet, it is their vivacity, and the violence of my love, that have doomed me. Go in search of her on my behalf, my friend; tell her about my dolor. Wait—I'll write to her to depict the despair I am in for having offended her...but no, stay; it's better that I see her; I want to die at her feet, if I cannot obtain pardon for an involuntary fault."

Petulant went to see Monime. She was alone, and doubtless thinking about him; she was not sorry to see him. The penitence she had imposed on him was beginning to annoy her. As soon as the Prince appeared, his sad and downcast expression touched her.

Petulant threw himself down at her knees; he embraced them for a long time, without being able to express himself other than by his expression, where passion was painted. He had no difficulty obtaining his pardon; Monime forgot her anger, had him get up, and showed him the satisfaction she felt at his marks of submission and his repentance.

I shall not report their conversation, which was very long; it concluded with new expressions of amity on Monime's part, and on the Prince's part with new assurances of the most vivid tenderness.

Monime finally made her lover understand that there are pleasures that the soul can savor, which, although detached from those of the senses, are no less keen.

"How sweet it is, dear Prince," she said to him one day, "to be entirely devoted to the person one loves, to make a duty of one's love, a merit of one's cares, to enjoy tranquilly the most delightful state of life, and to combine the charm of the union of hearts with that of innocence. Are not pleasures more perfect when amour is only introduced thereinto by esteem? At least if it disappears, it is only to give way to the mot tender amity. Is there any pleasure more touching than that of loving someone that one respects, and being cherished by them without division? And ought one immolate such a sweet felicity to the intoxication of the senses? It is necessary that no dread and no shame trouble our repose, and that in the bosom of true pleasures we can talk about amour without making virtue blush. I know that the majority of Idaliennes are far from that delicacy. Alas, my Prince, if you had snatched from me that which I am seeking to preserve from you, it would be your own happiness that you were ravishing."

"How cruel you are, divine Taymuras," said Petulant. "Do you think that I can be happy if you condemn my passion forever and annihilate all my desires?"

"No," said Monime, "but I only want you to learn to moderate them, in order not to exhaust them; that is the only means of not being their victim; for those who seek pleasure with too much avidity are prodigals, who can be accused of dissipating their funds, without giving themselves time to enjoy the income, and who ought to be regarded as individuals ready to fall to oblivion. It is therefore necessary, my Prince, to economize one's pleasures, in order to be in a state to savor them for longer."

Although Prince Petulant was very discontented with this morality, which he did not like at all, he seemed nevertheless to submit to it without a murmur, so true is it that veritable amour often causes the metamorphosis of difficulties into pleasure, especially when one regards them as means of pleasing the person beloved.

Petulant, who only recognized as true happiness that of paying court to Monime, gave her new fêtes every day, in which all the most delicate gallantry was seen to reign; there was nothing but balls, operas, comedies, concerts in various houses, for one can say that the Prince had at least as many of them as the Sun, and that all of them were true palaces, I which magnificence shone everywhere. In sum, he neglected nothing that might make a lover agreeable.

Although all the women of the court took part in these diversions, they nevertheless conceived a frightful jealousy against Monime; they all tried to discover some defect, either in her features or her figure; her beauty, they said, was not symmetrical; her graces were too simple and too natural; they found nothing so marvelous in her intelligence or in her fashion of using it, which was only distinguished by strange taste.

In spite of this criticism, if Monime invented some new adornment, the next day all the women had something similar; if she invented a new term, everyone immediately began using it appropriately. In a word, it was Monime who set the example for all the women of the court; they could not prevent putting everything to work in order to imitate her, convinced that by that means they would acquire as much grace as her.

Although Monime appeared to share the tenderness that the Prince had for her, he was no further forward, because she avoided with extreme care every occasion to find herself alone with him. Doubtless she blushed internally at the peril she had run by listening too closely to a penchant that might have carried her away in spite of herself, and which it would have been difficult to resist.

Finally, weary of being the incessant witness of their mutual love, I went to find Zachiel. "This will be my tomb," I said to him, "if you do not put an end to the cruel torments that I'm enduring by returning my Monime to me."

"What!" said the genius. "Is she not incessantly present to your gaze?"

"Yes," I replied, "but that only makes me desperate, since I see her ready to yield at any moment to the urgings of Prince Petulant, who is doing everything possible to seduce her."

"Have no fear," said Zachiel. "I agree that the air one breathes on the planet Venus produces an invincible inclination toward amour, and that it inspires violent desires, but Monime will have enough virtue to combat them and vanquish them. In any case, she only has one more week to remain in the body that envelops her, so I exhort you to be tranquil and moderate the agitations that are distressing you."

In spite of the assurances of the genius, incapable of deceiving me, I can say that I suffered the cruelest anxieties during that week; I feared some weakness on Monime's part at any moment; I did not want to leave her, blinded by jealousy and a thousand other different passions, which prevented me from reflecting on my impotence; for it is certain that the form in which I appeared would not be capable of imposing anything.

Chapter IV
The Consequences of Petulant's Amours

The Prince, whose amour was augmented every day by the conduct that Monime maintained with him, finally determined him to beg the Queen to consent to their marriage. Nothing seemed to oppose a union that appeared to be so well matched; Taymuras' birth ceded nothing to that of the Prince. Nevertheless, the Queen opposed it formally, even though Petulant employed everything of which he was capable to influence the Princess. He painted the excess of his amour with a great deal of vivacity, made the most of the brilliant qualities of the object of his flame, protested that he would die of grief if Her Majesty persisted in refusing him a grace on which the happiness of his life depended, and added that, as the birth of Princess Taymuras was not inferior to his own, he had been able to flatter himself that he would not encounter any obstacle to his desire.

The Prince's eloquence only served to make his amour manifest. The Queen was inflexible. However, in order to soften to some extent a refusal that might wound the princess, she assured Petulant that it was only because of the invincible opposition encountered by that alliance by virtue of one of the laws of the state, which forbade any person, no matter of what condition, to contact any foreign alliance. That law only tending to the wellbeing of her subjects, she would never permit anyone to dare to infringe it during her reign, and Petulant, as the first prince of her blood, ought to be the first to maintain it by example. Moreover, the prohibition that she imposed on him of marrying Princess Taymuras would never diminish any of the esteem that she had conceived for that person; she would always have the esteem for her that she owed to her rank and that which was only owed to the eminent qualities with which she was endowed.

That eulogy, which the Queen gave the Princess, softened slightly the dolor that Petulant felt at such an absolute refusal, and as a skillful courtier, he had the skill to dissimulate his chagrin. He pretended to respect the Queen's reasons and assured her that he would not mention it again.

In order not to arouse the suspicions of the court, the Prince thought that it would be politic to pretend to go to let his chagrin pass in one of his houses. He left immediately without seeing Taymuras—which gave rise to an infinity of speculations on the part of the women interested in the conquest of the Prince. Several courtiers followed him, but he was able to get rid of them and only to retain with him his most intimate favorites, to whom he confessed his chagrin and the resolution he had made to go to the object of his amour that same evening.

It is well-known that there are few favorites who dare to resist the will of a Prince; his applauded him as reasonable; they even took responsibility for hiding from curious and attentive eyes all the steps that it was necessary for him to take. That assurance tranquilized the Prince, and, the vivacity of his amour not permitting him to defer going to Monime in order to take with her measures certain to ensure his happiness, he left his house by a secret door and went to Taymuras incognito that very night.

Monime had not yet gone to bed when he arrived. Disquieted by the Prince's precipitate departure, without being able to divine the cause of it, she had taken the decision, in order to dissipate her disturbance, of having a casket brought to her containing all the letters he had written to her. Occupied in re-reading them, that agreeable pastime, far from provoking sleep, had, on the con-trary, reanimated her spirits and spread through her soul a sweet sensuality, ex-cited by the urgent expressions of love and tenderness with which the letters were filled.

Taupette, a confidante of Monime's, came to interrupt that rereading to an-nounce the Prince's arrival, asking to speak to her about an important matter. Surprised, Monime hesitated momentarily. "I can't receive his visit," she said, after reflecting briefly. "Why was he not told that I'm not visible?"

"That's true, My Lady, but the Prince seemed to me to be so anxious that I could not resolve to do it. Shall I send him away, then?"

"What are you saying, my dear Taupette? The Prince is anxious, and ask-ing to see me urgently. Alas, what can have happened? Heavens, can one refuse a quarter of an hour? No, I want to avoid anything suggestive of a ploy; that is too opposed to my candor."

Monime immediately left her cabinet to receive the Prince.

"Pardon me, dear Taymuras, if I dare to appear before you at this hour. Penetrated by the most violent chagrin, I cannot defer any longer making you party to my despair. The Queen opposes my happiness; she forbids me to marry you; your quality as a foreigner is the sole cause. But if you love me, if your tenderness equals mine and if the assurances you have given me have no flat-tered me too much, will you refuse to crown my flames? Consent, divine Prin-cess, that I give you the pledge of my faith, and that I receive yours, before an altar. Why hesitate? Amour has nothing that ought to make you blush; the flame is in nature, all hearts owe it a tribute."

Surprised and embarrassed, Monime made no reply.

"Object worthy of gods," the Prince went on, "you ought not to fear the proposal that I have dared to make; the heaven that protects you ought to guar-antee my good faith and the purity of my designs; you ought to recognize in them sentiments that you have taken care to purify." The prince softened his voice. "You're not replying; can it be that amour does not dictate to you any-thing in my favor?"

"It is true," said Monime, in a very serious tone, "that I have every reason to be astonished by the Queen's refusal; I even confess that I would not have expected it. But in spite of the refusal, which must separate us forever, be assured, my dear Prince, that the memory of your tenderness and that of your generosity can never be effaced from my heart, and that it is only my gratitude that can equal them."

"Alas," said Petulant, "how poorly you read my soul. Is it gratitude, then, for which you think that I am asking of you? Oh, you know only too well that that is not a tribute made for you, since nature has not created you so perfect only to grant its favors."

In expressing himself thus, the Prince looked at Monime with an expression so tender and so sincere, his gaze depicted so clearly the fears and purity of his sentiments, that Monime, who was only retained by the idea she formed that a secret union might tarnish his glory, only responded by an animated silence. It is necessary to agree that the mind always serves a tender heart poorly, but in recompense, when one has commenced to please oneself, it seems that one has been given the password. The mind, the heart and the eyes all collaborate to form the intelligence of the soul, and that delightful concert contains all the declarations, all the oaths and all the certainties of amour.

The Prince, perceiving Monime's disturbance and embarrassment, strove to reassure her by every seductive means that Amour was able to inspire in him. "Oh, divine Princess," Petulant added, with a kind of ecstasy, "the fire that I see burning in your eyes must be in your heart; it gives me a sure guarantee that, sensitive to my woes, you have finally consented to put an end to them, and the Amour himself will be your guide, to lead you at dawn tomorrow to the temple, where the sacred fire is preserved. Yes, my Princess, it is there that I want to assure you by the most solemn oaths that my fires will always be as pure and as durable as the one conserved there with care."

Monime, pressed to respond to the ardor of the Prince, felt obliged to represent to him the submission that he owed to the orders of the Queen; the danger to which she would be exposed if that Princess discovered their union; the shame of perhaps being sent away, rendering a marriage contrary to the laws of the nation null and void; and finally the dolor of losing him forever. She added to those a few further difficulties—which is to say, some of those which only served to nourish and augment his passion.

The Prince, whose ardor was extreme, eluded them all by apparent reasoning. "Reassure yourself, charming Taymuras," Petulant added. "Content with my rank, my ambition is limited to the sole desire to please you; agree, at least, that nature has made simple, easy and tranquil pleasures for humans; it is only to their disordered imagination that they owe those that are embarrassing, uncertain and difficult to acquire. You see that nature is far more skillful than we are; that is why we ought to repose on her the concern for our happiness; it is that good mother who ought to supply all our delights; without her, the insipid drowsiness of a cold indifference holds all of nature in a kind of universal torpor, contrary to human happiness. Let us leave those vain men to enjoy the ambition that they have only invented to poison their pleasures and trouble the repose of life; if my Princess thinks as I do, we shall savor without any disturbance the purest voluptuousness; it is a communicative force that draws great souls and raises them above others."

Monime, animated by the same sentiments, only responded initially with a smile. Her complexion was heightened by a rosy redness, the true color of amour; she finally yielded to the insistences of the Prince, but she made him understand that it was prudent not to precipitate their happiness, in order to render it surer and more durable. Petulant had difficulty swallowing that advice; he regarded the days that would postpone his felicity as so many centuries; however, he was obliged to yield to Monime's reasoning. She consented in her turn to come in a week's time at the appointed hour to the temple of Amour.

The next day, Monime was invited to a ball given by the Queen to the entire court. I did not follow her there, in despair at the projects that I had overheard; my withered and crushed heart appeared to be separate from me, plunged into the most profound lethargy. I had no sentiment, no fixed idea; my eyes wandered languidly over everything that ornamented the apartment of my inconstant Monime: I saw nothing; they were only the eyes of a machine, in which the soul was extinct; and I could have believed in that extreme disorder that I had two souls, one of which, sad and desperate, was reproaching the other for the loss and annihilation of past felicities.

Zachiel, anticipating the woes that would be overwhelming me, came to my rescue. He found me devoid of any movement and carried me to a terrace that was adjacent to the Queen's apartments. After having reanimated me with a divine breath, the genius made me sense forcefully the scant reason I had to render myself slave to my passions.

"Is this the way," he said to me, "that you take advantage of my advice? Ought you not have been reassured by the assurance I gave you that Monime would always conserve the preference for innocence that has never been extinguished within her? It is an immortal spirit that the divinity has placed in her heart, never to emerge therefrom. I agree that the proof is rude; however, you can see that she is sustaining herself without my help. But you, what would you have done if I had left you to yourself, prey to all the vehemence of your passions?"

"Alas," I exclaimed, interrupting the genius, "I have never loved anyone but her. Monime appeared to respond to my tenderness; I have lost everything; at present, I can only listen to my dolor; reason no longer has any purchase on my mind. Why expose me to such cruel proofs?"

"I ought," the genius replied, "in order to punish you for your incredulity, to surrender Monime to the prince's desires."

Those words made me shiver.

"Oh, my dear Zachiel, forgive my weakness, or take away my life; I cannot go on without Monime."

"Be reassured," said the genius. "I still want to be ready to calm your aberrations, because I'm convinced that the human heart is susceptible to all sorts of impressions; their force or virtue almost always depends on the manner in which objects present themselves; your deflected reason has just ceded its place to a violent passion, but when you have returned to yourself, the reason that you have sacrificed to unjust jealousy will recover all its strength. If the enlightenment of your mind has been unable defend you against these disorders, it is at least necessary to regard it as a resource from which I ought to expect an abatement of the tumultuous passions that have agitated you thus far. To complete the dissipation of your anxieties, I shall take you to the temple of Amour."

Chapter V
A Description of the Temple of Amour

It was with regret that I drew away from a place that contained Monime. It was not in my power to resist the will of the genius; a single word from his mouth annihilated all my projects. His presence deadened all my passions, but, still too forceful for him to be able to extinguish them, they resumed their vigor as soon as he left me to myself. At that moment my heart became similar to a vase filled with a loose and combustible substance, in which all the sun's rays were plunging like arrows of fire, to form fermentations there that were born and calmed down in the same instant.

The Temple of Amour is several miles distant from the capital; it is situated in the midst of a very agreeable landscape; beautiful groves of myrtles, orange-trees and lemon-trees ornament the roads and spread a delicious perfume in the air; all the pathways that lead to it are strewn with flowers. Zachiel came down in a spacious valley, where woods and meadows were mingled with a few habitations serving as retreats for travelers in stormy weather. All the roads are very safe, thanks to the safeguard that Amour has received from Mars on the recommendation of Venus; it is said that even the animals dare not make war, and that there is no fear that any other snares than those of Amour are set there.

We were stopped at the bottom of the valley by a Torrent of Anxieties that is precipitated very noisily from the height of a mountain, to come to lost itself in a sea of delirium, which, flowing in great waves, draws with it a few plants that grow on its banks. It is there that one sees nymphs and sirens incessantly playing and frolicking with the naiads. The harbors are covered with an infinity of little gilded boats, festooned and magnificently ornamented. A multitude of games and bursts of laughter fly incessantly around it, and thousands of little amours invite you, with their banter, to come and take your place there. Nevertheless, it is only persons who appear to be opulent that are received there to the sounds of the most melodious instruments; for the others, they are conducted silently to flat-bottomed boats, at the risk of being capsized by the waves.

I was surprised to see the prodigious quantity of persons of either sex approaching from all directions. Zachiel told me that the inhabitants of that world are obliged, but a law emanated by the Council of Amour, to come as soon as they have reached the age of puberty to be enrolled under the standards of the god, which results in a perpetual flow of people of all estates and conditions coming to embark.

We traversed that sea rapidly to enter a plain bordered by delightful shade. It is in the midst of that plain that the Temple of Amour stands. To the right is a spring whose bright, shining and silvery water is guarded by a dragon of enormous size, which forbids any approach. Zachiel told me that it is the Fountain of

Youth. In the earliest times of the world it was permissible for all sorts of people to come to drink from it, but the abuse made of that treasure obliged the gods to take away that usage, and Pluto, who is the Prince of all subterranean places, committed its guard to the monster.

To the left is another spring, whose waters have the same property as that of the River of Forgetfulness. It is in those waters that the inconstant fop and the fickle coquette come to purify themselves before entering the temple of Amour. One sees those two springs connected by a broad canal in front of the temple, in the middle of which is a statue of the goddess Venus, who is represented sitting in a shell, in the state of an individual emerging from the bath; one of the graces appears to be smoothing her hair, still damp, another is finishing drying her, and the third is holding a robe, ready to pass into her arms.

We then advanced under the portico of the temple, which forms various galleries, above which superb apartments have been built which serve as lodgings for the priestesses responsible for ornamenting the altars and transmitting to the god the rich offerings that are brought there. Further on are warm baths and chilled cabinets, where amber and perfume burn everywhere, and a thousand other places they have invented to satisfy sensuality. In those delightful places all the people who bring rich presents are received; as for the others, they can never be admitted there.

We passed through another gallery. In the middle stood a silver throne beneath an awning sown with pearls and diamonds. There a crowd of individuals of both sexes was gathered, who were impatiently awaiting the arrival of someone; they were agitated, and seemed to be in pain, when I saw a tall woman appear, clad in a bizarre manner. A crown of myrtle ornamented her head, and the various passions that agitate humans were depicted on his costume. Her manner was imposing, her stride proud and her gaze menacing. She sat down on the throne, and three women accompanying her placed themselves at her feet.

"Who is that Princess?" I asked Zachiel. "I cannot believe that it is the mother of Amour, and the three individuals with her do not bear any resemblance to the idea that I have formed of the Graces."

"You're right," said the genius. "The person you see on the throne is named Passion; her followers are Folly, Suspicion and Jealousy. One rarely sees Passion appear without the three women accompanying her."

That sovereign, addressing the whole assembly, told them about the advantages that her troops had just won over the empire of Reason. "You're not unaware," she told them, "that the Princess in question has never ceased to make war on me, always treating my faithful subjects as her cruelest enemies. The enmity that has reigned between us for such a long time, far from deterring you, has, on the contrary, encouraged you to sustain the glory of my empire. I consent to give you further marks of my benevolence, when you have renewed your oaths of fidelity and obedience and sworn between the hands of Folly that you will always conserve an implacable hatred from Reason, my greatest enemy."

The whole assembly rose up in a tumult, and to demonstrate to the Princess the zeal they had to carry out her order, there was a struggle to determine who would have the glory of approaching Folly first in order to pronounce the oath that she had dictated. At the end of the ceremony, a clock was heard to chime, which announced the shepherd's hour.[22] Then each man took his mistress by the hand and led her into the gardens in front of the temple, where all the pathways ended in cabinets decorated internally by the most beautiful paintings, which represented the various attributes of Amour. Those cabinets were surrounded by rose-bushes, jasmines, laurels, myrtles and a quantity of other bushes.

Not wanting to disturb the pleasures of those fortunate lovers, Zachiel took me toward the Temple of Amour. The first door was guarded by a man clad as we depict Mercury, with wings on his heels. The second was attended by a nymph of considerable and well-proportioned stature; I was struck by her brightness; the whiteness of her skin effaced that of snow. I could not help sighing, finding her so similar to Monime that at first I mistook her for her. The genius told me that her name was Beauty; she saluted him in passing with a gracious smile.

Having reached the interior of the temple, I was surprised to see, suspended in the middle of the edifice at a height of a dozen feet, a ship in which an Amour could be seen manning the helm.

"That ship," said the genius, "represents the human heart; the sails that seem to be moving it are the desires, and the winds that inflate them are hope; the tempests that it passes through are caused by anxieties and jealousies; the Amour guiding it is the pilot; it is he who commands the vessel in order to bring it to port, which is the enjoyment of all the pleasures that he proposes. The lantern that you see at the top of the mainmast enclosed his torch, to illuminate his favorites and alert them to take advantage of the wealth he is preparing for them."

On the prow of the vessel these maxims were inscribed:

1. No one can participate in my favors without loving. The foremost of the pleasures is loving and being paid in tender return.

2. Apply yourselves to know the humor of the person you want to render sensible, in order to serve her according to her desires.

3. If you want to please, combine the agreements of your person with a gentle, kind, attentive and thoughtful mind, tender gazes and eloquent speeches; with such advantages, the heart you wish to assault will have difficulty resisting.

---

[22] "L'Heure du berger" [the shepherd's hour] is a French euphemism for the moment favorable for a seducer to persuade his target to yield to pressure. It is so defined in French dictionaries of the seventeenth and eighteenth centuries, and crops up in numerous literary works, notably used as a title in a 1664 "*demy-roman*" [novelette] by Claude Le Petit and a 1673 *pastorale* by Charles Chevillet de Champmeslé.

4. The good conduct that one observes at first ought to determine the success of the enterprise.

5. Only say that which can be agreeable and never do anything that is not useful to the person your design is to engage; that is the means of making oneself loved.

6. Never buy the favors of a mistress; it is only when one is sure of being loved that one ought to render her mistress of your purse as well as your heart.

7. Never hide anything from one another; the good and the bad ought not to be divided under my empire.

8. Two lovers that I have united ought to confound their souls and accustom themselves to thinking, fearing and desiring in common.

9. Avoid avarice, dread, suspicion and jealousy, if you want to conserve my favors.

Zachiel told me to reread the final maxim, telling me to imprint it firmly in my mind, if I wanted to merit the god's protection. My only response was a sigh.

The temple soon filled with a host of people who had come to invoke Amour and beg him to be favorable to them.

Zachiel pointed out two young women whose pleas were very different; one complained that her lover was too enterprising, she asked that Amour should relent his desires in order to render them more durable. The other accused her own lover of a contrary fault. "Alas," she said, fervently, "Why, powerful god, have you permitted me to attach myself to such a timid and indifferent man. Why can I not take the initiative and let him know my desires? The ingrate does not reply to any of my advances. Amour, enable him to become more enterprising, or rid me of the fire that devours me. I am not content with him or with me. I wish I had never seen him; I wish I could see him always; I fear him; I love him; I hate him; and I do not know which of those emotions is the sweetest. So, all-powerful god, take away from me the idea I have formed of the pleasure of rendering him sensible."

Another, driven by jealousy, advanced to implore the god to punish her lover for the attention he was paying to her rival. "The traitor is punishing me for being too complaisant. Oh, divine Amour, by what barbaric love have you permitted that one cannot love too much without seeing oneself loved less?"

One woman complained of her husband's jealousy and begged Amour to inspire her to new ruses in order to deceive him and steal his money so that she could give it to her lover.

A widow enveloped in crepe came in with a lively and joyful step, to ask the god for the grace of taking full advantage of the time of her mourning without it being able to prevent her from achieving a second marriage.

A woman with a saintly and modest appearance followed, imploring the god to reanimate the fires of a flame that had directed her for a long time. "Determine," she said to the god, "that I shall always be beautiful, or put to sleep the dragon that forbids approach to the rejuvenating spring, in order that I can drink from that source, and by that means always have preference over my companions; determine too that my rival, who has attempted to dispute the heart of my lover with me, becomes hideous, that she appears as monstrous in his eyes as she already is in mine."

After that, I saw a quantity of young fops arrive, who came to ask to be preferred to their rivals. Some begged Amour to enable them to make the acquaintance of some old dowager who was very rich, and make them the depositary of all her treasure, in order that they could share it with their mistress. Other old graybeards full of self-love and always prejudiced in their favor, powdered, pampered and made up like women and perfumed from head to toe asked Amour for the grace of fixing young women without it costing them anything, and that their union should never be troubled by dread or jealousy.

We also visited the private chapels where the offerings are kept that have been sent to acquit vows made to Amour. There was a multitude sent by beautiful women and another by their lovers; some for secret favors received, some for marriages that has established their fortune; this one was for having removed a lover from his companion, that one for having been conserved to the age of sixty, with graces and pleasures, in an agreeable freshness, without the aid of any art.

I shall pass over many other vows, which intelligence will easily divine.

We emerged from the temple in order to go back into the gardens, where a host of Idaliennes were strolling. The genius went into a somber pathway; the trees to either side of it were garnished with little flax-gray flowers with a very pleasant odor. Curious to know the name and property of those trees I asked Zachiel.

"That is the tree of love," he told me, "which cannot grow in any other place in the world; it only flowers by night or in dark places; it provokes those who touch it to tenderness, and all its flowers close at sunrise; that is why it is revealed at sunset."

We then passed into a myrtle arbor, that tree being consecrated to love. The semi-covered arbor was full of fops and coquettes.

I noticed one who was showing in her actions and gaze some of the dispositions of her heart; her beauty, graces and an air of vivacity made me curious to know who she was.

"That," said the genius, "is the beautiful Aramire, who possessed the tenderness of Prince Petulant for a long time. That woman sacrificed to her ambition the love of a man who was uniquely attached to her; the glory of being chosen and preferred to all her companions, that of being reckoned the most beautiful, is sought by all the women of this world with more ardor, sleepless nights and cares than a man can employ in seeking to obtain the principal employments of the State.

"For a long time, Aramire deceived the Prince with a feigned love that she never felt; all that she loved in him were the rank and consideration he gave her by his credit; her complaisance was only intended to maintain her in a position that rendered her mistress of disposing of all the graces; she accorded solely to politics that which ought to be due to tenderness alone; but the Prince, who could not be deceived for long by a feigned love, finally opened his eyes. Enlightened as to Aramire's conduct, he no longer showed her anything but a sovereign scorn.

"That ambitious woman has only been sensible to the loss of her favor, and to compensate herself for having allowed such a fine conquest to escape, she has come here to sacrifice to Amour a part of the wealth she has amassed, in order to be able to engage someone else in her irons."

Chapter VI
The Story of Albion

When we returned to the palace, the genius permitted me to rejoin Monime. He knew my weakness, and that is why he engaged me to remain close to her beneath a bower of roses and jasmines that terminated a long terrace. The important individuals of the court and the city assembled there every day. In order to dissipate my ennui, Zachiel was also kind enough to amuse me by giving me accounts of the adventures of some of those who passed before us.

One young man made for painting and as handsome as amour attracted my gaze. "That is Albion," Zachiel told me, "the only one who can compare with Prince Petulant for the graces of his wit and those you can see of his person. Before veritable amour had subjected him to its laws, the grandeur of his birth and the elevation of his fortune had only inspired pride, arrogance and self-love in him; he was generous when he was offered opportunities to be, but he was so conceited that he would have thought it beneath his rank to anticipate someone in order to oblige him. Doubtless he feared humiliating himself by rendering himself agreeable. He only esteemed and placed himself in the number of those men who, by their birth and the titles that decorated them, those whose opulence put them in a state to link themselves in society with him; the others he regarded as people unworthy of his attention. Thus, the former were the only ones he obliged, because he only imagined the flattering gratitude they would owe him. It was only by the rank of those to whom he accorded benefits that he measured the pleasure of spreading them. The most touching misery was unknown to him, as soon as the unfortunate only presented to his generosity an obscure person who only offered him an unknown and unostentatious exercise.

"Albion appeared to be naturally sensitive, but his heart hardened against the shame of his soul, and his pride always wanted to find in the subjects of his generosity a vain gleam that advertised its benefits. He did not recognize the amiable fashion of giving that delights the soul, so to speak, of the man whose misfortune obliges him to receive while hiding the humiliating aspect thereof in order to preserve his self-esteem. That is what ordinarily gives birth to the keenest gratitude, whereas, in striving to extract a benefit, the unfortunate person who has seen himself in the dire necessity of having to beg often has need of all his virtue not to be indignant at the benefit itself, because of the difficulty he had had in obtaining it and the disobliging fashion in which he has been obliged to act in order to be granted it, as if one were fearful of giving his woes excessive relief.

"Albion was equitable, but he was not always good. One might say that he united in his character as many faults as perfections; he was a composite of a thousand contrary qualities, and one might be tempted to believe that nature, informing him, had taken pleasure in crushing and kneading two souls together that were entire different from one another. As soon as he was in love, he was no longer the same man; Amour worked a miracle; he was cured of all his defects.

"Lisis, a young woman devoid of wealth and birth, was nevertheless to fix him, and, so to speak, re-found the bad dispositions of his soul in pure and delicate sentiments. Raised by the cares of a tender mother, virtuous and filled with a rare merit, the education she had received had purified her heart and inspired a nobility of sentiment; until then, Lisis had not known Amour or his darts.

"It was during a stroll that Albion saw her for the first time. The richness of her figure and the graces of her face, combined with a lively and modest attitude, charmed him immediately; one might have thought that it was the sole prerogative of Lisis to imprint the laughter of pleasure and the tenderness of sentiment that the regularity of the features almost always excludes from a beautiful face. Albion, struck at the first glance, could not help admiring the young woman; a secret charm drew him toward her, and when she went away he had her followed in order to discover where she lived.

"The simplicity of her attire already made him regard Lisis as an easy conquest to carry off, presuming that a simple bourgeoise would not dare to resist him. Impatient to see the beauty again, Albion paid her a visit the next day, but Lisis surprised by the honor that she was receiving, seemed a trifle troubled at first; her face was covered by a blush born of modesty, and the laws that nature engraves on an incent heart obliged her to lower her eyes.

"'Be reassured,' said her lover—for he had become that at first sight— 'don't blush at your situation; indigence takes away nothing from merit. I've come to put my rank and my fortune at your feet, only too happy if I can merit by my cares and attentions the hope of one day being able to render your sensible to my love,'

"'I don't know," Lisis said, when she had had time to get over her disturbance, 'what idea you have conceived of me, but to respond to your abrupt declaration, I dare to assure you that my heart is not made for you, although born in an estate far beneath yours; content with my lot, riches and grandeur cannot dazzle me, and the heart you are intent on attacking so abruptly is formed in such a fashion that it can only ever yield to tenderness and not ambition. I beg you, therefore, to refrain from further visits.'

"Such a firm and positive response surprised Albion infinitely. Unaccustomed to meet resistance in his projects by the liaisons that he had always formed with women whose virtue was domesticated by the sight of a purse full of gold, he saw that it was necessary to change his tone. After having said to her all that gallantry could dictate to him of the most tender and seductive, he left her house much more amorous than when he had gone in.

"Albion continued his visits, in spite of the opposition that Lisis employed to put an end to them. He put to work everything with which his imagination could furnish him in order to seduce her: rich presents, tender letters; everything was sent, nothing was received. However, Lisis loved him; Amour had doubtless struck her with the same darts; but she feared his inconstancy.

One day, Albion presented Lisis with a casket full of diamonds, which she refused. He was penetrated by that. 'Why,' he said to her, 'are you obstinate in refusing the homages due to your beauty? I know that you need ornaments to make you shine. What do you have to fear from me? Be certain that the benefits that one receives on the part of a friend can never be humiliating.'

"'There is too great a disproportion between you and me,' said Lisis, 'for me to dare to take that quality.'

"'Oh, you drive me to despair,' said Albion. 'Does Amour not equalize everyone he submits to his power? But I am hated and envied for the joy of protecting merit and extending a benevolent hand to the unfortunate. I agree that if fortune had been as favorable to you as nature has been lavish, it would debase you to receive presents, but when I see you plunged into the cruelest indigence, to refuse the help of a friend who puts his glory into offering them to you is to show him hatred and scorn, to want to prefer your misfortune to the pleasure of obliging him.'

"Touched by her lover' dolor, Lisis reassured him as to his fears, and finally consented to receive from him all the gifts that he wanted to make her.

"Albion began by buying her a beautiful house, which he had furnished magnificently. Then he engaged her to receive his friends there. Soon, the finest companies in the city were seen assembling in her house, attracted there by her intelligence and good conduct. Albion, whose love was augmented every day, pressed Lisis to end his martyrdom and yield to his desires; his pursuits were incessantly renewed.

"One day, he employed the most seductive terms and the most urgent solicitations. 'Stop, cruel man,' she said. 'Are these the promises you made always to respect my virtue? Is it in seeking to seduce me that you pretend to be happy? What! Is the prerogative of beauty to inspire crime? Learn that veritable amour is only produced with modesty, and that it never acts other than in a fashion honorable to the object that gives it birth. If you continue to offend me with your discourse, you will oblige me to renounce seeing you; and if you demand as the price of your benefits an unworthy gratitude, you can take them back immediately.'

"Those words made Albion tremble; he promised to conform with her desires; the desire he had to fix Lisis' heart and attach it to himself forever caused his faults gradually to disappear; love purified all of them. It is true that Lisis employed all sorts of means to perfect her lover, and it was only by her tenderness, her attentions and her complaisance that she finally succeeded in causing him to renounce the excessive self-regard, conceit and obstinacy that enveloped all his good actions. It is to the cares of that amiable individual that he owes the esteem and admiration in which he is held today. The entire court saw with pleasure a union that would doubtless last as long as them.

"A few months before Monime appeared at court, Prince Petulant, who had heard mention of Lisis as a prodigy of intelligence, grace and beauty, who combined all imaginable talents, thought at first that he had only to appear in order to be loved by her. He rendered her his assiduous cares, but Lisis, whose mind was still firm and constant, fearing that the Prince's frequent visits might cause her lover some anxiety, assured Petulant, with as much nobility as generosity, that as it had never been the glamour of grandeur nor the lure of riches that had determined her in the choice she had made of Albion, but merely the inclination of her heart, she felt obliged to beg him to cease his pursuits, since nothing in the world would be capable of changing her, convinced that her lover would always have the same regard.

"Petulant, desperate that a single woman dared to reject him, having not yet found one as cruel, redoubled his efforts and employed every imaginable way to touch Lisis' heart. Veritable amour is almost always accompanied by jealousy; the assiduities of the Prince troubled Albion; not daring at first to make his anxieties known, he began by sulking and putting ill-humor into everything he said, but what threw him into despair was a ball that Petulant gave for Lisis, to which she could not refuse to go. He imagined that, dazzled by rank and grandeur she would finally yield to the Prince's pursuit.

"Troubled by jealousy, Albion's agitation was manifest the following day in all his actions; he threw himself into an armchair without saying anything. 'What's the matter?' Lisis asked him. 'I can't imagine what can have put so much trouble and alteration into your mind. For several days you've only seen me to quarrel with me; I've overlooked all your disparities, but they're finally beginning to annoy me.'

"'I believe it,' said Albion, 'and I'm not unaware that my presence is importunate to you; entirely delivered to the Prince, I've doubtless disturbed a tête-à-tête that would be much more agreeable to you than mine; for you can't imagine, perfidious woman, that I've been so long delayed in perceiving that you've sacrificed me for your new conquest; I have done myself enough violence not expressing anything when I only had indications of your treason.'

"'You ought to moderate your language,' said Lisis. 'Know that it offends me.'

"'It's of no consequence to me that I've offended you,' said Albion. 'My intention was not to pay you compliments, since it's impossible for me to constrain my resentment any longer. But if you believe that you have anticipated me by your change, I'm glad to tell you that I detached my heart from your bonds a long time ago, and I've come today to tell you that I'm going to offer it to a young woman who is at least as beautiful as you and will doubtless never be as perfidious.'

"Lisis, in despair at being accused so unjustly, told him with a great deal of bitterness that he was the master of his heart, and could take it back and give it to whomever he wished. 'But you ought not,' she added, 'to blacken with calumnies the one to that I have given you, and which I have the right to withdraw, since you have rendered yourself unworthy by such injurious suspicions. You ought to adopt another pretext for being unfaithful than that of accusing me of being so. Although you had not told me that you had begun to disengage your heart a long time ago, I am not sufficiently deprived of judgment not to have perceived by your somber and contradictory humor that your love was entirely extinct. It was therefore not necessary to insult the little merit that I might have. I have no doubt that the person you have chosen will be perfect, but whatever precaution you take, I believe nevertheless that it will be difficult for you to make the choice of one who will be as faithful to you; that in my turn, I am glad to tell you, less to disabuse you than to satisfy me. Do not be so vain as to believe that the fear of losing you makes me say that; be persuaded, on the contrary, that I am not seeking to regain the place that I occupied in your heart, but to make you acquainted with the state of mine and to make you see, at the same time, that it is well enough placed not to have to descend, with you, to the level of justification.'

"She then went into her cabinet and closed the door rather rudely, in order to avoid hearing to the numerous hurtful things that her husband pronounced with a great deal of volubility. He remained at the door of the cabinet for a long time, listening, although he was quite sure that there had been no one there when Lisis went in, and that there was no other way out except going through the window and its bars—for the windows were all protected by grilles. When a man is blinded by passion, however, he can no longer listen to the counsels of reason.

"Until then, Albion had not yet meddled in giving orders in Lisis' house, and although she owed all her wellbeing to him, he had always had enough respect for her not to make her sense the price of his benefits, finding himself well compensated by the preference she had accorded him over his rivals, and every present she had received had been regarded on his part as a new favor. Those principles of delicacy, from which he had not deviated, were annihilated; all the plenitude of his pride and self-esteem got the upper hand. He began by assuming the attitude of a master, had the door forbidden, and ordered that supper be prepared for him.

"Lisis, who could hear everything that was happening from her cabinet, allowed her lover to take as many impertinences as he pleased, resolved to punish him that night. Albion, after having given free rein to his bile, judged by the silence that Lisis was maintaining that whatever noise he made in her house she was determined to appear to pay no attention to it. That is why he finally made the decision to return home in order to despair at his ease.

"As soon as Lisis heard him leave, she sent for the maidservant who had the most affection for her, to accompany her to the home of one of her relatives, where she had been living when she made Albion's acquaintance. They both left without the other servants nothing. Caliste—that was the name of the relative—was surprised to see her arrive so late, and in attire that reflected the disorder of her mind. She asked her the reason, but Lisis could not satisfy her without bursting into floods of tears; her heart penetrated by the sharpest pain by virtue of her lover's unjust accusations, she could not sustain the weight; that same night she was afflicted by a terrible fever, which seemed likely to take her to the grave.

"As soon as it was light, Albion, who had not even thought about going to bed, and to whom the hours had seemed like days, driven by the desire that he had to reproach Lisis further for a infinity of things he thought he had forgotten and of which he did not think he ought to spare her a single word, went to her house with the intention of heaping further insults upon her. Lisis' domestics, who did not know that she had left the house, told him that she was not yet up. It was necessary, in spite of his air of authority, for him to be patience until it pleased his mistress to ring to announce that she was awake. The usual hour having been more than passed, however, they all began to get anxious. Albion, who sensed his disturbance increasing, pressed them to go into Lisis' apartment. 'Perhaps she's ill,' he said to them. His anger was already dying down; his love was about to acquire new force when, opening the first door of her apartment himself, he was surprised to find all the others open.

"Albion' desperation is easily imaginable; he ran through all the bedrooms dressing rooms, boudoirs and wardrobes twenty times over, but saw nothing except a portrait of Lisis that he had commissioned himself in twenty different poses. Unable to comprehend at first what decision she might have made, as lovers ordinarily take pleasure in giving birth to monsters in order then to have the glory of combating them, our furious lover got it into his head that she had departed with the Prince for one of his houses of pleasure. That idea determined him to attach himself to the Prince's footsteps, and he followed him like his shadow.

"Petulant, who was unaware of all the disorder he had caused, presented himself at Lisis' house several times. First he was told that she had gone out, on another occasion that she was in the country. The domestics were unable to tell him where she was, and he could think of no better way to find out than address himself to Albion. The latter, surprised by the question, was unable to reply, since he did not know himself, but, far from clearing away his unjust suspicions, he regarded the question as a ruse on Petulant's part, and redoubled his assiduity in following him.

"After a certain time, however, Albion, not perceiving anything that might denote any conspiracy on the Prince's part with Lisis, began to reflect on his conduct. A little better in accord with himself, he agreed that he might have been mistaken in the conjectures he had drawn from Petulant's frequent visits. Those reflections led him to the ultimate despair; he recalled all the insults that he had directed at Lisis, and promised himself to do everything in his power to repair them. But where could he find Lisis, who was so dear to him, but whom he had nevertheless insulted, to the point of driving her to renounce all the gifts he had given her? It occurred to him then that she might have returned to her former dwelling. He ran there with a disturbance and an agitation that is difficult to describe; he asked to speak to Lisis; he was simply told that she was not visible. He returned in the afternoon, and received the same response, and for several days he was unable to obtain any other.

"Without being put off by a procedure that he had so thoroughly deserved, he continued his visits. Finally, by dint of importunity, he was shown one day into a room where he found Caliste with an exceedingly sad expression. 'It is in vain,' she said to him, 'that you persist in trying to speak to Lisis. She is too irritated with you for you ever to hope to obtain forgiveness. She has told me to tell you that you will find in the house she owed to your benefits all the gifts that you were able to give her, that she renounces them and asks you for the final favor of forgetting her forever.'

"'How can I do that, my dear Caliste?' Albion cried. 'For pity's sake, grant me the favor of letting me speak to Lisis; I want to die at her feet if I cannot obtain her pardon.'

"'No longer expect to see Lisis again,' said Caliste. 'She is at the extremity, and it is you, cruel man, who have driven her to death; it is your injustices that have killed her.'

"'What am I hearing?' cried Albion. 'Lisis is ill; she is at death's door, and she has not said anything to me? I am lost in her heart and in her mind. Is the heart that I rendered sensible closed to me irredeemably?'

"'Yes,' said Caliste, 'since she does not want either to see you or to hear mention of you.'

"'Oh, this is too much!' said Albion. 'I cannot resist my grief.' His eyes glazed over and he fell down, unconscious.

"Caliste, frightened to see him in that state, called for help, and managed to bring him round, but as soon as he recovered the use of his senses it was only to ask for Lisis.

"To soothe his distress, Caliste finally promised to speak in his favor, and to do everything she could to obtain his pardon; that promise tranquilized him somewhat.

"When Albion had gone, Caliste gave Lisis an account of her lover's distress; she painted his repentance, his disturbance and his alarm in such natural colors that the tender Lisis could not help feeling sorry for him. 'If I believed that his repentance was sincere, my dear Caliste,' she said, 'I confess that I could find the tenderness to pardon him. Do you believe, my dear friend, that he still loves me?'

"'Have no doubt of it,' said Caliste. 'Agitations as violent as the one he experienced can only come from a heart penetrated by the keenest tenderness.'

"'Alas,' said Lisis, 'what injuries that cruel man has inflicted upon me! But I would like to forget them in favor of love; I permit you, my dear, if my health improves, to give him some hope.'

"Amour is a great physician; the pleasure that Lisis felt in learning of her lover's return served as a balm that soon reanimated her strength, and Caliste, who saw that there was no longer anything to fear for her life, wrote to Albion to tell him that good news, adding that Lisis was beginning to soften, and that it was on the conduct he adopted that his forgiveness depended.

"That assurance restored calm to our lover's heart; he ran to Caliste's house to tell her that he consented to submit to whatever proofs were demanded of him. Lisis, content with his submission, finally permitted him to be admitted to her presence.

"When Albion went into Lisis' bedroom, he advanced in a crestfallen fashion, gazing at her with eyes full of languor, but on encountering her gaze, in which love seemed to be keenly expressed, he stopped; a sudden tender and naïve joy animated his own gaze, coloring his face, and, inflamed by the desire to convince her of his joy, he looked at her more ardently.

"'Complete your reassurance' said Lisis, in a voice that emotion rendered even fainter, 'come and read in my eyes the pardon that they announce to you.'

"Albion, beside himself with joy, threw himself at her knees; too penetrated by desire to be able to speak, he expressed himself at first solely by the ardor with which he embraced them. That expression passed into Lisis' soul; she made her lover get up, and, forgetting all his injustices, she spoke to him with a great deal of tenderness.

"The peace between the two lovers was eventually cemented by their marriage.

"For a long time, Petulant has run from conquest to conquest, without being able to fix himself, nor ceasing to regret not having known Lisis before she had attached herself to Albion. That glory was only reserved for Monime; the resemblance that he encountered in her character would have enchained him forever, if destiny had not been opposed to his happiness. It is unfortunate for that Prince only to be able to attach himself veritably to women whom destiny is not to render him the enjoyment. So, my dear Seaton, you ought to cease exercising your unjust jealousy against him; I have only told you this story in order to engage you to feel sorry for him and to moderate a passion that appear to be subjugating all the impulses of your soul.

"I agree," Zachiel added, "that a heart strongly attached to an object full of charms cannot see without anger the object of its love favoring anther; but if spite excites it, amity soon appeases it, and when it believes that is hating, it is only loving more. If you take my advice, your torments will soon change into pleasures, and I assure you that, whatever happens, Monime will never belong to anyone without your consent. You ought no longer to be alarmed by the tender sentiments that she has conceived for the Prince; they are involuntary, merely the influence of this planet acting upon her heart; and to prove to me your docility in following my orders, I want you to stay with me until the day that Monime has chosen to go to the temple; then, if I find you sufficiently firm and reasonable to witness their oaths without showing either jealousy or weakness, I shall permit you to witness them."

Chapter VII
The Marriage of Prince Petulant and Monime

Soothed by the promises of the genius, I remained with him, almost without thinking about Monime, thanks to the care that Zachiel took to amuse me with further stories as instructive as they were interesting.

One day, we were strolling in the Queen's gardens when I perceived a young woman who appeared to me to be charming. Even though I was in the form of a fly, I could not protect myself from the influences of the planet, which doubtless extend over everything that breathes there, and I believe that I could gladly have consoled myself with her for Monime's scorn. Zachiel could not help laughing when he saw me fluttering around her, trying to steal a few favors from her; whatever he did to recall me, for a long time, I did not want to leave her.

"I admire you," said Zachiel. "At the same time as you complain bitterly about Monime and believe that you have the right to condemn her inconstancy, when she is bound to disagree with you, since she does not retain any idea of ever having been a fly, and has also forgotten everything that has happened to her in the course of her life, and thus, in consequence, cannot reproach herself for any infidelity....

"What right do you have, Seaton, who ought not to have lost your memory of the tender sentiments that she had made you know, and who ought to conserve the keenest gratitude to her forever, to demand that Monime renounces her good fortune? The sentiments that one has for a brother are entirely different from those that one feels for a lover. If I did not attribute your extravagant fashion of thinking to the malignity of the influences that dominate this world, I would already have punished you.

"Meanwhile, in spite of the violent amity that you incessantly bear toward Monime, that ardor does not prevent you from trying to please another object, without reflecting that you are rendering yourself culpable of ingratitude. Has the extravagance of your project already made you forget your impotence? Do you not fear making yourself seem even more ridiculous in my eyes? At least admit your weakness after this disparity, and that Monime is giving evidence of much more strength than you are showing; her virtue is sustaining itself without my help. What would your conduct have been if, like her, I had left you to your own devices? You would doubtless have run after the first object that was presented to your eyes."

The reflections of the genius caused me to blush internally; nothing occurred to my mind that could justify me.

"Do you know the person who has just charmed you?" he continued. "She is a woman of the upper class, a fashionable woman, of whom all the fops are in

180

pursuit, a woman who combines in her character a thousand contradictory qualities: to live to the extent of frivolity, sometimes to that of being carried away; excessively coquettish, her mind is not made to languish in indolent indifference, and the source of the fire that you see shining in her eyes animates all her actions. Possessed by the desire to please, she only knows how to calculate her glory by the number of her conquests, even if she has to purchase them by her weakness, when she sees no other means to arrest a lover momentarily or retain him in her chains. She is more tender and more passionate than another for the man who has found the art of rendering her sensible, however, and capable in moments of reflection of thinking with more justice and force than the man most distinguished by those two qualities. With that, she is generous, good, witty, clever without malignity, always ready to oblige by her services and her cares, as seductive by the pleasant quality of her humor as by the charms of her face. In sum, the woman is a free spirit disengaged from prejudices; she can say that she makes the reputation of all the fops, since she has lost her own."

It often happens at the Idalian court that the habit of seeing one another takes the place of love. People of quality enter into intimate liaison with women of their species, and, without scandalizing anyone, they occupy the same house and the same apartment; they have the same table, the same society, the same pleasures and the same occupations. It is by that commerce that they learn to know their faults and overcome them, and to free themselves from all kinds of decency and constraint. Often they make one another mutual confidences, in order also to put in common their satisfactions or their woes.

It is, however, neither interest, not the appetite for pleasures, nor that of society, not amour, that links them; the majority see one another without urgency, absent themselves without the slightest sign of chagrin, and it scarcely occurs to them to say a few tender words; they often refuse one another the simple gestures of politeness that one ordinarily makes to a stranger; they resemble animals linked together by the same instinct, without knowing the determining cause.

In spite of that singular fashion of living, one would try in vain to make them renounce the liaisons that they have formed, because in the totality of their lives they believe themselves to be necessary to one another, and that they are united by the most tender bonds. As they are not sufficiently delicate to know veritable amour, they are thus unworthy to sense all of its delights, and the pure voluptuousness that is the charm of true lovers.

When the week had expired, I begged Zachiel to give me the liberty to follow Monime to the temple. The genius took me there himself, assuring me that this proof would be the last.

I had to arm myself with new strength when I saw Monime appear. The incarnadine of her complexion effaced the brightest colors of the aurora. Prince Petulant, who had arrived in advance of her at daybreak, came toward her to offer her his hand. The fire of amour was shining in his eyes; it animated all his actions, and as they advanced toward the altar the prince assured her in the most tender and passionate terms of the excess of felicity that he was enjoying.

After they had said their prayer, the high priest, who was waiting for them, had them enter a private chapel, which surprised me by its magnificence. At the back of the chapel a statue of the goddess Venus could be seen, which seemed to me to be a masterpiece of art. The figure is made of porphyry; it is situated in a niche of black marble, between columns of the same color, in order to bring out its whiteness. Everything that I saw seemed to me to be in exquisite taste; every item there offered a eulogy to the skillful hands that had wrought it, and all the carvings were admirable in their delicacy.

When the high priest had pronounced a few mysterious words, which he had the two spouses repeat, he asked Heaven and all the constellations to pour down upon them the benignity of their most tender influences. A witness to their oaths, I could not hear them without sensing myself penetrated by the sharpest dolor. There were only two young lords, confidants of the prince, serving as witnesses to the wedding. When the ceremony was over, Petulant and Monime separated.

I followed Monime, who returned alone to her apartment. Taupette, the confidante of her love, had prepared a bed for her covered with petals of rose, jasmine, violet and a thousand other flowers; that is a custom long established among the Idaliennes; perhaps it is the perfume that those flowers spread in their bedrooms that occasions the vapors to which all the women of high society are subject, and from which the men who find glory in copying them in everything also suffer.

Voluptuousness has even introduced a new method there, which is scarcely practiced in the other worlds; it has spread among the great and the petty alike, who, when they go to bed, in order to invite sleep to expand its delightful poppies more promptly, and carry them away on the wings of agreeable dreams, have the soles of their feet, the palms of their hands and the underside of their chins tickled; that is done with such great delicacy that their eyelids close and they go to sleep instantly.

The Prince came to Monime's house in the afternoon; he would have been glad to find her alone, but she was surrounded by her maidservants, who were all striving to ornament her with the utmost care. "What is the point of these vain ornaments?" he said to her. "Your beauty effaces everything that art can invent, and I see nothing in these adornments that does not hide one of your attractions."

Petulant approached Monime's ear and begged her to send away her maids and go into her cabinet. She declined on various pretexts, but, vanquished by the ardor of the Prince and perhaps by her own desires, she eventually consented to wait for him in her apartment after midnight, and promised that she would be careful to send her maidservants away. The Prince, transported by that assurance, left her at dusk; joy and satisfaction were painted in his eyes.

The disturbance that was agitating me caused me to follow Petulant, without any particular design. When he went into his apartment he ordered his chief valet to prepare him a bath strongly perfumed with amber; his orders were promptly carried out. I left him in order to rejoin Monime, encountering her as she was going to pay court to the Queen. In spite of my trouble and agitation I could not help admiring the majesty of her bearing and the graces that accompanied it; one might have taken her for the goddess of beauty. It is true that nothing embellished her more than the interior satisfaction of her soul. Her eyes were shining with a gleam so bright that it was almost impossible to sustain its intensity. Her complexion was animated, and a cheerful and gallant attitude reigned throughout her person.

Far from suspecting that anyone had infringed her orders, the Queen heaped Monime with the most delicate eulogies and favored her with many caresses. The Princess, by that reception, doubtless wanted to make her forget the interior resentment that she might be harboring as a result of the opposition that she had raised to her alliance with the prince. At any rate, the praise with which she honored her set the tone for all the people who were present; the ladies paid her a thousand compliments on her adornment, as if to make it understood that it was only to those vain ornaments that she owed a part of her beauty, for they did not say a word about her or about her graces; but in recompense, the male courtiers did not forget a single one, and all of those graces, down to the slightest smile, obtained a particular eulogy from them.

When the Queen had had supper she went into her cabinet, where she was awaited by her prime minister in order to regulate a few matters of State. Everyone withdrew. As for Monime, she was accompanied to her apartment by a crowd of courtiers, all of whom were insistent on paying court to her. In order not to lost sight of her I settled on a diamond spray with which her head was ornamented.

As soon as Monime had gone into her cabinet she complained of a bad headache. Her maids seemed to be alarmed by that; they were all very fond of her. As for me, forgetting the assurances that the genius had given me, blinded by a thousand different passions, I imagined at first that it was only a pretext of which she wanted to make use in order to get rid of her servants. Imagine my surprise and despair, however, when I saw her fall unconscious. I uttered a cry—which, fortunately, was not heard by anyone.

Then, forgetting all the hatred that I had conceived for the infidel, I only remembered my love, Desperate in my condition as a fly, which robbed me of all the pleasure I would have obtained in giving her all the necessary aid, I nevertheless flew to her bosom and her mouth, in order to try to reanimate her with my breath, but I thought I would drown in the astral water with which her maids inundated her, in order to bring her round.

Monime had disappeared; nothing was able to recall her to that body, which she had abandoned. Alas, what would have become of me if the custom on that world had been to make use of vinegar? It would have been the end of my poor little person.

However, I still had enough strength to pull myself out, almost swimming, and reach the arm of an armchair, where I had time to fortify myself and recall my reason by means of serious reflections. More tranquil then, I remembered the genius' promise, and had no doubt that Monime had quit the pretty envelope that she had animated in order to resume the form of a fly; that idea suddenly changed by dolor into an inexpressible joy.

I shall not elaborate upon everything that happened at Monime's pretended death, or at least her separation from a body that only seemed to have been formed to make the delights of the person who had been able to render it sensible; I shall not depict the despair of her maidservants, who attracted a number of people into the apartment by their desolation and appeals.

Prince Petulant, full of his amour, advanced in the expectation of collecting the fruit of his tenderness and seeing himself at the peak of the most perfect felicity, but his hopes vanished, like the clouds that present agreeable and varied forms to the gaze, which one sees dissolving, dissipating and disappearing if they encounter an impetuous wind.

The Prince, approaching Taymuras' apartment, alarmed by the cries that he hears, precipitates his steps. He goes in; at the sight of him all hearts are gripped, everyone stands aside to make way for him. His soul, already stirred by what he sees, seems to announce his misfortune to him; all his senses are agitated, and his eyes, wandering everywhere, encounter nothing but images of dolor...but what is his despair when he finally perceives the body that he has idolized, lying motionless on a bed.

At that sight, he stops for a few seconds, as if petrified, and then falls upon her, doubtless thinking to reanimate her with the fire that is devouring him, saying the most tender and most touching things in the world to her.

When he sees that all his efforts are vain, and that there is no longer any hope of recalling her to life, he cries, in the frightful dolor that is tearing him apart: "Alas! Is there a mortal in the world whose lost resembles mine? Is it necessary that so many torments should fall upon me at once? I have no more pretention, then, to the expose or the happiness of life. What evil auspices presided over our union? May the hatred of the star that dominates me bury me in the bosom of the earth and take away forever the daylight I detest! Why must I be destined for so many horrors?"

He continued: "But I can free myself by means of a prompt death; I can still unite my soul with that of my Princess. I shall at least bear away in dying the flattering idea of having been the only one who had a share of her tenderness, and that the same tomb will contain us both."

Then the prince, animated by his fury, drew his sword, with which he would have pierced himself if a courtier, who had been observing all his movements, had not been prompt enough to stop his arm. "What are you doing, my

Lord?" he said to him, taking away his sword. "The Princess, who doubtless foresaw your despair, orders you to live; those were the last words she pronounced"

That speech, which the old courtier had supposed, seemed to calm the prince somewhat, but they had a thousand difficulties removing him from a place that could only serve to augment his dolor. He claimed that Princess Taymuras had been poisoned, and swore vengeance on the authors of such a crime. The physicians employed all their eloquence to cure him of his suspicions, although the majority of them knew nothing about it.

I will admit that although the Prince had been my rival, and a favored rival about to be heaped with the most precious favors of Amour, I was nevertheless sensibly touched by his distress. The Prince had an excellent heart, and a noble and generous soul. He was faithful to his word and all his engagements; probity and honor were his rules; with such sentiments, I was not surprised that Monime, whose qualities responded to those of the Prince, had become attached to him so promptly; it seems that a sympathy immediately links beautiful souls. I had been very far from rendering him that justice two hours earlier, which was difficult to accord to a beloved rival, but now I had nothing more to fear on his part.

The Queen and all her courtiers united their grief with that of the Prince; for the ladies I cannot affirm that the regrets they affected were sincere; I even believe, without wishing to offend them, that for the glory of their allure several of them blessed Heaven secretly for having delivered them of a rival who had effaced them all.

In order to honor the memory of Princess Taymuras, the Queen ordered that her body by carried to the tomb of the princesses of her blood; she was given a magnificent funeral—and, which is quite rare, Monime witnessed the procession herself.

Without waiting for all those ceremonies to be complete, however, I left Monime's apartment as soon as the Prince had gone, in the hope of finding her with Zachiel, who was ordinarily stationed under a bower of roses and jasmines.

"Approach, Seaton," the genius said to me. "Come and receive your Monime; I return her to you in all her purity."

"Alas," I exclaimed, "it was just in time!"

The genius smiled at my response. As for Monime, I could not perceive whether she had any reaction; flies scarcely blush, and she made no reply. Charmed to see her again, however, the sight of her caused me to enjoy that pleasure, and it was the kind of joy that spreads calm in the soul and serves as a balm soothes all woes. In the intoxication of that pleasure I could not help making a few remarks in jest about her coquetry, but she immediately seemed so disconcerted that I was very sorry to have reminded her of it.

"You're scarcely delicate," said Monime, "to seek to augment my shame and displeasure with your bad jokes. If Zachiel had instructed you regarding the force of the influences that agitate this world, perhaps you would not doubt that that they make such a great impression on the heart, and act upon the mind with so much violence, that they entirely take away the liberty to act in accordance with the principles of reason.

"How cruel you are," she continued, addressing the genius, "to have exposed me, because of a casual remark, to all the malignity of the air that one breathes on this planet! That is a reproach that I shall make to you as long as I live. You have robbed me of the pure joy that I enjoyed; a thousand scruples have come to poison my soul, and I sense that from now on, there will no longer be any true pleasures in life for me. Oh, cruel Zachiel, you have taken everything from me."

"Be tranquil, beautiful Monime," said Zachiel. "Put away forever the vain scruples that have come to trouble the sweetness of your days; dissipate the clouds that that they have spread over your soul; a heart as pure as yours has nothing for which to reproach itself; I want the serenity of your spirit to recover the cheerful humor that is the charm of society. You ought not to complain about my care, since the instant that I perceived that the star presiding over you was beginning to achieve too much empire over you, I hastened to free you therefrom. Furthermore, that which is involuntary can never imprint any stain."

"You reassure me as to the past," said Monime, "and your discourse causes a calm to be reborn in my soul that is being communicated to all my senses. However, I cannot remain any longer on a world where the examples are so contrary to virtue; and to engaged Seaton to support me, I also dare to assure you that my heart is keenly touched in favor of the Prince; the grief he feels in having lost me causes me a chagrin so sensible that I cannot forget it. At least ensure, my dear Zachiel, that he encounters some object worthy of occupying his heart; promise me that for the sake of my tranquility.

I supported Monime and asked the genius not to refuse his favors to a Prince who must be worthy, since he had been able to please Monime. Far from being jealous of the sentiment that she conserved for him, I was infinitely grateful for it; it justified the generosity of her heart, and I regarded it as a proof of the candor and verity that never abandoned her.

Chapter VIII
The Genius takes us to Various Islands

The genius wanted to lend himself to the haste the Monime expressed to get away; that is why he took us away from the court in order to take the road that led us to a port where on embarked for the Fortunate Isles, the name given to several small islands surrounding one named Gallantry, which collectively contain more than two thirds of the globe of Venus.

Having arrived in the port, Zachiel had us embark—or, to put it better, he enabled us to maintain our incognito by conserving our tiny forms. The vessel into which he passed was filled with young people of both sexes, all of whom seemed to be in a great hurry to enjoy the pleasures they hoped to savor when they landed on the islands.

However, the crossing was a long one; a north wind that had been blowing for a long time had already spread sadness through the hearts of all the passengers when transports of joy were suddenly heard; land had been sighted and signaled, and everyone trembled in case a wind rose that would dissipate the object and dissolve all their hopes, like the inconstant clouds in which one finds appearances.

Meanwhile, the almost imperceptible dot perceptible on the horizon begins to take on extent; illuminated by the Sun's rays, the combination of light and shadow made it sparkle with gold and azure. Shortly thereafter, the objects assembled there begin to present themselves in the forms and colors natural to them; plains descend before hills crowned with cloud, the enamel of meadows bursts forth everywhere; the forest seems to detach itself from the valleys that it favors with its shade; palms and fir-trees raise up their stems proudly, and seem to bear their tresses, agitated by the wind, toward the sky.

Soon, the uniform report of the senses confirms that we have almost reached the goal to which all desires aspire. Already, the myrtles and the lemon-trees are announcing themselves by their sweet perfumes, while the gently stirred air brings the ears the sound of the waves, which rise, curl and fold up, undulating as they die amid the little pebbles and silvery and that border the shore of the Island of Peace.

We have no difficulty landing there, in the calm and tranquility that reign incessantly in its ports; they are never battered by any tempest; they only feel the gentle breeze of zephyrs that agitate them night and day. One can compare that island to the banks of the Lignon;[23] like them, it is only inhabited by shepherds and shepherdesses, who, content to love and be loved, put all their glory into

---

[23] The river featured in Honoré d'Urfé's classic pastoral romance *L'Astrée* (1607-1627).

giving further evidence of it every day by means of innocent caresses. Suspicions, jealousy and a thousand other passions that ordinarily torment so many Idalians, never poison their pleasures. Those fortunate citizens are unacquainted with remorse. Guided by nature, they follow its laws; the same desires animate them, and it is only the art of pleasing one another that limits their cares. A grotto formed by nature is for them a palace; the fruits of Pomona enrich their gardens, and the florid countryside furnishes pastures. It is there that the young shepherdesses watch their flocks graze, and amuse themselves singing while spinning the wool.

Zachiel, who had rendered himself visible, advanced toward a group of shepherdesses, who received him with naïve and humorous expressions; and although a slight shame colored their faces with the vivid incarnadine that accompanies innocence, they responded with a god deal of common sense to the discourse of the genius, who made an effort to descend to the level of their intelligence and the simplicity of their manners. I admired their beauty and their simple adornment, which took away nothing from the brightness of their complexion—which, without the assistance of art, effaced the lilies and the roses. Naïve graces even more touching than beauty were spread throughout their persons.

The shepherds occupied with the care of watching their flocks amuse themselves instructing their dogs. One of them occasionally takes up his bagpipe in order to divert his shepherdess, singing to her about the innocent pleasures of rural life. If he leaves her, it is to visit his fallow fields and meadows, or to pick flowers with which he makes garlands with a crown to ornament his mistress—who, content with that present, grants him the recompense of a kiss that she allows him to take without resistance. It is thus that he sees the approach of sunset, which announces the time for supper to him, and the exercise of the day prepares him to find the frugal meal excellent that has been prepared for him in clay bowls.

Such is the common life of the inhabitants of that island, a thousand times happier than all the nobles, who, by dint of philosophizing over the means of achieving happiness while materializing everything, are only drawing away from it without being able to savor true pleasures.

After the beautiful shepherdesses had instructed Zachiel with regard to their daily occupations and the cares that the shepherds take to spread abundance and joy in their canton, and to do the work that procures them everything that is necessary to their life, a continual fête, they left him in order to go into the dense shade, where, in the dark pathways, the figures they have engraved in the bark of oaks have grown along with the trunk. We followed them for some time, Monime obtaining much amusement from their games.

Sometimes a shepherdess goes to sleep on a carpet of grass, confiding the care of the flock to her shepherd. Some sit down on the edge of a spring; one sees them looking at themselves in the crystal of the waters, and ornamenting their heads with a thousand little flowers that grow in the vicinity. Often, they dance to the sound of flutes and pipes, or songs that the shepherds compose; and in the evening, when they have put their flocks under cover, they come back again to tread the tender grass in the moonlight. It is doubtless at that hour that Amour favors them; sighs and the renewed oaths seem to authorize the shepherds' larcenies. But I shall stop there, in order to permit the imagination of my reader the pleasure of painting the rest.

We went on to the Isle of Complaisance, which is only inhabited by a colony drawn from the Isle of Politeness. I only remarked rather insipid individuals; everything they do, according to what they say, is with a view to obliging one another. They never carry out their determinations; they never experience any obstacles. I noticed that indolence was their dominant vice. Those inhabitants have an air of languor that irritated Monime from the first day. That is what obliged us to leave in order to go to the Island of Persuasion.

That island is very small; a genius commands it in the quality of a Viceroy of Gallantry. The employment of the genius is to maintain all the citizens in the respect that they owe to their sovereign; he is the one that seasons all pleasures; his intelligence is regarded there as a celestial fire that only appears brilliantly, which shines and diverts and invents a thousand new ways of pleasing every day. It is thanks to him that ugliness becomes agreeable; he procures the charm of life; he is the soul of the conversation, the friend of the arts; it is to his knowledge that those people owe all their happiness; without him, everything on the large island would languish; this one serves him as a college or university, where the ambitious come to obtain their qualifications, in order to receive some important position in Gallantry.

Having finally arrived at that large island, we were assailed by a troop of adventurers, whom storm winds had caused to run aground there. Uncertainty was at their head and had no other employment than to cause the hearts of citizens to float, in order to prevent them from determining anything useful to their happiness. Opinion, who wanted in his turn to draw them into his party, made them esteem only that which was worthy of scorn. Credulity sought to deceive them; Novelty arrived thereafter to make them adopt a thousand puerilities and to give nourishment to chimeras devoid of common sense. Reflection, with a grave and serious expression, introduced them to Remorse, who tormented them incessantly. Inconstancy fluttered around them, to make them spin like weathervanes; Flattery sought to send them to sleep with a dangerous poison. Curiosity showed himself like an eagle, ready to cleave the skies in order to excite a thousand desires incapable of satisfaction; Imposture only applied himself to deceiving them; Presumption attracted them, only to precipitate them into all imaginable misfortunes; and Error made every effort to seduce them. Such were the wretches who had just landed on the island, and were trying by their intrigues to render themselves its masters.

Amour, who reigns in that island in accord with Inclination, assembled their council in order to deliberate as to what course of action to take in order to oppose the progress of those adventurers. It was decided that they would send to combat them Anger, Hatred, Jealousy, Despair, Dread and Dolor, at the head of a corps of light infantry made up of Sighs and Impatient Desires. In order to assure them of victory, Amour advanced himself, guided by Good Faith, Probity, Value, Generosity, Compassion and Confidence—all battle-hardened troops accustomed to vanquish their enemies. The combat was obstinate, but the party of Amour and Inclination was victorious.

When calm had been restored to the island, all of the citizens were free to devote themselves to games and pleasures; Inclination led them by example. That Princess, whose birth remains unknown to anyone, has a despotic power over all her subjects, and although the greatest genii of the entire empire labored for a long time to discover Inclination's origin, they have not yet been able to fix it with any certainty; the most common opinion, which I believe to be the most likely, is that in following the research of their philosophers, one learns that when Amour lit his torch for the first time, a prodigious quantity of sparks emerged from it, which, instead of descending to the earth, rose up toward the sky and were changed into stars there; they affirm that since that time, as soon as two bodies are formed and prepared to receive a soul, each of those stars divides into two equal parts, and, detaching themselves from the sky at the same time, they come to preside over those two different bodies; but the two parts are very often in places separated by such long distances that it is very rare for them to join up again.

That is, I think, a very good explanation to justify the inconstancy of the fop and the fickle coquette, since it is natural for them to search for what ought to complete their felicity, which they can only encounter by the union with the veritable half-star that can alone ensure their happiness. So, in the island of Gallantry, and even throughout the world of Venus, one only sees people who bind themselves together without pleasure, and quit one another without regret; because each one is only occupied with searching for the cherished half, which is not easy to find. When hazard brings them together, however, a secret instinct forces them to love one another, and that is how grand passions are formed. From that comes the secret knots, the sudden inclination, and the sweet sympathy that binds hearts together and has so much power over souls that it never fails to attract them. Now, as it happens so very rarely that the two halves of a star encounter one another, that is doubtless the reason why there is so little perfect amity in the world.

Such is the birth of Inclination, which I report in conformity with what I read in the archives of the Princess' palace.

We visited all the beauties of the island, where one can see everything that art and nature can gather of the most curious. The island is fertile in elegies, madrigals, epistles, end-rhymes and vaudevilles; the greater number of its citizens obtain their ordinary nourishment therefrom. All of them are piqued by great sentiments, delicate thoughts, ingenious imaginations, generosity and grandeur of soul; they spend their lives in pleasures and joy; every day there are new fêtes at which Amour presides; it is on that island that he exercises a supreme power; everyone submits to his laws and everyone owes him obedience.

It is equally permitted to the two sexes to form liaisons of pleasure without any fear of criticism. The mother who remembers the ruses she employed in her youth closes her eyes to her daughter's steps, and the night hides them under the obscurity of its mantle. No one ever experiences the torments of love except at the commencement of an affair of the heart, when uncertainty almost always troubles the tranquility of the soul—but everyone knows that anxieties of that sort are much more pleasurable than bitter, and in any case, they do not last long on the island. We were, however, assured that it was not without example that women had taken delicacy and decency to the extreme of resisting the pressures of their lovers for three weeks; but that was contested by several scholars on the island, who sustained that it could only be done with a view to arrangements—which is to say, to put oneself in a state to conserve two or three lovers without exciting jealousy between them.

Chapter IX
The Story of Zelime

We were walking on the seashore one day with Zachiel when we saw two women in a small boat, one of whom, pale and discomposed, seemed to me to be suffering an extreme affliction. Both of them took the route to a somber cavern, which only received daylight through its entrance. The two women went in and sat down on a bed of grass.

Flies have many privileges; they can go anywhere without attracting anyone's attention. Monime and I placed ourselves to either side of the afflicted beauty. Profound sighs emerged from her breast, and one might have thought that she was ready to expire.

"Will I always see you prey to all bitterness and dolor, my dear Zelime?" asked her companion. "Why do you want to sacrifice the rest of your life to weeping for an ingrate who has abandoned you in the excess of your torment? If the perfidious man had loved you, would he have stopped seeing you? After the loss of all your hopes, believe me, my dear friend, forget a fickle individual who only merits a sovereign scorn on your part, or, if you remember him, let it only be to avenge yourself."

"It's easy to give such advice," said Zelime, in an almost extinct voice, "when the heart is not affected by any violent passion. Your amity for you dictates it, and that which I have for you, dear Agla, engages me not to hide any of my pain from you; it is in that quality that I'm going to reveal all the secrets of my soul to you. I agree that I would be unworthy of your amity if I still had the weakness of regretting Volins; he's a monster of ingratitude, whom I've detested for a long time."

"What?" said Agla, in a surprised tone. "You don't love Volins? You're young and beautiful, and have all the talents necessary to captivate the heart of the greatest lords of the court; what, then, can be the source of this despair that has made me fear for your life for some time and has obliged me to advise you to come and take refuge on this island, in order that the dissipation that reigns here might contribute to making you forget an ingrate?"

"Alas, dear Agla, I hate him too much ever to forget him, and I cannot retrace in my memory either pains or pleasures over which he has not presided. But I've kept you in suspense for too long; it's necessary to tell you the story of my woes, in order to convince you that it isn't the loss of his heart that I regret.

"I was consecrated in my earliest childhood to the cult of the temple of Amour. I passed the age of adolescence tranquilly enough, and I had already attained my fifteenth year without any man having yet been able to touch my heart. I lived in that peace and mildness that you have doubtless experienced; but that torpor of the soul was not made for the vivacity of my temperament; I soon perceived that my happiness lacked something. The things that had previously amused me became insipid; a somber melancholy took possession of my mind; I no longer sought out any but the most solitary places, in order to dream there are liberty; my ideas were confused, and in spite of my efforts to clarify them, I could not yet divine what it was that could render me happy.

"I was in that disposition when, walking behind the Fountain of Youth, I encountered a young man as handsome as Amour. My face was covered by a blush when he fixed his gaze on me; I perceived that a tender emotion was also agitating him. He approached me timidly; I wanted to flee, but an invincible force stopped me.

"'Why, beautiful Zelime, do you want to avoid meeting me?' he said. 'Are you afraid of giving me too much love? Oh, if that is your objective, cease to flee; your concern is futile. For more than two months I've been seeking an opportunity to find you alone, in order to tell you about the tender sentiments you have inspired in me. If your heart is not inflexible to the darts of Amour, you'll receive without anger the vows that I have made only to live and die for you.'

"I was so surprised by the appearance of the young man and his speech that I remained motionless for some time without daring to reply. He took advantage of my disturbance to talk to me about his passion. In sum, what can I tell you? He obtained a favorable response from me to his desires and I promised to meet him every day at the same time in the vicinity of the fountain.

"We enjoyed the sweet felicity that two hearts united by love savor, and I was approaching the moment that ought to have completed my desires by espousing my lover when Volins surprised us one day in one of the cabinets that are contained in the gardens of the temple. He came in with a lady of the court; we went out immediately, but not quickly enough for Volins to be unable to perceive us. The lady, occupied with the young man, could not remark the sharp impression that I made on the heart of her young lover.

"Not believing that Volins knew anything, I asked Lisimon to take a stroll under the covered arbor. Meanwhile, Volins and his mistress, both pensive and distracted, went some time without speaking, and then reproached one another for the state of coldness in which they found themselves, each one striving to preserve their humiliated self-esteem. They reproached one another and emerged from the cabinet quarreling.

"We were still under the arbor, and you can imagine, my dear Agla, how we were examined by that couple of chilled lovers.

"I went to the rendezvous the next day, but it was in vain that I waited for Lisimon. Several days passed without me hearing any news of him. The time having expired when girls are kept in the temple, my father was alerted by the priestesses that they had learned that Lisimon, who had asked for my hand in marriage, had disappeared, and that, having accepted that young man for a spouse, I could no longer, in accordance with established laws, hope to be admitted to the ranks of the priestesses, or, in consequence, remain any longer in the service of the altars. That order was also given to me. I confess that, in the hope of seeing my lover again, it only caused me a mediocre chagrin.

"My father, unfavored by the gifts of Fortune, annoyed by my return, initially showed me a great deal of ill humor at my emergence from the temple, even though it was forced. As you can imagine, my dear Agla, my first concern was to seek information about Lisimon. I was so far from suspecting infidelity that I thought a violent illness has confined him to bed. My design was, therefore, to inform him, to spare him any anxieties that my leaving the temple might cause him—but Volins, attentive to my every move, had me told by a woman that he had stationed that on the last day that I had seen Lisimon he had embarked that same night to go to the Isle of Gallantry with a woman with whom he had been keeping company there for some time. I was so sensitive to my lover's perfidy and the indignity of his action agitated me so much, that I fell ill.

"News of my adventure spread through the city. Melise, a rich widow whose house was opposite my father's, and who received a numerous company in her home every day, took pity on my lot; she asked my father for me and had no difficulty obtaining me, promising soon to find me a suitable establishment. I was, therefore, introduced into Melise's house. My languor touched her, and in concert with Volins they both strove to return my tranquility; the perfidious individual had no need of being spurred on to that. He rendered me assiduous cares, which won him credit with Melise, as an excess of kindness on his part.

"Prejudiced in Volins' favor the eulogies that Melise incessantly gave his slightest actions, he began to gain my esteem and my confidence. I ceased to weep for my infidel, and soon no longer thought about him except to detest the indignity of his actions. Volins took advantage of those circumstances, and eventually took the place that Lisimon had occupied in my heart. Several considerable suitors presented themselves, but, filled with my new passion, none had the advantage of pleasing me. Volins seemed sensible to the sacrifice of a brilliant fortune that I was making for him. Oh, my dear, how I savored the pleasure of making them? Incapable of any other attachment, I put all my glory into convincing him of my amour.

"However, the perfidious man was making a game of deceiving me, and the oaths he made to love me forever were merely a repetition of those he had employed to seduce a thousand others. I eventually discovered a part of his treasons and made him sharp reproaches, but one word from his moth had the gift of persuading me. Incessantly agitated by new anxieties, I wanted to break with him a hundred times, and a hundred times he was able to appease me.

"Hazard caused me to encounter one day a woman who, like me, had been the dupe of Volins' false protestations for a long time. That woman, irritated against him, gave me a long account of all his dishonest maneuvers; she ended by informing me that he had recently debauched a chambermaid that he kept imprisoned in his house, in an apartment into which he descended by means of a trapdoor, which was connected with his own. The woman, outraged at having

194

served for a long time as the pretext for their intrigue, swore to avenge herself in a manner that would make him repent for as long as he lived. For myself, my heart torn by a thousand overwhelming reflections, I promised never to see him again.

"On returning to the house I was told that Melise wanted to speak to me. I went into her cabinet. 'I ought to quarrel with you, Zelime,' she said, 'because of the secret you have kept from me, but the good news I have to bring you ought to suspend my reproaches. Know, then, that Fortune and Amour are in accord at present, joining forces to ensure your happiness. Volins has just told me about the new engagement that you have formed with Ariste, who has finally obtained his mother's consent to marry you.'

"Imagine, dear Agla, how surprising such a speech was to me. I scarcely knew Ariste, and I understood immediately that it was a trick that Volins was employing to undo me by causing me to quarrel with Melise. The emotion into which that knew knavery threw all my senses covered my face with a fire that it was impossible for me to hide. Melise was not surprised, believing it to be occasioned by the shame of seeing my intrigue discovered. She complained of the lack of confidence that I had shown in the affair; in order to correct her deception I protested that my disturbance was only surprise. I protested that I had never had any liaison of the heart with Ariste and I could not believe that he was pushing temerity so far as to dare to boast of such an imposture.

"Melise took offense at my speech, heaped me with reproaches, and was carried away to the extent of making use of injurious terms that I could not hear without bursting into tears. That day was to be the epoch of all my woes, for in taking out my handkerchief I dropped a letter that I had received from the perfidious Volins. Melise, believing that it was from Ariste, seized it in order to convict me of imposture, but what was her surprise on recognizing the handwriting. She read it several times avidly. That letter contained a few poor justifications for a new intrigue for which I had thought I had the right to reproach him; it ended with the most ample protestations of a sincere and inviolable attachment.

"After having read it, Melise looked at me with eyes in which fury was expressed, and without wanting to listen to any of my explanations she threw me out of her apartment. How can I depict for you the treason of that false and subtle man? What expressions can I use to characterize the scorn and hatred I feel for him?

"Meanwhile, Volins, in the first fire of his new intrigue, did not know what had transpired; he relied on the discretion of his servants. In that persuasion he came, full of confidence, to pay court to Melise; he had a sensible interest in not quarreling with her, because of the protection she accorded him and the considerable sums of money he obtained from her. I was also a resource for him, which he was able to draw on during the brief times that were not favorable for him with regard to Melise. I was, so to speak, a reserve supply of which he made use in times of dearth.

"Melise, who was meditating a resounding vengeance, first wanted to convince herself of his perfidy. She showed him the latter he had written to me. I was summoned, and in spite of the respect I owed Melise, I could not help reproaching him for all the blackness of his conduct. I then gave Melise a thick stack of letters from Volins, in which he employed the most seductive terms to corrupt my innocence.

"You might perhaps think, my dear Agla, that they should have made an impression on Melise's mind and serve in some fashion for my justification. No, the wily Volins still found the secret of appeasing her, by persuading her that the letters I had just given to her had been written on behalf of Ariste. I begged Melise to summon Ariste, but Volins opposed it, saying that it would compromise his person to descend to explanations, always humiliating for men of a certain rank. I was therefore sacrificed to Volins' inconstancy and the hatred that Melise had conceived for a rival who had long enjoyed all the tenderness of her lover. I was forced to return to my father and to live there in the obscurity of a fortune so mediocre that it scarcely furnished enough for our subsistence.

"So, my dear, you see that after having renounced the most brilliant establishments in favor of Volins, the only gratitude I received on his part was a total abandonment. My self-esteem, humiliated in every fashion, has cast me into the despair in which you have seen me; but what has completed my distress has been learning that Lisimon had only gone away because of the calumnies that the treacherous Volins had employed to blacken me in his mind; it is only with a view to justifying myself to him that I consented to accompany you to this island."

"I cannot get over my surprise," Agla said, "and give thanks to Amour for having avenged you on Volins. Perhaps you don't know that Melise, convinced of his new intrigue, has entirely withdrawn all her favors from hum and obtained from the court an order exiling him to the deserts of Reflection. But that's not all. The little creature for whom he sacrificed you, who caused him to lose the good graces of Melise, and whose libertinage was unknown to him, has finally gratified him with a present that is causing him a painful remorse, which it is believed that he will experience as long as he lives."

We left those two individuals to rejoin Zachiel, and as we had visited all the beauties of the island, we prepared to leave the planet.

Chapter X

Before quitting the world of Venus, I asked the genius to instruct us regarding the mores and the religion of its people.

The Idalians, he told us, worship fire, because it is the noblest of the elements; they regard it as a living image of the Sun, and when one sees in a few of the provinces of that world that the fire which they maintain perpetually is beginning to diminish, they are convinced that they are threatened by the greatest calamities. That is why they conserve it with such care in places closed by walls without roofs, and the submissive and credulous people come at certain hours of the day to beg the most qualified individuals to throw precious essences thereon, which they regard as one of the finest rights of nobility.

Those people claim to be the first to have discovered fire, so necessary to the multiple needs of life, without which the principal operations of the arts that depend on it, whose detail has become almost infinite, could not be perfected. That is why, in all their capital cities, one sees a superb temple destined to conserve the sacred fire; that concern is confided to young women, the most beautiful that can be found in the city, and that honor is sought after by the greatest, for the privileges that are attached to it. If, however, one of those unfortunate priestesses allows the fire to go out by her negligence, she is rigorously punished; neither birth, nor age, nor beauty can ever save her.

At end of each year, however, the fire is allowed to die in order to be reignited at the beginning of the next, with many mysterious words; for mystery, credulity and ignorance are, it is said, the pillows on which the majority of Idalians repose. I have noticed too that when their sovereign senses the end of her life approaching, she orders the fires to be extinguished in the principal cities of her empire, and it is only after her death and the coronation of her successor that the fire is reignited with pomp and magnificence; then the mourning of the nation is concluded by great rejoicing, and during the celebrations a prodigious quantity of pastilles and the most precious essences are burned; those fêtes cost enormous sums.

Those people also worship the stars; they believe in a species of astronomical metempsychosis, and say that their bodies, after having quit their bodies, are constrained to pass through a hundred consecutive doors, which must take several million years, before they can reach the Sun, which they regard as the abode of the blessed; each door is composed of a different metal, placed in the planet that presides over that metal.

As nothing is more mysterious than that metempsychosis, they represent it by the emblem of a very long ladder, divided into seven consecutive passages; that is what they call the great revolution of celestial and terrestrial bodies, or the entire achievement of nature. They are convinced that souls go to inhabit successively all the plants and fixed stars that circle the sun, and that they purify themselves in these passages by a secret virtue as they get closer to that star, which is the center of felicity.

The Idalians are also convinced that the Sun and the Moon, by virtue of their brightness and their light, render themselves worthy of the principal homages that are owed to the stars. They name the former the King and the Sovereign of the heavens, and say that the Moon is the Queen and the Princess. As they are only ever inspired by Amour, they believe, following their principles, that the Sun cannot see the Moon without becoming amorous, and without communicating his fires to her; that is why, in order to put more decency into that union, they have decided to marry them. That marriage of the Sun and the Moon is regarded among them as the source and origin of all production, because it is on the earth, rendered fecund and abundant by them, that the fruits of that union make themselves evident. The most considerable advantages obtained therefrom are metals and precious stones. It is certain that no celestial marriage can be better matched.

Those people, always inclined to inconstancy, did not want the Sun to be exempt from it; that is why they regard eclipses as adulteries, because it seems, while they last, that the earth wants to invite the favors of the Sun, in order to steal them from the Moon by preventing her from receiving the accustomed light; one can see that they strive to extend coquetry all the way to the stars.

In order to ornament the majesty of the two spouses, they wanted to give the King and Queen of the Heavens a court as pompous as it is brilliant; that is why they represent all the other luminous globes as their ministers, the guards, their army or their subjects; that is how their beliefs are composed. They are convinced that there are genii amorous of the most beautiful women, who, in the frequentations they have with them, have revealed all their secrets to them, and an infinity of other things that they would never have known without the help of those genii.

Monime thought them very gallant, and said that the Idalians ought to think themselves very fortunate to have had women sufficiently beautiful to achieve their conquest and clever enough to have extracted their secrets from them, which, veritably, ought never to be revealed to mortals, always made to admire and not to know.

Chapter XI

I shall not elaborate on the laws of the Idalians, which differ very little from those of the inhabitants of the Moon; their mores and customs also appeared to me to be the same; they regard the most superfluous things as necessities of life. There is a considerable expenditure on that world on a prodigious quantity of charming but useless items of every sort; I was assured that each of them was endowed with a magnetic virtue that attracts gold as a magnet attracts iron. The merchants in possession of these precious rarities always have their establishments full of the greatest lords and ladies of the utmost quality, who are doubtless drawn by the attractive force of the marvelous rarities, which must necessarily draw them away from the serious occupation of their toilette; it is there that one sees them exchanging their gold for puppets, trinkets, portraits of new form, all kinds of animals and a thousand other gewgaws, of which they tire a fortnight later.

It is certain that sensuality causes them to invent new fashions every day, which they can no longer do without, although they were unacquainted with them two months before. These fashions, born of caprice and inconstancy, probably originate among them, and it is also in that world that they have their ordinary abode: coiffures, clothes, colors, designs, gallant mannerisms, Greek ringlets like cabbages or artichokes, modish pleasures, new allures, games, talents, spices, and even the language that one sees reigning and declining at the whom of caprice; it is fashion that changes everything; it is what forces a fine mind, a philosopher, a poet or a great author to yield to the petty talents that it chooses to put in credit; it is what makes people forget their old friends only to occupy themselves with new acquaintances; finally, it extends its power even to the worship rendered to the gods, and usages change in that regard as in the most indifferent matters.

These variations in taste, combined with the luxury that reigns in that world, are decorated there with the title of good taste, the perfection of the arts and the delicacy of the nation, which ought necessarily to spread an amenity and a suavity that renders all its citizens perfectly happy Their self-love doubtless causes them to regard those vices, which attract an infinity of others, as virtues, in spite of the contagion they spread even to the least of the people, and one can say that the luxury in question, taken to excess, tends to the ruination of all the citizens, who, by virtue of an inconceivable abuse, believe themselves to have an obligation to copy one another.

The example that the ladies of the court authorize, by imitating the magnificence of the Queen, causes the wives of those who are elevated in dignity to strive to copy the ladies of the court; women of a mediocre estate want to imitate the great, and none renders herself justice; the petty flatter themselves by passing for mediocre. Everyone wants to shine, to emerge from her sphere, and everyone runs to her own ruin, some by ostentation and vanity, or in order to make the most of their wealth, others out of shame, in order to conceal their poverty—but those who are wise enough to condemn such great disorder are not sufficiently so to dare to reform the others or to set contrary examples. As it is only to ostentation and adornment that homage is rendered, they doubtless fear seeing themselves too humiliated if they present a simple and modest appearance in company; that is why they are obliged to allow themselves to be carried away by the torrent of prejudices.

Among them the conditions are confused; the passion they have for display and vain expense corrupts the purest souls; people only seek to shine; they borrow, deceive, and employ a thousand unworthy artifices to succeed in that.

Nothing deters the Idalians; they can combine everything; good and evil are equally appropriate; it is among them that one can say, with reason, that Pride, wanting to perpetuate itself, one day married Ignorance, and from that union was born Prejudice, Conceit, Self-Love, Presumption, False Glory and the ardent desire they have to please, all children worthy of their birth, who deliver themselves to idleness, and rest the care for their fortune on Amour.

It is that, undoubtedly, which has banished from this world verity, decency and modesty, which have neither altars nor worshipers; thus, the veritable Amour, disdaining to enlighten them, has long ago extinguished his torch; it is not in the perfidious and mercenary smiles of an unworthy coquette that he can take pleasure, since the favors she lavishes are always accompanied by treasons, and only leave the vain regrets of an infamous attachment.

It is certain that the most tumultuous passions have their interval of relaxation and silence; it is by that means that they leave time for an upright and enlightened reason to perceive the precipices to which they lead and to arm itself with new strength to combat them, or to escape therefrom when one has had the misfortune to allow oneself to be taken by surprise.

We saw nothing on the planet Venus but people devoted to amour, pleasures, sensuality and good cheer; their tables are served with extreme care for everything that is new, everything that came flatter the taste-buds, excite the appetite and warm the blood; they never wait for hunger or thirst and always anticipate those desires with a great deal of sensuality; it is true, however, that they are entirely ignorant of the true sensuality that can only be felt by virtuous souls and can only be savored after having been able to vanquish oneself.

Amour, in all the worlds, has always passed for the most perfect happiness that humans can experience; that is what determined them to make a god of it. In the earliest age of the world, modesty and decency were an essential part of his worship; innocent pleasures and games animates his fêtes. But when the reign of the passions commenced, they excluded the virtues, and only reserved themselves the pleasures, which cannot subsist for long without virtue, always inseparable from the veritable amour.

Those people, who doubtless find themselves dragged away by the force of the constellations that preside over them, do not want to employ their courage in resisting it, and their most glorious deeds are only counted by the number of sacrifices that they have offered to Amour. Unfortunately for those imbeciles, however, the season of their offerings does not last long; and what is even more unfortunate for them is that it often happens that those they have offered imprudently often cost them painful remorse. There are a thousand reiterated examples of an infinity wretches obliged, in order to relieve themselves, to have recourse to the messenger of the gods,[24] who is indubitably the most accredited physician on this planet. Nevertheless, these examples have not arrested their lubricity; doubtless it would be necessary, to moderate their intemperance, to change al their habits, in order to deaden the frantic appetite they have for pleasures, by reforming their customs—but I do not believe that any genius wants to take responsibility for such a difficult enterprise.

"In whatever province you travel throughout the globe of Venus," Zachiel told us, "you will find very few inhabitants occupied with their business affairs; they all think about nothing but their pleasures; the foremost avoid the poor, in the dread of becoming so by contagion; the others, in order to give themselves entirely to their diversions, are somewhat more human; they are accessible in more ways; that is why their mistresses, their confidants and those they associate with their pleasures can easily take advantage of the follies that are their whole occupation; in those moments their souls seem to open to benefits; it is up to those who surround them to seize those moments, for their uncertain conduct does not often present the opportunity. The avidity for pleasure and a thousand other passions always prevail over amity; they regard the duty of life as a hindrance, to which they ought not to subjugate themselves; thus, those who seek to be in liaison with them ought to conform to their idea, confide very little to them and extract what they can."

The most reasonable people on that world see themselves constrained, in a sense, to follow those maxims, for nothing is more futile than that wisdom bristling with the nails and claws of an infinity of people incessantly occupied in setting themselves up as reformers of the human race; it is true that they cannot sustain those personalities for a long time without rendering themselves ridiculous, offending everyone and making themselves universally hated.

Monime, discouraged by only having encountered in the various places that we had visited, in some nothing but folly, the love of novelty and coquetry, and in others nothing but self-interest, bad faith and knavery, but nothing capable of satisfying her intelligence, would have liked to limit her voyages to those experiences, which proved only too well that the corruption of human beings

---

[24] Mercury poisoning was the standard treatment for syphilis in the 18th century—a "cure" sometimes, but not always, worse than the disease.

extends through all worlds, but the genius encouraged her and reanimated her curiosity with a few words.

"The enterprise that I have formed of working to educate you both obliges me to engage you to visit the other planets. The universe belongs to all humans, and you are made to enjoy the spectacle that it presents to your eyes; thus, curiosity ought to excite in you a strong interest that links you to the objects that animate it, in order to render yourselves spectators of everything that happens; for it is certain that the imagination is the source and the guardian of our pleasures; it is to that alone that the agreeable illusion of the passions is owed, always in intelligence with the heart. It can, when it pleases, furnish that illusion with all the errors of which it has need; its rights also extend over time, because it recalls past pleasures, and also enables us to rejoice in advance in those that the future promises us; it seems, as someone has said, that it gives us all the serious joys that alone can make the heart and mind laugh. All of our soul is within it, and as soon as the imagination cools, all the charms of like disappear and one remains in a lethargic torpor.

"It is to avoid your falling into that condition that I want to furnish you with the means of its exercise; it is necessary to see whether crime and error extend throughout their empire, and whether verity and virtue are not relegated to some distant planet, occupied in giving to the mores of its inhabitants more humanity to some than others. You are presently in a state no longer to find yourselves strangers in whatever place I might take you.

"As you are not yet pure enough to go to the Sun, we shall pass under that globe in order to go to the planet Mars, which will give us new subjects of meditation. I expect that Seaton will be able to find compensation there for the annoyances he suffered among the Idalians. As for you, charming Monime, you will have no other occupation there than the interest you take in Milord's fate, and everything that will happen during the sojourn you make there.

As Monime was pressing us urgently to depart, it was necessary to yield to her impatience. That prevented me from visiting a few other provinces of the world of Venus, but the genius assured me that they were only inhabited by peoples who, entirely delivered to the vilest crapulence, consequently did not merit my attention. We hastened, therefore, to travel rapidly to the planet Mars.

THE FOURTH HEAVEN: MARS

Chapter I

We arrived on the planet Mars at nightfall. Dusk had already dressed the landscape in somber livery; silence marched in its wake; the animals and the birds had taken refuge in their places of retreat, the only one that remained was the nightingale, which, accustomed to amorous wakefulness, spends entire nights singing. Hesperus, the conductor of starry bands, was shining at their head; the firmament was sparkling with bright sapphires. The Moon was rising with a nebulous majesty, unveiling her tender light with the bearing of a Queen, extending her silvery mantle over the obscurity. The genius, continuing his rapid flight, took us down into a sandy and arid plain.

Monime, gripped by fear and scarcely able to breathe, begged the genius insistently not to stop on that planet.

"I implore you, in the name of the amity that you have avowed for us, to take us to another world. The name of Mars alone frightens me; I imagine that it is filled by barbaric and ferocious citizens, that everything only breathes for combat, blood and carnage. What do you expect me to do on such a world? Is a woman made to confront its hazards?

"Rid yourself, dear Monime," the genius said, "of these puerile and frivolous fears; my design is not to expose you to the fury of combats. But my dear daughter, do you not want anything done in favor of Seaton? It is only here that he can make his apprenticeship in the métier of war; you're not unaware that a Lord like him cannot be occupied with any other employment, nor achieve any other than military rank. If you love him, you can never give him greater evidence of amity than by stimulating him yourself not to neglect any of the means that present themselves to make the most of his courage."

"Which means that today," said Monime, with a kind of chagrin and impatience, "you would like me to resemble those women who only find pleasure in the choice they make of a soldier for a husband, and of seeing him leave for the army without being obliged to go with him. Content to be distanced from him, they enjoy the satisfaction, or at least the hope, of believing him to be more than a hundred leagues away for a long time. If they were deprived of that time of liberty, of which they doubtless take advantage, a warrior, or anyone else, would then become indifferent to them.

"In any case," Monime added, sardonically, "the strongest Hercules can never hold firm before an Omphale; one of our gazes is sufficient to change their club into a distaff. Let us therefore allow them to ornament themselves occasionally with the name of hero; we render them effeminate often enough. Finally, my dear Zachiel, if you are absolutely insistent on forcing me to make a long sojourn on this planet, I want to disguise myself; I declare to you that I shall don the uniform, the sword, the plume, the high collar, and the spontoon; I shall buy a regiment and become a colonel at a stroke. Perhaps you will tell me that in that accoutrement, which will rejuvenate me even more, I shall appear to be no more than a child—fine reasoning; I'm sure that I shall see more than one in this world who, having reached a superior rank, doubtless thinks himself important and believes himself more skillful than the most experienced, although less expert and more infantile than me."

Monime persisted for longer in attempting to make the genius take another decision, but it was a waste of time; her representations were futile, and it was necessary to set forth. After Zachiel had dissipated some of her fears with stories that were as amusing as they were singular, the charming young woman saw that she was constrained to vanquish her repugnance, no longer daring to oppose the will of the genius openly.

Our voyage was very pleasant; the roads were full of post-chaises, carriages, heavy wagons and mule trains, but especially of people, who seemed to be the most content in the world.

One said: "This is a campaign that will advance me to the head of the regiment; and if I'm rendered justice, I'll have every reason to hope for a good pension and a government post at the end of the war."

"The country is rich," said another. "We'll be able to obtain fine booty there."

Several of them wanted to wager that the war would be concluded by that single campaign. "It isn't possible," they said, "that the enemy can hold out even for two months."

In sum, all of them were marching with great confidence; they only talked about places taken, victories won. To hear them, one might have thought that the cities would advance to meet them that that the armies would take flight merely at the news of their approach.

Obliged to quit that road to take another, we encountered a few battalions returning to the army. They did not seem nearly as content as the first; as much as the others seemed enthusiastic, these appeared discouraged and weary. Monime mistook them at first for poor cripples, who were begging for alms on the highways. Officers soldiers, servants and horses were all equally fearful and pitiable. Their speech corresponded to their faces.

"We were led to butchery," they said.

The general had lost his head; the cavalry had advanced ineptly; the infantry, poorly commanded, had not done its duty.

"Why, said one of them, "before exposing us, did they not sent scouts to reconnoiter the position? If the enemy had been closely watched, their maneuvers would not have been hidden. Our spies are poorly paid; that's why they neglected to inform us."

In sum, each of those military men was only content with himself, and all had a desire to utter a thousand maledictions against a state of affairs with which they seemed extremely disgusted.

That sad spectacle was not calculated to renew Monime's courage; her fear and dread increased. "Let's leave this vile Mars, she said to Zachiel. "Let's take another route; I feel myself oppressed by the air, which is assuredly too keen for the delicacy of my temperament; the vapors are already overwhelming me and my heart is palpitating as we advance further on the planet."

Deaf to Monime's complaints, the genius continued his route without deigning to respond. We soon discovered the most eminent and celebrated place on the entire planet, the famous Temple of Glory to which all the citizens of the world flock.

"The grave and serious expression you adopt will never deter me, my dear Zachiel," Monime continued. "I even dare ask you for a favor, before you go on into this frightful country. Begin, I beg you, by taking us to that magnificent temple. A noble presentiment informs me that a sojourn in that admirable place might calm my senses, reanimate my courage and reconcile me at the same time to the rest of the planet. Gods, what do I see? You're frowning! You're going to refuse me again; I shudder; don't pronounce sentence on me."

"What you're asking isn't reasonable," Zachiel said. "It's not by way of the Temple of Glory that one succeeds in the empire of Mars; on the contrary, one has to pass through the most difficult ordeals and along the thorniest roads to arrive at that temple. I can't change such a just law in your favor; Renown, to whom the guard of the temple is confided, would be bold enough to refuse us entry; she only opens up to those she knows, and whose name has already been transmitted throughout the world."

"Do you think, my dear Zachiel," said Monime, looking at him with an enchanting smile, "that there are not devious routes here, as there are everywhere, by which one can introduce oneself through some false door? Personally, I think that one can make heroes, like doctors, by the fireside. The Renown of whom you speak does not have a very sound reputation for accuracy, and if she doesn't look any more closely in order to open the door than to blow her trumpet, it must be admitted that people often get in with more facility than you imply."

The slightest things sometimes determine victory; that reflection gave all the advantage to Monime. Zachiel gave in, and the carriage that as carrying us became the chariot of triumph on which our amiable conqueress led us like captives to the Temple of Glory.

That admirable edifice is situated on the summit of the highest and steepest rock there ever was. Once, it was enclosed by high walls, very difficult to approach, but several roads have been flattened; nowadays more accessible, one can arrive there easily from several directions, on roads that appear newly traced.

The temple gains considerably from being seen from afar; its beauties are developed successively; the further they are from the center, the more brilliantly they shine; their gleam is proportional to that distance.

Scarcely had we arrived at the foot of the rock than it confronted us everywhere with nothing but frightful precipices, Zachiel having maliciously guided us to the least accessible place. No well-beaten road presented itself to make the ascent. It was then that our courage failed. I had initially joined in with the genius to combat Monime's fears, but I began to tremble like her; shame prevented me from adopting her language, but in the depths of my heart I shared her sentiments.

Another sight, even more forbidding than the rock, inspired further repugnance in us. It was a pile of horribly disfigured cadavers covering the floor of the valley. Gripped by astonishment and horror, Monime and I looked at Zachiel without having the strength to speak to him, but it was easy for him to read in our eyes what was passing in our soul.

Looking at us with a serene expression, he said: "Those corpses that you see do no merit your attention or your pity; they are here in ignominy and forgetfulness, because they were never more than failed heroes, and falsely brave; several of them came to break themselves against the spur of rock you see to your left, which is known as the False Point of Honor; they are people who, in order to avenge an imaginary insult, have dishonored themselves by a shameful death, who have perished, not in battle, which ought to be the bed of honor of the truly brave, but in duels that are only appropriate to vile gladiators. There are hired assassins who put all their honor into taking men's lives; people who make honor, virtue, vice, infamy, truth and lies depend on the outcome of a combat, who have no other rectitude, no other justice and no other reason than murder, as well as the strongest and most skillful, who believe themselves the most worthy of immortality, all their virtue being measured at swordspoint.

"Some of those you see on the other side had received the most fortunate dispositions from nature to become great men one day, but, by virtue of the abuse they made of them, they were only pernicious men and great scoundrels. Such, in particular, is the one you see near here suspended by the feet, head down, covered in blood that seems recently shed and whose stain will never be effaced. Do you know him, my dear Seaton? It's the author of all the misfortunes of your fatherland, as well as those of your family in particular: Cromwell. You shudder at that name; you're right, my dear; England would have been happy if it had not given birth to that monster, who ought to have been its glory but will forever be its opprobrium. He began by soiling it with the blackest of assaults against its king, and after having engaged it to condemn him to death of a scaffold, he ended up usurping the crown and becoming its tyrant.

"Look a little further on and you will see Totila, King of the Goths, who rendered himself frightful under the emperor Justinian I. That Prince fought numerous battles, as many at sea as on land, where he always had the advantage, and in spite of the resistance of Belisarius, whom the emperor sent against him, he besieged and took Rome, destroyed it almost entirely, burned the Capitol and toppled half the walls, ordered the citizens to abandon the city under pain of death, and treated those who did not profess his religion cruelly.

"That big pug-faced fellow you see over there is Attila, King of the Huns, the scythe of nations; he had a subtle intelligence, was ambitious, full of cunning, finesse and treasons, cruel, arrogant, rascally and reckless. The seat of his empire was in Sicambria, on the Danube. He was called to the aid of Genseric, King of the Vandals, against the Goths, and same with an army of five hundred thousand men, ravaged all the provinces of the Roman Empire and put all the places through which he passed in Germany and Italy to fire and the sword; but the run of his victories was finally stopped in Gaul by Aetius, the chief of the Romans and Merovech, the King of the Franks, who destroyed more than a third of his army in a single day and constrained him to flee to Hungary. The Prince, after having crushed a number of provinces, demolishing all their cities, attacked Aquileia, sacked Milan and Pavia, and finally died of a flux of blood that suffocated him, occasioned by his execrable debauches.

"There is Nicocles, tyrant of Sicyon in the Peloponnese, who was expelled from his states and died of hunger and cold. To the right you can see Hermias, son of Artane Donien,[25] who fought a bloody war against Memnon—who, after having vanquished him, had him sown up in the skin of an ox to serve as a plaything, and made him suffer a thousand indignities.

"Look," Zachiel continued, "at those who men who seem to be tied together. They are Cassius and Brutus, two traitors who took up arms against the common father of the land—I mean Caesar. That Emperor was so fond of Brutus that he had named him as his heir, but the ingrate, believing that he would acquire immortal glory, took treason so far as to become the leader of a conspiracy, and although Caesar had received advice not to go to the Senate that day, Brutus took him there personally. As soon as the Emperor entered, sixty assassins surrounded him and struck him with their swords. Caesar defended himself courageously, but when Brutus had also struck him he ceased to defend himself. 'Oh, my son,' he said to him, 'in whom I have put all my confidence, is it necessary for you to give me death?' Caesar said no more, covered his head with his robe, and let himself fall against the statue of Pompey, pierced by twenty-three sword-thrusts, of which he died in the hall of the Senate. But Heaven avenged his death with that of all the conspirators, who are all buried here in the dust, and

---

[25] This name is enigmatic, although the slightly-misrendered reference is obviously to Hermias of Atarneus, who was tortured by Memnon of Rhodes. Ovid records that he was sewn up in an ox-hide, but not by Memnon.

that same Brutus, after having lost a battle near the city of Philippi, fell on his own sword, and died instantly, killing himself with same blade that he had employed in the parricide that he had committed on Caesar's person.

"I would never finish," the genius added, "if I name for you all those you see here. It is true that some performed fine deeds, but they soiled them by actions even more barbaric; brigands rather than conquerors, it was their ferocity that animated them and not worth; they only sought to vanquish in order to massacre and pillage, and the name that they left after them is only immortal in the horror and execration of men, because they did not know the true path that leads to the Temple of Glory and, although they took great steps in order to reach it, their faults and vices banished them from it forever."

"All these men horrify me," said Monime. "I find it repugnant to the society of reasonable beings that subjects dare to dictate the law to their masters and attribute to themselves to privilege of inflicting their punishments, since a sovereign is only accountable for the conduct to the tribunal of the divinity. However he disposes of our bodies and our wealth, one ought only to oppose to him submission and obedience; that has always been my way of thinking. I see it justified by the number of traitors, tyrants and the impious who, in seeking glory and immortality, have found nothing but opprobrium and scorn. One might think that tyranny is a species of rage, which is often pushed to the ultimate extremity. Oh, my dear Zachiel, let us flee, and no longer amuse ourselves with the contemplation of such monsters."

"I consent to that," said Zachiel, "but before going on, I want Seaton to look at this reef, which is scarcely confronted by except by those of his nation, and which is deadly to numerous Englishmen; its name is Suicide. Would you believe, my dear, that the greater number of all those you see are your compatriots who have been made enough to give themselves death? That kind of fury is regarded in England as a grandeur of the soul; it is a noble disdain for life, confusing despair with intrepidity, and that pusillanimity that allows itself to be felled by the slightest troublesome event, with the heroism that renders us superior to all the woes that surround us."

While Zachiel was making me that list, which I found very interesting, we saw a troop of individuals advancing toward us, very poorly clad and rather surly in appearance, who were holding large scrolls of paper, quills and writing desks. They saluted us in a pedantic fashion, and told us that they had come to offer us their services.

"I'm not dear," said one of them, who called himself a gazetteer. "For a small fee I promise to render you to the temple and sign you a distinguished place there."

Then a quantity of poets and historians presented themselves, to offer us immortality in verse and prose.

"Here, sirs," said one of the poets, "are poems that I have composed for the great conquerors, and here are some for great politicians; these are for the men of vast genius whose intelligence and enlightenment extend over all the sciences. I've left all the names blank; if you want to choose one, I'll immediately fill in yours, provided that you do me the kindness of making me a little present of a hundred guineas."

My curiosity excited by that singular compliment, I took one in order to examine it, but I only found it filled with enthusiasm and bloated verses; great words formed a complete collection of all the most anciently coupled rhymes: battles and chattels, sun and run, glory and victory, sublime and chime, hazard and Caesar, thunder and asunder, fights, mights, advantages, carnages, errors, terrors and many more. In the end, all those cadenced words, like a tune played on a pipe, which would be too long to reproduce here, appeared to me to signify very little. However, the poet offered nothing less than to put Monime at the rank of the goddess Pallas, and to make me occupy the place of the god Mars himself.

From the other side Monime was assailed by people presenting new pamphlets to her. "My Lady," said one of them, "this is new; if your grandeur will permit, I shall have the honor of dedicating this little work to you; it is bound in pink, which is the color in fashion."

"Take mine," said another, "it's in flax-gray, the delights of a tender soul."

"My Lady," said a third, "give preference to this collection; it's in green and yellow, to paint springtime; the book is sown with nothing but flowers and brilliant words; it's divine."

"Beautiful goddess," said a man with a languorous expression, "Allow me to present this elegy to you."

"And me these epistles, which are above those of Cicero."

Other brought odes, rondeaux and vaudevilles; those requested very little money. Afterwards however, came historians of great repute, who offered us the same services—which is to say, to have the most beautiful events in our lives inscribed in the book of bronze that is never erased. Oh, those were very dear!

I was tempted at first to place myself in that great book. The writer was already beginning to sharpen a fine quill, delicate and light, but when the hand posed on the paper, ready to trace my great deeds, he asked me under what title I wanted to announce myself. I confess that the question embarrassed me; I sensed internally that I did not merit any. After having thought for a moment, I said: "Give me whichever one you wish; perhaps hazard will enable you to encounter the right one, and if the zeal I feel to live up to it can substitute for merit, you won't be taking any risk."

Zachiel, who was present at that conversation, warned me that it was only by heroic actions that one could acquire the glory of occupying a place in the great book, without which whatever vulgar writers attempted to inscribe therein was easily erased by envy or jealousy, which pardon nothing, but the darts of which are blunt and cannot tarnish the reputation of individuals whom Heaven has endowed with true merit and invincible courage.

"The rank or the place that great men merit," added the genius, "can only be decided after their death, because there are some who lose in the last moments of their life a part of the glory that they acquired over several years, and others who become even greater in dying than they were when they enjoyed perfect health.

"Scipio, the father-in-law of Pompey, redeemed at the moment of his death the poor opinion that people had had of him; he showed by his confidence and boldness that the people who have seemed the weakest can sometimes raise themselves to the grandeur of soul of heroes. Having been cast up on the shore of Africa by a horrible tempest, and his vessel captured by enemies, Scipio wanted to save in his person the glory of his name, and could not suffer seeing the Africans, being accustomed to see them vanquished, put him in chains. As great as the vanquisher of Carthage, he tamed the horrors of death, by plunging his sword into his bosom. That example, my dear Seaton, ought to suffice to inform you that he last moments of life ought to be regarded as the touchstone that distinguishes the heroes and the true philosophers from those who have only usurped the name."

We were interrupted by a man, who came running toward us with a whip in his hand, saying: "Sirs, I am the English postillion; I guarantee to take you from here to the temple without spilling you; would you like a coach, a post-chaise, a two-wheeler, a cabriolet? Choose—we have vehicles of every sort here."

"Stand aside," said another, "you're nothing but a chatterbox. These gentlemen merit going forth on Pegasus; he's ready saddled and bridled, only waiting for you to depart; he's the gentlest animal in the world, and allows himself be mounted easily. Take advantage of it, beautiful goddess; I promise you that you'll arrive at the temple in the blink of an eye."

A runner advancing with a proud and audacious attitude told us, in a methodical tone, that he was the forerunner, who ordinarily matched his pace to the gifts that were made to him. He was followed by a quantity of scholars, who, all for a price of silver, cane to offer us immortality.

Aggravated by all these offers and that crowd of merchants of reputation, whose number was increasing at every moment, we made the decision to get rid of them, but we could only do so by accepting large volumes of praise, which they gave us very cheaply and which put us at least at the level of the most famous heroes and heroines of antiquity.

Renown immediately announced herself with her hundred mouths and her hundred trumpets, with which she intoned our pretended great deeds; at the same time her horse was hitched to our chariot; in a trice we were borne up to the clouds, and, without having touched the rocks, we found ourselves in the great square of the temple.

"I would prefer not to advance any further," said Monime, "with making a halt here. We're hungry, and I feel too weak to go on."

"What are you saying?" said Zachiel, interrupting her abruptly. "Is this the place to talk about eating and drinking? Know, beautiful Monime, that in the abode of glory, one only feeds on wind and smoke; one only gets drunk on one's own merit. Sleeping in the shade of those laurels, receiving incense, throwing dust in the eyes—that's the life and the sole occupation of immortal heroes."

Monime did not appear to have any appetite for that diet of immortality; she was already preparing to dip into her bag of dried fruits when we were suddenly invested by a swirl of exceedingly odorous smoke, Then came a gust of wind, which seemed to reanimate volcanoes of sulfur and saltpeter, which spread more smoke throughout the square. Combining with the other, it seemed to intoxicate all the spectators. Unable to sustain the force of that wind, Zachiel took us into a vestibule.

"Here you are," he told us, "in the midst of the most vaunted heroes in the universe."

Our astonishment at the sight of that singular company is inexpressible. Scarred faces, punctured eyes, slashed craniums, sliced ears, arms in slings, wooden legs, bodies covered in wounds and plasters, and women, one of whose breasts had been hacked off: such were the frightful sights that presented themselves to our eyes.

"Great God, where are we?" exclaimed Monime, utterly bewildered. "Oh, wicked Zachiel, you've deceived us; what pleasure have you gained in thus taking us for fools? Why have you forced me to undertake this long voyage? Why excite my curiosity with stories that have no kind of connection with what I see? Why, finally, have you claimed to be introducing us into the sanctuary of immortality, when I can see that all those magnificent promises have ended up bringing us to a hospital?"

The genius, smiling at her error, told her that he was sorry that these unfortunate officers had only excited her alarm, when they ought at least to inspire sentiments of admiration; and that it was only by way of such accidents that one could lay claim to glory."

"What!" said Monime. "You still expect to persuade me that we're in a temple here?"

"Assuredly," said Zachiel. "You're under one of its porticoes—but let's go into that vast colonnade on the left."

Frightened to see a large tower that was in the middle moving, Monime uttered a cry, dreading that it might fall on top of us. The tower, which machinery similar to our windmills was causing to rotate rapidly, showed us several figures that its movement appeared to animate. Monime's disturbance was augmented by that appearance, and in spite of the desire she had to discover what such an extraordinary decoration signified, I noticed that she would have liked to be much further away. However, Zachiel, attentive to all her movements, finally fixed her attention.

"Look at these different heroes," he said. The one that you see nonchalantly leaning on the arm of his squire is the great Cyrus, who transferred the empire of the Medes to the Persians, won an infinite number of battles and conquered entire provinces, who traversed Asia, Media, Hyrcania, Persia and, in sum, ravaged more than half of the world he inhabited."

"He was doubtless an ambitious Prince," said Monime, "who wanted all the earth to be submissive to him?"

"Not at all," Zachiel replied. "Amour alone prompted him to all that disorder. He only wanted to free the Princess Mandana, with whom he was passionately in love; but that Princess was snatched away from him eight times."[26]

"There," I said, "is a beauty that passed all proofs."

"That's true—but all her abductors were illustrious scoundrels, who nevertheless had virtue enough to respect her; they never dared even to lay a finger on her, and if her square could talk, he would recount marvels.

"The other who is appearing is Romulus, the first King of the Romans, whom he citizens put to death, and afterwards affirmed that he had risen up to Heaven. That one is Codrus, the King of Athens, who devoted himself to death for the service of the fatherland."

"I'd be curious," I said, "to know who that beauty is who appears with such a proud attitude."

"That's Cloelia, the most illustrious of all Roman ladies; she swam the Tiber in order to escape from Lars Porsena's camp."

"That one," said Monime, "appears to me to be a heroine very heavily armed; is she not some Queen of the Amazons?"

"That's the Maid of Orléans," said Zachiel. "You can't be unaware that she was the one who liberated France from the English yoke. The one that you see in the alcove is Zenobia, Queen of Palmyra, who governed that realm with as much wisdom and mildness for more than thirty years, until the time when Aurelian came to declare war on her. That Prince, after having vanquished her, took her

---

[26] According to Herodotus, Mandana of Media was Cyrus the Great's mother, while his wife was Cassandane. How Madame Robert acquired this misconception is unclear.

212

as a captive behind his chariot of triumph. He had her two sons, Hernianus and Timolaus, killed.[27] There's Elizabeth, Queen of England; her glory would have been perfect if it had not be tarnished by the death of the Earl of Essex and that of Mary Stuart, Queen of Scots. It is claimed that jealousy had a great deal to do with the reasons that determined the pronunciation of those two condemnations."

Then we heard something akin to a hurricane excited by several winds that were in conflict. The wind of glory and that of immortality appeared to be struggling against that of jealousy. Renown was blowing from the south. To the north, the winds of envy and calumny were making such a frightful racket, shaking the edifice with so much violence, that they were bringing down various figures from the paneling and the colonnades, which were still attracting out curiosity.

"There," said Zachiel, "is a King of Phrygia, who was the richest Prince of his time, and the one whose enlightenment, intelligence and politics were the most useful to his people, in enabling him to discover the secrets of his allies and the ruses of his enemies. That monarch profited so considerably from the gifts he had received from Heaven, in making them serve the glory of his realm, that he rendered his subjects perfectly happy. His name was Midas."

"What!" said Monime. "Is that the Midas who is depicted with asses' ears, and whom the indiscreet request he made of Bacchus to change everything he touched into gold caused him to die of starvation?"

"The same—which proves that posterity often spoils, by allegorical fables, the finest actions and embellishes pitiful ones; as witness the story of Lucretia, who has just fallen beside Midas; you're not unaware of the fashion in which her death was published; reading it ought to instruct you. Nothing, however, is as false as the story that is told of it; the truth is that Collatinus, her husband, having learned of her intrigues with the young Prince, stabbed her himself, and put about false rumors against the Tarquins, in order to take possession of the Republic conjointly with his colleague Brutus."[28]

"I suspected as much," I said. "Not that I presume that all women are coquettes, but that story of Lucretia always seemed to me to be a trifle apocryphal, in that it seems that it would have been more natural first to turn her weapon

---

[27] There appears to be no evidence of Zenobia having had sons with these names.

[28] The historical accuracy of the story of Lucretia's rape, which allegedly sparked the revolution that established the Roman Republic, as told by Livy and Dionysius of Helicarnasus, was always regarded with some skepticism; that did not prevent it becoming an oft-cited moral exemplar, employed by both St Augustine and Dante, and a significant theme in Renaissance art and literature; English writers who employed it include Chaucer and Shakespeare.

against the man who wanted to dishonor her, or at least not to wait until the crime had been committed to kill herself."

Aggravated by the fatigue of being obliged to struggle against the impetuosity of the winds that were blowing relentlessly, Monime asked the genius to take us into a building that was on the right.

The vault and pilasters of that building were made of glass; several columns of cardboard supported the edifice. On those columns, blackened by smoke and agitated by the winds, as in the other building, the great deeds of heroes—as many ancient as modern—were inscribed. It is true that when the gusts of wind became violent, some of those columns toppled, and although the poets and historian hired by the State to maintain the edifice applied an extreme attention to their reestablishment, it often happened, in the disorder, that they forgot a great many heroes, who, by virtue of that negligence, found themselves deprived of immortality in spite of the efforts they had made to merit it.

We saw several people walking there who seemed to us to be greatly predisposed in their favor. One of those men approached me and asked whether I was newly arrived, and what was being said about him on our world.

"When you've told me your name," I said, "perhaps I'll be able to reply to the question you've asked me."

"I am Mucius Scaevola, a noble Roman, whom seeing my city besieged by King Lars Porsena, took my leave of the Senate and went to his camp with the intention of killing him; but as I did not know the King I was deceived and mistook one of his favorites for him, whose life I took. I was immediately arrested and taken before the King, but, without being astonished by any of the threats he made against me for daring to make an attempt on his life. I showed him how little I cared about the cruelest torments by putting my right hand into an ardent fire, and suffered the pain constantly until it was entirely burned. Lars Porsena, astonished by my firmness, could not help admiring my great courage and sent me away without doing me any harm. Scantly sensible to that generosity, I declared to him that I was not the only one that had conspired against his person, and that there were another three hundred Romans who had sworn his death. That was what determined him to make an alliance with the Romans, fearing their intrepidity because of the example I had just shown him."

"You horrify me," I said. "How dare you boast of the blackest of all attempted murders? Are those your fine exploits? What! After a cowardly homicide, you claim immortality? It isn't be treasons that one attempts to vanquish one's enemy. The action from which you want derive vanity would only be regarded today, in our world, as a model of rascality and ferocity, and you would have no other glory at present than being placed in the ranks of those bandits who hire themselves out as assassins and put a certain price on each murder proportionate to the difficulties they encounter in committing the crime. For myself, I do not see anything great in voluntary homicide. The basis of all the virtues is humanity; it flows like a pure and salutary stream that fertilizes everything it

214

encounters; but you, vile assassin, if you have acquired any honors, they are illegitimate."

Mucius, very discontented by my reception, shrugged his shoulders and went away.

Soon afterwards I was surrounded by a large number of people. One of them told me that he was Achilles, another Caesar, and a third Alexander. I could not hear the names of a great many of those heroes because they were all speaking at the same time. As I saw that each of them was preparing to tell me his story, I interrupted them to beg them to explain themselves one at a time.

"I am Childebren," said a fat, wheezy man. "I would like to know what is being said about me."

"What is said about you? I can assure you that I've never heard your name pronounced on any world."

"And me," said another, with an air of generosity. "I am Montezuma."

"Ha! You, I know; you're an honest man to whom the Spanish did great injustice. But you, who announce yourself to be a Caesar, tell me what country you come from, which world you inhabited and in which realm you were born?"

"The question is singular; has there ever been more than one Caesar? You are an imbecile who only has a human face, and have not the intelligence of a carp."

"I have not learned to reply to invective, but I can assure you that there are at present on our earth more than a million Caesars and at least as many Alexanders, since the least of our officers, and even our soldiers, regard themselves as such."

I had no sooner uttered those words, which they doubtless took for as many blasphemies, than the entire crowd of heroes disappeared, to the great contentment of Monime, who was beginning to fear their petulance.

Zachiel then took us through a large hall filled with heaps of silk and cotton of different colors. Three old women seemed to be continuously occupied in spinning them. Monime and I looked at them very intently, without being able to discover the mystery. This is how the genius explained it to us.

"The three old women you see are the Fates who spin the lives of mortals. Humans can only remain on earth for as long as they take to finish each mass. When they have completed a skein, Destiny attaches a little gold, silver or lead plaque to it, which defines the good or bad qualities of person whose thread has just been cut; his name is engraved on the plaque and his virtues or vices traced in indelible characters. Then an old man, whose rapid course can never be halted, fills the flaps of his robe with them and goes to throw them in the river of forgetfulness, which you can see in the distance on the left flank of that hill.

"The old man comes back continually to take more, untiringly, without ever being able to diminish their number; but when, with an air of chagrin, he has discharged his burden, two swans whiter than snow, which float incessantly on the river, take care to detach with their beaks the names of the most illustrious mortals and put them in the hands of a nymph of ravishing beauty, whose unique employment is to carry them to the Temple of Glory, in order to consecrate them to immortality there. There she attaches them, with great care, to a simulacrum placed on a column elevated in the middle of the temple."

"It's easy to deduce," said Monime, "that the old man you have depicted for us is Time; but what do the swans signify, which, careful to detach the names of heroes from those of vulgar humans, prevent them from being swallowed up by the river of forgetfulness?"

"They represent the great poets and the best historians," said the genius, "who both, by their late nights and assiduous labors, serve to immortalize monarchs, princes, great politicians and all those who have distinguished themselves in the course of their life by heroic actions. The nymph depicts History, who, under that figure, represents the candor, purity, simplicity and above all the verity that a historian ought to employ in the pictures that he gives us in tracing the lives of the heroes that he sets out to put before our eyes."

After leaving that hall the genius took us across a large courtyard. We noticed that the sun, by the heat of its rays, had concentrated the smoke in the entrails of the earth; all the winds had dissipated; the only one that remained was that of glory, which, like all zephyrs, was only blowing to render the air milder and more agreeable.

"We have finally arrived," Zachiel told us, "at the Temple of Immortal Glory."

That temple, the dome of which appeared by its elevation to pierce the clouds, immediately fixed our gaze; we were enchanted by the beauty and the regularity of its architecture. Monime and I, dazzled by its majesty, felt a faint terror take possession of our souls; we approached it with the respect that divinity inspires.

Under the steps of the temple is a profound lair, in which we saw Vulcan forging, on an anvil, the redoubtable thunderbolts of which the Marcians[29] make use to sustain their rights and ensure the destiny of States. To one side of the door of the sanctuary was the divine Urania, a compass in one hand and a map in the other, one which were traced realms, cities, citadels, lakes and sea. On the

---

[29] The original text employs both *Marciens* and *Marsiens* to describe inhabitants of Mars, although the former is employed to refer to a regional population, contrasted with the Salians and Bellonians, and might be derived from the name of the Byzantine emperor known in French as Marcien rather than the name of the planet. When first introduced, the latter seems to be used in a more general sense, but is subsequently used in the limited one. In consequence, I have maintained the inconsistency, transcribing the two terms as Marcians and Marsians, rather than unifying them or substituting the now-standardized "Martians." Some early English scientific romances employed "Marsians" rather than the more familiar term.

other side, Calliope was holding a history book, using her finger to point out the finest features. Further away were ranged Intrepid Valor, Vigilant Toil, Tranquil Composure, Hope, Cunning, Deflection, Disguise and Imagination, who seemed to be occupied with a thousand brilliant projects that they were presenting to the confidant of Mars, whom Zachiel identified to us as Impenetrable Secrecy. The temple is surrounded by laurels, with which Pallas herself forms the crowns that Mars subsequently presents to his favorites.

Chapter III

"You ought not to be proud," said Zachiel, "of the unmerited glory that you are receiving today in entering this temple. Covered by my wings, I shall render you invisible to the eyes of all these heroes, and those of Mars himself; I only want to excite in you the martial ardor and noble courage that animates and forms great captains in order to render you worthy of one day occupying a place beside these demigods."

Mars, seated in the middle of the temple on an elevated throne, sustained on the wings of the genius of war, appeared to be gazing at a hero placed beside him to his right, obligingly showing him several passages in a large book that Destiny was holding in front of him. I dared not ask questions of the genius for fear of being discovered, but he anticipated my desires and gave me an indescribable pleasure by telling me that the person who excited my curiosity by virtue of the preference he had obtained over the others was Henri IV, the good King of France, whom Mars was enabling to read, in the book of Destiny, the glory of his race and the striking actions that were to be accomplished by all his descendants.

"O gods!" said Monime, in a low voice, "What an amity I feel for that hero! He is the one, then, whose memory will be perpetuated eternally from race to race among the people as well as the great and sovereigns, who will always have the glory of being taken for a model throughout the universe? But tell me, my dear Zachiel—I'm curious to learn whether he knows how much his memory is revered in all the nations of Earth, and whether he enjoys here the renown that he so justly acquired."

"I give you my word," said Zachiel, "that what makes his recompense, and the proof that the divinity created him in an eminent degree of superiority of intelligence and talents in order to reign over all men, is that those who were most jealous of his glory are forced to admit today that he alone merits commanding the entire universe, since Henri IV has been placed above the greatest men that Rome produced in her greatest elevation.

"I hate flattery and false praise," the genius added, "and only ever applaud true merit. Scipio Africanus is, without contradiction, the greatest that Rome produced, but Henri IV required much more strength of genius, grandeur of soul, intrepidity and courage to reach the goal of becoming king of France than was necessary for what the Roman achieved.

"Scipio, supported by good troops, expelled Hannibal from Italy, reassured the Romans frightened by the loss of the battle of Cannes and carried to the Carthaginian lands the furies of a cruel war with which they had shortly before set all Italy ablaze; in sum, he liberated Rome from that proud and dangerous rival. But what puts the glory of Henri IV above that of the Roman is that, at the head of semi-naked soldiers, devoid of money and without any other aid than his courage and his right, he sets out to recover the crown; he is obliged to make the conquest of his own kingdom, usurped by the member of the Ligue, the Spaniards and others even more redoubtable. In spite of all his oppositions, Henri IV carried through his plans, and after having reestablished himself on the throne of his fathers he made those same Spaniards tremble who, a few years earlier, had combined scorn with presumption in merely referring to him as "the Béarnois."

"You see, my dear Seaton, the affairs of Henri IV were in much greater disorder on the death of his predecessor than those of the Romans after the battle of Cannes, since they at least had money and the means of reestablishing their army. Far from the king of France having the same assistance, I recall a letter that he wrote to one of his generals, in which he indicated that his finances were in a pitiful state, that his cooking pot had been empty for a week, that his suppliers had not had a penny, and that he was obliged to eat with the officers of his army."

I would have liked Zachiel to add to that account and summary of the lives of some of the heroes that I saw assembled in the temple, but Monime, who was beginning to weary of such a long fast, assured us that she did not have enough strength to want to attempt to resemble those great individuals, and that being unable to imitate Henri IV in his great deeds, she would still find enough glory in resembling him in his humiliation by going to ask for supper from some officer whose turnspit was not dismantled. It was necessary to satisfy Monime.

When we emerged from the temple we encountered a large number of troops, whose officers, dressed in different colors, were carrying on their flags or ensigns the emblems of battles they had fought. On some the depiction of an honorable retreat was seen; others described an advantageous capitulation; this one showed the conquest of an entire province; that one the destruction of a well-fortified city filled with all sorts of munitions; that other a naval combat that represented an entire fleet that seemed to have been dissipated or sunk. Further away, the standard of victory shone, borne on a chariot followed by various other troops; in fact, I cannot describe or enumerate the prodigious quantity of ensigns hoisted by the multitude of claimants of immortal glory, for it is necessary not to think that only military men can make the claim; all estates have the same rights, and Renown blows her trumpet for the favorites of Apollo as well as those of Mars, thus forming a perpetual competition in the vicinity of the temple.

As we advanced into the country we discovered a manor house whose form and structure indicated that it had seen several centuries; Zachiel took us to it. The manor house was occupied by an old officer who gave us a good welcome, but during supper he began giving us a account of the battles in which he had been involved, the duels in which he had been employed, the wounds he had received, the injustices that had been done to him in gratifying men far inferior to him, and a thousand other things just as uninteresting for strangers. That conversation bored Monime so much that she had the vapors. We took our leave of our host in order to depart at dawn the next day.

Zachiel took us in the empire of the Salians, where the fire of war was ignited everywhere. As we approached one of their cities we were obliged to pass through the middle of a camp. The officers, helmets on their heads and fully armored, were preparing to leave; the movement of the soldiers was already producing a cloud of dust that was rising into the air and the trumpets, fifes and drums were already sounding the march, when a courier arrived, bringing a countermand that stopped them.

Monime, observing their movements, seemed disconcerted at first by the sight of the blades of their bristling pikes and the brilliant gleam of weapons, which dazzled the eyes. Gripped by fear and dread, she begged the genius in a tremulous voice to take us to some other world, unable to bear the sight of those men, who seemed to be respiring nothing but death, blood and carnage.

"I see that you are still prey to unworthy weaknesses," said Zachiel, in a severe tone. "Ought you to dread anything while I'm accompanying you? Is this the fruit that I must expect from my care and my complaisance? Rid yourself of these vain terrors if you want to merit the gifts that I intend to make you."

Monime blushed; ashamed and confused by having attracted the reproaches of the genius, she dared not reply, and was constrained to follow Zachiel, who took us through the camp in order to enter the city, where we obtained a room in a lodging-house. We spent the reminder of the day resting, while listening to the instructions of the genius.

"These people are very different from the Marcians. Among the latter, morality, candor and good faith form the most solid foundations of their empire, and among the Salians those virtues have long been banished. You will see nothing in this realm but a tissue of false pretexts, vain arguments, frivolous complaints, crude and borrowed colors, muted and hidden intrigues, and artifices suggested by individuals interested in finding means to continue the war in order to enrich themselves at the expense of the people."

"I find the condition of humans very deplorable," I said, "especially when they take their own passions or those of others as guides for their conduct. If war is proposed, the soldier, dazzled by the lure of pillage, delivers himself to it with enthusiasm, and the citizens, seduced by the false pretext of conserving the fatherland and their liberty, seem to animate the troops; the officer, guided by another interest, encourages them, while he often runs to his own doom."

"It's true," said Zachiel, "that nothing is more persuasive for the persons one wants to rally to one's party than setting an example; that is an inclination attached to nature; it seems that humans are only made to imitate one another; an entire province observes what its neighbors do; the fire spreads, is communicated, and soon becomes a general conflagration. It is from those kinds of muted mines that one often sees an evil spring gush forth, and the politics of those who foment them often employs al the artifices that it has put to work until the blood of the troops is shed. This realm has furnished a terrible example, since the war they have undertaken too lightly is reducing the State to cruel extremes. Imbecility, ignorance, corruption and debasement are the dominant vices of the Salians, the usual source of the poverty and misery of peoples; judge, my dear Seaton, whether they are to be pitied."

The next day we were visited by several officers. Monime's surprise was extreme when, instead of seeing robust men with martial features she only saw young Adonises, powdered, primped and perhaps painted, for they had complexions as fine as that of a woman who spends three-quarters of the day in her toilette. Those plumed demigods with red heels and doubly-ruffed sleeves did not have the slightest scent of gunpowder; ambered from head to toe they perfumed Monime's whole apartment. Those darlings of the god Mars doubtless made their principal occupation imitating him in his amours, leaving the care of their glory to hazard or fortune. They only talked to us about the favors they had received from their beauties, the feasts with which they had been regaled, and those they still proposed to give in the city, and invited Monime and me to take part in them.

That debut gave me a very poor idea of the prudence and talents of those young officers. However, curious to instruct myself regarding a profession of which I only knew the theory, which I soon hoped to put into practice, in order not to neglect anything, I asked them numerous questions about their manner of combat and certain rules that I thought necessary.

First I asked them whether they had a thorough knowledge of the map of the country into which they were about to go, and the character of the people they were going to attack, because I thought that knowledge very useful to facilitate the passage of their troops, taking precautions against enemy ruses and avoiding falling into the traps that might be extended for them. I added that I also thought that a good officer ought to know engineering, fortification, cartography and mathematics, especially the parts concerning the military art.

"Not a word of all that," replied one of the gentlemen, pirouetting on tiptoe. "Among us, courage and valor substitute for everything."

"But sir, valor that is not accompanied by prudence and composure becomes an impetuous courage that looks at danger from afar and wants to be at grips at the time when it is necessary to camp. Thus, I regard that valor as a false bravery or a blustering courage, instead of which a great soul, a penetrating genius and an intrepid heart sees peril at close range without being frightened by it."

"It appears to me," said the young officer, "that the men of your country are very phlegmatic; it's necessary to hope that a little of our way of operating can contribute to banishing useless reflections from your mind." Those words were pronounced in the most jovial tone, accompanied by a bow that announced their departure.

Surprised to see so much ignorance in an officer entrusted with an important position, I asked Zachiel whether the other officers were not more learned.

"It is necessary not to be astonished by the vivacity of the Salians," said the genius, "any more than that of all the peoples who inhabit this world. As this planet is much closer to the sun than the others, the influences that dominate them communicate the fire and petulance that often leads them to act without giving themselves time to reflect."

We spent a few days in that city, where we saw the most frenetic license reigning; pleasures—fine food, gambling, spectacles, concerts, balls and amorous assignations—were the sole occupations of a the officers; their tables, always served with profusion, represented nothing less than the calamities of war, always onerous for peoples. During those pleasures and that dissipation, however, the wretched soldiers who were camped in the vicinity of the city were exercising a thousand disorders therein, because of the poor discipline observed there.

Monime and I were invited to a great supper and to a masked ball that would be given thereafter by the steward of the province. That man, whom fortune had extracted from the most mediocre estate to raise him to the highest degree of favor, had rendered himself hateful throughout the city by the airs of grandeur that he effected with regard to the nobility and the scorn he displayed for the richest burgers. The women, piqued by the scant regard that he had for them, complained of it to the officers of the garrison, who promised to avenge them

The plan was to dress a dozen soldiers as women, magnificently dressed, who were to harass the steward all night long. The masque favoring that disguise, they had no fear of being recognized. We were only told about the comedy they intended to play two hours after the ball began. The pretended goddesses had already surrounded the steward, and were preparing to play a thousand pranks on him when a confused noise was heard of whinnying horses, men and women uttering frightful screams, and troops filing the air with bellicose roars. The alert was immediately sounded and the call to arms issued; the enemy had mounted a surprise attack on the city, and had entered through a passage that had not been guarded.

Then, all the young officers, without appearing to be frightened by the danger or the dolor of their beauties, calmly left them in order to run to give orders and assemble their troops. In spite of all their vivacity, however, and even though they deployed considerable bravery, their efforts were futile. The city was taken and put to contribution, in spite of all the efforts of the inhabitants, who defended themselves with courage and intrepidity.

Zachiel, who had anticipated that disorder, came to our rescue; he got us out of the city in order to take us to another province. I could not imagine that those pretty faces, which had been admiring themselves in all the mirrors a few

222

hours before, had had the courage to precipitate themselves at the enemy squadrons; that appeared to me to smack of enchantment.

"After having thought about that event," I said to Zachiel, "I find the conduct of those men very imprudent. Since the guard of the city had been confided to them, why did they neglect to fortify the places at which it might be attacked?"

"It's because the enlightenment of those men is very limited," said the genius. "The majority have only one marked point of view, beyond which they cannot extend their penetration. They are, so to speak, enclosed in the darkness of human politics, which makes them blind to everything presented to them. They arm themselves with specious pretexts to embellish good or bad arguments in order to find the means of engaging their allies by motives of ambition or chimerical concessions, with which they are not miserly, but the ruses they employ often rebound on them."

During the journey the genius instructed us as to the religions and mores of the Marsians.

"Their way of thinking is free," he told us. "All the great men of this world prefer what they imagine to what they have seen or learned; all their sentiments belong to them; they think that in matters of opinions one should always follow the mildest and most moderate, and those which tend to conciliate minds and maintain social repose.

"There is nothing more absurd, say their pretended philosophers, than to try to subjugate beings who ought necessarily to be happy, in order to oblige them to regulate the celestial spheres and combine all the events that happen on earth in order to make gods of them susceptible to hatred and vengeance, who allow themselves to be moved by tears and prayers, and who can be offended by our disorders even though several among them furnish more than one pernicious example themselves; ought we, after that, to regard them as veritable gods? We ought, therefore to believe that if the world is submissive to the power of true gods, it would be much better guided, and that everything would happen in a manner worthy of those wise and enlightened gods who governed it. As we see the contrary every day, that is evident proof that hazard alone presides over everything that happens here.

"In spite of sentiments so contrary to their religion, one sees them regularly in the temple of Pallas in the position of supplicants, offering the goddess prayers and incense. As they relate everything back to union, they recommend to all the citizens to lend themselves to public ceremonies and the acts of religion that their mythologies impose, even when they are not penetrated by them to the depths of the heart, since persons of intelligence can scarcely be convinced of the verity of all the fabulous translations presented to them; but because the people believe them, and whom it is dangerous to disabuse, since they serve to maintain peace and mildness among them, the great are obliged to put at least their external appearance in uniformity with that of their compatriots.

"The most reasonable among their philosophers are convinced that good and evil are only vain or chimerical things that opinion has introduced. Good is, according to them, that which really augments the power one has to act, and that which can pass for a greater perfection; evil is the contrary and is that which weakens the same power.

"What, then, can nature offer more convenient to these different views than to attach them to pleasure? Is that not what inclines the soul toward good with all the more force because good is much more desirable than evil? When humans abuse pleasure and run after it blindly without any moderation, those are their crimes. But is nature not sufficiently avenged for that abuse by the sharp pains engendered thereby and remorse even more terrible than the pains? In general, one of the greatest obligations of humans is to watch incessantly over the safety and conservation of their being; that is a concern nature has engraved in every heart, even though they are persuaded that their days are numbered and that nothing can change their destiny.

"This world is divided, like all the others, into different sects. Some put their confidence in idols that they fabricate themselves; others address their prayers to divinities that the foolish imagination of their ancient mythologies have fabricated in order to trick the good faith of people who cannot be cured of their prejudices; but all the nobles and the majority of their scholars recognize no other divinity than Nature, which they regard as the invisible soul of the world; they say that she has a supernatural virtue, which produces, arranges and conserves all the parts of the universe.

"Those scholars distinguish two wills in Nature, one of which they suppose to be good and the other evil. They believe that there is a kind of equilibrium that enables everything to be balanced and remain in an equal proportion, and that it is absurd to think that a bountiful being created the world and that, able to fill it with all kinds of perfections, he set out to do precisely the opposite. But argue with those false scholars, ask them what that Nature is, of which the term seems so vague, and they will reply to you that it is an active principle, an economical entity that regulates all things with so much art that good does not surpass evil; it is, they say, a superb divinity, full of ostentation, powerful, which tries above all to hide its secrets in order not to be discovered."

"So, according to their system," I said to Zachiel, "Nature, fate and hazard are all the same thing?"

"You will see here," the genius went on, "almost all the great lords cultivating the sciences; they have books of morality, philosophy and history, which they conserve without any change or alteration; the foolish love of novelty does not impassion them, and what distinguishes them from other worlds is that the same language has been spoken here since their creation. That kind of immobility of language enables them to understand their most ancient authors, who are often not very reliable, whereas on your earth one sees the language of a people change entirely in less than a century; one might think that others come to estab-lish themselves on the ruins of those that disappear.

"Music is regarded, throughout the extent of the planet, as a universal rem-edy capable of curing the worst diseases of the body and even of the mind; and the officers who command their armies draw infallible and incessantly present assistance from it, lifting the soul by means of noble chords in order to fortify courage and virtue, to govern and guide the passions at their will, to excite them and appease them at need. That is why all their exercises are preceded by agree-able and loud music that seems, in some way, to dispose the soul and render it bolder; for as the sound of the music penetrates it, they are transported, if one might put it like that, by a divine fervor, and believe that the god of war is enter-ing via their ears to animate them to combat and better enable them to obey.

"The men who are born on this planet feel its influences very keenly; they are all bellicose, and when they are not making war on one another they com-pensate themselves by making it on animals; furthermore, their manners are always simple, frank and uniform in their societies. They guard their speech religiously, because lies are severely punished here. An officer who has broken his word cannot avoid the scorn of the entire nation; he will be stripped of his rank, expelled from his corps and forced to seek to hide his shame and humilia-tion abroad."

We finally arrived in the realm of Bellonia, then governed by a tyrant named Tracius. That Prince, of a cruel and ambitious spirit, did not take pleasure in anything but blood and carnage. He was only occupied in seeking new ways of invading neighboring states and employing them to carry out the most unjust vexations there, while the legitimate sovereign, exiled, expelled from his kingdom, obliged to wander hither and yon in various states, groaned at the evils he saw overwhelming his people, especially those of which he anticipated that his unfortunate family would be the target.

Having arrived in the vicinity of the capital city, we were obliged to traverse a great plain strewn with dead and dying. One young woman whose sighs and sobs made the grief she was suffering manifest excited our pity and our interest in knowing her.

Monime, always full of zeal for the unfortunate, had our carriage stop and asked her what had occasioned the distress of which she was giving evidence.

"Alas, my Lady, you're doubtless unaware that a bloody battle took place on this plain yesterday. You see in me a spouse in despair, who bears in her womb the innocent fruit of a sacred union. Since daybreak I have been roaming this plain in vain; in vain I have visited all the bodies massacred by enemy fire; nothing has been offered to my frantic gaze, no hope has presented itself to my soul; disastrous fate has doubtless cut short my husband's days."

The young woman's tears redoubled. After having employed the consolations dictated by the generosity of her soul, Monime, touched by her distress, succeeded in calming her dolor somewhat. She invited her to take a seat in our carriage to return to the city, where we put her back in the hands of her family.

On the road we encountered a host of inhabitants who had come out in the hope of finding those who loss was exciting their groans.

There was an old man weighed down by the burden of his years; his organs, enfeebled by age, no longer permitting him to distinguish the objects surrounding him, he addressed himself to all those he encountered, asking them for news of his son.

"Alas," he said to one, his eyes bathed with tears, "the support of my old age has doubtless perished in the battle; I could not disarm or weaken his proud courage, but I lacked the strength to go with him and die beside him."

After those few words, suffocated by grief, his knees buckled and he was ready to fall, but, reanimating himself with a final effort, he approached the next stranger, and sighed as he gripped his arm. "Convey to my son," he said to him, "this last embrace; tell him never to forget an unfortunate father who only lived in him, and whom his absence has reduced to despair."

In other places, friends were searching urgently to procure some assistance for their friends. Elsewhere, young women could be seen running with great strides toward the plain, in the hope of encountering the young warriors who had promised them his faith.

When we reached the city, we learned the details of the battle, in which more than thirty thousand men had perished. To that bad news was added that of a complete rout of its navy. So many combined calamities spread consternation through all hearts. It seemed that such reverses ought to have corrected Tracius, or at least moderated his ambition, but in spite of those scourges, the tyrant could not resolve himself to abandon his foolish enterprises. Insensible to the calamities of the State, barbaric toward the people, he hid from them with a cruel concern the greater part of the disgraces that fortune had inflicted, and in spite of the number of troops already sacrificed in several deadly encounters, and the exhaustion of men and finances to which he was reduced, nothing could stop him.

An old officer whose acquaintance we had made assured us that for a long time, every step he had taken had always been stained with blood, obliged to go in search of the enemy in arid lands devastated by the number of troops who had already passed through it, who were accustomed to pillage because of the poor discipline maintains in the companies.

"To those difficulties can be added the misery of our soldiers, poorly paid, poorly dressed, poorly maintained and poorly assisted in their maladies by the fraudulent conduct of our entrepreneurs; that is what causes the defections in our armies; the majority of the soldiers, and even the officers, are going over to the enemy and increasing their numbers even further. All those malcontents then find themselves motivated by their own vengeance."

Dissatisfied with what we had been told, we left the city in order to continue our observations. As we advanced through the land, we encountered a multitude of poor peasants forced to follow a soldier what had just enlisted them, by surprise or by authority. Those wretches, in despair at quitting their cottages, even though most of the time they lacked the bare necessities of life, appeared to be in the utmost consternation.

I noticed one in particular who touched me sensibly; I approached him in order to ask him what reason he had to be so afflicted by following a métier that would at least provide him with the means of subsistence.

"Alas, sir," the young man replied, sobbing, "the excess of my despair will not surprise you when you know that I was snatched from the arms of a mother charged with eight children, of whom the oldest that remains is barely ten years old. In the eighteen months since I lost my father, I have at last been able to allow them to subsist by my hard labor; what completes my woes in that in taking me away from my family they have been deprived of all help, and I can assure you that very little can be expected from me in a métier that I do not know and for which I have no appetite—because, sir, I do not even know how to load a rifle, the sight of a sword causes me to treble and almost too faint. All my comrades are no braver than me; judge from that what troops can be opposed to enemies long accustomed to vanquish."

I left the young soldier after giving him all the money I had on me.

"It appears to me," said Monime, "that that troop of soldiers has no ambition to obtain a place in the Temple of Glory. I'd rather confront the enemy with a cardboard army, like those employed in our theaters."

"Which is to say," said Zachiel, smiling, "that you're comparing the Marsians to swarms of flies that one can frighten by presenting them with grotesque figures. But do you know that the Marsians are the most prudent men on this planet, the most judicious and he most intrepid in case of danger. Such are, my dear Monime, the enemies of the Bellonians. It is to their army that I am taking Seaton; it is there that I want him to serve his apprenticeship in the métier of war, under Prince Aricdef, who is the general commanding the army sent to combat that of Tracius. I presume, given the elevation of your sentiment, that you will not raise any objection to the design that I've conceived in order to enable Seaton to profit from this voyages."

Far from opposing the views of the genius, Monime, who only intended to render me worthy of one day occupying the rank destined for me, appeared, on the contrary to be charmed by the opportunity that was offered to me to distinguish myself by some action that would merit Zachiel's approval.

During our journey I could not help sighing at the thought that I was going to be separated from Monime.

"Why that expression of sadness?" asked the genius. "Are you insensible to the pleasure that a great heart ought to feel when it's a matter of acquiring glory?"

"Pardon the sigh," I said. "It does not come from a pusillanimous heart that fears danger, but may I give nothing to the dolor of being separated from you and Monime?"

"I dare not tell you that I am sensible to that separation," said Monime with tears in her eyes, "since it is necessary to your advancement."

"Calm yourselves, both of you," said Zachiel. "The separation will not be long; it's necessary, my dear Seaton, to show more strength and accustom yourself gradually to my absence; you will not always have me. I am only taking you into the midst of dangers in order to teach you not to be prodigal in shedding blood. Heaven has given birth to you in order to command one day, so remember that a good general ought to be model of all his officers; it is his example that animates the army. You will learn under Prince Aricdef to merit the title of a great captain.

"Remember, my son, that valor is perhaps only a virtue when it is regulated by prudence and moderation., without which it is merely an insensate scorn for life or a brutal ardor that only leads to doom. A man who cannot retain his self-possession in danger is more reckless than brave, because it seems that he needs in order to be animated to put himself beyond the dread that he cannot overcome by the natural situation of his heart.

"Know that by delivering oneself recklessly to dangers, one can trouble the order and discipline of troops; by giving an example of temerity, one often exposes an entire army to great misfortunes; so refrain, my dear Seaton, from seeking glory with too much impatience; the true means of finding it is to wait tranquilly for favorable opportunities. Remember, too, not to attract the envy of anyone; do not be jealous of the success of others, never seek to diminish its value; on the contrary, be the first to give praise to those who merit it.

"Consult the oldest captains; ask the most skilful to instruct you; show them meekness and docility in listening to their advice. It is necessary nevertheless to be on your guard, to convince yourself that even the most enlightened cannot see everything, and that the wisest often make gave mistakes when they only follow their impulses or their prejudices. Above all, avoid revealing yourself to certain flatterers who take pleasure in sowing division among the officers in order indispose the chiefs and profit from the disorder they create."

I listened avidly to these lessons from the genius, which seemed to pass into my soul like a stream of pure fresh water that one sees flowing between flowers. My tender Monime also appeared to me to be penetrated by the keenest gratitude. Until then I had only filled my memory with great names and great events, without giving myself the time to make any judicious reflection. That conversation—or, to put it better, the instructions of the genius—gave birth within me to an ardent desire to take as a model of my conduct the actions of illustrious men, to profit from their virtues and to avoid falling into their vices.

On arriving among the Marsians, we learned that their general was to leave the following day in order to put himself at the head of his troops. Without losing any time, the genius introduced me that same day to the Prince, who received me with marks of generosity that immediately attached me to him. He promised Zachiel to watch over my conduct, and to take care of my advancement. In order to begin giving me immediate proof of his benevolence he ordered that an apartment should be prepared for me to spend the night in his house, in order that I would be able to leave with him.

The genius left me after giving me a few more items of advice, and the strongest assurances that he would not abandon Monime—which tranquilized me considerably.

The sun had risen and was already gilding the summits of the mountains when Prince Aricdef departed to rejoin the army. I was by his side in the capacity of an aide-de-camp. When we reached the rendezvous, the Prince gave orders for the encampment. I had the advantage of being employed on several occasions that attracted praise on his part, and procured me his confidence and amity. I had the good fortune to accompany him into various actions in which the Prince gave evidence of his intrepidity and the invincible courage that never abandoned him.

I could not weary of admiring the advantageous situations that he was always able to chose for the encampment of his troops, either because of the forage or the necessities of fighting. I also admired the order and discipline that reigned in his camp, the intelligence and impenetrable secrecy necessary to the success of an enterprise, the care that he took in visiting his camp personally, the attention he paid to the least of the soldiers, in order that anything that could be useful to them, either for clothing or for nourishment, would not be lacking, and, finally, the obedience that they showed to the slightest indication of his will.

That first campaign had nothing remarkable except the capture of a few places that we took from the Bellonians. The Prince distributed his winter quarters and we went back to the capital city with a young officer who had acquired a considerable reputation among the troops. His modesty, his candor and the purity of his morals, rare qualities in a young man, had attracted all my esteem and confidence. We were soon linked by an intimate amity; I invited him to spend his winter quarters with me. I introduced him to Zachiel and Monime, who both appeared to confirm the choice I had made by the eulogies that they gave him. It is true that it seemed that he carried with him a charm that drew all hearts in his favor.

Out walking one day with that amiable chevalier, after a few vague remarks, I said: "How fortunate you are to have commenced so young a métier that has so often procured you opportunities to distinguish yourself."

"It's true," said the other, "that I entered the service very early, but my dear Milord, what do you expect a man of condition to do whom of fortune has, if I might put it like that, adopted the task of humiliating in the most sensitive places? The next campaign promises us a decisive battle; if I can only have the opportunity to acquire some glory therein! But what am I saying? Is it for me, alas, to dare to flatter myself? No, however things turn out, I shall retire after that action, and no longer think about anything but trying to procure a repose for which I've been searching in vain for a long time; for it's necessary to agree, my dear, that unless one has a great employment in the army, it's a métier that's scarcely attractive to those who can do without it. I can only regard it as a resource for poor gentlemen who have neither enough wealth nor enough authority to be considered, and the majority of whom don't know how to occupy themselves. It's assuredly the most honest profession that a man of condition can chose; I like it a great deal, and if it weren't for the annoyances I encounter at every step I'd have difficulty quitting it; pressing motives would already have forced me to make a different decision, if a secret penchant hadn't drawn me into Aricdef's army."

"You haven't always been with the Marsians?"

"No," said the chevalier, "I only arrived a short time before you did. I began serving with the Salians, but their service involved so many annoying things; one depends there on so many interested and ignorant people, incessantly the butt of brutes who are mostly scoundrels, debauchees, gamblers or drunks, that it became insupportable to me. In sum, those who have morals pass among them for pedants. Nothing compensates for the loss of one's wealth or repose. The injustices of the illicit favors are a more sensible aggravation. Among them, merit, great talent, prudence and valor count for nothing; all the positions are bought for money or by vile obligations—which means that in spite of the number of their troops and the superiority of their forces, it's often easy to defeat them, by virtue of the ignorance of their officers, who don't have enough prudence to be able to take full advantage of their strength. In any case, the alliance they've made with the Bellonians determined me entirely to go into the service of the Marsians.

"Don't believe, because of that, my dear Milord," the chevalier went on, "that the ambition or the desire to obtain a considerable post from the Prince attracted me to his army; I wasn't led there by any of those views, but only that of numbing myself to the misfortunes that had overwhelmed me. Yes, my dear, I want to try to vanquish the fortune that is the enemy of my happiness and my repose, which, in robbing me of the honors in which I was born, has been unable to change my heart. Powerful reasons don't permit me to tell you any more at present; let it suffice for you to know that it's neither the dangers nor the fatigues of war that have taken away my taste for it. I'm a man of sound constitution; I get by easily on very little; but I dread dependency and would greatly prefer death to renouncing my liberty."

"I feel sorry for you, my dear sir, and dare not enquire as to the reasons that occasion your distaste for military service; however, I find that war, in spite of the aggravations you've just represented, has many advantages that ought to counterbalance them; all the vices that you believe to be inseparably attached to it, are not innate, since there are laws that punish them severely, and you'll agree that the Prince who commands us is not stained by the vices that you say are commonplace in the officers at the head of the armies of the Salians and the Bellonians.

"What idea ought we to have of Prince Aricdef? Without pausing at that which only ought to dazzle vulgar minds, you can't disagree that one can't help admiring in him the true virtues that form heroes. It's not his invincible courage that charms me, not his scorn for death and danger that I admire; it's his presence of mind, that intrepidity, that coolness in the disorder of the most furious combats, the indefatigable activity that is the true character of a conqueror; the unexpected rapidity with which he falls on the enemy army and carries off a signal victory when he's believed to be dead or cut off in a gorge, or his entire army seems defeated.

"We've both witnessed in the last campaign that with a handful of men he rendered all the strength of the Salians futile and took from the Bellonians several well-fortified places. In sum, he has always denied his enemies the means to attack him. One can therefore say that it's by virtue of his talents and rare qualities that he has acquired the love and confidence of his troops. It's certain that the soldier who loves and can count on his general is invincible; instead of which, those who are commanded by cowardly courtiers that they cannot hold in high esteem, allow themselves to be defeated easily. It's only necessary to wait for the opportunity of some court intrigue, which sows division among their troops; then, when one has good spies that keep you informed, one can take advantage of their dysfunction. I've heard it said that Prince Aricdef never lets one of those advantages escape.

"One can also add to all his qualities his incorruptible probity, his love of justice, his liberality, his clemency, his inviolable attachment to his work, his good faith, his mild and amiable manners, his attention for the officers and his generosity to the soldiers. One cannot, therefore, without injustice refuse him the titles of great warrior, redoubtable captain, good politician and sage philosopher, since he's an honest and honest man and loyal to his friends. We see that he even cultivates with care those who are beneath him."

"I confess," said the chevalier, "that all these qualities are Aricdef's prerogatives, that he justly merits the praise and admiration of all men; the renown that has published them all over the world gave birth in me to the desire to come and participate in his glory; without that desire, my dear Milord, perhaps I would never have had the advantage of knowing you."

A sigh accompanied those last words, which, combined with those that had preceded it, appeared to me to enclose an impenetrable mystery. I dared not ask the chevalier the reason for it. Remarking a good deal of trouble and agitation in his eyes, I was anxious; in order to distract him from his melancholy I proposed that we should go to see Monime.

We were staying in the same house, and the chevalier rarely spent a day without seeing Monime; I even believed that I could perceive the pleasure he felt in her company, given the urgency that he showed to be near her. Monime also showed him a distinguished complaisance, which was only in accord with his true merit. The chevalier's character, mild without being insipid, attentive without any baseness, was combined with all the gifts he had received from nature and those that depended on a noble education; he possessed all sorts of talents, but he was naturally borne to melancholy. Zachiel, who was doubtless able to penetrate the reasons for his sadness, attempted, out of condescension for the chevalier and Monime, to give birth every day to new opportunities for amusement and dissipation.

We were scarcely approaching the welcome return of the season of flowers when Prince Aricdef was already preparing to reassemble his troops. I was ordered to join him near a frontier city belonging to the Bellonians, to which he intended to lay siege.

Engineers are surveying all the surroundings, drawing up plans; trenches are being dug and covered ways formed, and the Prince, always active, is supervising the work. He sees defects, he corrects them, doing everything that is to his advantage, following them and animating them in their labor, pressing the siege of the city with ardor, animating all his troops by distributing liquor to them, which he sometimes drinks with them, with the familiar air that, better than speeches and recompenses, often passes into the soldier's soul the noble ardor that animates the hero, who seems to be rendering himself their companion.

The enemy was unable to hold out against the valor and vigilance of Aricdef; the city was taken and he entered it in triumph at the head of his troops, received the oath of fidelity from the burgers, fortified the place, and, after having reestablished abundance and tranquility there, we emerged therefrom to follow the Prince, who went to take possession of an advantageous position in order to observe the enemy.

Surprised not to see the chevalier arrive, I began to fear that the secret chagrin I had remarked in him might have constrained him to withdraw. I was preparing to write to him when I received a letter from Monime which told me that he had been retained by a bad fever. Anxiety about my friend's illness, combined with the urgency I felt to see Monime, caused me to ask for a week's leave. I had difficulty obtaining it, at the commencement of a campaign in which our army, already victorious, was only waiting for a movement on the enemy's part to direct its march, pursue it or disrupt its projects, but I could not refuse myself the pleasure of seeing Monime again.

Her eyes, I said to myself, *will animate my courage; a word from her adorable mouth will fortify my virtue; Zachiel, by his sage advice, will contribute to enabling me to acquire glory; perhaps, too, I shall bring back the chevalier, who, I feel sure, is burning with desire to find a decisive action.*

I obtained relay horses, which I sent forth, and then presented myself to the Prince in order to receive his orders.

"I've just learned," he told me, "that the Bellonians are advancing, with the intention of forcing us back to our retrenchments. My duty is to anticipate them, and I presume that the battle will be bloody, so I believe there's no need to recommend you not to let any opportunity escape to signal your courage. I permit you to go where your affairs summon you, provided that you return by the time we set forth, in order to fulfill the duties of your employment."

After leaving the Prince I climbed into my chaise and traveled all night, in order to bring forward the moments of happiness that I anticipated. What sweeter charm is there in the world than that of the union of hearts?

Oh, dear Monime, you combine virtue and innocence with amity; no dread or shame troubles your felicity. I am sure of being loved without division by a sister, the most perfect of all women.

Those reflections enabled me to enjoy in advance the pleasure of surprising her.

I finally arrived at ten o'clock in the morning. I flew to Monime's apartment, where I thought I had been petrified. Great God, what do I see? The chevalier in her arms; she is holding him tightly, and seems to be reassuring him with regard to ill-founded dreads. She kisses him; I believe I can see their sighs confounded.

"Oh, perfidy!" I cry. "By what charm have you been able to seduce her? Your blood will wash away the shame I feel."

Those words, pronounced with vehemence, cause them to turn their heads. Surprised to see me, they both blush; I want to flee; the chevalier stops me without being able to pronounce a single word. Monime, trembling and bewildered, falls unconscious.

"I perceive only too well," I said to the chevalier, pushing him away with eyes full of the anger that is animating me, "by the disorder and trouble I am causing, that you have completed your treasons."

"No, my dear Milord," said the chevalier, in an emotional voice that was almost extinct. "In spite of appearances, refrain from daring to suspect two people who are equally attached to you. I shall leave instantly, and will tell you at the camp everything that is the cause of your surprise today. I shall wait for you there to give you the satisfactions you demand. Begin by helping Monime."

Zachiel, who appeared at that moment, followed by one of Monime's maids, extracted me with a single word from the new anxieties that that speech had just plunged me.

"No, my Lady," he said, stopping the chevalier, "you shall not leave. It's no longer in the danger of combats that you ought to seek glory; you've disguised yourself for too long; it's necessary to resume the clothing appropriate to your sex. Follow my advice and allow Zerbine to accompany you into this dressing room."

"Oh, my dear Zachiel," I exclaimed, "with what concerns are you occupying yourself? Alas, Monime is dying."

The genius went to her and made her swallow a spoonful of universal elixir. I was at her feet; I held one of her hands, which I moistened with my tears. She finally opened her eyes; her first gaze was for me; it was tender; its languor passed into my soul. I felt annihilated by the reproaches that she seemed to be making for my outburst.

"Is it really true, my Lord," said Monime, in a voice that was still ill-assured, "that you were able to suspect me? Alas, my heart is not yet known to you? But where is the Princess? She is the one who must justify me."

"You have no need of her, my adorable Monime; a single word from Zachiel has done that. But who will justify me to you for my unjust suspicions? Will you pardon me for an initial impulse of which I was not the master? It is honor that was responsible or my crime; that is what will judge me."

"Well," said Monime, "get up, amity pardons you."

"Oh, that admission restores calm to my soul," I said, kissing the hand that I had not released, delightedly.

"I agree," Monime went on, "that appearances must have alarmed you, not being disabused as to the sex of the pretended chevalier, whom you have always regarded s a man; so can I not support the idea of the suspicions that I perceive the situation in which you found us presented to our mind?"

We were interrupted by Princess Marsine, who came back in after having put on garments appropriate to her sex.

"You're doubtless surprised, Milord, only to rediscover in me an unfortunate woman, from whom fate has stolen everything. You have seen me fight in several encounters with some considerable advantage, which have attracted your esteem and amity to me. Do not reproach me for not having accorded you all my confidence at first; I know that you merit every regard, not only by your virtues but also by the thousand services that I have received from you on various occasions; be persuaded that I have always distinguished you from all the other officers. Had I told you about my birth and sex, however, it would have been necessary to explain my misfortunes to you, in order to justify in some measure the disguise that the austere wisdom that you profess might perhaps have disapproved. Besides which, I had promised myself never to reveal my secret to anyone.

"When the Prince's orders recalled you to him I was counting on joining you soon; stopped by a bad fever, I could not carry out my project. I owe the reestablishment of my health to the charming Monime; her kindness, her care and assiduous attentions, and that charm which enables the union of souls, finally extracted from me that which I believed was in my interest to bury eternally in a profound silence. She has repaid my confidence with a sincere attachment and the confession of the sentiments of esteem that link you to one another.

"Dispense me, Milord, from telling you the story of my adventures; I have hidden nothing from the beautiful Monime; I permit her to make you party to my secrets; the interest she has taken in my misfortunes, and the graces she puts into everything she says, will render them more touching, so I dare flatter myself that her account will reestablish me in your opinion."

Princess Marsine left without waiting for my response, leaving me at liberty to talk to Monime. After we had said all the most tender things that our two truly touched hearts could imagine, I begged her to acquaint me with the reasons that had engaged Marsine to maintain her disguise for such a long time.

Chapter V
Which only contains an abridged history of Princess Marsine

"Princess Marsine," said Monime, "is the daughter of Belus, King of Bellonia. That Prince chose for his favorite Tracius, whom one might deem to be one of those men born for great revolutions, who take and strikingly sustain roles on the world stage far above their birth. The King raised that favorite by degrees to the principal dignities in the realm. Tracius was so well able to take advantage of his favor and simultaneously hide the ambition that devoured him that the King did nothing without consulting him, regarding him as the most affectionate of his ministers.

"When Tracius saw that he possessed all his master's confidence, he got rid of all those who might clarify his conduct, and, making use of all his cunning, he succeeded so well by his insinuations, that he embarked the King on several false steps, the consequences of which he disguised from him with extreme care. His seductive intelligence even found the secret of causing him to envisage his treasons as signal services: the fatal blindness of a heart seduced by the poison of the most outrageous flattery, which unfortunately almost always surrounds a throne.

"The King, accustomed to the adulations of his courtiers, too prejudiced in favor of his favorite to listen to any complaints against him, was unable to perceive the precipice that was being gradually hollowed out in order to doom him. That monarch was ignorant of what the love of a people for their sovereign might be; he knew the art of vanquishing his enemies, of conquering cities, but he was entirely ignorant of that of winning the hearts of those he had conquered, which is the greatest advantage a Prince can obtain from his victories. He was all the weaker because he had too much faith in his strength and his own enlightenment—or, rather, those of his favorite.

"The newly-conquered provinces did not take long to revolt, and by virtue of the treasons of Tracius, several other more considerable cities followed their example. It was necessary to raise new troops to chastise the rebels and recall them to their duty. Those new recruitments occasioned excessive expenses; in order to meet them it was necessary to impose a number of taxes, which overburdened the people; but those impositions, far from swelling the public treasury, were merely torrents that carried away the substance of all Bellonians to disappear into the immense fortunes of those protected by Tracius—who were nevertheless obliged by secret treaties they had made to surrender three-quarters of it to him

"The tyrant employed a part of his wealth to win over the principal officers of the crown, who, seduced by his gold, had no difficulty in obtaining general command of the army for him. When Tracius was at the head of his troops, like

236

a vulture falling on a dove or a wood-pigeon and dissipating its palpitating limbs in the wood after tearing it apart, the tyrant began pitilessly murdering the king' subjects. His parricidal hands, confiscating their wealth, sacrificed them to his ambition.

"Prolonging the war by means of his covert intrigues and underhand maneuvers, Tracius augmented the misery of the people and found the secret of multiplying his treasures. The tyrant's politics had doubtless engaged him to allow himself to be defeated in several battles, but, seeing his credit increased by those losses, the same politics inspired new projects. He began spreading his wealth among his soldiers, and then affecting to have only a very mediocre table, cutting back all his expenses. That conduct succeeded in winning him the hearts of the soldiers.

"The tyrant put about the rumor that a number of prodigies had appeared in the kingdom; it was said that on the frontiers the angry heavens had been seen covered in fire, and that on a tranquil and serene day the sun had appeared all radiant with flames; it was added that thunderbolts had fallen in several places, including the temples of Mars and Pallas, and that a statue of Hercules had been toppled.

"In spreading these rumors Tracius added hypocrisy to his villainy, pretending to be frightened by them. Bribed augurs consulted on his orders responded that a great swarm of wasps had flown around the square all day and had gone to settle on the temple of Hercules; it was said that it was necessary to consult the books of the Sibyls in order to try to discover the cause of the prodigies, and Tracius, continuing his false zeal for the worship of the gods, ordered sacrifices in order to appease them.

"Things being thus disposed, the tyrant then had further rumors spread that were very disadvantageous to the King, cleverly insinuating that the ambition, bad conduct and excessive expenses of Belus, and his lack of love for his subjects, were obstacles that would always serve as a barrier to their happiness. That seditious discourse had all the success that Tracius expected; the troops began a mutiny, demanding their pay and wanting to lay down their arms.

Profiting from that disorder, Tracius distributed money to them, and, with a false zeal for the good of the State, ran through the ranks to encourage them. The soldiers, already won over by his liberality, seduced by his eloquence and the love he manifested for the public good, applauded him, and the army was then filled with a dull rumble similar to that heard after a tempest, when the recesses of rocks still retain the echoes of impetuous winds that have troubled the sea all night with their furious whistling.

"Such was the applause that they gave Tracius in choosing him for their King. He was first proclaimed unanimously at the head of his troops. In order not to let the ardor they had just manifested to die down, the tyrant advanced on the nearby city and had himself crowned with the ceremonies customary among the Bellonians. Then, pursuing his conquests rapidly, almost without encountering any obstacles, he came to besiege the King in his own palace. The unfortunate Prince was obliged to flee with Princess Marsine, the sole heir to the realm, who was then only four years old. It is certain that the monarch made an irreparable error in giving the tyrant time, by virtue of that flight, to fortify himself increasingly, and to engage several sovereigns in his party, which had become sufficiently strong to be feared.

"The unfortunate dethroned Belus, obliged to wander through various realms without being able to obtain any help, or even to dare to appear except under false name, finally terminated his sad destiny by a forced death. He commended his daughter, the Princess, to those of his faithful subjects who had accompanied him and who had never abandoned his party, preferring to sacrifice their grandeur and their fortune than to fail in their duty to their sovereign. They swore to the dying Prince to employ their zeal, their courage and their very lives in the service of the Princess, and to do everything possible to restore her to the throne.

"The unfortunate Marsine, reduced like her father the King to the sad necessity of hiding the majesty of the rank in which Heaven had caused her to be born, was thus forced to descend therefrom in order to drag out an obscure life in the world, subject to a thousand upheavals because of the intrigues of the tyrant, who took indignity so far as to put a price on the Princess' head.

"The resentment that Marsine conserved with so much justice, and the horror of the treasons that Tracius never ceased to exercise against her, had led her to adopt the disguise under which you have known her; it was in that costume and under a borrowed name that she distinguished herself in several battles, which acquired her a good deal of glory, while her faithful officers, dispersed in various provinces and States, tried by means of their friends to foment an uprising in favor of their sovereign, of which she might take advantage. Several were already ranged on the side of the Princess; they were only waiting for a favorable opportunity to allow their zeal and their submission to burst forth, when a countermove by a few traitors ruined al their plans; some were arrested and immediately executed; others more fortunate, took flight and Marsine did not know what had become of them.

"What completes the misfortunes of the Princess today, however, is that she has been unable to see Prince Aricdef without being touched by all the eminent qualities that shine from his person and all his actions. Although concern for her vengeance and her glory has never abandoned her, she has nevertheless admitted to me that she had only entered Aricdef's camp with a view to being noticed by him. Several occasions have arisen, when she might have been able to reveal herself without risk, if the dread of making known the sentiments that animate her in the Prince's favor had not retained her; but an unexpected event that caused today's disturbance and has augmented her despair forces her to retain forever a secret that was ready to escape her.

238

"A few months ago, Prince Aricdef was told that an envoy from Tracius was requesting a private audience. Marsine, who was engaged by more than one motive to inform herself carefully of the subject of that commission, learned from the Prince's squire that the Tyrant Tracius had offered his daughter the Princess to his master with the assurance of associating him with the crown, provided that he would immediately abandon the Marsian party and join his army to fight the Salians and the Ancides, with whom he had broken the treaties of alliance that he had contracted.

"The Tyrant judged the sentiments of the Prince by his own, not doubting that such a magnificent proposal would dazzle Aricdef and draw him into his party; but the Prince always unshakable in his duty, far from lending his ear to a treaty that could only be accomplished by a treason, could not help showing Tracius' envoy all the scorn and indignation that such a proposition excited in his soul; he sent him away, adding that if he ever had the audacity to show himself in his camp again, he would have him impaled.

"Marsine, who was entirely unaware of Aricdef's response, was in despair at the tyrant's plans; she feared that a general peace might contribute to their execution; her chagrin caused her to fall into a languor that soon damaged her health, and, her mind agitated by so many woes that had inflamed her blood, that is doubtless what brought on the malady from which she has just suffered.

"Although I still regarded her then as a simple officer, it was sufficient that she was your friend for me to take an interest in her fate. I begged Zachiel to visit her. The genius knew the subject of her woes immediately; he prepared for the soothing of her mind by making me the confidence. He revealed her sex to me, told me a part of what I've just told you, and advised me to see her frequently in order to try to reduce the bitterness of her troubles. I lent myself to that task with extreme care, and by that kindness, guided by Zachiel's advice, I acquired her full confidence, and was unable at the same time to refuse her mine.

"Alas, my dear Seaton," Monime continued, "when you came to surprise us it was at one of those frequent moments when reason buckles under the weight of her woes; the unfortunate Marsine, in a flood of the heart in which the soul is laid bare, appeared to be beside herself. As troubled as she was by the bitterness of her dolor, I employed all that amity could to do moderate its excess, convinced that a communication of hearts imprints on sadness something soft and touching that is the only thing capable of calming the greatest troubles.

"That, my dear Lord, is a succinct account of the disgraces of a Princess who merits, by her virtues, her talents and the grandeur of her soul, a more fortunate fate. Her beauty, although somewhat faded by her troubles, will resume all its brilliance when Zachiel has carried out his promises. I don't know what his views are for the happiness of the Princess, but he has assured her that her destiny will soon change. Marsine has for the genius all the deference that is due to him, but she is not informed of his quality; convinced that I owe my birth to Zachiel, as he has never assumed any other title, I often see her embarrassed as to those she seeks to give him. You have just been witness to the air of authority that the genius employed to engage her to quit her disguise. I know that her design was to go to the camp and do everything to try to distinguish herself in the case that there was a battle, or to conclude her sad destiny."

Penetrated by the misfortunes of the Princess, I went into her dressing room with Monime in order to offer her all the services in my dependency. We found her in her armchair, her head supported by one of her hands, plunged into a somber reverie; she looked up at us with languid eyes.

"I shall see you go with regret, Milord; alas, you are going to acquire glory while I am force to remain buried beneath the weight of my troubles."

"It is necessary, my Lady, "I said to her, "for you to make full use of the courage that has not abandoned you thus far. The grandeur of your soul ought to put you above the injustices of blind fortune. You have often honored me with your confidence; I leave you with a different self, who, penetrated by your woes, will employ all his care to help to support them. I also dare to combine my pleas with those of Monime, in order to determine you to follow Zachiel's advice. If his talents were known to you, I am convinced that you would have no difficulty in choosing him for the guide of all your actions."

The Princess, who was animated by a desire for glory and for vengeance, and perhaps even that of her love, seemed absorbed by her reflections; she did not think of making any response to me. Marsine was not unaware that a battle was about to be fought against the Bellonians; the hope of encountering Tracius, the author of all her woes, the advantage of fighting him, and the hope of defeating him, above all, were animated by despair. To those reasons was doubtless joined a keener sentiment: amour, the tyrant that respects neither scepters nor grandeurs, had also come to tyrannize her heart, in the hope of making herself known to Prince Aricdef by some striking action. All those thoughts were agitating the Princess when Zachiel came in, and, perceiving her trouble, hasted to extracted her from it.

"Moderate your anxieties, my Lady," said the genius, causing a divine fire to shine in his eyes. "Hide, if that is possible, the agitation of your soul. You know what I have promised you; rely on my word and my attachment until the complete accomplishment of your desires; the knowledge that I have of astronomy enables me to see distinctly that your troubles are about to come to an end, but if you are obstinate in wanting to risk yourself in combat, that same science predicts an inevitable death therein for you."

Such positive words produced all the effect that the genius had expected on the mind of the Princess. "I shall no longer resist following your advice," Marsine replied, "and will regard you henceforth as my father. My happiness and my glory are in our hands; I confide them to your wisdom and your experience. I only implore you to believe that everything I have attempted until now has merely been an enthusiasm caused by the ardor to die; I envisaged that as the sole means of delivering myself from a life that was a burden to me. What do I not owe to cares that are snatching me from a death to which despair was about to deliver ne! Fortunately, your discourse has imported gleams of enlightenment into my soul that have made me recognize that the benefits I receive from you are effective; I can only mark my recognition by an entire deference to your advice."

Zachiel told us then that Tracius' envoy, on returning to his court, had informed him of Prince Aricdef's response, painting in the blackest colors the scorn that he had showed for his alliance. That speech had thrown the tyrant into a fury; shame, honor, anger and despair had excited contradictory movements in his soul that almost caused him to lose control of himself. Fury got the upper hand and the barbaric tyrant, like those men who, for want to heroic virtues, have impetuous vices, abandoned himself entirely to all the sentiments that range cold inspire in him, in order to excite his troops to punish a proud individual who had resisted his power.

That news hastened my departure; it was necessary to tear myself away from Monime. The presence of the genius obliged me to constrain my dolor, but an expression of sadness spread over my face. My confused and inconsequential speech revealed more clearly what was passing in my heart than the most forceful eloquence could have done. Monime, whose trouble equaled mine, in spite of the efforts she made to try to hide it from me, could not help telling me, softening considerably, that she would renew her prayers to Heaven to augment my glory and conserve my days, to which her own were attached.

Without permitting me to respond, Zachiel drew me away to give me further instructions. "You're going to find yourself," the genius added, "in one of the most glorious occasions of your life. Never allow yourself to be frightened by the peril; let composure and prudence accompany all our actions. Above all, my dear Seaton, try not to be separated from Aricdef, and fight by his side; follow his orders; let false glory not prevent you from asking things you do not know; remember that the general is invested with all the power and authority of the Emperor, and that the authority in question is communicated like the sun's rays—which, immense and infinite as they are, do not diminish by their emanation the brightness of the star, the source of light. I shall not retain you any longer; go, my dear Seaton; victory will follow in your footsteps."

Chapter VI
Description of a Battle

I arrived at the camp at the moment when Prince Aricdef had just given the order to depart. The general had received certain news that the Bellonians were advancing with the design of fighting, that the conjunction of their army with the Salians would give them a numerical advantage, and that they had already taken possession of an advantageous terrain, which was a plain between two mountains, closed at the rear by a large wood, but spacious enough to contain an army in battle order. To that effect they had arranged all their troops in two lines; the first was backed up against the wood in order to prevent any attack from the rear; they also believed their right to be assured by a castle and the city whose masters they were; their left was closed by a chain of steep mountains that extended a long way. In addition to that, they had in front of them at the foot of the mountain a wide river and a substantial stream, which enclosed them on that side of the plain.

It was before that plain that the Prince led us, after several days of forced march. Aricdef began to reconnoiter the situation of the locale and the disposition of the enemy, which he could not attack from the right, because of the steep mountains, nor from the left, defended by the city and the castle. The only means of approach he could see was a defile alongside the city, which could scarcely contain four men abreast and was overlooked by the castle, so that one could only pass through it by taking control of the castle and the outskirts of the city, whose avenues were filled with market gardens, hedges, vines and little steams, which formed a marshy terrain in which foot soldiers would have great difficulty marching. All those locations were occupied by the Bellonians, who had stationed infantry there.

It was therefore necessary to expel that infantry, and pass over the stream and the river, which was deep, to reach the defile, at the far end of which it would be necessary to do battle on a very narrow terrain that was always rising, in which one could only deploy a front of six or even squadrons. It is true that the terrain broadened out after a certain distance, but also that the troops would then be within musket-range of the enemy. How could one have the audacity to form lines so close to a camp whose troops were still fresh, rested, and recently emerged from good winter quarters, while ours were extremely fatigued by a long march, without any rest and without carriages? Their cavalry was armored in metal; ours did not even have leather armor. Finally, from whatever direction one approached their army, it is certain that it not only had the advantage over ours of situation, but also that of numbers.

All these difficulties, far from stopping the Prince, only animated his courage. None of those advantages escaped his penetration; he envisaged them all, and also the dangers to which his troops would be exposed if they did not engage in battle before the conjunction of the enemy armies. The desire he had to signal himself in the campaign by a striking action determined him to fight, in spite of all the obstacles that seemed to deter him from doing so.

Such a bold resolution astonished all the officers, but the soldiers, accustomed to victory under the Prince, applauded the decision with cries of joy that were then regarded as a good augury; all of them zealously entrusted their destiny to the prudence, valor and great talents of their commander.

It was, therefore, that course that our general adopted. He arranged his troops in such a way as to provide mutual support, after having obtained an exact knowledge of the terrain. He was able to profit from his advantages, and the defects of the enemy, and to avoid traps with all possible activity.

Already he has taken possession of the heights overlooking the city and the castle, examined at the surrounding terrain, counted all the enemy's resources and discovered the points favorable for an attack. The night is destined to expel them from their positions, and the silence of that frightful night is troubled by the continual discharges of all our artillery.

It seems that the gods favor our designs; the sky is covered with clouds, lightning flashes mingle with the continual rapid fire of our batteries, and the noise of the cannons, combined with the increased outbursts of thunder, make the rocks resound; the ramparts crumble, and all the objects united in the obscurity of a dark night form a scene of horror and terror. The astonished enemy is forced to fall back to the torrent, felling after having surrendered all their riches to the flames.

Those unfortunates hastened to rejoin the bulk of their army. The vigor of the action spread alarm and fear in the Bellonian camp. We then attacked the castle overlooking the defile by mans of which we could reach the enemy army. When we had rendered ourselves masters of it, we dislodged them from all the heights, and the Prince passed his entire army, without any obstacle, into the terrain we had just gained, in order to take up battle order.

That terrain, closed on both sides by long hedges that extended all the way to the enemy camp, was guarded by our dragoons. The Prince had them advance to the left and the right of the infantry, which he placed in various locations, either in corps or detachments, in accordance with the disposition of the terrain, in order to cover the cavalry when it arrived, or to support it if the enemy charged. Those dispositions made, he had the cavalry units advance as they arrived, to arrange them in battle order. The restricted extent of the terrain forced us, initially, only to form very short lines.

The Prince then gave orders to the lieutenant generals who were each to command a position and placed himself in the center of the army, at the head of which he had placed his cannons. The Prince ordered that, above all, the cavalry should endure the initial enemy fire, and only charge with sabers in hand.

The Bellonians, who could see all our movements, came to fall upon us with all the advantage that the slope of the terrain gave them, and their infernal blades, quivering with rage, struck our soldiers, driving our first line back to the second. Confusion was already beginning to set in when Aricdef advanced his battalions, pikes lowered, to arrest the impetuosity of the enemies who were making every effort to make inroads into our lines; but those who were posted behind the hedge launched such furious discharges at them that they were unable to withstand the fire; they began to buckle in their turn, gradually retreating. We attacked them on the heights and gained enough terrain by the first impact to give a new form to our army.

Aricdef then placed his cavalry in the center, put four heavy battalions on the wings and platoons of infantry between the squadrons to support the cavalry when they came to blows. He placed his artillery at the head, made a third line, and ordered the other two to be extended.

Scarcely had our canons begun to fire than the Bellonians came back a second time, with the elite of their troops, folding us up and causing gaps to appear between several squadrons, which sowed enough disorder among our troops to cause fear for the outcome of the day, but the Prince had positioned his infantry so well that it found itself able everywhere to repair the disadvantage of the cavalry, with the result that our squadrons rallied. Aricdef set himself at their head, followed by his senior officers, who charged the enemy, swords in hand, with so much force and vigor that they folded up in their turn; that gave us the advantage again for the final action, which lasted until the end of the day, during which the Prince contented himself with going back and forth through the ranks encouraging the troops with words and gestures, animating them considerably by his example. The Prince was everywhere, not sparing himself any more than the least of his soldiers; he gave his orders with as much tranquility and composure as if he had been in his tent.

The Bellonians, dazzled by a phantom, followed the frightful death that covered their entire camp with funereal wings. At daybreak they offered us a combat far bloodier than the one the day before. Standards and flags were captured and recaptured on both sides. Our generals and other officers showed an equal courage in their conduct in the various encounters that took place.

The wind, which was then blowing impetuously, combined with the movements of the troops, raised such great amounts of dust that it was almost impossible to see, and the confusion almost inevitable in those circumstances contributed to the carnage. The battle was so furious that there were skirmishes everywhere. The fury unleashed became general; unusual clamors were heard; the noisy clash of weapons raised a frightful discord, and the scintillating wheels of the Bellonian chariots howled in their terrible impact. A multitude of flaming arrows was seen whistling frightfully through the air, covering the two armies with flames; and the noise of the cannons, similar to that of thunder rumbling in the clouds, added its threat to those who heard it at close range.

Meanwhile, our troops, animated by the presence of Aricdef, all knew when it was necessary to advance, to hold firm, to switch to the attack, to open or close their files; no one thought of flight or retreat; no action was marked with fear; everyone employed himself as if his arm were capable of deciding the outcome of the victory, In sum, everyone believed that they could see before them the death of their enemies getting closer.

That battle occupied an immense field; the face of the army was constantly changing, and fortunes still appeared equal, when Tracius, blinded by the fury and resentment that he conserved at the scorn Aricdef had shown for his alliance, advanced with the audacity that pride and presumption give; he was already envisaging the Prince as chained to his chariot.

"Tremble, perfidious one," said the tyrant, "at the horrors of this deadly war, which it only depended on you to end by advantageous propositions; these cruelties will only fall upon you and your accomplices; I shall send you fleeing to Hell to signal your furies there."

"Do not expect," Aricdef replied, "to intimidate by your bravado a man who is sufficiently scornful of you not to fear your blows. Have you put to flight the least of my soldiers? Do you think you can vanquish me any more easily, or do you have enough audacity to imagine that you can make me tremble? The justice that has put weapons in my hand is sustained by honor; such are my motives. Would you like to end this war by a single combat? Let us make use of our courage; it is for the god of battles to decide our fate."

They put an end to their discourse and, advancing toward one another with an equal ardor, they commenced a furious combat; they were seen to turn with equal rapidity, and their flamboyant swords traced horrible spheres of fire in the air.

That great spectacle suspended everything; the two armies, gripped by horror, fell back to either side to await the decision of that combat; their vigor, their skill and their agility seemed the same; but Aricdef had received from the hands of Mars a sword of such perfect temper that nothing could resist its trenchant blade; he broke his adversary's scimitar, and the second thrust inflicted a deep wound in his side. Tracius' buckler then became useless to him; he folded up and recoiled, tottering, and finally fell to the ground on his knees.

At that sight, the Bellonians, as if thunderstruck, shivered with rage and despair at the humiliating condition of their King. His bravest warriors ran to his aid, putting their bucklers over him and carried him to his tent, bewailing their misfortune. In fact, what a baleful augury for them, but what a triumph for us! Our soldiers uttered cries of joy that were simultaneously the signal for combat and the presage of victory.

The Bellonians, wanting to avenge the death of their King, did not remain inactive; their frightful cries were followed by a new attack. That last combat represented the image of Hell; iron and flames were glinting on all sides; they all fought, wounded and bloody, like ferocious beasts irritated by the sight of blood, unaffected by the fear of death. The cries of joy of victors were heard drowning out the plaints of the wounded and the moans of the dying.

We finally drove them back with so much vigor that they were entirely defeated, the majority hacked into pieces. A small number escaped by courtesy of the dust that hid their retreat from us.

Masters of the battlefield and their camp, which they were obliged to abandon, their artillery, their munitions and all their equipment were the prizes of victory. The soldiers made a considerably booty of them, which compensated them for the fatigue they had endured by a march of four days and four nights without having time to rest, followed by a battle whose second day lasted from six o'clock in the morning to five o'clock in the afternoon.

Prince Aricdef, without stopping, pursued his conquests with so much rapidity that he obtained the submission in very little time of all the cities that had allied themselves with the Bellonians, and those which had favored their passage through their realms. After having punished the chiefs for their rebellion, he no longer thought about anything but going to fight the Salians and the Arcians, whose army, he had learned was advancing rapidly to join that of the Bellonians, apparently unaware of their total defeat.

Aricdef caused his troops to retrace their steps, and in order to give them time to rest he took possession of an advantageous position, and distributed his army in various places from which it was easy to rally them, in order to attract the enemy into devastated terrains, to close the passages and be in a position to capture all the convoys coming after them. Those regions, inundated with blood by the ravages of the war, offered a frightful spectacle everywhere of the barbarity of Tracius. It was impossible for that multitude of poorly-hardened troops to resist an army of conquerors for long.

The Salians fell into the trap that Aricdef had set for them, and found themselves surrounded in spite of the number of their troops. The general of the Arcians, who perceived the mistake he had made, harangued his soldiers. He was eloquent, knew his men, and was able to exploit their weakness and master them, first appealing to their appetites studying them skillfully and adjusting himself artfully to the various movements that he observed passing through their souls.

The general was so well able to take advantage of his enlightenment that he made his troops see that the Salians had only been defeated by their own fault and the ignorance of their captains, who had not been able to make use of their numerical advantage or their strength. He gave reasons so manifest and so plausible for his sentiment that the officers and the soldiers were convinced; he invited them in consequence to make offers of peace.

"What augury," he went on, "ought we to take for the success of our forces and our courage, when the bravest of our allies have just been vanquished and reduced shamefully to flight? Are we, by our obstinacy, going to reignite the anger of the victors in the uncertainty of success? We have allowed ourselves to be seduced by the pernicious advice of Tracius, who has drawn us by means of the sights of ambition; we ought to have reflected further before taking up arms against such a dangerous enemy, but we delivered ourselves blindly to the impulses of our courage. You're not unaware that exile, ignominy and slavery are the inevitable woes of the vanquished. It is necessary to yield to fickle fortune and sue for piece; everything invites me to counsel peace, with regard to the condition to which you are reduced."

Scarcely had the general finished his speech than everyone applauded his advice. He was regarded as the pillar of the fatherland. Every soldier handed in his weapons, helmet, buckler and spear, in order to form a kind of trophy in his honor. One of the senior officers was delegated, with full powers to grant all the articles that Aricdef cared to demand.

The Prince received him as a generous victor, and although he was in a position to lay down the law, he accorded them reasonable conditions, and the peace was agreed at the foot of the mountain where the bloody battle had been waged against the tyrant Tracius.

The campaign ended with that peace; Prince Aricdef disbanded his troops and returned to the court, where I was constrained to follow him. After having received the honors of his triumph, the general introduced me to the King, and had the generosity to make my eulogy. The monarch heaped us with praise, and to conserve the memory of such a great success, he had a statue of Fortune erected facing his palace, holding a horn of plenty in one hand and a tiller in the other, at the top of which is a mural crown with these words around it:

The fortune of return brings us abundance.

Chapter VII
The Sequel to the Story of Princess Marsine

Hardly sensible of the praise I received from all the courtiers, I got ready to leave to return to Zachiel and Monime, from whom I flattered myself that I would receive the most sincere welcome. Marsine ought to have shared my concerns too, but I could not think about that Princess without feeling the most ardent desire to be of service to her being reborn within me. My urgency yielding to that desire, I did not want to quit Prince Aricdef without tell him the story of the woes suffered by the unfortunate Marsine, and to interest him more keenly in her favor I began by reminding him of the misfortunes of her father, the King.

"I'm not unaware," I added, "that the tyrant Tracius offered to share the empire he had usurped from Belus with you, by marrying you to his daughter, but the grandeur of your soul, your incorruptible probity and love for justice caused you to scorn propositions that could only be accomplished by unjust means. Permit me to dare to tell you, my Lord, that Fortune sometimes presents opportunities to us from which one can profit; such opportunities, far from tarnishing the glory of an illustrious conqueror, are only offered to make it shine with its full brilliance. You know all the treasons that the tyrant employed to render himself master of the realm of Bellonia, which belongs by right to Princess Marsine by virtue of the death of her father, the King."

"What are you trying to insinuate by this discourse?" said Aricdef, interrupting me. "I would have liked to be able to be useful to that unfortunate Princess, but since the flight of her father the King I have never heard mention of her; doubtless her misfortunes have precipitated her into her father's tomb."

"No, my Lord," I said. "She is still full of life; a disguise has hidden her for a long time from the unjust Bellonians; she is even known to you; her rare qualities cannot have escaped your eyes, since she has served in your army with the same employment that you have been kind enough to accord to me. Marsine and the Chevalier Meilly are one and the same person; you know what a reputation she acquired under that name."

"Gods, what am I hearing?" cried the Prince, extremely surprised. "Have I, then, been able to mistake for such a long time the heir to the throne of Bellonia? It is true that a secret penchant always led me to distinguish her from the other officers; I admired above all the candor, the verity, the generosity and the courage that are inseparable from great souls—but go on, and tell me what prevented her from joining the general action."

I then told the Prince about Marsine's illness, occasioned by the consequence of her chagrins, which I recounted to him in detail, combining them with the reasons that had engaged her to adopt that disguise, in order to evade the cruel tyrannies of Tracius.

"Why," said the Prince, "did she refuse to honor me with her confidence? Speak, my dear Lord; I implore you, in the name of our friendship, to tell me in what fashion I could have attracted her hatred—for what other reason could have prevented her from revealing to me the secret she confided to you? I know that you merit it, but in what way am I unworthy of it?"

"Oh, my Lord, how far away the Princess is from such an unjust way of thinking! It is true, my Lord, that Marsine permitted me to be informed of all her secrets. There is another that your generosity doubtless ought to have extracted from me, but permit...."

"I permit nothing," said the Prince. "Once again, speak, my dear Lord. I wish it; I demand it, not as a Prince but as a friend."

"It's too much," I aid. "I cannot resist that excess of bounty." Then I revealed to the Prince the tender sentiments that the Princess had conceived for his rare virtues, the renown of which was incessantly published throughout the world. Nor did I believe that I ought to hide from him the combats that had taken place in her soul between the desire to declare herself, the dread of saying too much, and that of a peace that might ruin all her hopes.

"I was unable to see that unfortunate Princess," I added, "without being touched. An impression of languor and abasement, extinguishing the vivacity of hr physiognomy, renders her more interesting; her eyes, tarnished by dolor, like rays of sunlight filtering through the clouds, launch, like them, the most piquant gleams; her humility still has the graces of modesty; one cannot see her without feeling compassion for her, or listen to her without admiration."

I had the good fortune, by my story, of inspiring Prince Aricdef with an ardent desire to see the Princess and offer her all the services within his dependency. The Prince went to take his leave of the King. That monarch, who loved him dearly, surprised by such a precipitate departure, wanted to know the reasons that obliged him to leave the court so soon.

Aricdef, who had been expecting the question, did not hesitate to satisfy the king. He told him all the details of the misfortunes that had afflicted Princess Marsine in the course of her life; then he begged the king by all the arguments he thought most capable of touching him to accord his protection to the illustrious unfortunate, who could not be abandoned without injustice.

The monarch, surprised that the Princess had been able to resist so many troubles, not only granted him what he desired but obligingly added that he could not give better recognition to the services that he had just tendered the State than by employing all his power and the most convincing reasons to determine Princess Marsine to share her crown with a Prince who would sustain its majesty with as much justice, prudence and glory as he had acquired by his courage and his talents in all his campaigns.

A grace accorded with such flattering eulogies on the part of a King full of justice and bounty, whose merit alone had a right to claim all favors, filled the heart of Aricdef with joy; his gratitude was manifest by assurances of a respectful attachment and an entire submission to His Majesty's orders. The King instructed him to assemble his troops and depart immediately, in order not to give Tracius time to form new intrigues in Bellonia.

After Prince Aricdef had taken his leave of the King, animated by a new desire for glory, and perhaps that of a nascent amour, the prince easily recalled the features and majesty of bearing of the false chevalier; he already sensed the seed of a passion attracting him toward her, which he would conserve until death. The lure of a crown that was almost on offer also had attractions for a heart made to reign.

His orders having been given to his officers to gather the troops, we got ready to leave. I dispatched a courier to the Princess to announce the Prince's visit and the grand designs that he had formed to reestablish her on her throne; but we proceeded with such great diligence that we arrived in advance of the courier by an hour.

As much for the sake of decency as amity, Marsine had continued to share Monime's apartment. The two charming individuals were together when we arrived; I introduced them to the Prince. Marsine seemed a little troubled at first, but Monime caused joy to shine in her eyes, and the Prince, surprised by their striking beauty, was rendered momentarily speechless.

Pulling themselves together, however, the two of them had a long conversation together, in which the Princess displayed the nobility of her sentiments, the grandeur of her soul, the extent of her intelligence and the courage that she had show in so many adversities. Aricdef, already prejudiced in Marsine's favor, conceived in that first conservation as much amorous sentiment as she desired to inspire in him.

While the Prince and the Princess were so agreeably occupied I retired with Monime to the embrasure of a window in order to be able to talk more freely. We said everything tender to one another that amity can inspire in two truly fond hearts that have not seen one another for some time. Monime expressed herself with the energy that characterizes the sentiment of a noble soul. She told me about all the care that Zachiel had taken to ensure Marsine's happiness.

The genius had made several journeys with the design of disposing the Bellonians to receive their legitimate sovereign, and in consequence of his moves those subjects who had remained faithful to the Princess and had been obliged to wander hither and yon in various realms had been reassembling when they learned of the death of the tyrant Tracius, which was followed by the defeat of his entire army. Their zeal enabled them to seek out all those whom fear, or perhaps interest, had caused to support the tyrant; the banished their fears, reanimated their zeal and their fidelity, so successfully that in very little time they were able to form a considerable body of troops.

Zachiel came in, and brought my joy to a peak by his presence; he received me with the love and cordiality of a father who cherishes his son. After certain conventional politenesses due to the noble, he confirmed to the Prince everything that Monime had just told me. That news reanimated the hopes of the Princess. It was decided to set out the very next day to join up with those troops and stimulate them by the presence of their sovereign.

Monime wanted to accompany the Princess; Zachiel, far from opposing it, seemed charmed by her resolution. He had no doubt that Marsine's example would serve to dissipate all fears.

Prince Aricdef, at the head of an army of thirty thousand battle-hardened—and even better, victorious—troops, soon joined the supporters of the Princess. Once the conjunction of the troops had been made, they entered Bellonia, but the Princess, who wanted to spare the blood of her subjects, sent a herald to announce her return and published a general amnesty in favor of all those who wanted to return to their duty and rally to the standards of their sovereign. That mark of clemency swelled her army considerably.

However, Princess Faustine, the daughter of Tracius, who had just been crowned, had a strong party; her generals employed all the forces of the realm to maintain her on the throne, but Aricdef took away all their means of taking him by surprise and obtained information about all their moves. The Prince distributed men in Faustine's camp, her court, her Council and everywhere else who observed, discovering her views, her designs and her projects, and then informed Aricdef. In spite of the rigors of the season the Prince advanced into the country, withstood several attacks, subjugated cities and pursued the rebels. The surprised Bellonians, confused by his audacity, fled precipitately, conceding him victory everywhere, and were finally constrained to surrender and ask for a pardon that they had no difficulty obtaining.

After having reconquered her realm, Princess Marsine received a magnificent embassy on behalf of the Emperor of the Marsians. The ambassador had orders to congratulate her on her fortunate accession, to assure her of his friendship, and to negotiate a treaty of perpetual alliance, the principle article of which was to accept Prince Aricdef as a husband.

Marsine gave the ambassador the most pompous reception and with the approval of all the nobles of the court she replied that she was delighted that the Emperor's wishes accorded so well with her own; that she could not better recognize the protection he had accorded her and the services that Prince Aricdef had rendered her than by sharing with his a crown that he had already acquired by his intrepid valor, his rare virtue and his talents, so worthy of reigning; that in addition, the prince having the honor of belonging to him by blood, she would always glory in the alliance that gave her the right henceforth to regard the Emperor as a father attentive to the happiness of his children. She added, with infinite grace, that she begged him to assure the Emperor that, in spite of all the advantages she found in the union, interest had less part in it than the choice of her heart. The Prince, a witness to that conversation, felt penetrated with the keenest gratitude; love and joy gleamed in his eyes.

The Queen did not want to send the ambassador away until he had witnessed her marriage to the Prince. The ceremony took place with a pomp and magnificence worthy of the two spouses. It was learned a few days later that Princess Faustine, in despair at her fall, had shut herself away in the temple of Pallas, in order to devote the rest of her days to the worship of the goddess. Finally, the amiable peace so long desired closed the temple of Janus, reestablished confidence, and banished envy and jealousy. Commerce acquired new energy, talents and the arts were reborn, the dismissed troops were no longer occupied in anything but combining myrtle with their laurels, and no one as thinking about anything except enjoying the fruits of glorious labor.

Aricdef and Marsine, peaceful in their estates, are only concerned with rendering their subjects happy. The Prince, ever humane and very wise in his projects, is attentive to all the parts of the economy, all the objects of public administration and everything that might ensure or augment the power, the glory and the wellbeing of his subjects; he could be compared to a Proteus, taking on a thousand different forms. His life is a book that all the generals, even the great Princes, ought to study.

That conduct makes him adored by his people, who count his days by as many benefit. It can also be said that the Fates, attentive to their common happiness, have been glad to elongate the weave of his days, in order to give his subjects time to admire his virtues and allow them to germinate in their hearts.

Chapter VIII

We could not refuse the pleasure of waiting for the return of spring to Aricdef's court. The Queen, attached to Monime by the bonds of the most tender amity, wanted to ask her to take up residence with her, and made her several brilliant proposals on that subject for my establishment. The King joined forces with Marsine, and it would have been very difficult to resist their urgency without the eloquence of Zachiel, who made them sense the necessity of our continuing our voyages.

Although lodged in the royal palace, we were nevertheless obliged to go through several courtyards and a prodigious number of apartments to arrive at the Prince's study. Those apartments were always full of people who had come to solicit pensions, a government post, or the guard of a fort; some were from companies, and a large number requested little gold plaques representing the face of the god Mars surrounded by glory; that plaque as a mark establishing their courage, which ennobled them and made them respected by soldiers and the people. That procession of petitioners formed a crowd that it was difficult to penetrate.

Others—old officers no longer fit for service, purveyors of news—assembled, cheerful or taciturn in spite of the rigors of the season, in platoons in the palace gardens; there, without fear of the north wind, they warmed themselves by regulating the State, arguing about the judgments that each one brought to all affairs. The extent of their sight pierced the cabinets of princes and seemed able to discover the most impenetrable secrets there.

Curious to hear them arguing, I went into the garden one day. I accosted an old military man, who seemed to me to be full of common sense. After a few turns around the path I asked him what the laws of the Bellonians were.

"Our laws," said the officer, "go back to before the war. Our legislators had no goal in mind but victory; that it why they recommend us always to keep our citizens occupied with military exercises, without permitting them to devote themselves to any other profession, except for those who had grown old in the métier of arms and whom the feebleness of age or the wounds they had received rendered them incapable of serving. So, when we were at peace, they had to study with the same diligence all the means of making war advantageously, by carrying out without delay all the orders of their commander—for troops are a body of which the general is the head; it is necessary that he animates his efforts, since their destinies are committed to his prudence and skill, which remain awake while they sleep. The safety of his soldiers depends on him alone. He has to establish good discipline and oppose cruelties. Any general who suffers carnage, who pillages, ravages and permits excess, even if he conquers half the world, is seen as nothing but a tyrant and a bloodthirsty tiger by the voice of people, united against him, forgetful of all his exploits."

"With such extensive knowledge of the military arts, sir, you merit a command."

"Those principles," he went on, "were never to the taste of Tracius; too full of pride, he didn't take advice from anyone; that was what led to his downfall."

"The King who governs you now has always followed those maxims exactly; he renders justice to merit, and only accords military honors to those who have distinguished themselves by striking actions, without regard to birth."

"I know," said the officer, "But I'm too old now to bother paying court to him. I yield to the young courtiers the precious advantage of meriting his benefits."

During our sojourn at the court we were regaled with several lavish feasts, in which Monime made her graces shine and captivated more than one heart. Occupied the rest of the time in paying our court, receiving visits or rendering them, it is certain that we did not have time to get bored.

In the number of Monime's suitors I remarked one who appeared to me to be more assiduous then the rest; he was a young colonel, very full of himself, who turned his eyes and mouth methodically, always equipped with little items of news and gossip, which he recited in terms typical of individuals of his species. We could not take a step without encountering him; I believe that he had the gift of multiplying himself.

One day he came to the house of a woman who had invited us to supper; after he had reeled off a tissue of nonsense devoid of common sense he got up to leave. "What," said the mistress of the house, "you're not saying for supper?"

"No," he said, "I have to go and see the marshal, who, as you know, honors me with his esteem. In truth, I'm in despair at not being able to take advantage for longer of such radiant company, but visits exhaust me; they petrify me, although no one renders or receives more of them than me; my secretary can't keep up with them and my horses, which I force to be martyrs to fashion and good taste, are dead on their feet, as is my runner."

"What do you think of that amiable cavalier," Monime asked, maliciously, of a woman who had never ceased applauding all his stupidities.

"He's charming," said the lady. "It's necessary to agree that he's an adorable man, full of wit, replete with graces, as amusing as possible, who sets off a tapestry nicely, matches porcelain astonishingly, has an exquisite taste in ornaments and is always radiant in his costume, his furniture and his carriages; in sum, he's divine."

"It's true," I said, "that those are rare and useful qualities in a military man."

I noticed that the occupations of almost all the young officers who inhabit the world of Mars resemble closely enough those that had just been offered for our admiration. Those occupations are analogous to their character. Their first concern on waking up is to think about their adornment. The morning goes by without their being able to determine what coat to put on; the choice of color embarrasses them. There are some that heighten pale complexions, others serve to diminish and soften the redness of those the previous days excesses in gabling, dining and other exercises. It is therefore necessary to consult one's mirror; one has difficulty making up one's mind. If one is spending the day with the beautiful Julie, whom the vapors cause to faint continually, one must necessarily put on something tender and serious, but is the amiable Dorine is encountered, one must also please her, and a sepulchral tone would amount to torture.

The valet, who does not understand any of this reasoning, is convinced that his master's irresolution is only caused by the embarrassment of choosing a coat that does not outshine the women to whom he intends to give preference today. He admires that expert delicacy in his master. Accustomed to speak his mind freely on much more serious matters, he extracts him from his anxiety. "Put on a blue coat, sir; that color goes equally well with a blonde and a brunette."

That oracle determines his decision; it is worth a part of his wardrobe to his domestic. The toilette continues; one gives orders to one's runner, whom one dispatches pitilessly to the four quarters of the city to pay compliments to women one quit at five o'clock in the morning and one is counting on seeing again in the evening. Meanwhile, one occupies oneself with one's purse, whose strings must be knotted in the latest fashion; but the wig, the arrangement of the curls, takes much longer than the coiffure of a woman who has a new net for her chignon.

When he has taken all possible trouble and care to decorate his face, all of the features of his visage being his own composition, the various attitudes of which that ought to render him more agreeable he has studied in mirrors, our young colonel believes himself to be more charming than Adonis. He departs like lightning in a magnificent carriage in order to have himself admired by several women, to each of whom he recites a epigram on all the others, relates an anecdote that he has just made up and which does not make sense; he mingles a few insipid compliments in the conversation, which he reels off with a distracted air, takes a hand, kisses it, while looking to see whether the kiss has made an impression, protests that he has never seen a woman as radiant, interrupts himself, sighs mechanically, bows and flies to the home of another in order to repeat the same comedy scene.

Monime's beauty attracted the homages of all the nobility. We were visited one day by one of those men that hazard has been pleased to elevate above their birth; his name was Doronte. His fortune had been established during the reign of the tyrant, who had raised him from a simple soldier to the highest dignities. Constrained to abandon them under the new regime, he nevertheless enjoyed certain honors and the immense wealth with which Tracius had heaped him. Full of pride and conceit, however, he was sovereignly scornful of people he had known in his mediocrity.

He had completely lost his reason, and was barely vegetating; his judgment gone astray, he recalled his initial condition dolorously; half of his life was, for him, a frightful torture that might cause him to die of vanity; in sum, he was seen to be succumbing under the weight of the pride that the post he had occupied had given him—but he was not the only one whom Fortune deprives of judgment by virtue her dangerous charms. There are few people strong enough to defend themselves from the traps that she sets for them.

Zachiel pointed out to us that experience shows us that in all times, the greatest of men have been subject, like the vulgar, to the fault of allowing their fortune to blind hem. They have justified what Hasdrubal said in the Senate when he established as a certain maxim that one very rarely sees judgment in company with good fortune. Those who have applied themselves most assiduously to knowing the human heart regard the union of wisdom and prosperity as something almost impossible. Self-esteem has too much influence over men not to persuade them very easily that they owe to their merit alone that which is often a pure effect of hazard. The greatest men are subject to the same faults. On examining ancient and modern history, one finds that the characters of those who have been favored by fortune almost always become more ill-natured as a result of the success they have had.

Alexander, on leaving Greece, was virtuous and humane; when he had defeated the Persians, he became debauched and cruel, had several of his captains put to death, ordered that Lisimacus be exposed to ferocious beasts,[30] killed his favorite Cleitus during a feast, and took the eunuch Bagoas, who belonged to Darius, in order to make him serve a shameful usage; in sum, the pride that inspired his good fortune rendered him sufficiently insensate to want to regard himself as a divinity.

Sulla only committed the cruelties that he exercised against his compatriots after having bee heaped by the favors of fortune in all the wars he had undertaken; the proscriptions with which he filled Rome and all of Italy were the consequences of his fortunate success.

"Several more examples could be cited," the genius continued, "but those ought to be sufficient to make you see that high birth does not always protect from the reefs those whom good fortune favors. A man elevated above others often believes that he in entitled to permit himself all kinds of excess; he forgets that his birth is an elevated rock, where he appears uncovered, where his designs and the motives that make him act are visible, and where the public, an impartial judge of his actions, pronounces sentence on him with impunity. The mask of virtue only deceives for a while; its penetration allows the depths of the heart to be read, and with a supreme air, the great are all condemned: dignities, wealth,

---

[30] In the tragedy *Lisimacus* (1755) by David Augustin de Brueys, an entirely fictitious story. Cleitus and Bagoas, on the other hand, are both cited in Plutarch's *Life Of Alexander*.

honors, nothing stops censure; their glamour decries them; a false step dooms them; informed of all their deviations, they are published; their virtue are effaced and the brilliant aurora that seemed to presage fortunate days is soon eclipsed by bad politics. There are few princes who carry to the tomb the regrets of the nation, whose attachment they warranted at the beginning of their reign.

The term that Zachiel having accorded to the King and Queen having expired, we got ready to follow the genius to the fifth heaven. I shall not report the final conversation that we had in taking our leave of Their Majesties. That somewhat halting conservation made us know the dolor that they felt at our separation by the violence they put up in contesting our departure. Indifference and coldness find words easily, but sighs, tenderness and tears are the true language of amity. Monime could not employ any others, and the sensibility of her heart had more impression on those of the King and Queen than the most eloquent speech.

We left that realm more flourishing than anyone had ever seen it. The throne had never been filled by a King as wise in the art of reigning. Uniquely occupied with the aggrandizement of his realm, he did not lose sight of the desire to extend its domination; his affability and the facility with which he expressed himself won him the hearts of all those who approached him, and his liberality attached them to him without return. The proofs that he had given of his intrepidity in danger, and his unshakable firmness in difficulties attracted their full confidence. The Prince was inexhaustible in his resources; one can say that he most complicated designs were, for him, merely the play of an imagination that, as vast as it was fecund, procured him the means of executing them with as much rapidity as ease of projection.

The arts, children of repose and abundance, reappeared at the court of a Prince who had become, by his conquests, powerful enough to protect them. He loved letters, and knew their price, recompensing those who cultivated them and often applying himself to them personally.

INVOCATION

Come, celestial spirits, which are resplendent in the brilliant rays of the Sun; I invoke you, luminous spirits; be complaisant, and yield to the petitions I make to you. And you, torch of the universe, inexhaustible source of light, who never cease to travel one or other hemisphere indefatigably; Apollo, Prince of Planets, god of scholars, sovereign of Parnassus; and you, charming Urania, who preside over the sphere of the starry firmament; you, brilliant Melpomene, who delight in that of the Sun; and you also, amiable Clio, who have invented history, come with divine Calliope, who presides alone over the harmony of the different spheres that compose the vast universe; bring with you Momus; I need him to suspend, for a time, his pleasures and his ordinary cares.

Amiable gods and goddesses, close your ears, I implore you, to the prayers of all those importunate individuals who only invoke you for vain or futile things; hasten to my aid, come reheat my imagination, come to ignite in my mind the fire that you are accustomed to pour into the bosom of those who implore you and who impart so many marvels to all our great poets; inspire me with what you have of the most touching; give me the graces and ornaments that are necessary for me to make a picture worthy of my subject; in sum, sustain the courage that has led me as far as the most elevated spheres, for fear that, like Bellerophon, I might fall from too high a region and, fearful and errant, lost and desperate, might only furnish half of my career.

Come, then, to contribute to the fortunate success of my enterprise; I beseech you, celestial spirits, to employ your virtues and your power to drive away the maleficent genii who might deflect the benign influences that I beg you to spread over my work; the help of the gods ought not to be lacking those who implore it with a zeal equal to mine.

THE FIFTH HEAVEN: THE SUN

Chapter I
Description of the Palace of Apollo

Placed on the wings of the genius, which easily pierced the air by their rapid flight, advancing amid the innumerable heavenly bodies that one sees shining from afar, like stars of all magnitudes, the heavens appeared to us to be sown like a field with all its luminous asters.

The genius, after having given us the time to admire that brilliant spectacle, then precipitated himself into the atmosphere of the Sun, and we descended to a place that Monime and I took at first for the Fortunate Isles of the Hesperides. We could not weary of admiring that beautiful star, which travels its immense course with such a dazzling apparel.

Zachiel pointed out to us the plains enameled with a thousand new flowers, the delightful woods, the florid valleys, of which the tender grass and verdure extended charming colors over the meadows. All kinds of newly blooming plants, developing their varied colors, appeared to be enlivening the bosom of nature and simultaneously perfuming her with the sweetest odors. Here one saw humble bushes and shrubs embracing one another, there majestic trees rising pompously into the sky; elsewhere there were springs whose banks were garnished with bouquets of salutary plants.

The variety, grandeur and beauty of thousands of new spectacles, birds foreign to all other worlds, bizarre and unknown plants: that assemblage formed an indescribable mixture for our eyes, the charm of which was further augmented by the subtlety of the air, which rendered the colors more vivid, the features more marked; on comparing all the points of view, the distances seemed less than anywhere else, where the thickness of the air seems to cover the earth with a veil.

In sum, one can say that the world of the Sun has something magical and supernatural about it, which delights the mind and the senses; the divine fire that animates you makes you forget everything; one forgets oneself, no longer knowing where or what one is.

Advancing into that luminous globe, we discovered a superb mountain, the supercilious summit of which was lost in the clouds; wild and tangled thickets defended its approached. Those bushes were preceded by a magnificent forest of cedars, pines and palm trees, whose branches, which embraced one another, formed by their ranks, disposed in stages, a superb amphitheater that presented a delightful view.

Above that enchanted wood one sees the Palace of Apollo. The first portal is erected on an alabaster rock. That palace, whose superb summit rises all the way to the heavens, encloses in its vast extent a park and admirable gardens. We had need of the aid of the genius, whose virtue prevented the splendor of those places from dazzling us.

We paraded our gaze in all directions without the sight of the eye encountering any obstacle or shadow; everything there shines with a brilliant light; the fires and radiance that the sun darts from everywhere are never interrupted by the encounter of any opaque bodies; the air, purer and more serene than on any other world, seems to bring the most distant objects closer, which was a new subject of admiration for us.

Uriel, one of Apollo's squires, the most enlightened mind in that world, knowing of the arrival of the genius, came to meet him in order to introduce him to his master. He conducted us into the palace of Apollo along a broad and superb road, the dust was of which was gold and the pavement diamond. The palace appeared to me at first to be a globe of fire; columns of light sustained arcades that might have been taken for rainbows, forming an architecture so brilliant that our gaze had difficulty sustaining the glare.

After having passed through several rooms, we entered a large gallery, at the end of which Apollo was seated on a throne, surrounded by all his glory; a golden and radiant tiara circled his forehead; his admirable hair floated over his shoulders at the whim of a slight wind that animated the zephyr; youth and grace animated all his actions and a divine fire was seen shining in his eyes, which penetrates all those who have the good fortune to approach that Prince. He was kind enough, at Zachiel's request, to temper the effulgence of his majesty, which our weakness would not have been able to support.

Arranged at the foot of the throne were all the intelligences that guide the different evolutions of nature. Those intelligences appeared to me to be placed by degrees, in accordance with the nobility of their origin and the dignity of their functions; their diaphanous bodies received all the impressions of the light that penetrated them and appeared, at the same time, as a light vapor tinted with fresh, bright and varied colors.

Apollo is regarded in that world as a sovereign prophet; he is the custodian of the art of divination. He presides principally over poetry, music and medicine; he is the chief of the muses, the sovereign of the Fates; his lyre represents the harmony of the heavens. Of the nine sisters that are submissive to him the first, whose name is Urania, presides over the sphere of the starry firmament; Polyhymnia presides over that of Saturn; Terpsichore that of Jupiter; Clio guides Mars; Melpomene is for the Sun; Erato directs Venus; Euterpe regulates Mercury; and Thalia causes the Moon to act; of those eight variously conducted spheres is born a difference of tones that forms a melodious harmony, comprise under the ninth Muse, whose name in Calliope.

As soon as Zachiel appeared, Apollo, who recognized him immediately as a genius of the first order, whom nothing ought to resist, had him approach the throne right away. That monarch, after having congratulated the genius on the extent of his power and his various enterprises, had a long conversation with him on all sorts of sciences. Able to hear what they were saying, their eloquence elevated my soul and spread an inexpressible charm therein; a sublime language expressed their thoughts—but I shall stop, unable to report a discourse that was animated by the divine fire comprising their being; it would be necessary to be inspired by Apollo himself to render it with the dignity that it is appropriate to employ when one makes the gods speak. Is it for me to want to sow such flowers? The lot of mediocre minds is to applaud in the secrecy of the heart and to leave to extraordinary men the concern of celebrating the gods.

After the genius had introduced us to the monarch, who gave us the most favorable welcome, Uriel came to collect us in order to take us to the Princess Caparisse, one of the Prince's favorites.[31] We found the Muses and the Graces in the Princess's apartment, who has assembled there to hear the performance of a piece of music composed by Terpsichore.

When he genius had informed them of the object of our voyages he asked the beautiful goddesses to be kind enough to accord us their protection, and favor us at the same time with a spark of their light. They seemed extremely surprised by the boldness of our enterprise, no mortal from the globe of the earth ever having appeared on that planet, any more than the others, so the genius was obliged to make them party to the means he had employed to take us there. He added that we had already visited several planets—which prompted the goddesses, who like to chat and are naturally curious, to ask us a hundred questions, hardly ever giving us the time to reply to them.

Clio, knowledgeable about history, because she is informed on a daily basis of what is happening in all possible worlds, asked us what were the most curious things we had seen on the worlds we had visited. "I have certain news," the goddess added, "that in several vortices the customs have not changed, that one still encounters there those pretended scholars devoid of erudition, the periodicals that preserve the sublime talent of mutilating all productions and dissecting them in order to render the shreds they report ridiculous. All the critics that can be seen pouncing on nascent merit in order to try to stifle it resemble screech-owls, which, by their shrill and discordant cries would like to annihilate genius that is attempting to take flight, and one often sees them carrying out analyses of books they have not read, which ordinarily end up with flat and in-

---

[31] Caparisse is cited in the entry on Apollon [Apollo] in Daniel de Juigné Broissinière's oft-reprinted *Dictionnaire Théologique, Historique, etc.* (1644) but seems to have no existence elsewhere.

decent mockeries that serve equally for all the works they have an interest in decrying."

"It's true," Monime said, "that we have encountered some who believe they have acquired letters of nobility by the worthy profession of literary criticism, although it's said the high sciences are an algebra to them, and the arts a grimoire. One enlightened author compared one of those critics to a furious Cerberus, whose mind is nothing but an impure exhalation of malevolence, and who only enjoys impunity in the shadow of the scorn in which all the savant hold his venomous darts."

"I agree," said the Muse, "that an author ought to blush at those bastard eulogies; a savant ought to pay attention only to these that depart from the judicious mind of a sage who thinks for himself, without having any regard for those microscopic critics who seek to magnify the smallest faults, counting the *which*es, *that*s and *but*s and citing errors of impression as faults of grammar; but I'm not unaware that common sense and reason have been banished from many worlds; the sages and philosophers dare not manifest their idea freely, and I doubt that, with that way of thinking, Princes can savor true pleasures; incessantly prejudiced by their favorites, they are ignorant of the happiness that is the charm of life, which is the certainty of being loved for oneself, without ambition or interest having any part in the zeal that is shown to them."

Continuing to interrogate us, Clio asked us whether taste still opposed the novelty of objects, whether the people who employed their time poorly were still those who had less of it than the rest, and whether the spirit of presumption and conceit was still the prerogative of fops; whether generals were presently more avid for glory than they were for money; whether one saw ministers preferring the good of the state to their own interest; whether people always listened to the harangues of senators; whether priests, pontiffs and corybants preached humility and charity by their examples; and a thousand other questions that surprised us infinitely, because we did not know the extent to which those amiable goddesses pushed the extent of their knowledge.

Clio continued to converse with Monime while Urania and Polyhymnia made me party to their knowledge of rhetoric and astrology. They talked to me with a great deal of eloquence, and I judged by their discourse that no one could equal them on those matters.

Princess Caparisse invited us to go into Apollo's cabinets in order to admire the curiosities with which they were ornamented. The first offered to our eyes several pieces of tapestry that Minerva had made; in one of them the three Fates, daughters of Jupiter and Themis, could be seen occupied in spinning the thread of each mortal. Another offered the renowned goddess who presents a throne of honor. Opposite were representations, in the nude, of Cyrene, Daphne, Hyacinthe, Caparisse and Branchus, favorites of Apollo.[32]

Then we passed into another cabinet, which contained the most curious things in the world. We noticed, among others, the famous tripod on which the Sibyl of Delphi rendered her oracles; Aesculapius' beard; Mercury's caduceus; Diana's quiver; Minerva's aegis; Cupid's bow and arrows; Venus' toilette; Vulcan's forge; and a thousand other curiosities that I shall mention in due course—but what we admired most was Apollo's harp, whose seven chords correspond to the seven planets over which he expands virtue and light, which simultaneously represents the harmony of the heavens.

The Muses took us into the library of the sovereign of Parnassus. First of all, I picked up a work by one of our philosophers, which treats attraction, or the theory of the world.[33] That work appeared to me to be written with so much force and enlightenment that one would have thought that the author had caught nature in the act. I scanned it avidly, and begged the genius to explain to me several passages to elevated for my feeble knowledge.

"Attraction and electricity are the causes," Zachiel said, "of all phenomena, both physical and mental. Attraction is a force whose action is evident throughout nature; it operates not only on all material bodies, in direct proportion to mass and inversely to the square of distance; it acts similarly on intellectual objects, following exactly the same laws. It is also the cause of memory, in which ideas are renewed by strong conjunction, or the prompting of the time or place where the things occurred. One can also attribute to attraction the causes of analogy and sympathy; it is what makes us incline toward one object rather than another; it is what engages two hearts or two intelligent individuals to link themselves together in narrow amity; it is also what gives birth to the secret penchant that leads the two sexes to unite. One might think that human beings are animated by a double attraction, one that draws them toward vice and the other toward virtue; education and circumstances give them all their activity and energy. In brief, it is the unknown cause, the secret agent with which nature sets everything in movement and maintains everything in equilibrium; which is to say that it

---

[32] All of these names appear in the same list in the previously-cited *Dictionnaire Théologique*, although three are misrendered in Madame Robert's text, probably because of typesetting errors.

[33] Isaac Newton's *Philosophiae Naturalis Principia Mathematica*, which is probably the text that Madame Robert intends to indicate, was first published in 1687, some time after the supposed setting of Seaton and Monime's voyages. Zachiel's bizarre account of the thesis of attraction is highly idiosyncratic, and might well be derived from one of the more tongue-in-cheek passages in Listonai's *Voyageur Philosophe*, whose protagonist reads a treatise at one point extending the Newtonian theory in this analogical fashion.

acts universally. Time does not permit me to give you a more detailed account at present; it's necessary to accompany the Muses in their walk."

We followed the goddesses, who descended into the gardens and headed along a broad path planted with laurels, palm trees and olives; between those trees, enchanted hills were visible, and the flowery gorge of a valley cut by several streams, which presented a thousand new beauties. It is in those charming places that roses grow without thorns. There are somber grottos there, which offer invitations by their coolness to take advantage of their shade to shelter from the ardor of the sun.

Those retreats are carpeted with ivy and vines, which hasten to deliver their red grapes with an agreeable fecundity; and those riches are distributed at all times with an equal profusion in the landscapes that Apollo warms benignly with his divine radiance. In another direction one sees streams descending the hillsides, murmuring softly, and precipitating into various channels, which eventually come together in a large basin, the surface of which presents its crystal mirror to the verdure of its shores. There, the humble rural shrubs and bushes embrace one another; further away, one sees majestic cedars rising up pompously and bearing on their branches birds of every species, which form melodious concerts there, and the zephyrs only enter the foliage to agitate it lightly.

It was in that delightful location that the Muses and the Graces, who still accompanied them, sat down to rest. The beautiful goddesses, who love playful banter, began to pick flowers with which they decorated one another; but those flowers appeared to me to be quite different from those produced by nature on other worlds. I could not identify their species, but Polyhymnia, smiling at my ignorance, relieved my anxiety.

"These flowers that you are admiring with so much attention, if which you know neither the form nor the image, are the flowers of rhetoric and metaphysics; it is from this hill that the scholars of all worlds take them. The slope that you see further away, which rises to the top of Mount Parnassus, is where the metaphors, fictions and hyperboles grow that poets so often employ in their works."

During this discourse Monime was playing with the Graces, who seemed to have become more familiar with her. That charming young woman, finding herself covered with a prodigious quantity of those flowers, wanted to throw them in her turn, when she saw a large number of animals approaching, which on other worlds only inhabit woods and deserts, or ordinarily retreat to lairs.

At the sight of those animals, the majority of which were unknown to her, Monime was gripped by alarm and fear; I saw her go pale and try to hide in the shade of a few bushes—but Polyhymnia, always attentive and officious, perceiving her disturbance, far from lending herself her weakness, stopped her and employed, in order to reassure her, a physical discourse that had so much force on Monime's mind that not only did it dissipate her fears but put her in a state to take part in the various amusements that those various animals often procured for the beautiful goddesses, who were immediately surrounded by lions, bears, rams, goats and scorpions.

Monime obtained a particularly singular pleasure when she perceived a bull bounding before her and a working elephant employing all its industry in twisting its flexible trunk in a hundred different fashions in order to make a crayfish advance and prevent it from moving backwards. We eventually discovered that all the animals in that world are tame, can make themselves understood, and respond precisely to questions that are put to them.

We followed the Muses, who got up to continue their walk. The goddesses took a broad and winding path that seemed to me to be filled with shiny stones. As first I mistook the stones for diamonds; I picked up a few of various colors, all of which were gleaming brightly.

"You like gems of wit, I see," said one of the Muses. "You only have to furnish yourself with all the species; it's in this tortuous path that they grow in abundance; it leads to the Hippocrene spring."

When we arrived at the spring in question, I could not resist the desire to taste the water at its source. Scarcely had I swallowed a few drops than I felt animated by a divine fire; a kind of enthusiasm gripped me, which, in elevating my soul, expanded the charm and brilliance of poetry in my mind. I immediately composed an exceedingly tender elegy, which I addressed to the Muses, who were kind enough to approve of it.

We resumed the route that led to the Palace of Apollo. That monarch, out of consideration for the genius, did us the honor of admitting us to his table; we were regaled there by the odor of the most exquisite perfumes; incense was fuming everywhere. That is the sole nourishment one can take on that world, but the nourishment in question, although very light, is nevertheless fortifying; it is certain that it does not overload the stomach, so the inhabitants of the world never suffer indigestion; that is why the majority of physicians are only occupied in composing books that might be useful on other worlds.

The genius was very willing to permit us to spend a few weeks at Apollo's court. During that brief interval, the nine sisters, always submissive to the desires of the Prince, took pleasure in instructing us, and combining their instruction with a thousand new fêtes, which, although they seemed designed solely to amuse us, were nevertheless useful lessons.

I noticed that those who are admitted to Apollo's court have bodies so subtle that the eyes of a mortal can scarcely perceive them, but, like genii, when they want to render themselves visible, they have the same faculty of taking on fantastic bodies, because subtle matter is immediately obedient to their will.

That court is filled with scholars of every species; one sees astronomers, geometers, chemists, cabalists, poets, physicians, oracles and musicians—all the persons protected by Apollo. Monime and I could not weary of admiring such a delightful abode. Zachiel warned us, however, that it was necessary to make ready to bid farewell to the sovereign of Parnassus, the Muses and the entire court.

The Muses generously expressed the chagrin they felt at quitting us. The beautiful goddesses lavished a thousand caresses upon Monime; they each endowed her with one of the sciences over which they presided; they added that, without the certainty they had of receiving her, she would not be permitted to distance herself from a court for which her birth had destined her.

Chapter II
The Marvelous Forest

The genius, whose intention was to enable is to visit the various countries that the luminous globe contains, and at the same time enable us to admire all its marvels, had us descend from Parnassus by a kind of covered way that serves as a route for the inhabitants of the planet when they want to go to the mountain to participate in the gifts that the sovereign of Parnassus extends to his people.

That path, which is filled with golden sand, leads to subterranean regions that one might take for the cavities of the fiery planet. That, doubtless, is what prevents the inhabitants from feeling the ardor of the sun's rays, because it seems that their force increases as they draw away from the star. That part of the Sun can be compared to our cellars, whose coolness seemed to increase in proportion to the heat. It is as well to note that there are no nights on that world; as it is the center of the universe, Apollo distributes the purest light there, but the coolness of the cavities tempers the air and renders it more serene than in any of the other worlds.

When we reached the bottom of the mountain we perceived a great forest, where, the genius assured, all that was most precious in nature was contained. The trees of that forest are a singular species; the trunks are gold, the branches silver and the leaves emeralds, which, above the bright verdure of their surface, represent as in a mirror the image of fruits that hang there, and which borrow none of their beauty from the leaves, since they are as many vials that contain the intelligence and common sense of all humans. Every individual, at the instant of birth, has an allotment of two vials, one containing intelligence and the other common sense; the names of the individuals are engraved in the glass.

"Take note," said the genius, while making us examine those vials, "that nature, ever judicious in the distribution she makes of her gifts, does not favor one person to the prejudice of another. All humans are born in perfect equality; education corrupts or perfects their benefits."

"If that is the case," I asked him, "why are the vials not equally filled?"

"That," said the genius, "is because of the bad usage that humans make of the graces they receive from nature. You must have noticed in the different worlds we have visited that common sense and reason have been almost banished therefrom. Everywhere people run after intelligence, everyone wanting to have it, everyone forming new systems, and the noble simplicity that common sense gives us, which reason dictates to us, is abandoned and seems proscribed on all worlds; people only demand witticisms, a great deal of free and vivacity, and hyperbolic phrases devoid of meaning, which those who compose them do not understand themselves. There are big words that are assembled to say trivial things, which nevertheless take up volumes; but common sense, so necessary to human happiness, is regarded as simplicity, stupidity, timidity or lack of understanding. That is what determines the difference you see between these vials; you can see many from which all the intelligence has evaporated, because that is not what is fashionable; common sense is conserved for a longer time.

"You ought also to notice," the genius continued, "that this forest is divided by as many routes as the sun illuminates worlds, and that in each of those pathways one can see several side-paths that designate the different provinces of those worlds; but, for the convenience of the ministers of Apollo charged with examining all the revolutions that are frequently seen arriving on the planetary worlds, the name of the planet whose intelligence and common sense are deposited in each sector has been engraved on the first tree of each pathway."

I followed Monime, who began by visiting the paths that designated the worlds we had already visited. I saw her searching with extreme care for the vials of people that we had met. Her searches would have been vain if Zachiel had not lent himself to the satisfaction of her curiosity. He showed her the vials of a number of ministers, generals, judges, corybants and an infinity of other people who passed in those worlds for superior intellects. It is true that the intelligence had entirely disappeared, but the vials of common sense were full.

Surprised by such a singular phenomenon, Monime looked with great attention to see whether they were equally stoppered, and whether air might not be communicated from one to another, but found no opening in any of them. "I'm at a loss in my research," Monime said, with an expression of irritation. "Intelligence must be much more subtle than common sense, for how can one by persuaded that the great individuals we have seen playing the leading roles in the theater of their world have always lacked common sense, especially when one sees them appointed to posts where it is so necessary to the guidance of a State? Tell me, then, my dear Zachiel, whether methods have changed since we left those worlds; doubtless the spirit of vertigo has succeeded common sense and reason."

The genius smiled, and without replying to her, he took us into winding paths where all the vials of common sense were gleaming like carbuncles—which it to say that they were all empty—and those of intelligence were half-full.

"I'm almost certain," I said to Zachiel, "that the proprietors of those vials only shine in a mediocre fashion in their own sphere."

"You're mistaken," said the genius, "since they belong to veritable philosophers, all individuals of a precise mind, profound and enlightened in all kinds of science. It's true that the majority live in poverty, but without being any more unhappy, because the wise never complain of their misfortune, simple necessity being sufficient for all their needs."

Those paths led us into the path of Saturn; almost all the vials here were empty, resembling pearls whose white gleam was dazzling.

"This announces to us," Monime said, "A world full of candor, reason and good faith."

"Your reflection is just," said the genius. "It's on Saturn that you will find the infancy of the world, the Golden Age, the probity of the ancient patriarchs, the good faith so vaunted and at the same time so scorned on the other worlds.

We arrived insensibly in the part of the forest that concerns our world. Curious to visit all the bypaths, Monime and I hastened to enter it. The genius willingly lent his aid to satisfying our curiosity, in order to give us a striking idea of the portion of enlightenment allotted to the various nations filling the earthly globe—or, to put it more accurately, the usage they make of it.

I was extremely surprised by the variety I remarked between different climes. None of the paths seemed similar; in one almost all the common sense had disappeared, in another it was only the intelligence. Monime would have liked the genius to give her some detailed instruction regarding the monarchs and sovereigns, their generals and their ministers, but he put off that instruction until we had returned to our own world.

Chapter III
An Extraordinary Encounter

When we emerged from the marvelous forest we traversed a great plain in order to reach the City of Philosophers. Some distance from that city we perceived several people who appeared to be arguing with a great deal of bitterness. In the middle were two old men, who appeared to us, by virtue of the density of their bodies, to be newly arrived from some distant planet.

Zachiel recognized them immediately. He told us that one of the two old men was Paracelsus, a Swiss philosopher who had treated the secrets of nature, and the knowledge of the genii and elementary spirits. The other was the great Avicenna, a famous cabalist.

"Although I never doubted," the genius added, "that those two great men would arrive one day in the sphere of the Sun, that being their destiny, and from which they doubtless obtained the full extent of their enlightenment, I am nevertheless very surprised to encounter them here without having previously satisfied the order of nature. I have no doubt that they had themselves transported here by some elementary spirits that they indubitably summoned by the force of their conjurations. I know the extent of Avicenna's science; it is only by his studies that he acquired the power to command genii; he once forced me to descend myself to assist him in various operations that he undertook, and which acquired him the great repute he enjoys among scholars."

The genius went forward then, parting the crowd that was surrounding the two old men in order to learn the subject of their dispute directly from them. Avicenna recognized the genius immediately and seemed delighted to see him again. After having expressed his joy and surprise he examined us momentarily; too occupied with his adventure to distract himself in our favor, however, he did not offer us the slightest politeness.

"In the name of the primal light," said Avicenna addressing himself to Zachiel, "get us out of the embarrassment we're in. Perhaps you're not unaware that I made the acquaintance of this philosopher some years ago, who, like me, has always been convinced of the existence of elementary spirits. In order to assure ourselves of their power, however, we formed the resolution together to force them to transport us to the sphere of the sun.

"The power of my conjurations is familiar to you; you know that I'm not unaware of any of the names of the intelligences, since even you were constrained to respond to my invocations. I therefore employed the most energetic conjurations of Radiel, Caracaza, Amadyal[34] and several others of our acquaint-

---

[34] These three names are cited in series is a conjuration allegedly contained in the grimoire known as the *Clavicula Salomonis* [Key of Solomon], although the

ance. All those genii, obedient to the name of the Primal Light, transported us to the sphere of the sun.

"Scarcely had the spirits gone than we found ourselves the butt of the jeers of a people whose science doubtless only consists of doubting the most natural events; for, in sum, these people that you see push their incredulity so far as to dispute our existence with us, and even have the audacity to sustain that our vials of common sense have long since fallen from the tree to which they were attached. Have such absurdities ever been imagined?"

The philosopher was no longer in possession of himself; animated by anger, his veins were swollen, his face inflamed and his eyes on fire; he could scarcely articulate anything, when one of the women who were there caused him to withdraw into himself and to blush at the same time at his weakness by means of a few words.

"If you were what you're striving in vain to persuade us that you are," the woman said, "you would be better able to moderate your passions. Know that the veritable philosophy is so pure that it extracts even the slightest roots of vice; that it washes and cleans the soul to render it worthy of the one who formed it; and finally, that it operates in such a fashion that the love of glory, vanity and the desire for praise can no longer be produced. Only philosophy can make human beings perfect, but you, who have probably been guided here by the ambition of being admired by feeble mortals, have been unable, in consequence, to elevate your spirit to the degree that would have destroyed forever the weaknesses of humanity, because your prejudices or your passions have obscured your reason, and have necessarily prevented it from acting freely. After this small lesson, it is up to you to examine whether your soul is presently at the degree of perfection that true philosophy demands, especially after the disparities that you have just shown us."

Avicenna appeared to be downcast by that reproach, which served nevertheless to calm him down. Confused to have merited it by his fit of temper, however, he left us without daring to utter another word, and we saw him take the route to the forest.

The dispute having concluded, everyone dispersed; only Paracelsus remained with us.

"I would be very curious," Monime said to the philosopher, "to be instructed by you in the enlightenment that you have acquired in the matter of knowledge of the genii."

"I consent," Paracelsus replied, "to make you party to a science that I only discovered by means of toil and late nights, but the genius who protects you must have instructed you regarding the essential party that composes the celes-

---

reproductions of the list accessible via Google Books are later than *Voyages de Milord Céton*, so it is not obvious where Madame Robert came across it.

tial court, and which fills the immense void that must necessarily be found between the Supreme Being and feeble humans."

"It's true," said Monime, "that Zachiel has neglected nothing that might serve for our instruction. I'm not unaware that the vast universe is filled with several kinds of genii occupied in different functions, but as you have investigated the matter in depth, you would give me pleasure by instructing me more particularly."

"I cannot resist satisfying your curiosity," said Paracelsus. "You ought not to be unaware that only the Supreme Being is perfect and complete; that it is to his omnipotence and supreme will that he created abysms of nothingness, an infinity of worlds filled with various creatures that were formed in the instant that he had appointed by his wisdom. His divinity produced, at the same time, a prodigious quantity of spiritual substances, separated from bodies and matter, and more excellent than humans, which are the genii. Those spiritual and invisible substances far surpass human forces; they are the motives of an infinity of things, of which the most ordinary effects are the movement of the heavens and the courses of the stars, because the animated heavens could not guide themselves with such a good order and such a well-regulated cadence. A savant philosopher has affirmed the discovery, by simple natural light, that there are motivating intelligences—which is to say, genii—that ought not to be occupied with anything but shifting the celestial spheres and guiding them in their daily courses. One can therefore conclude that the substance of genii is more spiritual that the most subtle and loosely aggregated of bodies, such as winds and tempests, which have so little body that they are invisible.

"Several philosophers have asserted that genii cannot be anything but meteors that form in the air, but the most constant opinion is the belief that genii have no bodies, because if they had them, it would necessarily follow that they would be large, in proportion to the importance of their employment, which could not be the case with their making a considerable noise in the air. The genii have only been created to obey the orders of the divinity; some in order to approach him and participate in the light of which he is the principle, which determines that they must be disengaged from matter in order to penetrate, understand and listen with more facility to the secrets and orders of the divinity. Now, as they are the ones who approach him most closely, they ought to be regarded as the most perfect creatures.

"A few scholars have been persuaded that the genii were created at the same time as the heavens and the elements were extracted from the void, but the most famous philosophers affirm that the divinity, by his omnipotent virtue, created both spiritual and corporeal creatures at the commencement of time, and that there are several orders of genii, each of which has particular virtues; like the stars that shine in the sky and distribute different light, they have different properties.

"Those different orders of genii are distributed in all the possible worlds in order to guide them in accordance with the order of their functions. They differ from one another in their nature and their essence, and are naturally endowed with the faculty of knowing and understanding by the grandeur and extent of their mind; that is why they can distinguish everything there is in nature; the greatest secrets are developed for them, the essence of the heavens, the properties of the elements and other animate and inanimate creatures. They are natural physicists, physicians, metaphysicians, astronomers, geographers and mechanicians. The origin of the winds is known to them, the causes of the tides of the sea, the courses of the stars and numerous other sublime sciences that the divinity imprinted in their minds at the moment of their creation, in order to render them more able to carry out is orders; they are also great theologians, and understand much better than feeble humans what the attributes of the divinity are.

"Genii of the first order know spiritual matters well as corporeal ones at a glance, and, without employing long discourses and vain arguments, they discover causes and effects at the same glance. Their minds are always open and active, incessantly occupied in some knowledge that represents to them as in a mirror the perfections they have received from the Supreme Beings. Far from making them proud, however, they only make use of it as a spur to exercise their charity toward humans.

"Those genii also have, by virtue of the extent of their knowledge, the motivating faculty—which is to say, the power to move themselves, and everything else, and to transport themselves from one place to another. Just as their substance is the most perfect of created substances, their faculties are also the most perfect, the most active and the most vigorous, since they act with an unparalleled speed and agility; birds do not fly more nimbly through the air, the winds are not so impetuous, nor launched arrows as rapid as the course of a genius across the universe, transporting himself from one place to another. In an instant he passes from one world to another, descends from heaven to earth and rises up to heaven again by the vigor of his nature, piercing and penetrating everything, without finding resistance anywhere, because the superior genii, in addition to their power of movement, also have that of acting on other spiritual substances inferior to them and which they have the right to command.

"That means that it is in their power to produce innumerable affects by applying the active and the passive—which is to say, by approaching the bodies that have the virtue of acting on those that can receive impulsion or attraction therefrom. It is also in their power to bring down the fire of heaven, to raise the waters of the sea, to cause floods, to transport mountains, to uproot trees and perform a thousand other prodigies, because here is now power on earth to equal them; but the love that they have for virtue drives them incessantly to perform acts of charity in favor of humans.

"Those genii are always in action, always ready to render us service, but not with the indolence that one remarks in feeble humans when they take up our interests; neither time nor distance cools their amity, because their particular quality is to obey the Supreme Being and everything that belongs to his divinity, by virtue of an invincible force that renders them persevering and unshakable.

"In spite of the power of those genii, they are never seen to abuse their strength; always mild and obliging toward humans, whom they regard with a paternal affection and love, they always exercise their power with a character of candor, and it is only by the mild attractions of their generosity that they guide their inferiors—which provides that mildness is the most amiable of virtues, and that it has a thousand charms to win hearts and subjugate them. Their ever-pure intentions defer all their actions to the Supreme Being, with no mixture of interests, nor any view to glory or ostentation. Thus, one can regard the genii of the first class as celestial princes, but very different from the princes of earth, who only have the apparatus of their grandeur in view.

"It is also necessary to remark that the divinity has destined those primary genii to the economy and the care of the daily affairs of the corporeal worlds—which is to say that they accomplish, finish and conclude all the distinctions and the various orders of celestial nature—and they are employed day and night in watching over all the worlds, without ever being weakened by the length of time.

"The evil genii, although submissive to the orders of the superior ones, are nevertheless solely occupied in troubling the harmony that ought to reign between them and humans. Traveling through all the worlds incessantly, in order to corrupt them by sowing discord therein and to prevent them from following the paths of virtue, they attack them with vehement passions and drive men to reprehensible extremes by giving credit to vice with new and false doctrines. But the good genii and those of the first order oppose all those disorders with their continual assistance; that is why it is prudent to link oneself in narrow amity with the superior genii, and try to render oneself propitious to the inferior ones, in order to engage them not to trouble that commerce by their malice and their evil insinuations. I shall not speak to you about other intermediary substances, of which you are not unaware of any of the qualities."

"You have doubtless found the secret," Monime said, "by means of your observations and your late nights, of attaching one of those intermediary substances, or one of the superior genii, to yourself."

"That is what I worked to do for a long time, in vain," said Paracelsus, "but Avicenna has been a great help to me and it is only by combining our knowledge that we have succeeded in making the elementary genii obey us.

"That philosopher is the most knowledgeable man who has ever appeared on the globe of the earth; he possesses all the secret sciences, by which one can explain the different operations of nature; a famous cabalist, he adds to those sciences chemistry; he has the secret of the philosophical stone, and that of the universal elixir; he can discover treasures and drive away the evil genii that have rendered themselves masters of them. No prodigy appears difficult of execution to him; he can, when he pleases, turn humans into quadrupeds or reptiles; no talisman can resist him; the most secret mysteries of the cabala have been developed for him; it is by that means that he reached the goal of summoning the elementary spirits and subjugating them to his will. He has composed a large number of books, which treat all the prodigies of the cabala, but those books are written in a style so elaborate that unless one is instructed by a genius of the first class it is almost impossible to penetrate their meaning; it was never his intention to instruct ordinary men.

"Avicenna is several hundred years old; when he feels his forces diminishing he repairs them easily by means of a dose of the universal elixir, which, in reanimating him, also gives him a new vigor.

"Pardon me," Paracelsus added, "but I am obliged to follow Avienna and I am going to rejoin him."

Chapter IV
Remarks on Astronomy

When Paracelsus had left us we went to rejoin Zachiel, who had gone on ahead to meet several astronomers. Informed of his arrival by various movements they had observed in the signs of the zodiac, all those scholars had come to meet the genius, as delegates of the City of Philosophers. The principal ones were Thales, Anaxagoras, Pythagoras, Democritus, Aristarchus, Hipparchus, Ptolemy, Copernicus, Galileo, Gassendi, Klinkenberg, Vilnius, Tycho Brahe, Kepler, Cassini, Descartes and Newton. The last-named addressed compliments to the genius on behalf of all the others.

When the philosopher's speech had concluded, Zachiel had us approach those great men, in order to give us an inkling of astronomy. The philosophers greeted us gravely, but nevertheless showing considerable surprise, and looked at us attentively. I confess that their examination focused on Monime; I was even tempted to believe that some of those scientists took her for one of the signs of the zodiac, which is named Virgo, for I saw them immediately arm themselves with their telescopes in order to examine that sign, still shining in the sky with a gleam s bright as the one they had remarked in Monime's eyes.

"In order to anticipate the intentions of the genius who had brought you to this sphere," one of the scholars said, "I shall acquaint you, with the help of one of our telescopes, with several stars newly discovered by our most skillful astronomers. For a long time we have been on the lookout for these stars, which seem to delight in teasing us with their frequent disappearances."

I therefore armed myself, following the example of the philosophers, with the instrument that was to direct my sight and enabled me to distinguish in the prodigious quantity of stars the different forms of those that interested the scholars, with the names and signs to which they ought to be attached.[35]

"Gentlemen!" cried one of them, with a great deal of enthusiasm, but with his eye still glued to his telescope, "there is the star for which we have been searching for such a long time; it is visible at the neck of the sign."

"I cannot imagine," said Monime, interrupting us, "how you can recognize, in the immensity of a sky strewn with stars, whose brightness and gleam seem to me to be almost identical, the names and attributes of each of these stars."

"I can see," the astronomer replied, "that you have no inkling of astronomy."

---

[35] Given that we have been told that there is no night on the Sun, it would appear to follow that conditions there are not ideal for astronomical observation, but the telescopes there are presumably more competent than ours.

"It's true," said Monime, "that that science has always seemed to me to be a little too abstract for me to apply myself to it."

"Be persuaded, my Lady, that the study of the philosophy diminishes none of one's beauty; here, all of our ladies apply themselves to it, and it seems that the enlightenment they acquire by that study gives even more brilliance to their eyes, and even animates all their actions, but without altering the mildness of their character or the gaiety that renders them so amiable. As I have no doubt that you desire to surpass them in science to the same extent that you surpass them in beauty, I shall give you a little lesson; we could not choose a more convenient place.

"Know," the astronomer went on, "that all bodies are susceptible to different modifications; movement is one of those principles. Galileo has instructed more than one world with the laws that bodies follow in falling toward the earth. Newton has recognized that the cause that makes bodies fall toward the earth, without being able to explain its nature, also causes celestial bodies to gravitate toward one another. But the rumor had just spread among us that an elementary genius, one of those who preside over the movements of the Earth and the Moon, has just revealed the nature of that famous cause to a physicist of your planet, who is not yet known, and we are assured that he is not a little embarrassed as to how he can make that admirable secret known to others, even though the genius has given him a very clear idea of it."

"That is not astonishing," said Monime. "The genii instruct by inspiration; they imprint directly in the soul, by a simple and entirely spiritual operation, the knowledge that they want to communicate, whereas humans require the ministry of their senses, which are material and primitive, to manifest their ideas to other humans, who, for their part, can only grasp it by the same means—which often tends to render the communication of knowledge between human beings very difficult and almost always imperfect."

"Your reflections are just," replied the scholar. "It is easy to recognize, by the clarity and solidity of your reasoning, that you have been instructed by a genius of the first order; but be persuaded that if the new physicist of whom we speak really possesses this knowledge, he will succeed sooner or later in making it understood. One sees that at the end of all great enterprises, when one is not deterred by the toil and care necessary to succeed, and one is never deterred when they might lead to immortality. You can learn the details of astronomy in our schools. You will be told that any astronomer must know how to distinguish the constellations and the movement that each star employs to complete its revolutions, as well as those of comets. A mind as penetrating as yours can presently listen without boredom to the instructions I shall give you."

During that conversation I had quit my telescope. Had I any need of it to admire the fire that was shining in Monime's eyes? I confess that would rather have limited all my observations to those two stars, but I was obliged to pick up the telescope again in order to follow my scholar in his further research.

"Notice the brightness of that star," he said to me, "which approaches he brilliance of Venus. The place where you see it is recognized among us as the chair of Cassiopeia. The one that appears a little further away, which has the brightness of a third magnitude star, seems to disappear periodically. It makes its revolutions in approximately six years. The star is never entirely extinct; it is in the neck of the Whale.[36] Here is another that we lost for some time, and which has caused us a great deal of anxiety, because it is extremely diminished. It is visible at present between the breast and he neck of the sign. But we have lost one that surpassed in its brightness that of Jupiter; it as of a species quite different from the others; nothing similar has been discovered since it disappeared; it can be seen close to the ecliptic; it is in the right leg of the Serpent-Bearer."[37]

The famous astronomer pointed out yet another new discovery, which, he assured me, completes its revolution in four hundred and four days two hours ten minutes and fifteen seconds, and which, although it rarely surpasses the fifth magnitude, nevertheless returns very regularly. It was discovered with a six-foot telescope.[38]

The scholar than caused me to observe a few luminous patches that he had discovered among the fixed stars. "It is," he continued, "a light that comes from a very large expanse in the ether, through which a lucid medium is distributed, which shins by itself. One cannot see any appearance of a star in these bright patches; the irregular form that they have makes it evident that their light does not come from a luminous center. Those bright patches are six in number;[39] the largest is in the middle of Orion's sword; it can pass for a single star of the third magnitude. Another can be seen in Andromeda's girdle, which resembles a pale cloud with a spoke extended to the north-east. The third patch is near the ecliptic, between the head and the bow of Sagittarius. I discovered the fourth by working with the catalogue of meridional stars; it is in the Centaur, and only gives a little light. In relation to its length that patch has no radii. The fifth appears near the right foot of Antinous. It is a tiny patch, obscure itself, but the star

---

[36] The reference to the variable star in Cetus [the Whale] is obviously to Mira, but it is unclear what the earlier reference to a star as bright as Venus signifies, no star in Cassiopeia being brighter than the second magnitude.

[37] The constellation Ophiuchus. The term used in the text, derived from Ptolemy, is *serpentaire*, whose literal reference is to the secretary-bird, but the constellation is normally imagined to resemble a man carrying a snake.

[38] Probably R Hydrae, discovered by Giacomo Maraldi in the early 18th century.

[39] The list of the six nebulae cited here was made by Edmund Halley in 1715. The fact that the speaker uses the first person when referring to the "discovery" of Omega Centauri—which he rediscovered in 1677—implies that he is the scholar who is reporting all the information to Seaton and Monime, but Madame Robert is more likely to have derived all the information he is communicating from Pierre Charles le Monnier's *Histoire céleste* (1741).

that shines through it renders it luminous. The sixth was discovered by chance in the constellation of Hercules; one can see it without a telescope.

"I have no doubt," the astronomer added, that there are several other luminous patches that have escaped our observations, and which must occupy immense spaces since they are among the fixed stars, for it seems that there is a perpetual light in those vast spaces—which can furnish naturalists as well as astronomers with material for speculation."

"Tell me, I beg you," I asked the scholar, "what a comet is."

"A comet," said the astronomer, "is a solid body, almost the same size as the Earth, which appears to be entirely ablaze. We have observed that its direction of movement is always falling toward the sun. Some have been seen that appear to have fallen into the star, emerge hereafter in flames and rise much more rapidly than they fell, until they re lost entirely from view. Their exhalation and their smoke, while they are forming or rising, forms the tail or hair that is seen. But if one of those comets finds its sufficiently far away from the sun again, that tail or hair can fall back upon the crust of the cometary body, and by that means it becomes a more beautiful planet than it was before. But in more than three thousand years that astronomers have been occupied in observing the movement of the stars and the planets, none of the known planets has yet been seen to fall into the Sun.

"In any case, if you want to learn the veritable theory of the movement of celestial bodies, and have a calculus in conformity with its movements, you have only to consult Kepler or the illustrious Newton when you arrive in the City of Philosophers; it is those two great men who have demonstrated it with the most clarity."

After having quit our astronomers, Monime, finding herself fatigued by that hotchpotch of abstract science, which had bored her horribly, asked the genius to allow her to take a short rest.

"Well," said Zachiel, "to dissipate your ennui, let's go into this orchard; we can breathe a country air that will chase way the irritation produced in you by a discourse that was slightly too elevated. The song of the birds, their little twittering, will recall your good humor."

"Do you know, my dear Papa," said Monime, "that you aggravate me with your teasing, and make me want to quarrel with you—but quite seriously, since you've been making a game of imposing them on me for some time, what are these birds? Perhaps they're only more scholars, for I recall that you've already told me about the metamorphosis of the first men, who must surely have arrived her ready feathered. No matter—I'll go with you; perhaps I won't hear any more talk of those villainous comets."

The genius smiled, glancing at me, and we went into the orchard.

The first object that presented itself to our eyes was a famous theologian of the Anglican Church, who had written a treatise on Hell, which he had placed in the Sun.[40] He made that star the abode of demons and the wicked condemned to suffer eternal torments. The scholar had doubtless based his theory on the fact that the Holy Scriptures had called Hell the torture of fire, comparing it to a lake of fire burning night and day. Monime could not help bursting into laughter on hearing talk of a theory so extravagant.

We approached the scholar, who seemed to be plunged in a profound reverie.

"Well," Zachiel said to him, "what do you think now about the empire of the Sun? Do you still believe that it's an abode prepared for the wicked?"

"Our enlightenment is so limited on Earth," replied the Anglican, "that one ought not to be surprised to find the majority of pretended scholars falling into new errors every day. I agree that the one into which I allowed myself to be drawn was one of the most gross. I did not know then that there are numerous worlds and that the immense spaces that form the great universe are full of them, or that the fixed stars are as many suns, which illuminate a world or several others; but since I have inhabited the abode of light, my more enlightened mind presently leads me to place Hell in the atmosphere, or on the surface of a comet set ablaze by the sun's rays; I am therefore quite convinced that it is in one of those places that Lucifer and the angels of darkness, accompanied by the impious and the wicked who are to emerge from the entrails of the earth, will suffer the punishment that is their due."

"That's more of your malice," Monime said to Zachiel. "Always comets!"

Without replying, the genius addressed himself to the scholar. "You are still in error," he said to him, "since you cannot deny that an intelligent being is the author of all the phenomena of nature. Do you still doubt that the air is inhabited by immaterial beings, whose bodies are too subtle or too loosely aggregated to be the objects of your senses? Know, then, that although comets do not appear to you to be very comfortable places to serve as the habitation of intelligent beings that have bodies or corporeal vehicles, because the heat there would be too sensible when they approach the sun or the cold too excessive when they are distant from it, be certain that comets have not been made merely to produce great changes, to excite conflagrations or deluges; you ought, therefore, to believe that comets, like planets, contain vast countries, lakes and rivers, an infinite multitude of humans and animals of every species; I can also assure you that all the worlds are very closely similar to the one you have quit—which is to say that they contain a sun in their vortices, more or fewer planets than there are in that of the Earth, the size of which is proportional to that of each world."

---

[40] Tobias Swinden (1659-1719), author of *An Enquiry into the Nature and Place of Hell* (1714), translated into French in 1728 by Jean Bion.

Chapter V
The Mores of the Inhabitants of the Sun

After leaving our theologian, Zachiel chided Monime a little for the impatience she had shown in listening to the discourse of the pretended scholar.

"I ought now to instruct you," said the genius, "regarding the mores, customs and way of thinking of those who inhabit this luminous globe. You must both have noticed, by the form of their diaphanous bodies, that it is easy to perceive through their brains what they are imagining or thinking, for it is certain that without their clothing one could distinguish, by the movements of their heats, the different passions that agitate them. In sum, one can regard all the citizens of this world as true living skeletons, in whom it is easy to distinguish the impressions that the passions might produce in human bodies. It is for that reason that it is very difficult for them to hide their thoughts, so they do not take the trouble.

"This is a world that is entirely populated by scholars; dissimulation, base flattery and politics have never been known to them; they think what they say, they carry out what they have promised. Almost all philosophers are enlightened by reason, the examination of their own conduct is regarded among them as the primary duty and their principal occupation. Furthermore, everything that surrounds them only serves for their recreation; always attentive to perfecting themselves, to retrenching their desires, repressing their passions, one does not see them tormented by the foolish ambition to augment their wealth.

"In this world, men have no superiority over women, unless virtue, science, common sense and reason gives it to them. It is certain that a woman can equally well possess all these gifts, especially when she receives the same education; these have that advantage; they are taught the same sciences and the same talents; it is by means of that education that they acquire the accuracy of reasoning in useful and necessary knowledge. From birth they are taught to think justly, to reflect and to speak reasonably about all things; one can say that there is scarcely anywhere except this world where their veritable triumph is established, because common sense, intelligence and erudition shine equally in all their expressions—which proves that the truth resembles light, and that it strikes all minds attentive to seeking it.

"Nature, always judicious and liberal in distributing to humans an equal portion of her gifts, has not had the pretention to favor one sex over the other. I do not know by what fatality women on other worlds have been forbidden an exact and profound knowledge of all the sciences; one can never offer them an insult more marked, the consequences of which are more deadly; for it is certain that it is only the ignorance in which they are raised that occasions their weaknesses, their superstitions and all their deviations.

"That is one thing you ought that you ought to have noticed on all the worlds we have visited. You are not unaware that the majority of pretty women almost always spend half the day on their toilette; they are seen to examine with expert care the relationship that foreign ornaments have with their face, and only settle on one or another embellishment after the most scrupulous examination of the effect that it ought to produce on their charms; what ought to be presumed of the time that the old and the ugly spend on it, especially when the graces contribute nothing of their counsels.

"You will not see here, either, those women who, with simple and stupid expressions, listen to the numerous discourses of numbskulls as frivolous as butterflies, who only deign to talk to them with a view to seducing them by the false impressions that they create in their minds. People are unaware, or seem to be unaware, on several of those worlds, of the utility that is obtained by giving women a suitable education, which would procure both sexes their happiness and tranquility. Those reflections, which are usually the prerogative of a genius, are self-evident to the way of thinking and acting of the inhabitants of the sun.

"The majority of the philosophers of this world," the genius continued, "far from lending themselves to the ignorance to the pretended strong minds who believe that hazard, at the birth of worlds, balanced the enormous masses of the fiery globes that traverse the immense spaces of the vast universe in the waves of the firmament; that it is hazard that directs them in their majestic and rapid course; and that it is hazard that fixes the circle of their revolutions and prevents them from colliding with one another and reducing themselves to the almost imperceptible elementary particles of the atoms of which they are formed. On the contrary; they regard nature as a superb divinity; they believe that there is a force distributed everywhere; that it is essential to matter; that it is maintained there by a species of sympathy that links all bodies together and sustains them in equilibrium; that there is a power which, without decomposing itself, has the marvelous secret of varying things infinitely; that one can, in um, regard it as a principle if order and regularity that produces eminently everything that can be produced in this vast universe.

"Know, my dear children," Zachiel said, "that everything there is in nature has need of being nourished and substantiated; the grosser elements nourish the more subtle; the earth nourishes the sea and the earth, jointly with the sea, nourishes the air; the latter, in its turn, serves as nourishment or the ethereal fires, commencing with the Moon, whose vapors also exhale in their turn from its humid continent, the nourishment necessary to the higher stars; and the Sun from which all light departs, receives in its turn from those stars a tribute of humid exhalations, in drinking in the evening from the waters of their Ocean. It is good that you know that the air is a fluid eight hundred times lighter than water. A man ordinarily supports a mass of air of twenty-six thousand pounds, and without the elastic faculty of that medium, a burden so enormous would crush him instantly. The weight of the air is a discovery owed to Torricelli, a disciple of the famous Galileo. Pascal has carried out famous experiments to demonstrate it.[41]

"The emblem of which these scholars make use to represent nature is a circle painted blue and speckled with flames, in the middle of which is a serpent with the head of a hawk; the flames, the serpent and the hawk's head represent the tributes of the divinity, and the circle divinity itself; they are convinced that nature cherishes its works equally, as she shares its benefits equally between humans and animals."

---

[41] As reported in Pacal's "Traité de la pesanteur de la masse de l'air" [Treatise on the Weight of the Mass of the Air] (1653)

Chapter VI
The Genius takes us to the City of Philosophers

Monime, little accustomed to exercise, feeling extremely fatigued by an almost continuous march, asked the genius to allow us to rest at the entrance to a valley formed by two hills crowned with verdant trees; a gentle zephyr moderated the heat of the place with its breath. Through a gap, we could see one of the gates of the City of Philosophers.

It was in that charming place that the genius, in order to restore our strength, gave us a few drops of the admirable balm that also augmented our desire for instruction. Perceiving that it was necessary to continue his observations without interruption, Zachiel engaged Monime to follow the road leading to the City of Philosophers, at which we soon arrived.

In the middle of that city stands a very spacious edifice; its foundations are made of the philosophical stone. Large galleries distribute the apartments, which the Graces have embellished personally with numerous paintings, in which they seem to be represented everywhere. A frieze ornamented with festoons crowns the superb edifice, which the genius named as the Palace of Philosophers.

The majority of those great men live together, and live in a tender liaison and a perfect unity. They do not recognize the base jealousy that degrades so many men of letters in other worlds, and is nevertheless only too commonplace among them.

"More than one example ought to inform you, charming Monime," said Zachiel, that envy is a kind of epidemic malady that is communicated in almost all hearts. "The malady easily passes from the great to the people, although it seems that there ought not to be any jealousy between people who seem so distant from one another by birth, condition, eminent positions or the great dignities that render the former illustrious; one can also add character, which education ought to have perfected. Are you not astonished that, in spite of the different ways that the spheres inhabited by humans, the air of which is purer, more fluid or heavier, ought to influence their humor, you have nevertheless remarked on all these worlds that the same self-regard seems to be engraved in all hearts? It is that self-regard which has always provoked envy among illustrious men of every kind; there are almost no worlds in which people only suffer with regret that a man still alive demands by his virtues, his merit and his great talents a species of veneration and respect that, in elevating him above others, seems at the same time to be lowering those who are forced to honor his virtues; that is what has caused some scholars to say that the glory of a living hero wounds the eyes of those who are his witnesses, because they draw too humiliating a parallel between his elevation and their pettiness."

When we had entered the palace, we remarked a great assembly of people of both sexes gathered in a very spacious room. Curious to know the reason for it, Monime asked Zachiel to inform us.

"Don't be surprised," said the genius, "by the enthusiasm of all these scholars. Know that each of them is honored to participate in the reception of Fontenelle, who has just arrived on the sphere of the Sun.[42] That scholar has furnished a rather long career on the globe of the Earth; he is one of the most agreeable great intellects that France has produced. His works are known to you; you have admired them on more than one occasion, and I can assure you that one of the genii of the first class has often presided over his labor; let us follow him into the hall of the Academy."

It was in that hall that we heard the celebrated orators, the thunderers of eloquence that no one can resist. Cicero, charged with making the speech that would sing the praises of Fontenelle, pronounced the harangue with the unction that touches and the vehemence that excites, and his rapid eloquence took possession of the hearts of all the great men; philosophers, jurisconsultants and poets all applauded a discourse that Apollo himself would not have disavowed.

I shall not indulge myself by naming here all the great men, as many ancient as modern, who ornamented that admirable assembly. The genius pointed out Cardinal Richelieu, who held one of the foremost places in that Academy; his physiognomy announced the grandeur of his soul and the vast extent of his enlightenment. Zachiel assured us that he had always been greater by virtue of his intelligence and talents than the dignities that he acquired.

On emerging from that hall we went through a long gallery that distributes the apartments of the philosophers who live in the palace, each of which consists of a bedroom and a study. In one such apartment was Homer, who seemed to us to be very busy making corrections to the Iliad. We thought at first that Aristotle was serving as his secretary, but the genius, perceiving our error, told us that Aristotle had brought light into the darkness of nature and is the father of criticism in art.

"Time, whose justice is slow but sure, has finally put truth in the place of error, and has broken the statues of the philosopher, but has confirmed the decisions of the critic; destitute of observations, he mistook chimeras for facts; formed in the school of Plato and by the writings of Homer, Sophocles, Euripides and Thucydides, he drew his rules from the nature of things and the knowledge of the human heart, and clarified them by examples of the greatest models. Two thousand years have gone by since Aristotle; critics have perfected their art, but they are not yet in accord as to the object of their endeavors. The true critic cannot dissimulate that his task is only to begin; he weights, he com-

---

[42] Fontenelle died in 1757, so the scenes set in the City of Philosophers apparently take place after that date, however anachronistic it might be with regard to the dating of the scenes set on Earth..

pares, he doubts, he decides; exact and impartial, he only yields to reason, or to the authority that is the reason of facts.

"The most respectable name," the genius continued, sometimes yields to the testimony of writers to whom circumstances alone give a temporary weight; prompt and fecund in resources, but without false subtleties, he dares to sacrifice the most brilliant and the most specious hypothesis and does not speak to his masters in the language of his conjectures; a friend of the truth, he seeks the kind of proof that suits his subject, and does not bring the scythe of analysis to the delicate beauties that are effaced by the slightest rude touch. Also not content with a sterile admiration, however, he digs down into the most hidden principles of the human heart in order to render reason to his pleasures and distastes; modest and sensate, he does not display his conjectures as truths, his inductions as facts, nor his probabilities as demonstrations. But that is enough talk on that subject; let's go into this study."

We followed the genius, and saw Virgil, who was reading a few passages from his *Aeneid*, with considerable emphases, to the Emperor Augustus. The Prince left, and Virgil, in order to oblige Zachiel, agreed to explain the antiquities—the flight of a band of exiles, the battle with a few villagers and the establishment of a hovel—that form the much-vaunted labors of the pious Aeneas, which the poet has ennobled, and who was able, in ennobling them, to render them even more interesting by means of an illusion too fine not to evade the common run of readers. That poet embellished heroic mores, but he embellished them without disguising them. The pastor Latinus and the seditious Turnus are transformed into powerful kings; all Italy fears for its liberty; Aeneas triumphs over men and gods. Virgil also causes us to reflect on to the Trojans all the glory of the Romans, and the founder of Rome causes the founder of Lavinium to disappear. It is a fire that ignites; so it sets the whole world ablaze. Aeneas, if one can hazard the expression, contains the seed of all his descendants. But Virgil never employs his artistry better than when he descends into the Inferno with his hero, seemingly liberating his imagination.

The genius made us look at the Georgics, which we read with the keen appetite inspired by the beautiful and the delightful pleasure that the amenity of their subject inspires in every honest and sensible soul. One can say that Horace and Virgil fixed the taste of the Romans.

We quit Virgil to follow the genius, who took us into another apartment, where Epicurus, Pliny, Lucian and a few others had gathered in order to discuss wit.[43] This is how one of those philosophers explained to us the sentiment one ought to have of it.

---

[43] The word *esprit*, here initially translated as "wit," is one of the broadest in the French language, also translatable as "mind," "spirit" and "intelligence." The consequent analysis, although certainly focused on wit to begin with, soon embraces the other overlapping meanings—eventually substituted in the transla-

"Wit," he said, "is a quality of the soul that elevates and animates common sentiments and simple expressions, by giving them the elegant and fine appearance that attracts admiration and simultaneously causes surprise; it serves to animate our thoughts, to render our expressions vivid, agreeable and new. Wit can only be the effect of a brilliant, fertile imagination enriched by a great variety of ideas. One ought to distinguish two sorts of wit; that which is filled with fire rises more rapidly, and goes further, but it rarely smiles in that elevation; whereas a brilliant wit, which has vivacity, amusement and justice, does not stray far from its subject; thus, one can be compared to an excellent cook who gives an exquisite taste to the simplest dishes, and the other to an admirable seamstress who embellishes the most common of fabrics with rich embroidery. There are such beautiful productions of wit that everyone appreciates then and admires them without knowing the reason. There are others that are so fine and delicate that few people are capable of noticing all their beauties. We also have some that, without being perfect, are nevertheless spoken with so much artistry, sustained and conducted with so much grace, that they merit being admired.

"The manner of forming ideas is what gives character to the human mind. The intelligence that only forms ideas on real relationships is a solid intelligence; that which is content with apparent relationships is a superficial intelligence; that which sees relationships as they are is a just intelligence; that which appreciates them poorly is a false intelligence; and that which does not compare at all is an imbecile; thus, the more-or-less great aptitude in comparing ideas and finding relationships is what makes humans more or less intelligent.

"True genius is simple; it is neither scheming nor active; it does not compare itself to anyone; all its resources are its own, it experiences itself without appreciating itself. One sees people who, by a kind of instinct, of whose cause they are unaware themselves, decide what to present to their intelligence, and always make the right decision; those individuals, guided simply by taste, only judge on their natural light; their reason is not obscured by self-regard; everything within them acts in concert, everything is in the same tone, and that accord enables them to judge objects soundly and form a veritable idea of them.

"Let us seek now," the scholar continued, "for the physical cause of intelligence, which I believe one can attribute to a well-composed temperament, in which is found an assemblage of extremely delicate fibers, combined with a great abundance of very subtle animal spirits; these spirits must have a very rapid movement in order to put the soul in a state to operate with more vivacity; it is perhaps only by that means that the imagination can travel easily throughout nature, in which it contemplates an infinity of objects, and, observing the resem-

---

tion—in a fashion that the more divisive English language cannot reproduce uniformly. The variegation is illustrated in advance by the individuals supposedly involved in the discussion, who include the satirical humorist Lucian, the natural historian Pliny and the philosopher Epicurus.

blance or the difference of their qualities, sorts out and recombines the ideas that suit it best. From that arise the striking thoughts, beautiful allusions, bold metaphors and sentiments that excite the admiration and cause the most common thoughts to appear in a new form, which never fails to excite a kind of pleasure in us that makes itself felt throughout our being."

We passed into Cicero's study. The genius made us examine several of his works, including his treatise on Friendship, on which the genius made some reflections.

"Human souls," he said to us, "need to be coupled in order to bring out their full value, and the combined strength of friends is incomparably greater than the sum of their individual strengths. Nothing has more weight in the human heart than the voice of recognized friendship, which only ever speaks to us in our interest; one can believe that a friend is mistaken, but not that he wants to deceive us; if we sometimes resist his advice, we are never scornful of it.

"Although one only needs oneself to repress one's inclinations, a friend is often necessary to help us discern those that it is necessary to follow. The amity of a wise person gazes from another point of view on the objects that it is in our interest to know well. Friendship is a keen and celestial sentiment, which gives warmth to the arguments of a friend; the expansions of friendship are retained before a witness, whoever he might be; one wants, so to speak, to fall back on one another; the slightest distractions are troubling, the slightest constrain insupportable; when the heart puts words into the mouth, it is not possible to pronounce them without hesitation; it seems that the presence of a single stranger retains the sentiment and represses souls that would understand one another so well without him. The charm of the society that reigns between two friends consists of the opening of the heart that puts all thoughts in common and makes each one sense himself as he ought to be, and show himself as he really is.

"A vulgar attachment can pass for good, but never friendship; it might be an exchange or contact like others, but it is the holiest of all. The word 'friend' has no other expression than itself. The progress of friendship is natural, it has its reason in the situation of friends and their character; as one advances in age, all sentiments become concentrated, one loses something cherished every day without being able to replace it; one thus dies by degrees until one eventually only loves oneself; one has ceased to feel and to live without ceasing to exist; but a sensitive heart employs all its strength against that anticipated death; when the cold reaches the extremities, it gathers around it all its natural warmth; the more it loses the more it attaches itself to what remains, and it clings to the final object by means of the bonds of all the others."

After this speech, the genius made us admire among Cicero's works his treatise on Offices, that on Laws, that on Old Age, the Philippics, and others in which that prince of eloquence speaks eulogistically about the theories of the Platonists, the Peripatetics and the Stoics, but shows much more scorn for other sects, which he attacks with force and vehemence.

Zachiel assured us that the eloquence of the great man had acquired rights over the hearts of his fellow citizens all the more certain because, as an enemy of all tyranny and all constraint, he never employed anything but persuasion alone to win them over. From his earliest youth he studied all the sciences with an indefatigable application, and he filled his mind with all the knowledge that might ornament and embellish it, but he only began to speak in public at the age of twenty-seven; that was for a cause that attracted the attention of the entire Republic to him.

The most prudent orators, fearful of offending Sulla, had abandoned the affair of Roscius, accused of parricide; Cicero alone had the boldness to undertake his defense against the dictator's favorite. The success that action had was the first step of his glory, but the advantage was too striking not to arouse Sulla's jealousy and inspire the animosity of Chrysogonus; the freed slave who had rendered himself master of the man who was master of the entire Republic provoked against Cicero by his underhand maneuvers a persecution that lasted until the dictator's death, with the consequence that Cicero was obliged to leave Rome in order to avoid the storm ready to burst over his head. He nevertheless took the precaution of putting around the rumor that he was only leaving on the advice of his physician, who had counseled him, in order to preserve his health, to suspend his studies for a while.

Cicero adopted that pretext in order not to diminish the glory of his action by an appearance of fear or lightness that might have been criticized by the very people whose approval he had gained. Thus, he spent some time at his residence in Athens, where, finding himself free and rid of any other care, he studied the various opinions of the different sects of philosophy that were then in vogue. The ardent thirst that animated him to instruct himself in all the sciences engaged him to visit all of Asia in order to converse with those who had the most reputation; it was by that means that he took advantage of his travels, delivering himself to a study much more organized and more assiduous than he had been able to carry out in his study in Rome.

In the course of his travels he met Apollonius Molon in Rhodes, who had been his teacher of eloquence in Italy. That orator, hearing him recite a few of his pieces in Greek, could not help saying: "Cicero will steal from the Greeks the only glory that remains to them, in surpassing others by eloquence, to the honor to the Romans, who have already carried off that of valor."

During his travels Cicero learned astronomy, geometry, ancient and modern philosophy, the theology of his religion, Athenian law and all the laws of Greece. Diodorus taught him the mystery of Pythagorean numbers and harmony; he studied the morality of the Stoics under Philo and Clitomachus; Zeno and Phaedrus showed him the doctrine of Epicurus, which he had criticized in his writings. Eventually, he returned to Rome after Sulla's death with a mind enriched with a wealth of beautiful knowledge and health fortified by the exercise he had been obliged to take in the course of his voyages.

Zachiel then took us to see Thucydides, whom we found with Demosthenes; the latter appeared to be studying the great author's works, whose narration is always simple, clear and natural; but that simplicity has something noble sustained by the beauty of expression and the verity from which he never strays— quite different from that of Herodotus, who preceded him, whose manner of writing is more diverting by virtue of its great variety and the turn he gives to events or matters related to them; as he is not constrained by the truth, it is easier for him to be amusing and to please.

The genius told us that Demosthenes had prescribed the usage of a kind of popular morality, all of whose maxims related to the public good, glory and the interest of the fatherland; it was by that conduct that he had acquired the confidence of people to such a high degree; his advice was heeded as salutary counsel and he was regarded as the tutelary genius of the fatherland, because everyone was convinced that he only opened his mouth to support the authority of the laws and in the service of the State; the honor and probity of which he made the profession, and the evocation of the Gods that he never failed to make in his speeches, had procured him the reputation of piety and religion that has such a powerful effect on the mind, because that virtue is the rule and measure of all the others.

Nothing contributed more to the credit of Demosthenes than the liberty he took in declaiming against Philip. It is certain that one cannot imagine anything more glorious to a simply citizen of Athens than the boldness he showed in declaring against a King so powerful in his republic that he was dividing all minds; but the power of that Prince, his armies, his threats and his promises were never able to shake him, and all the gold in Macedonia was incapable of dazzling him; he was always impenetrable to the offers that were made to him in the attempt to corrupt him, which caused Antipater, Alexander's successor, to say that if he had had a minister as incorruptible as Demosthenes, he would have been invulnerable. How many sovereigns could justly say the same!

What Antipater added gives an even greater idea of the virtue of that orator. "It was," he said, "solely the love of the fatherland that made him involve himself in the government of the State and enabled him to employ virtue in a position that others only ought with a view to increasing their fortune. What would one not give to have a man resembling him, in order to have his advice on present matters and to hear that vice of liberty in the midst of the applause of flatterers? I am only too conscious of how useful advice as sincere as his might be to me amid the disguises of the Court."

That prince, who had retained nothing of Alexander but his ambition, doubtless believed that he would soon have rendered himself master of the world with a minister so disinterested, because no one could corrupt him, deceive him or take him by surprise. What would he not have done to have him? But Demosthenes, by virtue of an unparalleled grandeur of soul, preferred death to all Antipater's caresses, and, taking poison in the presence of Archias, who pressed him to yield to the power of the vanquisher of Greece, said to him: "Tell your master that Demosthenes does not owe anything to the tyrant of his fatherland."

Such was the probity of the great man, of whom Lucian made a perfect eulogy. By his eloquence he had the art of rendering himself the master of the mind of the proudest, most inconstant and most intractable people there very was. That rebellious populace, jealous of the merit of those who distinguished themselves in its republic, nevertheless submitted its reason to that of Demosthenes, constrained to yield to the weight of such great authority.

Chapter VII
Further Observations

The genius conducted us then to the study of Aristotle, who was instructing several of his disciples on veritable eloquence. He said that it excites disturbance in the mind by overturning thought and taming reason, that it only progresses noisily, that its features dazzle like lightning and strike like thunderbolts; that it is similar to the whirlwinds that topple the tallest trees as easily as the weakest reeds; so that persuasion is a species of conquest won over the human heart. He added that an eloquent orator ought to apply himself to knowing the intellect and the interests of those he wishes to persuade, trying to match his attitude, his tone and is speech to their thoughts in order not to trouble their harmony with anything foreign.

It is true that the human heart is the most impenetrable thing in the world and that it requires great attention to be able to fathom the depths of that abyss, or to find the means of recognizing and disentangling the detours that it is necessary to take in order to enter into it and implant intelligence there, which can scarcely be accomplished without the help of the passions—which is to say that, like a conqueror, one can attempt surprises there, sometimes by fear or by hope, sometimes by exciting desires, by igniting anger or, in sum, by giving birth to any of the movements capable of interesting it in favor of the speaker; but unless one has a perfect knowledge of the heart one is attempting to reach, and can find the places that might render it sensitive, success will always be difficult.

But how rare that gift of touching hearts and mastering them is! The inconstancy of humans, the changeability of their inclinations, the alteration of their humors, the diversity of their interests, conjunctures, places and even of fortunes, often play a large part in the general disposition of minds, especially in the great events that ought to be subjects of perpetual attention, when it is a question of inspiring new resolutions in people one wants to convert to one's views or opinions.

After the instruction of that philosopher, we went with him to Pindar's apartment, where Socrates, Plato, Thucydides, Hyperides, Epicurus, Pythagoras and several other philosophers had gathered. I shall not report the conversation that those scholars had together, for fear of boring my reader with an overly long narration; I shall only say that Monime was greatly impressed by the precepts of Pythagoras.

That philosopher asserts that everyone who has a head capable of it ought to work incessantly to maintain the harmony that makes the happiness of individuals and families, and which even extents throughout the body of the State. To that effect one ought to spare no effort to expel ignorance from the mind, and intemperance and evil desires from the heart, dissension and quarrels from families, and factions and all partisan spirit from society. The philosopher recommends decency and modesty in particular; he criticizes any excess in joy and in sadness; he demands that one should be always equable in the various events of life, and advises never speaking or acting without careful consultation.

On emerging from the gallery of philosophers we traversed a vast courtyard, at the end of which was a large square building whose dome extended to the clouds. That building is inhabited by the greatest poets; Homer, Euripides, Seneca, Horace, Corneille and the tender Racine were lodged there together; Juvenal, Terence, Plautus, Anacreon, Marot and Molière were opposite. Aesop and the charming and naïve La Fontaine entertained one another with their fables, deploring the misfortunes of human beings, who cannot suffer the truth unless it is masked by the envelope of a fable or an allegory. Can one not say that the truth needs to borrow the face of the false in order to be agreeably received by the human mind? But lies naturally enter there in their own form. Boileau-Despreaux and the famous Rousseau occupy the same apartment there; Fontenelle and Crébillon, newly arrived,[44] had elected to share.

We remarked to the left a lovely edifice designed to accommodate illustrious women—which is to say, all those who have distinguished themselves in the other worlds by their science and their talents; a long terrace terminates that edifice, the exposure of which is admirable, and which leads to an arbor of myrtle and roses. Monime, enchanted by that charming place, asked Zachiel for permission to rest there.

When we arrived at the arbor, the genius pointed out Madame de Maintenon, who, with a majestic and tender expression, was showing Madame de Sévigné several letters that a skillful secretary had written in her name, but which she disavowed in part. Sappho, Deshoulieres, de Villedieu and several others were walking on the terrace, among whom the genius pointed out to us the ingenious du Châtelet, the Urania of a scholar of our world, whom Zachiel assured us is one of the greatest geniuses of our century.[45] He also pointed out Pascal, Labruyère, Fénelon, Bossuet, Montesquieu, Bayle, La Rochefoucauld and a large number of others whose merit had brought them to the sphere of the Sun.

The genius then took us into a large hall where all the citizens gathered in order to hear instructions that were given publicly. Those instructions, similar to rays of sunlight, were generously communicated to the great and small alike, all

---

[44] Prosper Jolyon de Crébillon died in 1762, the same year as the publication of the early volumes of the *Voyages de Milord Céton*.

[45] The references to the French female poets are to Antoinette du Ligier de la Garde Deshoulières (1638-1694) and Marie-Catherine Desjardins de Villedieu (c.1640-1683). The ultimate reference is to Voltaire—still alive and very active when the present text was published—who was famously housed for some time by Émilie du Châtelet (1706-1749).

of whom are able to participate equally in the radiance of the star, the immortal source of light and science.

Zachiel told us to listen attentively to the discourse that one of the scholars was about to pronounce, in order not to let any knowledge that might be useful to us escape, to put us in the picture with regard to various sentiments, and to give us, at the same time, an idea of their way of thinking.

"Let us make use of our reason," the orator said, "to seek the truth; but let us be wary of going astray in little-beaten paths; the enlightenment of the mind teaches it to doubt, and to stop when it cannot clarify its doubts. You might perhaps reply to me that doubt is devoid of action, which all humans need; however, since we are seeking to discover the truth, we cannot yet be sure of having found it, although people employ incredible courage every day in searching for things they are obstinately determined to find; they doubtless believe that what has escaped the enlightenment of others is reserved for their discovery, or at least they hope so—and that hope, although often vain, is always agreeable to them. In sum, if the truth is not evident to one or another, the pleasure of the same error consoles them; it is their due.

"Our most knowledgeable philosophers," the orator continued, "tell us that we are only dispersed fragments of the same divinity, or separate drops of his essence, volatile spirits of eternity, fixed by destiny or by hazard in the vehicles of time and matter. You ought not to be unaware that the entire mass of the corporeal universe is merely an extremely loose-knit fabric drawn from the entrails of an infinite being and worked by him with an inimitable artistry in order to take on forms, ideas and immaterial souls; such are the natural productions of the eternal intelligence. It is therefore certain that we are as many disguised particles of the divinity, reduced into bodies by certain hidden magnets or charms, with which we have a sympathy. But without settling on that opinion, we ought to agree that there is nothing firm and constant except the heavens and the stars that compose them, and which always persevere in the immutability of their courses, which never change their globe and never quit their posts. Apollo rises and sets at accustomed times; his sister constantly observes the periods marked out for her in waxing and waning; those two stars only vary like the seasons of the year—which is to say, with an admirable regularity and ever-constant and fixed recurrences.

"But it is necessary not to believe that all these worlds resemble one another. Since our observations have fixed on the vortex that contains the globe of Mercury we have remarked a perpetual transmigration of states and forms of government. By the observations that have been made, and examining the vials of common sense contained in the forest, it has been discovered that the world in question is presently agitated by a perpetual flux and reflux; the pachas, like chemists, are no longer occupied with anything except extracting the quintessence of the substance of their subjects, in order to make it pass into their coffers and those of their creatures, not leaving anything to poor people anything but the terrestrial matter, and to the sovereigns anything but the murmurs and plaints of the citizens. These calamities, which we ought not to ignore, ought to make us bless the divinity, offering him new sacrifices, in order to render him thanks for having brought us to a world filled with light, justice and equity, and that the prince who governs us wants to share his gifts equally among all his faithful subjects."

The philosopher, after having extended himself on politics and the fashion of good government, took his leave of the assembly.

The genius took us into another building, which he told us was the residence of the seven sages of Greece. When we went in, the first one who was offered to our eyes was Thales, a man of great intelligence, who nevertheless allowed himself to die of hunger and thirst rather than leave a theater in which he was watching a gladiatorial combat.

Solon appeared next, and we had a rather long conversation with him on the laws that he gave to Athens. "The establishment of a body of laws," the scholar old us, "is necessary to any administration. The project that I formed, in giving laws to my fatherland, was to establish rules that could combine public safety with the individual interest of each citizen. The administration of justice, that precious emanation of the divinity, ought to be based primarily on the forms appropriate to it: no individual can permit himself to violate them without attacking the fiber and sustenance of the State; justice would no longer be anything but arbitrary, nothing but a vain word, as little redoubtable to crime as useless to innocence.

"Thus, laws, so necessary to public economy, apply equally to all branches of society; they avoid many evils and procure many goods. If the law is only the will of the person who governs, it cannot be known with certainty; hence, a great many citizens will believe themselves to be authorized to violate the rule of the law written by the hand of the almighty in the living tablets of the heart, in the hope of not being exposed to punishment; and those who follow it will only experience the interior testimony of the security that ought to be found in the protection of the known law, when it is never violated.

"Now, if the offense or the crime is not fixed, nor the punishment prescribed, that is one motive less or probity, for which one must necessarily substitute, as much for those who might be tempted to commit the crime as those who might be victims of it; in any case, if a sovereign wants to dispense governing by written and published laws, he has to apply the government himself, and it is to be feared that he might succumb under a burden that no one is capable of sustaining alone; if it is by the ministry of some of his subjects, it is again to be feared that the inferiority of their rank might expose them, either to temptations from which one cannot hope that they will always have the strength to defend themselves, or prejudices that it might perhaps be impossible for them to overcome. Thus, to exercise administration with equity, there must necessarily be a law that fixes the offense and prescribes the punishment; then, integrity alone suffices and the sentence no longer depends on opinion but on facts. Justice will rarely be corrupted, and in the case where integrity might be lacking, the fault for that cannot be thrown back on any error; one ought at least to be given pause by the idea of the infamy and danger that will result from a manifest prevarication."

Solon added that he had left his body in Cyprus after eighty years of life on the globe of the Earth, instructing his principal officers to burn it and throw the ashes to the winds, dreading that they might be taken back to Athens, because at the sight of his relics the Athenians might have thought themselves freed from the oaths they had made to observe his laws, at least until his return. The sage gave us his epitaph to read, which he had composed himself to be engraved on the tomb he had had constructed before his departure; perhaps you will not be sorry to find it here:

> *I leave to my friends all care for my glory,*
> *And I do not want in my memory*
> *Any other tomb but their hearts*
> *Nor any eulogy but their tears.*

After quitting Solon we went into the apartment of King Periander, the Prince who tried in vain to cut through the isthmus of Corinth. Zachiel told us that Periander loved his wife the Queen so much that he had great difficulty quitting her after her death.

We joined Cleobulus, who was reputed to be the most handsome man in Greece. That sage had learned philosophy from an Egyptian; he assured us that the worship that the nation in question rendered to animals was only a civil and political ritual, without the foundations of their religion having any part of it. As they drew their principal subsistence from the cultivation of the soil, they made a law by which they declared that all the animals that served for labor, and those that destroyed vermin, were sacred and inviolable, and that anyone who killed them, deliberately or accidentally, would be punished by death, regarding the animals as instruments of the divine providence that had given them for the support of human life; it was only in that view that they were consecrated.

We then saw the famous Chilon, who died of joy when he heard news of a victory won by the sons of Olympus. These are the three dicta that acquired him his reputation as a sage: the greatest knowledge is to know oneself; never borrow for the sake of appearances; and never commence a lawsuit.

Chilon took us to the apartment of Bias, Prince of Priene in Ionia. That prince was so content with his intelligence that when the city was taken he left, swearing that he was carrying all his wealth with him.

The seventh sage is Pittacus of Mytilene, who liberated Lesbos from the tyrant Melanchrus, and who killed Phrynon, the chief of his enemies, in a duel.

"I can hardly believe," Monime said, "that they are the seven sages mentioned in all our histories. Agree, my dear Zachiel, that if such individuals appeared in our world nowadays, they might well be taken for fools—although I except Solon. But who is that I see coming. Is it not an eighth sage?"

"That is Scarron," said the genius, smiling, "who has translated a few morsels of Virgil's *Aeneid* and Ovid's *Metamorphoses* into burlesque verse."

"I'm charmed to meet him," said Monime. "I remember having read a few of his works, which amused me greatly, and I'm convinced that he's worth as much as all your sages on his own."

"Sir," I said to Scarron, advancing toward him, "here is a beautiful lady who prefers you to all sages."

"My Lady honors me greatly," said Scarron, "but I can assure her that I never composed any of those stout volumes that try to prove that malady, dolor or suffering, combined with lack of fortune, ought not to diminish the cheerfulness of a sage."

"However," said Monime, "you were much better able than anyone else to prove it, since all your works offer very convincing evidence that you have always conserved, amid an infinity of woes, the joviality and patience that is the best kind of wisdom—or, to put it better, the only one, for who can boast of being sufficiently independent of nature not to fear any surprise?"

"Unfortunately, however, in spite of the savant discourses of your philosophers, if they were to speak in good faith, they would confess that she always conserves her rights, that she has initial impulses that they never escape, unless they become true automata set up in unison."

Scarron left us after saying the most agreeable things to Monime, and went to rejoin Marot.

A little further on, we encountered several disciples of Pythagoras, including Philolaus, who was from Corinth. That philosopher had formed the republic of Thebes and had given it its laws; the Thebans regarded him as their oracle; they believed him to be descended from a daughter of Bacchus named Bacchea; his works were so highly esteemed that Plato, who was not rich, bought three volumes of his for a price of twelve thousand livres, which Dion of Syracuse had given him for his subsistence. That philosopher treated amour in an entirely metaphysical fashion, but some reproached him for not always having the mind alone for his subject and often having put the body into consideration.

Zachiel also pointed out Anaxarchus, whom the tyrant Nicocreon had had crushed in a mortar.

Chapter VIII
Further Observations

Suetonius, advancing toward the genius, complained bitterly of having been confused on the Earth with a host of historians that were accused of being liars—which is to say, those partisan flatterers or blind individuals who spoke the truth by caprice and slander and lies by inclination.

"It's true," Suetonius added, "that a poor historian often finds himself severely embarrassed by the constraint he has to flatter the sovereign, especially when he is charged with recording the events that occurred in his reign. However, it is the interest of the nation that permits a scholar to tell the truth without flattery and without dread, in order that posterity can, in reading the history of its ancestors, learn to imitate the good examples and distance itself, even with horror, for the conduct of the wicked. It's certain that a man who attempts to describe history ought to begin by ridding himself of the natural sentiments of love and hatred; he ought not to envisage fatherland, relatives or friends, since he is becoming the judge of the events he treats and the princes whose actions he describes."

That conversation was interrupted by Kepler, one of the astronomers who had come to met us on the plain. The scholar, recognizing me as one of his compatriots,[46] told me that he was glad to meet us in order to procure us some further lessons; he took us into a very large hall filed with various instruments useful to their art.

In the middle of the hall was a table on which were arranged spheres, globes, compasses, quarter-circles, astrolabes, Justebrigne's proportional compass, whose true inventor was Flaviogicia, a Neapolitan, Newton's telescope, a microscope, the barometer and thermometer of Farinmith, Volq's aerometer, Bayle's pneumatic machine, a gnomon, a graphometer, an electric machine and a thousand other instruments as useful as they are curious, with several charts full of astronomical observations.[47] Facing them was a venerable old man, atten-

---

[46] This presumably means that Kepler recognizes Seaton as a native of Earth, given that he was not English.

[47] I have left the names in this passage as they appear in the original text, although they are badly garbled, in a fashion suggesting that the typesetter had difficulty reading the author's handwriting. We know what Mme. Robert probably wrote because this paragraph is obviously copied from a list included in the text of the lunar fantasy *Le Voyageur philosophe dans un pays inconnu aux habitants de la terre* (1761; tr. as *The Philosophical Voyager*) by the pseudonymous "Monsieur de Listonai," which Mme. Robert evidently read and which might well have played some part in inspiring her to write an interplanetary fantasy of

298

tive to examining the course of the stars, who, with the aid of a telescope that Galileo had built with a great deal of care and application, was trying to discover whether the planets rotated on their axes, whether the routes of the air were composed of little stars, whether eclipses occur when the Mon has the whole of its obscure half turned toward the earth, or whether it has to be directly under the sun to form a eclipse.

That scholar, after long application, quit his telescope in order to write a kind of century, in which he announced that the heaven of Saturn and that of trepidation having not completed their course, another eighty thousand years would have to pass before the celestial globes completed their cycle.

"There," said Monime, smiling, "is a philosopher who is not unknown to me, and I'm much mistaken if his portrait isn't seen at the head of all the almanacs on our world. My God, how well they capture his face!"

"It's true," said Zachiel, "that that is the famous Nostradamus, one of the greatest astronomers who ever appeared on the globe of the Earth; it is him who predicted several things that have happened, and left such beautiful centuries, which everyone strives to fit to extraordinary events.

"I ought not to leave you unaware," the genius continued, "that in the East Indies of your world, their astronomers are firmly convinced that when the sun and the moon are eclipsed, they are driven to it by a certain demon that has exceedingly black claws, and which, in order to cause them distress, delights in extending the claws over the two stars, which it tries to seize, in order to deprive them of light; and the poor Indians, convinced of that folly, throw themselves into streams and submerge themselves up to the neck; their devotion causes them to remain there as long as the eclipse lasts, in order to obtain from the Sun and the Moon that they employ all their strength and skill to defend themselves against the malign demon.

"Others believe that the two stars have quarreled when they eclipse one another, and attempt a thousand extravagances to reconcile them. But nothing approaches the folly of the Greeks, who believed the Moon to be ensorcelled by magicians who make it descend from the sky in order to spread a certain malefi-

---

her own. Listonai also garbled the name Fahrenheit, as Farenreith, but correctly attributed the pneumatic machine to [Robert] Boyle, and grave the name of the inventor of a better aerometer as Wolf (meaning Christian Wolff). Mme. Robert presumably wrote those names as Listonai gave them, although they did not reach the printed text unscathed. Listonai rendered the name of Juste Brigge correctly, but recorded that Brigge really was the inventor of the proportional compass wrongly attributed to Galileo, and mentions (the fictitious) "Flavio Gioia" as the true inventor of a different kind of compass mentioned two lines further on, the intermediate text being skipped in Mme. Robert's list, either by her or her typesetter.

cent foam over their herbs; that is why they purify the air with perfumes as soon as the eclipse is over."

We then passed into another very spacious hall, where the majority of the inhabitants wanting to witness the instructions of the philosophers were indistinctly assembled. Ptolemy, Copernicus, Archytas and several others were there. A dispute arose between the first two, who had always had different sentiments regarding the course of the stars.

Ptolemy sustained that it was necessary for the Earth to be permanently at rest at the center of its vortex, that all the celestial bodies had to make their revolutions around it in order to illuminate it, which must naturally form different circles in accordance with their distance. But Copernicus, gripped by a noble astronomical fury, interrupted him and sustained in German that the Earth was not worthy to occupy the principal place among the stars, that that honor was only due to the Sun, that he was certain that all the planets had to describe their circles around that luminous globe and that, in consequence, it ought to be the center of the circle described by Mercury, Venus coming next, followed by the Earth, which, more distant, ought for that reason to describe a larger circle than the two preceding plants; Mars, Jupiter and Saturn ought to follow in accordance with their rank, but the last-named must take far longer to make its revolution than any of the other planets.

"Thus," Copernicus added, "all that remains to us is the Moon, which I permit to follow the Earth, always turning around it and gratifying it with all her variations."

Archytas, a Pythagorean philosopher, approved Copernicus' sentiment, and, in examining the vortex of the Sun, he considered that star as a fixed star burning with its own light. They wondered together what the composition of that globe might be, as well as that of the planets rotating around it, that of the satellites or moons that companied some of them; then they calculated exactly the distances of the heavenly bodies contained within the Sun's vortex, as well their rotation, both about their own axes and around the star that is their common center. They explained the different sentiments of the great astronomers, and the nature of the known comets, regarded as errant planets of a sort.

They also made an examination of the luminous spaces or clouds discovered among the stars. They concluded with a detailed account of everything that was known about the celestial bodies. The atmosphere of the Earth was examined attentively, known in this world as the region of vapors, considered as a particular planet rolling in the air; the composition of that globe was examined; its inequalities, which we call mountains; what it encloses in its bosom, the great quantity of fire and sulfur with which it is equally penetrated. Then there was talk of lightning, meteors, rainbows, the aurora borealis, the tides of the sea; they discussed the causes of tempests and other meteors; they measured the abysses contained in the seas, observing the nature of that element, the qualities that were common to it, those given to it by the diversity of climates, the inconstancy of the seasons and the difference of the winds.

We quit that school in order to go into another, where Seneca, Zeno, Chrysippus, Confucius, Pliny, Montaigne and Erasmus were conversing, along with several other philosophers whose names would be quite indifferent to my readers.

"I have difficulty conceiving why," said one of them, "in almost all worlds, the majority of humans are always combated by foolish passions and sage reflections, why they employ views so long for such a short duration, so much science for vain and useless things and so much ignorance for the most important; why the ardor for liberty and the inclination to servitude; and why, finally, they have such a great desire to be happy and such a great incapacity to achieve it."

"It is because," another of the philosophers replied, "their pretended wisdom is not an effect of their reason, and it is the sole prerogative of reason to govern humans and regulate their conduct. The human species ought to gain by instruction, but if the enlightened centuries are as corrupt as the others, it is because enlightenment has not yet spread equally enough, being concentrated in too small a number of minds, for the radiance that escapes from it to have sufficient strength to reveal to common souls the attractions and the advantages that are obtained from science and virtue, compared with the dangers of vice. Only the cultivation of the mind, the exercise of virtue and that of talents can distract us from our woes and console us in our difficulties; nature has shared needs and passions equally between the two sexes; reason could repress desires, but the first impulse, which is that of nature, always urges humans to yield to them.

"People seek to elevate themselves to the heavens to discover fixed points there; they want to know whether the it is the laws of attraction or those of impulsion that maintain the order that strikes us in the regular movement of the celestial bodies; they lose themselves in philosophical conjectures; they draw away from reason and what is known as a plan of study becomes nothing but a combination of reasoned folly that does not leave them the faculty of reflecting for a single instant about themselves."

I shall not report the rest of the conversation that those scholars had together; it covered the advantages and pleasures of union and amity, bounty and humanity, order, the admirable operations of nature, the conditions and limits of virtue, the advantages it procures, the inviolable rules of reason, the veritable philosophy, history and poetry.

Monime, finding herself a trifle weary, refused to go into another hall where enquiries were being made into the fashion of uniting physically the verities of every contradiction—for instance, blue and black, whether one can be and not be at the same time, whether there can be mountains without valleys, whether nothing is something, whether everything is nothing, whether one and two only make one, whether the smallest part is as great as the whole, whether an atom can appear to be an elephant, the manner of squaring the circle, perpetual motion and a thousand other items of knowledge as curious, of which I shall dispense with giving the list, inasmuch as several scholars of our world are very well extended on those matters.

The genius, perceiving that the air of philosophy was too heavy for Monime, took us out of the city; we reached a covered pathway, where we rested for some time. Zachiel, who did not want to waste any time that might be used for our instruction, told us that, not having been able to take us into all the halls of the Academy, because of the delicacy of Monime's temperament, he would substitute for that by reporting to us the various sentiments of the majority of those philosophers.

"Some of them," the genius continued, "assert that souls, after death, go by a principle of resemblance to join the mass of light that is the Sun, and that their sphere is formed by nothing other than the spirit of everything that has movement in all the worlds that surround it, such as Mercury, Venus and the Moon, Mars, Jupiter, its satellites, and Saturn, its moons and its great ring. They believe that as soon as a human, an animal or a plant expires, the soul of the former and the spirit of the others rises without being extinguished as far as their sphere, in the same way that one sees the light of a candle rising into a point when it reaches its end.

"When all those souls are united at the source of daylight, and are purged of the gross matter that enveloped them, they exercise functions far more noble than those of growing, sensing and reasoning, since they are united with the Sun to form vital spirits, and it is by means of the heat of thousand of millions of rectified souls that the Sun forms a kind of elixir that subsequently influences the matter of other worlds, in order to give them the power of growth and reproduction, along with that of rendering bodies capable of sensation.

"Those philosophers add that there are three forms of spirits distributed in the worlds, of which the most primitive come to animate the beasts within their sphere and cause the plants there to vegetate; that the most subtle insinuate themselves into the sun's rays, but that those of philosophers that have not contracted anything impure in their first habitation arrive entire in the sphere of day and are received there as citizens, because one ought not to doubt that the matter that composed them during their generation must have been mixed so exactly that nothing was able to separate it—similar to that which forms the heavenly bodies, all of whose parts are, so to speak, blurred by an infinity of connections that the strongest solvents would never be able to relax.

"In the vortex of this world, humans only end with natural death—which is to say that they are not subject to any malady, and normally live for eight or nine thousand years; but when by the continual excess of work and study, or their fiery temperament inclines them, the order of the matter is confused, nature, which senses that it would require more time to repair the ruins of the individual than to compose a new one, aspires to dissolve him herself—with the result that the individual is seen gradually to decay into particles similar to red ashes. That death is that of individuals of mediocre intelligence, for the philosophers claim that they do not die at all, and only change form in order to go and live again elsewhere—which, far from being a bad thing, only serves, on the contrary, to perfect their reason, their talents and their judgment, which leads them to an infinite number of new discoveries.

"However, it has been observed more than once that a philosopher, by dint of exercising his mind, fatiguing his imagination and heaping up images upon images, causes his brain to swell so much that the skull, no longer being able to contain it, is forced to explode; that fashion of dying is doubtless the most distinguished, so it is that of the greatest humans of genius.

"Almost all the inhabitants of this world enjoy a tranquility of mind and an inalterable peace; one does not see them exposed to inconstancy, nor to the treason of false friends, nor to the invisible traps of hidden enemies, because fraud is regarded among them as a crime as enormous as theft or murder; their Legislators have established as a certain principle that the care and vigilance of a ordinary mind can guarantee its wealth against the attacks of bandits, but that probity has no defense against the knavery and bad faith of humans.

"Here the philosophers live in great consideration; equally sought after by the great and all the citizens, the education of princes and princesses is confided to them; the advantage that they obtain from the education is the privilege of telling them the truth at all times and taking it to the foot of the throne, where one can safely say that it very rarely arrives on other worlds. Each of them is charged with treating the matters that affect them the most."

Monime told us that she had thought it very singular, during the visits we had just made to the schools, that Plato and Socrates had chosen for their part matters concerning amour, and that they had taken responsibility for instructing women, who, as I have already remarked, participate in the same education. Thus, one does not see them, as on other worlds, becoming victims of puerile illusion, nor slaves of prejudice; but the avidity that they have for the sciences serves to put them in a state to reflect on all the events of life, and, far from seeking to ornament themselves by ostentatious display, they only appear more modest.

These people have no temples, nor altars; they believe that it would diminish the majesty of the divinity, who fills everything by his power and his benefits, to confine that majesty, as it were, to the narrow bounds of a temple. The whole universe, they say, announces his power, his grandeur and his goodness; the entire universe, in consequence, ought to serve as temple and altar. Where can one better know and adore the divinity than in places where it is painted with most advantage? That is why they usually say their prayers in the most spacious plains or on the most elevated mountains, regarding the stars and penetrated with the divinity. Created beings are, they say, only parts of a prodigious whole, of which nature is the body and the divinity the soul; that is what shines in the stars, animates humans, flourishes in trees, lives in everything that is alive, extends everywhere without dividing, acts without being exhausted, and gives form to humans as well as animals; in sum, it fills, connects and animates everything.

Such is, in substance, a part of the education given to this people.

Chapter IX
An Encounter with Sephise, and her Story

Zachiel drew our attention to a young woman who, by virtue of the help of a genius of the first order, had just crossed the immense void that separates the planet Mars from the Sun. The two genii met without showing any surprise.

"Nelapha in this place!" said Zachiel. "I thought you had gone to Saturn."

"It's true," said Nelapha, "that the last time we met I was preparing to take that route, but in traversing the world of Mars, tender plaints reached my ears. Surprised to hear them, I descended through the clouds and I perceived by the feeble light of the stars a respectable old man who appeared to me to be in the utmost desolation. I listened to his plaints for some time without rendering myself visible.

"A confidant who accompanied him was representing to him the danger to which he would be exposed if he were discovered. The old man only replied with profound sighs; then, turning toward the sea and perceiving by its murmur that it was beginning to be agitated, he cried: 'Just Gods, will you always be insensible to my prayers? And you, impetuous winds, respect the fragile vessel that bears the object of my love; gentle zephyrs, blow away the storms, arrange yourself at the poop, gently inflate the sails; waves, flatten out, so that a light wake, skimming your placid boom, scarcely indicates the trace of her rapid course; rocks, move aside from her passage; clouds, form a veil that hides her from the eyes of those who would betray her; and you, silver-tinted moon, let your dubious light favor that fortunate flight; relent your course, refrain from reaching the horizon; wait, in order to disappear, until daylight lends her the aid of its torch.'

"Thus spoke the respectable old man, who withdrew after having lost sight of the ship that was the object of his dread and that of his hope. I followed him into his palace, where I rendered myself visible. I employed what I believed to be the greatest consolation in order to calm his dolor, promising to fly to the aid of the object of his tenderness. After having left him, faithful to my promise and guided by the desire to render to virtue the aid of which it is all too frequently deprived, I departed and traversed the sea in rapid flight; its roars made me fear that the vessel, after having been the plaything of the winds and a frightful tempest, might have broken against some rock.

"I descended, still flying over the surface of the sea, where I perceived the debris of a ship on the shores of a desert island. I advanced and found the young woman lying on the sand, rendered immobile by the sight of a frightful serpent that was about to devour her. My heart was instantly gripped by horror; an irresistible force drew me toward her; I drove the monster away and, seizing her in my arms, I enveloped her in a cloud.

"I rose up again, and cleaved the air with a rapid flight in order to come to deposit her in the Sun, where I was sure to encounter you; it is to your care that I confide her; she is worthy to accompany the amiable Monime; a spoonful of the elemental elixir that I have just made her take has entirely reanimated her spirits. The beautiful individual will tell you about her adventures. You're not unaware that I'm obliged to obey superior orders, and cannot defer the fulfillment of my mission any longer."

Nelapha then said a few words to Zachiel in a language unknown to us, after which we saw him take flight again toward the Palace of Apollo.

That encounter informed me that genii do not pay one another any compliment; they explain their desires and their will without supplication; as they never ask for anything but just things, they never find any kind of opposition.

Monime, charmed to have a traveling companion, approached the beautiful stranger, and made her a thousand tender caresses, to which she responded with abundant grace. Anxiety as to her fate was visible in her eyes, however. "Be reassured, charming individual," said Monime, taking her hands and squeezing them tenderly in her own. "If fortune has been against you until now, you ought no longer to fear its blows; the genius who has taken you under his protection is above all human powers; he will not permit you to succumb beneath the weight of your persecutions."

At his speech the young woman uttered a profound sought; her eyes filled with tears, which she tried in vain to hold back—which engaged Zachiel to confirm what Monime had said with further promises to protect her and procure her all the benefits necessary to her tranquility.

The beautiful individual, relieved by those assurances, began to show us a more serene visage; she ran her gaze over everything surrounding her, doubtless seeking to discover what the country was that she was about to inhabit, very far from thinking that she had quit the globe on which she had been born, not yet being instructed as to the plurality of worlds. But Monime, who ardently desired to learn the subject of hr distress, asked her insistently to tell us her story. Without having to be begged unduly, the young woman yielded willingly to Monime's urging and began the history of her misfortunes.

"My name is Sephise, and you see in me the unfortunate daughter of King Bolomine. My unfortunate father, forced to cede his kingdom to a man whose intrigues and underhanded maneuvers had rendered him the master of it, abandoned by his subjects, was reduced to leading a laborious life. The unfortunate prince lived for a long time in the voluntary exile that he had chosen, in the middle of a desert. I was the sole companion of his misery; my mother lost her life in bringing me into the light; a single domestic, with my nurse, formed our entire entourage, and the unfortunate Prince took responsibility for my education himself. Much greater than his woes, he instructed me of mine as soon as my reason began to develop.

"'My dear Sephise,' my father said to me one day, while holding me tenderly in his arms, "you alone are my joy and my woes; you are my felicity and my trouble; without you, life would be a burden, and it is only for you that it becomes a torment. Alas, all my philosophy abandons me when I think about the deplorable fate that hangs over us. Why must destiny, always contrary to my prayers, force us to live incessantly in the cruelest humiliation, while a usurper triumphs from our misfortunes?'

"Alas!" Sephise cried, interrupting herself, "perhaps at that moment I offended the gods, in thinking that they might have taken away my father's common sense and reason; I looked at him with eyes in which the dolor of seeing him in that state was doubtless painted. 'Oh, my father,' I said to him, throwing my arms around his neck and bathing his face with my tears, 'what, then, can trouble you at this point? Alas, quite content with my fate, I will always prefer it to all the crowns in the universe, and will never form any other wish than for the conservation of your days. I enjoy all your tenderness tranquilly; can there be any wealth comparable my respect proves to you every day? Cease, then, to poison a wellbeing so dear and precious to my heart with futile and vain regrets.'

"My father, further softened by my caresses, could not hold back his tears, which mingled with mine; that appeasement lasted for a few moments, after which my father, becoming troubled again, gave me a long list of all his misfortunes. Then he left me with Fenix, my nurse.

"From the depths of his retreat, however, my father had maintained a correspondence with a few of his subjects who had remained faithful to him. One of those officers came one day to tell him about the rapid conquests of a monarch to whom everything yielded, and who had expelled the usurper after having defeated his entire army; that the project of that Prince was to render himself master of all Bolomia, and that it was time to appear in order to reclaim the rights he had over the kingdom. Charmed to hear that news, my father did not hesitate to go with the officer, after he had assured him that he had assembled a large number of his subjects, who had remained faithful to him.

"We left right away, and arrived a few days later in the victors' camp. We were immediately introduced into the King's tent, who received us with all the affection one could expect from a Prince as generous as he was sensible to the misfortunes of a sovereign whose virtues merited a happier fate. The two Princes had a long conversation together, which terminated on the part of the conqueror with the strongest assurances that he would not return to his estates until he had restored my father to the throne of his ancestors.

"The effect followed close on the heels of the promises, and King Bolomine returned to his capital city in triumph, to the acclamations of a people ever avid for novelty. First, the King had himself taken to the temple of Hercules, to which I accompanied him in order to render thanks to the god for the favors he had just granted. But his dolor was extreme when he saw that the temple had been pillaged and all its riches had been stolen. My father regretted most of all two columns of an admirable beauty. The King had several sacrifices made, and after having finished our prayers we went to the palace to the sound of a thousand instruments.

"Two years passed, during which the King was incessantly occupied in trying to pacify the disturbances that were still rife in his states. The usurper, shamefully expelled, did not believe that he was beaten; he renewed his intrigues and plots, which provoked new troubles in spite of the King's precautions.

"Often deprived for entire months of the pleasure of embracing my father, I regretted the happy times when I had incessantly enjoyed the satisfaction of conversing with him, when his heart, full of tenderness, was only sensible to the pleasure of instructing me, perfecting my soul and forming it for virtue, which had them been the only wealth he desired.

"Baneful grandeurs, vain honors, frivolous wealth, why, did you steal the peace that I enjoyed? I was scarcely flattered by everything that surrounded me, because it is not in the bosom of grandeurs that one finds true felicity. Since I had been at court, what had I seen there? Adulatory courtiers who limited their study to disguising the truth from us, trying to penetrate the interior of our souls in order to extract a surer advantage from our weakness.

"Fenix, surprised to hear me incessantly regretting my desert, tried in vain to make the comparison with everything the Court had of the most seductive; those depictions only increased my distress; a black presentiment seemed to announce new misfortunes to me, and I compared my sojourn at the court to those frail dreams that the first light, forerunner of the day, brings on its gilded wings, and which fly away with the shadows as soon as the glare of the sun comes to strike our pupils.

"'What, my Lady!' Fenix said to me, one day. 'Do I still see you prey to that somber sadness? I was not surprised by it when you had reason to fear for the life of our father the King; now that he has returned, at least enjoy tranquilly the pleasure of seeing him again and the honors that surrounds you on all sides.'

"'How incapable these honors are, dear Fenix, of touching a soul like mine! I can only be sensible to the tenderness of my father; I know that nothing can take that away from me. Alas, he has just told me again that all the measures he is taking to secure himself on his throne and expel division and intrigues are only with a view to seeing me placed; however, my Fenix, a frightful presentiment that I cannot vanquish comes incessantly to poison the repose of my days.'

"My father did not enjoy that shadow of tranquility for long; the war flared up again more furiously, and to complete the disasters, famine came to join that scourge. Then, all the temples were filed; further sacrifices were offered every day in the attempt to appease the anger of the gods.

"During these calamities, a few fanatical ministers and hidden enemies of the blood of Bolomine inspired in the people the desire to consult the oracle of Apollo in order to learn by what kind of sacrifice the wrath of the gods could be calmed and deliver the state from the scourges that were desolating it. One of those ministers was charged with presents that were to be offered in order to obtain a favorable response from the oracle.

"During the minister's journey I accompanied my father every day to the feet of the altars. The Prince seemed tranquil to me; a pure soul pursued by unjust fate finds his consolation in the testimony of his conscience; he hopes that time, the faithful friend of truth and justice, will one day make his innocence shine. Meanwhile, the minister announced his return, but alas, it was only to fill the entire palace with trouble and horror.

"The perfidious individual took a secret pleasure in having it published to the people that when he approached the temple, everything there had resounded with a noise similar to that of thunder, that bright flames had been seen in the air, and that the priestess' lair had trembled, and that finally, agitated by the god that animated her, she had pronounced this oracle: *'The divinity, offended by the crimes of an ingrate people, can only be appeased by the blood of a pure virgin; Bolomine alone has that treasure.'*

"That response was at first hidden from me with extreme care, but when I was informed of the envoy's return I went to my father's apartment in order to learn from him whether the gods had finally explained themselves.

"I approach in the hope of receiving tender embraces, but what do I see? My confused father recoils at the sight of me; a mortal pallor covers his face; his eyes, extinct with dolor, turn away from me, and he raises them, along with his arms, to the heavens. 'Unjust gods!' he cries, and remains immobile. An instant later he orders everyone to retire except the princess his daughter.

"I was alone in his study; gripped by fear, my trembling knees could hardly support me, and my heart, palpitating with dread, almost took away my breath. 'Oh, Father!' I cried, in a halting voice, falling at his feet. 'Relieve your dolor, please, by telling me what new misfortunes menace us now. What, alas, can have caused the trouble that is agitating you? How the state I see my father in makes me regret the tranquil days we spent in retreat!'

"'In the name of the gods, get up, my daughter, and cease imploring the gods, whose superior power only serves to render them more unjust and more insensate.'

"Surprised to hear from my father's mouth a speech so opposed to the sentiments of piety that he had always shown toward the gods. I dared not reply. Both of us remaining in a bleak silence, I was waiting for my father's order in order to retire when, looking at me with eyes in which dolor, mingled with tenderness, was painted, he said: 'Well, my daughter, I consent that you return to our former exile; the cruel gods demand it; it is necessary to obey them, alas. Would that you had never left it! Go back to your apartment, my daughter; I will take charge of making all the arrangements for our departure.'

"Gripped by the most violent dolor, I obeyed the King without daring to reply to him or ask him to explain the causes of such an extraordinary resolution. Fenix, astonished by the trouble that was agitating me, hastened to discover the reason; the sole confidante of my distress, I had no difficulty telling her the motives that occasioned my despair. 'You know,' I added, 'the sentiments with which my soul is penetrated; you know the tenderness and respect that I have always had for my father; it is not, my Fenix, that I doubt his now; he has never ceased to give me new proof of it every day. Would you believe, however, Fenix, that my father is ordering me to go away, and is making arrangements for that disastrous separation at this moment.'

"At that account, Fenix, no better informed than me of the unfortunate fate that was destined for me, only sighed; her anxious gaze ran sadly over me apartment. 'You're thinking,' I continued, 'that I shall be alone for a long time; that saddens you; but in fact, why this abandonment? Will those lax courtiers, by whom I was still surrounded two hours ago, regard my voyage as an exile? In what way will I have merited it? Always submissive to the orders of the King, my father, I have never desired any other glory than that of being loved by him. Fenix, my dear Fenix, run around the palace, find out everything that is happening there; try, above all, my Fenix, to learn the oracle's response.'

"But what do I see? The King advances; what does that somber expression signify? Alas, what is he coming to tell me? Gods! At least watch over his days, so dear, and if a victim is required, accept the sacrifice that I offer you of my life and add my days to those of a King who has always respected you!

"'Oh, my Father, for pity, sake, for you and or me, cease to overwhelm an unhappy Princess tormented by dread a thousand times more cruel than death. By what frightful fatality am I obliged to go away from you? Who can have inspired a resolution in you so contrary to my repose? How have I fallen into the disgrace of my Father and my King? In the name of the gods, explain a mystery in which all my reason in capsizing and sinking.'

"'My daughter,' my father replied, hugging me tenderly in his arms, 'calm this agitation, which is completing my dolor; ever more worthy of my tenderness and my love, be certain that nothing could ever weaken those sentiments; but my daughter, it is necessary to yield for a while to our unfortunate destiny, while showing a soul even greater than the evils with which it is heaping us. May the gods whom you implore with so much zeal be more propitious to you and guide you to a place where you can enjoy the repose that they have always refused me.'

"'Alas, I said, 'what repose can I enjoy far away from you?'

"'My daughter, I dare not flatter myself that you will be deprived of my presence for long.'

"At that moment, Germinus, a confidant of the King, came to tell us that the ship was ready. My father tore himself from my arms then, and ordered his confidant not to neglect anything to ensure my flight.

"I was left alone with Germinus. He said to me: 'Princess, the King had doubtless informed you of his will; everything in the palace is calm, the winds are favorable; in the name of the gods, my Lady, don't defer taking advantage of this moment.'

"'I will undoubtedly obey,' I said, uttering a profound sigh, 'but Fenix has not come back; I cannot leave without her.'

"'What concern is occupying you, my Lady?' said Germinus. 'Fenix is not running any risk, the moments are precious; please abandon this deadly place and be persuaded that all the tranquility of a monarch who cherishes you more than is life depends on your flight.'

"Fenix appeared at that moment, her face bathed in tears. 'Well, my Fenix,' I said, 'what have you learned? What is this fatal mystery, so difficult to understand?'

"'Alas, my Lady, this is not the place to tell you; flee forever and unjust and ingrate people who are demanding loudly to immolate you to their unworthy superstition.'

"'What am I hearing? Someone wants my life! Oh, if my death can ensure my father's repose, I do not hesitate. Let me be taken to the temple, the gods have doubtless ordered it; if I am a worthy victim to be offered to them, please do not deprive me of the pleasure of making the sacrifice without repugnance.'

"'Princess,' Fenix said, 'you're forgetting that the life of your father the King is attached to yours. If you are obstinate in perishing, you will render yourself guilty of a parricide that can only irritate the gods, since the King has sworn not to survive you by an instant.'

"'How tender that oath is, but how cruel! Alas, what use is my life to me if I am obliged to spend it far from my father!'

"A rumor that made itself heard obliged Germinus to take me away in spite of my resistance; he reached the ship without any obstacle. Fenix, who had followed us, employed everything that reason could dictate to her to soften my woes.

"Scarcely two days had gone by, however, when the sky was covered with frightful clouds, horrible meteors were seen, the sea swelled and its bellowing waves presaged a tempest. The sailors, gripped by horror, announced by their cries an inevitable death.

"In that frightful disorder, tranquil in the midst of danger, I cried: 'Just gods, you are pursuing your victim, she cannot escape your blows; at least pardon these people innocent of my flight, prolong the days of an unhappy father who has always loved and cherished virtue, and finally receive the sacrifice of my life.' As I finished those words, I threw myself into the sea, but Neptune, refusing to receive me, cast me up on a desert island, where I remained unconscious.

"A stony and rugged terrain seemed to forbid the approach of anything other than the malevolent animals, venomous reptiles and monsters of which it was the abode; a torrent precipitated from the top of an arid mountain came to break noisily against enormous rocks; the seething waves covered in foam sprang up in the distance, and, by their uncertain and miry course, completed the horror of that frightful solitude.

"When I had recovered my senses I thought I saw nature expiring; nothing so frightful had yet been offered to my eyes: a vast plain deprived of verdure and surrounded by precipices retraced all my misfortunes.

"I retreat into myself, I interrogate myself, I demand fearfully whether everything that I recall is in conformity with the truth; I seek to flatter myself, but in vain; how can I refuse the conviction that is overwhelming me? I retrace confusedly the full extent of my misfortunes, the uncertainty of my present situation and the assemblage of evils by which I am still threatened. 'All of nature is unleashed against me!' I cry, at the approach of a frightful monster. Trembling and bewildered, I try to flee, but the strength is lacking, and I fall unconscious.

"I cannot tell you what means the young man employed who brought me to you in order to save me from the fury of the monster, nor what route he took to bring me to this place; I am also ignorant to the reasons that he could have had that obliged him to abandon me so soon."

"Have no fear, beautiful Sephise,' said Zachiel. "The Supreme Being, who knows the purity of your soul and who knows that it has never been soiled by any crime, has brought you to the abode of the fortunate, in order to enjoy here a joy that will never perish. You are in the sphere of the Sun, where you will be purified of all terrestrial matter, until, like a pearl, you finally go to ornament the necklace of the Virgin, which is one of the signs of the zodiac."

Surprised by what the genius had said, Sephise demanded an explanation from him. The genius satisfied her in a few words, and a short time later we saw her change form and fly toward the place that was destined for her.

Before leaving the planet, however, Zachiel enabled us to see, by means of a telescope, that the amiable Princess had been transformed into a star of the sixth magnitude attached to the necklace of the Virgin. I have no doubt that our astronomers will soon make the discovery of it, and that those who are born under the signs that are in a good aspect with that star will be endowed with the filial love that forms the first bonds between reasoning beings.

Chapter X
Which Contains that which will be Seen

To continue our observations, the genius took us to a quarry, which we visited with a great deal of attention. That place was filled with a prodigious quantity of chemists, whom Monime mistook at first for charcoal-burners, so black and smoke-stained were they. Those good people were working with an incredible ardor under the orders of Flamel; that famous philosopher was at their head and appeared to be directing all their labors. He encouraged them by promising them to fix the sun's rays on their operations, and those individuals, animated by the desire to learn, listened with respect to their director's instructions. They received Flamel's words—which I am almost certain that they did not understand at all—as so many oracles.

Scarcely had we emerged from the philosophical quarry than a grotesque figure presented itself before us, Monime seemed frightened by him at first, but Zachiel, who recognized him as an oracle, reassured her and gave her at the same time the curiosity to hear the account of his adventures, which might inform us of a few interesting facts.

"Where have you come from?" the genius said to him, approaching him. "You seem to me to be very weary."

"It's true," said the oracle, "that my travels have almost worn me out. For several centuries I've been traveling various worlds; I've had no lack of occupations. If you'd like to take a rest in the shade of these laurels, I can make you party to some of my prowesses." The oracle looked at Monime and me with a great deal of attention, and added: "But what do I see? Either I'm a poor oracle or the two people accompanying you are inhabitants of the globe of the Earth, who have not yet been subjected to the yoke that nature imposes on all mortals. How then, were they able to get here?"

"If your science were as sure are you dare to assert," said the genius, "you ought not to be unaware of the full extent of my powers, nor the means that I have used in order to bring them here. At any rate, I order you to tell them what happened to you on their world."

"I cannot dispense with obeying a superior genius," said the oracle, who began his account: "Having arrived on the globe of the Earth, I went to Greece, where I made myself known, after the death of Socrates, as his demon. I instructed Epaminondas in Thebes; then, passing among the Romans, I attached myself to Cato, and then to Brutus. No one is unaware that all those great individuals only left behind them the phantom of their virtues; that is why I engaged some of my companions to follow my example by retiring into temples, caverns or other depths; but the people were so stupid and so primitive that we soon lost all the pleasure we had previously taken in deceiving them; that amusement became insipid to us.

"It is as well to inform his beautiful lady that my comrades and I, acting in accord, carried out a thousand extraordinary things under various names that the fanaticism and superstition had brought into fashion, particularly those of oracles, gods of the hearth, Lares, lamias, farfadets, naiads, incubi, sages, Manes, specters and phantoms. We therefore made the decision to abandon the Earth during the reign of Augustus; that was shortly after Drusus appeared before me when he was departing to make war in Germany and I forbade him to go beyond.

"However, I've made several voyages there since. It was me who appeared to Cardan while he was a student; I told him several very curious things. Agrippa was also led by my advice. I guided Campanella in his operations. I approached a number of the scholars known by the name of the Knights of the Rosy Cross and informed them of a number of natural secrets that allowed them to pass for great magicians. It was me who stimulated several new sects of fanatics who wanted to arrogate the rights that we have always had to predict the future. I informed those scoundrels of a new species a thousand tricks of flexibility, habituating them in early childhood to bend their bodies in a hundred different ways in order to strike extraordinary attitudes with more facility.

"Finally bored by only encountering on the globe of the Earth men who were mostly mad, ignorant or imbeciles, who were nevertheless always guided by their self-regard, easily persuaded that they were of the nature of angels, I was getting ready to rise up to some other world when hazard enabled me to make the acquaintance of a sage who is the glory of his nation and the shame of those who know him, without deigning to recompense in him the virtue of which he was the living image.

"That sage possesses all the sciences and all the talents, of which one alone would be sufficient for him to be admired, but would you believe that the assemblage of such rare virtues could remain buried under the weight of the most frightful misfortune? 'Oh century of iron,' I cried, in admiring that philosopher, 'unjust citizens who are only pleased to recompense vice and cause virtue to languish under the burden of ignorance!' I said to him: 'Permit me, admirable man, to correct fate by extinguishing informing you of the means to render yourself fortunate; accept these three vials. One is filled with oil of talc, another with projection powder and the third with potable gold.' The sage refused my offer, with a disdain more generous than that of Diogenes when he received the offers and compliments of Alexander.

"'I do not know,' he said to me. 'the price of the present you are offering me; submissive to the decrees of the Supreme Being, my life passes in tranquil peace; content with my estate, I have no ambition; I merely mourn the fate of these mortals, who, always indigent in the bosom of opulence, seek pleasure and sensuality in vain, without ever being able to savor either.'

"I quit my sage after spending two days with him. I can't add anything to his eulogy except that he is perhaps the only philosopher and the only free man that is presently on the globe of the Earth, for almost everyone that I knew there seemed to me to be so far beneath that man that I've observed animals superior to them by their instinct. The majority of the other worlds are similar enough, and that is what determined me to resume the route to the Sun in order to enclose myself in my lair, unless Apollo's orders send me back to one of his temples."

When the oracle had left us Zachiel took us into the forest of Dodona. That forest is filled with oaks, which, when the winds agitate and shake their branches, pronounce their oracles in a sufficiently distinct voice. In the middle of the forest there are two very tall columns; on one there is a bronze bowl, on the other the statue of a child whose hand is holding a whip, the cords of which, also bronze, are so artfully arranged that when they are pushed on to the bowl by the wind, they make different sounds there. The Gorgons, who are three in number, each explain those sounds in a different manner, often giving several meaning, which always relate to the requests or questions made of them.

On emerging from the forest we entered a mountainous country filled with lairs and caverns, and consequently very appropriate to the habitation of sibyls and oracles. It was also the place that Apollo had designated to serve as the residence of the priests and priestesses he had endowed with the gift of prophecy, because of the commodity and that advantage they ought to find in the secrecy of their mysteries and also because of the divine exhalations that emerged there.

It is true that lairs and caverns seem themselves to inspire a kind of horror that prepares the mind to receive certain inspirations that are uniquely formed to strike the imagination. Humans, ever curious to read the future, see nothing but projects, chimerical illusions and hopes; consequently, they can only ever be happy in anticipation, since the human mind almost never passes from imagination to reality without losing three-quarters of its pleasures.

Those lairs are half way to Mount Parnassus; they are surrounded by rocks and frightful precipices. We followed a large crowd of people attracted to the place by the desire to satisfy their curiosity. Having arrived at the spot where the Pythoness rendered her oracles, we discovered her in a kind of obscure sanctuary, whose opening was covered with laurel branches. The pythoness was sitting on the sacred tripod.

The woman, after having filled her lungs with odorous smoke, appeared to be animated by a divine fury; a violent enthusiasm gripped her; her eyes blazed; her features became animated, her veins swelled and her hair was seen to stand on end. Violent convulsions agitated her and filled her mind with fury; she seemed to us to be out of breath. That terrible agitation lasted for more than an hour; then, returning to her senses with a more serene expression, she pronounced several oracles, some in verse and others in prose, which were delivered by means of a speaking-trumpet, the sounds of which were multiplied in the rocks and vaults of the tenebrous sanctuary, augmenting the voice, and forming a reverberation the imprinted terror and caused the most intrepid to tremble.

The tripod of the Pythoness is surrounded and covered by laurels; the perfumes burned in her lair spread a smoke there resembling a thick cloud, almost obliterating sight and simultaneously concealing the preparations of the Pythoness, who doubtless has more than one reason for denying knowledge of her mysteries.

When the ceremony was over, Zachiel took us by way of tortuous paths into the Pythoness' den. No mortal dares to enter it, which is why the woman seemed extremely surprised to see us. Her eyes began to blaze; perhaps she was about to pronounce anathemas upon us, when the genius stopped her by making himself known to her.

"To what," she said "should I attribute the honor of being visited by a genius of the first order?"

"You only owe it," said Zachiel, "to a desire to instruct these two individuals, who are under my protection, with living images of all that passes; so I order you to respond as accurately as you can to all their questions, which ought not to extend into the future."

Monime asked her first about the names of the most famous oracles. The one that was the most renowned is undoubtedly the oracle of Apollo that reigned for a long time at Delphi, where it was regarded as infallible. In the early days of its reign, the most beautiful of the girls who were who were consecrated to Diana were chosen to pronounce her brother's oracles there, and that continued until the days of a certain Echectrates of Thessaly, a man who had always had a great deal of devotion for the tripod but whose fervor soon changed its object and no longer held in honor anything but one of the priestesses, who formed his desires. The difficulty he found in presenting his offerings to her caused him to make the decision to abduct her, in order to sacrifice in her presence with greater facility and less dread.

That adventure alarmed all the priestesses. Apollo and Diana were consulted as to what ought to be done; both were deaf to the voices of the priestesses and made no reply, which caused them to judge that they ought to bury the affair in profound mystery, in order to avoid anyone finding out about a scandal that might have ruined the reputation of the oracle. It was therefore decided in a general assembly that no one would any longer be admitted into the sacred mysteries but spinsters who had passed the age of fifty, in order to prevent amour from coming to trouble their sacrifices and diminish the great confidence that people had always had in them.

"It is as well that you know," the Pythoness added, "that all the talent and science of oracles consists in knowing how to deceive cleverly. The most renowned have always been the most adroit in disguising their deceptions; it is only with equivocal words and gestures that they envelop the meaning of their responses in singular fashion, rendering them so obscure that they would need a further oracle themselves to explain them."

"It appears to me," said Monime, "that you excel in that art."

Another might have blushed at the compliment, but the Pythoness interpreted it to her advantage.

Then we visited the oracle of Themis and the two of Trophonius; although the later was only a simple hero, his oracles were rendered with much more ceremony than those of the gods themselves; two temples had been raised to his intention, one of which was in Lebadaea and the other at Thebes.

No one could be admitted into the lair of Trophonius without having spent several days in a kind of little chapel dedicated to good fortune and the good genii. In that place one received expiations of every sort, but it was necessary, in order to merit them, to abstain from warm water and to wash in the River Herkyna, after which sacrifices were offered in your name to the entirety of the hero's family. In the meantime, one was only nourished by the flesh that had been sacrificed, after having consulted the entrails of the victims in order to discover whether Trophonius thought it god that one could take the liberty of descending into his lair.

It was only ever the last victim, however, which had to be a ram, that decided the response; if it was favorable you were taken out of the chapel during the night in order to go to the River Herkyna, where two young children rubbed you all over the body with oil of myrrh, and then made you go upriver all the way to its source; there you were made to drink two kinds of water, the first from the River Lethe, of which you were made to take a large glass in order to efface from your mind all the profane thoughts that had occupied you during the course of your life. An instant later—which is to say, when it as judged that the water had taken effect—you were presented with a golden cup, that of Mnemosyne, which had the virtue of engraving in your memory everything you were to see in the hero's sacred lair.

After those preparations you approached the statue of Trophonius in order to say your prayers there; then, dressed in a linen tunic, your body was girdled by several sacred bands to which great virtues were attached; after which you were taken to the oracle. The oracle was at the top of a sheer mountain in an enclosure formed of white marble, in the middle of which rose the bronze obelisks that surrounded the entrance to the sacred cavern of Trophonius, the opening of which resembled the mouth of an oven. One could only descend into that cavern by means of a ladder, but when one had descended into it one found another cavern, whose entrance was so narrow that ne could only get into it by lying on the ground facing upwards; in that posture a venerable old man put balls into each of your hands composed of certain simples, which had the virtue of driving away evil genii; then one passed into the opening of the cavern and immediately felt oneself drawn into it with great force.

It was there that the future was revealed to you in different ways. For some the events were made to pass before their eyes that were the object of their curiosity; others heard the narration of the adventures that destiny had in preparation for them; others, finally, terrified by a thousand frightful phantoms, could not distinguish anything in the future, and those were incontrovertibly the greatest in number. However, you left the lair as one had entered it; you went to the Temple of Good Fortune, where you were left, still stunned by the marvels you had just seen.

After that story, Monime was asked whether she wanted to descend into the hero's lair.

"You make me tremble," Monime said. "I've never been curious to read the future, and if I had had that malady, your account would have cured me of it forever."

We continued our route and passed several caverns into which the majority of the ancient oracles had withdrawn. We noticed that of Ceres, who was making several curious events visible in a magic mirror; that of Jupiter Ammon, which was once located in Libya; that of the head of Orpheus, which was kept on the Isle of Lesbos; that of Hercules, which had long been in vogue in the Peloponnese on the coast of the gulf of Corinth; that of Venus, so renowned; and those of Latona, mother of Apollo and Aesculapius. We saw several more famous lairs, which gave the genius the opportunity to make further reflections.

"You ought to take note," Zachiel said to us, "that in all worlds, the most ancient, most inveterate and the most incurable malady that has ever reigned among the human race has always been the pernicious desire to know future events, without the obscure veil that hides their destiny from them, or the experience of several centuries, or an infinity of futile attempts for very little success, having been able to cure them of that unfortunate mania. They cannot be corrected of an error so agreeably received; always as credulous as their ancestors, like them they never cease to lend an ear to fraud and imposture; that which has disappointed thousands of times dos not lose for that the deadly right to deceive again.

"On Earth the Tuscans introduced to the Romans the method of predicting the future by means of meteors, lightning and thunder. They gave an exact list of their different species, detailing their names and the prognostications that could be drawn from them.

"When one makes use of reason one can scarcely comprehend how the human mind has been able to lend itself to such gross errors. However, these errors, absurd as they appear to us, have been received by the most enlightened peoples. Would you believe that philosophers were ever able to believe in gods whose examples could only inspire vicious desires, for in examining the mythology of the pagans, what is the conduct they attribute to Jupiter? What are the qualities that that they give to their god Mars, who appears proud, brutal and bloodthirsty? Cunning, flexibility and rascality are the prerogatives of the mes-

318

senger of the gods. Pluto only takes pleasure in hearing the cries of the unfortunate. Venus, whom they cause to be born from the foam of the waves, instantly becomes the mother of Amour, without anyone knowing who could have aided her in the making of that beautiful masterpiece; she is depicted as amiable, voluptuous and carried away by her caprices. Juno is jealous and vindictive. In sum, on surveying all the gods, I cannot find one to whom that title can judiciously be given.

"Then, each of the gods is charged with the various passions that animate the soul and all the events of life; and, as every nation wanted to be protected by them, the richest built temples to them; festivals were initiated to them; sacrifices were offered to them; ministries were formed to them, which soon became oracles. Doubtless those people were convinced of finding partiality in those divinities established by crafty, rascally or ignorant humans. Those gods, therefore, ought always to have distinguished within the crowd those whose tastes conformed with their inclinations; consequently, they owed them sentiments of preference, since the worship they rendered them was always relative to their characters.

"Human victims have been seen expiring on the altar of Mars; thousands of courtesans have devoted themselves to temples of Venus and a quantity of distinguished women in the city of Babylon immolated their modesty to a certain goddess in order to procure their fellow citizens the most precious favors of the goddess in question."

"But if false deities are also worshiped on other worlds," said Monime, "and the same sacrifices are also offered to the goddess or to other gods, it seems to me that the gods must be very embarrassed in settling the different interests of nations that are no less opposed to their mores; for how can one reconcile the quarrels of two peoples who are both asking for the same thing? I believe that must cause a great deal of division in Olympus."

"You must have seen, in the account that Homer has given us of the Trojan War," Zachiel said, "that the part the gods played in that war occasioned a general upheaval in the heavens. The Scamander saw Minerva's aegis shine; it was also witness to the flight of arrows emerging from Apollo's quiver; it felt the redoubtable trident of Neptune, which lifted up the entire machine that made the globe of the Earth rotate, and nearly dislodged it from its pivot. That is why it was agreed that only the inevitable edicts of destiny could reestablish peace between those gods animated by the most frightful vengeance, or they would have to agree mutually to remain neutral and not interfere with any quarrels of the human race."

"Could one not say," said Monime, "on examining the conduct imputed to these false divinities, that the majority of magnificent temples that were erected to them were only built to serve their gods as houses of pleasure—which is to say, what are called 'small houses' on the Moon—since they believe that they often come to inhabit them in order to relax from their occupations and amuse themselves at the same time at the feasts held in their honor? One can also presume that they wanted to recompense the piety of humans by causing to be born among them a large number of heroes, who participated by their birth in the divinity of those who gave them being; that is doubtless what firmed the multitude of demigods that are only owed to the charms of beautiful mortal women."

"It is true," said Zachiel, that several societies of slaves have awarded the title of gods to monsters unworthy of bearing the name of human. That was what was done at Alexander's court, in believing him to be the son of Jupiter. The Romans, who were enlightened, had no qualms about uniting in the person of Caesar a god, a priest and an atheist; temples were erected to his clemency; a colleague of Romulus, he received the prayers of the nation; his statue was placed, in the sacred festivals, next to that of Jupiter, whom a moment later he went himself to invoke. Domitian was also confused with Jupiter; flattery and adulation named him the benefactor of the earth; their rights to divinity were the same and their nature and power equal."

Chapter XI
The Genius takes us to the Mouth of Various Rivers

After we had rested long enough under the dense foliage, which branches full of fruits and interlaced with ivy rendered very agreeable, the genius took us through a very spacious valley filled with flowers destined to form the crowns and garlands of Zephyr and Flora. That valley led insensibly to the mouth of three great rivers that serve to irrigate the brilliant countryside of that luminous world.

The first and largest of those rivers is named the River of Memory; the second, narrower but deeper, is that of Imagination; and the third, much smaller than the other two, is that of Judgment.

"Neither of you can be unaware," the genius said, "that several subaltern faculties are found in the soul that ought to serve reason, which never ceases to be the sovereign. Among these faculties, the imagination always holds the first rank; that is what receives the impressions of the external objects of which the senses often feel the effect; it is what forms images and figures of those same objects, on the correspondence or discordance of which our reason has to found what we call verities or what we reject as lies.

"When nature delivers herself to repose, reason seems to withdraw from its seat, and it is then that the imagination, which takes pleasure in painting pictures, works more freely. For want of knowing how to sort its images, however, when it no longer has reason for its guide, one sees it very frequently producing bizarre mixtures during sleep and assembling carelessly things that are quite unrelated to one another, which memory conserves—and guided by common sense, it can sometimes make a useful choice. You know that memory is the garden of our thoughts, our pleasures and our pains; common sense and reason are thus absolutely necessary to direct the other two."

The genius then pointed out to us on the banks of the Memory certain amphibious animals that often seem ready to devour you. Monime did her best to tame some of them, but when she tried to bring them together they redoubled their cries and looked at her with furious expression. Those animals only nourished themselves on the water of the river and spent their days repeating in a hoarse and shrill voice everything that they had heard. Furthermore, we saw on the banks of that river parrots, crows, jays, magpies, starlings, linnets, finches and all the other species of birds, which formed a very discordant chorus. The water of that river seems sticky; it exhales a black vapor similar to a thick smoke, and flows very noisily.

The River of Imagination flows with greater rapidity; its light and shiny liquid sparkles everywhere, like a torrent of flashes; in its acrobatics it does not observe any certain order, but by fixing the attention on the permanently agitated waves on perceives that only the water flowing in its depths is pure and drinkable; its foam forms oil of talc. Monime was curious to taste it; I followed her example and we found the taste exquisite.

On the banks of that river a quantity of precious stones are strewn, mingled with golden sand. We noticed, among others, several of those pebbles that have the virtue of rendering those who carry them lighter; there are others that, if they are applied in a certain fashion, render you invisible. The river contains salamanders; eagles also come frequently to fly over it; one sees sirens there, and several other species of creatures that are pleased to float upon its waters. The banks are bordered by a magnificent wood of cedars and palms, whose branches are laden with phoenixes and nightingales, which form a delightful concert there. We also saw many fruit trees; Zachiel pointed out several to Monime on to which had been grafted fruits from the garden of Hesperides, where Discord collected the apple that sowed strife between the three goddesses, filled all Olympus with troubles, and did so much harm to the Trojans.

What is most remarkable about the course of those two rivers is that, as they flow alongside one another, it often happens that in places where the Memory is most extensive, the Imagination seems narrower, and when the Imagination extends with more rapidity and glitter, the Memory seems nothing more than a petty stream—as if each of the two rivers only nourishes itself at the expense of the other.

A little further on, on the right, is the channel of the River of Judgment. That channel, which seems to be extremely deep, presents to the eyes water that is clear without being brilliant; its waters seem to run very slowly, but when, by means of subterranean channels, the Imagination communicates with that river, its naturally cold waters take on a degree of temperate warmth, which changes its sand into diamonds of an inestimable value; hellebore plants grow in the mud of its bed whose rots clean and purify the water. That river, like the other two, distributes an infinity of tiny channels, which swell as they move away and flow together into a great lake.

The genius then took us along a road bordered with broad and superb pathways; we walked for a long time on gold dust, and finally arrived at one of the ports of a great Ocean, which the genius told us was the Sea of Hope. It was on that sea that we were to embark.

"You see," said Zachiel, "that nature has not spared any effort to furnish the inhabitants of this world with all the necessary resources to render themselves perfectly happy, since she has granted them hope, which is a treasure that one can possess even in the bosom of indigence. Hope softens woes, it serves to reanimate the heart, to sustain desires and console in all the disgraces of life."

Monime wanted to sample those waters too, which seemed to her to be as mild as milk and very pleasant to taste.

That sea contains immense riches; its tides are only occasioned by a prodigious quantity of Hopes that are lost in all possible worlds and come to throw themselves into that sea, their source, in great waves. It is often agitated by stormy winds that form great tempests; that is what renders its waters sometimes clear and bright and sometimes troubled and muddy; but when it is calm and tranquil, once can see that immense riches are always rolling in its bosom. It engenders a large number of singular animal species; one sees on its shores a quantity of simples that attract you by their perfume and whose leaves resemble the sensitive plant; myrrh and laurel form delightful groves there.

While walking along that shore, we met a young mariner who seemed to be in the greatest desolation because of the loss of a ship that he had been unable to save from the fury of the waves. The young man gave the most tender regrets to the loss of the brave officers who had served under his command.

Zachiel wanted to take advantage of the young man's ignorance to give us a few lessons on navigation. "If that young man had been instructed in the basic elements that ought to form a mariner," he told us, "he would not have exposed his vessel to an inevitable disaster.

"The principal object that ought to fix the attention of a seaman is to examine his vessels, to know their capabilities, their solidity, their proportions, their speed or slowness; that knowledge ought to regulate his operation. The winds that have been created by nature to purify the air by agitating it and to bring or dissipate rain, to spread the seeds of plants or to transport them, and, finally, to fortify vegetables by useful shocks ought to be his second study; they are what almost always decide the success of combats. It is therefore necessary to know them, in order to try to vanquish their obstacles by regulating the choice of positions to draw great advantage from them when they are favorable or to oppose them when they are contrary.

"The third matter, which regards the sea, is to estimate the action of the waves that continually impact his ship; it is necessary to obey the ever-agitated movements of the surface, know and take advantage of the direction of its currents, calculate the times of its tides, examine their strength and effects, in order to profit from them. All these multiple details can only be the consequence of a great deal of study and consummate experience. It is from those combined fields of knowledge that the pilot's art results.

"You ought not to be unaware, my dear Seaton," Zachiel added, "that humans need to learn even the simplest things. It is a gross temerity to dare to think that one can succeed without study, since that alone gives useful knowledge. Authority gives titles, nature produces graces, and often talents, but only morality, philosophy and history are capable of producing wisdom, justice, joy, pure pleasures and a stainless glory."

THE SIXTH HEAVEN: JUPITER

Chapter I
Description of the Empire of the Jovinians

Judging that there was nothing more to retain us in the globe of the Sun, Zachiel proposed that we take to the vortices again in order to reach the planet Jupiter—which is, as is well known, one of the largest and most distant from our world—or, to have us transported there by atoms. Monime preferred the latter comfort, not wanting to take the risk of being crushed by a collision of vortices, whose rapidity is capable of disturbing the firmest brain.

The genius put us on a group of hooked atoms which were aggregated as if linked together. Those atoms, which are not as frightening as vortices, conveyed us quite comfortably to the planet Jupiter.

The delight I felt during that voyage, in admiration of thousands of beauties, transported my soul more rapidly than we traversed them. My eyes scanned and embraced all at once an infinity of objects as varied as they were agreeable; the heavens presented me with new images incessantly, of which the ostentation, the magnificence and the majestic disorder drew all my attention; my mind delivered itself to them entirely; a delicious calm penetrated it and I was enjoying that vast universe as if it were mine when Monime uttered a cry that extracted me from my ecstasy. She had been unable to rectify a violent surge of fear excited by the view of the immense void through which the genius was transporting us with much greater rapidity than in any fall.

We eventually arrived on the globe of Jupiter at the moment when Aurora, awakened by the Hours that run incessantly, was getting ready to open the Gates of Dawn, and Night, pierced by her nascent darts, was obliged to flee before them. Then we began to discover the bushy tresses of forests and the gray peaks of mountains, and to respire an air that brings a mild sensuality into the soul and seems to give the inhabitants of that world an extra sense.

The genius transported us over a vast extent of terrain, which appeared to us at first to be very similar to that of Mercury, and Monime and I thought for some time that the genius had mistaken his way and that, instead of bringing us to Jupiter he had taken us back to Mercury by a different route. The resemblance between the two planets in question is so great that it is scarcely possible to tell them apart, and it was only after a good deal of time and many observations that we succeeded in glimpsing a few features of difference. In the rural areas the poverty is the same, and the unfortunates that live there similarly give the impression of people who are begrudged even the thatch which covers their huts and the air that they breathe.

As we approached one of the capital cities we noticed that the land, although rich and fertile, was similarly destined purely for the pleasures of sight—which is to say that instead of being prepared for useful crops, the fields everywhere presented nothing but superfluous ornaments, variegated beds of the most beautiful flowers, avenues whose trees were pruned into a thousand different shapes, parks of immense circumference, cascades, sheets of water, carpets of grass ornamented by exquisitely-carved statues, arbors and admirably well-designed labyrinths. In sum, one might have thought that the land, which ought to be the nursing mother of humans everywhere, is there merely a theater of pure representation and spectacle solely to satisfy the eye.

The mores of that world bear an even closer resemblance to Mercury: the same luxury, the same expense, the same usages, the same manners, the same air of arrogance and vanity, but principally, the same avidity to acquire wealth, the same profusion in dissipating it, the same facility in contracting debts and the same custom of not paying any of them.

"Would one not think," said Monime, "that their pride leads them to believe themselves formed of the parings of angels, since they cannot bear their inferiors to dare to express sentiments of amity; doubtless they prefer the sumptuous respect their dignity demands to the tenderness and amity that seem only to be fashionable among the gods. It is those false principles that deprive the great of the keenest sweetness of life, for it is certain that those whom a tender sympathy impels to link themselves in friendship are forced by the impression of prejudice to repress the impulses of their hearts in order to avoid giving to manifest evidence of their inclination, in the dread of only being repaid by a humiliating scorn instead of the gratitude that they have the right to expect."

Monime ended her remarks by trying to persuade me that the Jovinians must know the secret of crossing the immense spaces that separated them from the world of Mercury, and that the two peoples were in commerce together, but Zachiel disabused us.

"You cannot doubt," the genius said, "that I have a perfect knowledge of the character of both peoples; be certain, beautiful Monime, that it is in one respect completely opposite. The finance that reigns on Mercury can conceive of nothing more frivolous than nobility, while the nobility that is everything on Jupiter has only scorn for finance.

"However, sane individuals compare high birth to a pyramid elevated in the middle of a vast field, where everyone can examine its perfection or its faults at will. An aristocrat, by virtue of his elevation, similar to that of the pyramid, seems exposed; he is measured; his plans are penetrated, his secret motives divined, and the public, an impartial judge, pronounces its verdict with impunity; the mask of virtue only deceiving it for a while, it reads the depths of hearts; dignities, wealth an honors—nothing is protected from censure; informed of all his deviations, they are published and his brilliance often serves only to decry him; but that does not alter the fact that here, as elsewhere, the rich financier does not want to be compared unfavorably to the nobleman, and that the less well-to-do nobleman employs all his talents to approach the profusion of the rich man."

I had noticed on the planet Mercury that the greater number of citizens wear large rings, which are the distinctive marks that decorate persons of quality, although they have no title that authorizes them to wear that mark of distinction; on the planet Jupiter it is a kind of dagger similar in form to our hunting-knives, which they wear in their belts. That blade, which it is only permissible for those who have defended the fatherland to wear, by virtue of an inconceivable abuse, also serves as an ornament for those who are only occupied in its ruination. I could not conceive of a contradiction so striking, my English education having taught me that carrying a blade is a privilege that only belongs to warriors and noblemen; I had difficulty accustoming myself to seeing salesmen and doorkeepers infringing the rights of the nobility.

My sojourn in Jovinia gave me plenty of time to get used to that custom, so contrary to our English manners; I saw everyone there, without distinction of estate or condition, armed with the same blade, which they never take off, any more than their shoes; I was assured that many slept with them on.

After being invited to dinner one day in the house of a lord, Monime and I had ourselves conducted to the most popular spectacle, in which were represented not only all the marvels of nature but many other prodigies even greater, which no one can ever have seen in the theater, in which one saw, pell-mell, gods, goblins, monsters, kings, shepherds, enchantresses, enchanters, furies, fires, battles and a ball; that magnificent assemblage is represented in a great hall whose two sides are equipped with wings similar to the leaves of our screens, on which the objects that the scene is to represent re crudely painted. It is there that all the persons of condition assemble, because it is considered good form for a man of a certain society not to miss one.

After having run my eyes over everything surrounding me, I chanced to fix them on a young man with a rather handsome physiognomy. My attentive examination caused him to blush; I sought to recall his features and the place where I might have seen him before; in order to reassure myself I decided to speak to him.

"Your face is not unknown to me," I said to him. "Was it not in the house of Viscount de La Chimeradière? Were you not at dinner there?"

At first that question disconcerted the young man; he could not dissimulate his embarrassment. Immediately making a decision, however, he whispered in my ear: "Please, my Lord, don't ruin me with my master. I can't deny that it was me who came to fill your glass at Milord's table. I'll confess to you that I was gripped today by such a strong desire to play the fop that I couldn't resist it. Milord does me the honor of distinguishing me from his other domestics; I'm what is known as his griffon; it's me who normally accompanies him on his nocturnal expeditions."

"Which is to say," I said, "that he's Amphitryon and you're his Sosie."[48]

"Precisely, Sir," said the alert young man, emboldened by my joke. "As my master has just departed for the country, where he is to stay for two days, I wanted to profit from that time to see whether I could copy him in more than one role. I believe that it's easy for you to see that I'm only dressed in his plumage—but that's not the most interesting part of my story, and if Sir will permit, I'd be honored to make him party to a project that is on the point of conclusion."

The effrontery of the domestic amused me greatly. I consented to listen to him.

"You're not unaware, Sir," he went on, "that it is the dignity of a great Lord to have theatrical performers for mistresses. My master, who does not depart from that custom in the slightest, took a new one yesterday evening and wearied of her this morning. In order to avoid the reproaches of the beauty, my Lord, generous in all his actions, sent her two hundred guineas, which is doubtless the price she puts on her favors. As his most zealous servant, he put them in my hand to give to the nymph. The probity in which I glory does not permit me to remove any, but the gallantry in which I am also enthusiastic to excel, following my master's example, seems to invite me to make use of that same sum to try to obtain from the beauty a small share of her good graces. That is what led me to make the decision to write to her under the name of a foreign Lord. I won't hide it from you that I copied the note from one of my master's rough drafts, in order to show her a style so familiar that I count on going to supper with her when the spectacle finishes, bearing an offering considerable enough to render her sensible to my ardor. I received in response in conformity with my desires. You see, Sir, that I am not doing any wrong to my master, if I can, by means of the incense that he charged me to offer the goddess, participate in the same favors, not being able to obtain them in any other way."

I found the fellow's idea so amusing that I made Zachiel party to it that same evening. Far from being surprised, he assured me that such adventures were very common among the Jovinians. The majority of domestics, especially those of Lords, almost all have a bourgeois suit, if that of their masters cannot serve them, when they want to counterfeit gentlemen or copy their masters, to introduce themselves into a spectacle or other places where men in livery are not tolerated.

"Nothing is more abject, in the judgment of Jovinians," Zachiel continued, "than to have no other title than that of bourgeois, which means that one sees everything put to work to procure a more distinguished one, in order to make

---

[48] The chief character in Molière's comedy *Amphitryon* (1668), based on an original by Plautus from the second century B.C. Yet again, Molière's work seems to be familiar throughout the solar system.

oneself a name. A merchant is ambitious to raise his son to the magistracy; a tenant farmer, having become rich by his work, puts his into the military; and taking the figurative expression *to make a name* literally, seeks no other finesse than that of changing that of their family by removing a few letters or adding a few syllables. By that kind of combination, the son of a Pierrot is easily transformed into a Pirtori, which is one of the finest and oldest names in this empire. It is necessary not to forget to put the particule *de* or *du* before the name; that precaution is important, for one always passes for a very minor individual when one does not have a *de* in one's name."

It is true that that mania went so far as to cast doubt on the fact that I was a man of birth for the sole reason that my name was Seaton; that name was judged to be extremely bourgeois, having nothing in the least aristocratic about it and no means of becoming so. De Seaton would not have been much better, especially being alone, because it was another subject of scandal for those Lords to hear me say, quite naturally, that Seaton was my only name and that I had no others; they wanted me to have at least three or four, and thought that Seaton was too short and ought to be elongated.

I was therefore forced, in order to make myself distinguished, to yield to that bizarre caprice and to have myself named, for all the time we remained among the Jovininans, as Lord de Seaton of the Albions of Gloucester; all those names attracted a great deal of consideration and respect. Monime followed my example; like me she combined the first three names that came to mind and became de Monimont de Kaquerbec d'Hibernalk, to which Zachiel wanted to add Princess of Georgia, a quality that she had already adopted on the world of Venus, but without telling us the reasons that determined him to name her thus.

We began by visiting the most considerable provinces of Jovinia. When we arrived in one of their capitals we were introduced as very great aristocrats, for almost all the Jovinians want to pass for great; everyone wants to be noble at any price—because nobility is sold on that world as cloth is sold on ours. An artisan, a merchant or a financier traffics in nobility as an Englishman might charter a ship, so one sees nobility at all prices, and provided that one has the money, its achievement is almost complete. When one is able to buy some land, one thinks oneself a peer of the highest nobility; one is already an entire Lord, one talks about "my vassals," enjoys to right to hunt, mentions "my manor house," travels by carriage, bears the name of one's estate and is soon a branch of the family of its former possessors.

We were told the story of one well-off peasant who obtained the tenancy of the farm of an estate very cheaply. The owner, carelessly of his property, has let it go to rack and ruin, but the clever and cunning peasant, who knew its limits, made the most of them, cultivated it with great care, and made a few advances on his master, who, being a wastrel, died laden with debts. The farmer, on the contrary, who had built up savings during his tenancy, found himself the creditor of considerable sums, and pressed for their payment, threatening to go to court unless the land were ceded to him at a low price, which he offered to pay in cash. The heirs accepted the proposition in order to avoid the legal proceedings taking away everything else, each finding the bargain acceptable. The farmer became the owner of the land, his son soon acquired the pompous title of Marquis, and his grandsons succeeded in obtaining governmental positions; the greatest Lords in the land were honored to be acquainted with them.

Those sorts of usurpations of nobility are very easy there by means of a little-known but carefully-researched possession; one has recourse to makers of genealogies, who spend their life in an environment of dust and parchments deciphering old titles, which they can cause to say whatever they think appropriate without anyone being able to contradict them; one has only to pay them well and they will make you descend from any family you choose. This is an example of which we were eye-witnesses.

Monime had made the acquaintance of a pretty young woman full of distinguished merit; already very rich, the young woman had come to the city for the legal settlement of a considerable succession, believing herself to be the only one who had the right to receive it, when a villager came to annihilate all her hopes.

The man in question had left his village at an early age to enter the service of a lady in the capacity of "hussar." That is a common practice among Jovinian ladies, almost all of whom bring up little boys, whom they dress in grotesque fashion, in order to have them dance attendance on them. This one having been produced in that quality in the lady's house, she had him take the name of his village, which was Jarnac. Having grown up, and being intelligent, she placed him in the service of a fop who was said to be her lover. At any rate, Jarnac was so well able to insinuate himself into his master's good graces that he gained his entire confidence and amassed a considerable amount of money, which allowed him to live in the house with a kind of distinction

Hazard caused Jarnac to find himself one day in a place where his lord's heiress was pointed out to him. Surprised to learn that the lord had died without posterity, and simultaneously charmed by the young woman's beauty, he went back to the house very pensive. Immediately, amour gave birth to the idea of profiting from his name to pass himself off as the lord's heir. Sure of the amity of his master, he did not hesitate to confide his project to him, asking him to indicate the means to succeed in it.

The master, charmed to find an opportunity to make the fortune of the domestic without it costing him anything, began by joking about his new grandeur but ended up advising him to find a genealogist and tempt him with a considerable sum, for which he promised to answer. Jarnac had no need of his master's caution; the money he had saved up was sufficient to pay the genealogist. A purse full of gold, with the promise to pay twice as much in case of success, opened the eyes of the learned parchmenter so well that he fabricated several beautiful contracts, on the strength of which his client was said to be a direct descendant of the original ancestors of the Seigneur de Jarnac, and the rich inheritance belonged to him by full entitlement.

By virtue of a noble delicacy, however, and to satisfy his amour, Jarnac set out with a good grace to console the young heiress by offering to marry her and share his fortune with her. He had a pretty face and an admirable stature; he knew how to copy his master perfectly, and as soon as he belonged to the aristocracy he adopted all its mannerisms. None of these qualities escaped the young woman, so, either because she believed in good faith that he might belong by some descent to the house of Jarnac or because she was simply touched by his handsome appearance, she finally consented to unite her fortune with his, and we were witnesses to their marriage, which took place with the utmost pomp and magnificence.

Like the inhabitants of our world, the Jovinians have several kinds of armories and escutcheons, which serve to distinguish great houses, and one cannot better demonstrate among them that one is of the same stock than by making it seen that one has always and constantly borne the same arms. The most newly ennobled men glory in equipping their carriages with them as soon as the ancient nobility renounces them. Once, one never saw any carriage on which the master's arms were not imprinted on all four faces, but that usage has been entirely abolished; floral designs have been substituted, which signify nothing; genii, fabulous divinities or pretty landscapes have taken their place.

We were assured that the old method was found too inconvenient, and that it was utterly ridiculous not to be able to appear in public without announcing one's quality. One presumes that their pleasures require anonymity, and that is doubtless what has led them to choose that fashion of maintaining it; further confirmation of that conjecture is that several have changed their livery for the sole reason that it was too well-known. It is not rare either to see those who are decorated with ribbons, medallions or other attributes of Orders of chivalry hiding them, or putting them in their pocket.

On that subject we were told about an adventure that had happened recently to a Lord named Paragon, who, being encountered in an exceedingly suspect place without any mark of distinction, was grievously insulted by a few bravos, men of the people who had no other talent than that of knowing how to handle a sword. Paragon was warmed by the juice of Bacchus, and also by the aggravations of a nymph who, far from suspecting his dignity, regarded him as one of those old debauchees ripe for plucking; with that in mind she sought to make him lose whatever reason he had left in order to try to despoil him entirely.

His purse had already been taken and his jewels were being removed one by one, but when Paragon perceived that he as lacking a golden casket containing a portrait of his mistress he demanded its return urgently. The lady in the drinking-den initially denied having seen it. Paragon, who would have given part of his fortune to recover that box, got carried away and made use of epithets that, although appropriate to the woman's profession, nevertheless offended her;

she riposted with the same accompaniments of which Paragon had made use; the dispute became heated, the bravos got involved, a few blows were exchanged, swords were drawn—but Paragon, not finding his own with which to defend himself, would indubitably have been hacked to pieces if the racket they were making had not prompted the neighbors to call for help. The brigands escaped with their young lady by means of a secret door that opened into another street, and Lord Paragon found himself in the necessity of having to swallow the shame of the adventure in long draughts without being able to flatter himself with the possibility of obtaining any vengeance.

Chapter II
Portrait of the Jovinians

In Jovinia the great Lords and members of what are known as the Old Nobility are affable, humane, devoid of arrogance and pride, but the new nobles are braggarts and seem to have been suckled on the milk of vanity; they believe that they alone are respectable, demanding submission, scornful and envious one another, and hating one another. That world has doubtless caught from the air of the Moon the contagion of ostentation, and from that of Venus laxity and sensuality; there is nothing but magnificence in furniture, sumptuousness in carriages, profusion in meals and refinement in pleasures; they are scornful of merchants, and the latter often return the compliment. "You have your titles," they say to them, "and I have my strong-box, with which I can buy nobility whenever I wish."

The rich have charges that bring them honors and profits; the people call them "my lord" and give them other honorifics; they have vassals, beautiful peaks, beautiful manor houses, big town houses and the hope of achieving the principal dignities of the State. How many reasons to forget that they are only human! Thus, the majority only regard all those who approach them as insects with which the earth is covered. Like a certain King of the Molucians who said that he was the King of Hell and wanted his wife to be called Proserpine, his mother Ceres and his dog Cerberus, the Jovinians want to divinize themselves. Those Lords affected simplicity in their garments and have themselves accompanied by domestics whose clothes are decorated with gold and silver.

The majority of the nobility, although obsessed with their names, nevertheless leave to the people the concern of furnishing the State with new citizens. It is exceedingly bourgeois to have several children; a Lord ought to limit himself to a single son—the result of which is that the majority of great names become extinct among them, or would if they were deprived for long of the assistance of genealogists, whose sole occupation in reviving them by means of lies.

At one time, the nobility had no interest at all in science; all their studies were limited to the usages and protocols of society. They scarcely permitted themselves to know how to write; the ability to scribble their name was all that was required. For the same reason, they paid very little attention to the education of their children; they saw them once a day for two or three hours, before dinner, without enquiring as to what they had been doing in the morning or worrying about how they had spent the rest of the day; they were given a tutor, but only for form's sake; if he wanted to teach them anything it was feared that he might weary them; if he dared to complain about them he was an insupportable pedant who only gained the hatred of father and son alike.

In spite of that lack of concern, however, nothing flattered fathers and mothers more than the good dispositions they observed in their children—but nothing touched them less than the obligation they had to cultivate those fortunate dispositions; they imagined that they had fully accomplished their duty by handing over the care of their education to a tutor, until they had succeeded in learning a few items of literature parrot-fashion, which only served to enable them reason abstractly about trivial and puerile matters, and their best days were spent studying a jargon that only served to render them van and presumptuous. They went into society infatuated with themselves; they were convinced of everything, believed that they knew everything, even though they had learned nothing; people only spoke to them about the nobility of their birth, the grandeurs of society, the dignities to which they might aspire; they began by inspiring in them an appetite for wealth, but never spoke to them about honesty, disinterest, good faith or fidelity to their word, doubtless supposing—mistakenly—those sentiments to be innate within them.

The new nobles were not taught to limit their desires; they were not inspired with anything but an immeasurable ambition. Instead of attempting to make them honest and good, equipping them with good morals, showing them generous actions in order that they might acquire a desire to imitate them, and giving them a horror of vice, one only sought to make them men of the world—which is to say, true parrots who only repeat what they have heard said. Thus, far from inspiring in them the true principles by which the truth is reached—I mean enlightened and judicious taste, accurate and delicate discernment, which does not allow itself to be dazzled by appearances but seeks to penetrate matters and gasp their essence, and, in sum, the mentality that learns to know and appreciate the merit of others—that essential study was neglected, and they were only inspired with pride and the desire to please women, and all their instruction as limited to a few superficial duties in which the heart played no part. They were only presented with objects by means of which to become false; errors and dangerous opinions were communicated to them; their hearts were eventually spoiled and their minds filled with nothing but ideas of grandeur and establishment.

It would have been the height of ridicule for a Lord to pay any attention to his household affairs; those concerns are confided to a few stewards who can be regarded as their guardians and who made them pay dearly for the right to that guardianship; following their example, the other domestics rob them at their discretion. One day, I was in the house of one of those Lords, with whom I was acquainted, when his chief valet, an old domestic attached to the household for a long time and very affectionate to its interests—he was perhaps the only one who limited himself to the profit of his wages—sorry to see his master's household in such disorder, took advantage of my presence to warn him that he was being pillaged left, right and center.

"What do you want me to do about it?" said the master. "Do as they do and leave me in peace."

The domestic looked at me with an appealing expression, with a sign that seemed to invite me to remove the scales from his mater's eyes. I therefore said to Lord Periandre that he ought to pay more attention to the zeal of a man who was perhaps the only one who was veritably attached to him, that his advice merited investigation, and that I thought that one could, without being degraded, arrange one's time in such a fashion that, without failing in the duties of one's position, one could spend a few hours a day attending to one's affairs.

"Couldn't you examine your household accounts?" I added. "That would hold your servants in respect and prevent them from conspiring together to bring about your ruination."

"Which is to say," Periandre said, in a tone that bore a strong resemblance to impertinence, "that, in accordance with our noble way of thinking, it's necessary to reduce oneself to the condition of the pettiest bourgeois. I confess that such ideas have never entered the head of a man of my species, and that it would be the most utter absurdity to lower oneself to concerns so puerile."

I did not amuse myself by replying to Periandre's stupid speech, nor in combating his error and his poorly-extended vanity. As he did me the honor of taking my silence for a confession of my ignorance, he condescended to display the most beautiful flowers of his rhetoric to persuade me that his opinions had an infallible character of greatness, beauty and generosity—but his savant discourse only served to inform me that the spirit of order and arrangement is regarded among the Jovinians as a folly and a pettiness unworthy of their nobility. Nothing has greater influence among them than luxury; no one is esteemed except for people who are richly dressed; adornment makes people stand out at last as much as a good reputation. They are less concerned to know a person's morals than to discover whether his wardrobe is well-furnished, whether his furniture is elegant, whether his carriage is spick and span, whether his horses' tails are docked, whether his coachman has a moustache and whether his porter has the marks of distinction of a high-class porter.

In general, all Jovinians love splendor, their glory is to match that which birth and fortune have placed above them; they want to distinguish themselves from their equals; example seduces them and fashion entices them, but both often lead to lavish excess. They are not much given to love, and in just return are not much loved. All their affection is limited to three or four objects: their dogs, their lackeys, their horses and their carriages. They talk about their packs, making the most of the talents of their dogs, which they visit, and all of which they know by name; the loss of one of those animals is often more sensible than that of a mistress.

It is fairly common to see twenty or thirty domestics in a single house, who are as many idlers; far from fulfilling their service, they have themselves served with more arrogance and exactitude than their masters.

But nothing equals the lords' tender attachment to their horses; one would think that the attributes of their grandeur were attached to the number they possess and the prices they paid for them. They push their attention so far for animals of that sort that I have seen more than one lord travel in public carriages in order not to trouble them; they often die of obesity. Often, too, by a contrast that I can hardly conceive, although they so much to be of revive to them, they let them go at full rein. A lord of high quality is always in haste to kill his horse and his runner, if he must, in order to arrive somewhere a quarter of an hour sooner that there is often no urgency for him to reach.

The majority of nobles prove the antiquity of their family by a right to hunt that on other lord can dispute with them. One also produces one's title-deeds, cites one's fiefs, details one's tenures, displays the extent of one's lordships; in sum I cannot describe how jealous the nobility is of its rights, above all that of hunting, and the extent of the powers that they give to their gamekeepers, making them exercise a thousand unworthy vexations every day.

I have seen several fields devastated by the ravages that the hunters, their horses, their dogs and the animals they pursue inflict on the land, but the servitude in which they hold their vassals prevents them from daring to attempts to remedy such disorders. A man whose property adjoins that of a lord can be assured of not drawing any profit from his fields; no one dared dares infringe their rights, because of the penalties to which they are condemned even if they are only found culpable of having frightened off animals that come into their gardens to ravage their vegetables and the plants or bushes that they cultivate with so much care.

Monime and I were invited to spend a few days on the state of a lord named Ardillan. His vassals, notified of his arrival, came to met him with pomp and magnificence, all of them calling him "Milord," and praising his nobility and grandeur. The pressure on his table was great, and all the time he remained on his estate people hastened to pay court to him. The neighboring gentlemen assembled and several hunting parties were arranged.

One day, when it was a matter of putting a stag at bay, we departed early in the morning for the rendezvous. When everyone had assembled, the horn was sounded; the dogs were launched in pursuit of an old stag that gave them exercise for a long time by its ruses, during which everyone saw its skill and agility.

Monime, who took little pleasure in that diversion, and was, in any case, a little fatigued, quit the chase with a another young woman in order to take one of the routes through the wood in the opposite direction. I went with them, and we stopped in a charming spot where they wanted to dismount in order to rest.

After various remarks revolving around the trouble people took in tormenting various animals, the young woman asked whether we were going to be present at the celebrations being held on the occasion of the marriage of Lucinde and Amilcar. Monime replied that, not having the honor of being known to Lucinde, she did not think she would be there.

"You don't know the story of that beautiful person, then?" said the young lady. "I heard it from my brother, who was a witness to the commencement of the adventure, and who, as an interested party, being very smitten, took great care to inform himself of its development."

Chapter III
The Story of Lucinde

"One day, when my brother had been invited to join a hunting party, he was returning on foot with Ardillan. As they came through one of the gates of the park they found a young woman, her face covered in tears, who threw herself at Ardillan's feet. 'I've come, Lord,' she said to him, 'to implore your justice against two of your gamekeepers, who have just murdered my father; those wretches, not content with having fired two rifle shots at him, struck him with the butts.'

"Ardillan tried to lift her up. 'No, Lord,' she said, "I assure you that I shall not quit your knees until you have ordered the cruel murderers who have just taken my father's life to be brought before you.'

"Ardillan, surprised by the action and the firmness of the young woman, ordered one of his servants to summon all his gamekeepers. Then my brother offered her his hand in order to help her to her feet, and, perceiving by the pallor of her face that she was ready to faint, made her sit down on a nearby bench. 'Don't worry, my beauty,' said Ardillan, sitting down beside her and taking one of her hands, which he held in his. 'I give you my word that if your father in not guilty of any crime, I shall inflict an exemplary punishment on the wretches who have committed this injustice,'

"'I protest to you, Lord,' said Lucinde, 'that my father was tranquilly going about his business when those wretches attacked him.'

"Several gamekeepers appeared, but the authors of the crime, warned about the complaint that had been made against them, had taken flight. In the meantime, some domestics arrived to announce that Lucinde's father had just shown a few signs of life. Ardillan immediately ordered that he be brought to the manor house. At this news, Lucinde summoned up all her strength in order to go with the surgeon, who had been ordered to help him promptly.

"Amilcar, Ardillan's son, arrived just as Lucinde's father was brought. The beautiful girl was holding one of his hands, which she was bathing in tears. In spite of the change that despair had inflicted on her features and the disorder of an adornment whose simplicity did not announce opulence, Amilcar was nevertheless surprised by her beauty. Touched by her dolor he went to her and offered her his aid against the authors of her woes. Lucinde, although brought up in retreat, replied to him with a great deal of politeness.

"My brother, who had not quit her, perceived when they entered the courtyard that Ardillan changed color when he saw his son talking to Lucinde. He went to her to invite her to come into the drawing room, but she refused on the basis of the necessity of accompanying her father, in order to be able to give him any help that she could. Ardillan ordered his son to keep the ladies company, and, under the pretext of discovering whether the wounds Lucinde's father had suffered were dangerous, he gave his hand to the beautiful young woman to accompany her to the apartment destined for her.

"The surgeon, after having examined the wounded man, assured them that none of the injuries he had received were dangerous; he was ordered by Ardillan to remain with him until he had recovered entirely.

"The Lord then approached Lucinde. 'If the wound you have inflicted on me,' he said, in a low voice, 'were as easy to cure, I would have no subject for complaint; promise me, my beautiful child, to bring as much care to my relief, as I swear to you to employ for the cure of our father.'

"'I don't know,' Lucinde said, 'what injury I can have caused to your grandeur, but I know that gratitude engages me to employ all that is in my power to acquit myself, if I can, of the obligations that I have to you.'

"'Remember the promise you have made,' said Ardillan, 'and believe that I shall soon give you the opportunity to show me evidence of it.' The Lord left her without waiting for a response, and returned to join the company.

"As the season was already very advanced, they began to play cards, no longer being able to enjoy the pleasure of going for a walk. When Amilcar saw his father engaged in a game, he went out without being observed and ran to Lucinde's apartment, where her father had just fallen asleep.

"The hope that the surgeon had given her had stopped her tears and reanimated her complexion; nothing remained but a certain air of languor caused by the aftermath of the shock she had suffered on learning of her father's misfortune; but that languor rendered her beauty so touching that Amilcar, full of love and admiration, stood there for a few moments contemplating her.

"Lucinde, perceiving that, was slightly troubled; her face was covered by a blush that always accompanies innocence; she lowered her eyes, and that interval of silence was the signal for the commencement of their passion. 'Pardon me, charming Lucinde,' Amilcar said, 'if I dare to appear before you without being announced; anxious about the health of your father, I could not put off any longer coming to seek information.

"'One cannot be any more sensible than I am, Lord,' said Lucinde, 'to the care that you are taking; I'm told that his accident will not have any unfortunate consequence; however, I fear that we will be forced to inconvenience you for a little longer.'

"'Say rather,' said Amilcar, 'giving me a great deal of pleasure by your presence. Be certain, beautiful Lucinde, that if it were in my power to prolong your father's illness without him suffering any damage, there would be nothing I would not do to keep you here as long as I could. The impression you have made on my heart can never be effaced. Don't be surprised by my declaration; the moments are precious when it is a matter of conserving that which one loves, and if I did not fear being anticipated by my father, I would only have begun to make my sentiments known to you by my respect and my intentions. Pardon me, then, divine Lucinde, if I dare to declare a love that will only end with my life.'

"'I would have every reason to take offense at such an outrageous discourse,' said Lucinde, with an irritated expression, 'if I were not convinced that you are too honest a man to want to infringe the laws of hospitality by making mock of a young woman who is already too afflicted by the dolor of seeing a father whom your gamekeepers have almost robbed of his life. My Lord, I would like to believe that you love me, but as I can never respond to a love that can only be, on your part illegitimate, since I'm not unaware that your birth destines you a party more considerable in status, I beg you to contain it within yourself and to be persuaded that, although I am only the daughter of a simple gentleman, you and your father will try in vain to seduce me by means of vain speeches that can never make any impression on my soul.'

"'Cease, beautiful Lucinde,' said Amilcar, 'to accuse me of a perfidy of which I am incapable, and be certain that my intentions are as pure as it is true that you are the most accomplished person in the world. I have no other design than that of uniting myself with you by indissoluble bonds as soon as I am the master of my fate, content, in accepting my responsibilities, simply to await the time when I can give proof of the sincerity of my sentiments, and to adopt the conduct that I ought to maintain in order to convince you that nothing in the world is capable of changing me.'

"Somewhat embarrassed as to the response that she ought to make, Lucinde remained silent for a few moments. She feared offending Amilcar by showing doubts; already her heart was speaking in his favor. Finally, vanquished by that air of frankness, the true character of verity, she said to him: 'If I dared to flatter myself, my Lord, that my scant merit could attach you to me, I would gladly spend the rest of my life in the hope of such a sweet possession, but it would be on the condition of bringing all your care to the conservation of my reputation and my delicacy, in only making your love for me known by the attention you take in concealing the knowledge of it from anyone else.'

"'I submit to all those conditions,' said Amilcar, taking her hand, which he kissed respectfully, 'provided that you assure me that you will never belong to anyone other than me.'

"Lucinde swore that to him, and he left her, very satisfied to have assured himself of the heart of the beautiful young woman, and to have, by his urgency, anticipated his father, on whose part he could not doubt the tender sentiments that she had inspired in him.

"The following day, Ardillan, wounded by the same darts as his son, went to Lucinde's apartment. After asking for news of the invalid, he approached the young woman. 'I have come, my beautiful child,' he said to you, 'to summon you to keep the promise you gave me yesterday, to employ the remedies appropriate to my cure.'

"'Lord,' Lucinde replied, fearing a second declaration, 'As I do not know the kind of malady that afflicts you, it is quite impossible for me to remedy it.'

"'And when you know,' said Ardillan, 'will you not content me, my beautiful young woman, by curing me?'

"'I would be very ingrate,' said Lucinde, 'to refuse your grandeur any help that it was in my power to accord to you; but Lord, you have a surgeon too skillful not to have brought you all the remedies that might contribute to your health, and if the malady is incurable, I am not a good enough physician to attempt such a cure.'

'When one has confidence in a physician,' said Ardillan, 'the remedy supplied has much more effect than those of any other, and as it is in you alone that I put mine, it is also from you alone that I can expect health. Your beauty, charming me, has made a deep impression on my heart; if fortune had been as prodigal in your regard as nature, you would have no need of my benefits. If you care to respond to my love, I can repair the injustices that fate has done you; be content, then, my beautiful child, to render me happy.'

Lucinde, outraged by chagrin at being forced to hear such injurious propositions, nevertheless took the decision to pretend not to understand; that is why she asked in a naïve fashion what it would be necessary for her to do to contribute to his happiness.

"'To love me, my beautiful angel,' said Ardillan.

"'Love you, Lord? But nothing is easier, and on that point, I cannot believe that you have anything of which to complain of anyone. I protest to you that for myself, I have all the respect for you and gratitude that your generosity merits; I can guarantee that of my father, and can assure you of the sentiments we shall both conserve until the tomb.'

Amilcar came in, interrupting the conversation; he told his father that a courier was waiting for him, on the part of the Emperor. Very annoyed by that inconvenience, Ardillan went out, ordering his son to accompany him.

"The courier had brought an order from the Emperor summon him; he could not defer it for an instant, but in order to deny his son any opportunity to see Lucinde, he ordered him to go with him—which Amilcar dared not refuse, for fear of augmenting his the suspicions of his father, an old courtier very difficult to deceive. Amilcar only just had time to scribble a brief note and give it to the surgeon, who came to bid him farewell.

"Meanwhile, Lucinde, left to herself, had time to reflect on her adventure. To begin with she recalled Amilcar, with all the advantages with which he was endowed, and, comparing the respectful attitude of the son with the scornful tone and expressions of the father, she could not doubt that the latter would seek all the most humiliating means to dishonor her. That is why, as soon as her father was in a state to be transported without inconvenience, she begged him to return to their house—or, to put it more accurately, to the debris of an old building of which scarcely two rooms remained intact, and of which the dovecot had been conserved with the greatest care.

"Cilindre had some difficulty resolving to do that, finding himself much more comfortable in Ardillan's house than his own, but Lucinde, dreading that Ardillan's return would expose her to hearing his indecent proposals, or perhaps something more offensive, told her father that since she had been in the manor house she had not obtained any repose, and that the air must be absolutely contrary to her. That determined Cilindre to leave.

"Amilcar, in despair at not being able to obtain any news of Lucinde, not daring to confide in any of his domestics, whom he knew to be devoted to his father, asked my brother, who had become his confidant, to include him in a hunting party that he was due to undertake with several lords, in order to be able to go to see Lucinde without his conduct arousing any suspicion. The party was arranged for the following day.

"Ardillan, delighted to be rid of his son, took advantage of the opportunity to go to Lucinde; he departed in a carriage and arrived at his manor house at nightfall, but was chagrined to be told that Cilindre and his daughter had left a few days after his departure. He was given a letter which only contained expressions of gratitude for the good treatment they had received in his house. Ardillan, aggravated by that setback, lost his temper with his domestics, accusing them of negligence for not having sent him the letter.

"Frustrated of his hopes, he decided to go to visit Cilindre the following day, in order to try to find a few favorable moments to talk to Lucinde. While he was still on the perron giving orders, however, he heard two horsemen coming in sat a gallop, who advanced to the foot of the perron.

"Imagine the surprise of those riders, my Lady, when they recognized Ardillan. Amilcar and my brother—for it was them—remained for a few minutes as if petrified, unable to understand how Ardillan had been able to discover their plan, not having confided it to anyone. Amilcar, however, more familiar with his father's designs than my brother, told him that, having been separated from the hunt, hazard had allowed them to catch a glimpse of him on the road, and in the dread that he might have suffered some disgrace, he had asked Florian to accompany him in order to follow him.

"'You're too attentive, Sir,' said Ardillan, severely, 'and you could have saved yourself the trouble, without seeking to penetrate a mystery in which I didn't judge it appropriate to inform you. I advise you to retrace your steps if you don't want to irritate me further.' He turned his back on them.

"Amilcar withdrew without making any reply, and when he saw his father go into his apartment, he went to find the concierge to obtain news of Lucinde. When he heard that she was no longer at the manor house he was glad, knowing that his father was capable of anything in order to satisfy himself.

"My brother, although piqued that Ardillan had not shown him any politeness, nevertheless urged his friend to come and spend the night with me, which

Amilcar accepted all the more willingly because it would put him in a position to see Lucinde before his father, whom he assumed had only made the journey with that objective.

"It was then the end of autumn and in the shortest days of winter; the woods that it was necessary to traverse were not sure, and the night was very dark. They were marching in silence when they heard the stifled cries of a woman who was being forced to keep quiet by putting a handkerchief over her mouth. My brother, gripped by fear, found that he did not have enough bravery to battle brigands whose number he did not know, and was of the opinion that they should turn back, but Amilcar, far from listening to him, urged his horse in the direction from which the cries were coming.

"As the moon began to dissipate the nocturnal clouds, they say saw two men occupied in despoiling a woman whom fear had rendered immobile. The two wretches, hearing the noise, abandoned the woman in order to come and seize the bridles of the two riders' horses, and each took aim at them with a pistol. Amilcar and Florian, who were fortunately armed with their own, fired at the two thieves, who fell to the ground, and, causing their horses to pass over them, they dismounted in order to see whether there was still time to render some help to the woman, whom they found almost naked and motionless, her face covered in blood.

"After having tormented her a little, Amilcar, who felt an extraordinary agitation, placed his hand over her heart, and, feeling a faint heartbeat there, said, in a voice that shock rendered tremulous: 'She's not dead.'

"Florian approached and they both carried her to the place where the moonlight was brightest. Then Amilcar and my brother, equipped with flasks filled with different waters, tried to make her swallow a few drops. Having entirely emptied them over her face and neck, Amilcar, who had lifted her head, looked at her with more attention, uttered a piercing cry and let her fall back, falling at her feet himself.

"That rude shock recalled her to consciousness; she sighed, opened her eyes, and, as if waking up from a profound sleep, immediately looked around. Then she tried to stand up, but, lacking the strength, said, in a voice that as almost extinct: 'Alas, what are those two wretches waiting for, to rob me of the remains of a life that can no longer be anything but a burden to me? What, can pity still find a place in the heart of a barbaric murderer?'

"'Reassure yourself, dear Lucinde,' said my brother, bathing one of the unfortunate woman's hands with his tears, which pity, love, dolor and amity had caused to flow. He pointed at Amilcar, lying at her feet, unmoving. 'Your lover has just delivered you.'

"'Just Heaven!' cried Lucinde. 'Oh, to have returned me to life only to witness a spectacle that tears my heart!' Then, rolling over, so to speak, beside Amilcar, she took him in her arms, and that tender lover, feeling himself reanimated, finally opened his eyes—but the joy he felt at seeing Lucinde, who was hugging him to her breast so tenderly, was such that, forgetting the misfortune that had just occurred, he thought he had been transported to an enchanted isle. I cannot tell you, my Lady, all the tender and touching things that those two lovers said to one another.

"My brother, a witness to their discourse, forced to enclose his own amour within himself, unable to resist such a rude constraint, interrupted them to tell them that a longer conversation might do them harm, that it was time to think of examining Lucinde's wounds, which might require prompt attention. That is why he advised them, if they had strength enough to reach Lucinde's house or mine, to set out right away.

"Amilcar was of the opinion that they should retrace their steps and deposit his mistress in his father's house with the same surgeon who had taken care of Cilindre, in order that she might be treated with more attention.

"That resolution, which at first appeared foolish, was nevertheless carried out. Lucinde, perceiving the bodies of the two wretches, did not want to go without anyone having looked at them; that is why Amilcar approached them, and, finding that one of them was still breathing, asked Florian to help him carry him to a tree. On examining him, he was extremely surprised to recognize one of his father's gamekeepers, the same one who had previously mistreated Cilindre.

"'Wretch!' said Amilcar. 'So you also wanted my life? But tell me, monster, what do you have against this young woman to attempt hers?'

"'Lord,' said the rogue, in a faint voce, 'has she not one me a great wrong, since she was the cause of my comrade and I having to take flight and losing a position that enable us to live graciously; for it's necessary that you know that her father was not the first that we maltreated thus, but we acquitted ourselves by accusing them of rebellion, and were always believed on our word. It's true that those who gave us a few pieces of silver could hunt safely; we even indicated the places were the most abundant game was. That's the reason why we made the plan to avenge ourselves on Lucinde, and when she went out we kept watch for a moment when she would be alone; having learned that her father had left a few days ago for a long journey, we abducted her tonight, with the design of putting her in a cavern to serve our pleasures, but the girl's cries forced us to maltreat her, and I was preparing to thrust a dagger into her heart when you appeared.'

"Weakened by the blood he had lost, the man expired after having spoken those last words, without showing any repentance for his crimes.

"Amilcar and Florian shivered with horror at the danger that Lucinde had just escaped. It seemed to both of them that she had become even dearer to them, and that is why they hastened to take her to the surgeon, whose wife, who undressed her in order to put her to bed, assured him that her body was badly bruised. The surgeon, after examining her carefully, regarded it as a miracle that such a delicate person had been able to resist such ill-treatment. The barbarians, who had dragged her through the brambles and thorns, had turned her entire body into a wound. Imagine Amilcar's dolor when he saw her in that state; Florian's, although more moderate, was nevertheless keen. Both of them begged the surgeon and his wife to employ all their care to Lucinde's cure.

"The beautiful young woman reflected, however, than an old maidservant, the only domestic she had, surmised not to see her the next day, would not fail to utter loud cries and run all over the village. That is why it was decided to send the concierge, an intelligent and reliable man, to tell her that Lucinde had received an urgent message from her father, and had been obliged to leave immediately in order to obey his order. As Amilcar did not want to leave the manor house as long as Lucinde was there, it was also resolved in their petty council that Amilcar would go to bed immediately and that his father would be told that, while returning with Florian, they had been attacked in the woods by a band of brigands, who had dangerously wounded both of them, but that they believed that they had killed two and that the others had run away.

"Ardillan, sensibly touched by his son's accident, reproached himself for his harshness and ordered that the woods be searched to see whether the wretches were showing any signs of life, in order to extract some enlightenment that might allow their accomplices to be discovered. Then he went to his son's apartment, to whom the surgeon had given a drug that made it seem that his body was covered with contusions. Ardillan, in spite of his finesse, could not help being taken in, but what troubled the pretended invalid furiously was that he made the resolution to remain with him until he was better. The surgeon got out of difficulty by assuring Ardillan that his son's accident would not have any serious consequences, except for confining him to bed for a while.

"In the afternoon it was reported to Ardillan that the two men were dead, and that they had been recognized as the same two gamekeepers who had maltreated Cilindre, which threw him into a furious anger. As the evil was without remedy, however, and they had received the just punishment of their crimes, he ordered that scrupulous searches be mounted throughout the canton.

"After a few days, Ardillan, who could not absent himself from the Court any longer, was obliged to leave, but did want to go without seeing Lucinde, and therefore stopped at her door. The old domestic, hearing the sound of horses and carriages, came running. Ardillan demanded to see her master and mistress. The old woman, deceived by the concierge, told him that they had left a week before to go to the city. Although annoyed by that setback, Ardillan had no trouble consoling himself, in the hope of seeing them soon.

"The Lord having learned the Cilindre was involved a legal dispute that would last a long time, on the subject of a considerable inheritance, his right to which had been contested, was delighted by that circumstance, thinking to make use of that means to give Lucinde evidence of his love by employing his influences with the judges in order to obtain Cilindre a favorable decision. He continued on his way with the greatest diligence. Having arrived at his town house, his first concern was to seek information regarding Cilindre's residence. It took a long time to discover it, but a domestic who encountered him was able to inform him about the visit his master had rendered to hum and the pleasure he would have in seeing him.

Cilindre, his mind occupied with his lawsuit, was charmed by Ardillan's politeness, and as he was not unaware that he had a great deal of influence, he did not fail to go to see the Lord early the following day, who received him as one ordinarily receives the father of a young woman one loves passionately.

"After having made him a thousand caresses, pretending to be unaware of what had brought him to the city, he asked him the reason for his journey, offered him all the services he could provide, and then talked about the beautiful Lucinde, saying that if he had known of her design to come to the city he would have been pleased to offer the charming person a place in his carriage and an apartment in his house, which he begged her to accept, because he thought she would be more comfortably accommodate in his house than anywhere else. 'So,' Ardillan added, 'I shall give my orders to have her luggage brought and tell my coachman to be ready whenever you wish to fetch your daughter, whom I shall expect for dinner, with you.'

"Cilindre, who did not understand any of what the Lord was saying, assured him that he had not brought his daughter or given any order for her to come, having not thought it reasonable to expose her to the dangers of a little frequented road, much less to make her the target of the intrigues of a number of fops who would not fail to put everything to work to find the means of seducing her. 'I'm only a poor gentleman,' Cilindre continued, 'but I swear on the sword I wear that if anyone were dishonest enough to attempt the honor of my daughter, I'd avenge myself in a fashion to make him repent; so, to avoid such misfortunes, I can assure you, Lord, that my design was to never expose her to the risk.'

"At this speech, Ardillan could not help showing his surprise, and after having praised Cilindre's firmness, he told him about the response he had received when he had presented himself to visit him. The gentleman could not persuade himself that his daughter had run away, never having noticed anything to indicate a spirit of intrigue; nevertheless, in order to assure himself of her conduct, he determined to leave immediately in order to clear up the mystery. Ardillan, delighted by his resolution, persuaded him to take his post-chaise, with several domestics, who were ordered to accompany him.

"Meanwhile, we had left Lucinde in the surgeon's apartment, whose wife, no longer unaware of the passion that Amilcar had for the young woman, hastened to express to both of them the zeal she had for their service. She therefore took as much care of Lucinde as if she were already the mistress of the manor, and procured Amilcar every facility to speak to her in private. The two young lovers, ever more charmed by one another, swore a love and fidelity proof against anything, a hundred times over.

"Lucinde had recovered from her fright and the bruises she had received, although a few marks still remained on her body and her face was still swollen and filled with extravasated blood. The beautiful young woman, by means of I know not what presentiment, was absolutely determined to return home, and whatever Amilcar and his confidants could say to her, they had to yield to her insistence. She therefore arrived at her father's house just as he was about to enter it.

"As she was accompanied by Amilcar and the surgeon's wife, Cilindre, who was perhaps the most delicate and prudent man in the world, asked her very mildly what had obliged her to leave his house during his absence. Lucinde was not deceived by that feigned mildness; that is why, for fear of irritating him further, she began by making him examine the bruises with which she was still covered; then she described the misfortune that had overtaken her, and ended up by speaking at length about the new obligations that she owed to Amilcar, assuring him that without the help she had received from the young Lord, she would never have had the joy of seeing him again.

"Satisfied with his daughter's story, Cilindre could not help shivering at the danger that she had run. The tender father, penetrated by the keenest gratitude toward Amilcar, could only express it to him at first by moistening his face with his tears. The young lover, touched as he was, took advantage of the moment to declare the love he had conceived for the charming young woman's rare qualities, swearing to the gentleman that as soon as he was of an age to decide his fate, he would have no other desire than to be united with the amiable Lucinde, and begging him not to give his word to anyone else.

"Cilindre swore that to him, hugging him in his arms again. 'Be persuaded, Lord,' Cilindre added, 'that it is neither to wealth or honors that I am yielding, but to that noble generosity, that delicacy of sentiment and the sincere ardor that you have shown me, which, in assuring the felicity of my daughter, will also complete mine, for I have no doubt that she has the same sentiments for you.'

"That reflection made Lucinde blush, and the malicious Cilindre, perceiving her disturbance, said to her as he embraced her: 'I take your silence, my dear daughter, for a confession of your tenderness; you have placed it too well for me ever to have to complain of it.'

"The beautiful young woman, reassured by those words, judged that she ought also to inform her father of the amour that Ardillan felt for her, and the jealousy that he had conceived of his son, the ruses that the latter had employed to hide the knowledge of the adventure in the wood from him by making it fall only on Amilcar, and the constraint that he had shown in trying to retain within himself the desire that he had for her.

"The worthy gentleman could not help smiling at the folly of Ardillan, who, although certain of his son's amour, still had sufficient self-regard to dare to flatter himself that he might obtain preference with a young woman of sixteen. 'I want, my dear children.' he said to them, 'to punish him for his vanity and his foolish pride, and to be in concert with you. In order to avoid the ruses he might employ to abduct my ewe, I shall go this very day to shut her away in the temple of Helen—and I swear to you again, my dear Amilcar, that she shall never come out except to give you her hand.'

"Our young lovers, who had not expected this decision, were slightly disconcerted by it, but, far from showing their dolor, they were even constrained to thank Cilindre for an attention that would deprive them for a long time of the joy of seeing one another and conversing with one another.

"After the gentleman had thus assured himself of his daughter's conduct, he returned to the city, and rendered an account to Ardillan of the success of his journey—which is to say that he made him believe that Lucinde had returned of her own accord to the virgins until his lawsuit was entirely concluded.

"Ardillan, wanting to hasten that conclusion, employed all his power, and eventually succeeded in obtaining a verdict in favor of Cilindre, which gave him a considerable inheritance. That inheritance rendered the gentleman one of the most powerful Lords in the province, and, in consequence, his daughter became one of the richest parties there was—which led to her being sought by several individuals of great consideration.

"Religious in keeping his word, however, Cilindre waited until Ardillan had also entered the ranks; then, the fortune and the titles he had just acquired having made them equals, he told him that he would have received his proposal with honor if he had not given his word to a young Lord to whom he judged that his daughter had long ago accorded all her tenderness; that he was too good a father to oppose an inclination that was nothing but praiseworthy, the character, age, birth and wealth being well matched, and that he had in addition essential obligations to the young man and all his family, which he could not recognize otherwise than by his union with his daughter.

"Ardillan, who had not expected to find any obstacle to his happiness, was extremely surprised. 'Be wary,' he said, 'of rendering young daughter unhappy by this choice, by yielding too much to his desires. Young men are for the most part dissipated, they indulge in all sorts of excess and superfluous expense: gambling, hunting, pleasures, women and good cheer are ordinarily all their occupations, which often lad them to their ruin.'

"'I agree,' said Cilindre. 'I flatter myself nevertheless that the one I have chosen in not afflicted by those faults; I have known him for a long time and am quite convinced that you will be unable to dispense with approving when you know that it is Amilcar to whom I have given preference.'

"'Amilcar!' cried Ardillan, changing color.

"'Yes,' said Cilindre. 'What is surprising about that? Do you think them poorly matched? Believe me, my dear Lord, make this sacrifice with a good grace, for although you are his elder, it is nevertheless necessary to yield to him in this instance; let us leave to our children the care of making the torch of Hymen burn, which it is only appropriate for youth to light.'

"Ardillan did not appear to like that precept at first, but he has assuredly consented to the happiness of the two lovers, and has only returned to his manor in order to organize the celebrations."

Chapter IV
Further Observations

After the young woman had told us the story of Lucinde's adventures, we resumed the route to the manor house, where we found Cilindre and his charming daughter, who had just arrived there. Ardillan, informed of their arrival by his runner, abandoned the hunt in order to come and welcome them, and, going into the drawing room with us, introduced us to the father and daughter, adding that he hoped before long to see his son the possessor of that treasure.

"It is true," he said, casting an animated glance at Lucinde, "that I was reckless enough to compete with him for her, but the beautiful child's choice has finally rendered me sage; all my desires are limited now to the sole pleasure of being able to call her my daughter, and I flatter myself that you will be kind enough to honor with your presence the feasts that I am preparing to celebrate their wedding."

Monime excused herself on the grounds of the little time that we had to remain in the province.

We departed the following day to rejoin Zachiel, to whom we rendered an account of our journey. After having told him the story of Lucinde, Monime praised the young woman's charms greatly, and the probity and fine manners of Amilcar. She thought that no marriage was as well matched as that one.

"Those fortunate lovers," she said, "will finally enjoy in liberty the pleasure of loving and being loved, the mixture of tenderness and the return of esteem for which sensate people always ought to search in their marriages."

"It is true, beautiful Monime," said Zachiel, "but bonds so sweet can only be founded on virtue, and unfortunately, the majority of Jovinians employ nothing in their unions but disguise; one might think that they only reach accord in order to deceive one another more fully; enjoyment, complaisance, assiduity, concern, ostentation and expense are only employed to hide the eccentricity of their character, the inequality of their humor and the sorry state of their affairs. Nothing is to rare as to find among them two hearts linked by the most perfect esteem, the most sincere confidence, the most delicate respect and tenderness, and the mutual ardor to oblige one another and care for one another; everything ought to concur in those engagements of good intelligence, which adversity can never alter, and which become one bond more for those who are united in that way, as if it were a new duty that ought to end up making them a single individual.

"But the young people here glory in the license of their conduct; they display their vices ostentatiously and extract vanity from their dishonor. The majority deliver themselves to lust less to enjoy its pleasures as to have the means of depreciating themselves, glorying in the baseness of their sentiments. Born in the impure source of crime, nourished with all that is most contagious, delivered entirely to their appetites, virtue appears to them to be nothing more than a chimera; they only recognize evil; that is what uses them up before their time and cuts short their days."

We arrived in a large city, whose streets were filled with an infinite multitude of people. Monime asked Zachiel what that great influx of people signified.

"It is," said the genius, "to see the ceremony of a procession that is due to take place at midnight."

"Is it something very extraordinary, then?" I asked him.

"No," said Zachiel, "nothing is so ordinary as seeing death; nature subjects all humans to it—but nothing is as singular as the ceremonies that are employed among the Jovinians for their burials; here, it is only permitted to the bourgeois to have their relatives buried as soon as they are dead, without being divided, and it is part of the grandeur of a Lord to be kept for at least seven days; it is necessary for that for them to be embalmed. The corpse is laid out on a table, its entrails are removed and put into a lead barrel in order to be taken to one place. The heart is put into a golden box to be taken to another, and the body to a separate sepulcher in a third place.

"The three inhumations always take place at night; it would be too humiliating for humanity to bury a dead man of quality in broad daylight. How can one imagine that the souls of the great, which must assuredly be privileged, can escape ignobly with the crowd of the simple faithful? Their glory demands that extravagant ceremonies be reserved for them; hence the glare of torches multiplied to infinity and more brilliant in the obscurity of night, which renders the funeral pomp more magnificent and more beautiful.

"Everyone in the household, including the horses and carriages, must wear mourning for the deceased. I don't know whether it is very heartfelt, but in any case, it will not last long; this is the world where one is most easily consoled, and although the apartments are hung with black and all the carriages are draped without, people here nevertheless wear cheerful and elegant mourning; it is merely a conventional decency, because it would be shameful not to weep for those whom nature has joined to them by blood. That is why they copy the external appearances of a true dolor—but that hypocritical dolor is only to satisfy custom.

"A father whom death robs of a unique, tenderly beloved son, is obliged to confine his chagrin; he dare not mourn in public; but a husband who loses a wife whose enemy and persecutor he was must affect for a long time all the exterior lugubriousness of a dolor he does not feel.

"It is also part of the dignity of a great Lord to order by testament the construction of some new chapel, either in the temple of Juno or that of Jupiter, because one ought to donate in dying a part of the wealth that one can no longer enjoy; then one has a magnificent tomb built; epitaphs in a fine style ornament the four faces—which costs immense sums that might be better employed in paying creditors than raising a superb mausoleum to an insensible debtor.

"In sum, nothing is lacking in this funeral pomp but the grief of those who take part therein. They are still remembered, however, two or three months longer than the poor dead man, because custom requires that all his acquaintances are solemnly invited to come and hear a hired orator pronounce a eulogy that is commonly a tissue of counter-truths, which only serves to make the eloquence of the orator admired, to whom it suffices to paint the virtues of a hero and add the name of the deceased thereto."

The various provinces that we have just traversed had only offered me, as yet, very few examples that could inform me as to the customs of the Jovinians, because, in spite of what I have said about the manor houses so magnificently built, and the exteriors so carefully maintained, that we had found on our route, the Lord to whom they belonged had almost never put in an appearance. A great Lord only retires to his estates if he is disgraced, or for some pleasure that nature and art have contrived there; he does not like it there; he dries up with ennui and in the end is no longer alive, scarcely vegetating, and death soon comes to deliver him from that humiliation.

We continued our route toward the capital of the Empire. After a few days' travel, we entered into a beautiful avenue that formed a delightful arbor as far as the eye could see. Monime found the place so agreeable that she wanted to get out of the carriage in order to walk on a lawn that might have been taken for a carpet of emeralds.

Scarcely had we taken twenty paces than we perceived a man who was walking alone, in a profound reverie; in spite of a livid and jaundiced complexion, and a sad and languid expression, his physiognomy announced a nobility and something interesting.

"I'm surprised," I said to Zachiel, "that a Lord is left to himself like this in his convalescence, for it appears to me that he has just endured a serious illness from which he has not yet entirely recovered. The air of grandeur that one observes in his entire person leads me to believe that he ought to have a court, or at least a few friends, seeking to amuse him; dissipation puts a balm into the blood, which contributes a great deal to the reestablishment of health. Doubtless he has only left the Court in order to come here to fortify himself."

"You're mistaken," said Zachiel. "The cause of that Lord's dejection is not an order he has received to leave the Court, although it's true that it is a severe distress for a courtier to be forced to live in his estates."

"For what reason has he been exiled?" I asked.

"It's because he has insufficient skill to maintain himself in favor," said the genius, "because his intrigue was not superior to that of his enemies, because he was unable to bring down those who have brought him down, and because he made enemies of those he had obliged the most; those are his crimes.

"That Lord," the genius went on, "is naturally good; he was born obliging; he has a pure soul, the mores and conduct of a perfectly honest man. I know that he has only fallen into the Prince's disgrace for lack of having the ardent malevolence by means of which one dooms one's enemies; that is the masterpiece of the intelligence of a courtier. Among the Jovinians, everyone is solely occupied with his elevation and his fortune; that is what produces illustrious deceivers. A bad reputation is indifferent to them, injustice hardly touches them; love of grandeur alone takes possession of their desires. However, the avidity that they have to reach eminent positions torments them all their lives and it often happens that a man who obtains a few great dignities by means of intrigue lives in the perpetual anxiety of waking up to discover his fall."

"It appears to me," said Monime, "that this Lord ought scarcely to regret a position that puts him in continual anguish; he ought, on the contrary, to bless the Heaven that, in delivering him from so much embarrassment, puts him within reach of living tranquilly."

"I am sure, beautiful Monime," said the genius, "that that courtier does not regret overmuch the place he has just lost; that is not what has broken his heart. No, he has conserved his kindness and his generosity, but the habitude of honors has disturbed his mind; he regrets the turmoil in which he lived, the trouble that everyone took to reach him when he had his master's ear. The flatterers of which he made fun in the times of his elevation and who regarded it as good fortune to win his favor, are lacking; he no longer sees the timid and crawling expressions that amuse his vanity; he is no longer in a position to secure anyone's destiny; his false friends no longer have any interest in cultivating him. He is sighing for the place he occupied in the minds of others, for the fearful respect that it pleased him to inspire, for the incense with which people tried to intoxicate him, even though he employed the most obliging methods to dissipate it; in sum, he is sighing for a thousand similar phantoms, without which he can no longer live, because they have become the necessary nourishment of a mind poisoned by the pernicious venom of ambition."

"Whatever you say," said Monime, "I feel touched by that Lord's distress; his dejection penetrates the depth of my heart. Out of regard for his rare qualities, grant me, I beg you, the favor of curing him of his ambition, since it is the sole fault you recognize in him. You can do that, my dear Zachiel; make his chagrins disappear, I implore you; enable him to forget their causes it make him scorn them; enable his virtue to console him for the injustices he has received from fate, and let him renounce all the ideas of grandeur and elevation that are the source of his woes. Take away the disgust that he has for solitude, in order that he can savor its delights. I would like at least to think that I had seen one man among the Jovinians happy by virtue of the assistance of reason alone."

"I consent to satisfy you, charming Monime," said Zachiel. "The tender interest you take in the troubles of that illustrious unfortunate gives me further evidence of the generosity of your heart, and I shall employ the force of reasoning to convince him."

We advanced toward the courtier, whom the genius approached with a mild and majestic attitude. Their conversation revolved at first around vague matters, but what power a genius has over the human mind! He is always sure of leading him to the point that he desires. The Lord, drawn by a superior force almost in spite of himself, forgot his ordinary politics in order to show himself as he was; he opened his heart to the genius, who read his soul; what weaknesses did we not see! How petty humans are! How much they have to bemoan!

The courtier, his mind still full of his disgrace, recounted all his misfortunes to Zachiel; he complained bitterly of the treasons and unjust means that had been employed to bring him down, of which he had become the unfortunate victim. To console him, Zachiel first lent himself to his weakness and appeared to sympathize with all his reasons, but then he combated them with the intelligence that pleases, draws insensibly and touches the heart so well even it seems only to be speaking to the mind and its reason. He added that the innocence and purity of his intentions ought to reassure him for the future; that the Prince would recognize them one day and would avenge him on those who had dared to blacken him without his knowledge and engineer his fall; that he ought presently to regard his disgrace as a road that would lead him to perfection; that he only had one step to take to free himself from the yoke of the passions that dominated vulgar men; that with a little effort upon himself, he could render himself master of his penchants—and afterwards, exempt from weakness, he would enjoy a fate that undoubtedly ought to be envied by all mortals.

The Lord, penetrated to the depths of his heart by the reasons the genius had employed to console him, was immediately relieved. The speech resembled a shooting star that pierces the night and leaved after it a trail of light to show sailors the heading of their compass, in order that they can put themselves on guard against the impetuous winds that might break their vessel on jagged rocks; such was, I think, the sharp impression made on the soul of the courtier by the insinuations of the genius.

"I render thanks to fortune," said the Lord, "for having made use of the malice of my enemies to enlighten me as to the nature of good and evil; without their treasons and perfidy, perhaps I would never have had the good fortune of meeting you, and it is only from you that I have learned that adversity put to profit purifies the heart and submits it to reason. I confess that at first, I did not regard my exile with indifference, and only sustained it with a great deal of difficulty; sensitive to the insult I had received, a frightful melancholy, at being separated from the court and deprived of all society, had, so to speak, numbed all the faculties of my soul; my self-esteem, too humiliated by that fall, left me no liberty to reflect. You have suddenly removed the scales from my eyes, in making me sense the price of virtue, the danger of honors and the stupidity of the prejudices in which I was living; what thanks do I not owe you for so many benefits!"

"However," said Zachiel, "you have more than one motive for consolation; you know that men are not always the same; it would do too much honor to human nature to credit it with uniformity; so those who regard you with indifference or scorn today might perhaps seek tomorrow, for some extraordinary motive, opportunities to be of use to you. These changing men are always filled with bad qualities; that is why it is necessary to get out of them what one can; there are honest insinuations that even the most artful can use without scruple; there are complaisances that are as far from adulation as from rudeness."

The Lord invited us with such good grace to spend some time with him, in order to help him fortify the fortunate dispositions that the genius had just inspired in him, that we were unable to refuse, and the time that we enjoyed his hospitality was employed so usefully for the Lord that he assured the genius, when we left him, that he was completely cured of all the nonsense of grandeur and elevation that had troubled his repose for such a long time, and that whatever proposition might be put to him, he would not exchange the state of tranquility he had acquired for the foremost dignity in the Empire.

During our journey the genius took advantage of the example of that disgraced courtier to give us further instructions on the character of courtiers, their jealousy and their intrigues.

"You will see among the Jovinians," he told us, "nothing but perfidy and artifice. It is on this world that one sees flattery always crawling at the foot of the throne, overturning virtue, innocence and truth as soon as they appear; you will see envy ornamenting itself with the name of emulation or, of course, self-esteem; you will see arrogance taking on that of noble pride, ostentation that of magnificence and avarice that of thrift; in sum, you will see everywhere vices usurping the external appearances, titles and prices of virtues; probity, honor and innocence unknown, debased and persecuted. Courtiers compose nothing by a mixture of baseness, ridicule and impertinence; insincere among themselves, they only seek to betray one another; the majority only see through the veil of their passions; they see events as if in a distorting mirror that disfigures the objects it represents, always abandoning the truth in order to run after the phantom forged in their imagination by ambitious deigns, and mistaking their chimerical hopes for realities.

Having finally arrived in the capital of the empire, I began to instruct myself, but where I came to know the Jovinians in depth was at the Court. We went for some time without appearing there. That capital, which is one of the most beautiful and richest cities on the entire plane, is also the rendezvous of the entire Empire. The city, so vast, so rich and so varied, presented so many new objects to our curiosity every day that, charmed by all we saw there, I could not imagine that there could be anything more worthy of our attention—but the Court disabused me agreeably.

Chapter V
Description of the Emperor's Palace

The Emperor has his residence in the Palace of Taste. That palace surpasses in beauty and magnificence everything one can imagine of the most marvelous; broad and beautiful avenues lead to the first courtyard, which is closed by a gate in the middle of which is a golden sun whose rays serve as bars. Three sets of colonnades enrich the exterior of the palace; the first colonnade is bronze, the second porphyry and the third transparent jasper, which form the most beautiful view in the world.

The walls of the palace are a marble as white as alabaster. The Ionic order and the superb Corinthian have been employed to raise the pompous edifice all the way to the clouds. It is evident that the architect and the sculptor, both excellent in their art, have put all their glory and combined their talents in order to render the edifice one of the most perfect in the universe. The frontispieces are ornamented by numerous figures in relief, which represent a hundred beauties of which the history of fable boasts. They all appear on that marble with such optical perfection that each of them expresses there the most interesting phase of her life.

On the side of the colonnades are represented the various amours of Jupiter; to the right, Mark Antony is forgetting beside the Queen of Egypt the care of the Roman Empire; further away, the enchantress Armide is gazing menacingly at Renaud, who is fleeing with the Danish knight; here Artemisia is showing Clélie the fatal urn that contains the ashes of her illustrious spouse.[49]

On the left, one sees Helen, the beauty who did so much damage to the Trojans for having favored the shepherd Paris; one sees the apple that Discord had picked in the garden of the Hesperides, which the shepherd presented to Venus; the satisfaction of the goddess is painted on her face, and her smiling expression seems to be announcing to the shepherd King the protection she accords him; to the side one sees Juno and Minerva, who, although very wise goddesses, are nevertheless showing by their angry expressions that they are not immune to the deadly poison of jealousy, which will lead each of those goddesses to take sides in the Trojan War in order to signal her vengeance.

On the same side one sees Oenone, the nymph who, ordinarily living on Mount Ida, had espoused the son of Priam when he was only a simple shepherd;

---

[49] *Clélie, histoire romaine* (1654-61) is a ten-volume novel by Madeleine de Scudery, which became notorious for its invention of the allegorical Carte de Tendre [Map of Tenderness], which provides a geographical guide to amorous intent; it has clear links with some of Madame Robert's allegorical passages. Jupiter's presence in Scudery's novel is also allegorical rather than literal.

her dolor is so well represented that she seems to be complaining to the Nereids of the fickleness of Paris, who quit her for Helen, whom Theseus had already abducted. Cassandra, Paris sister, appears in the recess, her hair scattered and agitated by a spirit of prophecy, abounding the misfortunes that will lay waste to Troy.

On the right one sees Ariadne, the daughter of Minos and granddaughter of the Sun via her mother Pasiphae, the princess exiled from the island of Crete after betraying her father the King for love for Theseus, by giving him a thread in order that he could get out of the labyrinth containing the Minotaur, who was abandoned by that Prince on a desert island where she bemoaned his perfidy for a long time—but Bacchus, perhaps attracted by her plaints, became amorous of her; one sees the wedding of the god celebrated by the Bacchantes, and Ariadne raised into the heavens, where she forms a crown of stars.

Dejanira, the wife of Hercules, is on another side. It is known that Hercules, the son of Jupiter, after having fulfilled the dozen labors that had been imposed in him by Eurystheus, minister of Juno, allowed himself to be seduced by the charms of Omphale, and with her exchanged the club with which he had killed so many monsters for a distaff, and the skin of the lion he had vanquished for the young woman's girdle. Dejanira, only heeding her jealousy, allowed herself to be seduced by the insinuations of the centaur Nessus, who, seeing himself close to expiring from an arrow he had received, assured her that his blood had the virtue of reigniting the first fires; that is why Dejanira sent Hercules a shirt tainted with the centaur's blood, but, on learning that the shirt was poisoned, her fury drove her to hurl herself from the summit of a rock into the sea.

Dido, Queen of Carthage, is represented with a dagger in hand, driven by the despair of having allowed herself to be seduced by the promises of the perfidious Aeneas, whose ship she can see drawing away under full sail.

Hypsipyle appears to be reproaching her husband Jason for having left her for Medea; that sorceress employed her art to aid Jason when he went with the other Argonauts to conquer the Golden Fleece, which allowed him to overcome without difficulty all the dangers that lay in wait for him; he tamed the bulls consecrated to Mars, killed the dragon that was the guardian of the Fleece and carried that rich booty to Thessaly, taking Medea with him, whom he subsequently abandoned for Creuse—but Medea, to avenge herself, caused him to burn in his palace with his new spouse.

One also sees the amours of Ceres with Jason; that goddess, who presides over the crops, had retired to the depths of the woods, her hair was not ornamented with ears of corn; her heart conflicted by amour, was only occupied with the doom she had prepared for Jason, whom Jupiter caused to die out of jealousy; it is said that his amours gave birth to Plutus, who presides over wealth.

The other face represents the goddess Venus, who is seen sitting in the depths of a remote wood on Cythera; the goddess has just quit Paphos to weep for Adonis, whom a cruel monster has just snatched from life; the Graces, in mourning dress, are seated beside her; Laughters, Games and Amours, frightened by her despair, are flying to Paphos to spread the news.

Ornaments, in sum, cannot be distributed with more elegance and profusion; all the parts of that superb edifice are admirably well-wrought, and everything that genius, taste and art can invent of the most perfect is combined there; one can say that it contains the masterpieces of all the arts.

I shall not attempt to describe the magnificence and richness of all the furniture, the paintings, the mirrors, the busts, the vases as precious by virtue of their material as the perfection of their carving, and a thousand other rarities that ornament the Emperor's apartments and compose an accumulation of objects that please and dazzle the sight. Monime and I, gripped by delight and ecstasy, remained motionless for a few moments, with the result that we might have been mistaken for two new statues that had just been placed.

Nor shall I say anything about the beauty of the park or the diversity of the ornaments that embellish the gardens, in which the history of fable is represented in the midst of the great basins or beautiful expanses of water that are distributed in all the parts of those gardens. We cast a rapid glance over the beauties of that enchanted abode; we admired the crystal and murmur of the waters, several of which sprang into the air in sprays and fell back as rain; others descended in cascades or fled into the plain.

On another side the freshness of the arbors, the symmetry of the flowerbeds, and the side-paths embarrassed with labyrinths, and the agreeable mixture of flowers all fixed our attention for some time; one might have thought that the skillful artists who enriched them with ever-renewed masterpieces had also combined with their art the secret of connecting streams, and that, improving of nature, they forced them to launch forth toward the clouds, hurling millions of brilliant arrows into the air, and liquids driven by the marine gods or the naiads; on the other hand, they fall back in a thousand places marked by the artist.

Chapter VI
Their Reception at Court

Night was beginning to deploy its veils when Zachiel introduced us to Cassiel, who was one of the principal captains of the Emperor's guard. That genius—for he was one—was delighted to receive Zachiel, and made us very welcome, but he excused himself for not being able to stay with us longer, because he was on duty.

It is customary in that court for each captain to be unable to dispense, under any pretext whatsoever, with making his round of the palace, in order to make certain that the guard is maintained exactly at all its posts, and as it was time for him to make that round and he is a rigid observer of his duty, he handed us over to the Emperor's principal gentleman and the marshal of his lodgings, who took us to a superb apartment. The gentleman informed Zachiel that great revolutions had occurred in the Empire since the genius Samael, who is its protector, had absented himself.

"Everyone," he continued, "seeks honors and riches here, without putting any effort into meriting them; but your presence might bring us a few fortunate changes useful to the entire State."

He quit us then in order to inform his master of the arrival of the genius.

Zachiel was introduced at his *petit lever*; he had a long conversation with the monarch regarding the affairs of his State. The genius then talked about us, informing the Emperor of the protection that he had accorded us, the various voyages he had made us undertake and the ideas he had in mind for our establishment. That novelty excited the curiosity of the Prince, who had difficulty understanding how we had been able to cross the immense spaces that separate so many worlds. That secret, which the genius only confided to him, determined him to give us a public audience the very next day, wishing, by that favor, to demonstrate to the genius the pleasure he had in seeing him again, by allowing us to participate in the honors he disposed to all those who had the advantage of being admitted to his court.

The genius had Monime take the same name and qualities that he had given her among the Idalians, because, in order to appear with brilliance in any court, it is necessary to have a name that distinguishes you. Her house was soon built; the same gnomes were summoned to ornament it thereafter and to serve her, and the following day, we were introduced to their august majesties, who were on a golden throne enriched with diamonds. That throne, elevated by ten steps, was at the end of a long gallery bordered on both sides by several steps in the manner of an amphitheater, on which had been placed, on the Emperor's side, all the lords of the court, and on the Empress' side, all the ladies—who formed an admirable sight, for nothing is richer and more magnificent than that Court.

The Emperor was surprised by Monime's beauty; it is certain that, in spite of the splendor and brilliance of everything that surrounded him, she appeared as a new star; the genius has lavished everything upon her that might render a person accomplished.

Zachiel advanced between us, and presented us to the Emperor. "I have come, Lord," he said, "to put under Your August Majesty's protection these two young strangers, who have acquired, by their application to the study of the sciences, mores and customs of the different nations that fill the universe, the honor of being presented at your Court and of participating in the benefits of which you are the dispenser." Indicating Monime, the genius added: "This young Princess is named Thaymuras; she is the sovereign of a country on Earth, which is a world very distant from this one, which your astronomers only see as a dot in the universe. This young Lord is her relative; both having been brought up by my cares, I have judged them worthy of being admitted to the grandeurs and other gifts that might be acquired by your benevolence."

"I have always regarded you as a benevolent genius," said the Emperor. "It is to give me a signal proof of that to procure me the advantage of receiving in my Court a Princess who will be its entire ornament." The monarch added: "But my Lady, how were you able to decide to undertake such long and fatiguing voyages?"

"My Lord," said Monime, "Your August Majesty can easily be persuaded that, being guided by a genius of the first order, we are not running any risk, and our voyages have been made with all possible convenience."

The monarch asked her a few more questions regarding the mores, customs and usages observed on our world, to which Monime replied with sagacity and dignity. During that conversation, all the ladies and lords of the court had their eyes fixed on Monime; everyone was regarding her with admiration, unable to convince themselves that she was a mortal. When the audience was over, we were visited by all the nobles of the Empire.

That Court, although a little more serious than that of the Venusians, is no less amusing. Amour presides there; his temples are at least as frequented as in the Empire of Venus, but everything happens with much more decency; it is true that the etiquette is a trifle inconvenient; there is a continuous ceremonial, all the hours are marked there; and although we were strangers, we were nevertheless obliged to conform to the usages.

A few days after our audience, Zachiel introduced me to the Emperor's *petit lever*. The monarch received me generously, and asked me about the observations I had made on the different worlds that I had visited, with regard to their governments, their laws, their customs, the genius of the great men and the ministers, the extent of their enlightenment and the talents it was necessary to have in the courts to succeed to the highest dignities.

"Have no fear of telling me your reflections freely," said the Prince.

"I must obey Your August Majesty's orders," I replied. "I have noticed, my Lord, in the different worlds we have traveled, that the majority of men, with little merit, aided solely by hazard and fortune, nevertheless acquire glory and perform great functions without being great themselves. Virtue and true merit often remain in oblivion; there are people of very limited intelligence who are nevertheless distinguished; one sees brave men whose other quantities do not respond to their value; great captains but small intellects; others who have high intelligence and are regarded as wise heads, but whose souls are base and their hearts evil.

"I have seen, my Lord, many individuals whose intellect and merit does not have the good fortune to please, who have been unable to combine all the talents they have received from nature with that of making themselves loved. One sees others who shine in movement and action, but whom repose obscures and annihilates, because it is only employments and dignities that give them value, and who, in retreat, are no longer anything but the shadow of what they were. That is because, on the majority of all those worlds, persons of true merit are not employed in the ministry, and the greatest interests are only confided to people who do not even have the quality of leadership so necessary to a State.

"That method, it is true, seems very inconsequential, but when one reflects on the genius of those nations, of which the fire, the inconstancy, the fickleness and the spirit of intrigue are the motors of all their actions, one is no longer surprised by such conduct. In any case, the majority are deluded, and leave to their presumption the art of dissimulating their incapacity. But my Lord, I have perhaps gone on a little too long, and I fear that I might have fatigued your attention."

"No," said the Emperor, "I am very satisfied with your reflections, and I see with pleasure that your voyages have not been fruitless for you. It is certain that, aided by the enlightenment of the genius and listening to his advice, it will not be difficult to combine in yourself all the talents necessary to govern well, because the faults that you have remarked in humans will be incessantly present to your mind, to prevent you from falling into the same faults."

"It is true, my Lord," I said, "that one knows others better than one knows oneself; the defects of others wound us far more than our own; the familiarity that we have with our passions disguises them for us; nothing in ourselves is new, because it forms so to speak, a species of habitude between our reason and our weaknesses, which enables them to subsist together; it is nonetheless the same ones that we discover in others; the reason with which we like to ornament ourselves examines them, pursues them and condemns them, while it permits itself a thousand disorders that it does not have the strength to correct."

"It is easy," said the Emperor, "to recognize by your reflections that you have profited a great deal from Zachiel's precepts. That is why you are better able than anyone else to put a brake on your passions."

A profound bow was my response.

The monarch then chatted for a long time with the genius; I could not weary of admiring his generosity and familiarity.

When we had quit the Emperor, I told Zachiel how sensible I was to such an agreeable reception. "I know," I said, "that it is only in your favor that the Prince showed me so many marks of benevolence, but that does not diminish my keen gratitude in the least; I am so penetrated by it that I would shed my blood for his service."

"The better you know the monarch," the genius said, "the more you will like him. If Princes knew how many hearts they would gain if they cared to familiarize themselves with those who approach them, they would often quit the false grandeur that always seems grim and inaccessible. Remember, my dear Seaton, that true grandeur is free, mild, familiar, and even popular; it allows itself to be touched and loses nothing by being seen at close range. The better one knows it, the more one admires it; although it inclines generously toward its inferiors, it is soon seen to return effortlessly to its natural state; and if it sometimes relaxes its advantages, it is always able to take them up again and make the most of them; one approaches it with both liberty and restraint; its character is noble and facile; its inspires respect and confidence, and in sum, enables Princes to appear much less grand without making you feel small. Such is the character of the monarch who reigns over the Jovinians."

We then we to see Monime, whose beauty, intelligence and graces had already attracted a great many admirers, but none worthy of touching her heart; they were the kind of brilliant scatterbrains who, always convinced of their false merit, are convinced that they have acquired the right to master all the women they wish, and whose urgent attentions are so many insults. Never sensitive, never content, always perfidious, always ingrate, incapable of limiting themselves to a single conquest, they want to seduce all women, and employ the basest stratagems to succeed in that; tyrannical to their mistresses and even crueler to women who have the strength to resist them, one sees them boasting about the favors they have received and presuming similarly upon those they have been refused, which makes it rather difficult to shield oneself from their malevolence and calumny.

Those gallant fops could not cause me any kind of anxiety, and I was not attacked in that courting by the deadly poison of jealousy. As the influences that dominate that world only work upon the love of grandeur and wealth, I believed that I had nothing to fear for the interests of my heart; I was aware of Monime's noble sentiments; I had the pleasure of seeing her every day, and her attentions to me seemed to assure me of a tranquil fate.

However, the Emperor could not see Monime with indifferent eyes. All the perfections that shone in her gave birth in the heart of the monarch to the most ardent passion. First of all he wanted to lodge her in his palace, and lavished her with gold and diamonds in profusion, like Danae. Every day there were new presents of inestimable price, but what is singular is that very few women were jealous, perhaps because they feared the vindictive humor of the Empress, who, in spite of the Emperor's inconstancy and all his infidelities, had nevertheless acquired so much credit for her intelligence during the absence of the genius who was the Empire's protector that nothing was done without her orders— which was the cause of many troubles.

That Princess was not endowed with the enlightenment necessary to rule such a great Empire and her self-regard did not permit her to follow the advice of enlightened ministers who had worked under the genius Samael. Those ministers, either by virtue of dread or weakness, preferred exile to the noble boldness and love of the fatherland that ought to have encouraged them to make known to the Emperor the disorders that poor administration were introducing into his State.

Chapter VII
Seaton's Anxieties Regarding the Emperor's Love for Monime

Monime was the delight of the entire court, and the Emperor came to see her assiduously two or three times a day, delighted by the enlightenment of her mind, her talents, the tenderness of her character, and the candor and air of modesty that never quit her. Her heart, exempt from all ambition, and her conversation, sustained by the most extensive knowledge, charmed the monarch, whose admiration for her was further increased every day.

His assiduity soon attracted the homages of all the couriers to Monime; it was to her that they paid court; her apartment became the rendezvous of the finest individuals; it was the height of fashion to say that one was coming from the Princess Thaymuras' house, and a number of fops were seen there who not only went to pay court to the Emperor but also for the sake of vanity, in order to give themselves the reputation of being of the Prince's party, and in consequence well placed at court. It often happened that Monime's apartments were filled with a quantity of people of whom she did not know the face, the name or the quality.

Among the number of ladies who came to Monime's house, I noticed one who always contrived to place herself next to me and talked to me with an air of mystery. What she whispered in my ear was mostly trivia, but she did it in such a honeyed tone that she seemed only to want to speak to the heart. I confess that I did not understand, at first, what her intentions were; being little versed in the art of gallantry, in any case, and quite denuded of self-regard, I was the last to perceive the provocative glances of which a fop would not have failed to take advantage. As for me, perhaps I say to my shame, all her advances were a pure waste of time; my heart being entirely delivered to tender amity, I would have thought it a crime to flirt with a woman for whom I did not feel anything. I am sure that the people who perceived the advances that were made to me must have regarded me as a fool, but I have always thought that candor and good faith ought to reign in all our actions.

However, Nardillac—that was the beauty's name—had one distinguished merit; she as at the age when art embellishes, coquettish with intelligence, sensible with solidity, tender with sensuality and voluptuous with economy; the age when a man who pleases is sure to be fortunate, to be loved and to be conserved, provided that, in his turn, he can become amiable, amorous and faithful; the age, in sum, when a thousand advantages, very well known to men, are nevertheless a source of vivacity in pleasures, delicacy in cares, resources in the intervals and surety against loss of appetite, since sensuality consists in managing pleasures, tasting them with refinement making the most of the simplest things and finding satisfaction therein.

Tranquility, ease and purity in morals are normally the companions of sensuality: a mild, uniform, innocent and happy life can only be voluptuous; often solitude, the study of the sciences, a small number of friends, a frugal meal can still be susceptible of sensuality; one also finds it in the union of two hearts exactly faithful by virtue of the conformity of sentiments; the purity of their ardor, a reciprocal confidence, enables them to enjoy the sweetest pleasures of sensuality; in sum, it is certain that it is encountered everywhere that debauchery is not.

But I am straying from the subject, which is Nardillac.

I shall leave that beauty momentarily, in order to return to Monime.

One day, the Emperor came to spend the whole afternoon with Monime; as he did not admit anyone to that conversation I could not resist the sharp anxieties that were agitating me, and I waited impatiently for him to emerge, in order to make Monime party to them. It was not jealousy, but a milder and more delicate sentiment that I cannot define. It is true that I feared the monarch's love, but I had too high an opinion of Monime's virtue to be alarmed by their long tête-à-tête, and the candor of her soul answered to me for her conduct.

When the Prince emerged, I immediately went into Monime's cabinet.

"No one is unaware, beautiful Thaymuras," I said, approaching her with an anxious expression, "of the love that the Emperor has for you; the entire Court is admiring at present the change in his humor, and seems surprised by his constancy. As for me, who render your merit and your charms all the justice that is their due, I am not astonished; I know that Heaven has given you birth in order to subjugate all hearts; doubtless the monarch only talked to you for such a long time today to declare the passion he feels for you."

I could not help sighing; I would have like to hide the emotion that was agitating me in spite of myself, but Monime saw it. She looked at me, held out her hand and sighed too.

"I admit, my dear Milord," said Monime, "that the marks of benevolence that I receive from that Prince every day would give you cause for alarm if you were able to doubt the purity of my sentiments; I fear nevertheless that you are imputing a spirit of coquetry to the indispensable obligation in which I find myself to seemed flattered by his assiduities and gallantries. It is true that I cannot doubt the monarch's infatuation; it bursts forth in a thousand benefits and gallant gestures that succeed one another without interruption, with as much magnificence and sumptuousness as taste in the distribution he makes of them. However, if I believed that the complaisance that forces me to lend myself to all his amusements could give birth to any suspicions regarding my conduct, I would implore the genius to remove me from his pursuits."

"Sentiments so noble, so generous and so delicate can never inspire any suspicion in me," I said. "Furthermore, I only have over you the rights that a brother can have; united by blood and amity, your condescension for my desires can only be an effect of the tender sentiments that nature inspires in us, and all that I can desire for the advantage of my sentiments is that you conserve them for me."

I left her after that explanation, much more tranquil than I had been.

The next day I was present at Monime's toilette. What touching graces accompanied it! How beautiful I found her in her negligee, ornamented with simple attractions. I thought I saw in her the charming Euphrosine, the amiable inhabitant of the heavens and companion of Venus. *Alas*, I said to myself internally, *why am I forbidden to love the woman that I adore?*

"Come here, Milord," she said to me, with an enchanting smile. "I have a bone to pick with you over your lack of confidence; I believe that I have given you enough evidence of mine to be authorized to complain about the mystery you have maintained with me regarding the tender sentiments you have inspired in the beautiful Nardillac. It's no secret; the entire Court has observed the preference she gives you. Agree that she is charming and full of intelligence; if you have enough strength to resist her charms, one must regard you heart as insensible to the darts of Amour."

"A heart that is only devoted to pleasing you," I replied, in the same tone, "becomes insensible to any other object."

"That's very gallant," said Monime, laughing, "But will this note, which can only be addressed to you, not change your language? May one, Milord, without indiscretion, read the note?"

"It's taking the joke a little far," I said, "for I protest that it does not belong to me, and that those that people have sometimes been kind enough to write to me are too precious for me to risk losing them; thus, you may do with that one whatever you think appropriate; I have no interest in it."

"I'm curious," said Monime, "to know what it contains."

She opened it, and read these words:

Is it possible, Milord, that you do not understand the language of the eyes? One has a sensible interest in knowing the state of your heart; dare one flatter oneself that in a Court so gallant, no object has yet been able to touch you? Be at the entrance to the labyrinth at eleven o'clock tomorrow morning; it is there that someone wants to instruct you in a mystery that can perhaps only be confided to you.

That note was a complete surprise to me.

"Well, Milord," continued Monime, who perceived my embarrassment, "what have you to respond to such an attack?"

"Not a word," I replied. "I do not know who sent me the note, but I swear to you that I have no desire to go to the assignation."

"Be careful of what you do," said Monime. "You don't know the character of the beauty who has written to you. Remember that it is sometimes dangerous to offend a woman, whoever she is, especially if she is bold enough to permit herself to make the first advances. There is no enemy more dangerous; for a woman who does not have enough credit to harm the person she believes to have offended her often joins forces adroitly with someone in a position to assist her in her projects—and be persuaded that the most adroit minister is only a novice by comparison with an outraged woman in search of revenge. She is impenetrable in her secrets; a clever woman is as restrained with what regards her as she is unreserved with regard to the affairs of others; nothing escapes her; she follows a plan better and more surely than the most refined man, who, in spite of his pretended strength of mind, falls every day into the most primitive and the most injurious traps."

"You are displaying your eloquence in vain," I said. "As the note does not indicate the person who has written it to me, I believe that I can, without lacking politeness, dispense with going to the rendezvous."

"You don't feel, then," said Monime, smiling, "any disposition to establish commerce with the beautiful unknown? Or perhaps you don't want to confide in me?"

"Such remarks," I replied, rather hotly, "make me perceive only too well that you don't know the measure of my heart. It's accusing it of weakness to doubt its fidelity, and a poor response to the confidence I have always had in you."

Monime could not help blushing at that reproach, which she judged to relate to the Emperor, and to tranquilize me, she assured me that she believed me incapable of deceiving her.

That little cloud was soon dissipated by new assurances of an entire confidence.

In the afternoon I went to find Zachiel, who smiled when he saw me. "You have a conquering air," he said. "It appears to me that you haven't remained idle in this Court—but my dear Seaton, you're scarcely gallant to make the beauties wait, without thinking of giving them the satisfaction they desire."

"It would be difficult to deceive you," I said. "It's true that I've received a very pretty note, but I don't know where it came from."

"Are you anxious about it?" asked Zachiel. "That note contains more than one mystery, although it was written by the hand of Nardillac, who has offered you several provocations. She is, however, not its author; you can see her without fear of any bad consequences. She's an amiable woman, full of intelligence, who has possessed for quite a long time, without division, the good graces of the Emperor. It appears that she wants to employ the assistance of jealousy to bring him back into her toils. But as it is necessary to love in order to be caught, that strategy is of no use to her, and so long as the Prince's passion for Monime lasts, all the efforts she makes to bring him back to her will be vain. The monarch's way of thinking has changed completely; since he has adored Monime, his sentiments have become much more delicate; his appetite for amour is no less keen, but it is purer, and consequently more tender, more passionate and more sensual; he wants to be loved for himself. Princes are rarely sure of that advantage, especially in a Court where love of grandeur and that of riches are the only motives that make people act.

"Take note, my dear Seaton," the genius continued, "that a courtier who makes his usual abode next to a Prince immediately forms a particular talent for knowing him well; the Prince has no inclination that is hidden from him, no aversion that he does not penetrate, no weak point that he does not discover. From that come the insinuations, the complaisance and all the delicate measures that form the art of winning hearts and conciliating minds. The Prince, who is not on guard against those artifices, often mistakes for zeal what is actually interest or politics. All those manipulations form a skill that courtiers study, exercise and put into practice; tormented by ambition, it is rare that they succeed in satisfying it. The majority of courtiers are flatterers, treacherous toward those who need them, dissimulated, proud, ambitious and incessantly occupied in new intrigues to try to bring down their competitors and render themselves masters of disposing of the Prince's favor, while searching for the means to render suspect to him those who are endowed with real merit.

"However, the Emperor has acquired, in every respect, the love of his subjects; he has all the talents appropriate to a great monarch—which is to say, the veritable courage that consists of perfect self-possession; balancing reasons for and against and forming, without precipitation and with discretion, all the plans of his enterprises; executing them with prudence and firmness; and distinguishing what is appropriate to render his people happy, by treating them more like a father than a sovereign. In the midst of the splendor and ostentation of his Court, he has always conserved a heart incapable of perfidy, full of love for good faith and verity; he has protected it in all his treaties and preached it by example to his subjects.

"Remember, my dear Seaton, that all virtues stem from sincerity and candor. Such is the true character of the Emperor; but his fortunate qualities have been obscured until now by the invincible penchant he has for amour: by the number of his mistresses and the complaisance he has always had for the weaknesses of the Empress. That Princess, not content with the honors that accompanied her, has pushed ambition so far as to want to invade all authority, and her politics make her furnish new pleasures to the Emperor every day, in order to distract him from the interests of his State.

"he monarch, who likes variety in his amusements, yields to them easily, resting on the wise precautions he has taken to prevent in justices—but the new ministers that the Empress has placed, like those of the Cillenians, are only thinking at present of enriching themselves, and prefer their particular interests to the general good of the entire people. The same motives have made his mistresses act, combined with that of ambition; but the charm has now been broken; the truth has been announced to the Prince in a flattering and touching manner; it has entered into his mind by the route that leads there most agreeably—which is to say, via the heart. Everything is about to change its face, and those who have had that audacity to impose upon him will be rigorously punished."

"Who has worked this miracle, then?" I asked. "Doubtless some benevolent genius?"

"It is true," said Zachiel, "that it is owed to the return of Samael, who is the protective genius of this Empire, and to whom the fortunate disposition in which the Emperor is presently finding to employ all kinds of means to favor his people and render them happy, by repressing all the abuses that have been made on his authority during the absence of the genius, who, to obey the Supreme Being, has been obliged to visit several fixed stars that are also inhabited, in order to established laws and introduce more orderly mores."

"As I have no doubt," I said, "that you have visited these different worlds more than once," I said, "you would provide me with a sensible pleasure by giving an idea of their laws and their government."

"Although there is no world that I have not visited several times," said Zachiel, "I cannot satisfy your curiosity at present. Samael ought to come to Monime's house tomorrow, in accordance with a promise he has made me; so it will be that genius who will instruct both of you."

Chapter VIII
Which One Can Read if One Wishes

I did not fail to go with Zachiel to Monime's house the following day. Samael arrived almost immediately after us. That genius had adopted a charming figure. Introducing us, Zachiel said:

"Here are two people to whom I am very attached by inclination. You can see that I have done very extraordinary things in their favor, which none of us has yet dared to undertake for mortals, but you're not unaware of the scant docility that is to be found among humans; that is what prevents us communicating with the humans who inhabit the different spheres of the vast universe. This charming young woman and this young man, who is her near relative, have already traveled to several planets with my help. Their curiosity extends further, to visiting a few fixed stars; I flatter myself that the complaisance you will have of instructing them as to all you have recently seen might save them the trouble."

"With all my heart," said Samael. "Have no doubt that I will be delighted to spare the beautiful Princess and Milord voyages that would be of no use to them, and would be extremely tiring. You know yourself that I have nothing very curious to tell them. Since we last met I've been summoned to various worlds, one of which displayed nothing but monsters, hideous creatures reduced to an instinct more primitive than that of animals. Others only contained inhabitants in whom the human form is almost unrecognizable, who do not cultivate their land; they only nourish themselves by their hunting, and often push barbarity so far as to eat one another when they make war. Those people would horrify the charming Thaymuras; they do not merit her taking the trouble to seek them out. It's true that there are some that do merit being visited, but as she is not immortal and cannot spend her life traveling, I advise her to limit herself to the planets alone, where enough variety is found to be able to satisfy her curiosity fully.

"The world I have quit," Samael continued, "and that on which I spent the longest time, is presently one of the most civilized, thanks to the care I have taken to form subjects capable of governing themselves, but I was unable to cure them of their superstitions, nor the accumulation of mores, laws, customs, tastes and systems that are scattered there. Among those peoples, everyone thinks differently; instead of tolerating one another mutually amid that infinite variety of opinions and new systems, and suffering them meekly, I saw them tearing one another apart in cold blood.

"When I arrived, the amiable truth had lost its most precious advantages over the error that is its most dangerous rival a long time ago; both of them excited the same troubles, the same tempests and were sustained with the same obstinacy. In sum, that world has only become richer and more magnificent to be more vicious; it had only multiplied its laws to give itself the privilege of infringing them with more boldness. Its people only cultivate the fine arts in order to abandon themselves with more license to luxury and the deviancy that accompanies it; they only honor baseness, only raising mediocrity to the highest dignities and only recompensing poor administration by setting aside the advice of persons of intelligence and those whose talents are superior, claiming that they are too anxious and trouble the repose of the State.

"That repose, however, which they ought to compare to those calm periods that often precede the most violent tempests in nature, only serves to give birth to new tyrants who take a malign pleasure in dominating their life and their liberty, and who, in robbing them of their wealth, do not even want to take the trouble of deceiving them under specious pretexts. All the advantages that strength gives having been put to work to oppress the weak, the rich have become insolent, and their fortune, far from serving the good of the State, causes the misfortune of all the people.

"I was therefore obliged to break the talisman that rendered all those peoples imbecilic and to recall each of them to the reason and virtue they regarded as ancient chimeras, in order to prepare their minds to receive new laws and form more orderly mores."

The Emperor, who came in at that point, interrupted the genius. "I'm delighted," said the monarch, "to find you with the incomparable Thaymuras; her taste for the sciences is doubtless known to you, and I have no doubt that the charms of her conversation will often attract you to her company. Let me, I beg you, enjoy it in my turn; go, both of you, to wait for me in my study; I want to consult you about important matters on which the happiness of my people depends. I shall henceforth apply all my cares to procuring them a real happiness, by enabling them to enjoy a constant felicity. You can, while waiting for me, examine my projects. Go—I shall not take long to follow you."

I went out with the two genii. Monime remained alone with the Emperor.

"How charmed I am," she said to him, "to see sentiments so worthy of a great monarch shining in the heart of Your August Majesty. Permit me, my Lord, to praise you for not being inflexible, since you want to listen favorably to the wise counsel of genii who are devoted to you; the forgetfulness that you appear to make of your grandeur ought to encourage them not to hide anything from you; I am sure that in the depths of their hearts thy would like to everything in their power to return to you a hundredfold the grandeur that you so obligingly deprive yourself in their favor.

"What motives more noble than yours can motivate a great prince? You have nothing in view but the happiness of your subjects; you enjoy, my Lord, the rewards of a peace that ought to be durable; your numerous and formidable troops hold your neighbors in respect; your ships bring you all the treasures of this vast world; you dispense all honors and riches; finally, the truth, suffering for so long, is about to reappear in all its splendor.

"For me, in whom Zachiel has always inspired a love for the truth and the candor that consists of only praising the virtues that are worthy of praise, I can assure you, my Lord, that I shall publish in all the worlds to which destiny might take me that your reign is nothing but a continual chain of marvelous events, as clear and intelligible when executed as they were impenetrable before their execution, and that the Renown, as favorable to you as she has always been, has not yet said anything that is less than the truth."

"I would have interrupted you," said the Emperor, "if I had not found glory in being praised by a mouth as beautiful as yours. Is it possible, divine Thaymuras, that with sentiments that are so favorable to me, you take pleasure in rendering me unhappy? Why feign ignorance of the vivacity of my ardor? Know, then, my beautiful star, that all the grandeurs that surround me, these immense treasures, these honors that I can dispense at my whim, all became insipid to me, bored me, and became a burden to me, as soon as I could not touch your heart with them; that alone is what I want to complete my felicity. But what do I see? As soon as I speak to you about my love, you resume a cold and serious expression that intimidates me and drives me to despair. What is there in my person, then, that can inspire so much distance in you? You lower your eyes and make no response. In the name of the gods, divine Thaymuras, tell me what I ought to dread or hope? Oh, you sigh and turn away; speak, I implore you; this is too much suffering; I want to know my fate; I can no longer live in this cruel uncertainty."

"Your August Majesty," Monime replied, almost without daring to look at the Emperor, "is doubtless forgetting that the genii are waiting for him to hold council."

"What do I hear?" cried the Prince, carried away. "You're sending me away without deigning to give me a favorable glance or say a single word of consolation? I shall go, my Lady, and I shall go in despair at your coldness."

The Emperor went out, with a disturbance that all the courtiers observed. They followed him in silence, no one daring to interrupt his reverie.

I immediately went back into Monime's cabinet, and found her absorbed in a profound reverie; leaning over her armchair, she was supporting her head on one of her hands; her eyes, in which dolor and anxiety were painted, seemed to me to announce some great misfortune. I was seized to such a point that I remained motionless for a few moments.

"Dear Monime," I said, "what can have occasioned this trouble? Do we have some misfortune to hear? We are here under the protection of the genius, who certainly will not permit us to suffer any insult. Speak, my sister, can I not be informed of your chagrin? Whence comes this dolor into which I see you plunged and which penetrates me to my very soul?"

"Reassure yourself, Milord," said Monime. "This dolor only arises from the sensibility of my heart. You are not unaware of the love the Emperor has for me; until now I have always eluded the declarations that he has sought to make to me, but today, I was unable to avoid it. Left alone with him, he seized the opportunity to talk to me about his passion in terms so touching and so tender that, not being able to give the Prince a response that could satisfy him without wounding my glory, I could not find any other course at first than that of maintaining an obstinate silence, which appeared to put him in despair.

"He quit me in a trouble and agitation that I can't describe to you, but what confounds me and oppresses me is not having been able to have got a sufficient grip on myself to reply to the Prince. Perhaps a favorable word would have appeased him, but I feared nourishing a passion that I would rather destroy. Although penetrated by the Emperor's generosity, his benefits, his love, his tenderness and his complaisance, everything seems to reproach an ingratitude of which I am incapable. I confess that I love him; he is the best of Princes; he merits all my gratitude. What am I saying? I'm penetrated by him.

"Alas, if he could read the depths of my heart and be content with a pure amity and all the sentiments of the most perfect esteem, and even the admiration that his rare virtues have inspired in me! But I do not have the audacity to deceive him; it is amour that he demands of me, and that is the only sentiment I cannot accord him. My heart, destined for another, must conserve all its purity for him.

"My dear Seaton, the tenderness I have for you does not permit me to hide my sentiments from you; that tenderness, which is authorized by blood, gives you the right to read my soul; I cannot tell you more at present; the genius will instruct you one day of the choice that he has made in order to ensure my happiness. Go, Milord, inform Zachiel of the anxieties that I have; press him to take me out of them."

As she spoke the last words, Monime held out her hand; I took it in mine, and could not help applying a kiss to it—when the Emperor came back in and surprised us.

The agitation in which the Prince had left did not permit him to apply himself to any affairs; unable to bear Monime's indifference, nor live without seeing her, he had doubtless come with the intention of reproaching her.

Nothing can describe the surprise and astonishment of the monarch. All three of us remained immobile for an instant; but the Emperor, animated by the most furious anger, yielded to his first impulse. Already he was holding a dagger, which he would indubitably have plunged into my heart if the genius, who was watching over me at that moment, had not shielded me from his vengeance by transforming me into a butterfly.

The Prince, who saw me disappear, thought that I had run away in order to flee, and gave the order to have me arrested.

Monime, nonplussed and trembling, hardly dared look up.

"So that, my Lady," said the Emperor, "is the fortunate mortal who opposes my happiness; his life will answer to me for the scorn that you show my tenderness. Ingrate, since my benefits have not been able to touch you, I shall at least have the sad consolation of making you sense how far my power extends."

The Prince tried to leave, but Zachiel, who wanted to put an end to all his agitations, stopped him by seizing his hand.

Genii of the first order have the virtue, as soon as they touch you, of appeasing the most violent passions. The genius, then making use of all his power, spoke to him thus:

"Your Majesty is doubtless blushing at his loss of self-control. These strangers are not subject to your laws; they are two persons I protect, and over whom you can have no rights; it is in vain that you will have Milord sought; I have just shielded him from the sight of all mortals. This young Princess whom you have striven to seduce with your benefits can never give you anything but esteem, gratitude and veneration, while you see only her virtuous sentiments. Inclination, amour or tenderness are impulses of which one cannot dispose at will; they are born in the depths of the heart and maintained there with pleasure; in any case, you are not unaware that this young Princess cannot dispense with returning to the vortex of the world that gave her birth; it is there that she must choose a spouse who is worthy of her. The voyages that I have enabled her to undertake are solely with a view to rendering her worthy to reign over the people that will be submissive to her. However, she has just suffered an outrage by virtue of the rage that escaped you against one of her relatives, as if they had both been submissive to your Empire."

No one but a genius would ever have dared to speak so freely. Monime, judging by that discourse that she had nothing to fear for my days, sensed her courage and firmness reborn at that moment; the presence of the genius inspired a noble boldness in her, and, addressing the Emperor, she said: "I am in despair, my Lord, that my anxiety, my timidity, my lack of experience and my lack of enlightenment regarding the laws of your Empire have prevented me until now from revealing to Your Majesty the true sentiments that animate me. They are such that I will do everything in my power to respond in a manner worthy of you and those that with which you have been good enough to honor me.

"The laws of your Empire permit you to have several wives without failing in your duty to your religion; it would be a crime in mine to consent to the ardor of your desires; two invisible obstacles oppose your satisfaction: my religion and my glory; a third, even stronger is the indispensable obligation I have not to be able to spend my life in our court. Before being presented to Your Majesty, my Lord, I loved, and could be sure of being loved. Brought up in the care of the genius, he knows my heart and the obligation I have to unite myself with the person he has destined for me, and all the benefits that you have lavished upon me could never authorize me to break that faith.

"However, my Lord, if the keenest gratitude, the most sincere veneration and, if I dare to say it, the most tender amity, can still be agreeable to you, I shall render them with the pleasing idea of having at last merited your esteem by the purity of my sentiments. I am not unaware that it is a temerity on my part to dare to take the title of friend; however, my Lord, that title would be a thousand times more precious to me than all the honors and riches with which your generosity has helped me. Your esteem and your amity are the only treasures for which I am ambitious; if our sentiments are unable to accord with mine, permit me, my Lord, to withdraw immediately."

"You drive me to despair," said the Emperor, in a penetrating voice. "Why do you refuse my tenderness? Oh, you augment it by the nobility of your sentiments. Is it possible, divine Princess, that my love cannot touch you? Your soul, made to reign over all mortals, cannot be touched by grandeur or wealth; deign at least to accept the homage that I render to your charms, and grant, if possible, some glimmer of hope to my desires."

The Emperor continued: "My dear Zachiel, it will be to you that I owe all my happiness if you engage the Princess to remain in my court; allow me to have the pleasure of swearing to her incessantly that I adore her, and that it is only on that condition that I can pardon Seaton."

"I would never oppose Your Majesty's will if it appeared reasonable," said the genius, "but you are doubtless forgetting that it is impossible to separate two hearts that veritable amour has united forever. Permit me to add, too, that it does not befit the dignity of a great monarch to deliver himself with so much vehemence to his passions."

"Oh, let's leave my grandeur there," said the Emperor. "Can't you see that the man who possesses the heart of the Princess is a thousand times happier than I am; if he does not enjoy all the honors that surround me, he is well compensated by the certainty that he has of being loved. As for me, in spite of my power, I have never tasted that pleasure in all its purity. What almost always troubles the happiness of sovereigns is the cruel doubt they are in of not being able to be sure of being loved for themselves. They would be equal to the gods if they could flatter themselves that they possess the love and tenderness of those they attach to themselves, but ambition, the love of greatness, the lure of riches are only too often the sole attractions that make us sought out; I've had several experiences very prejudicial to my repose. Where can a heart like that of the charming Thaymuras be found? Doubtless a character so perfect and so rare can only be acquired by the cares of a genius as great as Zachiel.

"How happy I would be, divine Princess," the Emperor continued, in an impassioned manner, "if I could touch a soul as beautiful as yours! Will you allow me to ask you with insistence?"

"Your August Majesty," said Monime, "will always be the master of ordering what he pleases."

"Yes," said the monarch, "I know that I am the master of commanding everywhere that you are not; but when it is a matter of obtaining grace from you, I am the one who begs and can never obtain any complaisance but your amity."

"I shall obey, my Lord," said Monime. "I even dare to assure you that it is with the greatest pleasure, ever more penetrated by the new favors I receive."

"Favors! Oh, abandon that language; you cannot be unaware that it is only you who can accord them. So, beautiful Thaymuras, I will receive with much gratitude the favor you grant me of remaining in my court."

"The sojourn that I can make in your estates," said Monime, "depends entirely on Zachiel; always under his guidance, I am submissive to his will, and cannot, nor would ever want to, depart from it."

"I leave you, my Lady," the genius said, "the mistress of remaining here for as long as you wish. I am sure that Seaton would not oppose your will, provided that he is permitted to reappear at the Court."

"My Lord," said Monime, blushing, "he is my brother, and a brother I love tenderly; that is a grace I dare not ask of you, although sure of Milord's respectful attachment to your august person."

"Your brother, my Lady!" said the Emperor, excitedly. "How guilty I am! Why have I been left ignorant of that until now? Oh, divine Thaymuras, will you pardon me for my hastiness? Forget it, if you can, only to remember my passion, and never doubt that you have acquired a full power over my will. I am not unjust; let Milord reappear, I consent."

The Emperor left, much more tranquil, telling Zachiel to be at the Council the next day.

As soon as we were alone the genius caused me to resume my natural form. My first concern was to thank him for having rescued me from such a dangerous situation. "The astonishment and surprise into which the Emperor's suspicions had thrown me rendered me immobile; one word on my part might have calmed him down, but your presence, my dear Zachiel, remedied everything."

"That little adventure," said the genius, "ought to convince you that you ought to be incessantly on your guard. I do not criticize the attachment you have for one another at all; I merely recommend that you moderate its vivacity."

Tender amity is easily alarmed and persuaded; something trivial troubles it or renders it desperate; something equally trivial calms and reassures it; similar to amour, it augments its own torments, and in the same way, has the power to savor sweetness a thousandfold in the slightest of its pleasures. That is what I experienced that day during the various impulses that agitated the Emperor.

How happy I found myself in comparing my fate with his! *That Prince*, I said to myself, *although always obeyed, always feared and always respected, is nevertheless constrained to admit that he has not yet been able to taste the inexpressible charms that one senses when love or amity is equally shared. What a torment for a noble soul, to be incessantly delivered to the torture of uncertainty, without ever being able to work out whether it is duty, zeal or ambition that makes all those act who render their homage to sovereigns!*

Those reflections caused me to examine the courtiers. I was not duped for long by their submissive and crawling manner; I soon perceived that the desire to shine at court and supplant those who appeared to possess the favor of the prince is an epidemic malady that one catches by frequentation, for without that, how is it understandable that people who could live happily in the bosom of their family want to spend their best days in the antechamber of a Prince, or that of a minister, and buy at the expense of the most difficult servitude the glory of being the foremost at the Emperor's *petit lever*? And that is often purely motivated by vanity.

What also surprised me very greatly among the Jovinians was to see families in fashion, like carriages or new houses; the names of those illustrious families soon absorb all the others. If they lack nobility, favor substitutes for that by pompous titles, and those titles soon procure them the most distinguished alliances, which serve to cover the baseness of their origin and render their names more illustrious than those of the ancient nobility ever were.

Chapter IX
Nardillac Explains the Mystery of the Rendezvous with Lord Seaton

One day, I was in the house of the Empress, to which I had gone assiduously to pay my court, when Nardillac came in. The charming individual
blushed when she saw me and darted a mysterious glance at me that I did not
understand. I bowed to her in a rather distracted fashion, occupied in looking at
an exquisitely-carved box of bonbons, of which the Emperor had just made a
present to the Empress. The Princess, who appeared delighted with the new trin-
ket, was showing it complaisantly to her entire court. Nardillac asked to see it
and advanced toward the window-embrasure where I was standing.

"Come to supper at my house this evening," the lovely woman said, as she
took the box that I handed to her. "I have secrets to confide to you, which concern the good or ill fortune of my days, and perhaps yours."

Nardillac drew away immediately without giving me time to reply. I left
shortly thereafter to go to Monime's house. I found her clad in a dress that the
Emperor had sent her the day before; it was in blue satin embroidered with diamonds, and resembled in the light a sky strewn with stars.

"I'm expecting the Emperor," Monime said. "You see me still adorned
with his new benefits."

"He could not gratify anyone with them who merits them as much as you,"
I told her. "If I were not sure that riches and grandeurs are feeble attractions for
a noble soul, I'd have every reason to be alarmed by the traps that are being laid
for your virtue; but you're not unaware, dear Monime, that opulence is the idol
of the insensate, and often the embarrassment of the wise; it's true that it does
not entirely destroy virtue, but at least it weakens it and, so to speak, blunts its
point. But I believe, penetrated as you are by the principles you have received
from the genius, that you are not running any risk—and that he will get us both
out of the labyrinth in which we are, I believe, a little too deep."

"Although your reflections are very judicious," said Monime, smiling, "I
nevertheless find them a little too grave; they expand in the mind a certain serious impression that does not suit the matters about which I want to talk to you.
Permit me, Milord, to ask for news of your amours with the charming
Nardillac."

"I was about to mention that to you," I said, "and tell you about my pleasures and my good fortune. I left that beauty a little while ago; she has invited me
to supper, and I believe that I can't dispense with it. I'll wait here for Zachiel in
order to ask him to accompany me."

"What a child you are," said Monime. "Can you not go alone? I believe
that it would be paying your court very badly to take someone with you; be sure
that she does not want any third party but Amour—but as I have retained the

god first, it's at my house that he must preside over supper, and Zachiel will be the fourth. You'll have to excuse yourself; it's a settled matter."

"In truth," I replied, laughing, "that would be doing me a perfidious turn. How will I dare to present myself before that beauty?"

"Tomorrow, at her toilette," said Monime, "you can easily obtain pardon for that fault by telling her that you were violently retained, and could not get rid of the inconvenient Thaymuras."

Zachiel, who appeared at that moment, was ready to lend himself to Monime's pleasantries; she continued to chaff me regarding the good fortune that she was causing me to miss.

The Emperor interrupted the conversation with his presence. The Prince, full of new projects that he had formed with the genii for the wellbeing of his people, told Monime about them; she congratulated him on the paternal love that he was showing in favor of his subjects, and the new laws that he wanted to establish in his Empire.

"The most important of all," said the genius, "are those that are not engraved in marble or bronze but in the hearts of the citizens; those laws, so strong and solid, are mores, customs, often even opinions. There are very few politicians who make the attempt to know that part, on which the success of all the others depends, they alone being able to form the veritable constitution on the State, by taking on new strength every day and reanimating the ancient laws on the brink of extinction; they alone conserve in peoples the spirit of their institution, and insensibly substitute the force of habit for that of authority."

After having extended his reflections of that matter much further, the genius left with the Emperor. He soon came back, enthusiastic to take part in our supper.

Monime was giving birth to joy with a thousand quips that amused Zachiel when we heard a burst of laugher that surprised us. It was Samael, who, without rendering himself visible, had taken pleasure in surprising us.

"How bold these genii are!" said Monime. "They go everywhere without being announced. Do you know, sirs, that one is never safe when one is in commerce with you; one cannot flatter oneself with a tête-à-tête with anyone."

"It's true," said Samael, in the same tone, "that I didn't think that Zachiel would be an inconvenient third party here, and it would have been a true pleasure for me to surprise you without that witness, but it appears to me that he hasn't spoiled the feast, and that you're amusing yourselves well enough not to be embarrassed if the advancing hours announce the return of day. Is it not time, gentlemen, to leave the beautiful Princess the time to obtain the repose she requires?"

"Let's leave my principality out of it," said Monime. "You're not unaware that it's fictitious."

"I know," Samael replied, more seriously, "that you merit ruling more than anyone else in the world, and that the peoples submissive to your law would enjoy all kinds of wellbeing and felicity under your reign."

He left without waiting for Monime's response; she took the speech for a very flattering compliment.

The next day, I could not dispense with going to see Nardillac. I feared that tête-à-tête horribly, convinced as I was that I would have to defend myself against the reproaches I had so often merited. I went into her cabinet very ill-assured. My embarrassment surprised her; she divined its cause, but, without seeking to enjoy it she hastened to relieve me of it.

"It is very difficult to see you, Milord; what suspicions can you have formed against me? I beg you at least to banish from your mind all those that might be injurious to me. I'm not unaware of the amity you have for Princess Thaymuras, and you must know that which I conserve for the Emperor; I asked you to come to my house in order to combine our interests and to make you the depository of a part of my chagrins."

"You are very gracious, my Lady; I can assure you that you could not confide them to anyone more disposed than me to do everything in my power to oblige you."

"I know," Nardillac continued, "that constancy, honor and probity are the virtues that you cherish the most, and that you are far from imitating those men that a caprice and a perpetual contrariety always oppose to their interests and their principles and renders almost inevitably the injustice of which they are accused. Many employ the most tender care to undoing an innocent heart; they stun her with their dutiful attentions, seduce her, and when they have won her over, they accuse her and punish her for surrendering too soon. That is the sad fate that the Emperor is causing me to experience by his inconstancy.

"I am going astray, Milord; it is not with my woes that I wanted to begin this conversation. But what terms can I use to tell you what I have been ordered to say to you? However, whatever the role is that I have been forced to play, I beg you to believe that I have only accepted it in order to prevent the commission being given to someone else, who, less inclined to your interests, would make a glory out the enterprise by distracting your mind from all the dangers that ought infallibly to stop you.

"You're not unaware that for a long time, the Empress has honored me with her full confidence; it is on her orders that I wrote to you and have often conversed with you at her house and that of the Princess Thaymuras; it was also her who engaged me to speak to you today. Can you not divine now the rest of what I have to say to you?"

That beginning took me by surprise. "Explain yourself, my Lady," I said. "What do these detours signify? Has Thaymuras something to fear on the part of the Empress? I'm cognizant of her jealousy, and not unaware of the excesses that she has sometimes perpetrated against those the Emperor has distinguished with his favors—but my Lady, you can be assured that Princess Thaymuras has too much virtue and too much grandeur of soul to do anything that could tarnish her glory."

"How poorly you understand what I am saying, Milord! If the Empress is jealous, I can assure you that the gallantries of her august spouse have not made any impression on her heart; you alone, at present, can excite it by your assiduity toward the beautiful Princess."

"What are you saying, my Lady? What! The Empress could...but no, such suspicions are unthinkable; they would be too injurious to her."

"Listen to me, Milord. You're beginning to understand me—well, it's at that price that all dignities and honors are offered to you; it is necessary for that to renounce your other attachment. You have inspired the keenest passion in that Princess; the hope of touching you initially contained her desires within the bounds of duty; delighted to learn that the Emperor was impassioned by the charms of the beautiful stranger without your seeming alarmed, her passion has taken on new force. What can I tell you, in sum? Her imperious humor cannot suffer that anyone resists her; unaccustomed to moderating her desires, it is only by satisfying them that she finds the secret of vanquishing them. That is why she has instructed me to tell you that she wants to talk to you this evening in private.

"You see, Milord," Nardillac continued, "that I was right to tell you that the repose of my life depends on the secret that I have confided to you. The decision that you are about to make will ruin all my hopes or fortify them. If you decide to remain in this Court with Princess Thaymuras I shall lose forever any hope of regaining the tenderness of the Emperor, which I have long possessed; my amour and my glory are interested therein. I ought, however, to warn you that you would be running grave risks by refusing to respond to the desires of the Empress; that Princess would not support patiently the scorn you would be showing for her charms; the advances she is permitting herself announce to me only too clearly the danger you are in. The entire Empire is submissive to her orders; think about the course you ought to adopt. Tell me the response that it is necessary for me to make, and be assured, Milord, that it is only the interest that I take in your days that could have determined me to take responsibility for such a commission."

In the trouble that confidence caused me, I could only thank Nardillac by assuring her that I would do nothing that would be contrary to her views. I begged her not to tell the Empress that she had spoken to me, and to try to delay her for a little longer by insinuating that it would be much better to wait for the effect of her charms, which could not fail to take effect on a heart already inclined to tenderness. Nardillac approved of my idea, and I left her, my mind agitated by the sharpest anxieties.

I immediately went to see Monime; she had asked me to give her an account of the success of my visit. I could not hide my disturbance, and she hastened to enquire as to its cause. Embarrassed as to whether I ought to tell her what we had to dread, I was hesitating over my response when Zachiel came in. Emboldened by the presence of the genius, I told him about the conversation I had just had with Nardillac.

At that narration, Monime could not help showing a great deal of anxiety with regard to the consequences that such an immoderate passion might have, but the genius reassured us by telling us that the Emperor had finally opened his eyes to the conduct of the Empress, whom he had just repudiated and exiled to a desert island.

That crafty Princess had found the means of taking possession of the government during Samael's absence, the Empire's protective genius; her limited knowledge had been unable to distinguish the true from the false; her intelligence had only consisted of receiving all sorts of impressions, struck by all the images that the ministers she had chosen presented to her.

The scant enlightenment of the ministers was so complicated, so interrelated, so multi-faceted and so biased that everything appeared to their eyes to be opinions, prejudices, probabilities or hazards; it was nevertheless with such ideas that those great men congratulated themselves on the efforts of their imagination and had difficulty understanding how their minds were able to rise to such a high degree of perfection; but in order not to distract them from the good opinion they had of their merit, the Emperor sent them to a well-fortified citadel, where they could contemplate at their ease the full extent of their vast deigns without fear of being interrupted by any object that might distract them.

We were charmed to learn that news, not only because it tranquilized us with regard to our fears, but because it favored the glory of the sovereign.

Chapter X

The share that Nardillac had long had of the favor of the Empress caused her to dread being implicated in her disgrace; she confessed that to Monime in the most touching terms, giving her an account of the conversation we had had together.

"How could I refuse to obey my sovereign?" Nardillac continued. "I have often bemoaned her injustices. Attached to that Princess since childhood, she has always given me preference over my companions, and in spite of the amour that the Emperor has conserved for me for a long time I have been unable to betray the confidence of my mistress; treason has never found any place in my heart. Imagine, my Lady, the horrible position in which I found myself and the fears that must, with good reason, have alarmed me."

Monime, sensitive to the amiable woman's dolor, employed all that she believed to be most consoling to calm her, and the genius, who knew the depths of her heart, promised to protect her. I advised her to attach herself to the Princess, in order to profit from all the opportunities she could find to converse with the Emperor, who, in losing the hope of uniting himself with Thaymuras, might take on new chains.

Nardillac appreciated that advice, had had no difficulty effacing the slight impression of coquetry that we had formed against her. Her candor and sincerity acquired her the amity of Monime, who collaborated with Zachiel in order to make the Emperor aware of her constancy, her fidelity and the disinterested attachment that has caused her to refuse the best suitors in the hope of regaining his confidence. Such powerful protectors eventually ensured that the Emperor not only recovered all his tenderness, but that he subsequently accorded her the glorious title of Empress—a title that she sustained all her life with the nobility, virtue and purity of sentiment that ought to ornament those whom destiny elevated to that high degree of glory.

We spent more than a year in that court, and were witness to numerous changes that the Emperor made throughout his estates. Guided by the genius Samael, the monarch brought as much attention to recompensing merit as to punishing crime.

It would be desirable for that severity to be imitated on the other worlds; that would be the true means of establishing an exact probity there in the administration of finances and that of justice, of repairing injuries, keeping the peace, maintaining the good order and confidence of citizens and procuring the people the placid enjoyment of their property and their industry.

The Emperor's wealth was so considerable that it not only sustained the expenses of the State and the sumptuousness of the Court but also maintained several armies on campaign, either to suppress rebels and hold them in respect or to cover the frontiers and defend them against enemies. In addition to those expenses, which were immense, the Prince also found himself in a condition to put considerable funds into the coffers of his treasury, which he only permitted himself to touch on extraordinary occasions.

Samael also established a new law that tended to abolish all the intrigues of the courtiers, in order that the route that led to honors would be open to all those who distinguished themselves by virtue, probity and superior talents, and that when it was a matter of filling eminent posts, no regard would be paid to favor or nobility, on the grounds that it was unjust to prefer people who had no other merit to distinguish them but the actions of ancestors who had been dead for a hundred years, and that it was better to accord to present virtue the prizes that it had earned by hard work and late nights.

Such a sage regulation ought to encourage citizens to acquire talents that might be useful to the State. In order to establish that new form of government the genius Samael made the resolution to remain with the Emperor for some time in order to be able to assist him with his advice, and Zachiel has since assured us that the monarch, by the mildness of his reign, became the idol of his people. Guided by the enlightenment of the genius, he finally took up the reins of the Empire and governed with so much wisdom that he will serve as a model for centuries to come.

Not wanting to take our observations any further on that planet, it would have been easy for us to disappear as we had done on the other worlds, but it would have been poor recognition of the generosity of a monarch who had lavished us with his favors. The genius took charge of announcing our departure to him.

The Emperor concealed his chagrin when he learned of the resolution the genius had made to continue our voyages.

"I flattered myself," the monarch said to the genius, "that you would give me the pleasure of obliging me by permitting Princess Thaymuras to remain in my Court; I can presently offer her the principal place in my Empire. Why do you want to oppose my happiness and her glory? No kingdom can be compared to the vast extent of my estates."

"I know that," said Zachiel, "but I am not the master of destinies; it is the prerogative of the Almighty t dispose of them; that of the Princess Thaymuras summons her to another vortex; it is there that she must reign over the people who will be submissive to her. Submissive to the order that guides everything in nature, I have still to take them to one more world."

"So," said the Emperor, with a sad expression. "I'm going to lose you for a long time."

"You have nothing to fear," said Zachiel, "since Samael is not disposed to abandon you. I invite you to regard him as a sure friend, with whom the liaison is all the more solid because he is a genius of the first order; you will find pleasure and contentment in his familiarity; his conversation is always sensate and always satisfying; you will procure a thousand advantage from it. His brilliant mind is very different from that of the harsh men who once surrounded you, the majority of whom affected a gravity that importuned you.

"Those individuals wanted to be regarded as solid and essentially people, although they had nothing but a tedious ponderousness; their rigid attitude often made the insinuations of a courtier preferable to their austere fidelity; be certain that you will find none of those inconveniences in the amity and conduct of Samael; he is a benevolent genius, destined to protect your empire for as long as you have confidence in his counsel; but if he finds himself obliged to leave you in obedience to superior orders, I have given you a talisman which has the virtue of summoning us; you know how to make use of it in case of pressing need; be certain that I will come to your aid immediately. You ought not to be unaware that we seek neither wealth nor honors, nor authority in any of the worlds that we are constrained to visit. The divinity has created us to aid those who cherish and protect virtue, justice and truth.

"I shall never forget the marks of confidence that you have given me," the genius added, "nor the amity and benevolence that you have testified in favor of the two individuals in whom I am interested; and to recompense you, I wish that Heaven will lavish its most precious gifts upon you, that all the hearts of our subjects will be inclined toward you, and that the mere sight of you will be a benefit for them."

I shall not relate all the marks of benevolence that we received from the Emperor when we went to take our leave of that prince; suffice it to say that our hearts were penetrated by them. The entire court showed considerable chagrin at our departure; the beautiful Nardillac, above all, made it manifest how sensible it was to her; she assured us that she would never forget the services we had rendered her.

That monarch of the best of all princes; he is good, tender in friendship, compassionate, benevolent, entirely devoted to those he loves, and makes the delight of the people he honors with his familiarity; those are his admirable qualities, which touch hearts, soften them and dispose the to execute his will; but what completes the wining of the love of his all subjects and renders them so sensible to all is virtues, is the attention he has paid, since the arrival of Samael, to having the laws obeyed in all their rigor.

We finally departed after having bid farewell to all the nobles of the Empire. In order to travel with less inconvenience, the genius dismissed a number of our officers and the majority of our domestics, only retaining the gnomes.

Without stopping anywhere, we traversed the vast extent of that planet, which abounds in gold and silver mines, and where quantities of precious stones of inestimable price are also found. That world, which is immense in extent and wealth, seems to be the general store of all the treasures of nature.

The mores of the Jovinians are relatively mild, but their religion is, as on other worlds, divided into different sects. They have numerous temples, among others that of Hercules, in which the figure of the hero, raised on a pedestal, is represented with the pelt of the lion that he defeated in the Nemean forest; his twelve labors are detailed around the pedestal and his other equally famous exploits are engraved on several columns in the environs of the temple. We also visited that of Castor and Pollux, and that of Helen, but the temple of Jupiter surpasses all the others in magnificence and is the most frequented.

The majority of Jovinians address their sacrifices to unknown or anonymous gods, in the fear that, in describing or calling them by name, they might make mistakes or forget one of them, who, annoyed by their forgetfulness or negligence, might punish them by inflicting a great many woes upon them.

THE SEVENTH HEAVEN: SATURN

Chapter I
Pastoral Description

The genius raised us up by means of the waves of the air to cross the immense spaces that separate the world of Saturn from that of Jupiter. He caused us to pass between the five little planets and traverse the great luminous ring that seems simultaneously to crown and illuminate the world of Saturn.

When we had descended on to that globe, the genius, perceiving that we were almost stifled by the pressure of the air, rubbed our entire bodies with a spirituous liquid that fortified us, reanimated our minds and gave our senses a new vigor. Then he caused us to resume our natural forms, and, when the gnomes had arrived, equipped with everything necessary for the journey, we set forth, with the intention of not letting anything escape us that might be instructive.

First Zachiel took a road that led us into charming countryside. Sometimes, I saw a laborer who seemed to be devoting the final care to fields whose crops still seemed to be unripe; sometimes I heard the voice of a busy shepherd seeking to charm the duration of his toil by singing; here reapers were catching their breath and sharpening the blades of their scythes; there shepherds sitting in a vale were recounting their amorous adventures to one another.

In another place a vast landscape offered a thousand new objects to my gaze; I admired immense plains filled with ears of wheat, the precious gifts of Ceres; I saw meadows where flocks were wandering, the majority confided to the guard of dogs, while shepherdesses, ornamented by their rural advantages, danced a little further away to the sound of bagpipes to celebrate the pleasure promised by an abundant harvest. To see the joy that reigned among them, one might have thought that Zephyr and Flora had joined in their innocent games.

Further away, sterile mountains were visible, on the summits of which the clouds seemed to be reposing; lower down, there were long meadows dotted with flowers and irrigated by streams; in another direction, there were arbors formed by nature, surrounded by old oaks that one imagined that the ax had only spared out of respect for the deities that resided there, or to serve as retreats for the forest Nymphs when wind and rain forced them to take shelter.

On that world one breathes a heady odor that rejoices and satisfies the sense of smell, and one does not see any venomous plant germinating in that fortunate vortex. While admiring all those various views, I thought I was seeing nature in her springtime, giving impetus to new productions, and remarked that in her infinite caprices she surpassed the inventions of art infinitely.

Zachiel assured us that the inhabitants of the charming region spend tranquil days there; the plains are always full of laborers, the woods resound with a thousand aerial concerts, and the winged folk fly up to the summits of the oaks to announce the return of the god that illuminates them.

"It is here," Zachiel told us, "that I want to enable to you admire the grandeur of the Supreme Being; His power is manifest in everything that appears to our eyes. Look at that butterfly deploying its multicolored wings; little patches of red are distributed over a silver background, and on the edges of the wings a fringe of gold is juxtaposed with a beautiful green tint; a tiny silvery plume ornaments its dainty head. Admire that other insect that is passing by, buzzing; it is covered with black armor and bears on its bright red wings the juice of flowers that it has collected in that meadow you see ornamented with the most beautiful colors, which seems to be lulled by the zephyr.

"Notice that black forest of firs, whose ruddy trunks rise up like arrows through the dense branches. Look at that majestic and rapid river emerging from the bosom of a gray-tinted mountain, its silvery waves flowing noisily, and the weak streams that escape from it, murmuring through the long grass, whose blue flowers rise up above its surface, its waves accumulated around their tremulous stems, forming little sparkling rings; and he flowers seem to incline desirously, as if to embrace their courts. The limpid waters flow through their enameled vaults, shining with the reflection of their colors."

Further away, Monime perceived a broad meadow; she admired the rich variety of the shades of its verdure, illuminated by the sunlight.

Clumps of delightful plants can be seen there, extending their tender branches and variegated foliage between the grass. Violets can be seen, the symbols of true wisdom, which remain humbly confounded with the most common plants, and spread the sweetest perfume around them, while odorless flowers raise their proud heads above the grass, seeking ostentatiously to attract our gaze. A thousand tiny winged creatures can also be seen pursuing one another over the vegetation; sometime the eye loses sight of them in the verdant shade, sometimes one sees hosts of them agitating in the sunlight, or flying in legions and making a thousand brilliant evolutions in the air. The tumultuous and frolicsome play of the zephyrs precipitates others after one another through the grass, like waves that a gentle wind chases over the surface of a pond; the undulating stems bend and murmur, while the multicolored tiny folk to which they provide shelter fly away and contemplate their movements fearfully from mid-air.

Having passed through the vast countryside, the genius, in order to enable us to obtain a little repose, lodged us with an old man, who welcomed us with the hospitable zeal that makes the charm of coming together and seems, so to speak, to render property common. The amiable old man lived with a numerous family, whose members found their pleasure in work and their happiness in mediocrity, regarding the superfluous as an awkward burden that only serves to corrupt mores.

Those children love life without fearing death; they never allow themselves to be dazzled by ambition; tranquil with regard to the future, they only think of savoring the present. Their lives go by in unalterable peace; they recognize no other laws than those imposed on them by nature; one does not see them forming unfortunate relationships; neither interest nor honors ever presides over their choice; they adore virtue, beauty and graces in the very bosom of poverty.

That family represents those of our ancient Patriarchs; complaisance and badinage, always the companions of union, reign in their hearts and animate their tender caresses; they agitate with nobility; it is neither imitation nor laws that direct them; their hearts, full of honor and virtue, guide them effortlessly toward what is just.

"Notice," Zachiel said to us, "that benediction always reposes in the habitation of the just. The man whose heart is honest, and who puts his confidence in the divinity, need never fear his footsteps taking him into a deceptive marsh. When the just man offers a sacrifice, its smoke rises all the way to the throne of the divinity, who heeds and receives with pleasure the prayers and offering of virtuous men; he lives in repose beneath his placid roof, his favorable Penates hear his virtuous discourse and bless him.

"Content with their cabin, which shelters them from the rain and impetuous winds, it replaces for them a palace; although it is not surrounded by marble columns, it is surrounded by fruit trees and vines that are always green. The nearby spring furnishes them with clear water, they drink the wine of their harvest, nourish themselves on the fruits of their gardens and what their flocks provide. For want of gold and silver, their table is covered with odorous flowers; they know neither the anxious desires nor the mad passions that agitate other humans; they have no other cares than that of loving one another, lending one another mutual aid and seeking their happiness in common felicity.

"This family serves as an example to all those surrounding it; the peasants in their cottages find among them the assistance of reciprocal benevolence, the sincere counsels of the liveliest amity enable them to live in good intelligence. One sees the young men and women bantering together under arbors of vines; they detach the ripe grapes therefrom in order to reassemble under the thatch, where a joyful meal awaits them; it is there that rustic gaiety appears to be accompanied by bursts of laughter."

We spent several days with that amiable family. We visited their gardens, which seemed formed by nature; walnut trees circling it with vaults form pathways; gentle zephyrs, amiable coolness and tranquil repose dwell beneath their green foliage; at the end of the pathways, a spring of pure water murmurs under a trellis, and one seeks ducks and ducklings playing in its current. On the other side gentle doves stroll over the grass, craning their multicolored necks. Those gardens are full of fruit trees, which attract birds that call to one another with their melodious songs without fear of any traps being set for their liberty. Several hives are lined up there, whose bees, incessantly occupied with the concerns of their republic, seem by their labor to serve as an example for the inhabitants of the region.

Bees ordinarily settle in places where peace and repose reign; the meadows dotted with flowers attract them; it is there that they cheerfully take flight, where they chose and assemble their provisions, in order to swell the treasury of their republic on their return, all its members collaborating with an equal urgency to the commonwealth; never is any citizen idle; one sees them fluttering from flower to flower, and, in the course of their research, plunging their tiny velvety heads into the corollas of open flowers, or burying their entire bodies between the petals that are not yet open in order to extract the juice that they deposit in a separate place.

Further away is the farm-yard, to which various animals come in groups to request with seductive expressions the nourishment that one takes pleasure in distributing to them.

"You see," Zachiel said to us, "that happiness is not always encountered in the vain and inconvenient apparatus of luxury."

"I agree," said Monime, "that one does not often find sentiments that honor humanity in elevated ranks. One ought to mistrust the virtues of the great; it sometimes happens that their elevation can create a illusion; the distance there is between the aristocracy and people of humble estate only represents them with a deceitful microscope, but the petty, who are purified in the crucible of indigence, do not impose upon us. When a man has virtue, sound judgment and a heart full of honor, what point is there in examining his family? The glamour of rank is a vain title, if it is not accompanied by grandeur of soul, a stainless probity and all the virtues that ought to form a great man.

"Gold is often found in the sand, worms produce purple dye and oysters give us pearls; but it is not with citizens as perfect that one should make these reflections. You"—she was addressing the old man—"who enjoy in tranquility the most delightful way of life, who combine the charm of the union of hearts with that of innocence, enjoy a felicity that no dread or shame ever troubles, since the sentiment of wellbeing and peace reigns incessantly in the depths of your soul."

"How could we act otherwise?" said the old man. "We are submissive to the government of a Prince whose justice and equity form all projects, who puts into all his measures the unshakable firmness that always accompanies true courage; a Prince who only counts the days by benefits, who only employs his power to prevent crime rather than deploying his strength to punish it, who spreads wellbeing everywhere without seeing to increase the weight of the yoke of submission. It is the love that he has for his subjects that animates him to good. The resolutions of our monarch are a law for us, because we are convinced that he only seeks his own happiness in that which he can procure for us.

"That Prince, in taking the reins of government, made it the first of his concerns to give free scope of commerce, forming new manufactures; attentive to the application that is made of finances, he employs a part of it to the serve progress in the arts and to encourage individuals of talent. Here one leaves liberty to people of letters who unveil dangerous abuses, without permitting anyone to crush the talents of those who remove the blindfold of error. The liberty that our philosophers are given in their writings has taught our poets and our orators to make use of the noble eloquence that, in elevating the sentiments, simultaneously corrects vices.

"Our monarch has also obliged Judges to ensure the repose of the State by means of an integrity that has fixed jurisprudence. It is by all those talents in combination that the prince has formed the worthy object of our attentions. Far from having the blind confidence that some of his predecessors afforded their ministers, too enlightened to deliver his subjects to the conduct of a man who is often tempted to betray his interests and those of his people in order to occupy himself solely with his fortune, our monarch need have no fear of being obscured by his shadow; far from seeking to procure himself a borrowed glory, he alone expands it over others. As his principal goal is the wellbeing of his people, all his views are directed toward that object; the sages of the nation, his ministers, all applaud it, because the most powerful recommendation one can have to obtain the favors of that Prince is to think and act in conformity with his views."

Chapter II
The Mores of the Inhabitants

It is only on that charming world that simple art lends itself with docility to second the agreeable caprices of nature; one never sees artists, as on other worlds, rebelling against her, or regarding her productions as a servile material in order to warp them into bizarre and grotesque forms. A wall of hazel-trees forms the hedges that surround their gardens; bowers of vines serve as terraces and protect them from the sun's rays.

While admiring all those beauties of nature, I thought I was present in the youth of the world—which is to say, when humans had not yet been corrupted, the era of the first seeds of the nascent arts of nature, when the needs of innocence were not numerous. The magnificence of the countryside, the cabins surrounded by animals of every kind, attracted by the lure of nourishment; the birds living nearby amid dense foliage, enlivening the rural scenery with their melodious songs: audacious humans, how dare you undertake to ornament that nature by means of arts that can only imitate it distantly? You construct labyrinths, you contrive bowling-greens, you carve your trees into grotesques, you ornament your flower-beds with baskets, and you scorn the rustic fields and wild woods, where nature causes a hidden order to reign within confused variety, in conformity with secret rules of harmony and beauty, whose effect is felt in the soul as the sweetest delight.

We quit our old man and his family with difficulty in order to continue our route. Zachiel pointed out to us that those people, accustomed from infancy to work, have much more agile bodies. They also have more serenity of mind; their pleasures are less vivid, but their passions more moderate; they enjoy a tranquil voluptuousness that has nothing sensual about it, of an unalterable purity. Frugality enhances their strength, temperance maintains it, and virtue guides them in all their actions; one of their maxims is to prepare the young in advance for all the unfortunate accidents of the climate; that, they say, diminishes their intensity and preserves them from the baleful impressions that the elements cause weak constitutions; it spares them a thousand accidents to which the body is subjected more by lax education than temperament. It is certain that nature has constructed all beings to live in the fluid that surrounds them; it is foolish to withdraw them from it by precautions whose necessity is avoidable.

"You ought to remark," Zachiel continued, "that on this planet, people almost always follow the simple impulsion of nature; lying is held in horror here and punished severely; you must already have perceived that their raw judgment in superior to the politics of other worlds. One always encounters in their conduct the model of a perfect felicity, far from imitating the inhabitants of the worlds we have recently quit, who only dedicate themselves to disfiguring nature and wanting to reform it. What happened in consequence? They travestied the sentiments of humanity that she inspires in us, and gave entry, by a refinement foreign to the simplicity of her principles, to all the vices capable of troubling, corrupting and dishonoring that condition of society.

"Here the people are naturally grave, but that gravity is devoid of melancholy, without being deprived of the amiable gaiety that is not incompatible with reason; placid without indolence, the vivacity of their desires loses its sharp point and only leaves in the depths of their hearts a light and soft emotion. The passions of humans that are their torment elsewhere only serve for their felicity here; they hardly ever experience any violent agitation, or any of the mental maladies known on your world as vapors.

"You will see the taste for agriculture and commerce reign everywhere, regarded as the two pillars on which the edifice of their politics is posed; they are also the only ones that occupy them extensively. These people are not afflicted by the fatal prejudice that one sees reigning on other worlds, which keeps those who cultivate talents so necessary to the public good in a shameful obscurity; far from devaluing those talents, they attach marks of distinction to them, and humanity is among them a natural virtue. They regard their Prince as the image of sovereign intelligence and as their common father; they have a respect for him and an entire submission to his orders; bound by the oath of fidelity, they obey him by virtue of a sentiment of love and gratitude."

Chapter III
The Genius Takes us to the Capital of Abadia

It was spring, and I thought I could see Aurora in her purple costume bringing with her the graces of youth, merry banter, laughter, games and amour, and who, in running her gaze over the spinneys and the meadows, seemed to be smiling in advance at imminent victories. Already the god is deploying his bow and his redoubtable quiver, the Graces are augmenting his cortege, and the charming troop arrives on the first rays that the sun sends to the earth.

One then sees the innumerable swarm of day birds enjoying themselves among the columns of flame traversing the clouds, coming to salute the god of day with their melodious songs; one also sees young roses full of impatience hastening to emerge from their buds; one might think that each of them wanted to be the first to bloom, to exhale its sweet perfumes and open to the aspect of spring. The zephyrs announce it with their frolicsome games; one sees them launch forth from the hill into the valley; the flutter in the thickets, traverse the forest and return with mischievous smiles to the places where they reveal to the amorous shepherd the attractions of the beauty that charms them; they recognize with pleasure the places where they maliciously made the young shepherdess blush. Here there are flocks that bound through the tender grass; everywhere, one thinks one can see nature renewing herself, and one might think that she is taking pleasure in setting herself in opposition to herself, so different are her various aspects.

Monime interrupted my reflections in order to invite me to admire the beauty of the roads that led to the coastal city of Abadia. The roads were lined with iron, broad and comfortable, bordered with useful trees.

When we arrived in the city, Zachiel took us to the house of two young widows who lived together in a perfect union. Those two amiable individuals hastened to procure us all the commodities of life. We found in that pleasant house a sure and solid liaison, a familiarity full of mildness, a conversation that was always sane and always satisfying. We had not yet encountered in anyone a politeness franker and more natural, devoid of artifice and finesse, attempting to please but with a delicacy far from any kind of adulation. Floride and Cleontine did not know any other art of winning hearts and conciliating minds. They were kind enough to accompany us to show us the most beautiful places in the city.

That city is situated on the shore of a lake that empties into the sea; it forms a perfect square; the four principal gates are terminated by triumphal arches of simple but noble and majestic architecture; all the streets are broad and aligned; on each side are porticoes forming galleries where pedestrians can walk comfortably without fear of any accident; the houses are regular and interspersed with edifices serving public utility. One sees granaries there in which abundance reigns incessantly; fountains are distributed in an orderly fashion and decorated with emblems, and their waters flow into broad basins. One sees beautiful squares of vast extent, which form several blocks of buildings. The Emperor's palace is built in the Roman style; it is in the center of the city; it is only distinguished from others by its height and a colonnade that runs around it, on which the statues of great men have been placed and simulacra of all those who have worked to assure the wellbeing of the nation.

All the houses are built in stone or brick; they are well-vaulted, which renders them secure from conflagration. One sees aqueducts there that bring clear and pure water in abundance into all the streets in order to prevent the corruption of the air and maintain cleanliness; those waters flow by a gentle and imperceptible slope into the lake.

The public markets are vast and concave; in the middle are large gutters, and it is by that route that water released from the fountains draws away and precipitates all ordure, in order not to leave any vestige that might corrupt the air.

"The Prince who governs us," said Cleontine, "occupied like the father of a family with the felicity of his people, has ordered that children receive a good education, that they suckle with the milk the principles that tend to form good, faithful and useful subjects; that is why he wants the first concern of parents to have the temperament as its object, which often influences the way of thinking.

"From the cradle, the time when nature makes all kinds of impressions, children are exposed naked to the ardor of the sun and the insults of the seasons; they are also plunged into cold baths; it is thus that the body, accustomed from the most tender infancy, finds itself subsequently exempt from a thousand ills, to which it is too often rendered vulnerable by delicacy; it is by that means that it is habituated to the rudest exercises and the hardest labor."

She also informed us that public schools have been instituted for the education of youth; every child is received there as a citizen, without regard to rank or fortune, because they are convinced that the people is composed of human beings; one never sees there, as on other worlds, the forced laborers who are employed in cultivating estates without being able to enjoy the fruits of their labors. Here, a laborer is regarded as the most useful of citizens, peaceful in his habitation and the bosom of his family he enjoys the produce of his labor without dread.

The education of children is an essential part of government. The people regard youth as the most precious treasure of the State, and they consider its education to be a matter of great interest for society. Happiness and tranquility therefore depend on the care taken to form children in the duty that maintains harmony. The mind of a child, like soft wax, is susceptible to all the forms that one wants it to take on; the earliest impressions are hardly ever effaced, and the characters imposed therein influence their mores and their knowledge.

Human beings are often merely what education makes them; they owe their virtues or vices to it, their errors and prejudices, their ignorance or the development of their ideas, their idleness or love of work; like weak saplings devoid of vigor they need to be cultivated, nourished and grafted on to an appropriate tree favorable to their substance. What more worthy employment can one make of one's talents to render them useful to the good of humanity? Is it not to work for one's own wellbeing to bring up the young and form their virtues, give them a taste for knowledge, inspire them with a love of the fatherland, a desire for glory, an inviolable attachment to the sovereign and a dutiful respect for religion?

The first concern of those who preside over the schools is to inspire honest mores before ornamenting the intellect; they begin by enlightening the heart, by regulating all its movements, by developing its sentiments in order to purify them, disentangling all its inclinations in order to rectify them and by studying its passions in order to moderate them. They give the pupils lessons in constancy, firmness, temperance, moderation and all the virtues that form human beings, elevating the soul and putting it on guard against the illusions of self-love, in order to sustain it in hardship and avoid the intoxication of prosperity. Far from depicting virtue for them in sad images that only serve to inspire distaste, they show it, on the contrary, with all the charms of pleasure, in a fertile and cheerful setting, surrounded by games that lead toward it by flowery roads and facile paths; that renders it much more powerful over hearts inclined to cherish it.

After enabling us to admire everything that could interest our curiosity, the beautiful widows, who held a distinguished rank in the city, and moved in the highest social circles, invited Monime to make a few visits. Her beauty, her intelligence and her graces had always shone on all worlds; her mild and engaging character made her welcome in several houses to which Floride and Cleontine took pleasure in accompanying her.

One day, invited to dinner at the home one of the nobles of the Empire, where the company was numerous, we noticed that the honest and obliging Lord did not demand any of the respects that an affected arrogance usually demands. Content to merit the eulogies of reasonable people, he did not require any. We admired that noble and open attitude, and the discourse in which frankness announced the generosity of the heart, which is rarely encountered on other worlds. So, instead of the fine and alert complaisance whose piercing eyes see and seize upon all the passions of the great, in order not to lose any opportunity to flatter them, we only saw, on the contrary, old men whose geometrical minds seemed to be applying a ruler and compasses to the praise that they deigned to give.

Those grave individuals took possession of the conversation, talking about their youth; a few recounted military actions in which they had been involved, under the conduct of some commander or other; others repeated old stories they had already told in the morning; they talked about properties they had discovered in substances that ought to serve for the edification of brilliant theories, but which the slightest objection might cause to crumble.

The lord listened to all these speeches complaisantly, replied with justice and precision, making them see that the most enlightened among them could scarcely lift a corner of the veil with which nature covers herself, and that there are few truths susceptible of demonstration, even among those that are the most universally received. The sublime knowledge of humans is almost always reduced to being content with the probable, at which they only arrive by the way of doubt.

"What temerity is there, then," the lord continued, "in wanting to sound the depths of an abyss whose rim is unknown?"

No one daring to contradict a reflection so just, everyone applauded it, and the conversation ended.

We left in order to make a few more visits to persons who interested the heart and mind by a thousand virtues, the foremost is that of obliging—a virtue that, if it is commonly encountered among the Abadians, but is rarely found in our world, where one frequently sees indiscreet tongues divulging the services they have rendered, inflating their nature and the circumstances, exaggerating them without reason, to the point of revolting those who have been their object. They are monsters who dare to reproach them, and dispense them thereby of the gratitude they are entitled to have. One also often encounters ignoble protectors—which is to say, people who are only obliging in return for money, false individuals who always promise without any intention of obliging, or who are incapable of keeping their word. Those people disoblige you doubly, by making you miss the opportunity to address yourself to others who, franker and more zealous, might at least have informed you of the means to succeed. One can compare those people to bushes whose flowers render neither fruits nor odors.

Chapter IV
The Triumph of Amity

After we had fulfilled the duties of society, Floride and Cleontine invited us with such a natural grace to spend a few days at their country house that we could not refuse their urging. We departed at daybreak.

Scarcely had we covered a few miles than we discovered a cheerful valley formed by two hills crowned with green trees. A gap revealed to our eyes a habitation built on the side of a hill, a vast plain covered in the gifts of Ceres and those of Flora, surrounded by pleasant orchards that terminated the state of our beautiful widows. The air was pure, the sky serene, the earth shiny beneath the pearls of the dew, and the sun, scarcely a sixth of the way through its course, was only darting temperate rays that a gentle zephyr moderated with its breath.

The delightful location gave Monime the desire to repose there; a carpet of grass strewn with flowers served as a seat. The landscape inspired joy and confidence.

"Dare I ask these beautiful ladies," said Monime, smiling, "what can have engaged them to live together in celibacy, while still so young and ornamented with all the graces of beauty? You ought not to lack admirers; I have even thought that I distinguished several in the number of persons that assiduously pay court to you."

"It's true," said Floride, "that Cleontine has always had a number in her entourage, in spite of all the care she takes to distance them; but to respond to your question, know that, linked together by the most tender bonds of amity, we have renounced everything that might diminish its charm. Both raised in the temple of Cybele, the same education was given to us, and our sentiments are analogous: the same desires, inclinations, pleasures and love of liberty; it was there that the amity formed that has united us with indissoluble bonds. You know that inclination is a pleasant impulse that draws us together, and that impulse is all the dearer to us because it is born of the depths of our tenderness and is maintained there with pleasure. It is true that amity does not always have the fire and brilliance of amour, but its gaiety is simple, devoid of ornamentation and art; united by it, one only sees its own graces shining, without ever employing the adornment of wit.

"Cleontine's family, much more favored by the gifts of fortune than mine, took her out of the temple a few years before anyone thought of withdrawing me; that interval distanced us from one another without altering our sentiments. It is not difficult to imagine, in view of Cleontine's charms, that it did not take her long to attract the desires and homages of the most brilliant youth and the richest suitors in the city. Cleonbule, who only aspired one day to enjoy the pleasure of seeing his daughter well established, announced to her one day that it was necessary to fix herself, that he did not want to interfere and would leave her to make her own choice.

"'I am only seeking,' Cleonbule said, 'to render your felicity perfect, if it is possible; little sensible to the gleam of riches, nor that of grandeur, I will always prefer merit, talent and good faith to the vain glamour of honors. I only warn you that you ought not to envisage anything in the union that you are about to contract but pure pleasures, which ought only to draw their source from the admixture of souls that receive their perfection in a mutual confidence and complaisance. It is up to you to choose a man whose probity and mores can contribute to rendering you happy.'

"Cleontine, penetrated by the generosity and tenderness of a father she cherished more than her life, assured him, while thanking him, that his will would always be the rule and motive force of all her actions.

"After that conversation, Cleonbule, fearing that the timidity natural to her sex might prevent his daughter from manifesting her true sentiments, determined, in order to make sure of them, to study the character of the people who rendered themselves assiduous in his house. He examined the reactions of his daughter on their arrival, and thought he had discovered in her a tender penchant for a young man with an interesting face and distinguished merit. The young man focused his attention; truth reigned in his heart as well as on his lips. His name was Clitandre; he was the only one who had not yet dared to declare himself; that timidity came solely from his lack of fortune. However, Cleonbule determined, by virtue of a generosity scornful of riches, to give him preference, provided that Cleontine was not inclined in favor of another. What a man! What a father! What a tender interest he took in the happiness of his daughter and that of all those who surrounded her.

"I have a singular interest in giving you a portrait of Cleonbule. He was a man of about fifty, tall and well-proportioned in his figure; a thousand graces emanated from his entire person; he had a majestic air, serious without being grim, a common sense always guided by reason, and a keen but delicate taste for all that is called beauty in art. His politeness was a natural consequence of the desire he had to oblige; his generosity inspired him with a paternal concern for all those whom providence had put under his protection. He combined with those rare qualities the keenest attachment and the most unshakable fidelity to his sovereign. In sum, Cleonbule had always been the best of fathers and the most tender of spouses, complaisant and filled with regard and a warm amity that nothing could discourage. I have got a little carried away in order to render justice to the memory of a man who will always be dear to me.

"It was in those happy circumstances that my mother took me out of the temple of Cybele. My first concern was to go to visit Cleontine, who informed me by means of a thousand tender caresses of the joy she felt at my return; all my pleasures were combined from then on in her society. Although Cleontine's house was the rendezvous of the very best of society, I did not take long to perceive the preference she gave to Clitandre; she often talked to me about him eulogistically. I confess that he had also made a deep impression on my heart; the graces of an open physiognomy, masculine and animated, the vivacity of a mind that education had ornamented with a thousand talents, and a noble soul, liberal, benevolent, sincere and the enemy of dissimulation, put his virtues in broad daylight.

"The frequent conversations we had on his subject told me that my friend would gladly settle in his favor if the sentiments he had inspired in her were in conformity with those of her father. But how could she dare to think that Cleonbule was as sensible to Clitandre's merits as his daughter?

"Meanwhile, Clitandre had not yet made any declaration—but does one need words to express the tender fires that love inspires? Does everything not reveal them? A thousand hasty cares, gazes in which sentiment burns, the fear of offending, the timidity in his expressions, his distress at the slightest severe glance and a thousand other small observations that do not escape the sight of an interested lover are always the true interpreters of the heart.

"Cleontine was more pensive than usual; the anxiety she had regarding her fate gave a certain expression of languor to her eyes, which rendered her even more beautiful. For myself, convinced of her attachment, I only thought of fortifying her hopes with a view to tranquilizing her.

"Cleonbule, who had been observing the two lovers for some time, perceived with pleasure the tender penchant that had gripped his daughter and driven her to give preference to Clitandre. Charmed by that welcome discovery, he did not want to defer their happiness, and in order to assure himself of the sentiments and views that Clitandre might have regarding his establishment, he invited him to spend a few days at his country house. Cleontine was not in that party; her father exempted her, in order not to be distracted in the project he had formed to sound her lover's heart.

"On the very first evening Clitandre was impelled so impetuously toward Cleonbule that, in spite of the resolution he had made not to declare himself, he was finally forced to admit his passion; but Cleontine's name died on his lips; his disturbance prevented him from pronouncing it.

"'That's enough,' said Cleonbule, embracing him. 'Pull yourself together and have no fear of opening your heart to me; regard me as a father who loves you and who has been uniquely occupied with your happiness for a long time. Talk to me naturally. Is my daughter aware of your sentiments? Do you believe that she is sensible to them?'

"Clitandre blushed; it was neither shame nor fear of the research that might be carried out of his conduct; the blush was occasioned by a more delicate sentiment; he was not unaware of the empire that Cleonbule had over his daughter, but, although he loved her more than himself, he would nevertheless have renounced the happiness of being united with her if he had believed that she was only giving herself to him out of obedience. His anxiety increased and prevented him from replying, but Cleonbule, who read his heart and penetrated the motives of his anxiety, reassured him.

'You ought not to fear,' he told him, 'that I would ever constrain my daughter's inclinations; my authority could not extend so far as to force her to marry a man who had not touched her heart; it is, therefore, only you, whose probity I know, that I can consult on that matter. Your lack of fortune is not a sufficiently powerful reason to distance you from my alliance; a wise man is never poor. In two days you will see my daughter again; don't mention my sentiments to her, try to discover hers, and if they are such as I desire, I give you my word that nothing will ever be able to raise any obstacle to your marriage.'

"Clitandre, penetrated by love, respect and gratitude, in thanking Cleonbule for the graces he had shown him, employed only simple expressions, but the natural eloquence of which made all their energy felt.

"As soon as Clitandre returned, he went to Cleontine's apartment. She was alone. His arrival surprised her and his anxious expression intimidated her. Clitandre, perceiving the disturbance he had caused, did not dare to speak for some time. The sighs that escaped him made an impression on Cleontine; her soul, penetrated by anxieties, could not bear the silence any longer and she hastened to break it. 'What can have caused the emotion that I see in you?' she asked. 'Speak, hurry up and tell me.'

"'It's true, beautiful Cleontine, that no one can ever have experienced the perplexities I feel, but a favorable word from your mouth would change it instantly into a perfect felicity.

"'I don't know the species of your trouble,' said Cleontine, 'but if it depends on me to alleviate it, you ought not to doubt that I will apply myself to it with all the zeal of which I am capable.'

"Such a favorable response restored calm to Clitandre's soul, and emboldened him to declare his passion.

"There are souls that seem linked by secret chains, which understand one another implicitly. Cleontine was unaware of the art of pretence; her heart was simple and always guided by nature; coldness and constraint were banished from it. She would never have had the pettiness to abandon herself to suspicions; her lover's amour seemed as disinterested as her own; she listened to his oaths with a pleasure that she did not seek to dissimulate, and saw nothing in his response but the impression of his sentiments.

Clitandre then allowed the transports of his joy to burst forth in a thousand inconsequential statements. Could there be any better proof of his love? That evening he remounted his horse in order to go and inform Cleonbule that his amiable daughter was not opposed to his happiness, and they returned together in order to make the preparations for the marriage, which were concluded in a matter of days.

"Everything seemed to announce an endless happiness for the two young spouses, but is there anything on which one can count? Everything down here is fragile. We incessantly make plans for a durable felicity, but all our plans are vain; the edifice advances insensibly, our hearts quiver with joy in observing its progress; already, it is reaching the point of perfection that is in view, when the hurricane suddenly rises, topples the edifice, and destroys the most beautiful hopes in an instant.

"A year had scarcely gone by in the charm of a perfect union. Heaven had blessed the union by the birth of a son who would be the delight of the amiable family, when Clitandre was appointed to the government of the province of Gronor; his merit, his great talents and his integrity acquired that position for him without having solicited it. Clitandre, wanting to mark his obedience to the Emperor's orders, got ready to leave without waiting for his wife, whom Cleonbule was to bring, being unable to reconcile himself to be separated from his daughter.

"Cleontine made me party to the god news, but far from sharing her joy, I was sensibly afflicted by it; I feared that time and distance would cause her to lose the memory of our old friendship. Although I dared not show her all the grief that I experienced at a voyage that would put such a great distance between us, the dolor was expressed so perfectly in my eyes that Cleontine was touched by it. Her heart, divided between love and friendship, then made her envisage the voyage and the honors that awaited her with a great anxiety, which troubled her mind. Our discourse became serious; our separation was its subject.

"Cleonbule, who was present at that conversation, strove in vain to import more cheerfulness into it. 'Whence comes this disturbance, my children? You ought to hope for everything from time; perhaps you will soon be reunited, never to be separated again. Times change and events are submissive to their vicissitudes; a cloud can obscure the sun, but it never interrupts its course. Might it not happen that the amiable Floride will soon find an establishment worthy of her, which, in bringing the two of you together, will retighten the knots of the amity that has bound you together since the most tender age? I'm convinced that Floride is reasonable enough to prefer in a union a man who will find his happiness in rendering her happy. I don't presume that any object has yet succeeded in subjugating her young heart, so there is every reason to believe that reason will do for her what amour has the custom of operating for others.'

"That speech made me blush, and after having thanked Cleonbule for the advantageous sentiments that I believed to be dictated purely by the amity he had for his daughter, I embraced my friend, with tears in my eyes, and wished her a fortunate voyage.

"On my return to my lodgings my mother came to see me. That tender mother, as sensible as I was to my friend's departure, found no other consolation than that of lending herself to my dolor and gently combating the reasons I believed I had for my affliction. She combined with her discourse useful lessons for forming a new plan of life for me, the simplicity of which would be its basis and render me happy. I listened avidly to her advice, which passed into my soul like a stream of pure water flowing between flowers and serving to refresh them. It was thus that her admirable counsel served to tranquilize me.

"Several days had already passed without my having received any news of Cleontine; I believed that she had already arrived in Clitandre's government and was commencing to murmur at her silence when I received a note from Cleonbule asking me to me to see his daughter as soon as possible.

"I ran there instantly—but how can I depict the excess of my dolor when, on going into my friend's apartment, I perceived the father and the daughter plunged into an indescribable affliction? Seized, my legs trembling, I stood there motionless, scarcely breathing. I did not have the strength to pronounce a single word. Everyone maintained a bleak silence, and a baleful presentiment made me suspect that some terrible accident had happened to Clitandre.

"I made a movement to go to Cleontine, who, raising her eyes to the heavens, finally let them fall back on to me. Despair was painted therein; her gaze had something deranged, which chilled me with far. Then I seized her hands, which I bathed with my tears; hers had not yet flowed but, in gazing at me, her eyes moistened. 'I can see, my dear Floride, that you have guessed a part of my woes.' Her sighs stifled her voice.

"Cleonbule, who had doubtless dreaded irritating her despair but telling me immediately what its object was, informed me in a few words that during Clitandre's journey, his horse had reared up and had precipitated him into an abyss, that the fall had broken his entire body, and that he had died a few days later of his wounds. 'I asked you to come, my dear daughter,' Cleonbule added, 'to help me console your friend, and also to bring some relief to my woes.'

"'Alas, sire,' I cried, 'what can I do, except to share your affliction?'

"'I know,' said Cleonbule, 'that indiscreet consolations only sharpen violent dolors. Indifference and coldness can easily find words, but sadness is the true language of amity; the vulgar do not recognize violent afflictions, and great passions almost never germinate in feeble souls.'

"I sent word to me mother begging her to permit me to spend a few days with my friend; not only did she give me her permission but she also made it a duty to share our affliction. Cleonbule did not leave us, and although he was overwhelmed by distress himself he nevertheless found enough mental strength to hide the greater part of it; he employed all the consolation that his natural eloquence could provide to soften his daughter's pain.

"His cares succeeded; the sweetness of her character, her filial tenderness and her piety toward the divinity, which had no affectation, finally procure her a little more tranquility, so true is it that virtue sets aside all chagrin, filling our souls with an interior softness that is the charm of our being. It also purifies our pleasures in rendering them more sensible to the charm it adds to them.

"Always tender, attentive and obliging, Cleonbule said to his daughter one day that she ought no longer to occupy herself with anything but giving birth in her son's heart to all the virtues that had ornamented her husband's, by inspiring in him the energy of sentiment that characterizes noble souls.

"'It's necessary, my dear daughter, in giving him a taste for the sciences and a love of work, to put economy into his studies, in order not to charge his memory with a thousand useless things that might overwhelm judgment beneath the weight of a fatiguing erudition that does not enlighten the mind or the heart, and to avoid any prejudice for any particular system; it is for reason to enlighten him, when the time comes, as to the choice he ought to make. Let us try to enable him to resemble his father, whose mind was so perfect that he transformed, so to speak, those of others in himself; one could not know him without striving to imitate him; his enlightenment was so sublime that it penetrated all those surrounding him. All his virtues combined ought to be a new motive of consolation for us, since they assure us that the divinity, ever equitable in His judgments, has received your spouse in his bosom, and that he is enjoying the glory promised to all those who are faithful to His laws.'

"Cleontine appeared to heed those consolations; the love she had for her son gave rise in her to the desire to see him one day become the worthy successor to his father's virtues.

"I did not let a day pass without seeing Cleontine. Her dolor gradually dissipated and the time of her mourning expired; she reappeared in society more striking than before. Several suitors declared themselves, but Cleontine announced the resolution that she had made to renounce any new engagement for life.

"Obliged to undertake a journey with my mother that kept me away from my friend for more than a year, I often had news of her, in which she never ceased to give us proofs of her tenderness and always pressed us to return. Flattered by her insistence, I persuaded my mother to conclude her affairs. When I returned, my first concern was to go to see Cleontine, who welcomed me with an amity that allowed me to judge that absence had not diminished the tender sentiments that united us. Cleonbule also made evident the joy he had in seeing me again.

"After a short time, I perceived a considerable alteration in Cleontine's humor. A somber melancholy had taken possession of her heart; I often found her sad and pensive. I was anxious, and pressed her to open up to me. 'What holds you back,' I asked, 'from confiding to the bosom of a friend the troubles that I can see all too clearly penetrating your soul? Can there be anything in the world more appropriate than sharing them with a friend who has always been devoted to you?'

"'Alas, my dear,' cried Cleontine, embracing me, 'I know your sentiments and I don't doubt your amity, but will you have enough to determine yourself to change my afflictions into delight?'

"'How offensive that doubt is!' I said.

"'Wait,' said Cleontine, looking at me fixedly. 'You don't yet know the full extent of the sacrifice that I dare not demand. Listen to me, Floride, and reply without prevarication to my questions. I've suspected for a long time the quality of the sentiments that my father has for you, but his amity resembles amour so strongly that I feared that I might be mistaken.'

"'What!' I said, astonished. 'You dare to suspect Cleonbule of a weakness injurious to his glory and mine?'

"'Why would that suspicion be injurious to my father? Why would it be injurious to you?'

"'Because,' I said, 'Cleonbule is far too reasonable to attach himself to someone who cannot be his,'

"'You have a poor understanding of amour,' said Cleontine, 'if you believe that it always allows itself to be guided by reason; but that would never cause my father to abuse it, since he would find in you a subject worthy to fulfill all his desires. But you, my dear Floride, what could prevent you from responding to Cleonbule's sentiments? Is your heart so strongly attached to Filidor that nothing can any longer break the bonds, and can you have made a mystery of that for me, who has always uncovered my most secret thoughts to you?'

"'Alas, Cleontine,' I cried, dolorously, 'how you abuse the power that you have acquired over my soul! Me, hide anything from you! Could I do it, and would I not be unworthy of your friendship if I were capable of it? Have I not made you party to the tender sentiments that Filidor has always had for me? I have talked to you a hundred times about his passion and have not hidden from you that I was sensible to it? Why pretend not to know?

"'Cruel friend,' I added, 'has not the first of my sentiments always been that of loving you? Since my most tender years my heart alas been confounded with yours; I no longer love and feel except through you; you regulate all my sentiments and I have only lived until now in order to be your friend. Even before your marriage to Clitandre I consulted you about Filidor's passion. He is young, handsome; he has virtue and morality; he is honest, attentive, obliging, and he loves me; my heart was free when he addressed his ardor to me; what can I tell you? I sensed the contagion and I could not refuse him a portion of that heart, which, but for him, you would still possess in its entirety.

"'But what am I saying? That heart is not divided, since you reign equally in his, and to dissipate your suspicions entirely, know that Filidor's father will shortly make the proposal of our marriage; my mother consents to it, and I flatter myself that it will soon be concluded. So, my dear Cleontine, have no fear that I shall ever betray the sentiments that delicacy inspires in me, in consenting to a union that I fear more than you, and I swear to you....'

"'Stop, cruel individual!' said Cleontine, swiftly. 'Let that fatal oath not become the instrument of my woes! Oh, Floride, how poorly you understand my sentiments! Is it thus that you know the force of amity? What reason would I have for fearing your union with my father? On the contrary, it alone could complete my desires. My dear Floride...alas!....how can I say this? Would I have been capable of such a great sacrifice? However, I demand it. Yes, dear and tender friend, I demand of your amity that you renounce the sentiments that Filidor's love has inspired in you, in order to crown my father's, in making his happiness and mine—and I dare to flatter myself that it might also make yours.

"'I am aware,' Cleontine continued, 'that my conduct is contrary to delicacy; forgive that, in favor of a father that I adore, and who will be unable to live if he has the misfortune of seeing you enter the arms of another. I know your virtue, and have no fear of precipitating you into misfortunes without resource; my father loves you, and the passion he has for you can never be weakened by any other; it has only become stronger, and has found no counterweight to lessen its strength. The reason that governs, when it is alone, is not strong enough to resist the slightest effort; it is only souls on fire, like yours, that are able to conquer and vanquish; all great efforts and all sublime actions are their work; the sacrifice that I am demanding is worthy of you, and worthy of our friendship.

"'It is, you will perhaps tell me, a ridiculous pretention to believe oneself to be loved for oneself. I confess that my amity is very interested; it is my own happiness that I am seeking in yours; but my dear, you're not unaware that amity, that sentiment so pure, only founds its preferences on personal interest. Birth, fortune, talents, youth and beauty are only the effects of hazard; it is, nevertheless, all those embellishments in combination that render us lovable; but that is only the canvas of the tapestry, the embroidery makes the whole price; all those gifts are loved in us, they are confounded with us; we ought not, therefore, to flatter ourselves with the distinctions they give us; it's necessary to regard them simply as a currency whose alloy often makes all the consistency, and which loses its value to some degree in the crucible. It's into that crucible that I that I want to put yours.

"'You know, my dear Floride, the tenderness that my father has always had for me; you have shared that tenderness, and far from being jealous of that, it has only ever augmented that which I have for you. Cleonbule is not unaware of Filidor's passion, but he does not know that it is paid in tender return, and he cannot see the object of his amour pass into the hands of a rival without the sharpest dolor; his heart, oppressed by the chagrin that is experiencing, has not been able to resist the pressing solicitations that I have been making incessantly to persuade him to disclose his troubles to me. He has finally resolved to confide them to my bosom; sure of the keen interest that I would take, he has entrusted me with the care of contributing to his happiness and counting on your friendship for me. I have promised him everything, flattering him with a fortunate outcome.'

'Oh, Cleontine!' I cried. 'To what proof are you putting the price of your own? Is it necessary, then, that I sacrifice Filidor, his love, my tenderness, or that I lose irredeemably a friendship that is so dear to me?'

"'No, you will not lose it,' said Cleontine. 'I know your heart much better than you know it yourself. Amity will triumph over love, and I shall announce to my father that my friend finally consents to render him happy, in order that we can enjoy in advance the pleasure that we shall have in spending the rest of our days together.'

"'Stop,' I said. 'At least give me time to draw breath.'

"'What objection do you have to make to me?' that dear and tender friend went on.'

"I confess that, stunned by her vivacity, nothing presented itself to my mind at that moment that could combat her reasons; the empire that she had acquired over my heart, the natural eloquence that she always employs successfully when it is a matter of persuading those she attempts to bring round to her sentiment, transforming the, so to speak, into herself—all of that, as I say, robbed me of the strength to respond.

"Perceiving that I was maintaining a bleak silence, Cleontine redoubled her caresses. As if she wanted to make me ashamed of the resistance that it was necessary to overcome to adhere to sentiments so contrary to my desires, Cleontine, without seeming to perceive the disturbance I was in, went on: 'Don't you remember, my dear Floride, having heard Clitandre say that three sorts of love between humans can be distinguished? The first, which is coarse and vulgar, they have in common with the animals, which is only guided by the attractions of need and pleasure. The second, which is pure and celestial, brings us closer to gods; that one is, I believe, the depiction of keen and tender amity. The third, which participates in the first two and occupies the middle ground between gods and brutes, seems most natural to humans because it is the bond of souls cemented by that of the senses. I would like to know,' Cleontine added, 'to which of the three kinds of love my friend will give preference.'

"Stunned by that question, too subtle for my feeble enlightenment, I did not hesitate in giving my suffrage in favor of the second love. 'You're vanquished, my good friend,' Cleontine cried, embracing me with a kind of transport that surprised me. 'You yield in the end to tender amity.'

"'I confess,' I said, 'that it's impossible to resist it when it's you who is determined to assert its rights.'

"But to cut short a story that might become tedious for you, I shall only add that after much conflict, I consented, not without difficulty, to yield to Cleontine's persistence. My mother, who found great advantages in the marriage, completed my determination with her sage advice. The sacrifice was all the greater because, in spite of the amity that Cleonbule had always shown me, I had an antipathy for him that I found difficult to vanquish. I can say nevertheless, truthfully, that during the five years I spent with him, we both enjoyed a peace that was untroubled by any kind of anxiety; his kindness and attention triumphed over my heart; love had taken the place of indifference when death separated us.

408

"I confess that, delivered then entirely to Cleontine, the rights of the spouse prejudiced those of friendship for some time, but the dolor we experienced, one for the loss of a father and the other for that of a tenderly beloved husband, united our sentiments, reanimated our hearts and fused them again. I have long shared Cleontine's; it has taken possession of the greater part of mine; there was a double theft that I had made from my friend, a debt that I had contracted for which I owed her restitution and which I engaged to pay throughout the course of my life.

"Content to spend the rest of our days together, Cleontine only being occupied with the education of her son, I share with her the cares that we regard as a duty; it is also what forms our pleasures and causes our days to go by in an unalterable peace."

Chapter IV
Depiction of the Court

After having thanked Floride for her complaisance, Monime got up and we took a little path that led to the house of our beautiful widows.

That simple but comfortable house is furnished with everything that might serve for honest amusements; one sees gardens there in which art is so cleverly combined with nature that the human handiwork can hardly be perceived. The house is made to be inhabited; nothing can be seen there that is not cheerful and agreeable; everything respires cleanliness and nothing reeks of luxury; there is no apartment in which one does not find all the necessary commodities. Instead of the multitude of idle individuals that is called "good company" in our society, Floride and Cleontine only assembled in their home persons who interested the heart in a thousand advantageous fashions, and who redeemed a few petty defects with an infinity of virtues.

Those beautiful individuals also found amusement in the conversation of peasants, which often has charms for elevated souls. It is certain that one finds characters more marked in village naivety; more people think for themselves than behind the uniform mask of city-dwellers, in which everyone shows themselves as others are rather than as they are themselves; one also finds in them hearts sensible to the slightest caress, which are glad of any interest taken in their wellbeing. Neither their hearts nor their minds are fashioned by art; they have not learned to form themselves on the model of people in society, and it is only in them that one finds natural human beings.

"Take note," Zachiel said to us, "of the laborer who, at the decline of day, sees the end of his task and returns cheerfully, whistling a pastoral tune, to his dwelling. His appetite, excited by labor, devours the frugal meal that his wife has prepared for him. That meal disposes him to sleep, but, in spite of its short duration, daybreak announces the agreeable moment of return to his work. He invokes Ceres, and in his condition, he counts more happy moments than the nobles of your Earth, who, when they get up, are unaware of most of what they are going to do and how they will employ their day—whereas to the laborious villager, with the sensibility of his heart wide awake within him, the entire world offers nothing but objects of tenderness and gratitude. Everywhere he sees the benevolent hand of nature, collects her gifts in the productions of the earth, sees his table covered by his cares, goes to sleep under her protection, and owes to her his placid awakening; her lessons make themselves felt in disgraces and her favors in pleasures; the benefits that he enjoys, and everything that is dear to him, are as many further homages that he renders to nature; although the god of the universe escapes his weak eyes, he sees and adores the common father of humans everywhere; in honoring his supreme benefits thus is one not serving the infinite Being as best one can?"

After we had taken our leave of our amiable widows, the genius took us to the Palace of Nature, where the Emperor has his usual residence. In that palace is a drawing room that exceeds in its grandeur and its regularity everything that I have ever seen; it is in that room that the Emperor renders justice to all his subjects. A throne is placed in the middle, and to either side are seats destined for those whose merit has brought them the dignities that earn them the right to occupy them. I thought, in admiring that illustrious assembly, that I was seeing Saturn holding council in the midst of gods.

We had no difficulty in obtaining an audience. That Prince, whose mildness and affability cause his other virtues to shine, received us with the air of generosity and candor that rendered him master of all hearts.

"Never," Zachiel told us, "has the throne been filled by a Prince more expert in the art of reigning. That monarch combines all the talents and qualities that form a hero and a conqueror. He combines those rare talents with the most majestic bearing and a masculine beauty which the nobility of his features renders even more striking. That charming exterior, combined with the facility of his expression, wins the hearts of all those who approach him, and his liberality attaches them to him forever. Intrepid in dangers, firm and unshakable in adversity, inexhaustibly ingenious in resources and penetrating, the most complicated designs are mere child's play for his imagination, as vast as it is fecund, and he executes them with all the more rapidity because he projects them so easily."

The Emperor's Council is composed of people of consummate experience in military art, the administration of laws and that of finances. The monarch has always paid equal attention to recompensing merit and punishing vice. Any lack of integrity in the ministry is punished by death; there are no slight faults for those exercising public responsibilities. The Prince, always attentive to the well-being of his people, makes secret enquiries in order to be informed of their conduct. If a similar severity were observed on some of the worlds we had visited, it would perhaps have been the means of conserving an exact rectitude in the administration of justice and maintaining peace and tranquility among the citizens.

In that court, where equity has always reigned, it is regarded as dishonor to incur debts to procure the favors of the prince, which can only be the reward of virtue and talent. Nothing is granted to intrigue; no ostentation, opulence, titles or the exploits of ancestors can obtain preference; virtue alone has the right to present itself. Thus, one never sees those idle and disdainful courtiers who, always envious of favors that justice only accords to virtue, are solely occupied in diminishing the value of fine actions or seeking a means to render them suspect. Nor does one see men who, out of pride, interest or baseness, seem to make it a duty to protect vice and rapine.

In that fortunate world, one never sees the old nobility stifling that which is only acquired by merit; made to represent virtue in all its luster, it is, as one of their scholars says, neither the decoration of vice, nor the entitlement of indolence, nor the pedestal of pride; content to merit eulogies, it is not by base intrigues that it seeks to obtain dignities; without ostentation in their actions, without arrogance and vanity in their discourse, they leave to renown the care of measuring their worth.

That court seems to be the abode of liberty; one does not respire there the air of slavery that makes itself felt on so many other worlds; one is not vexed there by tyrants. The nobles of the Empire combine with the mildness of their mores the tender benevolence that is the charm of society. Never does interest counterbalance honor there; the pleasure obtained from tenderness and generosity is the sweetest of sentiments; when the heart is capable of it, how can it devote itself to any other?

When officers are commanded to place themselves at the head of an army, one does not see them taking with them the luxury that it practiced on many worlds, where the table, gambling, spectacles and assemblies fill all their time; these are occupied with plans and maps, or studying the books that have the greatest relevance to their métier, personally making use of geometrical instruments to trace their plans; one sees them examining all the works of the army, passing along the lines, advancing into the trenches and inspecting the batteries; that is how great generals are formed.

In times of peace, on returning to the capital, they visit the arsenals, the construction yards, the workshops and exhibition cabinets, because among these fortunate people war is merely a temporary fermentation, and if they limited themselves to the sole talent of making it, they would become useless to the state. That is why one sees those same officers applying themselves to the quest for new ways to extend commerce, to establish new factories, to render the soil more fecund, to augment the population, impede luxury and give free scope to the circulation of money, in order that it can furnish the multiple needs of the State.

Never does one encounter there one of those lords of finance whose luxury effaces that of the nobles of the court. People on that planet believe that virtues and talents are as useful to the State as armies; the negotiations and administration of the public treasury are their most serious occupations. Moderate in their pleasures, they only lavish their wealth in favor of the poor, in order to lighten the burden of their labor; those whose fortunes have been overturned by disasters find in their benevolence assistance all the more precious because it is always accompanied the consolations dictated by virtue. They are good and humane; they love everything that bears the imprint of honesty and truth; the agreeable never distances them from the useful. Their upright and well-made hearts are only occupied in working for common wellbeing, in order to merit the esteem of the wise, sustaining worthily the title of friend of humanity, because people are only esteemed in proportion to the good they do.

They believe that humiliated poverty often becomes the source of crimes; that is, they say, the fruit of the shame inflicted on those who suffer. A thousand people will endure indigence patiently, if they have no other pains than the privations associated with it; they will not be seen delivering themselves to criminal enterprises to extract themselves from their misery if they are only afflicted with fatigue; but if they are heaped with scorn and shame, they cannot sustain the weight. A honest man can eat poor food, dress very simply, be poorly lodged and poorly warmed; all those disagreements are tolerable; but if his indigence is known to a multitude of fools who only measure merit in luxury and expense, he will soon endure the humiliating scorn that drives him to despair, and eventually to base actions that make him forget virtue.

The effect of their morality is to prevent vice in weak souls, to excite them to virtue by the exercise of honest sentiments, and to affirm the same sentiments in virtuous souls that sometimes have need of reawakening; it is a fire that it is necessary to reanimate from time to time and nourish in order to prevent it from going out. It is neither in prosperity nor in elevation that one needs to learn to love virtue, but in abjection and misfortune.

The Emperor puts his glory into maintaining peace in his estates, and it is by his virtues that he obliges his subjects to combine love with the obedience that they owe him. There is nothing that he may not expect from them; their wealth and their lives are always offered as soon as he has the slightest need of them, and that zeal goes as far as their being only too glad to find opportunities to give him proof of their love and their attachment; all hearts fly toward the Prince and the sight of him is a benefit for them.

The monarch has sustained wars without seeing himself in the harsh necessity of vexing his people; the treasure of his savings alone furnished the expenses that such calamities always involve; a prudent and enlightened conduct terminated them in a short time. At present, however, a perfect harmony reigns over the entire planet; the same intelligence guides the various peoples who inhabit it; the same laws of equity, rectitude and god faith animate them, like streams that, after having gone astray for a while, finally return to reunite with the Ocean from which they escaped.

The capital of the Empire's revenues only consists of a single tax: a levy on all the wealth of every citizen of a tenth of the income from their lands. The majority of which return it of their own accord, without being obliged to any other imposition. Merchants and various kinds of artisans pay the same tax in proportion to the profits they make, and are obliged to bring to the treasuries named by the court the contributions they are due to pay, which they do without any constraint, recognizing their dependence by that persona service. That fashion of levying taxes is of great utility to the Prince, in that it spares him the considerable sums that he would have to give an infinity of people charged with collecting the money. In any case, the multiplicity of taxes always leads to a large number of abuses that tend to run peoples without the Prince finding relief in his pressing necessities; and his people, vexed, no longer address to the heavens anything but complaints and murmur, which only aggravated their woes further.

It is by virtue of that economy that the coffers of the State and those of the citizens are similarly full. The peasant cultivates his lands carefully there, in order to render them more fecund, without fear of new taxes. The treasurers, loyal to their prince, do not seek to enrich themselves at the expense of the people. The cities, ornamented with beautiful edifices, are all full of happy citizens delighted to live in them; others please themselves no less in the country, in order to enjoy the abundance and liberty that reign there.

The Court, the abode of the aristocracy, offers something that I had never observed on any other planet—which is to say that, following the example of the Prince, all the courtiers conserve an air of candor and verity; base flattery never poisons their discourse; not at all attracted by the desire to accumulate titles and honors, which, as I have already said, are only accorded to virtue. There is a disinterest proof against anything, a scrupulous probity, a sage, firm, profound intelligence far from the ridiculous self-esteem that believes itself infallible in its judgments; an affability that captivates hears, attaches and subjugates the confidence of all those who approach it; and an enlightened generosity and a noble equity that exposes to the monarch the fine actions of his officers.

In brief, those nobles appeared to me to be veritably noble, in that they are endowed with all the virtues that form perfect human beings.

Chapter VII
The Character of Women

In that Court the ladies conserve an air of modesty that serves as an example to the women of the city. Fashions are unknown in that world; for several centuries the same mode of dress has always been conserved there. One never sees them occupied with frivolities or bagatelles; intelligence ornamented by various knowledge renders their conversation interesting without taking away any of the vivacity of their wit. Their reflections always have a great and sublime character proportionate to the subjects under discussion; the serenity of their minds enables them to savor a pure and tranquil delight that has nothing bitter or sensual about it, and which raises them above ordinary women; nor do they recognize base sentiments—one might think that in this world the soul contracts an unshakable purity.

Abadian women, always following the first principles of nature, do not blush in recognizing amour as the motive of all things—by amour I mean the honest love that one could easily mistake for simple amity. That amour, as I say, is the rule and the brake of the penchants of nature; it is by virtue of it that, except for the beloved object, one sex is no longer anything to the other. One ought to suppose that love possessed of several estimable qualities, without which one would not be able to feel it. Abadian women often abandon themselves to those pleasures; they glory in loving—not the impetuous and inconstant love that the senses engender and disappears when it commences to weaken, but a tender and solid love inspired by the heart, which reason and honor direct and which can never be diminished by the certainty of being loved. Verity reigns in their hearts as well as on their lips; they are ignorant of the criminal art of deception; they do not feign a love that they do not feel and have a sovereign scorn for any abuse of the weakness of a credulous lover.

One can, therefore, believe that true love is the most chaste of all bonds; its ardor purifies the natural penchants by concentrating them in a single object. The truly smitten heart does not flee the senses; it guides them and covers their deviations with a delightful veil. That ever-timid and modest love, far from snatching favors, only seeks to merit them; silence and mystery sharpen and conceal the sweet transports, the purity of the ardor honors and purifies its caresses, and in the very bosom of voluptuousness, decency and honesty accompany it—and one can say that it alone causes everything to accord with desire, without modesty being offended by it. Take away from love its greatest charm, however, which is to esteem the beloved object and lend it perfections, and as soon as that honesty abandons it, it is no longer anything. Innocence combined with amour is the sweetest joy and the most delightful condition of life; neither shame nor read troubles the felicity of two virtuous lovers; they have no reproaches to make to one another, and can talk about virtue without blushing.

It is thus that beautiful Abadian women depicted love for us. "Would it not be," they added, "a rare phenomenon to offer to nature for a woman to call herself happy without any pleasure of the heart? The mechanism of such a statue would not be easy to analyze. The pleasure of the heart ought to be the interior satisfaction that one feels in loving what is honest. Can the mind be satisfied when the heart languishes in sadness? The lack of confidence puts it in shackles; one dares not explain one's thoughts with persons one mistrusts, the interest of the conversation is limited by that mysterious reserve, a cold monotony chills it, and it no longer contains anything but commonplaces, incoherent words, and in spite of an accumulation of frivolities, pleasure drains away into its lacunae; whereas, in composing a society of friends who interest the heart, sure of one another's discretion, it is then that the wit sharpens, and the conversation becomes animated and interesting, creating the desire to recommence it frequently."

Among those fortunate people, faithful in keeping their word, a simple promise is as good as a contract. Hardly sensible to the gleam of riches, they always prefer an amiable character to a considerable dowry in their alliances. Merit, virtue and good faith are their rules; but if it happens that two individuals of an entirely opposite character are joined by a marriage that parents have negotiated without consulting the union that ought to make the bond of souls, the law permits them to request letters of divorce that are rarely refused, because they think that it would be inhumane to force a man and a woman to live together for the rest of their life when their humors are incompatible and they can never reach accord.

They are permitted to remarry; then it is up to the spouses to make a match; mutual penchant must be their primary bond, the heart their principal guide; those are rights of nature that nothing can abridge. For a marriage to be happy, the man must have knowledge and principles, the woman reason and an attentiveness to detail, and in the harmony that reigns between them, everything ought to tend to the common good; each ought to follow the other's impression and each to obey; both being masters.

One recognizes everywhere on the planet the vigilance and attention of the government, in order to ensure people of security, comfort, ease and the free exercise of their industry. Their highways, maintained with care, are bordered by a double row of trees, and one sees woods on the sea coasts appropriate to the construction of ships, in order to procure abundance by the facility of commerce. That sage government has also provided for all the needs of travelers; one does not encounter there those mercenary refuges established by interest, but one sees large house that rich citizens have founded in out of the way places. Those houses are furnished with all that one can desire, and are gratuitously open to all travelers; but in the cities, people compete for the privilege of entertaining guests. I thought, in admiring that humanity, that I had been transported to the age of our patriarchs and those times of love and innocence when all people were simple and lived contentedly.

Those who have procured by their talents property useful to the State are immortalized by pyramids, obelisks or statues; those monuments are reserved for glory, superior talents and outstanding actions, in order to excite the emulation of the people and encourage them to contribute to the public good; but incapacity and lack of experience in generals and ministers is punished severely, always being prejudicial to the repose of the State.

Their views are attentive to commerce, agriculture and population. Canals and highways facilitate the transport of merchandise and food. As credit is the soul of commerce, the motive force of fortunes and the resources of the State, the government has wisely provided everything that might maintain confidence and ensure the fate of creditors by establishing a lending bank, where the citizen can deposit his money safely, certain of having it when it is needed. Every bankrupt is punished by death, because a default of conduct entails that of probity by an abuse of confidence equally pernicious to the wellbeing of society.

Among those people one does not see anything false in their way of thinking, their tastes or their conduct; they show themselves as nature has formed them, and only judge thins by the light of reason. That ensures that one always finds justice and proportion in their views and their sentiments; their taste is true and simple; it comes from them; they follow it by choice and not by custom or caprice; their language is straightforward, devoid of art and pretention; one never sees them intoxicated by a chimerical vanity; content to dress simply and without any ornament, they have no desire for magnificent palaces that art has decorated at great expense with a thousand luxuries useless to the happiness of a reasonable man. A rural refuge is all that they desire, a stream whose freshness makes its banks attractive and whose silvery ripples flow in serpentine fashion to moisten the foot of a meadow and render its enamel more brilliant.

After having traveled through vast provinces, we only remarked in the different people who inhabited them the candor of their mores and their conduct, and love for the commonwealth of the fatherland; their obliging manner is so gracious and so god, extended in such a tender fashion, that they are never ingrate.

We had difficulty quitting such a charming abode; one can judge that by this feeble sketch of their mores, their simplicity, their even temper and the plausible tranquility that renders them happy, by exempting them from troubles rather than by a taste for pleasure; but what I cannot depict or cease to admire is their disinterested humanity, the hospitable zeal that they have for all strangers. Everyone comes with such a tender urgency to offer you his house, exhibiting joy when he obtains the preference.

Chapter VIII

One only encounters agreeable scenery on that world: cheerful landscapes, meadows strewn with flowers, linden trees and a thousand others stirred by the zephyr; everything respires simplicity; everything is cheerful and forms their amusement; enjoyment, calm and freshness bring back, at the decline of day, young women with their lovers, who gather in the ferns in order to swear eternal love. Beauty never reigns with more empire than in the midst of country fêtes; it is there that one sees the Graces on their throne, clad in the simplicity that joy and gaiety animate. One only enjoys true benefits in innocence and candor; amour, amity and constancy are only content where liberty reigns.

"O beauty of nature," Monime exclaimed, "which alone has the right to touch the heart! You only require simple actions, naïve individuals, interest without complication, gaiety without grimaces and without effrontery; truth and candor are your natural virtues.

"O privileged mortals! The gods favor you; you are unaware of those ostentatious names that the nobles of our earth spawn in vain, but you have humanity; you possess little, but you share it without avarice and without mistrust; you are sensible to the difficulties and misfortunes of the poor; content with your lot, you spend your days in repose, without ambition, without desire and without envy. You are able to repress a blind transport; exempt from bemoaning the faults of the previous day, nothing troubles the peace of a tranquil slumber. For those whom indigence lays low, ever full of concern and politeness, you strive, at last by your caresses, to soften the rigors of their lot; you have no fear that cupidity will seek to rob you of the treasures that you find in labor and innocence. An amour exempt from turbulence unites you, you see its pledges growing without any anxiety, in the hope of seeing them one day share your labor; they will be the support of your old age; they will close your eyes and collect in peace the inestimable heritage that you will leave them, which is our virtues, your mores and your candor.

"My dear Zachiel," Monime went on, "grant me one favor; let us end our voyages here."

"I consent to that," said the genius, "but before returning to your world, it is necessary for your happiness that you complete the visit to this one, in order that you can both profit from the good examples that are encountered here."

"Why, my dear Zachiel," Monime asked, "do you want to oblige us to return to a world where we have experienced nothing but disgrace? Can we not fix our abode here?"

"Have you already forgotten," the genius said, "that it is only by a singular grace that I have been able to conduct you to the different worlds that you have visited? It is necessary, my dear children, to follow the order of nature and finish

418

on your own world the term fixed by the decrees of destiny. The favors that you have received will perhaps never be accorded to anyone else; it is only to instruct you and perfect you that I have enabled you to see a living display of the different passions of humans and the inconsequence of their conduct, in order for you to savor what is good, useful and honest and to avoid what is bad.

"The world of Saturn forms such a great contrast with the others that it seems that the natural virtues and simplicity of its people ought to be rendered masters of all hearts, and the soul that is struck by that ought to make it a duty and even a pleasure to imitate them. It is in order that these good examples should remain engraved in your mind that I chose this planet to be the terminus of your voyages. You ought to have remarked throughout Abadia, which is the most extensive part of this vortex, a charming mixture of rural life with that of cities; a mild equality reigns here, which, in being established on the order of nature, forms an instruction for some, a consolation for others and a bond of amity for all."

We then visited different regions of the planet; everywhere we remarked a singular mixture of wild nature with art. Near a cavern where one only expects to find brambles, one can pick ripe grapes; in another place, excellent fruits are encountered on rocks from which one can see brilliant cascades descend.

On advancing into those fertile regions we did not see any uncultivated land; we were making a comparison with those of other worlds when we were surprised, at the entrance to a city, to see a great affluence of people, who were running toward a nearby mountain.

Monime, curious to know the reason, asked Zachiel, who told us that a species of astronomer had come from the great ring that seems to cover Saturn, to predict that the time was approaching when several catastrophes would occur in their vortex because of the encounter with a few blazing comets, the violent impact of which might cause their globe to describe an orbit different from the one it presently described, and that they ought to fear a universal conflagration. Those good people, frightened by the news, were running to the mountain to implore the divinity to deflect the misfortune away from them.

The people in question follow the natural law; they have several temples dedicated to Cybele, whom they honor a great deal, and where young women are brought up with great care.

They still worship a Supreme Being, but they regard nature as a divinity whose force is distributed everywhere, and is essential to matter; they think that she is like a kind of sympathy that links all bodies together and holds them in equilibrium, and which, without being decomposed herself, has the marvelous secret of varying things infinitely; which one ought to regard as a principle of order and regularity; and which produces eminently everything that can be produced in the vast universe.

They believe that the souls of the blessed are distributed in the air and that they enjoy a complete liberty there; but that those of the wicked are enclosed in the entrails of the earth as in a prison, where they expiate their faults until the resurrection, when some will join the blessed and resume subtle and diffuse bodies.

Chapter IX
A Brief History of Monime's Family

After Zachiel had pointed out to us the most interesting things on that planet, he told us that it was essential for the execution of the projects he had formed to ensure our common happiness to return to our own world. That news did not please Monime; she would have liked, as would I, to spend the rest of her life with citizens so perfect—but the genius, without listening to her arguments and without deigning to respond to them, attached us both to a group of hooked atoms that took us away and caused us to traverse the immense universe, by means of a gentle slope, all the way to the Palace of the Genii, where Zachiel, after having reanimated us by means of a divine breath, caused us to resume our bodies.

Then the genius told us that the time for him to leave us was imminent.

"I cannot always be with you," Zachiel told us, "but I shall not abandon you until I have reestablished Princess Thaymuras on the throne of her ancestors. You are surprised, my dear Seaton, and perhaps annoyed by the mystery that I have made of the birth of our dear Monime. Both raised since your earliest years by the cares of the Quaker, who was ignorant himself of Monime's birth, you have always lived together in a fraternal union, which has maintained the tender amity that I have seen growing with pleasure.

"It is true that under the name of amity, marks of the keenest passion have sometimes escaped you, incessantly forced to combat sentiments that Monime shared, but with the difference that since her entry into the Castle of the Genii she has been instructed of her birth by the first of her race; since then the penchant of her heart has been directed to revealing it to you if, forced to live with you incessantly, she could not repress that penchant.

"Her heart, always guided by reason, finally determined to hide her birth from you, not with a view to testing your sentiments—she has never doubted them for an instant—but her delicacy would have been alarmed if the knowledge you had of her elevation had been capable of dividing your heart between amour and ambition. The mixture of those two passions would have been more difficult for her to disentangle, whereas the ignorance that you have always had of her birth leaves her in no doubt as to the purity of your sentiments.

"That passion, which has manifested itself in spite of you, on Venus and Mars, far from alarming her, has only served to augment the esteem that she had for you, and the delicacy of your sentiments that developed on the world of Jupiter, your generosity in refusing a thousand advantageous establishments in the sole dread of being separated from her, are an indubitable proof of your attachment to her person. In sum, your love of the sciences, your application to instruct yourself in all sorts of talents and your combined virtues have acquired you rights so precious over Monime's heart that all the monarchs in the universe could never take her away from you."

Surprised by all that the genius had just told me, I remained motionless for a few moments, and without reflecting on those final words, I threw myself at the feet of the Princess.

"Oh, my dear Monime," I cried, taking one of her hands, which I kissed respectfully, "you are not my sister, and I can now love you without committing a crime. Alas! Why did you not disabuse me sooner? How many conflicts you would have spared me! You're not unaware of my passion, or the efforts that I've always made to combat it; I believed it to be criminal; it will henceforth be the destiny of my life—but what am I saying? When heaven accords me a change so favorable to my destiny, is it necessary for me to renounce my amour? Is it for me to pretend to a hand that ought doubtless to be reserved for a sovereign?

"Yes, adorable Monime, you merit in every way being elevated to the highest rank; a soul so beautiful, so great, so virtuous, the extent of whose enlightenment is unlimited, must be made to command the universe. Who are the fortunate people who will be submissive to your law? I am losing you, divine Thaymuras! Alas! If my heart murmurs in consequence, I shall at last be able to enclose within the bounds of respect and submission a love that I sense clearly it will be impossible for me to vanquish.

"The sole grace that I beg you to accord me, as the greatest favor I can receive, is to suffer me to remain with you, to regard me as the most faithful of your subjects, the one who is the most attached to your person and who will always be devoted to you, until the tomb. Fatal ignorance!" I added, with a sigh "How dear you are going to cost my repose!"

"Be tranquil, my dear Seaton," said Monime. "Cease plaints and regrets that might end up offending me, if I did not attribute them to the emotion you are feeling. It is true that the blood in which Heaven has given me birth has developed in me since my entry to the Castle of the Genii. That vivid amity already formed between us when I believed you to be my brother has changed into a keener sentiment since I have discovered new perfections in you, and the solid qualities with which your soul is ornamented have finally tightened knots that I now regard as indissoluble. No longer envy me, then, the glory of being as generous as you; in any case, you are not unaware that I shall owe all my benefits to Zachiel, without whom it would be impossible to have myself recognized by my people, and consequently to mount the throne of my ancestors. It is therefore just, and I can even add that it is absolutely necessary to my happiness, that you participate in the favors of the genius, by sharing a throne that you will help me to conduct with equity."

"Oh, divine Thaymuras," I cried, "can my life be sufficient to merit such great benefits? What am I saying? Would there not be more grandeur in refusing an honor of which I feel so unworthy? Zachiel, for pity's sake, design to support my weakness by assisting me with your advice. Ought I to cede to the penchant that is drawing me? Alas, what should I do? I shall die if I must renounce my love, but I cannot live tranquil if my union with my Princess is contrary to her glory."

"Calm your disturbance," said the genius. "I would have opposed your passion if I had not judged your alliance necessary to the happiness of both of you. A secret penchant determined me to act in Monime's interests, but when I perceived the one she had for you, far from opposing it, I have always contributed with all my power to fortifying it. I've promise to employ that same power to making you happy; it's time to complete my work by giving you further instruction.

"I approve of your delicacy regarding Monime's glory, but it ought to cease on learning the misfortunes that have overtaken her family. However, it's to those misfortunes that you will owe all the wealth that awaits you, and it is in consequence of those same misfortunes that Prince George, heir to the realm of Georgia, was taken to your homeland, where destiny caused him to find in marriage to Lady Seaton, your father's sister, a shadow of tranquility that he had sought in vain in various climes; but it's necessary to give you a succinct account of the misfortunes of that illustrious family.

"Thaymuras, King of Georgia, was murdered some fifty years ago by Abas.[50] The monarch, forced to sustain several wars against the Great Turk, the Sophi of Persia and the Great Khan of Tartary was eventually betrayed by his favorite Abas, who had risen by degrees to the position of head of the army. That traitor, whose views were focused on taking possession of the throne, excited several uprisings, and finally succeeded by means of dangerous insinuations in forming a conspiracy against the life of his sovereign. His people, long

---

[50] In fact, the 17th century Georgian monarch Taymuras, or Teimuraz I, who was involved in a long war with the Persian Shah Abbas I following the latter's invasions of Georgia in 1614 and 1616, the second of which compelled a long exile, was not killed by him, and outlived him. With the aid of various allies, Teimuraz reclaimed his throne in 1625, although his reign was plagued thereafter by internal disputes. The "Sophi" to whom the present text refers was Abbas' successor as Shah of Persia, whose name is nowadays more commonly rendered as Safi, and whose marriage to Teimuraz' daughter temporarily ended hostilities from that direction. Teimuraz was expelled again in 1648, after a battle in which his last surviving son, David, was killed, but tried hard to recruit Russian aid to recapture his throne. Shah Abbas II renewed Ottoman ambitions in the Caucasus and began settling Turkish migrants in Georgia, provoking an uprising in 1659. Teimuraz returned to Georgia in 1661, but was imprisoned by Abbas II and died in 1663. The Bargrationi dynasty to which Teimuraz belonged continued to reign in Georgia until the 19th century, although perennially under the domination of either the Ottoman Empire or Russia.

weary of incessant wars, yielded furiously to Abas; pernicious counsel, and the unfortunate Prince was murdered in his own palace. Abas, then at the head of his troops, had himself proclaimed King of Georgia, Mingrelia and Turcomania. The tyrant returned to the capital triumphant, took possession of the palace, and after having himself crowned, sent all the members of the royal family he could discover to perish miserably in obscure prisons.

"A single child escaped the tyrant's fury; that child, named Prince George, had for a tutor Erasmus, who was from one of the oldest families in the realm, well-known for his probity, and whose attachment to the prince was proof against anything. Erasmus combined all the sciences and talents useful to the art of good government. As soon as he learned about the troubles that Abas had fomented throughout the kingdom, he foresaw their consequences, and warned the King, insisting on the danger to his security, the necessity of punishing the rebels and of putting himself at the head of his troops; but the monarch, far from listening to Erasmus' advice, imprudently fell into several traps that Abas had set for him. Erasmus, then foreseeing all the danger that the royal family was running, had the King consent to sending the young prince to Mingrelia, and his diligence in taking him there saved George's life.

"The wise tutor, informed of the cruelties that the tyrant was employing for the total destruction of Thaymuras' family, and finding no safety within the kingdom, hastened to embark with the young prince, passing him off as his son.

"After wandering for some time in various realms, trying to form a party in favor of Prince George that might procure him the means to recover his throne, but seeing no success in the various attempts he made, fearing that he would eventually be discovered and betrayed to the tyrant, Erasmus, in that cruel perplexity, persuaded the young prince to take refuge in England. But that kingdom too was beginning to experience the upheavals that burst forth a short while later, and the prince was unable to obtain any help there.

"Erasmus, who had known the reputation of your father, Lord Seaton, for a long time, and was not unaware that he was one of the foremost peers of the realm and one of those most advanced in the confidence of the King, had no difficulty in confiding the identity and misfortunes of the young prince to him. Seaton, the most generous and compassionate of men of the world, initially employed his credit and that of his friends to try to engage the peers in his interests, but the kingdom's troubles were getting worse every day and he was unable to succeed. In order to soften the prince's displeasures somewhat and help him pass the time that he had to wait for revolutions favorable to his views, he introduced him to his sister, the widow of Earl Pimbrock, who lived in one of his properties a few miles from London.

"The young widow combined immense wealth with beauty, talents and al the graces of youth. The identity and misfortunes of the Prince were confided to the young Countess, and she put to use all the seductions that decency permitted her to extract him from his melancholy. George yielded without much effort to the Countess' charms, and Erasmus, far from opposing that nascent amour, worked to tighten its knots himself by means of a marriage that was secretly contracted in accord with Lord Seaton.

"The two young spouses lived together for some years in a perfect union; then death took the Princess, who died giving birth to Monime—which plunged the Prince back into a melancholy that he was never able to vanquish. His despair initially led him to banish everyone from his presence; even the light of day seemed to become unbearable to him. Only Erasmus, who had always retained a sort of empire over his mind, had the right to enter the Prince's apartment at any moment. The affectionate tutor, sensible to his grief, shared it for a long time without attempting to diminish its force; it was by means of that adroit strategy that he was able to employ the counsel that reason dictated to him. Perceiving that nothing soothed his woes, however, he tried instead to reanimate his vengeance against the murderer of his father and the destroyer of his entire family.

"George emerged then from his lethargy, seemingly struck by Erasmus' discourse. Glory had always reigned in his heart; the sentiment in question combined with the desire for vengeance, which, far from weakening over time, had only been fortified. That is why, hatred and vengeance being supplemented by ambition, he pressed Erasmus to convert the greater part of his assets into cash and to employ all imaginable resources to equip a fleet that might procure him the means of returning to his kingdom in order to make one last effort to reclaim the throne of his ancestors.

"Erasmus employed everything that his customary prudence suggested to him to carry out the prince's orders, and son put him in a state to embark. Lord Seaton, Monime's uncle, was asked to take charge of the young Princess. George wanted to confide her to him as the most precious pledge of his amity. Seaton placed her in the hands of his wife when he too was forced to abandon his homeland to flee Cromwell's cruelties. In conformity with the Prince's orders he begged her not to reveal the secret of her birth until the Prince was entirely established on the throne of his fathers.

"George, tranquil with regard to his daughter's fate, embarked for Georgia. Having arrived in the region of lower Armenia, he never strayed from the wise advice of Erasmus, who, by virtue of his prudence and the correspondence he had maintained in different provinces, finally succeeded by their intrigues in causing the greater part of the nation to rise up by spreading the news of the arrival of Prince George, the sole and unique heir of Thaymuras, their legitimate sovereign, and the only one they ought to obey.

"That news caused the old love that they had always conserved for the family to be reborn in the hearts of all the people. Many came to range themselves under the Prince's standards, proclaimed him king and marched behind him, but the Sultan, to whom the treacherous Abas was submissive, leaning that the Prince was advancing rapidly, and that he had already taken possession of several large towns, sent a powerful army to support Abas. The Prince's army, considerably augmented, soon found itself in confrontation with the enemy, the battle was engaged.

"That battle was one of the bloodiest. The Georgians, animated by the presence of their Prince, fought with an intrepidity inspired by confidence in their general and love for their Prince. George, also animated by more than one motive, made his valor admired, but, his courage having taken him too far in advance of the melee, he found himself surrounded by enemies who were competing for the glory of capturing him. The unfortunate Prince, perceiving the danger into which his valor had taken him, killed himself in order to avoid slavery.

The Georgians, overwhelmed by that despairing blow, lost their courage entirely and ran away in disorder, abandoning the battlefield, their equipment and al their munitions to the Turks, who made a considerable booty of it. Shortly afterwards, the people submitted to the tyrant again, in spite of the advice of Erasmus, who, after having rendered the last rites to the prince, has rejoined them to assure them that a child of Prince George still remained who ought to govern them legitimately one day. But the people, naturally timid, refused to believe him, and Erasmus was obliged to flee himself, in order to avoid the cruel death to which the tyrant would not have failed to subject him.

"Attentive to Monime's interests, I have just learned of the death of the tyrant, who has been massacred in a new revolt fomented by the jealousy of the noblemen of the realm. Let us hasten to embark, my dear children, and go to show those people the sole surviving member of a family they have always loved."

Chapter X
Monime is Recognized as the Heir to the Realm of Georgia

Nothing any longer retaining us in the Castle of the Genii, we left to go to the nearest port. A ship was waiting for us; we embark; a favorable wind promises us smooth sailing; the sailors utter cries of joy, the anchor is raised and we depart. Zephyrs inflate the sails, the ship flies over the bitter sea, her agile hull cleaving the foaming waves and leaving a long wake behind. Everything responds to our impatience; hope and the desire to vanquish occupy us. We finally arrive, after a few months of the most fortunate navigation, in a port in Mingrelia.

When we disembarked, we learned that the entire kingdom had been broken up by the factions formed by the aristocrats, who had formed different parties. Some were attached to the family of the tyrant, who had left no child, wanting to recognize as king his nearest relative; others wanted to change the form of government entirely in order to establish a republic of sorts; and others who formed the largest party, proposed to put themselves entirely under the dominion of the Sultan and ask him for a governor.

Zachiel, informed of all these troubles, judged them very favorable to his views; he began by spreading the news of the disembarkation of Princess Thaymuras, the only daughter of Prince George, the sole heir to that house and, in consequence, their legitimate sovereign, and the only one to whom their homage and obedience was due.

That news had a surprising effect on the minds of the people. Their affection for and attachment to the house of Thaymuras appeared to take on new force. The genius, profiting adroitly from that benevolent disposition, brought its power to bear so effectively that he brought all minds into unison. Like one of those popular torrents in which the most indifferent and those from whom the most opposition is feared are carried away by the general movement and give themselves with a blind zeal to the sentiments of the majority, we saw the fury of the aristocrats disarmed, their spirit divided between despair and hope, ceding to revolutions that thy judged that all their efforts could never impede the success.

The entire weary nation had been sighing for repose for a long time; in addition, the tyrant had delivered himself to such violent excesses, and those excesses had produced such bloody scenes, that the memory of them still caused shivers of horror. Thus, the tumult of passions, weakened by reflection, began to give way to the spirit of fidelity, love and obedience to the legitimate sovereign. Everyone demanded the Princess with loud cries, and nothing was heard in the capital but the name of Thaymuras, which soon spread through all the provinces of the realm.

However, the principal functionaries of the State were not without dread; all their multiple crimes—the death of the king and his family, the execution of a large number of lords, the imprisonment of numerous people distinguished by their merit and their talents, all of whom had perished miserably—were represented to their eyes, and the fear that they might be pursued and punished by the most implacable resentment engaged the to implore the pity of their Queen. On the advice of the genius, she granted all her subjects a general amnesty.

That public declaration immediately extracted them from the cruel uncertainty that had suspended them for a long time between dread and hope, and their agitations were transformed into an unalloyed joy, which burst forth in collective transports that individual prosperity, no matter how perfect it might be, never inspires to the same degree. The effect of the declaration that the Queen had made was calculated to sustain a public satisfaction; she could not have offered anything more in conformity with their hopes than a general amnesty, without any exception, for those who returned within a week to the obedience they owed their legitimate sovereign. The prospect of the imminent reestablishment of order united all the sentiments of the various classes of the realm.

After having made sure of the dispositions of the aristocrats and the people, the genius assembled all the troops, to which he presented Thaymuras. "This is your Queen," he said to them. "No one is more worthy to reign over you. The misfortunes of her family ought to be still present in memory; they ought to render her dearer to you. Do you recall the mildness of the government that her ancestors exercised over you, the peace, repose and tranquility that your forefathers enjoyed? Compare their virtues and the paternal generosity that they never ceased to employ to render you happy with the cruelties and vexations of Abas, who established nothing in the empire he usurped by blood and carnage. Devoid of faith principle and honor, Heaven gave you to his wrath to punish you for your injustices and your ingratitude; that same Heaven, touched by your woes, wishes to deliver you from them and give you at the same time the means to expiate your sins, by submitting you to the obedience of your sovereign. You can now signal your zeal by working to affirm her situation on her throne, but you can only do so by shrugging off the infamous yoke of the domination of the Sultan to whom the weakness of the tyrant delivered you. That glory is reserved for you; do not be alarmed by the dangers; numerous brave warriors will join you; but before commencing the exploits that ought to cover you with glory, it is necessary to go to the temple to give thanks to the divinity and also to crown the Princess."

The genius spoke for a long time with pleasing eloquence, touching unction, compelling vehemence and subjugating force. All the officers surrounding him were dazzled by the divine fire gleaming in his eyes; his discourse seemed to them to be above anything that one might hear from the greatest of mortals. The charm of his words lifted up all hearts; officers and soldiers were equally penetrated by it. Then a murmur of applause was heard, the air resounded far and wide with the sound of drums, and the strident blast of trumpets. Everyone disputed the honor of rendering the first homage to the Queen. The soldiers, to mark their delight, repeated with increasing loudness: "Long live Princess Thaymuras! May her name reign over us forever! May her power and her glory extend over the whole world!"

Zachiel, taking advantage of that ardor, took us to the temple, after having summoned all the noblemen to go there. The people distributed in the streets uttered a thousand cries of joy, ad when we entered the sanctuary, an artillery salvo produced a sound like thunder. A dais was prepared for the Queen, after which she was crowned, and received with abundant majesty the oath of fidelity of a large number of her subjects. She was conducted to the sound of a thousand instruments of war back to the palace of her forefathers.

Although the Princess was a trifle fatigued by such a difficult day, she nevertheless spoke to all the people surrounding her with the bounty and affability that subjugated all hearts.

The next day, I was the first to pay my court to the Queen. Several ladies were surrounding her, and although Georgia has always produced the most beautiful women in the world, the Queen, in a simple negligee without any ornament, eclipsed them all with the splendor of her beauty. Surprised to see, on entering her apartment, the same furniture that had ornamented the one she had occupied on the world of Jupiter, I thought at first that the genius had transported us during our sleep.

The Queen, suspecting my error, smiled as she said: "You see, my cousin, all the scrupulous care that Zachiel takes. Would one not think that I were still in the empire of the Jovinians, since I find here all the immense riches with which I was heaped there? I can presently surpass all the powers of Earth in magnificence, but this wealth ought only to be precious to me in order that I might distribute it to me subjects."

Zachiel, who had just come in, applauded that generous sentiment. "You need have no fear," said the genius, "of exhausting your treasures; the most precious wealth of all, and the one that you ought to value most highly, is to reign in the hearts of your subjects; that is what ought to define your grandeur, your strength and the glory of your reign. I shall take advantage of the little time that remains for me to spend with you to give you my final instructions on the matter of reigning well. I have no doubt that you will employ all the enlightenment of your mind and all the care that your reason and judgment can dictate to you, in order to perfect yourself. The voyages that I have enabled you to undertake ought to have enlightened your mind, and I have remarked with pleasure that, attentive to examining the different passions that self-love and false glory bring into play every day in the theater of the world, you have learned enough about the different mechanisms that are employed there. You have observed the good and bad qualities, in order to profit from the examples of virtue that are encountered there, and avoid the false steps.

"You are not unaware, my dear children," the genius continued, "that I have only enabled you to undertake such long journeys in order to put you in a state to distinguish the good from the bad and the true from the false with judgment and solidity, in order that you can discern the best path to follow and attach yourselves o it inviolably. Apply yourselves, both of you, to knowing the courtiers who surround you; study the character of your ministers; try to disentangle their interests; correct, if it is possible, their errors and their passions. Distance from responsibility those who do not put tenderness and humanity in the ranks of the essential virtues; do not allow favor or recommendations to be sufficient to determine your choice of those you want to put at the head of affairs or place in the tribunals of justice. Before rendering them depositaries of your authority, examine them yourselves, in order to know the usage they will make of it.

"Be incessantly on your guard against flatterers and those who expect some recompense from you; those people, uniquely occupied with their fortune or the establishment of their family, will make every effort to hide the truth from you. Remember that the number of good people is very small; it is a matter of being able to distinguish therm. You also have to defend yourself against the ambitious, who sacrifice everything to their elevation and power, of lax and flattering courtiers who have no scruple about betraying the religion and their fatherland.

"The misfortunes that have afflicted your family," Zachiel continued, "ought incessantly to keep you on your guard against them. Alexander wished that he might reawaken for a time after his death in order to learn what people thought of him. 'I am not astonished,' that prince said to his favorites, 'that I am praised now; some fear me and others want to gain my good graces.' If the sovereigns who are always flattered when people compare them to that conqueror thought as rationally, they would not take the trouble to have triumphal arches erected or statues that flatter their vanity; content with governing their subjects well and employing all means to make them happy, they would fearlessly leave the care of immortalizing their name to their beneficiaries.

"What is the point of the monuments that the vanity or adulation of a few interested friends erect to them? As they unaware that a free historian who accords nothing to fear or hope, amity or hatred, who does not belong to any party, who gives actions the price they merit, without worrying about pleasing or offending, will doubtless render visible with a single stroke of the pen the ridiculousness of their pride and the baseness of their adulators? But you, my dear children, have acquired in your travels a depth of experience and enlightenment that when it is guided by reason, will doubtless be able to contribute to protecting you from al the traps that are being prepared for you.

"But as you presently have no need of your ministers to administer your estates, I advise you only to trust your own enlightenment henceforth, and that of a person I shall make known to you before the end of the day. I engage all three of you to consult one another when it is a matter of any importance; weight the reasons for and against without haste, and when you are absolutely sure of the course to take, follow it wisely, with prudence and above all with discretion. Do not entrust your state secrets to anyone; the only means of succeeding in your enterprises is never to allow yourselves to be divined.

"I do not intend by this discourse to suggest that you should reject the advice of your Council; there will be much in it that will be useful to you. Above all, do not disdain that of officers who have grown old under the weight of arms. They can often open possibilities to you of which your ministers would never think. Do not forget that the manner of reigning well is that the will of the ruler must always conform to the laws; never allow them to be infringed in any way whatsoever. Never burden your people with taxes that are too onerous; that is the means of attracting their blessings and the favors of Heaven. Never favor any but people eminent in the sciences; always listen to their advice, in order to learn to govern worthily.

"Always have as a principal maxim that the authority of a sovereign ceases to be legitimate as soon as he neglects to render justice to his subjects. Virtue, torpid for a long time, is about to be reanimated by the aspect of a virtuous Princess; her presence can be compared to that of the sun when its light pierces and dissipates the dark clouds that cover the earth, and which reanimate and vivify everything in nature.

"As it is absolutely impossible for you to be able to enter into every detail that concerns the government of your estates, you must apply yourselves to choosing personally those who will be responsible for the detail of affairs, in order to determine the different employments for which each of them is most apt. Knowing how to choose ministers and officers, placing them with discernment in the appropriate positions, correcting them when they stray from their duty, and moderating and inspiring good conduct by your example, is the true talent of reigning well. I have often said that in order to form great designs it is necessary to have a liberated mind entirely disengaged from puerile operations, in order to be able to think maturely and extend its view into a distant future, to invent, foresee and read in the past. It is necessary to arrange projects promptly, to prepare them far in advance, to maintain them incessantly in a state to struggle against fortune when it runs contrary to them, and to be attentive day and night to leave nothing to chance.

"Heaven is confiding the government of this people to you as a precious deposit, but it intends that by your wisdom and your moderation you will occupy yourselves incessantly to ensuring its felicity. All the grandeurs and riches that surround you should only serve to imprint respect and love for their sovereign. The grandeur of a realm ought to consist primarily in the multitude of its subjects, who are ordinarily its strength, above all when they are attached to a prince by love and the sentiments of the heart. You ought to maintain them in military exercises in order not to let their courage weaken; you ought also to maintain the peace, union and liberty of all the citizens, maintain the abundance of necessary things and show scorn for the superfluous. Accustom them to labor and instill them with a horror of idleness, emulation in virtue, submission to the law and respect for the divinity.

"It is also necessary to banish luxury from your estates, which often serves only to impoverish the citizen and ruin the aristocrat; by that conduct you will diminish needs, by reducing them to the simple necessities of life. Luxury, pushed to a certain extent, corrupts almost all mores; it often poisons an entire nation by the refinements of voluptuousness; people become accustomed to regarding the most superfluous things as necessities.

"Always be affable and often show yourselves to your people; let your virtues and your good deeds be the ornaments of your adornment, that they might be the shield that surrounds you, in order that your subjects learn from you of what true happiness consists. Remember that all the good you do will extend into the most distant centuries, and that evils can multiply until the remotest prosperity.

"Above all, never stray from the dread, respect and love that you owe to the divinity; it is only by courtesy of the divinity that you possess all treasures; it is the divinity that produces wisdom, justice, joy and pure pleasure, and also produces true liberty, sweet abundance and stainless glory.

"That, my dear children," the genius added, "is a brief sketch of the duties that your estate imposes upon you; but it is time to introduce you to the person that I have destined to aid you in the administration of the affairs that concern your estates; it is also appropriate that the person in question witnesses the celebration of your marriage. You are awaited in the Council; go there with Seaton and never forget, either of you, the principles I have just given you."

The genius left immediately, without wanting to hear the tender expressions of our gratitude.

Chapter XI
Monime's Marriage

I accompanied the Queen to the council chamber; the nobles and ministers were assembled there. Her majestic bearing, her beauty, her grace and the charms of her intelligence soon gained all hearts. She listened attentively to the reports that her ministers gave her on the present state of the realm; she then gave her orders will a great deal of wisdom and prudence.

Then the nobles invited her, on behalf of the state, to accord them the grace of choosing a spouse who could contribute to ensuring and perpetuating their happiness. The Queen stood up, promising that she would let them know her decision shortly. I noticed that the whole assembly seemed very anxious at those last words, each of them doubtless aspiring to the honor of sharing the crown.

Having returned with the Queen to her apartment, we found the genius there with an old man, whom I approached with a great deal of emotion. The Queen, her eyes fixed upon him, waited, before speaking to him, until Zachiel introduced us to him. Taking each of us by the hand he said: "Here are your children, who were confided by your orders to the care of the Quaker. In order to save them from the tyranny that was attempting to cover them, I removed them from the new dangers threatening their heads."

"What do I see?" I cried, throwing myself into my father's arms. "Oh, Zachiel, I owe all my happiness to you; nothing more is lacking to my felicity."

My father held me in his arms for a long time; his tenderness was manifested at first by tears. Recovering his self-possession, he made it his duty to render his first homage to the Queen, who embraced him with a great deal of tenderness.

"I shall never cease," the Princess said, "to regard you as my father; you have long substituted for him, and the services that you rendered King George will be eternally engraved in my heart."

The first moments we spent with my father were employed in demonstrating the joy we had in seeing him again, but I found him so downcast that I could not help expressing the anxiety that I felt regarding his health. The Queen, who shared it, asked him several questions about his disgrace.

"If I did not fear," the Princess added, "renewing your pain, I would ask you to recount to us the adventures that brought you to this realm."

"They are simple," my father said, "and I can satisfy your curiosity in a few words.

"After having quit England, I wandered for a long time in various parts of the world, always obliged to disguise myself under borrowed names. Banished from my homeland and not daring to reappear there, I employed all imaginable means to make contact with a spouse who, in addition to the tenderness I have always conserved for her, had become even more dear to me by virtue of the precious deposit I had confided to her; but all the enquiries that I was able to make were in vain. Desperate in being unable to discover any race of her, having no doubt that I must have been pursued even to the extent of my family, I thought that she might have taken ship in order to shield you from further vexations. With that idea in mind I embarked again, with the design of traveling in various parts of Asia.

"I enjoyed good fortune for some time; after having endured a few tempests, hazard finally conducted me to this kingdom, where I did not take long to learn of the unfortunate death of Prince George. I shall not talk about the dolor I felt at that news; suffice it to say that I have lived here in the obscurity of a private life; an isolated house formed my entire domain. It was there that I began to reflect with a little more tranquility on the objects that once surrounded me.

"I have discovered that human reason, examining at leisure the details and vicissitudes of life, combined with the help that nature is able to lend to the world to render it happy, is incapable of procuring a real felicity, independent of the blows of fate and entirely appropriate to our most natural desires and the objective for which we were created. I understood then that good air to breathe and the simplest aliments are sufficient to maintain our life, and that it only requires clothing appropriate to defend us from the insults of the air, with the liberty to take as much exercise as is necessary to conserve health.

"I confess that grandeurs, authority and riches can procure us pleasures and a great many charms, but, on the other hand, those pleasures have a terrible influence on our passions and seem, so to speak, to fertilize our ambition and our pride, our sensuality or our avarice; those dispositions of the heart, criminal in themselves, contain the seeds of all our vices, and have not the slightest connection with the talents that form a wise individual, nor the virtues that constitute the character of an honest man.

"Deprived for a long time of that exterior good fortune and distant from those brilliant foundations, I am fully convinced that virtue alone has the right to render us veritably happy; it is thus that my life has been spent for some years in the scorn or honors and the ostentation that surrounds them, avoiding the company of men and only waiting for the death that I believed to be imminent to put an end to all my troubles.

"I was in that disposition when Zachiel introduced himself to me; I opposed his arguments for some time, but who can resist the insinuations of a genius of the first order? Vanquished by the eloquence of his zeal, I was unable to forbid myself to accompany him. It was from him that I learned of the death of my wife and the cares that he had taken to perfect your education, those he has taken in order for you to be able to resume the throne of your ancestors, and, finally, the glory to which you intend to raise my son.

"All those reasons, combined with the attachment and, I dare add, the tenderness that I have always conserved for you, finally determined me to abandon

434

my retreat. I shall say more: they have reawakened in me the natural love of life, and I have not been able to prevent myself from bemoaning my weakness and the little time that remains for me to employ myself in your service. But Zachiel, who puts his glory into making people happy, has been kind enough to make me take an elixir whose strength will gradually be communicated to all the parts of my body, reanimating them as it penetrates them, and I presently feel by virtue of your presence that my being is renewing itself.

"I shall be glad if the knowledge that age, experience and my misfortunes have allowed me to acquire can at least contribute to giving you enlightenment that might be useful to you in the administration of affairs concerning your estates, and prove to you at the same time my zeal and attachment to your person.

"Zachiel," my father continued, "has also informed me of the supreme rank for which you have destined my son; I am quite convinced that he has procured him enough enlightenment to enable him to relieve you of the burden a thousand matters of detail concerning the government. Although the genius has doubtless lent himself to that alliance, it is nevertheless the choice of your heart, guided by reason, that ought to guide you in a matter of that importance; do not listen to any other motive, and let the intelligence of souls be your guide."

"After having thanked my father, the Queen added: "Be persuaded, my Lord, that Zachiel, by his counsels, has only confirmed the choice that my heart, in accord with my reason, had made a long time ago. The alliance that is already between us, combined with the cares that you have devoted to my father and those that you have devoted to me during my childhood, merit at least as much gratitude on my part. At any rate, the laws of the realm permitting me to choose a spouse, what choice could I make more worthy to fulfill my desires, which is also that of my heart? I will not hide it from you that I have tested Seaton on several occasions and I can assure you that his virtue and probity have never faltered.

"So," the Queen continued, "The genius is completing all the favors that we have received from him in rendering Milord a father and me an uncle and a friend, who will henceforth be the delight of our life. It is by that means that he is attempting to repair the void that we would have experienced by virtue of his departure—a void all the greater because, accustomed to allowing ourselves to be guided by his care, it would have been much more difficult to march alone; you shall therefore be our guide and our support now."

A few days after the arrival of my father, the Queen, pressed by her Council to choose a spouse, declared in a full assembly that, wanting to satisfy the desires of her subjects in full, without deviating from the laws established in her estates, she had made the choice of one of her relatives, worthy by his virtue and the great talents with which Heaven had endowed him, of occupying the place that she destined for him. The greater number applauded the Queen's discourse, but when she named me, I saw several, who had doubtless flattered themselves that they might obtain her hand, display their discontentment. That did not prevent the ceremony of our marriage being fixed for the following week, in order that the celebration might have more pomp and magnificence.

That week was spent in regulating, in concert with the genius, all the affairs that concerned the administration of the realm. Zachiel made the choice himself of the individuals who ought to fill the most important posts, and we had every reason to be content with the consequences, each one being placed in accordance with his particular talents, which is essential to the conduct of a State, and, what is even more so, all of them being men whose virtue, temperance and humanity was evident.

When the day of our marriage arrived, troops, all newly dressed, were commanded to form a double rank from the palace to the temple. The procession commenced with the queen's household, followed by the first officers of the crown and the nobles of the realm, preceding a magnificent carriage. At the back was the genius, to the right of the Queen, and my father to her left. I was at the front beside the minister who was carrying the book of the law. The most important ladies of the court surrounded the carriage, and the Queen's maidservants followed; all we mounted on richly-ornamented horses. The procession was closed by a large number of troops. It was in that order that we were taken to the temple to the sound of a thousand instruments of war, with which the air reverberated everywhere.

I shall not attempt to describe the ceremonies that were observed there. Suffice it to say that they were very long and very mysterious. When they were concluded, we returned to the palace in the same order, and we add the additional satisfaction of hearing all the people who prayed to Heaven, by means of redoubled cries of joy, to lavish us with its blessings.

Chapter XII
War Against the Turks

In spite of the fêtes that everyone hastened to hold in our honor every day, we were unable to vanquish a somber melancholy that took possession of our hearts: a sad presentiment of troubles we had yet to endure. Nothing was apparently missing from our common felicity when the genius announced to us that he was obliged to obey superior orders that summoned him to another world.

"However," he added, "I do not want to abandon you until you are entirely secure on your throne; I warn you that your kingdom is still threatened by great perils. The Sultan, to whom you have refused to render tribute, is advancing at the head of a formidable army. Hasten to assemble your troops; combine them with those of your allies; justice is on your side. Pray to the divinity; He alone can assure your victory; He it is who, balance in hand, regulates the fate of combats. Remember that you can do nothing without wisdom, justice and prudence; it is those virtues that must be your guides in all the actions of your life, and with those guides alone you ought never to have anything to fear."

My father came in, and confirmed the sad news. "You have no time to lose; the Sultan is advancing rapidly. I've just received the news from an extraordinary courier, and I'm in haste to give orders to your officers to assemble your troops. I flatter myself that within a week my son will be ready to march at their head."

"Although I am convinced of Seaton's courage," said the Queen, "I'm not without dread, if Zachiel cannot assist us with his advice. Trembling for my husband's life, frightened by the dangers to which my people will be exposed, I want at least to share them with them, and I charge you with the regency of the kingdom during my absence."

I tried in vain to alter the Queen's resolution. Frightened by the dangers to which she was going to be exposed, I begged Zachiel to support me. I was unaware of the help he was preparing for us and the services he intended to render us, which is why I was very surprised when he told me that, far from opposing the Queen's design, he could only approve of the resolution she had made to put herself at the head of her troops; that it was just that she share with her spouse the perils of a war that ought to cover us both with the greatest glory; that her soldiers, animated by her example, would become invincible; and that all her subjects, struck by such a courageous resolution, would publish everywhere her heroic and truly regal qualities.

At the moment of our departure we found weapons that Zachiel had had prepared for us by gnomes in the smoky caverns of Mount Etna. Those weapons were polished like mirrors; they shone like the rays of the sun. Easily visible on the Queen's shield were the fertile fields of Ceres; the goddess appeared to be assembling several men searching for their nourishment and showing them the art of cultivating the earth and extracting from its fertile bosom all that was necessary to them. Also visible were the gilded crops that covered fertile fields, and the iron destined for so much labor only appeared to be employed in preparing abundance and the renewal of all pleasures. On mine were engraved the exploits of Mars. The two shields were the emblem of all the favors that we had received on the part of the genius.

Guided by Zachiel, we found ourselves, at the first rays of daylight, at the top of a hill overlooking a plain that seemed to us to be covered with chariots, men and horses. The enemy was preparing to make camp there; everything was in motion, and a confused noise was audible, similar to that of angry waves when Neptune agitates them from the depths of the abysms of black tempests. It is thus that Mars commences with the clash of arms the quivering apparatus of war, by sowing rage in the heart of the enemy.

Then the genius ordered me to arrange our troops in battle order, and then, advancing into their midst to harangue them, I saw something divine shining in his face; his voice appeared to me to have the sound of thunder, his gaze had the gleam of lightning, and the fire that animated them passed into the hearts of the officers, setting them ablaze with a martial ardor and simultaneously awakening the thirst for a legitimate revenge.

Then courage, zeal and fury bore them to attack, and blinded them to all the perils that might inhibit the approach. Already, a cloud of dust could be seen rising; horror, carnage and pitiless death seemed to be advancing with great strides, when the Queen, penetrated with fear and horror, suddenly stopped, raised her arms to the heavens and cried: "Great God, protector of humans, be our judge! It is with regret that we are forced to do battle; we would like to spare the blood of men; we cannot hate our enemies, although they are cruel, perfidious and unjust. Decide between us; our lives are in your hands; if it is necessary to liberate Georgia from slavery, it can only be by striking down our enemies, and it is only by your power that we can hope for victory. Glory, O my God, will be due to you alone." Then addressing herself to her troops, she said: "It is to assure you of a tranquil happiness and a durable felicity that I am fighting for you today. Second my designs, and by a noble ardor to follow me, signal your courage."

The generous Princess ordered a simultaneous discharge of all her artillery; then, surrounded by the senior officers, she drove her horse into the most heavily armored ranks of the enemy, smashed through their advanced guard, and pierced to the very heart of their army. Her troops, animated by her example, followed her, and made a frightful carnage of everything their blows encountered. I commanded the right wing, which also fought with enormous courage.

Perceiving that her left wing was beginning to buckle, however, and hearing the cries of the enemy, who believed themselves already victorious, the Queen quit the place where she had come to do battle with so much danger and glory, and advanced, full of indignation, to rally her troops. Although she was covered in the blood of a multitude of enemies whom she had laid in the dust, she fought again with as much force, recalling her soldiers with loud cries, reanimating their strength and their courage by her example, simultaneously renewing the warrior audacity in their hearts and chilling the enemy with fear and terror. They were seen to pass rapidly from blind confidence to the most stupid panic; they threw down their arms, abandoning themselves tumultuously to flight, seeking a refuge on the heights of the mountains.

It seemed, after so many signal exploits, that Victory had not ceased during the course of that battle to cover the Queen with her wings, and that she held a crown suspended above her head; a gentle and placid courage animated her beautiful eyes; one might have taken her for Minerva herself, so sage and measured was she in the midst of grave perils. Thus it was that the powerful army that had menaced all Georgia for so long was destroyed.

Thus it is that an unjust and deceptive power, whatever prosperity it acquires by its violence, hollows out a precipice beneath its own feet. Deceit and inhumanity gradually undermine the foundations of an unjust authority, and cause it to collapse under its own weight, because it has destroyed its true supports, good faith and justice, with its own hands.

After we had taken possession of the battlefield, the Queen ordered that all the booty be abandoned to the soldiers, who made a considerable profit of it. We did not amuse ourselves pursuing the enemy over devastated terrain. The humiliated Sultan sent his grand vizier to negotiate articles that would render a general peace; the genius drafted them personally, and when they were signed by both parties, we dismissed our troops and returned in small stages to the capital city, into which we entered triumphantly. The temples were resounding with the prayers and thanks of the people, and the altars were charge with offerings that were presented to the divinity in actions of grace for the favors that had just been accorded to us.

Several days passed in rejoicing, during which we were complimented by the different orders of the State, all of which hastened to testify their gratitude to us, and the part that they had in the common joy. My father marked his own particular gratitude to the Queen by the most delicate praise, which appeared to embarrass her slightly, and caused her to ask that in subsequent speeches addressed to her, everything suggestive of adulation and flattery should be suppressed.

"It is not," the Princess said, "that I am insensible to praise, especially when it is given to me by such a good judge of virtue, but I fear coming to like it too much, and I must not forget that it often corrupts, rendering us vain and presumptuous. I ought, therefore, to employ the time of my life in meriting it; but that which is most agreeable to me and the best that you can give me will always be that which you publish in my absence, if I am fortunate enough to merit it."

A few days later, anxious about the absence of the genius, whom we had not seen since the day of the army's return, I complained of it bitterly. I was alone with the Queen.

"Is it possible," I said to her, that Zachiel has cruelly abandoned us without warning? Can we never again savor pleasures without their being mingled with bitterness?"

"I cannot believe it," the Princess said, "even though he had warned us about his departure. He is not unaware that, unsteady in the art of reigning, we still need his advice. We are both his work; it is him to whom we owe the talents that are necessary to attempts at self-improvement."

"Very few things remain for me to add," said the genius, suddenly appearing in our midst. "I believe that nothing is any longer lacking to your felicity, and I have come for the last time, to announce my departure."

"You leave me in despair," said the Queen. "Accustomed to allow myself to be guided by your care, how can I do without it so soon? Scarcely have you reestablished me on the throne than you are already leaving me to my own devices. It's not that I doubt Milord's talents, nor the knowledge that his father has acquired by a consummate experience, but I hope for your amity and your zeal in more detailed concerns."

"What more can you expect?" said Zachiel. "My cares are presently unnecessary to you; your timidity is making you fear things that might not happen; in any case, I cannot remain with you any longer; superior orders that I am obliged to obey summon me elsewhere."

"At least grant me that favors that I am about to ask," said the Queen. "The first is to agree to be the protector of this realm, and to come to our aid whenever some unexpected event occurs; the second is to dispose the hearts of my subjects in favor of a spouse that you have chosen yourself and whom I yearn to see reigning with me. You have also promised to give me an infinity of secrets that might be of great utility in future."

"I cannot refuse you anything," Zachiel said. "First of all, I promise to warn you of all the dangers that might threaten your estates. With regard to the secrets that you desire to learn, I presume that the universal elixir is the one that might be most useful to you. Let us go into your laboratory; we shall find there everything necessary for our operations."

The genius carried out several operations in our presence; among others, he filled a large jar with universal elixir and then made us write down the names of the plants and metals composing it.

Then, wishing to profit from all the moments that remained to give us his final instructions, Zachiel said to us:

"I am leaving you a kingdom in which peace and tranquility will reign throughout; remember, during that happy calm, to devote a part of your day to study; try to render yourself knowledgeable in all the arts, and reflect on the utility that you might obtain from them.

"Occupy yourselves with maintaining order; keep watch incessantly on the discipline of the troops, who, in peace-time almost always tend to become enervated. Let your example serve to produce generals who are worthy of command and who, far from changing war into a shameful traffic, will be lavish with their own wealth in recompensing the value of the troops.

"Never neglect anything that might contribute to the happiness of your people. Apply your cares to enabling commerce to flourish, and augment the quantity of their manufactures. Be incessantly attentive to the population; it is a concern that you should never neglect, and which will always be the strength of your estates.

"Accord privileges to foreigners, when you believe them to be capable of encouraging your people and rendering them more industrious. Far from thinking of oppressing them, always listen to their complaints, and never fail to remedy them as soon as you are informed of them.

"Both of you, cause to shine in all your actions and conduct the august and amiable character of a wise, just and debonair prince. Follow in everything the objects that monarchy ought to pursue, having only been introduced for the repose and prosperity of peoples.

"Philosophy, morality and history," Zachiel continued, "can spread further flowers over your footsteps. You are presently in a state to choose your tastes and decide on them; deliver yourself to letters in your quarter-hours of leisure; continue to sow in your minds the knowledge whose harvest will be the joy and pleasure of your old age.

"Lord Seaton is a model that ought to serve as an example to all men; he has endured in his youth all the calamities that can strike human nature, but he has been fortunate enough to store up resources that have served as consolations through all his tribulations, which a man who is the enemy of the fine arts never finds, who often has for his perspective nothing but shame, ennui, fear of the future, dolor and the tomb.

"You must also mistrust the vanity of certain scholars who measure the force of nature by human weakness, and who regard as chimerical the qualities that they do not feel themselves in their prideful reasoning: the frightful source of incredulity, of the inversion of the laws of nature and the disorder of society. Mistrust those who proscribe sentiment; who wish to subjugate everything to the laws of calculation; those who want to analyze everything and who, in searching for the proofs of evidence, fall into the abyss that robs them of the truth and deflects them from the true path that a scholar ought to take, since the true of objective of philosophy is to regulate our mores, purify our tastes elevates our soul and put us on our guard against the illusions of self-love, by giving us lessons in constancy firmness, temperance and moderation in pleasures, in order that we cannot deprive ourselves of them by tasting them more avidly, because the habit of enjoying pleasures enervates their attraction.

"Never forget that the surest way of ensuring the reign of virtue is to avoid opportunities for vice." Those were the last lessons that we received from the genius, who disappeared immediately thereafter, without appearing to listen to the tender expressions of our gratitude.

We spent days discussing the benefits that we had received from Zachiel and the singular favors that the benevolent genius had never ceased to lavish upon us. In order to dissipate our ennui, the Queen encouraged me to write an account of our singular adventures; she worked on it herself, and as we then enjoyed a fortunate calm, they were soon finished. I will only add that a short time after the departure of the genius, the Queen assembled her Council to deliberate on the services that I had rendered the State. She declared her intentions, and it was decided that they could not be better recognized than by enabling me to share her crown, in order to affirm their power in case the Queen died without children, which might excite new conflicts and draw them into new perils.

"In any case," said one of the ministers, "nothing we can do is more in conformity with the wishes of our Sovereign than confirming her choice by crowning the spouse she has chosen; he is wise, he is valiant, he is a friend of God, because he loves and fears Him; he is a true hero of our age and appears to be above humankind; he is good, he is a tender friend, he is compassionate and entirely devoted to those he ought to love; he is the delight of those who live with him; that is what ought to touch our hearts, soften us and render us sensible to all his virtues."

I only report all that praise in order to make known the motives that determined the Georgians to allow me to share the crown; all the nobles of the realm assembled and came in a body to offer it to me, bringing me, in accordance with their customs, the book of the laws, in order to have me swear upon it never to infringe them. Then they renewed the oath of fidelity in the same form that they had observed it at the coronation of the Queen.

"I am not unaware," I said to them, "of the obligations to which I am engaging myself; the first of my duties is to work for your happiness; I shall not propose any other to myself; my glory will henceforth be attached to the felicity of my people and I shall only believe myself to be our king when I have rendered you happy. In accepting the crown, I give you a pledge of the desire I have to work for that with all the zeal you ought to expect."

The Queen expressed to them how sensible she was to the justice they were rendering me, and I was crowned with the consent of all the nobles of the kingdom and the satisfaction of all the people who came from the most remote provinces to participates in the celebrations that were held for the occasion.

Since then we have had to sustain several wars against the Turks, but fortune eventually enabled us to triumph over all their efforts. At present we enjoy peace, savoring its fruits; tranquility and abundance reign among our subjects; a prince and a princess are the fruits of our union; may Heaven enable us to enjoy for a long time the happiness of seeing them grow up in virtue!

THE WATER-SPRITES

A Moral Tale

PART ONE

Chapter I
Introduction: The Birth of Tramarine

Lydia, which contains a part of Africa,[51] was once governed by Ophtes, a bellicose prince. Several wars were fought against him by various petty sovereigns jealous of the extent of his estates. The monarch battled them all, successively winning complete victories, and finally rendering them tributaries to his kingdom.

After having pacified the troubles that those princes excited over a number of years, the monarch no longer thought about anything but enabling his people to enjoy a peace that ought to bring back abundance and tranquility to his kingdom. In order to cement it further, however, his minister proposed that he make an alliance with the king of Galata by marrying Cliceria, the daughter of that monarch.

Ophtes lent himself readily to that view; he was charmed by the beauty of Cliceria, whose portrait he was shown. Ambassadors were sent to the King of Galata; they were charged with proposing the marriage of the Princes with the king of Lydia. A proposition so advantageous was accepted joyfully; both parties hastened to sign the articles and the marriage was only deferred for the time required to make the preparations with the pomp and magnificence that it was appropriate to employ in those kinds of celebrations.

Princess Cliceria had scarcely entered her fifteenth year; she was endowed with an intelligence superior to all women, and a ravishing beauty; she was received by the King, her spouse, with all the sumptuousness and gallantry that

---

[51] This Lydie [Lydia] is evidently not the actual Iron Age kingdom in Asia Minor, nor a misspelling of the African kingdom of Lybie [Libya], but an entirely hypothetical realm.

can be expected of a great monarch, especially when amour is combined with reasons of state. For more than a month, the days were marked with further celebrations. The King, although already of a certain age, took great pleasure in the diversions of his court; in addition, he wanted by that complaisance to make known to the Queen, as well as to the princes and princesses who had accompanied her, the satisfaction he had in seeing her embellish his court. The courtiers, in their turn, in order to mark their zeal and their attachment to the King and their Queen, strove to imagine new diversions that might amuse and please her.

Several years passed thus in pleasures, without them being troubled by any anxiety, except that the King appeared to have no successor. The desire to obtain one eventually caused prayers and sacrifices to succeed laughter and games; the King and the Queen went to offer them in all the temples, where they both did so with a piety worthy of example.

The prayers that the heart had formed could not fail to soften the gods; they were eventually granted; the Queen declared that she was pregnant. The joy that the news spread through all hearts is indescribable; the King ordered prayers in actions of grace; the people flocked to the temples in order to ask the gods to grant them a prince who would govern them with a much sagacity, reason, justice and mildness as the one who presently reigned over them; that he should be the inheritor of all his virtues, his clemency and all his talents as well as his estates.

The gods were deaf to their prayers; the Queen gave birth to a princess. There was, nevertheless, much rejoicing at the birth of the princess, who was named Tramarine.

Ophtes, curious to know the destiny of a child so long desired, ordered his prime minister to go to consult the oracle of Venus. He charged him at the same time with rich presents that were to serve to ornament the temple of the goddess.

When the pythoness had set herself on the tripod, she seemed to be immediately agitated by the divine spirit, which filled her; her hair stood on end; the entire lair resounded with a noise like thunder. Then a voice was heard, which appeared to emerge from the depths of her bosom; it pronounced that the child, in taking on a divine form, would not see her father again until after his ruin.

That response, which a second oracle would have been required in order to explain, afflicted the minister sensibly. He returned to the court with a consternated visage, not daring to announce to the King the response that the goddess had pronounced by means of the mouth of the pythoness. To begin with, he searched for some phrase that might clarify the oracle's response by giving it a more favorable meaning; but the king, judging by his sad expression that the prediction was not favorable to the princess, ordered him firmly not conceal anything, under pain of death—which the minister saw that it was necessary to obey.

"It is with great dolor, Sire," he said to him, "that I am constrained to announce to Your Majesty the baleful decrees that the oracle has pronounced regarding the destiny of Princess Tramarine. I wanted to spare Your Majesty the distress of hearing them. Here it is: 'The child, in taking on a divine form, will not see her father again until after his ruin.'

"However, Sire," the minister added, "Your Majesty is not unaware that the gods only ever express themselves with a great deal of obscurity; doubtless that is only to deceive the curiosity of feeble mortals who want to penetrate too far into the future, of which they alone are the depositories. It is prudent and wise to summit to their decrees, without seeking to penetrate the meaning, which they always hide by means of ambiguous responses to which it is easy to give several interpretations. Forgive my zeal, Sire, and the boldness of my reflections, but I am obeying Your Majesty's orders in not hiding any of my thoughts."

It is true that the reflections in question were those of a wise and prudent man. His soul was deployed therein and the interest he had in the tranquility and repose of his master were legible. But what can opinion and prejudice not produce? Neither the King nor the Queen wanted to take their minister's sage advice. The oracle's response was examined in full Council; several sinister consequences were drawn from it, which increased the King's distress in not being able to divine the meaning of the prediction.

It took a long time to decide the course of action that ought to be taken, but a second pregnancy on the Queen's part decided the fate of the Princess. She was sent to the kingdom of Castora, then governed by Queen Pentaphile, the sister of the King of Lydia. That Princess was an Amazon, who devoted her realm entirely to her valor, and had banished all men therefrom.

It was said that the hatred the Princess in question had conceived for men came from the bitter memory of having been deceived by a Prince in whom she had put all her confidence. It is true that the choice one makes of a favorite in youth is hardly ever enlightened by reason. It is neither the most zealous nor the most estimable who obtains preference, because one does not reflect on the price of virtue; glamour seduces, a scatterbrain presents himself with the brilliance and vivacity of his quips; one yields to him without reserve and without taking the time to examine him; one does not distinguish in him the reality from the appearance; one is almost always the dupe of an imposing exterior; and unfortunately, men only make use of the gift they have to please in order that their indiscretion and perfidy might triumph. It is to be presumed that it was very similar reasons that determined the Queen of Castora to banish all men from her estates.

As she was the best Princess in the world, the love that she had for her subjects and the desire to render them perfectly happy caused her to convene a general assembly of all the nobility—I mean all the noblewomen, for the men had been excluded from it. It was in that assembly that several questions were raised regarding the advantages that female society might obtain, by comparing them to all the evils that resulted every day for that same society. After many sessions in which everyone offered her opinion—which I shall not describe, because I was not summoned to that Council, and besides which, I dread attracting the censure of both sexes by composing a discourse that would doubtless be too simple for the importance of the matters that must have been proposed there—it was finally decided, by a majority vote, that the Queen should establish an explicit law by which it would be forbidden for any man, no matter what his quality or condition might be, to remain for more than twenty-four hours within the entire extent of the State, under pain of being sacrificed to the goddess Pallas, the protectress of the realm.

One has some difficulty in being persuaded that young women had the liberty of expressing their opinion in that assembly, into which a great deal of partiality appears to have entered; it is quite probable that the old dowagers had taken sole possession of the deliberative voices—which appeared to the men to be glaringly obvious. "For after all," they said, "ought one not fear that, by the observation of such a rigorous law, the realm might find itself depopulated in a very short time?"

At any rate, the entire Amazon people submitted to it without putting up any resistance—and the goddess Pallas, content with the sacrifice that had been made to her, wanted to recompense them by giving them a striking mark of her powerful protection. In order to perpetuate that population of heroines by procuring them the means of multiplication, the goddess suddenly caused a spring to appear in the middle of the realm, which a few scholarly mythologists took at first for the one into which the handsome Narcissus plunged when he fell in love with his own face. That spring was, for a while, the subject of much reflection, and it became the source of several disputes; everyone wanted to discover its origin, although they were entirely ignorant of its property. That discovery was only due to hazard; this is how it happened.

Several young women attached to the Queen's service fell ill with a kind of languor; the art of medicine was entirely exhausted in the attempt to procure them relief, but the malady, about which nothing was known, seemed to get worse every day. That determined the doctors, doubtless inspired by the goddess, to prescribe the waters of the new spring, hoping that the dissipation of a long journey might contribute to the reestablishment of their health.

The voyage succeeded as perfectly as they had wished; the young woman, on their return to the court, recovered their plumpness and their natural gaiety, and even something more, which immediately gave the spring a great reputation. All the Amazons, those of the highest rank along with the others, made daily journeys in order to bathe there and render their complexion fresher. Imagine the Queen's surprise, however, when, nine months later, each of the young women gave birth to a daughter. An event so singular made the virtue of the spring known, and such a prodigy augmented the respect and admiration of the noblewomen and the people for the goddess.

In order to mark her gratitude to the goddess Pallas for the new favor that she had granted her, the Queen ordered that a temple should be built on the site of the miraculous spring.

A few critics might perhaps think it ridiculous that women should set out to build a temple; my response to that is that a woman who receives an education similar to that given to men can undertake anything. Do not swallows match us in the art of building?

At any rate, the temple was finished in a short time. It is supported by twenty-four columns of white marble; in the middle is a pedestal twelve cubits high and eight square, representing the attributes of the goddess, whose golden statue enriched with the most beautiful diamonds is placed in the center. Around the temple is a cloister, which distributes several apartments designed to lodge the young women consecrated to the worship of the goddess Pallas. To begin with, the Queen named fifty young women, who were chosen from the noblest families, who would be solely occupied for ten years in singing the praises of the goddess. At the end of that time they were permitted to emerge, in order to join the army. All the children born to those priestesses would be brought up in the temple, their birth giving all of them the rights and privileges of their mothers.

Pentaphile, whose vast vision extended into the most remote times, felt obliged by that new establishment to make another law that tended to increase the population, and ordered all her subjects to visit the temple of the goddess at least once a year and to take salutary baths there, in order to contribute, to the extent that they could, in multiplying the number of the Amazons, which ought always to be the wealth of a state, by virtue of the competition in which everyone engages to procure the necessities and even the luxuries of life, and to contain the people in their duty. It is necessary to add that all those who contravened the law, either by neglecting the worship that they owed to the goddess or by seeking the company of the sex long banished by law, were condemned to be imprisoned for the rest of their lives in the Tower of Regrets, without regard to their youth, birth or dignities.

It was more than twenty years after that great event that the ambassadors of the King of Lydia arrived at Queen Pentaphile's court, where they were received with a magnificence worthy of that Princess. As, in accordance with the laws of the realm, they could not stay long in her estates, they were granted an immediate audience. After having granted their request, the Queen sent them away with rich presents, charging them with letters full of tenderness for her brother the King and Queen Cliceria.

Charmed by the proposition that the King of Lydia had made her to permit that Princess Tramarine should be brought up in her court, Pentaphile appointed the foremost ladies in the palace to go to meet the young princess at the frontier, in order to bring her with the women of her retinue. A numerous cortege of Amazons was ordered to accompany them. During their journey the apartment that

447

the young process was to occupy was prepared, which was next to the Queen's, Her Majesty wanting to supervise personally the conduct of the women charged with the education of the princess.

A few critics might perhaps think that there ought to be no danger of seduction in a court, and even in a realm, where no man dared to appear, and that it can be compared to a republic of bees whose drones have been driven away with darts. Although the Queen had liberated her people from dependence on men, however, while making them envisage the domination to which they had been subjected as a tyrannical yoke, and in spite of the despotism that she had established, she nevertheless reflected maturely on the abuses that might be introduced, either by means of disguises or other intrigues on the part of the women of the court. She was not unaware that their society sometimes becomes as dangerous as that of men, especially when ambition, interest or jealousy takes possession of their mind. Those different passions act with so much empire over a heart that is wilted that they often cause the most essential duties to be neglected. It is true that where there are men, those passions are felt with much more force; they are fomented and animated of their own accord; but the habit that men form of profound dissimulation ensures that they are infinitely more able to hide their faults, especially when it is a matter of deceiving a sex that is too weak and too credulous. At any rate, new sects had been introduced into her estates that augmented her fears; she could not, therefore, take too many precautions to protect the young princess.

When Tramarine had arrived at Pentaphile's court, Her Majesty took charge personally of her instruction in the religion and laws of the State, destining her for the throne that she occupied and forming the project of resigning the crown to her as soon as she was of an age to reign. That could only happen, however, one the young princess had given proof of her fecundity by taking salutary baths in the spring of Pallas.

Tramarine had scarcely reached her twelfth year when she seemed a prodigy of beauty and intelligence; all the graces and talents were united in her person, it seemed that her prudence was in advance of her age and nothing escaped her penetration. Her intelligence and enlightenment, however, only served to make her aware of the fact that she was not made to spend her life with those who surrounded her, and, without having a determined objective, she was already experiencing the melancholy that one could place in the rank of pleasures, although it often serves only to sharpen desire. Already Tramarine was sighing, already she was taking pleasure in solitude, in order to have time to sort out her ideas. Her reflections, dictated by ennui, gave her an air of melancholy that worried the Queen and the rest of the court; Celiane, a young princess related to Tramarine, who had accompanied her, was the most alarmed of all.

Amour, however, the passion whose driving force is the most extensive and causes the most trouble, ought to have been banished forever from a realm inhabited by a single sex. One no longer saw there those temporarily agreeable individuals who amuse a court by their continual persiflage, an occupation well worthy of the frivolity of their minds: those gallant fops with their honeyed tones, whose different inflections of the voice appear to be in accord with their gestures, and who, charged with a thousand baubles, often ornamented with beauty-spots, rouge and bouquets, mount an assault of charms on the most co-quettish of women; all those Adonises were proscribed in Pentaphile's estates. What a pity! I doubt, however, that it was much of a loss. But let us leave those reflections and pass on to more interesting things.

Chapter II
Princess Tramarine's Journey to the Spring of Pallas

As soon as Tramarine reached the age of fifteen, her household was organized. Celiane was appointed her chief lady in waiting. She was a woman of
keen and brilliant intelligence and, as I have said, a relative of the princess on
Queen Cliceria's side. Tramarine loved her dearly; she had accorded her all her
confidence; it is true that no one was more worthy of it, by virtue of her merit,
her zeal and her attachment.

Judging that the Princess was now ready for the novena prescribed by law,
the Queen assembled her Council to order the baths that Tramarine could not
dispense with taking in the miraculous spring. She wanted the journey to be
made with all the pomp and magnificence appropriate to a princess destined to
occupy the throne of Castora. Four thousand Amazons were commanded to escort the young princess, and the most qualified ladies competed artfully for the
honor of accompanying her; each of them hastened to pay court to her, not unaware of the fact that she was to reign as soon as she had given proof of her fecundity—a favor that they did not doubt that the goddess would grant her.

When the Princess arrived at the temple, the priestesses and young women
dedicated to the cult of the goddess came to meet her, and, after having received
her from the hands of her ladies in waiting, they introduced her into the enclosure of the temple to the sound of a thousand instruments. Tramarine then presented to the goddess Pallas offerings worthy of the rank that awaited her; she
said prayers in accordance with the accustomed ritual, to which the daughters of
Pallas added their delightful chorus.

When all the ceremonies observed for the reception of the Princess had
concluded, she was conducted to the spring in order to take the salutary baths
therein, which continued for nine days, without it being permitted to the princess
to speak to any of the women of her retinue, who had retired to tents set up in
the environs of the temple; the priestesses served the Princess themselves and
never quit her by day or by night.

During the Princess' novena, it was forbidden for anyone to approach the
spring, in order to avoid her mixing with the vulgar, and also with a view to observing the favors that the goddess would grant her. In consequence, all the Amazons who came to present themselves, in the hope of participating in the benefits of the goddess, were obliged to wait for Tramarine's departure, and none of
her women could take advantage of the opportunities of the journey.

When the novena had finished, the high priestess returned the Princess to
the hands of Celiane, who was the first to express the pleasure she felt in advance of her accession to the throne. Her other women surrounded her and took
their places in her carriage for the return journey to the court, where they arrived

at nightfall. The princess was greeted in the city by the acclamations of the entire Amazon people; the Queen's guards were all under arms, and the palace so brightly illuminated that it might have been mistaken for a globe of fire. The Queen welcomed Tramarine with a joy and magnificence that is indescribable; celebrations of every sort were invented to amuse the princess.

When there was no longer any doubt of the favor she had received from the goddess, the joy was redoubled; odes, epistles, elegies and songs were composed, all of which were addressed to the Princess, in order to predict the gifts that the gods ought to lavish upon those who gave birth to the favors of Pallas.

In all of Tramarine's actions, meanwhile, a languor and depths of sadness were observed, which she could not vanquish, in spite of the endlessly varied celebrations that were incessantly held in her honor. The melancholy in question was, however, attributed to her condition. When she entered into the ninth month, the Queen invited several sorceresses, who were particular friends of hers, to be present at the princess' delivery.

The realm of Castora is full of enchantresses and sorceresses, because of the lairs and mountains that surround it. Besides which, the terrain produces an abundance of all the plants that are necessary to the composition of their potions; it is even claimed that it is to this region that Medea sent all the women most adept at her enchantments.

Bagatelle, Petulante, Minutia and Légère, whom the Queen had not invited, fearful of their science, and even more so of their malevolence, were nevertheless the first to arrive. Each of them was in the most brilliant cabriolet, drawn by swallows. Folly, dressed as a runner, came on ahead of them. The Queen, who feared some malice on their part, went to meet them, in order to offer her apologies for not having invited them; Her Majesty blamed her Chancelleress.[52]

The others having arrived, they were taken into the princess' apartment. Légère, Petulante, Minutia and Bagatelle began by taking possession of the four bed-posts, although that honor was due to the enchantress Bonina and the principal ladies of the court; but it was not a moment to argue about rights.

Lucina, having approached the young princess, had no sooner received the child than Petulante and Légère both cried out at the same time that Tramarine had infringed the laws of the State. Camagnole and Bonina, who could not believe it, each put on their large spectacles to examine the matter; but, unable to dissimulate the sex of the child, the enchantress Camagnole assured the Queen that she would take charge of the education of the Prince, and that she ought not to worry about it. Fortunately, Bonina, although annoyed at being anticipated by Camagnole, began by endowing the Prince with wisdom, science, valor and prudence. The other sorceresses endowed him in their turn in accordance with their

---

[52] In 1768 English did not have a feminine equivalent of chancellor into which the French *chancelière* could be readily translated, but thanks to Angela Merkel, we have now been forced to invent this one, which I have gladly appropriated.

genius, but they could not destroy the good qualities with which Bonina had endowed him. That enchantress was the best and most prudent of all magicians, and she only ever employed her art to enable happiness.

Bonina remarked the dolor of the Queen, who seemed to be in despair that such an accident had happened to Tramarine, regarding it as the worst possible insult that could be offered to her authority. Her Majesty could not imagine that the young princess could have contrived such a crime on her own, and took Bonina into her study in order to try to discover its authors. The enchantress was of the opinion that they should first approach the sorceresses, the sole witnesses to the misfortune, in order to engage them to keep a secret that it might be very useful to conceal from the whole court, by simply declaring that the Princess had only delivered a tumor.

Petulante, however, who was Bonina's enemy, had only brought Bagatelle, Minutia and Légère, who were utterly devoted to her, with the design of blocking all her designs. They therefore declared that they were formally opposed to Bonina's ideas; that Pentaphile, having established the new laws herself, would be attacking the foundations of the State by tolerating such abuses; that a striking example was required; and that it ought to fall heavily upon the Princess, who, although better educated than others, had perhaps counted a little too much, for the impunity of her crime, on the grandeur of her birth, which rendered her even more culpable. The sentiments of the others were divided, but the majority opined in favor of exile.

Bonina, however, who was of the most savant, and the one in whom the Queen had the most confidence, employed her eloquence to combat the sorceresses' arguments, and finally succeeded in putting off the judgment of Tramarine until she was fully recovered, since they could not, without glaring injustice, condemn her without being heard. The Queen appreciated her reasoning, and granted a delay of two months.

Bonina then went into Tramarine's apartment, where she found her in a lethargic torpor. Lucina was occupied in preparing remedies for the Princess' relief. The enchantress talked to Celiane, and informed her of the misfortune that had just overtaken Tramarine, the news having not yet spread through the court.

Celiane, surprised and desperate, could not comprehend by what fatality the baths had produced an effect on her so contrary to the wishes of the entire nation. Her first impulse was to think that the goddess, by means of that alteration, wanted to punish the pride of the women who had taken possession of the government in order to cause it to pass into the hands of the Prince who had just been born. She communicated that idea to Bonina, who thought it very sound, and promised to make use of it herself when it was a matter of pleading the princess' cause, but that she dared not voice it while she was in danger, which might last for six weeks.

While Bonina was fully occupied in appeasing minds in favor of Tramarine, the evil magicians took a malign pleasure in publishing her adventure. The Queen, overwhelmed by dolor, was very embarrassed as to the decision she ought to make. She assembled an extraordinary Council, but could not prevent the sorceresses from presiding over it. Bonina continued to support Tramarine's interests there ardently, and it was finally decided to have all the women who had accompanied the princess to the temple arrested, without distinction of rank or quality. Four Council members were appointed for that examination. The order troubled the court and the city, and everyone argued about it according to the range of their intellect.

The report of the arbiters, however, exonerated the princess; everything was found to have been in conformity with the laws of the State. There was then a visit to the temple and the priestesses, in an attempt to discover whether some abuse might not have been introduced there. In order that no one could escape the examination, Amazons were commanded to surround all the avenues of the temple, with a precise order that in case of contravention, the guilty party should immediately be sacrificed to the goddess.

During that research, Tramarine, gradually recovering her strength, often complained to Bonina and her dear Celiane about the indifference of the Queen, who had not visited her. As everyone avoids those whose disgrace is almost certain, for fear of being dragged down in their fall, the entire court had also abandoned Tramarine.

"Alas, I can perceive only too well what is being done to me," said the unfortunate Princess, "Although I don't know what can have occasioned that coldness. I believe, at least, that no one is unjust enough to impute to me anything that might be contrary to my glory. Why am I refused the feeble satisfaction of embracing my daughter? Must that young princess also share my disgrace?"

Celiane groaned internally at Tramarine's error, but she dared not tell her yet what had occasioned the troubles by which the court was agitated. She was therefore constrained to repress her dolor, in order to soothe the bitterness of Tramarine's heart, but without giving her too much hope.

When the two months expired, the enchantress Bonina came to see Tramarine to inform her of the fate that was destined for her, unless the arguments she could put forward in her defense were strong enough to obtain suffrage in her favor.

"It is with much grief," said Bonina, "that I am forced to inform you of the greatest of misfortunes, but my dear Tramarine, it would doom you completely if it were hidden from you any longer. It is in vain that you ask every day to see the child to whom you gave birth; the child is no longer in my power, the enchantress Camagnole having taken possession of him. Nevertheless, you have nothing to fear for his life; that enchantress would employ all the force of her art in vain; I have anticipated her in preventing her from being able to do him any harm.

"But my dear, it would have been much better for your repose and that of the State had the child died before having seen the light of day. How, with the intelligence and reason that have always been remarked in you, after having infringed the laws of the empire, have you had the temerity to expose yourself to all its rigor? Was it necessary for you, my dear, who ought to have been an example to the entire realm, to become its scandal by your imprudence? A little more confidence in me might have saved you; you're not unaware of the influence I have over the Queen's mind. I would have prevented her from convening the assembly of sorceresses; left alone with you, with Lucina, it would have been easy for us to disguise the sex of your child."

"What do you mean?" said Tramarine, interrupting the enchantress. "What is your injurious discourse implying? Have you forgotten who I am, and what my rank is owed? Me, infringe the laws! What reason is there to accuse me of it?"

"Princess," the enchantress continued, in a severe tone, "is it to me that speech is addressed? You're doubtless unaware of how far my power extends; but to punish you for your temerity, I shall withdraw and abandon you. Others will instruct you as to your fate."

It was lucky for Tramarine that Celiane was present at that conversation. "What, my Lady," she said to Bonina. "Would you, who are goodness itself, be so cruel as to abandon the Princess? Far from being annoyed by her vivacity, you ought rather to draw conclusions therefrom favorable to her innocence. Agree, at least, that it is very humiliating for a young Princess, whose conduct has always been stainless in the eyes of the entire court, to find herself unjustly accused."

Upset to have irritated the enchantress against her, and judging by Celiane's speech that the accusations made against her were very grave, and that she might perhaps need the enchantress' help more than ever, Tramarine apologized for her vivacity and begged her to explain the crime with which someone had dared to blacken her name. Bonina, judging, by virtue of the princess' ignorance, that she could not be guilty, softened in her favor, and promised to help her, after having informed her of what had happened and the resolution that had been taken to banish her from the court.

The Princess, whose heart was pure, assured Bonina that she had nothing for which to reproach herself. "Undoubtedly," she said, "the goddess wanted to test my constancy; I should have suspected as much because of the dreams by which I was agitated in her temple. It is also true that the face of which I formed the image has been present in my mind ever since."

"In truth, my dear Tramarine," said the enchantress, "you surprise me infinitely. It's necessary to assure you that you have a very vivid imagination; are there no other arguments to put forward in your defense?"

"No," said Tramarine, suffocated by her dolor. "I have nothing else to add. It is not the exile that will cause me pain, since it will liberate me from an unjust court, but the shame of the unworthy suspicions that have spread through all minds. I can no longer count on anyone but you, my dear Bonina, and the attachment of Celiane; your amity will take the place of all the grandeurs I am losing."

Celiane could only reply with tears. What could she have said that would have soothed Tramarine's distress? Only time can efface the memory of great dolors; all advice and consolations weaken against the blows of fate when they have recently struck. Nature has rights that she does not care to lose, until chagrin has exhausted its strength; then, by virtue of a wise dispensation, reason regains the upper hand, to reanimate within us the faculties of the soul.

Chapter III
The Judgment of Tramarine

The following day, Tramarine was taken to the Council Hall to be interrogated. The enchantress Bonina, who no longer left her, spoke first on her behalf, and told the assembly of sorceresses that the process had no other defense to offer for her justification than the power of the imagination; that she protested that she had never seen any of the mortals proscribed by the law since her entry into the realm, except in a dream during the novena at the spring of the goddess Pallas.

Such a declaration surprised the Queen and her Council infinitely; it caused them to postpone the decision of the affair until the return of the council members charged with the visit to the temple.

Meanwhile, Tramarine was in an unbearable perplexity. Death appeared to her to be a thousand times preferable to living under the accusation of a crime of which she could not prove her innocence. In order to remedy to some extent such cruel woes, Celiane advised her to write to her father the King to inform him of the insult that she was on the point of suffering, by virtue of an exile that could only be injurious to her glory.

Following Celiane's advice, Tramarine wrote to the King of Lydia, but because all her women were entirely devoted to the Chancelleress, her letters were intercepted, and that enemy of the princess had sufficient skill to spread a venom of which she alone was capable.

When the council members had returned from the temple, the Queen assembled a Great Council, in order to be able to examine the princess' case. All the noblewomen of the State who had been delegated to examine the priestesses, after having made their report in favor of Tramarine, declared that they had found nothing that was not exactly in conformity with the law. The princess' defense was then exposed.

Conspiracies had been formed within the Council. Tramarine had few friends there; the vivacity of her intelligence made her feared. The Queen, enfeebled by age, did not involve herself much in government, and those who held the most important positions feared, with reason, the solid and penetrating intellect of the Princess. In sum, the cruelest envy of the Eumenides took possession of all hearts, determined to pursue Tramarine all the way to her exile.

Several Amazons, however, still offered opinions in her favor; they even insisted that a new law ought to be made that admitted the force of the imagination. It is easy to imagine that they were young women who offered that opinion, of which the Queen approved, being naturally inclined toward clemency.

The monarch would have been delighted if it had furnished a means of saving Tramarine; but the old Chancelleress and all the old dowagers of the court, who had a greater share in the government, rose up with a common voice against such a law, which was, they claimed, capable of overturning the order of the State. Besides which, it would tend to abolish entirely the virtue of the spring of the goddess Pallas and encourage the young to neglect the worship that was owed to the goddess, from whom new favors were received every day. Anything that might irritate the goddess against the realm, of which he had declared herself the protectress, had to be avoided, in the fear that she might avenge herself with calamities that would ruin the State entirely, robbing the Amazons of the strength to defend themselves against their enemies.

I shall only offer that abridged account of the Chancelleress' speech, which was found worthy of the eloquence of Demosthenes or Cicero; she finally rallied all the voices to her sentiment.

As the means the princess had employed for her defense had leaked out, the Amazons who loved Tramarine dearly were ready to rise up. They were already assembling in the squares; they even came in a tumult to the palace to demand the release of the princess and also that the power of the imagination should be established in law. But the Chancelleress, always firm in her resolutions, opposed yielding anything to the mutinous people; she advised the Queen to make the full weight of her indignation felt by punishing severely those who had contributed, by their seditious discourse, to spreading trouble in the city.

The sorceresses, devoted to the Chancelleress, supported her opinion, and the Queen, dragged away, so to speak, by the torrent, felt obliged to issue a decree by which she declared that her supreme will was that the laws must have their entire accomplishment, and that all her subjects were bound, under the penalties previously announced, to visit the temple of the goddess Pallas once a year, in order to take the baths salutary to population, and also forbidding anyone to employ, in any fashion whatsoever, the power of the imagination. In consequence, Princess Tramarine was condemned to imprisonment in the Tower of Regrets, although her exile, by way of clemency, would be limited to twenty years.

A judgment as rigorous, pronounced against a Princess of Pentaphile's blood, made the Amazon people tremble, but could not prevent them murmuring against such a severe sentence. The Tower of Regrets was known to be a frightful place, filled with terrible monsters that forbade entry thereto.

Thus in spite of the influence that the enchantress Bonina had over the mind of the Queen, the Chancelleress employed so many intrigues that she triumphed over her on this occasion, and under the vain pretext of the good of the State, she contrived to remove from the court a young Princess whose rank summoned her to the throne, in the fear that, had she mounted it, she would not have given her any part in the government. To suppress sedition, she assembled hardened troops and distributed them through all the quarters of the city in order to keep the people in check.

Bonina took responsibility for informing the Princess of the sad news; the latter received it with a great deal of confidence, and showed, on that occasion, that the grandeur of her soul was above adversity. Her heart, like a rock on to which the waves come to break during a tempest, was not broken; she heard the devastating sentence that her enemies had passed against her tranquilly.

Chapter IV
Tramarine's Departure for the Tower of Regrets

Of all the women in Tramarine's service, only Celiane remained faithful, which made the Princess see that the demonstrations of attachment and devotion that had always been shown to her by her servants could not hold up against her disgrace. In that encounter she experienced the ingratitude of individuals who are attached to highly placed individuals by interest alone. Always ready to follow the fortunate, they forget you as soon as fortune turns against you; that is why one ought not to carry the torch of truth into the depths of the cavern in order to learn to discern the subtle motives that lurk and hide between those of candor and blow away, so to speak, the sublime phantom of appearances in order to reveal beneath it the frightful monster that mortals often mask.

Tramarine sent Celiane to the Queen to ask her for a private audience, but she had the cruelty of refusing it. Tramarine, seeing herself deprived of the hope she had conceived of softening the Queen, asked Celiane to go back again, to beg her not to impute to her a fault of which she could not admit herself to be guilty; to remember that she had never failed in the submission she owed to Her Majesty's order; and to say that she flattered herself that she would at least be permitted, in order to make her exile more bearable, to take with her the child whose birth had caused her misfortune, whose destiny, given that he could not be brought up in Her Majesty's court, ought to be indifferent to her; that it would be the greatest consolation that she could receive to be able to inspire in her son the respect and veneration that she had never ceased to have for the virtues and eminent qualities that shone in Her Majesty; that she dared to hope of her clemency that she might be accorded that last grace, as a favor for which she would be grateful as long as she lived.

The Queen replied to Celiane that Tramarine ought not to be unaware that her son the Prince was in the power of the sorceress Camagnole, and that it was impossible to remove him from her until he had fulfilled his destiny; that she could nevertheless assure the Princess that it was only with regret that she saw herself constrained to cede to the force of the law, and that she ordered her to be ready to depart at dawn the following day.

Tramarine was sensibly afflicted in enduring so much rigor on the part of the Queen, to whom she was veritably attached, not only by ties of blood, but also by those of tender amity. But what can seduction not achieve? Can one not say that it covers with a thick veil the brightest lights of reason, and that, closing the eyes that might be enlightened thereby, all movements become like those of a blind horse that one sets to turn the wheel of a press, turning in a narrow circle while it believes that it is traveling the world entire.

The enchantress Bonina came the next day, in accordance with the promise that she had given the princess, to take her to her place of exile. Her chariot was harnessed to eight turtle-doves. Tramarine and Celiane climbed into it with the enchantress, and the birds immediately cleaved the sir with such rapidity that the Chancelleress, who was on a balcony with a few Amazons of her party taking a malign pleasure in watching them depart, lost sight of them in an instant. We shall leave them to rejoice in their triumph in order to follow Tramarine.

As they approached the tower, the enchantress, who wanted to hide the horror of the view from the princesses, caused her chariot to rise above the clouds, which came down thereafter in a vast courtyard, where twelve damsels dressed in green appeared, who, after helping the princesses to get down, took them into a superb drawing room, in which there was a rich dais destined for Princess Tramarine. Then music was heard, whose chords were delightful.

Tramarine, surprised by such a reception, felt herself penetrated by new obligations that she had to Bonina. When the concert had finished she descended from her throne into another room, where she was served the most delicate dishes. The enchantress, sitting down at the table between Tramarine and Celiane, asked them whether they thought that the abode that had been prepared for them was capable of softening the rigors of the Princess' exile.

"I have been unable to oppose your destiny," Bonina added, "but what I can tell you is that you are under the sway of a great genius, to whom my power must cede. I will protect you to the extent that I can; destiny has condemned you to sleep in the tower, but to reduce the rigor of your fate I have raised this palace alongside it; the gardens you see are attached to it, and although you must sleep in the tower every day, it will be easy for you to get out by means of a secret door that I shall open for you, in order that you can enjoy, without constraint, all the amusements that will be carefully procured for you. I hope that they can banish from your mind the somber sadness that I have observed there for a long time. I would have told you in the Queen of Castora's palace about the favorable intentions that I shall never cease to have to contribute to your wellbeing, if I had not feared that Turbulente, who is your cruelest enemy, might have countered them by means of some dark plot, which, in spite of my help, would have heaped a thousand more misfortunes upon you."

Tramarine thanked the enchantress, assuring her of a boundless gratitude

"I recognize," the princess continued, "the full extent of your power, and I perceive already that you have expelled ennui from this abode, for I can scarcely persuade myself that I am in the terrible fortress of which the mere idea filled me with horror. I see, on the contrary, that I shall be treated here as a sovereign, and far from regarding my exile as a punishment, I shall be glad to forget, in your presence, the woes that preceded it."

"I would like that," the enchantress said, "and will devote all my cares to it; follow me now, without any fear, into my park, to which I shall guide you."

Tramarine and Celiane followed the enchantress, who first took them into the tower, and then down a hidden stairway, at the bottom of which was an iron door. She opened it, and gave the key to Tramarine, recommending that she keep it on her person at all times. They traversed the enchantress' gardens, which were the most beautiful in the world, where they admired, above all, the statues of gods and goddesses, distributed in an admirable order.

Bonina led them into a pathway bordered by lemon-trees and orange-trees, which filled the air with a delicious perfume. Tramarine found the place so agreeable that she proposed to the enchantress that she rest under an arbor that terminated the pathway, where there was a spring whose gentle murmur, combined with the chirping of birds, inspired a mild reverie.

They sat down on the bank of a stream formed by the waters of the spring, which broadened out as it drew away from its source. Celiane, naturally cheerful and playful, who was always on the lookout for opportunities to amuse the princess—who had appeared for some time to be overwhelmed by a languor that was beginning to take root in her temperament—proposed to Bonina that they spend the rest of the day in that delightful spot, and even have supper there, if possible.

A thousand zephyrs immediately appeared to agitate the trees surrounding the stream, whose silvery waters formed rippling waves, which seemed to be mocking the joy that had been expressed in the beautiful Tramarine's tender sighs. Dusk had scarcely covered the sky with a somber veil than, in response to a signal from the enchantress, the twelve damsels appeared, and set down a table laden with the most rare and delicate dishes. They remained at table for a long time, and Celiane amused the princess greatly with the remarks full of wit that enjoyment always inspires in people of intelligence.

More than six weeks had already passed, during which the enchantress had taken care to provide new entertainments for the princess every day, without their being able to dissipate her melancholy. Celiane never ceased to make her tender reproaches, but Tramarine, embarrassed by the presence of her women, who had been ordered not to leave her, only responded with sighs.

A matter requiring the attention of the enchantress obliged her to absent herself for some time. She informed Tramarine about the journey that she would have to make, which she could not avoid. Tramarine was disappointed, and because of a presentiment of the misfortune that might overtake her, did what she could to prevent the journey and to engage Bonina not to abandon her.

"I absolutely cannot dispense with attending the assembly of enchantresses," Bonia told her, "which is being hosted by the redoubtable Demogorgon, one of the greatest magicians in the world; your interests too require me to do so. I shall keep my absence as short as I can; have no fear of the enchantress Turbulente. Here is the means of shielding yourself from her malevolence; so long as you carry this protection it will keep you safe for the traps that

Turbulente might set for you, provided that you are careful not leave the tower without having it on your person. You will lack nothing during my absence; I have given the orders necessary for your safety, and in addition to the dozen women that are at your service, I shall give you two others, in whom I have every confidence and who are sufficiently instructed in the art of magic to be able to protect you from unexpected dangers that the negligence of the others might occasion. Only suffer, beautiful Tramarine, that they are never far away from you."

Bonina then embraced the Princess and Celiane, who escorted her to her chariot, which disappeared momentarily.

Chapter V
The Abduction of Tramarine

In order to dissipate the chagrin caused to them by the departure of the enchantress, Celiane proposed to the princess that they go down to the garden, and Tramarine, not wanting any other company than Celiane's, forbade her women to follow them. The two that the enchantress had left to watch over her safety, however, told her respectfully that, having received precise orders from Bonina not to lose sight of her, they could not, without contravening them, dispense with accompanying her everywhere, but in order not to inconvenience her, they would remain at a distance. Tramarine, obliged to consent to that, went alone the path of the orange-trees to the covered arbor, and at down on a grassy bank perfumed by a thousand little flowers, where, yielding completely to her melancholy, sad reflections plunged her into a profound reverie.

Celiane, wanting to distract her from that somber sadness, sat down at her feet.

"Princess, she said to her, "I flattered myself that you had only come away from your women in order to relieve your troubles by confiding the reasons for them to me, but since my Princess does not hold me in high enough esteem to honor me with her confidence. I beg you at least to listen to the concerts that the nightingales are performing for her."

Tramarine, her eyes fixed on the stream, was paying very little attention to what Celiane was saying. The latter continued: "Don't you admire the happiness of those birds, whose only law is pleasure? For myself, I find that nature, in only according instinct to them, seemed to favor them much more than us. What use is the reason that the gods have reserved for us, which only serves to trouble our pleasures? In truth, the condition of those little animals enchants me, and the state of depression in which I see my princess almost makes me desire to resemble them. What if we were nightingales? How happy they are! No anxiety or regret ever troubles their felicity, they never have any desires that they cannot satisfy, and their joys never costs them any remorse. Why does the enchantress Bonina, who has so much power, not have that of allowing us that metamorphosis? At least I could amuse my Princess with my songs and the vivacity of my caresses, and perhaps please her."

Perceiving that nothing could distract Tramarine, Celiane finally adopted a more serious tone. She had the eloquence of rhetoric; she resumed that of sentiment, and succeeded in touching the heart of the Princess, who decided to confide her secret to her.

"Alas, Celiane," she said to her, sighing, "all your talk, far from easing my pains, only serves to renew them. Is it necessary that we should pass the most beautiful of our days like this? It's high time that I opened my heart to you; always harassed by my women, I have not been able to find the moment.

"I shall not remind you of my childhood; you remember well enough the honors for which it seemed that Heaven had destined me. You see, however, my Celiane, that everything has been reduced to spending my life in solitude, and in spite of your amity and the attentions of the enchantress Bonina, I cannot resist the ennui that is oppressing me. These gardens, whose beauty delights and enchants you, the waters of this stream whose crystalline quality you admire, redouble my distress at every moment, and, by a fatality that I cannot vanquish, and I can no longer distance myself from it. That doubtless appears to you to be a small problem, but when you are informed of my woes, you will no longer be surprised.

"Do you remember, my dear, the journey I made to the spring of Pallas? You know that during my novena, I remained within the enclosure of the temple, where I was served by the priestesses consecrated to the cult of the goddess, a grace only accorded to women of my rank; but the entire court is ignorant of what happened to me there. It is only to your zeal and your amity that I am going to confide a secret that has trouble the repose of my days for such a long time.

"Know, then, that when I had said my prayers to the goddess and had presented my offerings to her, the priestesses took me to the spring, where, after having undressed me and put me in the bath, they went away respectfully, leaving me at liberty. When I was alone, a felt the waters rise up; a slight movement agitated them, and a young man, such as Amour is depicted for us, appeared to my eyes. Timid at the sight of him, I shivered in dread, but, approaching me with a majestic and tender gaze, he took me by the hand and put his arms around me.

"Alas, how seductive it was! I cannot describe to you, my Celiane, the disturbance that was born in my soul. His first glance engraved forever the keenest passion; I know no crime except that of having been able to displease him, and all my misfortunes stem from that of having lost him; it is in vain that I search for him every day in the depths of thee waters.

"But what am I saying, my Celiane? My passion is leading me astray; I cannot think about it without disturbance. I mentioned that which he had spread through all my senses, which prevented me from fleeing; my gaze, attached to such a seductive object, seemed to have taken away all my strength to defend myself from his caresses when the priestesses, coming back, caused him to disappear, and I noticed that as he drew away he placed a finger over his mouth, doubtless to make me understand that I must not reveal what had just happened to me.

"The next day, scarcely had I entered the bath then the same movement that made itself felt the previous day announced the arrival of my vanquisher to me. He approached me, and spoke to me tenderly and passionately. Animated by his presence, my dear, I do not know what I replied, which appeared to transport him with pleasure, because he suddenly took me in his arms and the gleam emerging from his eyes was communicated to my veins, and I felt that I had been set ablaze by a devouring fire. I wanted to flee; my strength abandoned me, but in the midst of my disturbance I thought I perceived that he wanted to take me with him.

"The waters were already swelling, and I felt that I was about to perish. Gripped by fear, a piercing scream escaped me, which attracted the priestesses; but in spite of the shock that was afflicting me, I could not help looking again to see what had become of my vanquisher. I saw him plunged beneath the water, and I distinctly heard a voice that told me that my life and my honor depended on my conduct, and that the felicity of the Prince with whom I had just united myself was attached to the silence that I must maintain. I understood then the sin that I had committed.

"Alas, my dear, it was no longer in my power to repair it. Trembling and desperate, I fell unconscious into the arms of a priestess who had advanced to help me and to discover what had alarmed me. I refrained from confiding the reason to her; I only told her that the rapidity of the waters had frightened me— which caused her to make the resolution to have one of the young women destined to the cult of the goddess enter the bath with me thereafter.

"I confess that I was annoyed by that resolution, foreseeing that it would deprive me of the sight of my dear Prince. I was not mistaken; the rest of my novena passed without me seeing him. Since that day he has been ever present in my mind, but it is in vain that I have searched for him. In spite of my lack of hope, however, I cannot be content except on the edge of waters, which nevertheless only nourish my distress, without the ingrate who is its cause, and perhaps is witness to it, ever deigning to take pity on me."

"In truth, my Lady," said Celiane, "your adventure is one of the most surprising. You will permit me to criticize you for having neglected to employ those reasons, which are more than sufficient to justify you. It's quite certain that Queen Pentaphile could not have refuted their evidence, for it is doubtless some marine god who took on the form of a young man and united with you in the spring. Perhaps it was Neptune himself; and I have no doubt that if the Queen had known all these circumstances, far from ordering your exile, she would unfailingly have placed you on the throne she occupies. You should at least have consulted the enchantress Bonina about such a delicate affair, one which the repose of your days depends."

"What are you saying, my Celiane?" said the princess. "Are you forgetting the silence that was imposed on me? Perhaps at this very moment I'm offending my spouse in daring to confide my secret to you, although he ought to pardon me for that feeble relief. In any case, even if I had not made a vow to sacrifice my repose to him, what proof could I have given of the verity of my adventure? I would have risked my life, and lost all hope of seeing my Prince again. Besides which, you're not unaware of the ennui that afflicted me at Pentaphile's court, and that ennui has been greatly increased since my union with the Prince of the Waters.

"What could I have done in Castora's court, incessantly carrying the image of a Prince who doubtless does not approve of any of its laws? I assure you that I would always have lived in dolor and bitterness; you know how constrained one is there even in one's way of thinking, incessantly harassed by women whose bigotry and falsity renders their commerce unbearable; those women would rather renounce life than their opinions; they only take pleasure in excavating the sentiments of people they want to blacken. Nothing is lacking in their portraits; their scrupulous detail easily reveals the hand that held the brush. At least in this retreat I enjoy the relief of complaining, without fear of the criticism of my enemies."

"I agree, my Lady," said Celiane, "but it is the sole liberty that remains to you, and my princess cannot deny that, dissipation not being the surest remedy against chagrin, yours is nourishing itself and maintaining itself by solitude. I don't know anything as cruel as being incessantly prey to dolor, but permit me, my Lady, to add one more reflection regarding your divine spouse. If it were permitted to criticize the conduct of the gods, I would accuse the one who is the author of your troubles of injustice, for, after all, why has he abandoned you? Such conduct would surprise me less on the part of a mortal; it is so rare to find a sincere attachment among them that I had thought until now that constancy was a virtue that the gods had reserved to themselves, but your adventure has changed my sentiment; it has made me see that, like humans, they lose their appetite for the one they have loved the most as soon as they have satisfied their desires."

"Let us not criticize the gods," said Tramarine. "They doubtless have their reasons when they make us feel the effects of their wrath. It is not for feeble mortals to penetrate the causes, and we ought to submit without a murmur to all that it pleases them to order in our destinies, which are in their hands."

"My Lady," said Celiane, "I can only admire the piety of your sentiments."

"Alas," said the princess, smiling, "How far I still am from the blind submission that they demand from us!"

Lightning and the sound of thunder was heard then, interrupting the conversation, and they made their way back to the tower.

Tramarine, still tormented by the desire to see her spouse the Prince, found herself very agitated during the night. Unable to enjoy the sweetness of slumber, she proposed to Celiane that they go down into the gardens, in order to respire the coolness of a delightful early morning. Dawn was beginning to break, to announce the return of the sun.

Celiane had difficulty putting on a dress in order to follow Tramarine, who was already in the gardens when she traversed them in long strides in order to reach the path of the orange-trees. Perceiving that the Princess had neglected to bring her protective charm, she was about to beg her to go back to the tower when she heard her utter a piercing scream as she turned around.

Celiane, who could not see anyone, could not imagine what had caused her fright; she precipitated her course toward the princess, and fell backwards on perceiving the enchantress Turbulente, who, after having seized Tramarine, forced her to climb into her carriage, and disappeared instantly.

The tender and faithful Celiane reproached herself for her complaisance in following the princess without having alerted her women, or at least the two whom the enchantress Bonina had commissioned to guard her. The tender friend uttered cries that attracted the enchantresses, but while they are running to help her and to share her dolor, we shall follow the unfortunate princess.

Chapter VI
Tramarine's Entry to the Empire of the Waters

Although distressed by the latest cruel blow of fortune, the princess did not appear any less firm in her adversity. Indignant at the evil methods of the perfidious sorceress, she demanded to know, with a great deal of firmness, what could have made her bold enough to dare to come into Bonina's gardens to abduct her, since she could not be unaware of the protection that the enchantress had accorded her.

"It's that protection that offends me," Turbulente replied, "and it's in order to punish both of you that I intend to subject you to the punishment your disobedience merits. Bonina was greatly mistaken if she thought she could impose on me, but in order that she won't seek to surprise us in future, you'll remain under my guard."

At that impertinent speech, Tramarine was content to look at the sorceress with a sovereign scorn, without even deigning to respond. Having arrived at a lair adjacent to the tower, the sorceress ordered the princess to take off the dress she was wearing in order to put on a kind of brown canvas sack, but she pretended not to have heard her, which obliged Turbulente to serve as her chambermaid. Then she made her descend into a dungeon full of venomous beasts, leaving her nothing but a little poor flour steeped in water.

Left alone, Tramarine yielded to all the bitterness of dolor. Several days passed without her being able to close her eyes, but finally, overwhelmed by trouble and anguish, and no longer waiting for anything but death, she fell asleep.

A pleasant dream came to charm her mind, and made her see the Prince, her spouse, as tender and passionate as he had seemed in the spring of Pallas, showing her a door by which she could emerge from slavery.

Calmed by a little repose, Tramarine reflected on the vision she had just had, and, by the light of a lantern that spread a feeble glow, she explored the whole cellar. She did indeed discover a door, which she approached with a disturbance that soon changed into a frightful anguish, on finding it closed by several padlocks.

All her firmness crumbled before that last blow of her misfortune; seeing herself frustrated of the hope she had formed, she could not help bursting into tears, on reflecting on the sequence of disasters that had succeeded one another without interruption.

As everything in life dries up, however, and often gives way to more useful reflections, the Princess, after having exhausted her tears, remembered that she still had the key to Bonina's gardens, the sorceress having neglected to take away everything that she had on her person. She approached the door then, in order to try to open it.

She had no sooner put the key into a padlock than the door collapsed of its own accord, and the dungeon disappeared, by virtue of the power that the enchantress had attached to the key.

Tramarine, surprised to find herself alone on the shore of the sea, racked by pains, fatigue and needs, advanced toward the edge with the design of hurling herself into it. But Prince Verdoyant, who was watching all of Tramarine's movements from the bottom of the sea, saw her gazing at the waves and uttering profound sighs; he feared then the effects of a despair that overlong suffering might have excited. He instructed several undines[53] to stay close to the shore and to keep their eyes incessantly on the princess, ready to receive her in their arms and carry her to a grotto hollowed out under a rocky point, where no mortal had yet dared to take refuge.

The undines obeyed Prince Verdoyant and rendered in considerable numbers to the place where the beautiful Princess was, without attempting to guess their Prince's designs.

Tramarine, believing herself to be alone, and not perceiving in the distance any trace that could suggest to her that the place was inhabited, surrendered to the horror of her situation.

"Alas," she said, sighing, "I perceive only too well that this is the place that my husband has chosen to put an end to my woes; it is, therefore, in the waters that I must end my life; and the last wish that I shall form in dying is that that torture will at least be agreeable to you.

"O Neptune," the Princess added, "if it is true that I have been able to offend you, you ought to pardon my ignorance; do you not have proof enough of my constancy, and have you not avenged yourself by the woes that you have made me suffer for such a long time?"

Then she cast herself into the sea—but the undines, attentive to all her movements, received her in their arms and transported her to the grotto.

Such is the folly of the human mind: the individuals who misfortune overwhelms often prefer death to the services that can be rendered to them.

---

[53] Undines, the water elementals of the document apocryphally attributed to Paracelsus annotated in *Voyages de Milord Céton*, are usually imagined as being invariably female, like the nereids and oceanids of Greek mythology, but the French term has both a male form, *ondins*, and a female one, *ondines*, much as the usually-male *gnomes* are provides with a female equivalent in *gnomides*. English also permits "mermaid" to be supplemented with "merman," and when entire undersea realms are imagined in any language, the presiding figure is usually imagined to be male. As there is no English "undin," however, I have been obliged to make use of the more generic term "water-sprite" in the title of the story and to describe Verdoyant.

Tramarine, believing herself to be surrounded by naiads, allowed her head to fall languidly, sometimes on one of them and sometimes another, warming their bosom with her tears.

The beautiful undines did everything consoling that they could to calm her dolor; finally, they took away the wretched canvas smock with which the evil sorceress had covered her, in order to dress her in a sea-green gauzy robe decorated with silver, pressing her hair between their hands, which they allowed to fall back in waves on to her bosom; then, perceiving by the rising of the waters the arrival of Prince Verdoyant, they withdrew respectfully.

Tramarine, surprised to see them return to the sea, perceived an extraordinary agitation in the waves, and saw a superb chariot rising out of them, made in the form of a seashell, drawn by eight dolphins that appeared to be bounding over the waves. That chariot stopped outside the grotto; then Tramarine saw the young Prince who had been the object of her desires for such a long time, who descended from it, came into the grotto, and lifted her to her feet.

Seizing one of her hands, which he kissed delightedly, he said: "I have finally found you again, beautiful Tramarine, and I swear that I will never abandon you again. The time has come to tell you that I am the Prince of the Water-Sprites; my father's estates are at the bottom of the sea. As I can only live in the waters, I could not rejoin you sooner. Be certain, divine Tramarine, that it has not depended on me to enable you to avoid the woes that you have suffered since our union in the spring of Palas. Forced to abandon you then, I have shared your anguish without being able to abridge it.

"As it is not permitted to us to unite ourselves with a mortal, I have endured many contradictions before being able to determine our people to consent to accord you immortality; and it is only by proving your constancy and discretion that the favor has finally been granted to me. My father the King has demanded that you must pass through the most humiliating ordeals; he is satisfied with the firmness that you have shown on the various occasions when the jealousy of the Amazons has exercised them against you. Will you forgive me, my adorable Princess, for the woes that my love has caused you to suffer?

"But you're lowering your eyes, and making no response. Is it dread or amour that is making you sigh thus? Are you distressed by the idea of uniting yourself with a genius?

"Perhaps," Prince Verdoyant added, "The abode of my empire frightens you. It's true that until now, no mortal had descended into it without losing their life, but Princess, be reassured; I've obtained from my father the King, whose power extends over all the water-sprites, that in favor of a passion that I have been unable to vanquish, you will be admitted to immortality, and receive in his empire the quality of Princess of the Water-Sprites."

Tramarine was still overwhelmed by the emotion of the latest adventure that had happened to her; joy, dread and shame were all agitating her soul in turn, and robbing her of the strength to reply to the Prince, who continued thus:

"However, beautiful Tramarine, even though everything is ready to receive you, and I am sure of the favorable sentiments that you conserved for me, at least until the moment when you confided them to Celiane—don't blush, my princess, to have made that confession of a legitimate ardor; I was present to your eyes at that moment, and from the depths of that stream, formed expressly to renew the memory of the knots that amour ought to tighten, I admired your candor, the piety of your sentiments, and was ready to show myself twenty times, but in addition to the obstacle presented by Celiane's presence, I had not yet obtained from my father the place that I propose you enable you to occupy— I cannot be absolutely happy if you continue to show reluctance to unite yourself forever with my fate."

Tramarine, simultaneously surprised and flattered by the speech of the genius, but unable to convince herself that she could live under water, finally replied to the prince, while gazing at him with an expression that expressed both love and dread: "Forgive me, my Lord, if I have difficulty believing you; I don't doubt the extent of your power, and that is what makes me doubt that such a great Prince would want to lower himself to the extent of uniting himself with a feeble mortal, and that he would prefer her to the beautiful undines with which his empire is full. I do not know the laws of the genii, but I know that when they have chosen a companion, it is no longer permissible for them to change her, unless that law has an exception for women of my species; that would render me the most unfortunate of all creatures, since I would lose by immortality the only resource that the unhappy have in the excess of their woes, and I would be obliged to drag out a life that would become unbearable to me if you cease to love me, no longer being able to die of the dolor of having lost the heart of a prince who could alone attach me to life."

Prince Verdoyant, transported by such a tender confession, employed the most convincing arguments to reassure the Princess, giving her a thousand praises and taking as many kisses.

"Have no fear, divine Tramarine," the genius said. "I swear to you by this heart, which has never loved anyone but you, and by the vast extent of the waters, that no undine will ever share my tenderness henceforth; I also swear to avenge you for the insults that Pentaphile has made you endure by her injurious suspicions; I shall bring down her pride by submitting her realm to the Prince to whom you have given birth, and I shall punish the King of Lydia for the injustice he did you in expelling you from his court."

"Stop, dear prince," said Tramarine. "Remember that it is my father the King that you have just sworn to ruin. Far from complaining of his injustice, ought I not, on the contrary, to bless the day when he banished me from his presence? Is it not to that exile that I owe the joy of being united with you forever? In any case, deceived by the oracle, he doubtless believed my exile necessary to the repose of his people. How many reasons for daring to ask for grace

471

on his behalf! I flatter myself that I might obtain it in the name of the love that you have just sworn to me."

"I can refuse you nothing," said Verdoyant, "and I see with pleasure that the generosity of your heart is manifest in all your actions; I cannot revoke what I have pronounced against the King of Lydia, but I shall soften, in your favor, the rigor of his fate.

"Let us go, dear Tramarine," the genius added. "It is time to descend to the realm of the water-sprites, in order to introduce them to a Princess as worthy of reigning in all hearts by her virtues as by the purity of her sentiments."

In response those words, Tramarine was not able to conceal her fear at the sight of an element that she had always regarded as very dangerous, and although, two hours earlier, despair had driven her to cast herself into it, what had happened to her since had renewed the appetite that one has for life when one can flatter oneself with entering into an eternally durable happiness.

The young princess, at the sight of the danger that she thought she was running, fainted in the arms of the genius, who, without being astonished by her weakness—the final mark of her humanity—made her take a few drops of elementary elixir, which had the virtue not only of recalling her to her senses and fortifying her, but also of taking away the puerile dreads attached to the fate of mortals. Then Tramarine recovered her spirits, and, like a rose struck by the brilliant rays of the sun, reborn from the coolness of a beautiful night, which, extending its petals to a vivifying dew, stands up on its stem and seems to salute the beneficent dawn that has resuscitated it, the heart of the Princess opened to the sweet transports of joy; that joy reanimated her enfeebled senses, and her extinct eyes reopened to the light, shining with the flame of pleasure.

"How ashamed I am of my weakness," she said to the genius, with a tender and animated gaze. "But what has so suddenly dissipated my fears? Dear prince, henceforth, you may command me; I'm ready to go with you." Then she offered him her hand, with the smile of amour.

Verdoyant took her to his chariot, and the dolphins, which seemed charmed to be carrying away such a beautiful Princess, pranced over the waters, dived as they accelerated their course, and arrived a few hours later in the capital city of the water-sprites, where the King made his usual abode. To enter into the palace they traversed several large courtyards paved with emeralds and passed under an arcade sustained by twenty-four columns of ice. Several officers of the court were lined up there, who made speeches to the princess on behalf of the entire estate. There was no artillery salute; although the water-sprites are perfectly familiar with cannons, they make no use of them.

To begin with, Tramarine, along with a numerous cortege, was taken into a large gallery ornamented with monochrome paintings on the most beautiful glass imaginable; the frames were made of diamonds of different colors, whose assortment made an admirable view. At the end of the gallery was a throne made from a single diamond, which might have been taken for the chariot of the sun when it appears with its full brightness; it is certain that if Tramarine had not participated in her husband's divinity, she would never have been able to sustain the glare.

On the throne, the King of the Water-Sprites was sitting, with a trident in his hand, the sole ornament of his grandeur. To his right were the principal officers of the crown, to his left the beautiful undines who were the ornament of the court. The genius Verdoyant, having approached the throne with Princess Tramarine, introduced her to His Majesty, asking him to accord her all the favors that she had acquired by her virtues, her merit and her suffering.

The young Princess, educated in the mythology of the pagans, did not know any other religion or any principles other than those she had received. Convinced that she was in the presence of Neptune, she addressed him as such.

"Great God, sovereign of the waters, whose empire commands the whole universe...."

"Stop, Princess," said the king, interrupting her mid-sentence. "I am not a god. It is true that I enjoy immortality, but I obtain all my power from a singular divinity, whom we all worship and who formed everything there is in the universe. It is by courtesy of his omnipotence that we reign over the waters." Then, addressing his son in a voice that made the vaults of his palace tremble and, in swelling the entire ocean, announced a furious tempest, he said: "How, Prince, have you dared to surprise me by choosing a pagan to participate in immortality by a union that can no longer be broken?"

Prince Verdoyant, who perceived that Tramarine, nonplussed and trembling, no longer dared raise her eyes, said to the King of the Water-Sprites, in order to appease his anger: "My Lord, you're not unaware that amour is a sentiment born involuntarily, which is nourished by hope. That passion establishes its domination over everything that breathes in this vast universe, its choice often made at first glance. Amour examines nothing and puts no difference between the heart of a pagan and that of a genius, both burning with the same fire and seeking only to nourish it. It is true that I have not examined the beliefs of Princess Tramarine; her misfortunes have touched me, her virtues, her graces, her talents and her beauty have charmed me, and I have judged her worthy of a happier fate. It is for that reason that I have sought all the means of liberating her from the yoke of death; but my Lord, I can answer to you for her docility in listening to the instruction you want her to be given, and she will submit without a murmur to all your wishes."

After confirming the word that Prince Verdoyant had just given to His Water-Sprite Majesty, Tramarine added that she promised to conform to anything that was demanded of her, convinced that such an enlightened genius would not seek to mislead her.

The King seemed satisfied with that response and ordered that she be taken to the apartment destined for her.

Chapter VII
Tramarine is taken to the Hall of Marvels

The genius Verdoyant accompanied Tramarine to a crystal pavilion illuminated by carbuncles that appeared to be as many suns. One of the faces of the pavilion overlooked a flower-bed enameled by a thousand kinds of flowers unknown on land, which spread a delightful perfume through the air. A concert of a new kind was heard; voices were singing the praises of the genius Verdoyant and those of Princess Tramarine. When the concert ended, she was taken into a hall of magic mirrors that had the virtue of representing everything that was happening in the world.

Surprised by that marvel, the Princess told the genius that she would be very glad to know what had happened to Celiane since the malevolent Turbulente had so cruelly separated them.

"Fix your attention on the mirrors," said the Prince, "and all your desires will be fulfilled."

Tramarine looked into one of the mirrors, which first showed her the enchantress Bonina's gardens. Celiane appeared there, fainted, and the women commissioned to guard the princess hastened to help her. Their distress and anxiety were evident in their eyes. Tramarine saw her, after recovering from that weakness, recounting her misfortune; her speech was interrupted by sobs, and tears flowed in abundance; it seemed that her words were traces on the mirror. All the Princess' women present at that narration appeared to be in despair, but the deplorable state that the unfortunate Celiane was in did not permit them to scold her for her negligence.

Then she saw the enchantress Bonina arrive, who, informed of Tramarine's abduction, went into her study to consult the great books there. She spent a long time leafing through them with a singular attention; then, she drew several figures, with the great pentacle of Solomon, in order to oblige one of the genii inhabiting the air to descend in order to inform her of Tramarine's fate.

By means of her conjurations she eventually compelled the genius Jael to inform her that the Princess was united forever with the genius Verdoyant, Prince of the Water-Sprites, and had been admitted to the fate of immortals. The enchantress, content to learn such good news, hastened to make Celiane party to it, and gave her the option of remaining with her or being transported to the realm of her choice. Celiane preferred the society of Bonina to all the other advantages that the enchantress offered to give her.

"Look now," said Verdoyant, "at the despair of Turbulente; it ought to serve you as a comedy."

Tramarine saw the disheveled sorceress running in response to the loud sound that struck her ears when the genius broke and overturned the dungeon that she had built by the force of her enchantments. That Megaera tore out her hair in despair, and uttered howls similar to those of Cerberus, imploring the Furies to support her rage and fury, and uttering a thousand imprecations against Bonina, whom she believed to be responsible for liberating her captive.

Then she was seen mounting her chariot, which was harnessed to six monstrous rats, in order to go consult Pencanaldon, a famous magician.[54] As she was entirely preoccupied with her vengeance, however, she abandoned herself to the conduct of her rats by leaving the bridle around their necks and they tipped her into a precipice where she and her vehicle were smashed, and they saw her serve as pasture for the rats that had been hauling her.

Tramarine, whose heart was excellent, could not see that spectacle without horror, in spite of the evils that Turbulente had made her suffer. She turned to another mirror, which enabled her to see Queen Pentaphile, who, after having been told that she had departed for her exile, appeared to repent of the harsh judgment that she had, so to speak, been forced to pronounce against the daughter of the King of Lydia. The sovereign shut herself away for several days without allowing anyone into her presence.

Finally, no longer able to contain her dolor, she sent for the Chancelleress, made her ardent reproaches for having deprived her forever of the sight of a lovable princess who ought to have been the permanent ornament of the court and to whom she had intended to hand over the government of the state shortly, sensing her own forces fading by the day.

"Would it not have been punishment enough," added Pentaphile, "to be unaware of the fate of her son, without ever being able to hear any news of him? Besides which, the King of Lydia might repent of having deprived her of the rights she has to his crown; might he not also ask me to return her in order to form some alliance useful to his kingdom? It is against my will that her exile has been pronounced, and insufficient regard was paid to her rank and birth."

The Chancelleress, judging by the Queen's regrets that she was in danger of losing her favor, wanted to make one last effort at least to conserve her position; that is why she replied that if Her Majesty desired to see the Princess again, it would be very easy to bring her back to court; that the enchantress Bonina, who had taken her under her protection, would take pleasure in returning her; and that the sentence that Her Majesty had passed would serve all the same to maintain her people in their duty, which was the sole objective that her Council had had in mind in the condemnation that they had been obliged to pronounce in order to subjugate her subjects to the observation of the laws that Her Majesty had established herself.

---

[54] This sentence appears to be mistaken; Pencanaldon subsequently features in the plot as the king of a realm neighboring Lydia, and it seems likely that the magician Turbulente wanted to consult is actually Philomendragon, to whom Camagnole has taken Tramarine's son.

"It required a striking example," the Chancelleress added, "which could intimidate them; but Your Majesty always has it in her power to grant mercy to persons she thinks worthy of it. I will only dare to observe to Your Majesty that, in recalling the Princess to your court after the fatal sentence that it was necessary to pronounce against her, it is to be feared that she will conserve a bitter memory of it and that when authority is in her hands, she might change the entire form of the government, giving entry into the realm of new customs."

This adroit discourse did not save the Chancelleress from disgrace. Her enemies, jealous of the power she had usurped, did not fail to take advantage of the circumstances to finish blackening her in their sovereign's mind. Several memoirs were presented to her, in which there was evidence that the Chancelleress had animated the sorceresses against the Princess with a view to taking possession of all authority, and of the intrigues that she had long been fomenting among the troops, tending to put the administration of the realm in her hands. All the accusations were proven, and it was also remarked that the principal responsibilities of State were no longer occupied by any but her creatures.

The Queen, surprised to discover that he had been deceived by a woman in whom she had put her full confidence and whom she had every reason to believe to be attached to her by virtue of all the favors she had never ceased to lavish upon her, immediately issued an order for her to be taken to the Island of Ennui, finding her too culpable to deprive her of her life. The order was promptly carried out, and all the treasures she had amassed were confiscated, to the profit of the troops.

Tramarine was curious to learn the location of the Island of Ennui, of which she had never heard mention. The mirror immediately showed her a marshy place, perpetually filled by a dense fog, where the sun's rays never made themselves felt: an arid terrain filled with frightful monsters, which, by virtue of their venom, emitted a pestilential atmosphere; nothing grew on the island except poisonous plants. It was in that horrible place that Tramarine saw her enemy arrive, but what she could not see without shivering with horror was what those monsters did, in seizing the criminal and devouring her entrails, one attaching itself to gnaw her heart and others attacking the various parts of her body. By an unusual prodigy, far from those creatures robbing her of her life, they seemed to renew it by means of her suffering.

"It is thus," said the genius Verdoyant, "that all the criminals of state who have abused the confidence of their master by vexing the people ought to suffer for several centuries."

The Princess, continuing her observation of the realm of Castora, remarked that to replace the Chancelleress, a woman of distinguished merit had been appointed, who was strongly attached to her interests. As soon as she had taken the oath of fidelity, her first concern was to propose to the Council the recall of the Princess, whose virtue and superior merit were a sure guarantee of her good conduct. She added, addressing the Queen, that after having given an example of

476

severity in the person of Princess Tramarine, Her Majesty could not give one of clemency in any object more worthy, and at the same time more agreeable to her people.

The Queen yielded without difficulty to this sage advice, and, in order to favor the person who had given it she appointed her to inform the Princess of the mercy that she was showing her in ordering her recall. A detachment of four thousand Amazons was commanded to honor the princess' triumph.

Tramarine, satisfied to learn that they had finally been forced to render to her birth and virtue the justice that was their due, unembarrassed by the regrets that her loss might occasion, and impatient to know what had become of her son, passed on to another mirror. There she saw the sorceress Camagnole, who, after taking possession of the young prince, climbed back into her cabriolet, which caprice took to the abode of Philomendragon, one of the greatest magicians there was. He was a furious, malevolent, rascally and bloodthirsty man; he had instructed Camagnole in the magic arts, and one could say that she knew almost as much as he did.

As soon as she arrived they examined the little prince together, and Philomendragon, after having traced a few figures on a large ebony table, made such a frightful grimace as he showed them to Camagnole that Tramarine, trembling for her son, turned her eyes away from the mirror with a terrible alarm and looked at the genius.

"Dear Prince," she said to him, agitated by anguish, "Will you suffer that abominable sorceress to dispose of the life of the prince your son?"

"Have no fear, dear Tramarine; it is not in the power of the magician to attempt the life of a child who owes his birth to a genius, and the grimace you have just seen him make is only occasioned by the knowledge he has acquired, by means of his art, that he can never harm him."

"But is it not in your power to take him out of the hands of those two monsters," said Tramarine, "who will henceforth be solely occupied in spoiling the mind of the young Prince by giving him false principles and a very bad education?"

"Your reflections are just," said Verdoyant, "but I have foreseen all the inconveniences that might arise, and I can assure you, in order to tranquilize you completely, that one of my friends, a sylph, has taken responsibility for watching over the conduct of your son."

"I thought that your power was limitless," said Tramarine. "At least tell me his destiny."

"I cannot satisfy you on that point at present; be content with the promise I give you that he will be very fortunate."

Tramarine persisted, and the genius, by refusing to content her, irritated her. Women, like men, are naturally curious; the desire to know seemed to be innate within us, and the great ought not to neglect anything in the care they take for their education; talents, sciences and humanity ought to serve to sustain the dignity of their rank, although birth often does not give intelligence and judgment; one might think that nature sometimes compensates those she has caused to be born in a mediocre estate—but that is enough moralizing.

Tramarine persisted with a great deal of ardor; she employed everything she could imagine to vanquish the resistance of the genius, but, in spite of her insistence, seeing that he would not give in, she took his refusal for pure obstinacy, made him a thousand reproaches, complained of his lack of amity, and that she was very unfortunate to have had so much confidence and sentiments so tender for a Prince who responded so poorly to them. Tears and sighs were combined with these reproaches, which softened the genius to the point that he was ready to yield to her impatience.

"What are you demanding of me?" he replied, in an impassioned manner. "Know that my silence is attached to the happiness of the young Prince; if I speak, his fortunate destiny will be changed to one of frightful misfortunes.

Far from yielding to his arguments, Tramarine, convinced that what the genius had said was simply to avoid satisfying the desire she had to learn her son's fate, redoubled her insistence. "At least give me," the Princess added, "this mark of confidence. What fear do you have of my indiscretion? Are not my son's interests a sufficiently powerful motive to enclose within myself a secret that might harm him? Besides which, since it is no longer permissible for me to live on land, the deposit cannot be contrary to him."

What can Amour not do? His power is manifest in the heavens, in the air, on land and under the sea. The genius was about to yield to the insistence of the Princess when the King of the Water-Sprites suddenly appeared in the hall. His presence surprised the Princess infinitely; her disturbance was manifest in the blush that covered her face. She feared that the King might have overheard the altercation she had just had with Prince Verdoyant; she did not know yet that a genius has the power to read what is happening in the heart of a person by looking at her.

The King of the Water-Sprites, judging, by what had just happened as a result of Tramarine's indiscreet curiosity, that she was not yet sufficiently purged of the terrestrial substance that had enveloped her, and that the dose of the elementary elixir that Verdoyant had given her when he enabled her to descend into the empire of the waters had not been sufficient for her repose, ordered her to take another large glass. That completed the process of rendering her entirely similar to the undines, enabling her to envisage the things that affected her most with a Stoic tranquility; and, without losing sight of everything that interested her on land , she only spoke about them henceforth with the modesty appropriate to a Princess of the Waters.

Several months went by, after which the King, content with the dispositions in which he saw Tramarine, engaged the Prince of the Water-Sprites to take her on a journey throughout the immense extent of his liquid estates, in order to make herself known to al his subjects, and at the same time to instruct her in the religion and the laws of the empire. He accorded fifteen years for her voyage, in order that she could stay for a while in the most curious places.

Perhaps that seems like a long time to people uninstructed in the usages of that world, but let them be informed that in the realm of the waters, that time passes like a single day. The voyage that the King of the Water-Sprites ordered Tramarine to make can be regarded as an aspect of his politics. The Princess was the first person of the land he had admitted into his empire without being subject to the yoke of death, which changed entirely the way of thinking of the inhabitants of our hemisphere. The monarch feared, perhaps with reason, that in spite of the double dose of elementary elixir that Tramarine had been made to take, she might fall back into her former weakness, especially if she found herself within range of admiring every day the singular beauties contained in the Hall of Marvels. It was, therefore, in order to fortify her in their maxims and their laws that the voyage was ordered.

It is to be presumed that, although Tramarine was the most perfect of women, she had not yet acquired the virtues and gifts with which the genii are endowed at birth, and that, in spite of the great dispositions she had for the sciences, it was only after many years that she would be filled with the admirable talents that are only accorded to genii of the first order. The King, occupied with the preparations for the voyage of the Prince and Princess, and wanting it to be made with all the pomp due to aquatic majesty, ordered that their retinue would be composed of ten thousand male water-sprites and three thousand undines.

Perhaps one might think that such a numerous cortege would be a great embarrassment in such a long voyage; that is why I ought to inform my reader that water-sprites do not experience any; as they are genii they have no need of any provisions, air being sufficient for their subsistence. Tramarine, having become immortal and, in consequence, participating in all the virtues of water-sprites, was also dispensed of the needs to which human nature has subjected feeble mortals.

Chapter VIII
Voyages in the Empire of the Waters

On the day fixed for the departure of the Prince and Princess, they took their leave of His Aquatic Majesty, after which they mounted their carriage, which their retinue followed in vehicles of mother-of-pearl shape in the form of seashells—which must have been the most beautiful sight in the world for those who had the privilege of witnessing it.

To begin with, the genius headed southwards. He stopped in a place where frequent battles took place, which often only served to populate the empire of the waters.

"I see," said the Prince, "that you are gazing in surprise at that multitude of new inhabitants, who have been unknown to you until now. Know, my dear Tramarine, that these people you see arriving at every instant are individuals who have just been subjected to the fate attached to all mortals, death, and that they have been condemned by the Almighty to live among the water-sprites for a number of years, proportionate to the sins they committed on earth. Although I am already informed of their conduct, I shall nevertheless interrogate a few of them, in order to make you aware of how far the malevolence of the humans who presently inhabit the earth can go."

At the same time, the genius summoned a man who appeared clad in a very singular fashion, and asked him why he had been condemned to drink forty pints of elementary tea every day for a hundred thousand years.[55]

"Prince," said the wretch, "although my penitence will be long, I give thanks to the Almighty for not having given me one more rigorous; the hope I have of a happy future will enable me to support it without murmuring, because nothing is so consoling for an unfortunate as to be persuaded that his pains will one day be changed into pure and real pleasures; for it seems that one anticipates one's happiness in the certainty one has of arriving there.

"This, then, is my history in brief, in order not to weary the attention of the Princess who is accompanying you.

---

[55] "*Thé elementaire*" [elementary tea] can be found in two works by the offbeat moral philosopher Jean-Baptiste de Boyer d'Argens in the context of posthumous rewards and punishments. In *Lettres juives, ou Correspondance philosophique* (1737), however, it is not a punishment but a solace given to mild and virtuous women who join the company of water-nymphs, in contrast to the fate of proud and arrogant ones, who go to dwell in fire with the salamanders. In *Lettres cabalistiques* (1754), by contrast—which is presumably Madame Robert's source—drinking sixty pints of it per day is the punishment inflicted on a bad cardinal.

"Elevated to the foremost dignities of the state by the bounty of a great monarch who had accorded me all his confidence, far from employing my talents to merit his generosity by my gratitude and a sincere attachment to my master's interests, the sudden elevation of my fortune only augmented my pride. Having become insolent after the success of a few enterprises, I thought I could risk anything. I began by dissipating the finances, and was then obliged to overburden the realm with onerous state debts; in order to hide the bad employment I was making of the immense sums levied on the people every day, I provoked unjust wars in which the bravest officers and the best soldiers perished, and which spread desolation in all spirits. Then I engaged the Prince in false steps capable of diminishing his power, because they would increase mine. Conduct so opposed to the justice of government eventually attracted the hatred of the public to me; my actions were revealed and the disabused monarch had my subjected to the penalty due to my crimes."

Tramarine, surprised by the ingratitude and bad faith of that favorite, asked the Prince whether one could put any trust in the speech of a man accustomed for so long to lies and intrigue, and whether he was not still trying to impose on them.

"No, my dear Tramarine," said the genius. "when humans have quit the bodies that envelope them and bind them to the earth—as those you can see are only fantastic—it is no longer in their power to disguise the truth or to seek to deceive us. Sent here, in order to execute the sentence of their condemnation, nothing can diminish the rigor of their fate."

"Tell me, I pray you, whether all these people I see arriving in a crowd, and who are said to have died for the defense of their liberty, are condemned to the same punishment; those people seem to me to be full of candor and good faith."

"It's true," said Verdoyant, "that they are simple and devoid of malice; but here punishments are proportionate to the sins one has committed, and all those you see are only descending into the waters in order to be purified there. Less culpable than the others, their punishments will be much lighter and shorter, and they will not be obliged to drink the tea."

Tramarine demanded a much more extensive explanation from the genius, to which he lent himself gladly, for the sake of the Princess' instruction; but as that conversation was very long and perhaps a trifle tedious, we shall pass on to other matters that are perhaps of greater interest.

PART TWO

Chapter IX
The History of the Great Ogress

After Verdoyant had instructed Tramarine on the principal articles that ought to interest her, they continued on their way, and paused on the edge of a river that served as the boundary between two nations subject to great revolutions. The Princess was surprised to see a host of people camped as if in battalions, whose various garments formed a rather singular tableau.

"What do those disguises signify?" Tramarine asked. "Doubtless they're preparing to play some comedy and have chosen this location to serve as their theater."

The genius, smiling at Tramarine's error, told her that the different costumes she could see only served to distinguish the regiments composing the army of a sovereign very respectable for his virtues, whom they had served for a long time with much zeal and attachment.

"One of these peoples is guided by a liking for novelty, the other by that for riches. Ambition dominates some, others permit themselves to be carried away by weakness; the largest number have joined forces in order to shake the authority that ought to hold them in respect—but to explain their dispute to you it's necessary to begin by telling you how it originated.

"In one of the republics of this empire, a daughter was born of discord and lies, whose seductive intelligence was able to win over the principal officers of the reigning Princess, who, seduced herself by deceptive appearances, had her come to her court. At first no one thought of opposing the progress that the young woman made in the heart of their sovereign, but as she gradually grew up she became an ogress who was so well fortified in the mind of the Princess that she invaded a part of her authority, and in spite of the obscurity of her birth she nevertheless procured a quantity of admirers who, in order to captivate her good graces and obtain her favors, hastened every day to compose elegies, eclogues and epistles, which were presented to her with great ceremony; it was by that means that she was able to discover those who were most attached to her.

"As she is vain, ambitious, proud and arrogant, and has completely captivated the mind of the Princess, she has had the skill, in order to augment her authority, to change the entire form of the previous government in order to establish new laws; in sum. nothing is any longer done except on her orders; no one is as audacious as those who execute her wishes; they are set to attempt the most extraordinary things every day, without anyone being able to oppose their designs. By virtue of a species of consideration that is believed to be owed to the eminent titles with which they are adorned, they are emboldened to undertake anything—but what is even more singular is that they carry out with assurance what other people would never have dared to imagine.

"The faithful subjects of the Princess, repelled by all these actions, and even more so by the blind submission that the ogress wants to demand of them, have revolted. The boldest have attacked the ogress personally, saying that she is a daughter whose name and birth are unknown; some claim that she is a bastard. That has formed different parties in the estates of the Princess, and many of her subjects are seeking to shake off the yoke of the adoptive daughter, especially since she has attempted to invade all governments and attribute to herself graces that previously ought only to be accorded to the Princess. It is even claimed that she wants to distance the subjects from the obedience that they owe to their sovereigns, by means of new constitutions that seem contradictory and entirely opposed to the old morality. Many corybants have refused to submit to it, and the majority have rallied to the standard of rebellion, giving rise to perpetual wars. The different nations that you can see have assembled here in order to demand the head of the ogress."

"Tell me," asked Tramarine, "what reasons the Princess can have for wanting obstinately to compromise her authority, by leaving it in the hands of a daughter who might set all her estates ablaze? Ought she not rather relegate her to some distant island, in order to reestablish the peace that every sovereign ought to desire in order to ensure the wellbeing of her people? Could she not marry her to some foreign prince powerful enough and firm enough to reduce her to obedience? The Great Turk or the great Khan of Tartary appear to be sufficiently capable of it."

"That's true," said Verdoyant, "but they have refused. However, plenipotentiaries have just been appointed to negotiate a peace; they have orders to propose the marriage of the ogress to Philomendragon, who, as you know, is a great magician and one of the most monstrous ogres ever to have appeared. It is hoped that the Princess will be able to yield to the wishes of her people and that the marriage will deliver them from the tyranny of the young woman, all the more so as the magician's estates are at the antipodes of those of the Princess, which should ensure that there is no reason to dread such a union."

"For myself," said Tramarine, "I fear it, since our son the Prince is in the power of that magician, and I regard his union with this evil ogress as a superabundance of misfortune for the dear child."

"I've already told you, Princess," the genius went on, "that he cannot attempt anything against my son; but to set your mind completely at rest, know that the sylph who is charged with his education presently has him in his power."

The Prince and Princess were interrupted then by noises of conflict that became audible. All the soldiers were running to arrange themselves beneath their standards, and a black swarm of auxiliary troops, advancing in a disorderly fashion, came together and formed into a huge square battalion.

Then the ogress appeared; she resembled one of the pyramids of Egypt. Her head, which was triangular, had three faces; in one she seemed mild and modest; that was the one she showed when she wanted to subjugate new peoples; she showed the second, painted with arrogance and pride, when she had achieved her objectives, and the third face as marked with a furious and menacing expression. Her arms and legs were as many serpents that enabled her to move.

Tramarine, frightened by the sight of such a hideous monster, did not want to stay any longer by the bank of the river; that is why she never knew the outcome of the battle that took place there.

Chapter X
The Accomplishment of the Oracle

The genius, yielding to Tramarine's desire to go away, took her to the shores of Lydia. The princess, catching sight of an old man whose majestic air seemed to inspire respect, felt very emotional.

"My dear Prince," she said to the genius, "I can't resist the tender emotions I feel for that venerable old man. Grant me, I beg you, the satisfaction of conversing with him."

The Prince of the Water-Sprites complaisant, as all amorous genii are, told Tramarine that she was free to interrogate him, and simultaneously beckoned the old man to approach; although he was not unaware that it was the King of Lydia, he wanted to give the Princess the pleasure of discovering that for herself.

Tramarine, sensing an increase in the interest she was taking in the monarch—for she had no doubt that he was one—asked him, very gently, and in the tone that tenderness and pure amity inspire, who he was and what country of the land he had inhabited before descending to the realm of the water-sprites.

"I am Ophtes," the King replied. "I reigned for more than sixty years in Lydia."

At those words, if Tramarine had not enjoyed the prerogatives attached to great genii, which never permit the experience of any weakness, she would surely have fainted, but she got away with a slight shock.

"Oh, my Father!" cried the Princess. "I can therefore enjoy the happiness of seeing you again; but have you nothing to regret in what destiny has procured for me?"

"My daughter," said the King of Lydia, observing in her the tender emotion that one feels at the sight of an unexpected pleasure, "you will learn, by the story of my adventures, the fatality of my destiny and the accomplishment of an oracle that, until now, has always appeared to me to be impenetrable.

"I know," the King went on, "that you have been instructed in the home of the Queen of Castora of the principal events that had happened in Lydia before the time of your exile. I shall therefore pass over rapidly the first years that went by thereafter, since nothing remarkable happened to me.

"I was enjoying a perfect security; my crown having been ensured in my family by the birth of two princes that the gods had granted me, when I learned that Pencanaldon, whose estates are adjacent to mine, had made an irruption into one of my provinces. I learned at the same time that he had taken possession of one of the strongest places in Lydia. Surprised by such a move, sure that he had no complaint to make to me about anything whatsoever, having never had any quarrel with him, I hastened to have my troops assembled, with a view to opposing the rapidity of his further progress. I departed at the head of fifty thousand men, all hardened soldiers, in the hope of expelling the perfidious Pencanaldon and punishing him for his audacity, but Fortune, who had until then always been favorable to me, made me sense keenly, in that encounter, the scant trust that one ought to place in that inconstant goddess.

"As disorders were increasing by the day, I was constrained to force my march in order to halt my enemy's progress, I finally arrived a short distance from the army of the treacherous Pencanaldon, who was waiting for me in good order in order to do battle. I had resolved to try to avoid combat, in order to give my troops time to rest, but my soldiers were incensed themselves by the bravado of the enemy; I was no longer able to arrest their impetuous courage; the battle was gradually engaged; it was one of the bloodiest. I maintained the advantage for a long time, but just when I was about to render myself master of the battle-field, by a fatality that I cannot comprehend, fear suddenly gripped my entire army; my troops broke up, the greater number taking flight, and in spite of my efforts, I was never able to rally them. In the end, what can I tell you? My defeat was complete and I also had the misfortune of being taken prisoner, with the Queen, who had followed me in the expedition.

"Pencanaldon, glorious with the success of his victory, took us to his capital city, attaching us to his triumphal chariot like miserable slaves. Then he imprisoned us in a tower built on a rocky point that seemed to project far out to sea. What augmented my despair further was that he had the cruelty of separating me from Cliceria.

"I learned a few days later, from two officers commissioned to guard me, who were chatting familiarly together, believing me to be asleep, that the cause of all the disorders that had just occurred was simply the love that the perfidious Pencanaldon had for the Queen, because he flattered himself that, having vanquished me, he would have no difficulty in seducing Cliceria, by proposing to share his kingdom with her and allowing her to dispose entirely of my estates, which he wanted to unite with his crown, having no doubt that, being his prisoner, he could force me to repudiate it when I thought that I could only obtain my liberty at that price.

"Thus, blinded by his passion, he thought that he would find no obstacle to his evil designs, and even dared to declare them to the queen without any hesitation. Cliceria, indignant at the proposition that he had the audacity to make of marrying her once he had succeeded in making me sign the document that would return her freedom of action, marked the scorn that she had for such sentiments as his with so much pride that, far from wanting to hear him out, she went to shut herself in her cabinet, forbidding him to reappear in her presence unless the honor, virtue and probity that he had banished from his court returned to animate his soul and inspire in him new sentiments and procedures worthy of being adopted by Ophtes and Cliceria.

"For a long time, the unworthy Pencanaldon employed the most tender pleas and supplications in trying to seduce the Queen, but, perceiving that they were only augmenting the scorn that she had for him, he changed his conduct, substituting the most terrible threats if she would not yield to his desires. All those different assaults were in vain; Cliceria, fortified by glory and virtue, sustained them with a firmness worthy of her rank.

"I was informed of some of her troubles by one of the Queen's women, who, enjoying a little more liberty, had found a means of winning over one of my guards, who introduced her into my apartment by night. Although the woman strove to diminish somewhat the frightful situation in which Cliceria found herself, my mind, always industrious in tormenting me, enabled me to see it as it was.

"Overwhelmed by dolor and, unable to do anything to help in her distress a princess who was all the more dear to me because I was convinced that she owed all her woes to the affection she had always had for me, I might at least be able to reduce them. It was difficult to imagine that subjects I had treated more as a father than a king would be so little interested in my fate as not to form the design of delivering me from my captivity; in consequence, I could only exhort the Queen to suffer constantly tribulations that she could not avoid.

Pencanaldon, who did not want to leave the Queen, gave his generals orders to take possession of all of Lydia, which they succeeded in doing in two campaigns, no one opposing their rapid conquests. I learned the sad news that my people had surrendered, without any resistance to the perfidious tyrant, and what completed my despair was the loss of the two young princes that I had left in my palace, under the guidance of their tutor, a man whose probity was known to me. I had feared, rightly, the cruelties of that enemy of humanity, but that was the final blow of his perfidy.

"The Queen, who was pregnant when we were taken prisoner, had hidden her condition with extreme care, Celinde, the maidservant in whom she had the most confidence, offered to deliver her of a princess that she was disposed to conceal from the sight of the cruel Pencanaldon, when he came into the Queen's apartment unexpectedly, and, seizing that innocent victim, took her away himself to give her to his daughter, named Argiliane, with orders to have her exposed in the forest to the voracity of wild beasts.

"Far from obeying her father's orders, Argiliane, shivering at such an inhuman sentence, took the little princess to the Craintive Island. That island had been given to her as her privilege, with the power of command there. After having endowed the child with all imaginable perfections she gave her the name Brillante, and, to protect her from Pencanaldon's research, in case he discovered her disobedience, she placed her in the hands of the wife of a shepherd to be nursed, instructing her not to let anyone see her on any pretext whatsoever.

"The Queen learned that Princess Argiliane had taken charge of her daughter. She knew that the princess was a great sorceress, but she did not know that she only applied herself to the sciences, and especially that of Chiromancy, in order to do good, and with a view to impeding her father's cruelties. Cliceria, whose woes were increasing every day, ordered Celinde, a woman of great intelligence, to employ all her means to reach the princess. Celinde, full of zeal for the service of her mistress, insinuated herself into Argiliane's presence with great ingenuity; she had the art of gaining confidence, and depicted the misfortunes of the Queen in such a touching fashion that she was softened in her favor, and eventually promised to take a keen interest in the unfortunate Cliceria.

"Argiliane, whose heart was excellent, groaned every day, without daring to make her complaints known, over her father's barbaric conduct; that is why she was easily determined to do everything in her power to help the oppressed queen, by procuring her a thousand assistances to sustain her against Pencanaldon's pursuits and help her to support her woes—but without daring to declare herself overtly for fear of irritating her father.

"For a long time, Pencanaldon had been planning to marry his daughter to Prince Corydon, his nephew, who paid court to her assiduously. Although Argiliane recognized qualities in him superior to the other princes of the blood, however, the aversion that she had for dependency always made her distance herself from that union. In the fear that her father would one day constrain her, she made the resolution to propose to the princes that he should marry the Princess of Lydia, who had the reputation of being one of the most beautiful princesses in the world.

"'I know that your sentiments are too delicate,' Argiliane added, 'for you to make use of the influence that you have acquired over my father's mind. I can never be yours, in spite of the preference that I admit I have always given you over your rivals. If I could determine myself to make a choice, you alone would be capable of fixing it, but the resolution I have made to spend my life in independence determines me to beg you no longer to think about our union.'

"Prince Corydon seemed devastated by those words; he could only respond with a sigh, and although he had never felt any great passion for Argiliane, the habit he had formed of seeing her and conversing with her frequently about science and the interests of the State, and perhaps also the hope of acquiring by the marriage one of the most beautiful kingdoms in the world, caused him to suffer the Princess' speech impatiently. He complained bitterly of her indifference and employed all the eloquence that could be formed by an ambition founded on hopes that the King had nourished for a long time. Eventually perceiving that he could not touch Argiliane's heart, however, he limited himself to getting her to conserve her esteem for him, adding that he would always put his happiness and his glory into meriting it.

"It was after that conversation that the Princess advised Celinde to see Prince Corydon, in order to praise the charms of the Princess of Lydia, who ought to be at the court of Pentaphile, Queen of Castora. 'I know,' said Argiliane, 'that she is ravishingly beautiful, that she had all the virtues worthy of a throne, and that Pentaphile has destined her own for her. You ought then to ask him to liberate the Queen of Lydia, and tell him that Tramarine will be the price of the services he will render to that princess. Add, on my part, the assurances of reigning in Lydia after the death of Ophtes, and that I promise to do everything in my power to assist him.'

"The Queen informed me of that negotiation via Celinde, whom I ordered to follow Argiliane's advice exactly. That clever woman had no difficulty persuading Prince Corydon, who had already heard mention on numerous occasions of the advantages that Tramarine had acquired over other women; he was charmed by the prospect that Celinde offered him of an alliance that might satisfy both his desires and his ambition, since he saw himself forced to renounce that of Argiliane. Those advantages, combined with the promises she had made, completed his determination.

"The Queen, delighted to learn that Celinde had succeeded so well in her negotiation, sent her to give me the great news. Celinde therefore came one night to tell me that Corydon had promised to liberate the Queen and then take her to Pentaphile's estates, on condition that I ratified the agreement that the Prince had made with Queen Cliceria. I had, therefore, to engage myself by that treaty to accord to Prince Corydon Princess Tramarine, who, by virtue of her birth and the death of her brothers, had become the heir presumptive of the Kingdom of Lydia. By the same treaty, I had to declare him my successor to the crown in the case that Tramarine had disposed of her hand in favor of some other prince. On those conditions, the Prince promised to return with a powerful army to deliver me from my captivity, and then help me to reconquer my throne.

"As you can imagine, I accepted, without hesitation, propositions that, in the circumstances in which I found myself, appeared to me to be very advantageous. Deprived of all help and languishing for ten years in the most cruel captivity, I consented without difficulty to everything that was demanded of me, and had the Queen told that I gave her *carte blanche* and left her free to act according to the opportunities that presented themselves, trusting myself entirely to her prudence in the various negotiations that she would be obliged to make in order to engage our allies to furnish the necessary resources for me to be able to return to my estates and expel Pencanaldon's troops.

"When the articles of our negotiation were signed, Celinde took them to Princess Argiliane, who was so content that, in order to facilitate their entire execution, she sent the Queen a talisman composed of seven metals that had the virtue of rendering invisible the individuals who wore it around their neck. It was by means of that talisman that the Queen escaped from Pencanaldon's palace, where she had been kept prisoner for such a long time.

"In spite of the natural urgency one has to enjoy liberty, especially after such a long captivity, however, the Queen did not want to leave the castle without expressing to Princess Argiliane how sensible she was to all her evidences of generosity and all the services she had rendered to her, especially what she had just done to facilitate her escape, the first use of which she made was to beg her to extend her benefits to her husband the King and everything belonging to us.

Argiliane promised her that with a very good grace, and the two Princesses, after having given one another a thousand reciprocal assurances of sincere amity, separated full of esteem for one another,

Cliceria then came to surprise me with Celinde, who said to me as she entered my cabinet 'I've finally come, my Lord, to inform you of the deliverance of the Queen. She left the castle without any of the guards seeing her, and that miracle only occurred with the help of Argiliane, who wanted to help the Princess by removing her from her father's power.'

"'I render thanks to the gods,' I cried, 'and ardently wish that they will favor the justice of our rights, in order that I can enjoy the satisfaction of soon being reunited with her.'

"'A part of your wish is granted this instant,' said Cliceria, throwing herself into my arms.'

"Seized by joy at the sight of a Princess that I had always loved passionately, I could not understand how she had initially been hidden from my eyes, but the talisman that she showed me, turning it over several times, caused me to admire the virtue of that masterpiece of the art.

"Celinde left to tell Prince Corydon that the Queen would not be long in coming to him. I took advantage of her absence to express to Cliceria how sensible I was to this last proof of her tenderness, since she was, so to speak, risking her life, or at least the liberty she had only just recovered by a kind of miracle. Finally, after we had given one another a thousand testimonies of our mutual tenderness, I communicated to her all the information I thought necessary for her to make representations o the Queen of Castora and to engage our other allies to aid us with their help. Celinde came back in to tell us that it was time to separate. It was necessary for us to yield to circumstances, but it was not without shedding many tears.

"Accompanied by Celinde, Cliceria went to Prince Corydon, who was waiting for her, and, everything being prepared for the voyage, they left at daybreak. The Prince, in order to avoid the suspicions to which his absence might give rise, had adopted the pretext of visiting the fortifications of Strong Island, belonging to Princess Argiliane. Meanwhile, Pencanaldon, resentful for a long time of the scorn that the Queen never ceased to show her, after having employed the secrets of magic in vain to make her condescend to his infamous projects, finally took the decision of absent himself, on Argiliane's advice. That was what gave the fugitives time to get away, and with Argiliane's help, they arrived in a matter of days in the realm of Castora.

"During the journey, the Queen informed the Prince of the laws that Pentaphile had imposed on all foreigners. Corydon seemed charmed at first, flattering himself that, if he did not have the good fortune to please, at least he would not have any rivals to fear. His joy was soon turned to a profound sadness, however, when he realized that he would not be able to stay in the realm without exposing himself to a thousand dangers.

"Cliceria, who perceived his chagrin and did not want to be deprived of his advice in the various negotiations that she anticipated having to make in the circumstances in which she found herself, and who was no longer forced to conceal herself from the eyes of the curious, offered the Prince the talisman that rendered invisibility. Corydon accepted it with such abundant expressions of gratitude that the Queen was convinced of his attachment to her interests.

"Equipped with the talisman, which enabled him to go anywhere without fear of being discovered—and, in consequence, to see Princess Tramarine, with regard to whom he had formed the most charming ideas, at any hour—the Prince hastened his march, scarcely giving the Queen time to get any rest. When they arrived at the court of Castora, the Prince did not think it wise to appear there, although he accompanied Queen Cliceria in all the visits that she made to Queen Pentaphile.

In the first meeting of the two princesses, Pentaphile seemed at first to be slightly disconcerted when Queen Cliceria asked for news of Princess Tramarine and the reasons that might have prevented her from seeing her. The Queen of Castora could not help manifesting a good deal of disturbance at that question, but, being unable to avoid answering it, she told her the story of Tramarine's adventures, and ended up by expressing an authentic dolor and finding herself unable to give her any news of her.

"Cliceria could not understand any of the story she had just heard, being unable to convince herself that the power of the imagination could produce such surprising effects. She believed, therefore, that everything she had been told was a fable invented to seduce her, and that Pentaphile had perhaps made some secret treaty with her enemy, of which her daughter had been the price. She did not want to make her doubts known, however, and withdrew to the apartment that had been set aside for her in order to confer with Prince Corydon there, whom she seriously feared might have been put off by that first hitch, and, annoyed by the delay, might abandon her enterprise.

"That is why, after having talked to him for a long time about Tramarine's adventures, presuming that it would never be possible to obtain any news of her, she told him that a young princess still remained, whom she offered him in order to fulfill her engagements. 'It's true,' the Queen added, 'that I don't know exactly what has become of her, but as she is in the hands of Princess Argiliane, I flatter myself that it will not be difficult for me to find out.'

"Corydon, who had only attached himself to Tramarine because of the reputation she had acquired of being one of the most accomplished Princesses in the world, had a great deal of difficulty reconciling himself to the exchange that was being offered to him. However, he persisted in the advice that he had given the Queen to employ all means imaginable to discover the place that Tramarine might have chosen for her retreat.

"Although the Queen was very annoyed by Pentaphile's conduct, not only in the matter of Tramarine but that of her own unfortunate captivity, of which I was still experiencing the deplorable fate, she nevertheless told the Prince that she did not think it would be prudent, in the present circumstances, to risk irritating the Queen of Castora by conducting searches that would doubtless be fruitless. The need she had for her help in assisting her to reconquer Lydia caused her to think that it would be more appropriate to dissimulate their subjects of complaint until I had recovered my throne. Those arguments were too good for the Prince not to yield to them.

"As it would take too long to report all the negotiations that it was necessary to make in order to engage my allies to furnish the necessary troops, however, suffice it for you to know that, in spite of the efforts of Pencanaldon, who had made himself hated by all my people because of his cruelties, the Queen returned to Lydia, and I was finally delivered from my captivity.

"It was only after that great event that I learned about your adventures. As little inclined to believe them as the Queen, I was, nevertheless, in despair are having contributed to the disaster by my foolish credulity—or, to put it better, my stupid vanity in wishing to penetrate the secrets of the gods, and banishing you from my court by virtue of an injustice for which I had long been punished by my remorse. I wanted to repair my fault, by doing everything that was in my power to discover your fate, but what I was able to learn completed my despair when I was told that it was not possible to obtain any news of the princess, and that it was presumed that she had thrown herself into the sea. That frightful suspicion caused me such a furious upset that, after having sworn the doom of Queen Pentaphile, I fell victim to an apoplexy, which immediately brought me here.

"I do not regret a life that would only have prolonged my inevitable woes, by incessantly retracing for me the memory of my faults. I flatter myself, on the contrary, that the honors you enjoy in their empire, by virtue of your happy union with the Prince of the Water-Sprites, might have made you forget all the tribulations that preceded them, and that you do not conserve any resentment on their account."

Tramarine assured her father that he was just in his estimation; that, although she had missed his presence for a long time, she had no reason to complain about the rigorous sentence that he had pronounced on her; and that, in order to show him that she did not conserve any memory of it, she would henceforth do everything she could to have him rendered the honors due to his rank and procure him all the satisfactions he might desire.

No one is unaware that when one has quit one's mortal body, all ranks are confounded, and that there is no longer any distinction between souls, especially in the empire of the water-sprites. However, Princess Tramarine obtained from General Verdoyant, by a singular grace, that her father the King would be admitted to the Court, and that he would enjoy the same privileges there as the water-sprites. She also asked that he be dispensed of drinking the elementary tea, but she could not obtain that last favor, for reasons that I have not been able to determine, but which are doubtless unanswerable.

They continued their route thereafter with King Ophtes, with the design of visiting all the parts of the world. Reflecting on her father's adventures, the story of which had informed her that she had a young sister who must still be on the Craintive Isle, Tramarine wanted to know more about her, and made the request of Prince Verdoyant that he should direct his march toward that isle in order to procure her, if possible, the satisfaction of seeing her without it having to cost the life of the young princess.

"I can easily satisfy you," said Verdoyant, "and to dissipate the tedium of a long journey, I shall relate to you, and to your father the King, the adventures of the Princess, which will surely interest you both."

Chapter XI
The Story of Brillante and Amour

"Princess Argiliane, still not daring to declare herself in favor of the Queen of Lydia, thought that she could serve her most usefully by affecting to submit to her father's orders. She knew his cruelty, and fearing, with reason, that in one of those moments when the Queen's scorn drive him to despair he might give orders contrary to the desire she had to save the little princess, being accustomed to avenge himself by means of such cruelties, when she had taken her to Craintive Isle she returned to the court and told the cruel Pencanaldon that the child had been exposed, and devoured almost immediately.

"Brillante was, therefore, brought up as the daughter of a shepherd. I shall pass over her childhood rapidly, which was of no interest, because she was not known to be a Princess, the least actions of whom are ordinarily admired. When Brillante had attained her sixteenth year, however, Argiliane thought that it was time to begin informing her of the advantages of her birth, and as she came to the island quite often, in order to give lessons to the little girl—who, by her docility and gentleness, had entirely acquired Argiliane's heart—the Princess remarked with pleasure the beauty and touching graces of her young pupil. She saw germinating within her the talents that nature produces and education perfects; she admired most of all her charming modesty, a true sign of innocence and purity of heart.

"Argiliane, for particular reasons, did not dare allow Brillante to appear in her father's court, but she feared that the young Princess, whose heart seemed disposed to tenderness, might form some engagement whose consequences might trouble her repose. That is why she began to talk to her about the disorders that amour causes in al hearts. 'You ought, my dear Brillante,' Argiliane said in the latest conversation, 'always to be on your guard against the attacks of men, who, for the most part, are only seeking to seduce our heart; conserve the modesty that is the most precious attribute of our sex; it ought always to be the faithful guardian of the purity of the soul. Avoid sacrificing to Amour that which is your dearest possession; Amour is a restless, perfidious and tumultuous god, who is only constant in his frivolity; that god make a cruel sport of the misfortunes and despair of those who follow his laws; often, one sees him confusing male and female lovers and exciting the most tender friend against the person he loves the most; the furies that Amour inspires recognize neither rank, nor duty nor nature; there is nothing sacred so far as he is concerned, especially when jealousy or vengeance animates him, and it is only by avoiding him that one can avoid those woes.

"'Never forget, my dear Brillante,' the Princess added, ' the advice I am giving you; the time is approaching when that god will seek to seduce you; there is no form that he will not take in order to succeed; for, when the endeavors to please, he appears charming and full of attractions that only serve to subjugate reason; Desire and Voluptuousness march in his footsteps, Hope almost always accompanies him, and he seems only to make his happiness out of the felicity of mortals. You ought not allow yourself to be surprised by him now, after the portrait I have I painted for you.'

"It was by means of similar instructions that Argiliane strove to make Brillante experience the joys that one experience in a tranquil state, but youth only seeks pleasure, solitude seems tedious to it, and it is only age and reason that can cultivate a taste for the counsels of reason.

"Brillante began to sense ennui, and her heart told her that there were pleasures that she might savor. Already she was forming desire without knowing where to direct them, and sighs that escaped her caused the Princess to fear that she might form some inclination unworthy of the blood that had formed her. That is why she told her, before leaving her, that Heaven had caused her to be born far above the estate in which she had been brought up, and promised to reveal the mystery of her birth at their next meeting.

"Brillante, raised as a simple shepherd's daughter, was nevertheless not very surprised by the overtures that Argiliane had just made to her regarding her birth; the nobility of her soul had doubtless informed her that an illustrious blood must flow in her veins and animate all her actions. The impatience to know to whom she owed her existence caused her to desire to see the Princess again soon, and as if the desire could bring forward her return, she did not fail to go for a walk every day at the entrance to a forest through which Princess Argiliane had the custom of passing in order to go to her palace.

"One day, Brillante, finding herself much more agitated than usual, had not been able to sleep during the night, which caused her to get up before dawn in order to go to the entrance to the forest. Scarcely had she arrived there than she perceived a carriage in the distance, the splendor of which surprised her and fixed al her attention. It was a caleche upholstered in satin, scented with the most agreeable odors. The imperial of the caleche formed an image representing the goddess Venus, lying nonchalantly on a bed of flowers, her head leaning on the knees of the god Mars, watching the Graces, who seemed to be occupied in making crowns of myrtle to ornament the heads of the happy lovers. On the back of the caleche could be seen the shepherd Paris choosing Venus from the three goddesses in order to present the apple to her; the sides represented the different attributes of the goddess.

"Amour, in the depths of that admirable vehicle, seemed distracted and pensive, his head tilted slightly to the right toward Modesty, gazing with indifference at Favor, who was sitting to her left. Enjoyment, with a submissive expression, was sitting next to Amour, and seemed to be asking him whether he deigned to select her. The Graces were in front, one of them holding the god's quiver and golden arrows, the other two teasing him in order to renew his good humor, appearing to be solely occupied in playing pranks. The Shepherd's Hour served as postillion, holding the reins of eight swans whiter than snow. The Games, Laughters and Pleasures surrounded the charming caleche.

"It was Venus' carriage that Amour had taken, with her entire retinue, in order to hold a party in his new little house, but the retinue still did not know who was to be the heroine of a celebration that Amour had been preparing for a long time; because since the burn that Psyche had inflicted upon him by her indiscreet curiosity, no one had heard any mention of the god having had another mistress; it was even said that, in the dolor that he felt, he had sworn wrathfully, if not on the Styx, never to attach himself to anyone again. But perhaps one ought to mistrust the oaths of a god who puts all his glory into rendering them vain.

"Although Amour was then occupied with Brillante, and the god's apparatus, vanquisher of everything that breathes, was prepared solely for her, as he had not expected her to appear before dawn, he could not help blushing, initially mistaking her for his mother. He was soon disabused, however, on looking at her; her modest expression caused him considerable emotion. He had his carriage stop when it drew level with her, descended from it precipitately, and then approached her with a timid expression, almost not daring to raise his eyes to look at the young Princess, who was solely occupied in gazing at the magnificent spectacle offered to her gaze. Because of that, she did not perceive that Amour was at her feet, in the posture of a supplicant.

"A sigh that escaped the god, as he took her hand, extracted Brillante from her ecstasy. She blushed, and tried to withdraw it, but seeing that he kissed it in a tender and submissive manner, her disturbance increased.

"'Get up, my Lord,' she said, emotionally. 'What can you want from a young woman that hazard has caused you to encounter in this forest? Speak—can I be useful to you in some way? What has obliged you to descend from that beautiful carriage, and to quit the beautiful ladies with which it is filled?'

"'It is to offer it to you,' replied Amour, 'and these ladies, if they have the good fortune to please you, are destined to serve you. Suffer, then, divine Princess, that I lay my quiver and my arrows at your feet; I swear to you that I shall only occupy myself henceforth with the care of pleasing you; you alone can make my happiness. Too long have I reigned over the hearts of feeble humans; today I renounce the empire that I have always exercised over the world. Come, my adorable princess; enjoy the triumph that Amour is preparing for your charms.'

"'What!' said the young Princess, in a tremulous voice, her face covered with a rosy red hue. 'Is it possible that you are Amour? No, I can't believe it, given the frightful portrait that has been made of him for me.'

"'Is my name so frightening, then?' said the god. 'Yes, undoubtedly, I'm Amour; I don't seek to hide myself, like a seducer, who has no other objective than to deceive.'

"At these words, the Princess uttered a cry and wanted to flee, but she did not have the strength, and fell weakly into the arms of Amour. That god was temeritous; he made a sign to Favor, who ran nimbly to help Brillante—but Modesty, who got there ahead of her, caused her to step back, and that goddess, aided by the Graces, put all her efforts into helping the Princess recover from her weakness.

"Amour, who had remained at her feet, asked her, passionately, what could have caused such a great alarm. 'What do you have to fear from me?' the god said. 'Regard me as a child who adores you and will always be submissive to you; my intention will never be to do you any harm. Listen to Favor, yield to her advice; it is only by following it that you will enjoy perfect happiness.'

"Brillante, attentive to Amour's discourse, had not even dared to rest her timid gaze upon him, and, recalling to memory the sage lessons that she had received from Argiliane, anxious and pensive, she looked at Modesty with eyes that the tenderness and ardor of Amour appeared to animate, and sighed without daring to say anything.

"Amour, who was examining her, perceived her disturbance; he ordered Modesty to withdraw, believing that she alone was opposing his happiness. That order redoubled Brillante's dread; she threw herself into the arms of the goddess. 'In the name of the gods,' said the Princess, fearfully, 'stay and help me. What will become of me, alas, if you abandon me? Amour is nothing but a deceiver who is doubtless seeking to seduce me; for pity's sake, help me to flee.'

"'Who, then, has inspired such a bad idea of Amour in you?' said the god, angrily. 'But I can use my power, in order to convince you that I am not seeking to deceive you.'

"'Stop' said the young princess—and seizing the arrow that he was about to shoot, she threw it with so much skill that the god was pierced by it. Far from causing Amour any distress, however, the blow that he received one served to increase his ardor. Withdrawing it from his bosom, still burning with his own substance, he plunged it into Brillante's, without the young princess perceiving immediately the dart that had just been hurled at her.

"Modesty, who saw the trick that Amour had just played on Brillante, wanted at least to favor her with all her power, in order to render their union eternal; she took advantage of that favorable moment to engage Amour to recall Constancy, whom he had long since banished from his presence.

"The god, satisfied with his choice, consented to that without difficulty, and in order to cure entirely the suspicions that might remain in the mind of the Princess, he also permitted the Graces and Modesty to accompany her permanently, on condition that those goddesses were joined by Favor. 'I cannot live without her,' Amour added. 'Her conversation amuses me; she is the one who must always entertain me with a thousand little sallies; but it is time, my adorable mistress, to enjoy the pleasures that have been prepared for you.'

"At the same time, the god signaled to the Shepherd's Hour to approach. Modesty, who was still sustaining Brillante, opposed Amour's designs. The god seemed a trifle annoyed, but he dared not let his chagrin show, in order that he might gain the confidence of the princess by his complaisance; he presented his hand to her with an enchanting smile.

"Brillante, without being fully aware of what the disturbance agitating her was, finally allowed herself to be guided by the god, who had her climb into his carriage and sit down beside him, with the Graces, Modesty and Constancy. Favor sat down behind them, accompanied by a tall woman that Brillante had not perceived before. She asked Amour who she was and why she seemed so pensive. 'That is Enjoyment,' said the god, 'who is waiting anxiously for a favorable moment to make your acquaintance, in order to resume her usual cheerfulness and gaiety.'

"Amour ordered that she be taken to his little house, which might have been mistaken for one of the Sun's, by virtue of the riches that shone there in every part. A troop of Pleasures were detached to announce the arrival of Amour and the princess, who were received in the palace by the Laughters, the Games and the Pleasures. Amour conducted Brillante to a room of mirrors, and ordered the Graces to put her on a bed of roses, which Voluptuousness and Delicacy had prepared for them. Those two favorites of Amour never left that room; they were both charged with the responsibility of ornamenting it, maintaining a temperate air within it and spreading the most exquisite perfumes therein. The Games, Laughters, Pleasures, Favor and Enjoyment followed the princess into the room.

"Favor and Enjoyment lavished a thousand tender caresses on Constancy to congratulate her on her return; gaiety ornamented all the actions of Enjoyment, who flattered herself, with reason, that the reunion of her companion with Amour would finally allow her to triumph over her cruelest enemy. For, before the god had become sensible to the charms of Brillante, although Enjoyment had always been in his retinue, it had often happened, by a fatality that drove her to despair, that in spite of the orders of Amour, Repugnance, that enemy of her repose, had drawn him toward another object. She flattered herself that he had now been vanquished; the mild and complaisant character and the perpetually even humor of the young Princess would contribute a great deal to her winning the most complete victory over her enemy.

"Brillante, occupied with everything that surrounded her, was not devoting herself to reflection; she forgot Modesty, who had not come in with her, Amour having excluded her from that room, thinking to avoid, by her absence, a thousand petty quibbles to which she was strongly subject. That is why he had appointed the Shepherd's Hour to be the usher of the cabinet.

"In spite of his precautions, however, the god was not expecting to find Decency, a faithful companion of Brillante, who, in order not to abandon her, had hidden under the young princess' dress; when he tried to approach her, that imperious goddess declared to him that she would only cede her place to the god Hymen.

"Amour, inflamed by that further resistance, consented that his brother Hymen could come to light the nuptial torch, in order to illuminate his union with Brillante, which he swore to be eternal.

"Amour, having become constant by virtue of his union with Brillante, presently enjoys a perfect happiness, and his ardor, far from diminishing because of the continuous presence of Favor and Enjoyment, seems to increase; the pleasures that he experiences with their aid appear to him to be always new. It is easy to presume that Brillante has fixed him forever; it is therefore in vain that one will search for him at present in the world, since he has only left his shadow there.

"That, dear Tramarine," the genius Verdoyant added, "is the fortunate fate that your sister the Princess is presently enjoying on Craintive Isle, which the veritable Amour has chosen for his residence, because a perpetual spring reigns there."

When they arrived off the shore of that island, Verdoyant perceived Amour frolicking with Brillante and the Graces, who were out for a stroll accompanied with their entire court. The genius pointed them out to Tramarine, taking his chariot closer to the shore. After helping the princess to descend, he advanced with her toward Amour, who, recognizing Verdoyant at the Prince of the Water-Sprites, came to meet him.

"What brings you to this shore?" asked the god. "You have no more need of me to make you love the charming Tramarine; Esteem and Amity, who are accompanying you, leave me in no doubt of the happiness you are enjoying."

"It's true," said the genius, "that with your help those two divinities have joined us, in order to tighten the knots of a union that ought to be eternal. My primary object, in visiting you, is to express my gratitude to you, and to congratulate you, at the same time, on the fortunate choice you have made of the charming person who is accompanying you. It is so rare to see a sincere attachment on the part of Amour that, if it were known in the world, it would presently be considered as one of those phenomena that only appear very rarely, to announce the happiness of humans. That great victory was only reserved to Princess Brillante, who, by all appearances, ought not to fear your inconstancy."

"I confess," said Amour, "that I had banished Constancy from my retinue for a long time, but, finding her inseparable from Brillante, I recognized that it is only with her that one can experience true happiness, and I can no longer detach myself from her."

"What!" replied Verdoyant. "Have you abandoned mortals forever?"

"They haven't even perceived that I've quit them," said Amour. "Content with the shadow that I've left them, they can't distinguish it from me. Why? It's because the majority have neither morality, nor virtue, nor sentiment; delivered to brutality, changeability and repugnance, what use do they have for a god they cannot recognize? I agree, however, that there are some who merit being distinguished from the vulgar, so those are under my protection, and it is only to them that I distribute my most cherished favors."

"Since when has Amour learned to moralize?" said the genius, laughing.

"Since I took off my blindfold," said the god.

"It's easy to see that," said the Prince, "by the choice you've made of the amiable Brillante, and the greatest eulogy that can be given to her is that of having been able to fix Amour by her charms. But tell me, have you renounced Olympus forever?"

"I don't have any great desire for it," said Amour, "for nothing is more tedious at present than that abode. You can't be unaware that company is only amusing as long as one encounters amiable women there, and that's very rare to find there. Old Cybele no longer does anything but talk nonsense; as for Juno, her jealousy always puts her in a bad mood; Ceres is too sensible of her provincial divinity, and doesn't have the elegant air that the court provides. Minerva is incessantly armed as a Don Quixote, always ready for combat, and Diana only enjoys hunting, and ripping our ears with her horn; it's true that one can amuse oneself making occasional excursions with those two goddesses, but they're so grim that one daren't say a single gallant word to them. Hebe has become a trifle sugary since she had ceded her employment to Ganymede; the occupations of Pomona render her hands too rough, in spite of all the ointments she uses to soften them. I agree that Flora is very amiable, but she's too fond of gardening; besides which, she only enjoys herself with that little fool Zephyr. Aurora gets up so early that one can never catch her, and no one knows what becomes of her for the rest of the day. Venus is charming, but she's my mother; we're not always in accord on many points, which causes us to quarrel often; besides which, she never stays in residence long in one place, sometimes in Paphos, at other times in Cythera, Amathante or elsewhere, and the Graces are often with her. Thetis is only occupied in pleasing the god of day; the Muses are precious and overfond of philosophy; the Fates are spinners who show no mercy to anyone; the Hours run incessantly; and Folly only inhabits the earth nowadays. What can one do at present in Olympus? One dies there of boredom—for I can't amuse myself with Momus since he's giving himself airs and criticizing all the gods."

During this conversation Tramarine, after giving Brillante a thousand tender caresses, told her about the adventures of the King of Lydia, and the two amiable princesses, charmed by one another, would dearly have liked not to be separated again.

"You've troubled my repose," said Brillante, tenderly, to Princess Tramarine. "Since I've been united with Amour, I thought I'd never desire anything again; I was entirely ignorant of what blood and amity might do. In spite of the pleasure I feel in seeing you, though, and that I'd have in spending my life with you, I don't have either the strength to quit Amour or the courage to go with you. If you could live among us, my pleasure would be complete; at least,

Tramarine, grant me a few more days, in order to engage Prince Verdoyant to let me talk to our father."

"I'm in despair," said Tramarine, "at being obliged to refuse you, but I can't yield to your desires without breaking our laws. King Ophtes, after having lost the life that attached him to the earth, is veritably welcome among the water-sprites, but he doesn't enjoy the privileges of genii, who can reveal themselves to mortals when they please. I promise, you, nevertheless to come to see you as often as I can."

The genius approached the two princesses then, and told them that it was time to part. After tender farewells, Amour escorted the genius and Tramarine to their chariot, and promised always to be faithfully attached to them.

That separation was the first chagrin that Brillante experienced. It rendered her pensive for some time, but without putting her in a bad mood; she never had one of those, and when she experience dolor her plaints were always tender and touching. Amour, to dissipate her sadness, gave birth to new pleasures. It is even claimed that it was of his union with Brillante that the multitude of little frolicsome amours was born, and I am inclined to believe it.

The genius Verdoyant and Tramarine continued their voyage, informed the King of Lydia about the happy marriage of Amour and the princess, and painted him a vivid picture of the pleasures they enjoyed incessantly in their union—pleasures all the more desirable and sensible because time could never diminish them.

Chapter XII
The Story of Prince Nubecula, the Son of the Genius Verdoyant and Princess Tramarine

Verdoyant, wanting to procure the princess Tramarine one of those surprises that always agitate our senses impetuously, took her to a country where the majority of the citizens were only occupied with the future. Those people, although incessantly in dispute, seemed nevertheless to be trying to enjoy an eternal peace; in the midst of that pretended peace, however, they were almost all unhappy; they were suffering ennui and languishing, because they did not want to recognize amour, which alone is capable of enlivening the mind and occupying the imagination agreeably. For without amour, is one not deprived of the pleasure that gives splendor to grandeur, and sumptuousness to wealth? The charms of glory count for nothing and the attractions of the most touching beauty become insipid. How I pity them!

It was to the land of those people that the genius Verdoyant took Princess Tramarine and the King of Lydia. They arrived at a time when they were preparing a spectacle customary in that nation when it is a matter of the marriage of the eldest daughter of their king, because it is neither rank nor quality that can obtain her; it is to valor and the intrepidity of courage that she is accorded. That spectacle had been announced for a long time in favor of Princess Amasis. The princess in question was not endowed with graces or beauty, and the deformity of her body seemed to render her union less precious.

It was customary to submit to terrible proofs in order to obtain the alliance from the King. No one had yet asked for the hand of Amasis. Her repulsive portrait, which was not permitted to flatter her, had not tempted any sovereign prince to submit himself to the inevitable dangers. However, the King had so great an affection for Amasis that it often degenerated into weakness, and her sisters, although endowed with all imaginable perfections, were unable to obtain any favors if Amasis did not join with them to ask for them.

The Princess who was intensely annoyed at being deprived of life at court, fell into a languor that caused anxiety for her life; that was what determined the King to permit any foreigner to present himself to the proofs to which it was necessary to submit in order to render himself worthy of the princess.

All the King's daughters were brought up in a temple dedicated to the Sun, from which they only emerged in order to marry. The temple is built on top of a rock, its dome rising into the clouds, and the sea serves as a channel to the gardens that surround it. Before arriving at the temple, one has to pass through seven doors, which are as many proofs, which it is necessary to endure without interruption; they are knows as the Portals of Favor, because those who have the courage to pass through them are regarded as the favorites of the Sun, are worshiped and placed among the number of the gods. It is true that without a particular grace it is almost impossible to be able to get through all the difficulties that one encounters. It is, however, only in overcoming them that they can acquire the glory that immortalizes them.

Those seven doors are made of seven different metals, which correspond to the seven planets, and the last, which opens to the enclosure of the temple is made of gold, as the metal over which the Sun presides. No one has the right to enter the temple except the King, and that is only by a secret door to which he alone has the key, but all the princes and gentlemen of his retinue are obliged to camp in a wood behind the temple.

Scaffolding was erected in the form of an amphitheater facing the first door, which led to all the others. Magnificent lodges were also built in order to house the King and the entire court. It is as well to inform the reader that in those climes, the days are much longer than ours.

The genius Verdoyant, Tramarine and their retinue reached the foot of the rock at the moment when the King and all his court arrived to see the ordeals commence. The Prince of the Water-Sprites had his wife's carriage placed in a gulf near the temple, in order to enable her to see the marvels, which appear to many people to be incredible.

Scarcely were they in position when the King appeared, preceded by his elite troops. Thousands of ensigns standards and deployed flags were fluttering in the air, which served to distinguish the orders and ranks. The troops arranged themselves in order around the King's lodge; he then appeared, with a majestic expression. As soon as the king was in the lodge, the signal was given, which the drums, fifes and trumpets announced with strident sounds.

Then, several champions presented themselves to be admitted to the proofs; but some were unable to get through the first door, and the most determined were checked by the second. They were beginning to despair when a tall young knight appeared; the knight was clad in green armor and on his escutcheon was the figure of Pallas, which seemed to have been engraved by a masterly hand. The death of those who had preceded him did not intimidate him.

Tramarine shivered at the sight of that knight; her heart palpitated with the dread that he might meet the same fate as the others.

"What a pity it would be," said the Princess to the genius, "if foolish ambition were to cause that young knight to perish! That is what vain honors can produce; one runs after a chimera of which death can rob you in an instant; for it cannot be love that makes him desire the possession of a princess who, in spite of her deformity, would perhaps only have the utmost arrogance and scorn for him. Alas, what will his destiny be?"

"Have no fear for him," said Verdoyant. "He will be victorious; his weapons are invulnerable and a superior genius protects him."

The knight advanced immediately, in a proud and intrepid manner, to the first door, entrance to which was defended by a dragon of enormous size. The monster had three heads, which it was necessary to sever, and their combat lasted nearly four hours. Although the monster had lost two of its heads, it still had the strength to lift itself up on its feet in order to devour the knight—who, far from recoiling, thrust his spear into its side. That was the only spot where it could be killed, because of the thick scales that covered it. The furious animal fell, uttering howls that made the rocks and mountains tremble, and the first door opened noisily. Then the knight went into a large courtyard, where he rested for a while.

Not far from there was a mount whose frightful summit was vomiting swirls of flame and smoke, and where the ground shone with a yellow crust, indubitable evidence of the sulfur that formed in its entrails. Above that mount was the second door, guarded by fiery horsemen.

When the knight had rested momentarily, he fought them, and was able to drive them away and pass through the second door.

A giant defended the third, but he severed both his legs with a single sweep.

That victory cost him little; he then marched toward the fourth door, where there was a winged serpent. The animal ejected a venom through its nostrils that infected the air; the monster was twenty cubits long.

The knight could not help shivering at that sight; his heart quivered with dread and horror, stirred like waters agitated by a violent fire, and the decisive moment caused him to recoil momentarily. Blushing at his weakness, however, he reanimated his courage, took firmer hold of his sword and advanced toward the monster, which, hissing in a terrible fashion, caused Tramarine to tremble for the life of the knight—who, having shown his valor and the intrepidity of his great heart, was beginning to despair of his ability to vanquish the furious animal. With a desperate movement, he threw his sword at the moment when the monster, opening an enormous maw, launched itself forward to devour him. The sword opened its throat, and such a great abundance of venom emerged therefrom that the air, which was infected by it, caused the knight to fall unconscious.

Tramarine, penetrated by anguish at that accident, begged Prince Verdoyant to help him, which he did without rendering himself visible.

First, the genius took off his helmet, in order to make him take a marvelous elixir, which reanimated his vigor and simultaneously fortified his courage. The knight, recovering consciousness, was extremely surprised not to see anyone.

"To whom do I owe," he said, "the fortunate aid that I've just received? Undoubtedly a genius is protecting me, and perhaps it's only to him that I owe my victories. I can only attribute such marked favors to the protection of Pallas."

The fortunate conqueror advanced toward the fifth gate, surrounded by a broad ditch that, by virtue of its depth, presented a frightful abyss, into which he was seen to leap with an intrepid courage.

He was soon seen, however, taking the route to the sixth gate, guarded by sirens, who employed their most flattering sounds to charm him with their agreeable music. At first, the knight could not resist such touching accents; he stopped to listen to them; his head was already yielding to the pleasure of hearing them, his strength was weakening and his tremulous legs could hardly support him. It was visible that he was on the brink of losing the fruit of all his labors. That proof is the most difficult to overcome—but, perceiving his weakness, he suddenly armed himself with a new courage, and by means of a singular inspiration, he took his sword in his hand and fled with an extreme speed.

He finally arrived at the seventh door, defended by a bird of monstrous size, which was said to be the phoenix.

Tramarine, attentive to all the knight's actions, thought she would never see the end of such a singular combat. The bird did nothing but flutter incessantly before the knight; it seemed that it was only seeking to blind him with its wings. A hundred times he was seen to strike it down; a hundred times it was seen to reproduce itself.

The knight, not understanding the singular creature at all, realized that he would never be able to vanquish it with his weapons, and that it was necessary to employ cunning in order to try to take it by surprise. After the bird had circled around him thousands of times, doubtless fatigued, it finally came of its own accord to perch upon him, and he immediately seized it.

It was then that the vaults of the temple shook; the seventh door opened with a frightful din, and cries of joy were heard everywhere.

The victorious knight, holding his bird, traversed a great courtyard, at the far side of which was an exceedingly deep lake, which it was necessary to swim across in order to purify himself, but without letting go of the bird, which would have made it necessary for him to engage in a new combat.

The agitated waves of the waters of the lake were making a noise similar to a torrent precipitated from the top of a steep mountain.

After the victor had been subjected to that final proof, he advanced toward the Temple of the Sun. The temple is surrounded by a double row of columns of jasper-lined marble. In the middle of the temple, on a pedestal, is a statue of the god, whose head is ornamented with a crown in the form of rays, garnished with carbuncles.

Under the vast portico formed by the double row of columns surrounding the temple, young girls were lined up to either side. Those children, all chosen for the most agreeable faces, had long curly hair that floated over their shoulders. Their heads were crowned with flowers and they were all dressed in celestial blue. Several were incensing the altar with admirable perfumes; others were singing the praises of the Sun. Their perfect notes were heard everywhere, along with the melodious sounds of several instruments, moved by delicate and light fingers, until the moment when the star of Venus, favorable to lovers, appeared over their hemisphere. Then the Chorus, followed with ardor and delight, lit the nuptial torches, invoking the god Hymen, to whom Amour furnishes gilded features; it was with the torch of the latter god that he lit the durable lamp, and, sustaining him on his crimson wings, he was glad to share his reign with him. It is only by means of that accord between Amour and his brother Hymen that one finds reason, fidelity, justice and purity; and it is only by means of Hymen that the ties of blood, the gentle liaisons of father, son and brother, can be formed, he alone preserving them from sources corrupted by crime.

The sound of trumpets was heard when the high priest appeared, followed by Amasis and her priestesses. That venerable old man, throughout the time of the sacrifices, always had his head covered by a crimson veil. He finally advanced to consult the entrails of the victims that were still palpitating, and whose blood was fuming everywhere.

"O gods!" he cried. "Who, then, is the hero that the heavens have sent to performs such great marvels here?"

As he spoke those words his expression became grim, his eyes sparkled and he seemed to see other objects than those appearing before him. He was troubled; his hair bristled; his face was inflamed; and, raising his arms, he held them immobile. His voice halted; he was hardly breathing any longer, and he appeared no longer to be able to contain within himself the divine spirit that was agitating him.

"O fortunate Princess!" he said, in his enthusiasm. "What do I see, and what is your happiness? Gods, crown your work!" He turned to the knight. "And you, noble stranger," he continued, "whose labors have surpassed those of all mortals, may the God you implore lavish you with the most precious favors!"

The high priest gave them a sign to approach the altar simultaneously. The knight, who was disarmed, presented his hand to Princess Amasis. The princess was still covered by a thick veil. They both advanced to the statue of the Sun, at the base of which the high priest was standing, his hands bearing the nuptial cup. The priestesses were lined up to either side of the high priest, who, after he had made the two spouses drink what was in the cup, took their hands and joined them together, making the knight pronounce the following words:

I swear by the Sun, the father of nature.
Who gives life and fecundity;
And by you, lovely Moon, sole divinity
Who delights in the obscure night;
You, who give birth beneath your paces
To voluptuous and delicate pleasures,
Inflame the heart of the princess forever;
Enable her to respond to my tenderness;
Let her not fear that my flame
Will ever relent one day,
Since the same amour, incessantly
Will reign for her in my soul.

The priestesses and the daughters of the Sun repeated in chorus: "Inflame the heart of the princess forever."

That was repeated several times, with the accompaniment of delightful chords.

Princess Amasis then added, in a silvery and sonorous voice:

May the gods expand in our hearts
The torrents of pleasure that are sweetness;
May my spouse, always covered in glory;
Be incessantly accompanied by Victory,
And may his courage be celebrated forever
Beyond time and throughout the ages;
And may a union so fine be engraved in history
In golden letters in the Temple of Memory.

That was repeated several times by the choirs. The two spouses were then conducted, to the sounds of a thousand instruments, to the door of the temple, where the knight climbed with the princess into a magnificent carriage, which was immediately lifted up by eagles, and transported to the palace of the King.

The Prince of the Water-Sprites, wanting to procure Tramarine the satisfaction of seeing the end of that ceremony, took her with the King of Lydia along a broad channel, whose waters, artfully distributed, spread out through various small channels in a great gallery to form delightful cascades at both ends, into which care had been taken also to make waters distilled with the most exquisite odors flow. It was in one of those cascades that the genius Verdoyant placed Tramarine and her father the King.

In the middle of the gallery was an elevated throne, on which were seated the King and the Princess, the mother of Amasis. That day was a day of triumph for them. The two sides were occupied by the King's other wives and the princes of the blood.

Then the two young spouses appeared, who advanced in a noble manner and came to kneel at the King's feet. After they had kissed them, the monarch, all of whose actions were guided by wisdom, prudence and reason, embraced them both, and took a crown from the Queen's hands, which he placed on the knight's head, in order to render him by that mark of distinction the equal of the princess. She then took off her veil, showing herself for the first time to her illustrious spouse and the entire court.

As soon as Amasis had removed the thick veil that covered her, a murmur of confused voices was heard. All of them went up at the same time, the princes in particular complaining loudly that a considerable wrong had been done to the Princess Amasis by distributing portraits so dissimilar to her, since no one could refuse her admiration and a thousand other sentiments that her virtues, her beauty and the majesty of her figure inspired.

It is true that Amasis appeared in that court like a new star; it seemed that Amour and the Graces had taken pleasure in forming her; a slender and lithe figure, an admirable profile, fine and delicate features in which goodness, candor and modesty were painted, which rendered her even more beautiful. She did not have the grim expression that causes love to flee and tarnishes beauty, but the gentle, innocent and childlike decency that inspires respect at the same time as it inflames desires.

When Princess Amasis saw all gazes fixed upon her face was covered by a divine blush. She looked tenderly at her spouse, her eyes expressing the sentiment that animated her, seeming to say that it was him alone that suffrage ought to flatter, because her heart, obedient to the laws of the kingdom, had immediately attached itself to the young hero, whom it seemed that only some divinity could have formed.

Meanwhile, the King's surprise appeared to be extreme; he was nevertheless unable to dispense with replying to the princes, who begged him to explain the reasons he had had for not giving an accurate portrait of the charms of the princess. The King replied, with the expression of candor that so well befits the majesty of a sovereign, that unless the gods had performed a miracle in favor of Amasis, he agreed that he could only recognize, in the person that was presented to his eyes, the voice of his daughter the princess.

That confession by the monarch only increased the confusion, and as entry to the temples was only permitted to His Majesty, the monarch was humbly begged to transport himself there with the Queen, in order to visit the interior and interrogate the other princesses, to ascertain whether one of them had had the audacity to substitute for Princess Amasis some daughter of the Sun.

The Princess, however, surprised that anyone should seek to cast suspicion on her birth, begged her father the King to permit her to justify herself. "It is not," the Princess added, "that I want to prevent Your Majesty from making the journey that has been proposed; on the contrary, my glory is interested in that visit, in order to dispel all suspicions that might tarnish my birth and leave doubts in minds injurious to my husband; but if Your Majesty cares to recall the various conversations with which he has honored me in the course of my life, perhaps I can convince him that only Princess Amasis is able reveal to him secrets confided to her alone.

"In order to assure him of that," she continued, falling to her knees, "I dare to beg my father to accord me a private audience."

The King, moved by the princess' speech, got up immediately, and they went into his cabinet, where they remained enclosed for a long time.

The entire court waited impatiently for the result of such an extraordinary event. Only the prince, Amasis' husband, seemed tranquil; in the midst of so much disturbance. But the King, who emerged from his cabinet followed by Amasis, calmed all minds when he spoke.

"I am now convinced," the monarch said, addressing is entire court, "that this is Princess Amasis; I recognize her as my daughter, and you should regard her henceforth as your sovereign, since no one else in the world can have had knowledge of the secrets that she has just revealed to me. Although the journey to the temple I have to make has become unnecessary for the justification of Amasis, however, I cannot dispense with fulfilling the promise I have made. I shall therefore go there with the Princess, to thank the gods for the graces they have just accorded to the person of Amasis. I shall offer further sacrifices, and order at the same time that in recognition of the miracle that has just been accomplished in favor of my daughter, on the same day every year, a celebratory fête will be held in honor of the Sun, in order to eternalize the memory of such a great day.

"As for you, Prince," the King added, addressing Amasis' husband, "I associate you with my royalty; you will henceforth share my crown; I believe you to be all the more worthy of it because the gods seem only to have performed such a great miracle in favor of your labors. I recognize now that truth, reason, wisdom and moderation will always be your rules, so our sentiments can never be opposed."

The Prince could only respond to that eulogy with a profound bow.

The King was then escorted to his carriage with Princess Amasis in order to go to renew their offerings and sacrifices in honor of the Sun, to which the magnificent carriage that had conveyed Amasis and her illustrious spouse was dedicated. The King had all the details of the story engraved on tablets of bronze, in order to conserve the memory of it until the remotest centuries.

During the absence of the King and Princess Amasis, it was noticeable that all the courtiers who, before the Prince had been associated with the throne, had hardly deigned to look at him, hastened to pay their court to him. But the Prince, whose intellect was superior to all those mercenary flatterers delicately made them aware of the scorn he felt for their insipid praise, and, advancing toward the Queen, expressed to her, with a great deal of dignity, how sensible he was of the honor he was about to enjoy—a happiness all the greater because it procured him the advantage of dividing his cares between two princesses so worthy of one another, and of obtaining for both a liberty that he was convinced that they would only use to enhance the delights of the union formed by the gods themselves.

When he returned from the temple, the King returned Princess Amasis to her illustrious spouse, heaping him with a thousand marks of esteem and amity, to which the Prince responded with a great deal of respect. With amour painted in his eyes as he gazed at Amasis, who offered him her hand, they prepared to leave the gallery in order to return to their apartments. The pages were already preceding them in order to accompany them when they were stopped again by a venerable old man who suddenly appeared in the middle of the gallery.

The old man advanced in a grave and majestic fashion, but, perceiving the disturbance that his sudden appearance had excited in all minds, he fixed his eyes on the young spouses for a few moments, doubtless to give them time to recover from their agitation. Then he turned to the King.

"Calm the disturbance that I can see you are experiencing, my Lord," he said. "I only have agreeable news to announce to you. I am the genius Carabiel, sent on behalf of the Sun to inform you that the spouse of Princess Amasis owes his birth to the genius Verdoyant, Prince of the Water-Sprites, and Princess Tramarine, the daughter of the King of Lydia, presently associated by her union with the Empire of the Waters, by the protection that her virtues have been able to obtain from the goddess Pallas, daughter of Jupiter, who personally named that young prince Nubecula. You ought to have known, by the striking labors that he has just performed, that the Prince could only owe his origins to a favorite of the gods, and it is only in his favor that the Sun has consented to perform the miracle that has transformed Princess Amasis. That god is content with the election you have made of that young hero to reign with you over all the peoples dependent on our empire. He has charged me with announcing to you that he will extend its limits by joining to it the realm of Castora, and that he will extend his most precious influences over all your posterity. The flourishing land will render your fields always fertile and abundant; peace and concord will reign among the citizens, and the descendants of Prince Nubecula will enjoy his favors for innumerable centuries."

Then the genius turned to the Princess. "Prepare yourself, charming Amasis," he added, "for the departure of your illustrious spouse. Do not attempt to delay the glory that he must still acquire in the conquest of the estates of the Queen of Castora. Pentaphile has offended the gods by establishing unjust laws there, and it is to punish her that they have ordered that the kingdom will pass into the power of Prince Nubecula."

"Respectable Carabiel," said the Princess, "do not refuse me the grace that I dare to ask of the Sun's envoy, and at least permit me to accompany the Prince, my husband, on his new expedition."

The genius consented to that, and disappeared immediately, leaving the King and all his court in a surprise mingled with admiration at all the marvels they had witnessed. It is true that it seemed that had not had time to collect themselves, because the prodigious events had succeeded one another so rapidly; the courtiers, above all, seemed relieved by the declaration of the envoy of the Sun; their self-esteem, which had been under pressure for some time, suddenly recovered all its plenitude; their humiliation disappeared when they learned that it had required nothing less than a demigod to have carried off such great victories in such a short time. Thus, all the marvels that the Prince had accomplished increased his value in their eyes, and the stranger, whom they had found it humiliating to obey at first, could only cover them in honor and glory in future, as soon as the recognized him as the grandson of the King of the Waters.

Then the joy and satisfaction that an unexpected happiness had produced in Amaris' soul were seen shining in her eyes, and that happiness excited in her heart sentiments of the most perfect gratitude toward the gods. Her heart, already disposed to amour, caused her to say to the prince her husband the most tender and witty things in the world—but I shall not attempt to report that conversation, which was doubtless one of the most animated that love can inspire between two young hearts.

Although the King was extremely fatigued by all the events that had just succeeded one another, he was unable to defer for long hearing the adventures of Prince Nubecula; that is why he dismissed a part of his court and went back to his cabinet, followed by the Queen, the young spouses and the corybants most elevated in dignity.

"You ought not to find extraordinary," the monarch said to Prince Nubecula, "The haste I am in to learn the slightest circumstances of the life of a Prince like you; don't delay informing me for a moment."

At that order the Prince could not help sighing. He gazed at Amasis with impassioned eyes, and she knew by that gaze how sorry he was to be obliged to delay the moment of his happiness by yielding to His Majesty's urgency; but a smile from Amasis, similar to that of Amour, appeared to console him and simultaneously to invite him to satisfy her father's desire promptly. He therefore began his story, which he told very briefly.

"At the moment of my birth I was put into the hands of a famous magician, who, constrained by a superior power not to abuse his authority over me, abandoned me to a faun, who cared for me in my infancy. The faun lived in a cavern near the Temple of Ceres, and at the age of four he consecrated me to the goddess, in order to serve her cult at her altars. I had scarcely reached the age of fifteen when I felt penetrated by a poetic fury. Animated by the spirit of the god who protected me, I pronounced several oracles, and spent a few years in that occupation; but the priestess summoned me to her lair one day. "Young man," she said to me, in one of those enthusiasms that the goddess had the custom of exciting in her, "learn that you are to be the most valiant of mortals; it is time to quit this abode in order to go forth and signal your courage; a thousand various exploits are offered to your glory. Go; the god who protects you will take care of your glory, and your triumph will be admired throughout the Universe.

"Those words, dictated by the goddess, gave birth within me to the noble audacity that must always accompany heroes. I went out tremulously and found, under one of the porticos, the armor that has just served me to carry out the exploits of which Your Majesty has been the witness."

Although Their Majesties and those who had been admitted to the conversation would have liked to know the Prince's adventures in much greater detail, no one could complain about his complaisance, and the King postponed demanding those details until another occasion, perceiving that the Prince was burning with impatience to retire with Princess Amasis.

Tramarine and her father, both charmed to have been witnesses of the triumph and glory of Prince Nubecula, expressed their gratitude to the genius Verdoyant, and thanked him at the same time for the agreeable surprise they had experienced at the appearance of the envoy of the Sun, and learning by virtue of that favorite's discourse that the young prince was her son.,

"Undoubtedly," Princess Tramarine added, "it was to the genius Carabiel that you confided his education. I was unjust, alas, when I was able to doubt his fate! He is your son; you love him; you have secured his glory and his happiness."

"His destiny is now known to you," said Verdoyant, "and I believe that no doubt ought any longer to remain regarding the honors that he will enjoy. That is why, as we are very narrowly lodged here, I think it would be appropriate to rejoin the fleet, in order to continue our journey."

Tramarine, whose curiosity was replete with all the objects that might have excited it, perhaps feeling the ennui of such a long journey, and keenly impatient to introduce her father to the King of the Waters, begged the genius to take the fleet back in the direction of the capital, which they reached in a short time.

I shall not attempt to describe the celebrations that were held on their return; suffice it for my readers to now that His Aquatic Majesty, after having examined Princess Tramarine, seemed quite content with the change that had taken place in her. King Ophtes was introduced to him, and he was quite willing, in favor of his son's spouse to confirm the honors of the court that Prince Verdoyant had granted him. His Majesty added to that grace that he be given lodgings in the palace, adjacent to those of Princess Tramarine in the Pavilion of Mirrors.

By virtue of that new favor it was permitted to Ophtes to visit the Cabinet of Marvels frequently. Tramarine judged for herself the urgency that the King might have to learn what had happened in Lydia since his entry to the world of the Water-Sprites, and especially to have news of Queen Cliceria, the fashion in which she was governing his kingdom, and a thousand other matters of interest. That is why, after having given the King a detailed account of the attributes of the marvelous cabinet, she took him there to admire its singular beauties.

Ophtes, remembering his indiscreet curiosity when he had attempted to interrogate the gods regarding Tramarine's destiny, hardly dared raise his eyes to the mirrors. Doubtless he feared irritating the monarch of the Waters against him; but the Princess reassured him, telling him that when one did not form any desire the mirrors did not display anything.

Ophtes thought that he no longer desired anything, but thought is so prompt that one cannot stop it, and desire follows it closely. Ophtes thought, he desired; and the mirrors showed him what, in the depths of his heart, he desired ardently to learn.

He saw, therefore, the Queen of Lydia, who, after having mourned his loss for a long time and having tendered to his memory the honors and respects that could not be refused to a monarch who had only been occupied throughout his life in making the happiness of his people. He saw the amiable Cliceria, who, finding herself overburdened by the weight of guiding his vast estates, and fearing new irruptions on the part of Pencanaldon, sharing that burden with Corydon, the only one she thought worthy of filling the place that Ophtes had occupied for so long and with so much glory.

Without jealousy, Tramarine's father witnessed the union of the Queen with Prince Corydon; he contemplated their happiness in their posterity; and there were further subjects of satisfaction for him and for Tramarine, which they were to enjoy eternally.

SF & FANTASY

Adolphe Alhaiza. *Cybele*
Alphonse Allais. *The Adventures of Captain Cap*
Henri Allorge. *The Great Cataclysm*
Guy d'Armen. *Doc Ardan: The City of Gold and Lepers*
G.-J. Arnaud. *The Ice Company*
André Arnyvelde. *The Ark; The Mutilated Bacchus*
Charles Asselineau. *The Double Life*
Henri Austruy. *The Eupantophone; The Olotelepan; The Petitpaon Era*
Barillet-Lagargousse. *The Final War*
Cyprien Bérard. *The Vampire Lord Ruthwen*
S. Henry Berthoud. *Martyrs of Science*
Aloysius Bertrand. *Gaspard de la Nuit*
Richard Bessière. *The Gardens of the Apocalypse; The Masters of Silence*
Chevalier de Béthune. *The World of Mercury*
Albert Bleunard. *Ever Smaller*
Félix Bodin. *The Novel of the Future*
Louis Boussenard. *Monsieur Synthesis*
Alphonse Brown. *City of Glass; The Conquest of the Air*
Émile Calvet. *In a Thousand Years*
André Caroff. *The Terror of Madame Atomos; Miss Atomos; The Return of Madame Atomos; The Mistake of Madame Atomos; The Monsters of Madame Atomos; The Revenge of Madame Atomos; The Resurrection of Madame Atomos; The Mark of Madame Atomos; The Spheres of Madame Atomos; The Wrath of Madame Atomos* (w/M. & Sylvie Stéphan)
Félicien Champsaur. *Homo-Deus; The Human Arrow; Nora, The Ape-Woman; Ouha, King of the Apes; Pharaoh's Wife*
Didier de Chousy. *Ignis*
Jules Clarétie. *Obsession*
Michel Corday. *The Eternal Flame*
André Couvreur. *Caresco, Superman; The Exploits of Professor Tornada* (3 vols.); *The Necessary Evil*
Camille Debans. *The Misfortunes of John Bull*
Captain Danrit. *Undersea Odyssey*
C. I. Defontenay. *Star (Psi Cassiopeia)*
Charles Derennes. *The People of the Pole*
Georges Dodds (anthologist). *The Missing Link*
Charles Dodeman. *The Silent Bomb*
Harry Dickson. *The Heir of Dracula; Harry Dickson vs. The Spider*
Jules Dornay. *Lord Ruthven Begins*
Alfred Driou. *The Adventures of a Parisian Aeronaut*
Sâr Dubnotal *vs. Jack the Ripper; The Astral Trail*
Odette Dulac. *The War of the Sexes*
Alexandre Dumas. *The Return of Lord Ruthven*
Renée Dunan. *Baal; The Ultimate Pleasure*
J.-C. Dunyach. *The Night Orchid; The Thieves of Silence*

Henri Duvernois. *The Man Who Found Himself*
Achille Eyraud. *Voyage to Venus*
Henri Falk. *The Age of Lead*
Paul Féval. *Anne of the Isles; Knightshade; Revenants; Vampire City; The Vampire Countess; The Wandering Jew's Daughter*
Paul Féval, *fils. Felifax, the Tiger-Man*
Charles de Fieux. *Lamékis*
Fernand Fleuret. *Jim Click*
Louis Forest. *Someone is Stealing Children in Paris*
Arnould Galopin. *Doctor Omega; Doctor Omega and the Shadowmen* (anthology)
Judith Gautier. *Isoline and the Serpent-Flower*
H. Gayar. *The Marvelous Adventures of Serge Myrandhal on Mars*
G.L. Gick. *Harry Dickson and the Werewolf of Rutherford Grange*
Delphine de Girardin. *Balzac's Cane*
Léon Gozlan. *The Vampire of the Val-de-Grâce*
Jules Gros. *The Fossil Man*
Edmond Haraucourt. *Daah, the First Human; Illusions of Immortality*
Nathalie Henneberg. *The Green Gods*
Eugène Hennebert. *The Enchanted City*
Jules Hoche. *The Maker of Men and His Formula*
V. Hugo, P. Foucher & P. Meurice. *The Hunchback of Notre-Dame*
Romain d'Huissier. *Hexagon: Dark Matter*
Jules Janin. *The Magnetized Corpse*
Michel Jeury. *Chronolysis*
Gustave Kahn. *The Tale of Gold and Silence*
Gérard Klein. *The Mote in Time's Eye*
Fernand Kolney. *Love in 5000 Years*
Paul Lacroix. *Danse Macabre*
Louis-Guillaume de La Follie. *The Unpretentious Philosopher*
Jean de La Hire. *The Fiery Wheel; Enter the Nyctalope; The Nyctalope on Mars; The Nyctalope vs. Lucifer; The Nyctalope Steps In; Night of the Nyctalope; Return of the Nyctalope*
Etienne-Léon de Lamothe-Langon. *The Virgin Vampire*
André Laurie. *Spiridon*
Gabriel de Lautrec. *The Vengeance of the Oval Portrait*
Alain le Drimeur. *The Future City*
Georges Le Faure & Henri de Graffigny. *The Extraordinary Adventures of a Russian Scientist Across the Solar System* (2 vols.)
Gustave Le Rouge. *The Dominion of the World* (w/Gustave Guitton) (4 vols.); *The Mysterious Doctor Cornelius* (3 vols.); *The Vampires of Mars*
Jules Lermina. *The Battle of Strasbourg; Mysteryville; Panic in Paris; The Secret of Zippelius; To-Ho and the Gold Destroyers*
André Lichtenberger. *The Centaurs; The Children of the Crab*
Maurice Limat. *Mephista*
Listonai. *The Philosophical Voyager*
Jean-Marc & Randy Lofficier. *Edgar Allan Poe on Mars; The Katrina Protocol; Pacifica; Robonocchio; Return of the Nyctalope;* (anthologists) *Tales of the Shadowmen 1-11; The Vampire Almanac* (2 vols.)

Ch. Lomon & P.-B. Gheuzi. *The Last Days of Atlantis*
Xavier Mauméjean. *The League of Heroes*
Joseph Méry. *The Tower of Destiny*
Hippolyte Mettais. *Paris Before the Deluge; The Year 5865*
Louise Michel. *The Human Microbes; The New World*
Tony Moilin. *Paris in the Year 2000*
José Moselli. *Illa's End*
John-Antoine Nau. *Enemy Force*
Marie Nizet. *Captain Vampire*
Charles Nodier. *Trilby and The Crumb Fairy*
C. Nodier, A. Beraud & Toussaint-Merle. *Frankenstein*
Henri de Parville. *An Inhabitant of the Planet Mars*
Gaston de Pawlowski. *Journey to the Land of the 4th Dimension*
Georges Pellerin. *The World in 2000 Years*
Ernest Pérochon. *The Frenetic People*
Pierre Pelot. *The Child Who Walked on the Sky*
J. Polidori, C. Nodier, E. Scribe. *Lord Ruthven the Vampire*
P.-A. Ponson du Terrail. *The Immortal Woman; The Vampire and the Devil's Son*
Georges Price. *The Missing Men of the* Sirius
Edgar Quinet. *Ahasuerus; The Enchanter Merlin*
Henri de Régnier. *A Surfeit of Mirrors*
Maurice Renard. *The Blue Peril; Doctor Lerne; The Doctored Man; A Man Among the Microbes; The Master of Light*
Jean Richepin. *The Crazy Corner; The Wing*
Albert Robida. *The Adventures of Saturnin Farandoul; Chalet in the Sky; The Clock of the Centuries; The Electric Life; The Engineer Von Satanas*
J.-H. Rosny Aîné. *Helgvor of the Blue River; The Givreuse Enigma; The Mysterious Force; The Navigators of Space; Vamireh; The World of the Variants; The Young Vampire*
Marcel Rouff. *Journey to the Inverted World*
Léonie Rouzade. *The World Turned Upside Down*
Han Ryner. *The Human Ant; The Superhumans*
Frank Schildiner. *The Quest of Frankenstein*
Pierre de Selenes: *An Unknown World*
Angelo de Sorr. *The Vampires of London*
Brian Stableford. *The Empire of the Necromancers (1. The Shadow of Frankenstein; 2. Frankenstein and the Vampire Countess; 3. Frankenstein in London); Eurydice's Lament; The New Faust at the Tragicomique; Sherlock Holmes and The Vampires of Eternity; The Stones of Camelot; The Wayward Muse.* (anthologist) *News from the Moon; The Germans on Venus; The Supreme Progress; The World Above the World; Nemoville; Investigations of the Future; The Conqueror of Death; The Revolt of the Machines; The Man With the Blue Face; The Aerial Valley*
Jacques Spitz. *The Eye of Purgatory*
Kurt Steiner. *Ortog*
Eugène Thébault. *Radio-Terror*
C.-F. Tiphaigne de La Roche. *Amilec*
Simon Tyssot de Patot. *The Strange Voyages of Jacques Massé and Pierre de Mésange*
Louis Ulbach. *Prince Bonifacio*

Théo Varlet. *The Castaways of Eros; The Golden Rock.; The Martian Epic* (w/Octave Joncquel); *Timeslip Troopers* (w/André Blandin); *The Xenobiotic Invasion*
Pierre Véron. *The Merchants of Health*
Paul Vibert. *The Mysterious Fluid*
Villiers de l'Isle-Adam. *The Scaffold; The Vampire Soul*
Gaston de Wailly. *The Murderer of the World*
Philippe Ward. *Artahe ; Manhattan Ghost* (w/Mickael Laguerre); *The Song of Montségur* (w/Sylvie Miller)

Victor Margueritte. *The Bacheloress; The Companion; The Couple*

MYSTERIES & THRILLERS

M. Allain & P. Souvestre. *The Daughter of Fantômas*
A. Anicet-Bourgeois & Lucien Dabril. *Rocambole*
A. Bernède. *Belphegor; Judex* (w/Louis Feuillade); *The Return of Judex* (w/Louis Feuillade); *The Shadow of Judex* (anthology)
A. Bisson & G. Livet. *Nick Carter vs. Fantômas*
V. Darlay & H. de Gorsse. *Arsène Lupin vs. Sherlock Holmes: The Stage Play*
Séamas Duffy. *Sherlock Holmes in Paris*
Paul Féval. *The Black Coats (The Parisian Jungle; Heart of Steel; The Sword-Swallower; 'Salem Street; The Invisible Weapon; The Companions of the Treasure; The Cadet Gang); Gentlemen of the Night; John Devil*
Émile Gaboriau. *Monsieur Lecoq*
Goron & Émile Gautier. *Spawn of the Penitentiary*
Paul d'Ivoi. *Around the World on Five Sous* (w/Henri Chabrillat)
Rick Lai. *Shadows of the Opera: Retribution in Blood; Sisters of the Shadows: The Curse of Cagliostro*
Steve Leadley. *Sherlock Holmes: The Circle of Blood*
Maurice Leblanc. *Arsène Lupin vs. Countess Cagliostro; Arsène Lupin vs. Sherlock Holmes (1. The Blonde Phantom; 2. The Hollow Needle); The Island of the Thirty Coffin; 813; The Many Faces of Arsène Lupin* (anthology)
Gaston Leroux. *Chéri-Bibi; The Phantom of the Opera; Rouletabille & the Mystery of the Yellow Room; Rouletabille at Krupp's*
Richard Marsh. *The Complete Adventures of Judith Lee*
William Patrick Maynard. *The Terror of Fu Manchu; The Destiny of Fu Manchu*
Frank J. Morlok. *Sherlock Holmes: The Grand Horizontals; Sherlock Holmes vs Jack the Ripper*
Jean Petithuguenin. *The Adventures of Ethel King*
Antonin Reschal. *The Adventures of Miss Boston*
P. de Wattyne & Y. Walter. *Sherlock Holmes vs. Fantômas*
David White. *Fantômas in America*
Pierre Yrondy. *The Adventures of Thérèse Arnaud*

SCREENPLAYS

Mike Baron. *The Iron Triangle*
Emma Bull & Will Shetterly. *Nightspeeder; War for the Oaks*

Gerry Conway & Roy Thomas. *Doc Dynamo*
Steve Englehart. *Majorca*
James Hudnall. *The Devastator*
Jean-Marc & Randy Lofficier. *Royal Flush*
J.-M. & R. Lofficier & Marc Agapit. *Despair*
J.-M. & R. Lofficier & Joël Houssin. *City*
Andrew Paquette. *Peripheral Vision*
Robert L. Robinson, Jr. *Judex*
R. Thomas, J. Hendler & L. Sprague de Camp. *Rivers of Time*

NON-FICTION

Stephen R. Bissette. *Blur 1-5. Green Mountain Cinema 1; Teen Angels*
Win Scott Eckert. *Crossovers* (2 vols.)
Randy Lofficier. *Over Here*
Jean-Marc & Randy Lofficier. *Shadowmen* (2 vols.)

ART BOOKS

Jean-Pierre Normand. *Science Fiction Illustrations*
Raven Okeefe. *Raven's L'il Critters; Rave's Faves*
Randy Lofficier & Raven Okeefe. *If Your Possum Go Daylight...*
Daniele Serra. *Illusions*

www.ingramcontent.com/pod-product-compliance
Lightning Source LLC
Chambersburg PA
CBHW030923020726
47498CB00001B/85